**Malcolm Hamer** ~~~~~~~~~~~ y
and then worked in ~~~~~~~~~~~~~~~~~~~ l
multinational comp ~~~~~~~~~~~~~~~~~~~~ l
AMF International ~~~~~~~~~~~~~~~~~~~~~ s
agency in London ~~~~~~~~~~~~~~~~~~~~~ g
stars as Arnold Palmer, Tony Jacklin, Rod Laver, Jackie
Stewart and Gary Player. He formed his own agency in
1971 and has dealt with many top sportsmen including
Muhammad Ali, Sam Snead, Johnny Miller, Severiano
Ballesteros, Lester Piggott, Nigel Mansell, Denis Law,
Bobby Charlton and Gareth Edwards. In the 1970s he was
the licensing agent in Britain for the Olympic motif and for
soccer's World Cup motif.

His experiences led him to begin another career as a
writer. Since 1991 he has written four in the Chris Ludlow
series of golf thrillers: *Sudden Death*, *A Deadly Lie*, *Death
Trap* and *Shadows on the Green*. His account of the celebrated series between the golfers of Europe and USA, *The
Ryder Cup – The Course Book* was published the following
year. Together with his wife, Jill Foster, he has written a successful series of guide books – *The Family Welcome Guides* –
now in their fifteenth year of publication.

Malcolm Hamer is an enthusiastic golfer with a moderate handicap, and lives in Barnes, London.

I would like to thank the following for their unstinting help and advice: Jon Coleman, Alison Finch, Fred Macdonald, Martin Tyler and Abe Wilson.

# Predator

## MALCOLM HAMER

WARNER BOOKS

*To Jill, with love.*

A *Warner* Book

First published in Great Britain in 1996 by Little, Brown and Company
This edition published in 1997 by Warner Books

Copyright © Malcolm Hamer Books Limited 1996

The moral right of the author has been asserted.

A CIP catalogue record for this book
is available from the British Library.

ISBN 0 7515 1886 7

Typeset in Garamond by M Rules
Printed and bound in Great Britain by Clays Ltd, St Ives plc.

Warner Books
A Division of
Little, Brown and Company (UK)
Brettenham House
Lancaster Place
London WC2E 7EN

# Chapter One

It was Betty Lynagh's favourite time. Sunday brunch was a ritual in her home: bacon, kidneys, mushrooms, scrambled eggs, wholewheat toast and several pots of strong coffee, accompanied by a browse through the many sections of the *New York Times*.

The occasion was even more enjoyable when her beloved daughter was with them. She looked fondly at Suzi. She was a beautiful girl; everyone said so. She had brains, too. She had just finished her final examinations at the Harvard Law School. Betty and Joseph Lynagh were immensely proud of their only child. Suzi had never seemed happier. All her bounce and vitality had returned.

Steven Shaw, the handsome young man who was sitting next to Suzi and was busy tackling a second helping of bacon and eggs, obviously had much to do with her happiness.

Joe Lynagh tutted in irritation as he read about the widening boycott of the Moscow Olympic Games, which were due to start later that year, 1980. President Carter had taken a tough line following the Russian invasion of Afghanistan.

Steven, feeling Mrs Lynagh's eyes upon him, looked up and grinned contentedly at her.

'Wow, what a way to start the day,' Steven said.

'You deserve it, my boy,' Lynagh said. 'You played like a professional yesterday.' He turned towards his wife. 'You should've seen Brad Carrol's face, Betty. It's a long time since I've taken his money on the golf course. All thanks to Steven.'

'Not at all,' Steven replied modestly.

It was the second time that Steven had visited the Lynaghs' home in New York and he was trying hard to adjust to a style of life of which he had formerly only dreamed.

Joe Lynagh had sent the tickets for Steven's first trip to New York with Suzi. At JFK Airport they had been greeted by a tall black man with a fine head of crinkly grey hair. With his chauffeur's hat under his arm, he led them to a stretched Cadillac and stood attentively by the door as they climbed in. As he sank into the leather seat and surveyed the television and the radio, the drinks cabinet and the thick pile of the carpet, Steven knew that he had made the right decision to let his relationship with Suzi and her family develop for a little longer. Maybe for a lot longer. This was reinforced when they drew up outside a five-storey house just off Park Avenue. Steven recognised it as close to the apartment owned by the parents of Charlie Tomlin, who had become his closest friend at the Harvard Business School. It was in one of the most prestigious and expensive areas of the Upper East Side.

As Arnold, the chauffeur, with their bags under his arms, led the way to the front door, Suzi said, 'We call these houses brownstones, as you probably know. They're sweet, aren't they?'

The door was thrown back before they reached it. A tall and beefy lady in a flowing blue dress stood with raised arms into which Suzi deposited herself. When they disentangled themselves, Steven was introduced to Betty Lynagh and was ushered through the hall and into a drawing room which looked over a small square garden at the back of the house. Even to Steven's unpractised eyes, the room seemed to be a treasure chest of fine antique furniture. There was a collection of silver snuff boxes on one table and of paperweights on another. Oil paintings in heavy gilt frames were interspersed with bright splashes of colour from contemporary artists. The contents of this room alone were worth a fortune.

Steven swallowed hard and said, 'What a beautiful room, Mrs Lynagh! Are you the collector or your husband?'

Mrs Lynagh eyed the good-looking young man approvingly. 'Oh, both of us, Steven. We root about for things when we're on our travels. By the way, please call me Betty. Now, it's just past four when I'm sure you're used to having tea . . .'

Mrs Lynagh gestured towards a round table under the windows. A silver tray was laid with a teapot and a selection of sandwiches and biscuits. Oh yes, thought Steven facetiously, just like home.

'In honour of our English guest, tea is served. Now, Steven, tell me all about yourself.'

Not bloody likely, he thought, as he smiled at her.

Shortly after tea ended, Joseph Lynagh entered the house. After hugging his daughter noisily, he grasped Steven's hand and shook it long and hard. A squat man, with a square face on which thick glasses perched and magnified his deep-brown eyes, Lynagh was an even more ebullient presence than his wife. His voice was a boom and he threw comments and questions around the room with unceasing energy. As Steven answered his queries about Harvard and England and his parents, he had time to notice more about Lynagh. The man had a healthy crop of grey hair, but Steven guessed that it hadn't been near a comb since that morning; his clothes looked expensive but they were crumpled; his tie was loose and the top button of his shirt was undone. Lynagh was clearly not a vain man.

That first evening the four of them had dinner in a
neighbouring Italian restaurant. Although it was only a
couple of blocks away, Arnold drove them there in the
Cadillac. As they entered Leone's the *maître d'hôtel* and
several of the waiters greeted the Lynaghs enthusiastically
and Steven saw Joseph Lynagh press some money into the
*maître d'hôtel*'s hand.

Lynagh winked at Steven. 'I've been coming here for
over twenty years. But a little tip up front never does any
harm.'

Although Lynagh plied him with wine, Steven was careful not to drink too much. Occasionally he caught Betty
Lynagh watching him and she always smiled at him and
then at her daughter. He and Suzi's father achieved an
immediate rapport on the subject of sport.

'Suzi tells me that you play golf and tennis. And some
squash, too. That's great. My tennis days are over but I'd
love to take you to Westchester for some golf. What's your
handicap?'

'I was down to two for a while. But Harvard keeps me
busy, too busy for golf.' Steven shrugged modestly. 'It's
more like four or five these days.'

'Hey, you're on. You can help me win back some of the
money I've lost over the years to those bandits up there.
Next time you're over, I'll arrange it.'

Saturday was organised like clockwork. Suzi took Steven
to see the sights during the morning and they met Betty
Lynagh for lunch near Central Park. Lynagh was at meetings all day with some clients from Los Angeles and, as
Suzi pointed out, it was just as well the New York Mets
weren't playing that afternoon.

'Baseball?' Steven asked.

'You bet,' Mrs Lynagh said enthusiastically. 'He's been a

fan since he was so high. Now he's got a box at the Mets. It's paradise for him.'

The two women had planned to go shopping during the afternoon and Steven was taken in the Cadillac to the New York Athletic Club where one of Lynagh's younger colleagues was waiting to give him a game of squash. Steven felt rather sorry for the man; no doubt he had been told to volunteer by Joseph Lynagh. But they had a reasonably brisk game, even if Steven was several standards better than his host.

After the game, over a beer drunk in the almost empty bar, Steven asked Paul to tell him a little about Lynagh.

'He's a good lawyer, but his strength is bringing in business for the firm. He's an entrepreneur, people like him, but he's tough, you wouldn't want to cross him.'

'He's a New Yorker, I assume?'

'Oh yeah. Born in Brooklyn, went to New York University, then did law at Yale. He's infatuated with the Mets. I'm a Yankees man myself,' Paul said with a dismissive smile.

On the Saturday evening the Lynaghs had taken Steven to the Metropolitan Opera House to see a performance of *Turandot*. A bulbous Italian tenor was the star of the show and it was bizarre to listen to such an angelic voice issuing from such a gross body. Steven had to fight hard to stay awake and he noticed that Suzi fidgeted for much of the performance.

Afterwards the Cadillac took them to a fashionable and remarkably expensive restaurant, where Joseph Lynagh was well known to the staff.

Although Steven had been reminded several times to call Suzi's parents by their first names, he continued to address them respectfully as Mr and Mrs Lynagh. He was punctilious in his attention to Mrs Lynagh: he handed her in and out of the limousine and held her chair as she sat down in the restaurant.

The stretched Cadillac, in Arnold's skilled hands, whisked the two young people off in style to JFK Airport after brunch on Sunday. After waving farewell, Joseph and Betty Lynagh shut the door on a suddenly quiet house. They sat in companionable silence in the main sitting room.

'Well?' Betty Lynagh asked, after a while.

'I like him.'

'So do I. Nice manners – and that accent! I love a British accent.'

'He's bright. You don't get in the top twenty per cent at the Harvard Business School without being smart.'

'Suzi loves him.'

'She's got over the Peter episode then?'

'Yes, Steven's her man.'

'How can she know that so soon?'

'She knows, Joe, just as I knew as soon as I met you.'

Betty Lynagh stretched across the sofa and gave her husband a kiss.

'We'd better have him here again after the exams, in that case. And he plays golf off five,' he added.

The onerous demands of his final examinations lay in wait. Steven felt confident because his classroom work, which was given the same importance as the examinations by the Harvard Business School, had been consistent. He and Charlie Tomlin had analysed the techniques of classroom discussion and decided that it wasn't the frequency of the contributions that mattered but the weight.

'Be like a counter-puncher,' Charlie had said. 'Make every blow count.'

They had choreographed their own discussion routines:

they had devised argument and counter-argument for use on the following day. It was a risky device, since such collusion would be frowned upon by the presiding professor, but they had pulled it off on several occasions.

It was the objective of them both to finish the course in the top 20 per cent, as they had done in the first year, and thereby to pass with distinction. They set themselves a punishing schedule and felt ready when the days of reckoning arrived.

After a frenzied few days it was all over. Steven felt a great sense of relief and, despite the many celebrations, of deflation. Suzi, who had been sitting her finals at the Law School during the same period, was also subdued.

In the following days, Steven questioned his classmates about their plans. Most of them had already accepted jobs, usually with well-known multinational corporations. He made careful notes of their destinations and promised to keep in touch. He meant it. These people would eventually be in positions of power in business and Steven intended to make the maximum use of his connections.

Assailed by his own uncertainties, Steven was also prey to Suzi's anticipations. She was keen on jogging and he often kept her company on her runs along the Charles River. It was relaxing and he enjoyed loping along beside the lithe Suzi. He knew that they looked good, two beautiful people with rose-tinted futures.

'Are you going to take the job with the oil company?' Suzi asked.

'Maybe.'

'It's in New York.'

'Yes.'

'I'll be working in New York.'

'Yes.'

'So what's holding you back, dummy?'

'I must talk to my family first.'

'You told me that your parents have no conception of business or of what you're trying to do,' Suzi said with exasperation. She'd had to force Steven to tell her anything about his family, about where he lived, about anything in his background.

'I don't know what I want to do yet,' Steven replied. He increased his pace to try and stop Suzi interrogating him. They had already talked about getting married and Steven had computed the advantages that would accrue both in his social and his business life. The Lynaghs were rich. They made the Macaulay family, whom in his youth in Brighton he had regarded as unattainably prosperous, look like paupers. Apart from the brownstone house on the chic Upper East Side, they had a house on the west coast at Pebble Beach and an apartment in Florida. Their effortlessly affluent style of life encompassed visits to expensive restaurants, the opera and the theatre, and membership of exclusive clubs such as the Westchester Country Club. Steven wanted all of this.

A little breathless from striving to equal Steven's stride, Suzi said, 'What's the problem? Surely it's simple. We can be together in New York. That's what I want. Don't you?'

Steven pulled up and put his arm around Suzi, 'More than anything, Suzi, you know that. But I owe it to my parents to tell them my plans. I'm their only child, I'm all they've got.'

'I understand that, darling,' Suzi said with a surge of love for him that was so powerful it was painful. She was so lucky. She had a man who was not only honest but had a proper respect and a deep-seated affection for his family.

'But, before you go home, please spend a few days in New York. We'd all like you to be with us. Will you do that? For me?'

Suzi rang her father's secretary, who booked the air tickets to New York for two days later.

On Friday Suzi took Steven on the famous Circle Line boat which takes sightseers around the island of Manhattan. Since he had seen the Statue of Liberty in hundreds of photographs and frequently on the screen, he expected it to be corny. But he was moved by its grandeur and he marvelled at the audacity of the city's buildings; and Suzi saw the familiar sights afresh, through his eyes.

On the following day the Cadillac made its stately way to the Westchester Country Club with Joseph Lynagh and Steven on board. A game of golf had been arranged with two of Lynagh's friends, another lawyer in his fifties called Jimmy Franklin and an investment banker who was introduced as Brad Carrol.

Some golf clubs were hired for Steven, and Lynagh pressed him to buy a pair of golf shoes and a shirt from the shop, as well as several balls. The purchases duly went on to Lynagh's account.

Steven could not help being impressed by the sheer scale of the Westchester club, with its many bars and restaurants. It was a busy and bustling place, alien in its atmosphere to the cosy conservatism of golf clubs in Britain.

The stakes were declared for the match, a fifty-dollar Nassau. Lynagh explained the wager to Steven.

'It means fifty bucks on the first nine holes, fifty on the next and fifty on the result of the full eighteen holes. I'll stake you, young fella, don't worry about it.'

Lynagh turned to his opponents and said, 'Ten bucks for birdies, boys, is that OK? Steven plays off a five handicap, so he's giving shots all round.'

Steven's handicap at his club in Britain had lapsed since

he had played so little during his time at Harvard and the estimated figure of five was reasonable. Joseph Lynagh played off twenty and needed every one of his shots, while their two opponents were competent players off handicaps of twelve apiece.

It took a couple of holes for Steven to find his rhythm, and the generous width of the fairways encouraged him to go for his shots. He and Lynagh won the first nine by one hole but, helped by three birdies from Steven, they won the second nine and the match with ease.

The debts were paid over a round of dry martinis and Steven was grateful to pocket 180 dollars.

'I want that money back, young man,' Brad Carrol growled in mock irritation. 'You were much too good. We'll have to look at your handicap if this happens again.'

The banker returned his money clip to his trouser pocket and said, 'Joe tells me that you've just left Harvard and that you may settle in New York. If I were your age and had the good luck to know Suzi Lynagh, I wouldn't hesitate. She's a really lovely girl.'

Steven muttered something about his plans being unclear and that he had to talk to his parents. Carrol produced a business card and dropped it into Steven's shirt pocket.

'Give me a call if you're looking for a serious job. We can always use a Harvard man. I was there myself. Some of the best days of my life.'

'Brad was on the football team,' Lynagh explained. 'We reckon that's all he did at Harvard.'

With noisy promises of a return match, Lynagh ushered Steven into the Cadillac and they headed south towards Manhattan.

'Great golf, Steven,' Lynagh said, as he settled back in the leather seat. He pressed a button and the glass partition hissed shut behind Arnold's head. Lynagh opened the refrigerator and popped the cork off a bottle of champagne.

'It's great to beat those two, especially Brad. I don't see the colour of his money too often.'

Carefully, Lynagh poured out the champagne and clinked glasses with Steven.

'Here's to many more outings to Westchester,' Lynagh said. 'It was a lot of fun. Now, while I've got you on your own, I hope you don't mind my talking to you, man to man. It's obvious to me and Betty that Suzi's fond of you – real fond.'

In his seat opposite, Steven nodded his agreement and wondered where this conversation would go.

'People tell me that I'm impatient,' Lynagh continued, 'unsubtle. Sure, I'm a hustler, but why hang around on first base if you can steal second? Suzi's certain in her own mind about you but where do you stand? I can't tell how committed you are. I sense that you're still hesitating, or is it just that famous British reserve?' Lynagh chuckled and drank deeply from his glass. His eyes shrewd and expectant behind the thick lenses of his glasses, he looked hard at Steven.

'It's my family,' Steven said. 'I've got obligations to my parents. I must talk to them. It's a big decision to move to another country. And there's the question of a job. I've had an offer or two but—'

'If it's any help,' Lynagh interrupted, 'I've got a proposition for you. I'm a major shareholder in a business consultancy firm. They're located in my building. We feed them business and occasionally they send us clients. It cuts both ways. They could use someone like you on the marketing side. I'd make sure that their offer was favourable, better than the one from the oil company or that California outfit.'

Lynagh leaned forward. 'You see, Steven, I'm all up front, no subterfuge. I want my little girl to be happy. She's had one disaster with that faggot, Peter, and I couldn't bear it if she had another. I respect your wish to talk to your parents about everything. But sometimes, my boy, your heart should rule your head. Maybe you'd be OK as a son-in-law. Sure as hell you'd be a great golf partner.'

Rumbling with laughter, Lynagh refilled their glasses.

# Chapter Two

Open on to the rear garden, the wide windows of the Lynaghs' living room let in the mild warmth of an early June day. Steven felt totally relaxed as he anticipated several carefree days in Suzi's company. In every sense, it was all a very long way from his own parents' sparse two-bedroomed terraced workman's cottage in a dingy Brighton back street. At times he thought he was dreaming. On his first date with Suzi in Boston, she had arrived in a smart new BMW car and he'd guessed that her family was wealthy. But that hadn't prepared him for the reality.

When the doorbell rang, Suzi jumped up and volunteered to answer its call. It was the housekeeper's day off.

On the doorstep, Beverly looked up at the imposing house and assumed there must be a mistake. She had read about the brownstone houses around the upper end of Park Avenue and knew that only the very rich could afford them. It was a marked contrast to her hotel which was in a dirty and noisy street in the Garment District. The air conditioning had made a racket and she had barely slept. That morning, her eyes gritty from her restless night, she had taken a long shower and then strolled around the corner for breakfast in a delicatessen, but she had been too nervous to eat.

The door was opened by an alarmingly attractive young woman. Although she was wearing informal clothes – jeans and a T-shirt – Beverly recognised something different about her. At first she thought it was the classy cut of her jeans, but later she realised that it was the indefinable poise that attaches itself to people who have known nothing but prosperity and privilege.

'Oh, do Mr and Mrs Lynagh live here?' she asked, the words hesitant.

'Yes, they're my folks.'

'I have this address for Steven Shaw. I got it from the people at Harvard.'

Curious about the identity of the unexpected Sunday caller, Betty Lynagh appeared at her daughter's side. Suzi could tell that the visitor was British: she had a nice accent – it was like Steven's.

'Steven's staying with us,' Suzi said. 'Who shall I say—?'

'I'm Beverly Shaw, Steven's wife.'

'Is that some kind of joke, lady?' asked Betty Lynagh, who hadn't sloughed off all the elements of her tough upbringing in Brooklyn.

'It isn't a joke to me,' Beverly replied with spirit. She added, 'I don't suppose Steven told you about me, nor about our daughter.'

Suzi sat down heavily on a chair near the door and let her head drop into her hands. For once at a loss, Betty Lynagh let her good manners dictate her actions. 'You'd better come in for a moment.'

She paused and then shouted down the hall, 'Joe, can you come here, please?'

Joseph Lynagh patted his lips with a napkin and smiled at Steven. 'What the hell is going on out there? No peace, even on a Sunday.' For a minute or two, Steven heard the disjointed bursts of conversation from the direction of the hall, the rumble of Joseph Lynagh's voice and the subdued tones of a woman. Its rhythm sounded vaguely familiar, but he was more interested in a profile of a young amateur golfer who had confounded many of the professionals by finishing in the top ten in the Masters at Augusta. The handsome face of Sam Rhodes, the American amateur champion, smiled confidently from the page.

Steven's own smile, as Joseph Lynagh reappeared in the doorway, faded on his lips as he registered the man's look of anger. Lynagh's squat body was taut and his eyes fierce behind his spectacles. He shut the door with studied care, as if afraid that his emotions were about to get out of control.

'I don't know what you've been up to, Steven, but you'd sure as hell better have some kind of explanation for me.'

Steven stood up and was waved into silence as he attempted to speak.

'I've just met someone who claims to be your wife. Beverly. I'm praying that it's some kind of sick joke. I'm praying nearly as hard as my daughter. Suzi is devastated.'

'Mr Lynagh, all I can say—'

'What you can say is the truth. That's all I want from you. Is Beverly Shaw your wife?'

'Yes, but—'

'No buts, young man. I suggest you get out of my sight before I do something foolish. I also suggest that you try and make your peace with your poor wife. Now, get the hell out of here.'

Lynagh threw open the door and marched away. Steven picked up his jacket and trudged in his wake. He was glad that Suzi was nowhere to be seen. There was only Beverly, standing forlornly by the open front door.

'Thanks a million,' Steven said bitterly as they walked away from the Lynaghs' house.

'You're a bastard,' Beverly said in a matter-of-fact way. 'You've led that poor girl and her family up the garden path. You make me sick. I knew you were up to something but I didn't think you'd behave in such a shitty way.'

They had stopped on a street corner and one or two passers-by registered their quarrel and looked at them with interest. Beverly was surprised at how calm and strong she felt. 'I suppose I could've coped with you having a bit on the side, a passing fancy. But not this.'

'Beverly, I want to marry her. I want a divorce.'

'You just try. I'll make it so bloody tough for you.'

'Don't push your luck. You suckered me into marriage, you bitch. You deliberately got yourself pregnant so that I had to marry you.'

'You're loathsome,' Beverly said fiercely. 'I'm going to catch the next flight back to London. If I were you I'd take a long, hard look at myself. If you decide to come home, then we can discuss where we go from here.'

Beverly hailed a taxi and headed south. Steven walked aimlessly in the same direction. Like hell he would return to England. His only concern was to win back the trust of the Lynagh family.

He counted his money, realised that the dollars he had won at Westchester on the previous day would now come in useful, and booked himself into an hotel in mid-town Manhattan. The receptionist looked closely at Steven when he admitted that he possessed neither luggage nor credit card but accepted cash in advance for one night's accommodation.

Stretched out on his bed on the twenty-eighth floor, he analysed what he had to do. It was simply a business problem and he would apply the principles he had learned at Harvard. It was clear that the way back into the bosom of the Lynagh family lay with Joseph Lynagh. He was the key to his future.

The first point in his favour was that, until Beverly had made her unscheduled appearance, his stock with the

Lynaghs had been very high. Steven knew that Joe Lynagh liked him and he guessed that both Suzi's parents viewed him as their future son-in-law. There was no question that Suzi loved him. At the moment they all felt betrayed by him, but Steven calculated that, in their hearts, they wanted him to explain his conduct. It was just a matter of selling himself again, of overcoming their initial resistance. An essential marketing tactic, lovingly taught at Harvard, was to rubbish the opposition. The opposition in this case was Beverly.

As she settled into her seat for the long flight back to Heathrow, Beverly Shaw tried to still her rage. She asked herself how the all-consuming love she had once felt for her man could change to such hatred. It was his betrayal of her, so blatant and so calculated.

When Steven had telephoned her to tell her that he had changed his plan to return to Britain immediately after his examination, Beverly did not hide her disappointment.

'But, Steven, we'd planned a little celebration for you. And it's all Emma talks about, about her daddy and how he's coming home.'

'Don't make it worse, Bev. My friend, Charlie Tomlin, he's asked me time after time to visit his family. He wants to show me around. It's only a matter of a few days.'

'Well, I'm disappointed, but . . .' Beverly paused and changed tack. 'What about your results? Have you had them yet?'

'Not yet. Any moment.'

'Will they send them here?'

'Not unless I ask them to. I'll have them sent on to Charlie's place in New York. I'll call you as soon as I know anything.'

Beverly had known her husband was lying. The fear that

unsettled her stomach told her that something was wrong. It was the same emotion she'd experienced at the end of her first real love affair. She'd hardly been able to eat for a week. This time she would do something. She worried away at the problem for a couple of days and then made her decision.

She telephoned the Harvard Business School office, posed as Steven Shaw's sister and told them that she had to contact him as soon as possible. Their mother was seriously ill.

'Mr Shaw isn't on campus at the moment, ma'am,' said the friendly voice.

'Oh, that's right,' Beverly said, 'he's gone to New York. Do you have a forwarding address?'

'I'm afraid not. Our students have no obligation . . .'

'No, of course not. But Steven said he'd left an address with you. Where you were to send his results.'

'Well, we're not supposed—'

'Please, I'm his sister and I must talk to him about Mother.'

A few minutes later the kindly lady in the administration department of the Harvard Business School gave Beverly the address in New York of Mr and Mrs Joseph Lynagh.

Ten minutes later Beverly had booked herself on to the following day's British Airways flight to New York.

'I've got to see Steven urgently,' she told her mother, who was going to look after Emma. 'I just have to sort something out with him.' She refused to say more and Louise Seabrook wisely refrained from pressing her; but she guessed that something was seriously awry.

Awry. That was hardly the word for it, Beverly thought sadly, as she sipped at a glass of wine and looked blankly at the aircraft seat in front of her. As soon as she'd met Steven, she'd wanted him to herself; and she'd been determined to get him. And she'd done it by resorting to the oldest of tricks. He was right – she had deliberately got herself pregnant.

Aghast, Steven had suggested an abortion, or that the child be adopted, but Beverly had stood firm and told him that she was determined to have the child and keep it.

'Is this an ultimatum?' Steven asked. 'Get married or else?'

'No.' Beverly was far too subtle to issue an ultimatum. She would achieve her objective by playing on Steven's love for her. 'I love you and want to marry you but not if you feel you're being forced into it. I promise you I'd rather bring the baby up on my own than do that.' She took his hand and kissed it gently. 'No, my darling, no wedding bells unless you really want them. Of course,' she smiled at him, 'we could try living together, I suppose.'

'Babies cost money,' Steven said quietly, 'and you wouldn't be able to work for a while. How could I earn enough to keep the three of us?'

Beverly knew then that she'd got the man she wanted. 'Perhaps my parents will help. Do you want me to talk to them?' She knew her parents would fall in with her plans even more easily than had Steven.

Perhaps she had been too calculating by half and the Fates had taken their revenge. But Beverly consoled herself that she had done it all for love. She wished to God that she'd insisted on going to live in Harvard with Steven. Maybe she would have kept her man.

For nearly an hour Steven lay quietly in his room. Then he picked up the telephone and dialled the Lynaghs' number.

After many rings and just as he was on the brink of putting the receiver down, he heard Joe Lynagh announce himself.

'It's Steven here.'

'You probably want your things. They're packed and waiting in the hall. Where shall I send them?'

'I didn't ring about my things, Mr Lynagh. I just want an opportunity to explain myself to you and to Suzi.'

'I don't think she wants to hear anything from you. I can't believe what you've done to that poor girl,' Lynagh finished angrily.

'I love Suzi. I want to make things right. I want to explain. I got myself into a hell of a mess. Everything went so fast, out of control, and I just didn't have the courage to hold my hands up and tell the truth. I was so scared of losing Suzi. Please let me explain. I never had a real marriage with Beverly, it was a marriage of convenience and now it's over. Can I see you, Mr Lynagh?'

'My office at nine tomorrow.'

The call was terminated by Lynagh. Steven ran his hands through his hair, stretched and then smiled briefly. He had cleared the first hurdle; his foot was again in the Lynaghs' door. The sale could be clinched on the following day.

He went down to the bar and had a celebratory beer.

It was halfway through the first term of his final year at London University that Steven met Beverly Seabrook. He had seen her in the Students' Union bar on other occasions and asked a friend who she was. Tom, who was on the Students' Union Committee, knew everyone.

'She's not your type,' Tom said. 'Reading English, in with the theatrical set, darling.' He flapped his hand limply at Steven and grinned.

Steven looked across the room at her. Her oval-shaped face had a slight olive tinge to it and was framed by dark, curly hair; he noticed how animated she was, involved in several conversations at the same time.

'She is my type,' Steven said decisively. 'I'm going to buy her a drink.'

He strolled across the bar and edged into Beverly's group. She watched his approach with interest: he seemed a little more serious than most of the male students she knew and was certainly much more attractive. She smiled encouragingly at him and he said, 'Haven't we met somewhere before?'

Beverly giggled slightly at the corny opening gambit and then stopped as she saw his cheeks go pink.

He said, 'Not an opening remark that Oscar Wilde would be proud of but I wanted to meet you.'

Within a week the two were spending all their spare time together and had embarked on an affair that surprised both of them with the happiness which it brought to their lives. In comparison, Steven's other affairs had been mere passing fancies. Even the one with Araminta Macaulay. At the time he had been made miserable by Araminta's dismissive treatment and had vowed not to become involved with another woman for some time. But Beverly was different and he had fallen head over heels for her. She echoed his passionate feelings; they were delighted with each other, to the bemusement of both sets of friends.

Invited by Beverly to spend Easter with her family, he had been welcomed into their home on the outskirts of an appealing village in Surrey. This was commuter-land and Beverly's father was one of an army of people who took the train to and from London on every working day. Dick Seabrook was a partner in a large firm of accountants whose headquarters were near Victoria.

Despite another younger child who was at a boarding school, the Seabrook family was prosperous. Steven took note of the five-bedroomed detached house, part of a smart executive development, and the two cars in the double garage. This was middle-class suburban affluence, comfortable and taken for granted.

On learning that Steven played golf, Dick Seabrook took him off to his club on the Sunday morning, fixed him up with a set of borrowed clubs and was delighted when they hammered two of his friends.

In the bar afterwards Seabrook proudly introduced Steven to all his cronies as 'a friend of my daughter's, he plays off a six handicap'.

When they returned to the university, Beverly and Steven knew that they had to get into academic overdrive. Their final examinations were looming and it was a tense time for everyone.

Steven noticed that Beverly was rather withdrawn, nowhere near her usual level of ebullience, but he put it down to the imminence of their final examinations. In the flurry of the final revision, he hardly had time to worry. Then the exams were upon them both and, mercifully, soon over. Steven had few worries: the inevitable *post mortems* convinced him that he had performed adequately.

It was a few days after the final paper that Steven's world was thrown into disarray. Beverly suggested that they had a meal out to celebrate the end of their labours at the university and she chose a restaurant not far from the Euston Road. It specialised in English cuisine and made great play of such basic dishes as sausages and mash, Lancashire hotpot and roast beef. Simple food but far from simple prices.

Over the coffee, Beverly had shattered his optimistic world by announcing that she was pregnant. He had wondered whether she had deliberately tried to conceive in order to blackmail him into marriage. But that wasn't Beverly's style.

Steven remembered how she had told him that, after the initial shock, her parents had proclaimed themselves in favour of a marriage as soon as it could be arranged.

They were upset. They had envisaged their daughter getting married one day, but at a proper wedding, a joyous occasion for all their friends and relations. But at least Beverly wanted marriage. She would abide by the conventions of her parents rather than embracing the more liberal ideas of the mid-seventies generation.

Dick and Louise Seabrook discussed the problem at length and, as anticipated by Beverly, they devised an attractive solution for Steven and their daughter. After all, he was a fine young man, intelligent and ambitious, and a super golfer. They would make a delightful couple.

Mr Seabrook took the two young lovers to a wine bar but stopped short of ordering champagne. It wasn't appropriate.

When they had settled in their seats, Seabrook, cheerful and pragmatic, said, 'This isn't a time for recriminations or any nonsense like that.' He filled up their glasses with wine. 'So, before you two decide anything let's be practical. You need somewhere to live and you, Steven, need a job. First of all, we've got room for you in our home.'

As Steven began to speak he held up his hand and said, 'Don't worry, we don't want you under our feet and you won't want us cramping your style. We'll make a little flat for you, it'll be easy enough to do. You'll be independent.'

It was difficult to take any interest in food but Steven ate some of his salmon paté. He noticed that Beverly hadn't touched her salad.

Seabrook ordered another bottle of wine and said, 'As for a job, Steven, there are some vacancies in my firm for trainee accountants. Again, don't worry, we'll hardly see each other and I wouldn't even suggest it if I didn't know you to be exactly the right material for our firm. This isn't nepotism, I assure you, it's self-interest on several levels. In three years you'll be qualified and then it's up to you what you do.'

After a good swig at his glass of wine, Dick Seabrook leaned back, satisfied with the package he had offered. Beverly was looking expectantly at Steven, who gazed across the table at father and daughter. He felt trapped, even though he was sure he loved Beverly. But he didn't want to get married yet. There was so much to do and see, he hadn't even started yet. But it would be difficult to desert her, to walk away from his responsibilities. Yes, he was trapped all right, especially by the decent man opposite him. If only he had assumed the role of an outraged father, then he might have had the strength to reject both him and his daughter. It was clever of him to be so sympathetic, to offer so much support. But Steven knew that the implication was clear enough. If he accepted the package, it would have to include marriage.

'I don't know what to say, Mr Seabrook,' Steven began slowly. 'You're being more than kind. I'm sure Beverly and I can make a go of it—'

'I wouldn't be sitting here, if I didn't think that,' Seabrook interrupted eagerly. 'We like you and trust you and I'm well aware of Beverly's feelings for you.' He smiled at both of them and pressed his daughter's hand tenderly.

Steven had an uneasy feeling that he'd been outmanoeuvred by Seabrook, but he reviewed the practicalities of his situation. He was being offered a home and a job and, when the baby arrived, Beverly's mother would be on hand to help out. What was the alternative? Severe emotional stress, recriminations and some harsh financial problems.

With a deep breath and a smile Steven spoke directly to Beverly. 'If you'll still have me, I would like to marry you. Will you make an honest man of me?'

Beverly hugged and kissed him and Dick Seabrook

ordered a bottle of champagne. Thank God, he thought to himself. He was happy for his beloved daughter and had no doubts about her handsome young husband-to-be. One of the first things to do was to propose him for membership of the golf club. With someone who could hit a golf ball as well as Steven he ought to be able to win the summer foursomes at last.

# Chapter Three

At five minutes to nine Steven walked through the doors of a skyscraper office block not far from his hotel on Fifth Avenue. It housed Joseph Lynagh's law firm and several other companies.

To Steven's surprise the receptionist led him, not to the lift, but along a corridor to the back of the building and through a carved wooden door.

'The senior partners work in here,' the receptionist said. 'It's a town house, late nineteenth-century vintage.'

A smartly dressed, middle-aged lady took Steven into her charge in the hallway, the walls of which were panelled in dark wood. She led him up a wide and curving staircase into Joseph Lynagh's office.

Steven registered first the scale of the room. Lynagh, seated behind a vast antique desk, was speaking on the telephone and waved him towards a Chesterfield sofa. A chandelier dangled from the ceiling on which an extravagant scene from Greek mythology had been painted. Steven's bag sat ominously on the carpet near the door.

Lynagh put the telephone down.

'I can give you a few minutes. For Suzi's sake. No recriminations, but if I smell bullshit, you're outta here. OK?'

With a nod Steven acknowledged the conditions and made his pitch.

'I married Beverly under duress. She became pregnant when we were in our final year at university. I had no money and I was offered an easy way out by her father. A job and a home with the Seabrook family.'

Steven paused for a moment and then said, 'Above all, it was my parents' wish that I faced up to my responsibilities, that I fronted up and was a proper father to our baby.'

'You still have those responsibilities.'

'Yes and I'll do my best to discharge them but I can't go on with this sham of a marriage. It's crucifying me. I realised how false it all was when I fell in love with Suzi.'

Hoping for some sign that he was putting his message over to Lynagh, Steven looked earnestly at the lawyer, who gazed sombrely back.

'But you were a married man, Steven, with a child. How could you play with the emotions of another woman? It wasn't right.'

'No, sir. And I wouldn't have got so deeply enmeshed if I'd had a real marriage. These things happen. I fell in love. And the right moment to own up to Suzi about my marriage never came.'

Steven risked a short smile.

'Have you talked to your wife about a divorce?' Lynagh asked and Steven knew he was winning.

'I've asked Beverly for a divorce and she's promised to be as obstructive as possible. It's as simple as that.'

Both men were silent for several moments and then Lynagh asked Steven to wait in the outer office for a couple of minutes. The cheerful lady who was Lynagh's secretary told him how much she loved England and then he was beckoned back by Joseph Lynagh.

'First things first, Steven. My daughter has agreed to talk to you. It's her life, after all. I'll have my secretary book you into the Belvedere for lunch. On my account. Be there at one.'

For the first time during their meeting Lynagh smiled at Steven. The older man stood up, shook his hand and wished him luck.

Suzi was determined to maintain a patina of cool reserve when she met Steven. Whatever her father said, Steven had to make his peace with her and convince her of his love. She knew that she looked unnaturally pale, even though she had paid unusual attention to her make-up and had applied blusher to her cheeks.

As soon as she saw Steven across the restaurant her resolution began to weaken. He looked unnaturally hesitant as he rose to greet her and she wanted to reach out and comfort him.

By the time that they had picked at their first courses and sent them away mostly uneaten the atmosphere had warmed considerably. Steven pursued the same theme as he had with Joseph Lynagh. Halfway through the main course they were chatting about Steven's prospects of securing a quick divorce.

Steven realised, with joyful relief, that he had carried the day. They went back to his hotel and made love.

After Suzi left, he fell into a deep and contented sleep and was eventually awoken by the buzz of the telephone.

'Darling, it's me,' said Suzi. 'Did I wake you? Sorry, but it's important. Can you meet Daddy again? Tomorrow at nine o'clock? It's getting to be a habit, isn't it?'

Suzi went on to tell him that everything was going to be all right, that her father would resolve everything. And, by the way, he had arranged to pay Steven's hotel bill.

Once again seated in the hotel bar, Steven ordered a cocktail and asked the barman to put it on his bill; or rather on Joe Lynagh's bill. By using the well-proved methods of the Harvard Business School – analysis and negotiation – he had insinuated himself back into the affections of the Lynagh family. He should now have no difficulty in closing the sale, once the problem of Beverly was resolved. That should be easy for a top lawyer like Lynagh.

His thoughts turned to the woman who had encouraged him to seek a place at the Harvard Business School: the beautiful Clare Sims. Clare had changed his life.

When Steven and Beverly returned from their honeymoon, their flat within the Seabrook home was almost finished. The room over the garage had been converted into a large bed-sitting room with a small kitchen in one corner and a separate bathroom. Fortunately the Seabrooks' bedroom was on the other side of the house, but the young couple's only access to their flat was through the main door of the house. From the start Steven felt constricted, his comings and goings apparent to his parents-in-law.

On the first Monday in September Steven began his job at Dick Seabrook's accountancy firm. He travelled to Victoria with his father-in-law and home with him at night. That became the pattern of his days, interrupted by games of golf at the weekend.

Steven found the accountancy work easy and repetitive; he realised that being a trainee amounted to a gentle form of slave labour. He welcomed the breaks in his routine when he visited clients of the firm as a junior member of the audit team. The other lulls in his monotonous existence came when Beverly travelled to London and they saw a play or a film.

Emma Louise was born in the early part of February and, when Beverly brought her home from the hospital, the Seabrook household was thrown into turmoil. Friends and relations, including Steven's parents, arrived in numbers to see the baby, and Dick Seabrook, as proud a grandparent as there could be, always had a bottle of champagne in readiness to celebrate the birth. Steven received the congratulations which were offered with aplomb but wondered what all the fuss was about; Beverly seemed to have orchestrated the event on her own.

Emma was a pretty baby and although Steven's paternal feelings were meagre, he understood Beverly's deep-seated maternal instincts. They were reinforced by those of Louise Seabrook whose bonds with her daughter and granddaughter grew ever stronger. They spent much of their time together, each delighted by the other's company.

As winter turned into spring Steven felt more and more excluded, an outsider within his own family whose main focus of interest was the baby Emma.

He spent more time at the golf club and his handicap moved down to three. He was much in demand for club matches and local amateur tournaments and remained a regular partner of Dick Seabrook's in weekend fourball games.

When spring arrived and the hours of daylight increased, Steven began to visit the club in the early evening to practise. That was how he met Clare Sims.

He was working on his putting, that infuriating game within a game. He had given himself a simple exercise. He placed ten balls around a hole at a distance of four feet and had to putt them all. If he missed he had to start again from scratch.

From the verandah Clare Sims had been watching him for several minutes. She knew that he was one of the club's better golfers but that was of secondary interest. He was attractive, he had a super body. As he crouched over his putter, she gazed at him. What a lovely bum, I'd love to get my hands on that, she thought.

Starting his third attempt to hole the ten putts, Steven became conscious of a figure on the edge of the green. He knew Clare by sight. She was far and away the most attractive woman in the club. His friends all fancied her but, as far as he knew, none of them had propositioned her. She was fine to fantasise about but her self-possessed elegance was rather frightening. Steven smiled politely at her and addressed another putt.

'I'm looking for a partner for the mixed foursomes next week,' she said in her plummy accent. 'I'm Clare Sims. I think you and I would make a dangerous pair. How about it?' She arched one eyebrow at him.

'That's one way of putting it,' he replied. 'What do you play off?' As she strolled towards him, Steven appraised her figure. She was slender but had surprisingly large breasts.

'I've just gone down to twelve,' she said. 'Is that OK? Not too much of a hacker for you, I hope?'

'Not at all. Thank you for asking me. I'll see you next Saturday.'

A few days later Steven mentioned his golfing date to his father-in-law.

'The lovely Clare,' Seabrook said. 'Don't be deceived by her film star looks. She's very bright indeed. Was a stockbroker, got a golden handshake and multiplied it. Now she writes about the financial markets for newspapers and magazines. Divorced of course. She's the sort of person you should get to know, Steven. But not too well.'

Seabrook smiled at him but Steven heard a warning in his voice.

The mixed foursomes competition took place on Saturday afternoon and attracted a crowded field which included Dick Seabrook. Steven was grateful that he hadn't been drawn to play in the same group as his father-in-law; he would be free to enjoy Clare's charms without measuring every phrase and modulating every smile.

After playing the first hole Steven realised that Clare was a competent golfer. She had a slow and rhythmic swing which produced an unexpected amount of power. She was also as competitive as he was. They were well matched.

While their opponents, both off high handicaps, zig-zagged from one area of rough to another, Steven had time to chat at length to Clare.

She was self-derogatory about her job. 'I made sure I kept in touch with all my contacts in the City. For one thing I was and still am an active investor in the market and I needed to keep my finger on the pulse.'

She hit a shot down the middle of the fairway to the fringe of the green. 'You would be amazed, Steven, at what supposedly sophisticated businessmen are prepared to tell over a long lunch. Directors of public companies, partners in major stockbroking firms, merchant bankers.' She looked provocatively at Steven and added, 'Especially when they think there's something extra-curricular for them after-wards.'

Steven chipped their ball to within a few inches of the hole and asked quietly, 'And is there?' Clare walked away to mark their ball and didn't answer.

Later in the round Clare explained how she'd drifted into financial journalism. 'I started writing for one of those stock market tips magazines and then I did a few pieces for one of the Sunday papers. It all took off from there. It suits me because I work when I want to work. But the most important thing is that I'm paid to try and keep on an inside track in the City. Naturally I keep the best informa-tion for myself, not for my readers.'

'Presumably if they all charged in, they'd spoil the mar-ket,' Steven said, remembering a part of his university course which had covered the workings of the stock market.

'Exactly. The City's a small world where only the insiders make big money.'

They won the competition by several shots and each received a set of cut glasses: whisky tumblers for Steven and wine glasses for his partner.

As the male half of the victorious partnership, Steven braced himself to make the traditional speech of thanks. Sensibly, he confined himself to complimenting everyone concerned with the organisation of the event and to extolling the skills of his partner.

The conclusion of the prize giving was the signal for the members to begin the really enjoyable part of their day. To most of them the golf was secondary to the entertainment available in the bar.

Clare made her way through the scrum and reappeared with two bottles of champagne. Dick Seabrook was one of several who drank to the health of the mixed foursomes' winners. He kissed Clare on the cheek and pumped Steven's hand enthusiastically and asked him if he needed a lift home in his car.

'Louise and I are out to dinner so I thought you'd like to get home to Beverly,' Seabrook said.

Steven felt a gentle tap on his ankle. It must have come from Clare's foot since she was standing beside him.

'No thanks, Dick,' Steven replied, 'I'll have a couple more drinks and then get a lift from one of the boys. Tell Beverly not to worry. A little celebration, that's all.'

Shortly afterwards Clare said quietly in his ear, 'I'm going to slip away in a moment. Meet me in the car park. It's a white Mercedes.'

As they left the car park Clare said, 'I think it's appropriate for the winners to have a final drink together, don't you?'

Steven smiled his agreement and, after a short drive along country lanes, they arrived at Clare's home. It was a sprawling one-storey building of whitewashed brick and glass and the interior was designed in the same effective way. The plain brick walls were enlivened by richly patterned rugs and by an eclectic choice of paintings.

The living room was massive with a wall of glass overlooking a long stretch of lawn scattered with trees. Steven could just see a swimming pool in one corner.

'Make yourself at home,' Clare said. 'I'll organise some drinks.'

Steven wandered around the room to look at the paintings. He didn't recognise many of the names of the artists but realised that Clare was primarily a collector of twentieth-century art.

'One of my hobbies,' she said, as she entered the room with a bottle of champagne in one hand and two glasses in the other. 'I look for up-and-coming painters, but I've also got some that I bought as investments. Jasper Johns, Warhol, Hockney, you know the sort of thing.'

Steven didn't, but nodded as if he did and offered to open the champagne. His father-in-law had showed him how to do it without spilling a drop.

'Here's to us,' Clare said and they clinked glasses.

She stayed close to him, looked into his eyes and said, 'I didn't ask you here to show you my paintings. Let's take the fizz into my bedroom.' She took his hand and, laughing, turned and said, 'Let's see whether your holing out technique is as good there as on the golf course.'

Steven found himself hugely excited by her cheerful approach to sex. He couldn't hold back for long, quickly entered her and came sooner than he wished. He felt selfish but Clare understood. She smiled as he explored her body with his hands and mouth. As he gently nipped the

inside of her thighs with his teeth, she encouraged him:
'Harder, darling, bite harder.' She turned over and he bit
her buttocks while she groaned with pleasure. It was some
time before he lost himself inside her for the second time.

He wasn't keen on being awarded points but grinned
when Clare murmured, 'Nineteen exemplary holes.' They
lay in each other's arms, their bodies sticky from their exer-
tions.

'So you like some pain with your pleasure, do you?'
Steven asked tentatively.

'They always go together as far as I'm concerned, darling. As long as the bruises don't show.'

She took him to within a few hundred yards of his home
in her other car, a small and unostentatious saloon. Steven,
as he answered Beverly's questions about the golf and about
his partner, felt a faint spasm of guilt. But it was tempered
by a deeper feeling of satisfaction and of pleasure.

That night he made love to Beverly with fervour, but it
was Clare's body in his mind's eye.

During the next few months Steven made love to Clare on
many occasions. At first tentative in inflicting pain on his
lover, Steven soon began to join in the many variations
with enthusiasm. They rarely met at Clare's house. They
were both aware of the proximity of Steven's own home
but, above all, of their golf club, a hothouse of rumour, gossip and innuendo. It was necessary to be discreet and they
met on many occasions at Clare's apartment in London. It
was close to Regent's Park and Steven was able to scamper
up there in his lunch hour or after work.

It was on such an occasion that Clare, as she watched
him dressing, said, 'You're bored, aren't you?'

Startled, Steven replied, 'Not with you, I'm not.'

'No, darling, that goes without saying. You're bored with

your job, with your routine existence. Up and down on the train with your father-in-law every working day. Up and down with Beverly occasionally. You want more from life, don't you?'

'Yes, but at the moment I've got you.'

'Quite. But you don't want to be a boring accountant. It's a waste of your talents. I could open one or two doors in the City, if you like. Arrange some interviews.'

'I'd be interested to meet some of your old flames, Clare. We could compare notes. I can just imagine some smooth City bastard saying "Clare, oh yes, one of the best blow-jobs in town, old chap."' Steven affected a strangulated posh accent.

'Don't be childish, Steven, those people are always on the look-out for talent.'

'I'll bet,' he replied drily. 'No, I'm not cut out for the City, it's not my scene at all.'

'There's a lot of money to be made there, as I well know. That's what you want, don't you?'

'You know I do, but not by pushing paper around a desk.'

'I've another suggestion for you in that case, a longer-term one. You're interested in business, so why not go to the Harvard Business school? Their Business Administration course is one of the best in the world. It has real prestige.'

'How long does it take?'

'Two years.'

'It must be tough to get a place there.'

'It is but it's easier when you know who to talk to. I can help you there, darling. I'll speak to a friend of mine.'

'Hang on,' Steven said, 'this is going too fast for me. What about money, how do I pay for it all? What about Bev? Can I take her and the baby?'

'You'll have to get a grant. There are plenty on offer and you'll get one. There's also a loan scheme, if you need it. As for Beverly, you can certainly take her and the baby but why bother? You'll be coming home in the vacations and she's in the bosom of her family, after all.'

Staring out of the bedroom window at the park, Steven said, 'What d'you think? Should I have a go?'

'You know you should,' Clare stated. 'Harvard is all about money, that's their culture. It'll suit you down to the ground.'

She didn't want to lose Steven but sensed his frustration. He was capable of so much and she was determined to help him realise himself.

Steven knew that his lover was right on all fronts. Such a plan would also enable him to escape from the Seabrook household. Despite their having a separate flat, they were far from enjoying real independence and Steven felt that he was little more than a lodger. Beverly seemed to spend more time with her mother in the main part of the house than she did in their flat. Her parents were pleasant people but their proximity inhibited Steven; he felt as if he were under constant review. He almost expected a formal written report from them every few months.

Of course, he was fond of Beverly and their baby and didn't want to desert them, even for a few months at a time. But an MBA from Harvard would give him a great advantage in the future. It would benefit them all. After a term or two he could take them both with him to Boston.

On the Friday evening Steven took Beverly to a local restaurant. Although he could ill afford the treat, he wanted to discuss his plans in a congenial atmosphere, away from the constrictions of the Seabrook home.

As the first course was taken away Steven said casually, 'I've been looking at one or two business courses recently.

I'm not sure I can go through with this accountancy training. More than two years to go and getting more tedious every day. How would your father take it, d'you think, if I left his firm?'

'He'd be extremely upset, you know how keen he is for you to do well.'

'There are other ways of doing well apart from being an accountant.'

'I dare say, Steven,' said Beverly sharply, 'but Daddy had to pull strings to get you into the firm.'

'Come off it, Beverly, it suited him. It was all part of the package, wasn't it? A job and a flat and marriage to his daughter. All neat and under control.'

'What a cynical way of looking at things.'

'Realistic, I'd call it. Anyway, let's get to the point. I've got my eye on the Harvard Business School, their MBA is the best in the world.'

'What's wrong with an MBA from a British university?'

'There's no comparison. The Harvard Business School is *the* place, it can open so many doors for me.'

'So could accountancy.'

'I don't want to be an accountant,' Steven said harshly. 'There's more to life than the seven-thirty train to Victoria every day and the golf club dance.'

'You've made up your mind already, haven't you?' Beverly said accusingly, 'without any thought about me and the baby.'

'That's unfair, Beverly. The reason we're sitting here is to discuss it.'

Beverly fiddled with her wine glass and a waiter stepped forward and refilled it.

'I wouldn't do anything as important without your agreement,' Steven lied. 'But Harvard is the way forward for me, accountancy isn't.'

'How do you expect to pay for everything? What about Emma and me? Do we have any part in your plans or are you just going to abandon us?' Although the questions came challengingly from Beverly's lips she knew that she didn't want to exchange the comforts of her Surrey home for the less agreeable surroundings of a university campus.

'There are plenty of grants and we'll survive somehow,' Steven replied, sensing his wife's uncertainties about uprooting herself even on a temporary basis. 'Assuming I get on the course, I'll settle in first and you can join me later. You'll love it, it'll be good for both of us.'

Steven Shaw left London Heathrow for Boston early in September. Beverly's parents, who had driven them all to the airport to see him off, had withdrawn to a discreet distance while he made his farewells to his wife, their daughter clutched in her arms.

They kissed and hugged each other awkwardly with Emma balanced on Beverly's hip, gurgling and blowing bubbles.

'You will write and telephone, won't you, Steven?' Beverly said anxiously. 'We'll miss you terribly.'

'I'm only away for a few weeks,' Steven replied. 'No sooner gone than it'll be Christmas and I'll be back.'

He kissed them both once more, gulped back his emotion and, using the excuse that he hated farewells, walked away towards the passport control barrier. Steven turned and waved as he went through and felt an unsettling flutter of loss as he saw Emma, coached by Beverly, waving her pudgy arm in his direction.

Then he was through into the departure lounge. In those mundane surroundings, he was surprised when he felt a decisive lift in his spirits. He was free again, liberated from the confines of his job and the constraints of his

domestic life, at large to face the challenge represented by
the Harvard Business School. He looked ahead with confidence to the day when he would reap its rewards.

The euphoria stayed with Steven even through the flight
to Boston and for several days afterwards while he found
his way around the campus and the surrounding area.

Harvard was sedate after the incessant noise and hurly-
burly of London. On his first day there, after settling into
his small and spartan room, Steven strolled along the tree-
lined avenues between the stately brick buildings. He
relished the atmosphere. Concentrated into a small area, it
was reminiscent of Oxford or Cambridge rather than the
scattered nature of his old university in London. This was
the real thing. He was going to be happy here.

In gentle sunshine he walked on to North Harvard
Street and crossed the road to look at the football stadium.
It was an impressive structure with steeply raked seating.
Many soccer clubs in Britain would have been thrilled to
play in such a setting, but the ground was used only a few
times a year for college football, that peculiarly American
ritual which attracts the same degree of devotion as soccer
in Brazil or Italy.

Near the stadium he saw that there was an indoor running track and some tennis courts. He need not fear for his
fitness.

On the Anderson Bridge he stopped and looked back at
the fine buildings, bathed in early evening sunshine. To
his left were the steep roofs of the Weld boathouse and
Steven watched a rowing eight coast under the bridge
below him. As they feathered their oars in leisurely fashion,
he glanced at the emblems painted on their blades. He
looked again in disbelief. Dollar signs on the oars. That was
the half-satirical, half-serious motif of the Harvard Business
School.

What had his lover, Clare, said about the place? 'Harvard's about money, that's their culture': that was it.

Steven Shaw knew that she was right, and he knew that he was in the right place.

# Chapter Four

When Steven arrived at Joe Lynagh's office the day after making it up with Suzi, Joe greeted him in his accustomed cheerful way. Coffee was already laid out on one of the antique tables and the two men sat opposite each other in deep bucket armchairs.

'Now, Steven, I need some information about Beverly and her family. I'm going to try to persuade her not to be awkward. It'll be better, I think, if I try and quarterback this, not you. I can keep the emotions and the recriminations out of it. I can talk business to her and her father.'

'You're being very kind—'

'Practical. Suzi's happiness is at stake and, incidentally, yours.' Lynagh smiled widely and took the sting out of the remark. 'First off, tell me about Beverly's father. You say he's a partner in a significant firm of accountants. With a bit of luck, we'll find some connection with my firm. We do a lot of business in London. All we need is an edge, a lever we can use against him and, therefore, his daughter. I expect they taught you all of that at Harvard.' Not half, thought Steven.

On instructions from Lynagh, Steven reported back to his office just before lunch.

'We got lucky,' Lynagh said. 'We've found our lever. One of our clients here in New York is a multinational in the leisure business. All sorts of stuff, golf clubs, motorcycles, skis, parking meters, stadium construction, you name it. Well, Dick Seabrook's firm does the accounts for their UK operation. It's a big client for him.'

Lynagh leaned forward eagerly. 'Business is all about exerting the right amount of pressure at the right time. I'll mention our mutual client and then sell him on the idea that it's in his daughter's best long-term interests to let you go. And of course we'll make a settlement on your daughter, for her education and so on.'

'Darling Emma,' Steven said. 'I'll miss her so. She's . . .' His voice tailed off theatrically and he put his head in his hands.

'I'm sorry, Steven.' Lynagh's voice was gruff with emotion. 'But we'll take care of her. We'll put a good sum in trust for her. You and Suzi will have your own children one day.'

Dick Seabrook was tidying his desk before leaving the office for the day, when the telephone rang. He sighed wearily. He had spent a testing day with some clients in the City and wanted to get off home to see how his daughter was faring. On the previous evening Beverly had poured out all her anger and resentment at the way her husband had betrayed her. He was getting too old for all this drama.

Seabrook was at once disarmed by the warm American tones of the man who was calling him from New York, but he went on the defensive as soon as the man announced himself as Joseph Lynagh.

For several minutes, however, Seabrook was hardly permitted the chance of more than a 'yes' or a 'no' or a murmur of agreement, as Lynagh expounded the problem which faced them all and suggested its solution.

When their conversation ended, Seabrook sat still for some time and stared blankly out of his office window. He realised that he had committed himself to help the persuasive Mr Lynagh. If he were not careful he would be ground between the logical force of Lynagh's arguments, which were reinforced by thinly veiled threats to the well-being of Seabrook's business, and his daughter's fiercely expressed desire for revenge on Steven.

It was no contest. Beverly had to be persuaded to let go of Steven. He hoped that the offer of a settlement of £100,000 on Emma would prove to be the most potent of arguments.

A straightforward man, with no palate for dissembling, Seabrook told his daughter of Joseph Lynagh's proposals as soon as he got home that evening.

'Whatever you may feel now,' he concluded, 'it's the best and most practical solution. Agree to a divorce, take the money for Emma, and get on with your life.'

'I'll never forgive that deceitful bastard,' Beverly replied.

'You will, in time. Life's too short to harbour feelings of revenge.'

'I hope he realises that he'll have no access to Emma. I don't want him anywhere near her.'

As soon as she said that, Seabrook knew that Lynagh had won the day. 'We'll make that clear to him,' he said with a sigh of relief.

After a few days, Steven was received back into the Lynagh household. Betty Lynagh may have been guarded in her attitude towards him but the warmth of Joe Lynagh's welcome more than made up for her reserve.

When he received the news that Beverly had agreed to a divorce, Lynagh marked the occasion by opening some bottles of vintage champagne and said that he was working on the problem of speeding up the formal processes.

'I know you two don't want to hang around for a couple of years and I may have a solution. Quicker even than going to Reno. That takes several weeks, after all. No, I think that one of our associates down in Tijuana can do the trick.'

The trick was turned in no more than a week, much to Joe Lynagh's delight.

'It's amazing what you can do by putting the right amount of money in the right hands,' he said. 'Steven, you can come into the office tomorrow and sign the papers. Then you'll be a free man again.'

'Not for long,' Suzi said, as she planted a proprietary kiss on Steven's cheek.

As far as Steven knew, his parents were unaware that his marriage to Beverly was about to be unceremoniously ended, although he guessed that one of the Seabrook family might have contacted them. They did not possess a telephone and Steven did not want to duck the issue by telling them the news by letter, or even telegram. His solution was to telephone his father at his local pub; on the dot at six o'clock every evening Bill Shaw ordered his first pint of beer.

After some delay, he heard his father say a hesitant hello into the receiver. Steven could hear the usual noises of an English pub: shouted greetings, the clink of glasses. For a moment he had a sharp feeling of nostalgia for his home.

'Hello, Dad, it's Steven. I've got some news for you.' He told his father about the forthcoming divorce and that he was planning to marry Suzi Lynagh in the next few months or so. He was deliberately vague about a date. 'It'll be a quiet ceremony, as you can imagine,' Steven lied. 'In and out in five minutes, you know how it is over here.'

He said that his mother could make a call to his hotel and reverse the charges.

'No, she won't do that, son. You know her. She'll write to you, I expect.'

'I'll give you an address,' Steven said but Bill Shaw had already said goodbye and replaced the receiver.

After the date for the wedding was settled, one of Steven's problems was to explain his parents' absence from the celebration. He had no intention of inviting anyone from England and certainly not his parents. He told himself that they would be out of their depth socially but he couldn't bear the prospect of the embarrassment they would cause him.

To his great relief the Lynaghs didn't question his story that his father was reluctant to travel to the wedding because of his uncertain health and that his mother would not leave him, even for a few days. Joseph Lynagh offered to fly them over in first-class seats but Steven said that the stress and the excitement might be too much for his father. It would be better if he took his bride to see them as soon as it could be arranged.

Two days before the wedding Steven sent his parents a telegram to tell them that he and Suzi were getting married quietly in New York.

It was over two years before Steven again set foot in Britain.

The Lynaghs had dreamed of a great society wedding for their daughter at the magnificent St Patrick's Cathedral on Fifth Avenue, but Steven's status as a divorcé and a non-Catholic forbade it. Instead the couple were married at a civil ceremony, although a Catholic priest was present to give his blessing. No doubt a suitable donation had been made to the priest's church.

The reception at the Plaza Athénée was sumptuous and the Lynagh family, their friends and business associates were there in force. Steven invited a select few friends from Harvard and Charlie Tomlin was his best man.

When he tried to calculate how much the whole affair

had cost his father-in-law, Steven gave up because it made him feel nervous.

The honeymoon, one of the many gifts they received from Joe and Betty Lynagh, probably cost just as much. It encompassed a month-long tour of Europe and took them from one five-star hotel to another around the capitals and resorts of the continent. Steven kept them away from London. His argument was that any dutiful visits to friends and relatives were to be avoided. This was their time together and he would show Suzi the great city on other occasions.

When they returned to New York their rented apartment, on the Upper East Side and not far from the Lynagh home, had been refurbished. The starting salary which Joe Lynagh had arranged for Steven was generous enough to enable him to pay the considerable rent without strain. It was all a far cry from a flat in the Surrey suburbs and the endless drudgery of the commuter's life.

# Chapter Five

Scott Thomson was one of the founders of a firm which had built up an excellent reputation in the business consultancy field. He had opposed the take-over by Joe Lynagh but, an honest man, he admitted that their association had increased his turnover and profit dramatically. The lawyer had a knack for finding business and providing high-level contacts in large companies.

The two men were poles apart in looks and manner. Lynagh was square and feisty whereas Thomson was tall and spare of frame, with thin sandy hair atop a narrow face; his speech was considered, almost hesitant.

The arrival of a Harvard Business School hot-shot in the company would not normally have concerned its Chief Executive. After all, Thomson had been a Rhodes Scholar at Oxford University and done postgraduate work at Princeton. He felt intellectually secure.

Nevertheless, the presence of Steven Shaw made him uneasy. He was now under the eye of a member of the Lynagh family, someone who might even be regarded as his potential successor. Not only that but his new employee's salary was within spitting distance of his own.

Steven registered his boss's aloofness and tried to ignore it.

A telephone call from Joe Lynagh a few months later was to release both Scott Thomson and Steven Shaw from their uncomfortable relationship. Lynagh asked his son-in-law to drop into his office for a few minutes.

'What do you know about Sam Rhodes?' asked Lynagh without preamble.

'Amateur champion. Finished high in the Masters. Fine golfer.'

'Golf's next superstar,' Lynagh said emphatically. 'He's coming here for lunch tomorrow. I want you to meet him.'

'I'd love to meet him, but what's he doing here?'

'His father is a client of ours. Young Sam needs some advice. Should he turn pro or leave it for a while? His father wants him to hang on until next year so that he can play for the old country in the Walker Cup. It's at St Andrews. The reason I'd like you there is because you're young and you know about sport. Maybe he'll relate to you and that'll be helpful.'

'I suppose Sam fancies the professional game and all the money he might make.'

'Not *might* make, Steven. It's guaranteed. There've been agents beating on his door for over a year and talking telephone numbers to him. Of course, he doesn't trust any of 'em. One and all, they're shysters and con-men, and those are the good ones.'

'So where do we come in?'

Lynagh handed him a list of names and telephone numbers. 'Here are some of the big players in the sports business. Manufacturers of golf clubs, clothing, the people who put their names on the pros' golf bags and visors, car makers, airlines, the camera people. I want you to drop everything – don't worry, I'll square it with Thomson – and research the market for Sam Rhodes. What's his value? What's he worth, standing on the first tee as a pro at the Greater Milwaukee Open or whatever? Talk to the people on that list and let's have some projections for the boy tomorrow. And remember, Steven, golf needs someone like Sam Rhodes, it needs an American star, it's waiting for someone as marketable as he is.'

'As long as he's a winner.'

'He's a winner, all right.'

On the following day, having spent several hours soliciting opinions about the fees on offer for professional sportsmen's endorsements, Steven put all his figures together and went through them with Lynagh.

After half an hour in the company of Sam Rhodes, Steven revised the figures upwards by a conservative 25 per cent. Although he was only in his early twenties, Rhodes already had a presence that marked him out as someone special. It was partly his looks. The angular planes of his features signalled strength and determination. Below a straight nose, Rhodes had a generous mouth with dazzling white and perfectly spaced teeth. Deep-blue eyes looked expectantly out at the world and his square face was crowned with thick black hair.

He had the perfect physique for golf and looked fit enough to be an Olympic champion. Steven could picture him modelling all the gear: shirts and sweaters, trousers, sunglasses. He was a natural, the women would love him.

Above all, Rhodes was articulate and had an effortless charm which was abetted in no small way by his slight Southern drawl.

The man was a formidable package and Steven warmed to him from the outset. No wonder Lynagh had spoken of him as the star for whom golf longed. Any professional sport would have fallen over itself for such a talent.

While they ordered their lunch at a restaurant near the office, Rhodes summarised his background. His family originally came from Georgia, which accounted for his accent, and he had just finished his final year at the University of Texas. He had won the National Collegiate Championship and then the American Amateur.

'Why the University of Texas?' Lynagh asked. 'As I recall it, your father was at the University of Georgia.'

'It was all to do with golf. There's a great golf teacher at Texas and my dad also thought that those Texas golf courses would make me more adaptable. It's so windy out there, you've got to learn to improvise, hit different kinds of shots.'

'It's like playing links golf, I suppose,' said Steven.

'I guess,' Rhodes replied, as he sipped his glass of water, 'and that brings me back to the Walker Cup. It's over a year away, at St Andrews, the home of golf, and I can't decide whether to hang on and play in it or turn pro.'

'I gather that you've decided to make golf your career,' Steven said.

Rhodes nodded and Steven continued. 'So why not get on with it? You've won the Amateur and that's much more important than the Walker Cup. You've done what Bobby Jones and other great players did. The Walker Cup would only be a footnote to your career. Why not aim to be with the big boys in the American Ryder Cup team in three years' time? You could do it.'

With a modest shake of his head, Rhodes said, 'I don't know about that, Steven, but I agree your point about getting on with my profession. Do it sooner rather than later. It's those agents and business managers that worry me and that's mainly why I'm here talking to you. Several of them have made serious pitches to represent me and quite frankly I didn't take to any of them.'

'They promised you the earth, no doubt,' Lynagh said with a laugh.

'The earth, the moon and the stars. And it's money,

money, money with them. Sure, I want good contracts, I'm interested in the rewards but what I'm interested in first and foremost is having a good career in the game, pacing myself and trying to win a major championship.'

The three men discussed the various agents who had approached Rhodes, and Steven summarised the results of his own researches into the young golfer's value as a professional.

'It seems to me,' Steven concluded, 'that you'd be worth a minimum of half a million dollars in endorsement fees during your first year as a pro. If you start winning tournaments, a lot more.'

'Well, it'll be interesting to hear what Don Greenberg has to say.' Rhodes glanced at his watch. 'He's the best of the bunch and I'm due at his office in twenty minutes. He looks after a lot of golfers. That's what worries me because I don't want to be just one of the herd.'

'We'll check him out for you,' Lynagh offered.

When he returned to his apartment that evening, Steven stood by the window for some time. He looked at, but did not see, the flow of rush-hour traffic along Park Avenue.

Suzi was not due back for another hour from the fitness club and he was able to give his full attention to Sam Rhodes. He knew that Joe Lynagh was right and that the American public was waiting for another sporting hero. Rhodes certainly had the looks and Steven was well aware of how the public identified authority and even integrity with sporting prowess.

In a minor way he had himself been something of a sporting hero.

His first few days at Dean Grammar School had left Steven

dazed; everything was so much bigger, there were so many more boys and, after his cosy primary school, the teachers were frightening figures who asked impossible questions.

Steven tried to remain as inconspicuous as possible in the classroom but had no such inhibitions on the sports field. He was amazed at the wealth of the facilities and at the organisation that went into the various team sports. There were house and school teams at all the different age levels and Steven's abilities as a footballer were quickly spotted: he was chosen not for the school team of his year but for the one above, the under-thirteen team. It didn't take him long to realise that many of his classmates treated him with a new kind of respect because of his sporting talents.

In the subsequent terms he displayed his prowess in athletics and cricket and, after a few rudimentary lessons on the tennis court, showed a real flair for the game. It was clear that Steven Shaw found any game relatively easy. By the time he was fifteen years of age he was playing for the school's senior teams in all the major sports, as well as for the county junior teams at football and tennis. With some friends he even joined a coaching scheme for young golfers at a local club and uncovered an enviable ability to hit the ball hard and reasonably straight.

Steven did not have to court popularity. It was freely offered to him by his peers who admired his sporting skills, and he was a hero to the younger boys. He thrived on it at the expense of his academic progress. He had no wish to taint his popularity with any hint of studying too hard; he coasted along, a middling student content to do just enough. The more acute of his teachers realised that he was far from fulfilling his scholastic talents; but even they bestowed a sympathetic eye on him because of his athletic potential.

Steven remembered also how the golfing friends of his first father-in-law, Dick Seabrook, had paid surprising respect to his opinions. He realised that it was mainly owing to his ability to hit a golf ball with great power and accuracy. Tentative offers of jobs were made, come the day when he qualified as an accountant.

Just as he heard Suzi unlock the front door, Steven strode decisively to the telephone and dialled Joe Lynagh's number. When his father-in-law picked up the receiver, Steven said, without preamble, 'Joe, I reckon Sam Rhodes could be very big in golf. If he has the real gilt-edged talent to go with his looks and his personality, he could represent a great business opportunity.'

Lynagh's voice was sharp, 'What d'you have in mind?'

'Setting up a company to manage him. I don't know the business but—'

'Yes, you do. You've got an MBA and your specialty was marketing. The boy likes you and his father trusts me. Let's meet for breakfast in the morning.'

'I know how these sports agents work,' Lynagh said firmly on the following morning. 'You could beat the salary you're getting from Scott Thomson just by looking after Rhodes. Twenty or even twenty-five per cent of his endorsements and maybe ten per cent of his winnings. It's a great idea. As soon as you're up and running you can take on other clients. You know about sport, you know about marketing and you're on the same wavelength as people like Rhodes.'

'I'd certainly like to give it a try . . .'

'That's the style, Steven. One of the quickest ways for a business to grow is through diversification. I'll provide the finance and of course I'll give you all the legal back-up you need. Let's get hold of Rhodes. Maybe you can take him up to Westchester tomorrow for a game. Just the two of you.'

The game was arranged and Joe Lynagh's limousine took the two young men up to Westchester Country Club on the following day. During the journey doubts assailed Steven. Sam Rhodes looked the part, but you could never tell with sportsmen. The professional golf tour was littered with thirty-something journeymen, anonymous and embittered, who had once glowed with youthful promise.

After a few shots of their match it was clear to Steven that Rhodes had a singular talent for striking a golf ball. The sound of his shots was different: the crack of wood and the ring of metal on balata was more resonant. Steven couldn't properly describe the difference because he had never before registered it. But he recognised it. Rhodes was also well schooled in the basic grammar of the game, at ease with all the essential shots and they included a beautifully controlled putting stroke. Steven watched his elegant and unhurried swing with pleasure and knew that Rhodes, with his good looks and easy manner, was born to be a star.

As they played their round, Steven realised that the man had a lively intelligence which roved beyond the game of golf. It was his passion, and he had a wide knowledge of its history, but Rhodes had more than a passing interest in American literature and the theatre. Along with their mutual enthusiasm for sport, Steven guessed that he could use that interest to cement their relationship.

They had tea on the terrace and Steven cleverly told Rhodes that it was Lynagh's idea that he should offer to manage him. 'I don't know the business,' Steven said self-deprecatingly, 'but I do know about marketing. You would have my individual attention, which is more than Don Greenberg would give you, for instance.'

'Maybe, Steven, but Don is a good agent. He does great deals, whatever people say about him.'

'Fine. Everyone should reap the right rewards for their talent. But, from what you told me and Joe over lunch, money isn't everything to you. You have a wider vision and I'm glad about that. Because anyone who makes the pursuit of money and material possessions his passion will be unhappy. In the end, he'll destroy himself as a human being.'

Steven sipped at his tea and said, 'You want to be a great golfer and you want to retain your integrity. To use the cliché, you'll put as much into the game as you take out. More, I would guess.'

Rhodes nodded eagerly and Steven continued. 'So, you need a business manager who'll respect your integrity. I'll encourage you any way I can. I love sport and sport needs its heroes. Pele adorned football and he talked with humility about "the beautiful game". Sport needs men like Pele. Do you think you can be a hero, Sam? Are you one of those who's been "admitted through the ivory gates where most must enter through the gates of horn"?'

The young golfer looked seriously at him and Steven sensed that his words had won him his first client. He owed the remarks about the futility of material things to the man who had taught him English at his Brighton grammar school and had quoted them verbatim. Jeremy Knight, with a profound love for the English language, had peppered his pupils with apt quotations. Steven had stored many of them away for later use and found that they added an impressive depth to his arguments. It was Knight, too, who had played the game of dividing great men into heroes and others.

'Are you Byron rather than Wordsworth, Dylan Thomas rather than Eliot, Evelyn Waugh rather than Graham Greene?' Steven persisted.

'Eugene O'Neill not Arthur Miller, Joe Heller not Norman Mailer,' Rhodes said quietly.

'That's it.' Steven looked solemnly at Rhodes and continued. 'You probably know Byron's poetry better than I do, Sam. He's one of my favourite writers.

> "There is a pleasure in the pathless woods,
> There is a rapture on the lonely shore,
> There is society, where none intrudes,
> By the deep sea, and music in its roar."

I would trade all the wealth in the world for the ability to write like that.'

'Yes, Steven, I agree. I hope I can live up to your vision of the world.'

Got him, Steven thought.

Sam Rhodes gave him the dazzling smile which would one day be projected from newspapers, magazines, posters, shop windows and television screens all over the world. Then he thrust a sunburnt hand across the table and they shook hands on their deal.

In the years to come Steven, in his many interviews, usually referred to that handshake as the foundation of his and Sam Rhodes's business success. 'My agency was founded on a handshake with someone who became the greatest name in golf,' he would say fondly. 'That's all it took.' It became a part of the powerful mythology which Steven constructed around himself and his agency. He never added that a representation contract, which ran to thirty pages, was delivered to Sam Rhodes within a week.

On returning to his hotel, Rhodes telephoned his father and told him excitedly about the man who would manage him when he turned professional. 'He's exactly right for me, Dad. He's really bright, Harvard Business School and all that and he's a real fine golfer. But it's not just that. He didn't rub his hands and talk about all the money we'll make. He talked about my career and my responsibilities to the game. And hell, Dad, we talked about books. He's got a wide perspective on life, that's the important thing. I feel real comfortable with him.'

That evening at a local restaurant, Steven celebrated with Suzi and her parents his first step on the long road of a new career. It was a pleasurable occasion as they all gave a free rein to their optimism.

In high spirits when they got home, Steven and Suzi went straight to their bedroom and began to make love. Steven had given up trying to interest Suzi in any violence, however mild, and she had also rejected his pleas for anal sex.

As he entered her from behind, Steven tried again. 'Darling, how about the other place,' he whispered.

'No, it'll hurt me.'

'Only a bit and you'll like it, I promise.'

'I don't . . .'

'Do it just once, for me.'


A few days later Suzi Shaw met her mother at their favourite Italian restaurant, which lay midway between the Lynagh house and the Shaw apartment. They tried to see each other at least once a week – sometimes for lunch and occasionally to wander around the shops together.

After they had chatted for several minutes about mutual friends, Betty Lynagh asked after Steven. It was an obvious way, as Suzi knew, to air one of her preoccupations. She was longing, as was Joe Lynagh, for the day when Suzi announced that she was pregnant: the thought of having grandchildren was a continuing source of pleasurable anticipation to both of them.

'Is everything OK between you?' Betty Lynagh asked.

'Sure, Mom.'

'Bed OK?' Betty Lynagh was a firm believer that a happy sex life was one of the foundations of a successful marriage.

For her part, Suzi had always confided in her mother, who knew that she had only had one lover before Steven.

'Yes, Mom, he's wonderful but there is one thing I wanted to ask you.' Suzi paused, drank some water and leaned closer to her mother. 'Sometimes he asks me to . . . you know . . . do things that I'm not certain are, er, normal . . .'

'D'you mean oral sex, dear? Well there's nothing unusual—'

'No, Mom,' Suzi could usually discuss anything under the sun with her mother but found this very awkward. 'I mean, er, anal sex.'

'Oh,' Betty paused. Joe had certainly never suggested such a thing to her. 'Well, I know some couples do that, but I wouldn't think it's advisable too often, darling. Of course, you must keep your husband happy . . .' Betty Lynagh's voice trailed off doubtfully.

'Yes, well, I've some good news for you, anyway. I think I'm going to have a baby.'

Thank the Lord, thought Betty, Steven does it the right way sometimes. Her face grew pink and bright with joy. Suzi hushed her. 'But don't say anything yet, it's bad luck. I'm only a couple of weeks late and I want to be sure.'

True to her daughter's wishes but with much difficulty, Betty Lynagh said nothing to her husband about the pregnancy when he arrived home that evening. But she steeled herself to ask him about anal intercourse. Despite her tough upbringing, she was reserved about sexual matters and wondered how to broach a subject about which she had only read.

When they had settled with their pre-dinner drinks, Betty Lynagh said tentatively, 'Joe, is off-beat sex acceptable these days?'

'Off-beat sex? What's that?'

'Oh, you know, anal sex, that sort of thing.'

Trying not to show how startled he was, Joe Lynagh put down his glass of wine.

'You mean what the faggots in Greenwich Village do?'

'Well, yes, but men and women do it, too, don't they?'

'You want to try it, Betty?' he asked teasingly. 'At our age?'

'Be serious, Joe. Is it normal between men and women?'

'Not in my book. But what's got you going on this subject?'

'Oh, just an article in a magazine, that's all.'

When they went to bed that night Betty was surprised when her husband made love to her with an ardour he had not employed for a long time. As she drifted into sleep, she thought smugly that she ought to talk dirty to him more often.


Within the next month a separate company was set up for Steven Shaw and his agreement with Sam Rhodes was finalised.

A suite of offices was rented in the same building as Lynagh's law firm, and Shaw Management went into business.

At a Sunday lunch at the Lynaghs', Suzi announced to her parents that they were now expectant grandparents. On the following day, Joe Lynagh called into Steven's new office and offered to increase his investment in the new company to a quarter of a million dollars.

'It'll set you up for the first year. You'll have a lot of expenses, travel and so on. I don't want you to cut any corners. I'm so delighted about Suzi's news and I want to give you every chance to build up the new family business.'

Sam Rhodes turned professional and won the second tournament in which he played.

# Chapter Six

A special invitation allowed Sam Rhodes to play in the Southern Open. The sponsor knew that the journeyman professionals would complain that he'd favoured 'another poxy college kid who can't hit the ball out of his own shadow' but he didn't care; he knew class when he saw it. Rhodes repaid his faith by winning the event in style. His victory also ensured that he was accepted for the professional Tour without having to undergo the onerous chore of the qualifying school at the end of the year.

It was a dream start for Rhodes and for his manager who was handed some heavy ammunition in his battle to finalise his first client's main endorsement contracts. It wasn't as if Rhodes had come to him as a professional golfer with contracts already in place. The figures on those contracts would have given him some guidance; all Steven had were the estimates he had garnered before his first meeting with him.

As soon as Rhodes had announced his new status as a professional, Steven had tested the water with the company which had supplied his client with golf clubs and balls throughout his amateur career.

'I'd like to stay with Jack Burrell,' Rhodes said. 'They make great sticks and they've always looked after me well. Whatever I wanted in the way of equipment, it was there.'

Burrell's company, Parbreaker Equipment, was a prominent manufacturer of clubs and balls. They had dozens of professionals under contract in the hope that one of them would win a major tournament – preferably the British or American Open or the Masters at Augusta. That was when the company would cash in, when it would tell the world that *their* professional had won a major championship playing with *their* equipment.

A few sets of golf clubs and a few dozen golf balls given to Rhodes was small change compared to the huge investment they made in the professional game. It was a clever piece of marketing, nevertheless, to play the beneficent patron to a promising young amateur.

It took Steven over a week to reach Burrell in his Chicago office. He was in a meeting, he'd popped out for an early lunch, he was with a client. The excuses went on until Burrell at last accepted his call.

'Hi, Steve, what can I do for you?' Steven heard the synthetic friendliness in the man's voice. He didn't like to be called Steve, and certainly not on first acquaintance; and he had already explained the reason for his call to Burrell's secretary on two occasions.

'I'm Sam Rhodes's business manager and I'm calling to discuss a contract to play Parbreaker clubs and balls.'

'Steve, I've known Sam since he was in short pants. I'll look after him, as I always have. We'll put a few grand in his pocket, to help him along. We'll see how he does. I'll have a word with him.'

'Any business talk should be done with me, Mr Burrell.'

'Look, sonny, I've never heard of you and, until Sam tells me other, I'll deal direct with him. He doesn't need a goddam agent leeching on him. I'll look after his interests.'

'I'm not an agent, Mr Burrell. I'm Sam Rhodes's business manager. Since you don't believe me, I'll ask Sam to call you and confirm that it's so. Good day to you.' Steven rang off. Sonny. That would cost Burrell another ten grand.

After talking briefly to Rhodes, Steven made another call to a Japanese company which had recently launched an extensive range of golf clubs. They wanted to get their share of the huge American market. An up-and-coming player like Rhodes, whom they could use to give their clubs an identity and a touch of glamour, was a vital part of their sales strategy.

In assessing his client's value, Steven had applied some of the lessons he'd learned at the Harvard Business School. What was a realistic figure for Rhodes's services? What was the bottom line? What was the highest figure he thought he could achieve? Carefully he wrote the figures down for the various product categories and for periods from one to three years. That wasn't the end of it; there would be bonuses for tournament wins and a break clause in the contract if Rhodes won 'a major': the contract would then be renegotiated.

It was an agreeable surprise when the American chief executive of the Japanese company offered a golf club deal which was poised between Steven's highest and his realistic estimates. It was a promising start.

That afternoon Rhodes did his manager's bidding and told Burrell that all negotiations were to be conducted through Shaw Management in New York. Burrell turned to his marketing manager and said, 'OK, we'll have to deal with that smart-ass limey. He's just set up as an agent. Now's the time to screw him, phoney accent and all.'

On the following day, Steven, content in the knowledge that he already had a better offer for Rhodes's golf club contract than he'd anticipated, spoke to Burrell just before lunch.

'OK, Steve, let's talk sensibly,' Burrell began.

'I already have been.'

'Hey, Steve, we have to be careful. There're all kinds of

con-men ringing us up and saying that they represent this player or that player. They're just trying to broker deals on the side, we have to be wary. Let's start afresh. We like Sam, he'll never be an Arnie or a Jack but we'll help him out. Let's do a deal on clubs and balls.'

Burrell's offer was well below Steven's minimum for clubs alone.

'The competition has offered way beyond that for Sam's golf club endorsement,' Steven said, after a lengthy pause. 'Why don't you think about a significant increase in your offer for golf balls and we'll look at it?'

It was Burrell's turn to stay silent. Then he said, 'You're new to this business, Steve, and I suppose you've got to talk a tough game to impress your client. But I've been in the business a long time and I deal in realities, so let's talk realities, not bullshit.'

'If you'd like to make another bid, Mr Burrell, for golf balls only, go ahead. Why don't you call me before the end of the week? Thanks for your time.'

He put down the telephone and smiled to himself. During Thursday and Friday, Steven instructed his secretary not to accept any calls from Jack Burrell.

On the Friday Rhodes was three shots behind the leaders in the Southern Open. On Sunday evening he won the tournament by two shots with a final round of 66.

At nine o'clock on Monday morning, Jack Burrell telephoned Shaw Management's office. His marketing manager, who had long ago championed Rhodes's potential, had repeatedly urged him to make a positive offer for the young golfer's endorsement.

'You've missed the boat now, Jack,' the marketing man said with relish.

'Hey, Stevie,' Burrell said. That's another ten grand, thought Steven. 'I've been talking to my marketing manager and we're able to make a new proposal.'

'Yes, Mr Burrell?'

'My friends call me Jack.'

'Yes, Mr Burrell.'

The new proposal met with Steven's approval but he turned the screw a little more. 'You will of course pay Sam's bonus for the Southern Open, won't you?' he said.

When Burrell agreed, he told him that he'd let him know his decision before the end of business on the next day.

Shaw Management was up and running strongly, with two substantial contracts already negotiated.

The immediate success of Rhodes on the professional circuit, and the consequent publicity he attracted opened many of the commercial doors on which Steven had planned to lean heavily. He swiftly concluded contracts for clothing and shoes and arranged for his client to wear a particular brand of watch. An agreement with a car manufacturer, an airline and an international bank soon followed and most of the main planks of Rhodes's commercial platform were nailed into place.

Publicity for his client was abundant and Steven determined to siphon off some of it for himself. He knew that the media and the public were obsessed with the money that celebrities, and especially sportsmen, made and decided to feed that obsession for his own ends.

It was easily arranged. He contacted a reporter on one of the golf magazines. She had been in touch a couple of times to ask questions about Rhodes and he liked the sound of her. She was sharp but friendly.

Joni Postel was eager to talk to an agent like Shaw who had a client like Rhodes. If she hit an inside track with them, who knew where it might lead her?

From a window seat in the bar of a hotel near Central Park, Steven spotted Postel as she strode busily along the pavement. She was carrying a copy of the magazine for which she worked. She was tall and tubby – he guessed that she was at least a couple of stones overweight – but she had an attractive face. As she reached the hotel entrance she paused and gave money to a beggar who had his pitch there. She should be a push-over, Steven thought.

Over the first drink, he told her of his carefully considered plans for Sam Rhodes's future.

'Quality,' he said in summary. 'Every product or service must be the best of its kind. We'll be highly selective, we don't want to overwhelm Sam and distract him from his real purpose which is winning golf tournaments, especially the majors.'

Although she had heard the same refrain from other agents, Joni thought she caught the true note of sincerity in this man's voice. She could listen to him all day. And how about those beautiful grey eyes!

She looked down at her notepad. 'Tell me about Sam's contracts so far. You've set him up very well, or so the locker room gossip has it. What sort of figures are we talking here?'

'You know I can only give you approximations, Joni. Confidentiality and all that. But Sam, if he continues to play well and win tournaments, will be secure for life in a couple of years.'

Steven ticked off various deals on his fingers and gave the journalist his 'ball park figures'. In one case he quoted the payments for three years as if they applied to only one year, and in another case he added in all the possible bonuses as if they were part of the basic contract. Otherwise, he simply exaggerated the payments. The result was to inflate Rhodes's value many times over.

In the following month's edition of the magazine, Steven
was rewarded by a banner headline in the news section:
'MILLION DOLLAR RHODES'. The report went on:

Sam Rhodes has the personality to become one of
the hottest properties in golf, according to Steven
Shaw, a Harvard Business School alumnus who is the
newest agent on the golfing block. The New York
based Englishman told me, in an exclusive interview,
that his first client has already amassed prestigious
deals that will earn him well over a million dollars in
his first year as a pro.

During the week after the magazine appeared, Steven
had calls from over twenty professional golfers who wanted
to sack their present agent and acquire a better one.
Eventually he agreed to represent five of them. His tactic
had worked better than he'd expected.

The name of the new company had caused some lively
discussion. At first, Joe Lynagh didn't want the agency to
carry Steven's name. 'It'll be identified with you too closely,
it's too personal, especially if we decide to sell it one day.
We need some sort of zappy, get-up-and-go name.
Foremost or Headline International, that kinda thing.'

Steven pointed out how long it would take to clear and
register such a name even if they could think of something
appropriate, and he stressed the double meaning of Shaw
Management. It tipped the balance in his favour and the
Lynaghs insisted on hosting a small celebration to launch
the company.

The two men saw each other almost every day and
Lynagh, a dedicated sports fan, was ever prepared to talk
about his favourite subject. Despite his enthusiasm, his
advice was generally conservative. 'Stick with the sports

you know,' he said on one occasion. 'Golf, tennis, athletics, they've got international appeal. Don't get involved with baseball and American football, you'll be out of your depth.'

Steven argued that he was just a maker of deals, that he didn't have to understand the traditions and the lore of America's national sports.

'As long as I can quote Babe Ruth's sixty home runs in a season and Joe DiMaggio's fifty-six game hitting streak, that's all I need,' he said flippantly. 'Anyway, I thought you'd like the agency to get into baseball, it's your sport, isn't it, Joe? A part of the American heritage. "I see the boys of summer in their ruin" and all that romantic stuff.'

'Sure, I love watching the game, but you can forget the romance and the literary flourishes. Somebody said that if baseball was half as complicated as the writers make it out to be, baseball players couldn't play it, and I go along with that.'

Steven recognised the sense of Lynagh's comments. He would concentrate on the sports which were played around the world and build his business on an international platform.

'What about boxing?' he said to Lynagh one Sunday evening as they sat down to dinner with Suzi and her mother. He knew that Lynagh occasionally went to the fights in New York and Las Vegas. 'Big money, lots of television coverage, very much an international sport.'

'Ugh,' Suzi said. 'Men beating each other senseless. It's not a sport, Steven, it's organised brutality.'

'The noble art,' Steven replied, 'and it has a long tradition.'

'There sure as hell isn't much nobility about it these days, if there ever was,' Lynagh said. 'Perhaps a kind of desperate nobility about those poor dupes slugging it out in the ring. But the whole sport is run by con-men and gangsters. They fleece everybody: the public, each other when possible, and above all, the fighters. Don't touch it, Steven, we all want you to retain the use of your legs. Stick to the civilised sports.'

To call international sport civilised was a gross misinterpretation, as Steven quickly learned.

Having devised a strategy for his business, Steven pursued it: he concentrated initially on golf and then on tennis. He knew that the key to his future in the latter sport lay in discovering the tennis equivalent of Sam Rhodes. Suzi was a keen follower of the game and with her enthusiastic help he studied the results assiduously, watched matches on television and, when he went to tournaments, he talked to coaches and journalists. Over a period of several months he made short-lists of players, both male and female, in whom he was interested. Although he was in no hurry, he was conscious that tennis was experiencing a great upsurge in popularity. The middle classes, in America and Europe, were taking to the game in their droves. They had to have the right designer clothing, the right footwear and the best rackets. Steven knew that he had to get into that market. There was huge endorsement income to be generated for the right client; not only that, but the prize money was soaring skywards and he wanted to get his cut from that as well. Above all, he had heard that exhibition matches were very much in vogue, with sponsors paying six-figure fees for the best players.

His first target was a young Californian, Ray Gerrard. He had recently left the University of Southern California and was already ranked in the top ten in his own country and in the top thirty in the world. He was a future Wimbledon champion, if Steven had ever seen one. Well over six feet tall, Gerrard was a superb athlete with a blazing, knock-'em-down-and-drag-'em-out serve and volley game. He blasted his opponents off the court in brutal fashion. It wasn't pretty but it was vibrantly exciting. And Gerrard had the looks, too. Olive-skinned and with glossy black hair, he had the presence of an old-time matinée idol. With such physical attributes he might have been overwhelming but, fortunately, Gerrard had an abundance of self-deprecating charm.

Steven learned that his quarry was also being hunted by two of the biggest agents in tennis, and he arranged to meet him at an indoor tournament in Boston. He relished the idea of returning to the city and booked himself into one of its best hotels.

On the Saturday afternoon he watched his potential client demolish his semi-final opponent with the loss of only three games. He showed a degree of ruthlessness that was almost chilling and Steven was more than ever convinced that he had seen one of the tennis champions of the future.

He recognised the killer instinct without which no winner's armoury was complete. 'Show me a good loser and I'll show you a loser', as an American coach once put it succinctly.

# Chapter Seven

Steven had discovered his own killer instinct at the tender age of sixteen. After undergoing the ordeal of his O-Level examinations, Steven had to face the family's summer holiday which was always taken during the first two weeks of August. He knew that he would be at his mother's mercy.

At the start of the 1970s, many of Steven's friends went abroad, and he had lobbied hard for a package holiday to Majorca or the Costa Brava, but his mother had reacted with horror to the idea. The usual booking was made at the Marine View Private Hotel. 'We're not made of money, you know,' had been her final and emphatic rejection of his proposal.

Their neighbours, the Kyle family, had gone off to Torremolinos for three weeks. Danny, who was nearly a year older than Steven, had said: 'The lager's dirt cheap and I'm going to get in the discos and find myself a bird. Get 'em on the pina coladas, they're the best leg-openers in the business.'

Danny had grinned as Steven blushed. His Irish friend already had a steady girlfriend whereas Steven had not yet progressed beyond some tentative kissing with girls from the tennis club.

The Shaw family travelled by train to Margate and were picked up at the station by the cheerful proprietor of the Marine View Private Hotel. It didn't have a view of the sea, it couldn't be described as private in any sense of the word and it wasn't a hotel. It was a guest house and the guests were expected to vacate their rooms after breakfast and not to return until dinner, which was served at six o'clock sharp. The twelve bedrooms shared three bathrooms and four lavatories and there was a considerable shortfall in the facilities needed for nearly thirty guests.

In deference to his sixteen years Steven had been allotted a single room next to his parents. It had the dimensions of a cupboard and a tiny window which looked over an alleyway at the side of the building. But it was his and his alone for the two weeks of the holiday.

Every morning, shortly after nine o'clock, the Shaw family joined the rest of the holidaymakers who had been bundled out of their hotels for the rest of the day. Rain or shine, it made no difference. Fortunately, the weather was forgiving and the promenade and the beach filled up as the mornings wore on. The sun came out on several occasions and Steven swam and dived and floated in the sea. His father joined him while Mary Shaw guarded their belongings on the beach; she only cared to paddle, and only when it was really warm.

'I'll bet it's warm in Torremolinos,' Steven said and wondered what the Kyle family were doing. His mind flicked back to a golden fun-filled day he had spent with them at Hayling Island when he was a child. Through the haze of his recollection, he heard his father say, 'Maybe we'll go abroad next year.'

'Oh, yes, are you planning to win the football pools?' asked Mary Shaw sarcastically.

'If I do, I won't tell you,' her husband muttered to himself.

Lunch was eaten at one of the many cafés which clustered on the promenade and the nearby streets. It was an opportunity for Mary Shaw to make a careful scrutiny of the various prices, since they had to stay within their daily budget. Visits to the cinema and to the various variety shows that Margate had to offer were major items of expenditure and three of each were built into the budget. Steven enjoyed the shows with their mixtures of conjurers, singers, comedians and dancers. He was fascinated by the chorus girls and speculated about the delights that his friend, Danny, had said such women could offer. He understood more of the jokes, too, though he pretended not; his father's gusts of laughter induced enough glares from his mother, her lips thin with distaste.

The first week of the holiday meandered slowly to its close and, on the following Monday, Steven saw a poster on the promenade which advertised a junior tennis tournament at a club in Margate. There were four age categories from eighteen downwards with 'substantial' prizes available. Competitors were told to turn up and register before ten o'clock on the following day; tennis rackets would be provided if needed. His father encouraged him to go along and overrode Mary Shaw's protests that it was a family holiday and they should enjoy it together.

'Let the boy have some fun with people his own age,' he said. To Steven's surprise, his mother capitulated.

The courts were only a couple of bus rides away from the guest house and Steven was at the club shortly after nine o'clock. There were nearly a hundred children to register, many of them in expensive-looking tracksuits and bearing several tennis rackets. It took until midday to register everyone, and Steven, just turned sixteen, was placed in the senior category. In his grey shirt and a pair of shorts which he had been wearing on the beach, Steven felt inadequately equipped, especially when he was issued with a battered Dunlop racket for his first match. His opponent, in sparkling white tennis clothing and with a pristine metal racket, intimidated him only for the first minute or two of the warm-up. Despite the vociferous support of his parents, his opponent was despatched without winning a game.

During the next day and a half Steven forged through to the semi-finals. The only opponent to give him trouble was a boy from north London. Jerry Holmes wore even tattier kit than himself: ragged khaki shorts which had been cut off just above the knee and an old Aertex shirt which had started out white and had changed to indeterminate shades of grey. He had a whirlwind style, covered the court quickly and hit the ball very hard. The two boys had a tough contest until Steven realised that his opponent was vulnerable on the backhand. After Steven's victory they had glasses of lemonade together and Jerry Holmes wished him the best of luck in the rest of the tournament.

Steven killed time before his semi-final by watching the other contestants. For several minutes he lingered by one of the courts in order to watch a very pretty girl, with slim and suntanned legs, her bottom tightly encased in a pair of white shorts with red trimmings. She was battling hard against a tall and square-shouldered girl with a short haircut and spots. When the pretty girl won the first set, Steven found himself applauding enthusiastically; the girl flashed a smile of thanks at him and he grinned back. Her large green eyes glowed from an oval face framed by tightly bunched black curls. Her teeth were perfectly even and showed dazzling white against her lightly tanned skin.

After a few more games, which she won comfortably, it was clear to Steven that she was on her way to victory and he wandered off to see a few of the other matches.

Steven was keyed up for his semi-final, but the match was an anti-climax. His opponent was so paralysed by nerves that he could hardly lift the ball over the net. Steven felt sorry for him but blasted him off the court anyway. He stayed to watch the other semi-final. A tall and athletic boy, who seemed to Steven to be way past the age limitation of eighteen years on 31 March of that year, won easily. Steven watched him carefully; he was immaculately turned out and wore a sleeveless white sweater with blue and yellow markings that no doubt denoted a public school. To Steven's eyes he seemed not to have a weakness in his game: a powerful first service was backed up by a heavily cut second service to a good length; he had excellent ground strokes on either flank and was an exceptional volleyer. He seemed to be on very friendly terms with the umpire and commended his outclassed opponent with several shouts of 'Oh, fine shot' on the rare occasions that the ball was returned to him.

In between games the elegant boy in the sweater chatted in a relaxed way to a group of people who were sitting level with the net: two parents, a girl of about twelve and the suntanned girl with the remarkable green eyes.

As he was finishing a cup of tea before his bus journey back to the guest house, Steven felt a hand on his shoulder and looked up at a man with a rather long face and thinning fair hair. He wore a navy blue blazer, a striped tie and grey flannels. 'I'm Captain Wycherley,' he said. 'I help organise the tournament.' His voice was thin, as if the vowels were being filtered through something clenched anxiously in his wide jaws.

Wycherley sat down opposite Steven, who noticed the dandruff on the man's shoulders. 'You're in the final tomorrow against young Waring,' he stated. 'We must smarten you up. You won't be out there long,' he said with a smirk, 'but you must look at your best. New socks, shorts and a shirt. No need to return them afterwards. Courtesy of one of our sponsors. And I'll find you a decent racket, too. But you'll have to give that back. You're on court at three o'clock. The last match. See you then.'

With a nod, Wycherley strode briskly away. Steven looked at the shiny blue material which covered his receding back. So he wasn't expected to do much against young Waring. He could understand why: he looked a very classy tennis player. Steven wondered how he'd react to real pressure, the sort of relentless harrying that the junior county coach had taught him and the other young players from Brighton. Therein lay Steven's chances of an unexpected success. He was the underdog, so he needn't worry too much; but he was determined to be an underdog with very sharp teeth.

Steven mentioned the forthcoming final as casually as he could to his parents after dinner that night. They had eaten packet vegetable soup, shepherd's pie with frozen peas and carrots and tinned peaches; all of which his mother had pronounced to be 'very nice'.

'Would you like us to come and watch?' his father had asked.

'No, it's all right,' Steven replied. 'It won't take long, I'm up against the favourite. You won't want to see me take a hammering.'

Bill Shaw shrugged. He wasn't interested in tennis; football was his game, although he had watched his son play only a couple of times.

Mary Shaw interrupted. 'Just a minute, I think we ought to support Steven. D'you think there'll be a report in the papers? I'll put it in the scrapbook.' For some time now she had been keeping cuttings whenever Steven's name appeared in a report of a school or a county match.

As they settled down in the lounge, with its battered and mismatched settees and armchairs, to watch 'Coronation Street' Mary Shaw turned to her immediate neighbour and said, 'My son is in the final of the tennis tomorrow.' The other guest made no acknowledgement since the programme titles, accompanied by the familiar signature tune, were filling the television screen. 'I expect he'll win,' Mrs Shaw continued, 'he is a county junior player. In Sussex, you know.'

She smiled sedately, her husband lit a cigarette and an embarrassed Steven tried to retreat as far as possible into the refuge of his chair.

On the bus journey to the tennis club Steven tried to work out some tactics to unsettle his opponent. He reckoned that he would have to play a retrieving game, keep his own mistakes to a minimum and grind away at Waring's self-confidence.

They arrived with half a hour to spare and Steven was at once collared by Captain Wycherley. 'You haven't got much time,' he said self-importantly. 'We'll sort out some gear for you.'

As he was hurried off, Steven told his parents to go and find themselves a seat by the main court. When he reached it ten minutes later, feeling ill at ease in a new cotton shirt that was too large for him, he searched for them amongst the four rows of wooden chairs that had been laid out around the court. In their self-effacing way they were sitting in the back row near one of the corners.

Waring had his school sweater on top of a crisp white shirt. After tossing for service, he shook hands firmly with Steven, wished him the best of luck and smiled confidently.

If the shirt wasn't the right size, Captain Wycherley had found him a beauty of a racket, well-balanced and with the strings at just the right tension. The first six games in the opening set went with service and Steven noticed how Waring's attitude, initially relaxed and bouncy, began to change. He made him stretch and run hard to the corners and Waring's sporting cries of 'Oh, great shot' began to dry up, especially when Steven deceived him with a passing shot and then beat him with a top-spin lob. Nevertheless, Waring took the first set 6–4.

When they crossed to change ends Steven took a careful look at his opponent: he was puffing hard and sweating heavily.

In the second set Steven continued his war of attrition. There were no more cries of 'good shot' from his opponent, who even politely queried a couple of line calls. Steven broke his service twice to win the set 6–2.

With a three-game lead in the final set, Steven thought that the match was his until he lost his own service twice in a row and went 4–3 down when Waring held his service game. His opponent was puffing and blowing and had even removed his sleeveless sweater, but he had found some reserves of strength and was playing his best tennis of the match. It was Steven who was now feeling under pressure. The hundred or so spectators, who until then had been no more than politely attentive, at last became involved. There were some gasps at the speed with which Steven covered the court and stifled applause at the power of Waring's shots.

Steven knew that he must not lose the next game on his own service because Waring, adrenalin surging, would undoubtedly take the final game and the match.

The vital game went to deuce and then advantage to Waring. The shadow of defeat lay bleakly on Steven's face as he bounced the ball and tried to relax. Waring was poised eagerly on the far side of the court. Relax, take your chances, Steven told himself. Over went the first service and it was in play. Both boys played it safe with a succession of baseline shots, and then Steven played a poor shot into no man's land well short of the baseline. Waring smashed it to Steven's backhand and he replied with the only possible shot, a lob. Waring hit a good volley across court and

Steven put up another lob. It was short and his opponent went in for the kill. In his eagerness, Waring hit a false shot off the top of his racket and it ballooned up near the net. As Steven raced in for his volley Waring tried to turn and scamper for the baseline. He half fell over his own feet, recovered and realised that his only chance was to try and cover the net.

As the ball reached its highest point and began to spiral down, Steven was in position and could see Waring's difficulties. With cold intent he took careful aim at the scrambling body of his opponent. He caught the ball dead centre with perfect timing and it hurtled the ten feet straight into Waring's upper arm – his racket arm.

He dropped his racket and fell heavily to the ground. His first reaction was half-shout and half-scream and Steven threw his own racket down, jumped over the net and crouched down by Waring, his hand on his shoulder.

'Are you all right? God, I'm sorry, I thought you were moving across to cover the backhand side.'

The umpire, a line judge and Waring's parents had arrived and were crouched around the fallen boy. They lifted him to his feet and the umpire, who seemed to have some rudimentary medical knowledge, massaged Waring's arm and made him move it this way and that. After several minutes, the umpire asked Waring if he wanted to continue and Mrs Waring said: 'You don't have to, darling, it's only a game.'

It's much more than that, Steven thought, as he once again apologised to his opponent. Waring tried a few practice serves and said that he would try and finish the match. It was a forlorn effort and Steven won the remaining games and the match with ease.

Once again Steven apologised: 'Very sorry. You deserved to win, it was a great match until then.'

'Yes, well played,' Waring muttered as he draped his sweater over his shoulder.

The prize-giving ceremony was held immediately, and Steven stood in his sweat-drenched shirt while the winners of the various categories received their cups and their vouchers. Steven was pleased to see that Waring's green-eyed sister had won her section. He smiled at her as she passed him, though unsure of her reaction. She winked at him and grinned widely.

At last it was Steven's turn to shake hands with the Mayor, raise his cup in modest triumph and smile for the cameras. A reporter scribbled his name down and asked him what school he attended. He spotted his parents on the fringes of the crowd and waved at them. He had his picture taken with Waring and then with all the prize winners.

As the photographer tried to sort them all out into a coherent group he found himself next to Waring's sister. 'I'm Sam,' she said, 'Samantha Waring. It was deliberate, wasn't it?'

'What?' Steven asked.

'That shot in the final set. You lined Nick up, I watched you,' she said quietly in his ear.

'Right, boys and girls,' said the photographer, 'look at the camera. Smile, look like winners.'

'No, it was an accident, I'm not that accurate,' lied Steven.

'I don't mind. Serves him right, conceited hound. He's going to Oxford in October, thinks he'll get a blue.'

'He's a good player,' Steven said.

'Um, well, I must go. Mummy's waving at me. We're staying at the Grand in Sandwich, why don't you come over tomorrow for a game of tennis?'

'Well, I . . .' Steven hesitated.

'There're plenty of buses. Eleven o'clock. We can have lunch. 'Bye.'

Steven was still holding his trophy, but not for much longer. Captain Wycherley removed it from his grasp.

'Well played,' he said in his peculiar voice. 'I'll take the cup. You ought to get changed.' He led the way towards the changing rooms and continued, 'Er, about that voucher. Twenty quid at the local sports shop. I expect some cash would be more use wouldn't it? I can give you a tenner for it.'

Wycherley put his hand in his inside pocket and produced a wallet. They both stopped by the changing-room door and Steven handed over the voucher.

'Oh, and the racket, please,' said Wycherley.

About to take the ten pound note, Steven paused and said: 'Why don't I keep the racket? It's a good one. I like it.'

Wycherley grinned, returned the money with the voucher to his wallet and said, 'You learn fast, don't you, Shaw? OK, it's a deal.' He strode off.

Steven changed quickly and went in search of his parents who were still standing by the tennis court.

'Well played, son, I thought you were a gonner at one stage,' said Bill Shaw.

'Where's the cup, Steven?' asked his mother. 'It'll look well on the television.'

She looked disappointed when Steven told her that it went back into the safe keeping of the organisers, but seemed pleased that he'd acquired a new racket. As they waited for their bus, she said sharply: 'Who was that girl you were talking to?'

'What girl, Mum?' Steven replied in order to irritate her.

'The one with the very short skirt. Showing everything she's got. If I was her mother . . .'

'Oh, Sam. I'm playing tennis with her tomorrow. At the Grand in Sandwich,' Steven said airily.

'That's the stuff, Steven,' his father said, as they boarded the bus. 'You go and enjoy yourself.'

'Hmph,' said his mother, seating herself carefully, her handbag clasped to her lap. 'They're not our sort of people.'

After his mother's strict admonition that he must be back at the Marine well before the evening meal because it was the last night of their holiday, Steven set out on the Friday morning for Sandwich.

The Grand had a pair of dilapidated hard courts at the back of the hotel. Steven and Sam played some not very competitive tennis for an hour and then he offered to give her a few tips to sharpen up her game. Finally, he tried to teach her the rudiments of the top-spin forehand. It was a chance to grab her around the waist as he showed her the contours of the stroke. She was slightly damp from running around the court but she smelled of something clean and fresh.

'Come on,' Sam said, after hitting a few shots to his satisfaction, 'a quick change and then we'll have lunch.'

A dribble of tepid discoloured water from the ancient shower in the wooden shack that comprised the men's changing room ensured that it was a quick change, and they strolled through the gardens toward the hotel dining room.

'We'll have to be polite and join the family,' she said. 'It's a buffet lunch, you can eat as much as you like, so don't hold back. Daddy's paying.'

Minutes later they were faced by the mountains of food which were laid out on a long table; Steven had never seen such profusion, except in the movies. He felt intimidated by the waiters in white coats.

He wasn't sure what to choose, so followed Sam's lead exactly; his plate was piled high with smoked salmon, other fishy things that he didn't recognise, roast beef, baked ham and hummocks of salad.

He and Sam joined the rest of the Waring family at a corner table and there were introductions and smiles all round, though he noticed that the greeting from Nick, his opponent of the day before, was more grimace than smile.

'How's your arm?' Steven asked politely.

'Oh, I'll live,' he replied.

'You played splendidly, Steven,' said Mr Waring, a fork full of smoked salmon halfway to his mouth. He was a broad-shouldered man, with a shock of grey hair. He had a pleasant voice with a low-pitched rumble. 'It'll teach him to be a bit nippier round the court.' Mr Waring wore a faded blue, short-sleeved shirt with a crocodile motif on the breast.

Steven had hardly ever seen his father sit down to a meal 'in company', as his mother put it, without donning a jacket and tie. Even when they went to the beach he wore his tie and his habitual grey flannel trousers. Certainly he would never have sat in a posh hotel restaurant casually dressed, like Sam's father.

'How was your game this morning, darling?' asked Mrs Waring of her daughter. 'Did you and Steven have a lovely time?' She was a solid-looking woman with rather large breasts beneath a white blouse. Her hair was gathered behind her head in a French pleat. People in Steven's part of Brighton would have called her accent 'far back' and she sounded rather vague. But her eyes, widely spaced like Sam's, were sharp enough, as Steven discovered when he looked up in answer to her question: 'Where are you staying in Margate?'

Through a mouthful of roast beef, Steven mumbled, 'At the Marine, Mrs Waring.' He blushed as he found the eyes of the whole family on him.

'I don't know it. Is it nice? Where is your home?'

'Brighton.'

'Oh yes, we have friends there. Near the golf course. Are you on that side of Brighton?'

Mr Waring interrupted, 'For heaven's sake, Diana, let the young fellow enjoy his lunch. He doesn't want the third degree from you.' He poured himself what remained of a bottle of red wine and advised everyone to dive in for some pudding before it all disappeared. 'Come on, Diana,' he continued, 'we'll go and have coffee in the sitting room. Let's leave the youngsters to their puds.'

Samantha suggested that they went to the terrace and had a cola but Steven, determined to appear grown up, asked for coffee. She ordered the drinks from the waiter with assurance and asked him to put them on her father's bill. Steven thought briefly how nice it was to be rich enough not to have to worry about the odd lunch or bottle of wine rather than having to scour the weekly budget to find the means to pay for them.

He looked at his watch and realised that he would have to get his bus back to Margate.

Samantha volunteered to walk with him to the bus stop. As they strolled around the side of the hotel Steven reached out for her hand. He didn't know what to do; he felt over-awed by her family and wary of her. But she grabbed his hand and drew him close to her side. As they reached the corner of the building, she stopped and turned, her body close to his. Her bright green eyes looked up at his and she said: 'You can kiss me, if you want to.'

Until then Steven's kisses, shared with girls as hesitant as he, had been received under protest rather than with enthusiasm. But Sam was as eager as he was and their lips and tongues joined feverishly together. They heard a car arrive in the car park around the corner and pulled nervously apart.

'I'd better get the bus,' Steven said shyly. They walked the few hundred yards to the bus stop, carefully keeping their distance, their conversation desultory. As the Margate bus approached, Samantha produced a scrap of paper from her pocket.

'That's my address and phone number in Bath. Come and see us when you're next passing.' She kissed him on the cheek and then turned and ran back towards the hotel.

'When I'm next passing?' Steven wondered how Samantha envisaged the life he led. It would be a complicated journey by coach from his home to Bath.

But the vision of her suntanned legs, the glow of her green eyes and the taste of her kisses stayed with him for many a day.

Still jaunty with thoughts of Samantha, Steven chatted politely to his parents during the special homegoing dinner for the guests who were leaving on the following day: shrimp cocktail, roast chicken with bacon rolls and bread sauce, and fruit salad.

The proprietor had provided a bottle of Blue Nun wine for each table. Mary Shaw had two small glasses from it and Bill Shaw drank the rest.

Games had been organised for the evening and they started with bingo, which pleased Steven's mother. Then six teams were formed for a quiz and Steven knew all the answers on sport. The owner of the Marine took to the piano and led a sing-song and several of the adults stood up and sang songs which had been popular just after the war.

Bill Shaw sang 'Trees' and was rewarded with a burst of applause. He made several trips to the little bar in the corner of the room for bottles of beer and managed to persuade his wife to have a couple of glasses of sherry. When they all formed teams again to play charades Mary

Shaw was the hit of the evening, especially with her mime for *Seven Brides For Seven Brothers*.

The owner put some records on the record player and the adults began to dance. Steven said he was tired and would go to bed.

'What about that nice girl over there, Steven? I'm sure she'd like you to dance with her.' His mother nodded at a girl of about his age who was sitting quietly with her parents. She was overweight and her frock, with shoulder straps, did nothing to disguise the fact.

'No, Mum,' Steven said, 'I'm really tired. All that tennis and so on.'

As he drifted into sleep, the image of Samantha was engraved on his mind's eye. Perhaps he would take that journey by coach one day soon.

The noise of his parents' door opening disturbed Steven. He twisted into a more comfortable position on the narrow bed. He heard his parents open the door of their adjacent room. He heard their whispers and a suppressed giggle from his mother. He registered the creak of the bed as they got into it and then more whispers and more creaks. Surely they weren't doing it? Steven hauled the bedclothes firmly over his head and went back to sleep.

At the end of their holiday in Sandwich, the Waring family were most of the way through their final meal at the Grand. The parents, with only a little help from Nick, were well down their second bottle of claret. They had chatted animatedly throughout the evening: plans for the rest of the school holidays, Claudia's extra French lessons, tennis lessons for Sam and whether both parents would drive Nick over to Oxford for his first term.

Mrs Waring spoke to Samantha, who had made very little effort to eat her *daube de mouton*: 'Darling, either leave that meal or eat it up. Please don't fiddle with it.'

'She's missing her friend from Brighton,' Nick said sarcastically.

'Yes, well, he's a very pleasant young man,' Mr Waring said, 'and he's a super tennis player. If he gets to Oxford he'll walk his tennis blue, I'll be bound.' He looked teasingly across at his son.

'Yes, he beat you, Nick, and he's two years younger,' Samantha said nastily.

'Now then,' said Diana Waring, 'he's a good-looking boy, but there are plenty of those in the world. Your father was handsome once—'

'Thanks very much . . .' Mr Waring muttered.

'—but darling, he's not really your type. Now, what shall we have for pud? The summer pudding is lovely, but I expect your father will have the *crème brûlée*.'

When they returned home, Mary Shaw waited eagerly by the front door each morning for the postman. The results of Steven's O-Levels were due to arrive sometime from the middle of August onwards. On the frequent occasions that no letters were delivered she could not hide her frustration.

At last a buff envelope arrived, addressed to Mr S. Shaw. He was cleaning his teeth at the time and was startled to hear his mother yell, 'It's arrived!' She rarely raised her voice.

He ran downstairs, ripped the envelope apart and, with his mother craning over his shoulder, read his results: eight subjects and eight passes. Better than he'd hoped.

# Chapter Eight

The meeting with Steven's quarry, Ray Gerrard, was scheduled for ten o'clock at the player's hotel. Steven arrived at two minutes past the hour and a receptionist told Gerrard that his guest had arrived.

Twenty minutes passed and the tennis player did not appear. Steven sent another message. A further quarter of an hour went by on leaden feet and he was thinking of going up to Gerrard's room, when the doors of the lift opened and there he was. With a bundle of rackets under one arm and a large hold-all on his shoulder, and with his Swedish coach by his side, Gerrard didn't look as if he had a business meeting in mind.

Steven sprang to his feet and intercepted the two men as they headed across the lobby.

'Ray, I'm Steven Shaw. I'm here to have a chat with you.'

Gerrard stopped and smiled at Steven, who noted his perfect teeth. 'Oh, yeah, Steven. Hell, I'm sorry but something's cropped up. You know, I've got a final later and my backhand's a bit loose. Anders here wants me to work on it. Look, can we meet tomorrow?'

'I've got to get back to New York, I'm afraid. Can't you make some time for me? It's important.'

Gerrard looked doubtfully at his coach, who shook his head dismissively.

'Steven, I really am sorry,' Gerrard repeated. 'Can you

write me? We'll get together real soon. I'm very interested, but the tennis comes first, you know how it is.'

'No problem. I was here in Boston on business anyway,' Steven said, to save his pride. He forced himself to smile as if he'd just won the New York lottery and said that he'd drop him a line. He watched Gerrard and his mournful-eyed coach get into their courtesy car. When Gerrard became a client, one of Steven's first tasks would be to put the skids under Anders. And the day would come when the roles would be reversed: he would pick and choose his clients, rather than be pissed about by the likes of Gerrard.

Never mind. He'd get him and he'd make a bundle of money out of him.

Before he checked out of his Boston hotel, Steven jotted down the main points of the letter he intended to send. He emphasised to Gerrard that he only planned to have a select number of clients in a limited number of sports. He would give them his full personal attention. He made a note to remind himself to enclose a copy of the magazine article about his successes on behalf of Sam Rhodes.

Two months later, by which time Gerrard had climbed up the world tennis rankings, Steven at last managed to pin him down to a meeting. It was irritating that the rendezvous had to be in Dallas and even more unfortunate when Suzi's birth pains started at six o'clock on the morning of his departure. Betty Lynagh had given him strict instructions to call her as soon as there was any sign, however slight, of the imminent birth. Like most mothers in such situations, she doubted her son-in-law's competence.

Nevertheless, Steven first telephoned the private clinic where Suzi was to have the baby, and then Betty Lynagh. She arrived at their apartment within minutes, bursting with maternal concern, just as Steven was coaxing Suzi to drink some herb tea.

The intercom buzzed in the hall and Steven went to answer it.

'It must be the ambulance, Steven,' Betty Lynagh said. 'Just in time.'

'It's probably my taxi,' he replied. 'I'm due at JFK in an hour.'

Startled, Betty Lynagh asked him where he was going, and he told her about his meeting with Ray Gerrard.

'But you'll postpone it, won't you?' she said. 'Surely you're going to be with Suzi?'

'Of course I want to be with her. But I've been trying to meet this guy for months. It's too important to miss, this may be my only chance.'

Grimacing with pain, Suzi intervened. 'It's OK, Steven, you must get on with your work. It doesn't matter.'

They all knew that she didn't mean it. She desperately wanted Steven's presence and support while she gave birth. He hugged her and kissed her gently on the cheek.

'You'll be fine, darling. I'll be back tonight. I'll call the clinic from Dallas.'

As he descended the building in the lift, Steven reflected that things had turned out well. He had never had any intention of being anywhere near the clinic when Suzi gave birth. In fact, he had a plan in place for his secretary to call him away on a spurious emergency, if necessary. He couldn't understand why men wanted to be present when their wives gave birth, it seemed a bizarre idea to him. As he stepped out of the lift he remembered that a couple of years previously a leading American golfer had pulled out of the Ryder Cup match so that he could be present at the birth of his child. He wouldn't have done it if he'd been a client of Shaw Management.

Steven had felt the keen disapproval of Betty Lynagh as he'd left for his meeting, but he guessed that this would be balanced by Joe Lynagh's more practical attitude that 'business is business'. He reckoned that any discontent felt by Suzi would be forgotten in the euphoria which would claim her when their child was born.

Ray Gerrard was only half an hour late for their meeting and was full of apologies.

'It's my training schedule,' he said. 'Anders keeps me hard at it, day in and day out.'

'Well, it's paying off, isn't it?' Steven replied, smiling. 'You're about to move into the world top ten, aren't you?'

'Yeah. And this is when it gets really hard. The other guys won't take anything for granted any more. They'll be studying my game, trying to work me out. It'll get tougher.'

It was time to get down to business and Steven went into his well-rehearsed and assured sales pitch: his marketing expertise, his integrity, his wish to treat every client as if he were his only client, even if that were not literally possible.

Gerrard stayed silent throughout. His lean body was stretched out on a sofa and, if he had not been toying with a can of cola, Steven would not have known whether he was awake or not.

Steven summarised the complete managerial service he would offer. Not only would he guide Gerrard's career and maximise his income but he would also offer legal and financial advice and watch over his investments.

During a brief pause Gerrard sat up, stretched and said, 'I talked to Sam Rhodes about you the other day.'

'And what did he tell you?' He's not just a pretty face, Steven thought.

'That I should sign up because you'll do a great job for me.'

'I can't fault his opinion.'

'No. I'll bet. Look Steven, I've looked at your draft contract and I'll sign up for three years with an option for two more years after that. I need a professional in charge of my business. Anders has been doing the deals and well—'

'Would you come to me for advice on your forehand?'

'Er, no. Exactly. Send me the contracts and I'll sign them.'

Knowing how sportsmen could dither for months over signing anything, let alone a contract, Steven produced the representation agreement and its duplicate from his briefcase.

'Let's do it now,' he said. 'I want to get on your case tomorrow.'

The two men spent another hour discussing Gerrard's future plans and then Steven got a taxi to the airport. With his head full of ideas for promoting his new client's interests, it was only after he had checked in for his flight back to New York that he remembered to telephone the clinic to ask about Suzi.

The honeyed tones of a nurse told him that he was the father of 'a beautiful baby boy'.

Straight from the airport he went to the clinic. The bunch of flowers which he bought *en route* seemed a poor offering when he entered Suzi's room which was overflowing with blooms, a kaleidoscope of bright colours.

Steven was allowed briefly to hold his child, a ruddy and wizened creature, its eyes tightly shut. As soon as he decently could he handed him back to Suzi, via Betty Lynagh who was clearly in charge of Suzi, the room and possibly the clinic itself.

Early the next morning Steven returned to see Suzi, who, after a night's rest, looked wonderfully relaxed. He lingered for an hour or so and then made his excuses. He had a busy day ahead and his first task was to issue a press release to announce his representation of Ray Gerrard.

Steven had a hard time untangling the various deals made on his new client's behalf, and Anders was as unhelpful as he could be. The Swede knew that his days of wine and roses at Gerrard's expense were about to be terminated: the monthly retainer plus expenses and the chance to skim a good proportion of the endorsement fees. All Anders could hope for was a golden handshake and then get his hooks into another promising player.

Fortunately, Steven discovered that the agreements were mercifully short-term. After explaining his findings to Gerrard, he took great pleasure in firing Anders, whose deadpan expression did not flicker, even when the terms of his dismissal were outlined: $25,000 compensation to walk away immediately; no comment to the media; and a signature on a piece of paper which indemnified Gerrard and Shaw Management from any future claims.

Ray Gerrard was glad to see the back of his coach whose joyless attitudes had begun to depress him. He'd come to rely on him, nevertheless, but now a lively American, who had won the US Open title twice in the early 1970s, took over as his coach.

Suzi, who followed tennis and its players with interest, was overjoyed when she heard that Gerrard had become a client. 'He's got the sexiest legs in tennis,' she told Steven.

Within a few months, Steven had turned the same trick in tennis as he had in golf. He gathered together a stable of twelve tennis players, male and female.

Steven owed another breakthrough into the tennis market to Suzi who pointed out an item in one of the magazines about a tennis academy at Boca Raton in Florida.

'This is rather sad,' Suzi said. 'Kenny Crane, who runs

the academy, says he may not be able to keep going much longer. You remember him, Steven? Very attractive.'

'For an Australian, you mean. You're going back a bit, aren't you? He was around in the seventies, a great doubles player, wasn't he? Got to the singles final at the American championships, too, but was stuffed by Ashe or Connors.'

'That's right. He says he's got a future champion under his wing. Francesca Zanini, she's only just twelve years old. Wow, that's awfully young, isn't it?'

'Well, girls can go on the circuit at fourteen, Suzi, if they want. Let's see that article. I might go and see Kenny Crane.'

Two days later, Steven was greeted in the reception area of the Kenny Crane Tennis Academy by its founder. Lean and suntanned, Crane was clad in a green and gold tracksuit. He had a guarded manner and a laconic way of speaking, but, as Steven soon discovered, humour lay near the surface.

A one-storey wooden building housed the administrative resources of the academy. Although newly painted white, Steven could see how tired the structure was. There were four tennis courts and another wooden building which, Crane told him, housed changing rooms and a small gymnasium.

'I suppose you're interested in Fran, are you?' Crane said.

'Yes, and also in Kay Ferraris. She was mentioned in the article as having potential. But it's not just that, I'm interested in your set-up. You reckon you can produce tennis champions, is that right?'

'Sure, if I can get the right raw material.'

'Like Zanini?'

'Yeah. Come and look at her. She's on court in a minute.'

They walked the few yards to the tennis courts and

Steven saw a tiny girl whose racket seemed almost as big as she was. A short, tubby man was talking earnestly to her.

'That's Mauro, her dad.'

'What's his role?'

'He calls himself her trainer. He's as ambitious as hell for her.'

'She's very small.'

'You watch her hit tennis balls. Maureen Connolly was small and so's Billie-Jean. It didn't stop them.'

While Mauro stood aside and watched intently from the sidelines, Crane fed balls to Francesca Zanini: forehand, then backhand, volley and half-volley, lob and drop-shot. She went through her routine and Steven could see that her technique was superb, a tribute to Crane's coaching.

Then the girl went through her repertoire of services. Mauro, who had been darting glances in Steven's direction, at last waddled towards him. He gestured towards his daughter. 'You a reporter?' he asked. 'You do story 'bout Francesca?'

'No, Mr Zanini,' Steven replied. 'I'm a business manager. I represent Ray Gerrard, amongst others, and Mr Crane suggested I had a look at your daughter.'

'I'm agent for her. She can trust me.'

Oh yeah, thought Steven. 'Well, I'm just thinking long-term,' Steven said. 'When she plays the circuit, she'll need expert help.'

'Not for twenty per cent, she won't. I manage her fine.'

Mauro walked away and Steven went back to the office and got himself a cup of insipid coffee from a machine. He made a call to Joe Lynagh's office and talked quietly to him for several minutes.

When he went outside, Crane was working with another girl, who was at least a head taller than Fran Zanini. Crane shouted across at Steven: 'This is my other star, Kay Ferraris.' The girl made no acknowledgement of Crane's remark but concentrated on her next shot.

Some sandwiches and some cans of beer were brought into Crane's cramped office for lunch. Steven bit into his tuna mayonnaise, chewed and said, 'How much do I have to pay you and Mauro to sign up Zanini?'

'You don't have to pay me, mate, but Mauro'll want his pound of flesh.'

'How much?'

'Think six figures, if I were you. She's had plenty of agents trying to sign her.'

'What about Ferraris?'

'Fifty grand and her parents would be your friends for life. They'd probably piss it up the wall within six months.'

'Nice people, eh?'

'That's tennis. The kids are just meal tickets to their folks.'

'And for you?'

'Sure, but I enjoy it, Steven. I love the game.'

'Obviously. But who pays for all this? Who pays for the kids? Not their parents, that's for sure.'

'Oh, I've got various sponsors and grants from here and there. But I need an injection of cash or it'll all go down the tubes. I'm mortgaged up to my eyeballs. If I don't get a break soon, it'll be back to coaching rich kids at some country club.'

'D'you really think Zanini can make it?' Steven asked.

'Oh, yeah. She's got everything it takes.'

'OK, Kenny, let's have dinner tonight and we'll discuss a proposal. I think I can help you, if you'll help me to get Zanini as a client.'

The deal with Crane was relatively easy to strike. Steven

would raise sponsorship money for the academy but, instead of taking a commission, would acquire a stake in the business. It was agreed that, depending on how much money Steven generated, his share of the academy could grow up to, but not beyond, 45 per cent. Most important to him was Crane's agreement that all his pupils would in the future be optioned as clients to Shaw Management.

The negotiations with Kay Ferraris's parents were even more straightforward. Jack and Marie Ferraris were two obese people who were only too eager to sign their daughter up to anyone who could offer what they regarded as serious money. In return for a cash payment of $35,000 dollars the agreement was signed, with Kenny Crane as a witness. Steven took care to designate the money as an advance against Kay Ferraris's future earnings.

Mauro Zanini was by no means as easy to persuade. During the course of four meetings spread over two days, Steven became sick of the sight of the tubby Italian, his creased and sweaty face, his greedy eyes. At one point he was ready to give up the negotiations and catch the next flight to New York. But Francesca Zanini was one of the critical factors in Steven's attack on the tennis market. His deal with Crane would look valueless without her.

Mauro demanded an advance of $150,000 and Steven countered with an offer of $85,000. In small increments, he raised the amount to $95,000, guessing that a figure of $100,000 would be Mauro's realistic objective. The greasy bastard would relish the thought of boasting to his friends, if he had any, of how he took the hot-shot agent for a hundred big ones.

After more wrangling, Steven shrugged. 'Let's settle on $102,000, Mauro. That's my final offer.'

'Cash,' Mauro said eagerly. 'And you pay today.'

Steven nodded his agreement, touched hands briefly

with the Brazilian and the deal was done. As with Ferraris, the money would be set against future earnings and Steven was confident that, well before Zanini joined the professional circuit, he would have enough endorsements in place to repay his investment many times over.

Before he left for New York, Steven spoke at length to Crane about the training regime which his pupils underwent. 'What about diet and vitamin supplements?' he asked.

'I programme that for them,' Crane replied.

'Fine, but I'll get a specialist medical adviser for you. Zanini needs a bit of extra help.'

'OK, Steven, you call the shots on that side. I'll get on with the coaching.'

Within a week, Steven had appointed a doctor, well known in athletics circles, as the medical consultant to the academy. In the care of Doctor Bertram Rexel, Francesca Zanini rapidly grew taller and stronger.

# Chapter Nine

Although he was twenty yards away on the other side of the ground floor of Tiffany's, Eva Rosen was sure that she recognised him. It was partly the cut of his jacket and partly the way he stood: upright, shoulders back, he looked athletic. She moved a few paces closer and caught his reflection in a mirror. Yes, it was that newish agent, Steven Shaw. He was already handling a lot of good talent in golf and tennis. They were members of the same fitness club; she'd seen him working out. He had a beautiful wife, and rich, too. Some people had all the luck.

Steven was looking at a silver pendant when she tapped him on the arm.

'For your wife or your girlfriend?'

The voice was low and clear and Steven swung round and looked into a pair of wide, black eyes. They were unblinking under raised brows and her lips were slightly parted, humorous.

'Neither, actually, I want a little gift for my secretary. She's leaving me.'

It was true. Marion Carmody had joined him on a temporary basis, seconded from Joe Lynagh's firm. She was slim, attractive and very efficient. She had become a problem, though one of Steven's own making. One morning, a few months back she had arrived late for work with a black eye and a swollen lip. Steven's sympathetic enquiry had caused the tears to flow from her eyes and the story to tumble from her lips. She had a boorish husband who spent most of his time in their neighbourhood bars and sometimes he beat her up.

Steven had taken Marion out to lunch and given her some advice ('kick the bastard out – you're too bright for a low-life like him'). On their return to the office her tearful and slightly drunken thanks progressed from a kiss to her going down on him.

'It beats dessert,' she said afterwards.

Steven knew that he was stupid to get involved with an employee. He decided that he must get rid of her and alleviated his pangs of conscience by telling himself that the real reason was that Marion was Lynagh's creature, sent there to spy on him. It was a ridiculous notion because he discussed most aspects of his expanding business with his father-in-law.

When he suggested that she returned to work for Lynagh's law firm, he used the excuse that he needed someone with public relations skills to help him. Despite the generous bonus Steven gave her, Marion was upset, and he decided to confirm his nice-guy image by buying her a present from Tiffany's.

'That's very pretty,' Eva Rosen said, pointing at the middle of three pendants which he was considering. 'Any girl would be happy with that.'

Steven's memory had now retrieved what he knew about Eva Rosen. She worked in the sports department of AAN, one of the big three television companies. She had the dark, slightly exotic looks which made some Jewish women so attractive.

With a nod to the assistant, Steven bought the pendant and asked her to gift-wrap it.

'Do you have time for a quick drink?' Eva said. She was intrigued by this man. He was already talked about as a smart operator in sport; and he was thoughtful enough to buy his secretary a parting gift. He had class, and that was rare in her world.

A quick glance at his watch told Steven that it was midday. 'A coffee?'

'Whatever you like,' she said.

When they were settled in a nearby bar, Steven with a cappuccino and Eva with a glass of wine, he asked her what she was working on at AAN.

'Nothing mainstream, you have to be a man to do the big sports. No, bits and pieces, volleyball, swimming, women's tennis, you know the kind of thing.'

'You sound bitter.'

'Do I? It's over a decade since *The Female Eunuch* and men's attitudes to women in business are still as one-eyed as ever. Especially at AAN and especially in the sports department.'

'You picked a tough business if you're a feminist.'

'I'm not a professional feminist, I just want a fair deal. Those so-called executives in AAN sport are nearly as bone-headed as the morons they show on the screen every week.'

'Oh, come one, Eva, sportsmen aren't as bad as the media paint them,' Steven protested. 'They're under the microscope: no wonder their behaviour patterns get a bit strange at times.'

Eva Rosen leaned closer to Steven. Her eyes glittered with passion. 'Strange, Steven? That's not the word I'd use. I was stupid enough to go to a party after the World Series last year. You know that AAN have had the rights for years. There was enough coke there to get a full house at the Shea Stadium stoned for days. Well, OK, that's not my bag and the boys must have their fun, eh?'

Steven shrugged and she continued.

'After about an hour one of those shit-brained baseball

players got up on a chair and said "if there're any dames here who don't wanna fuck, they'd better go now". Then he got his dick out.'

Steven laughed and said, 'You stayed, of course.'

'No, I didn't.' Eva began to grin. 'Mind you, the fella had a lot to offer, I have to admit that.'

She drained her glass of wine and signalled to the waiter. 'Why don't you join me in a glass?'

'I don't drink during the day. But, since it's you . . .'

'OK, Steven, let's talk a little business. You've got some tennis players in your stable, haven't you? And I've got a slot for something a little different, a fun event. We could play it over a couple of days. Any ideas?'

'How about some mixed doubles?'

'Yeah, that's a thought. That's the only thing you Brits ever win at Wimbledon, isn't it?'

'A pro–celeb event?'

'Yuk. I've got enough trash-sport to hide in the schedule already. Yeah, I like the sound of mixed doubles. But we've got to have Ray Gerrard in it.'

'You've got him.'

'OK, let's talk about it some more.' Eva Rosen produced a diary from her handbag. 'Can you do dinner on Friday?'

'Yes, I'd be glad to.'

'Bring that lovely wife of yours, too, if you like.'

'Well, er, she's going to the opera, I think.'

'What a pity. I'll call you.'

The French restaurant chosen by Eva was not far from the Pierpont Morgan Library. When Steven arrived, she was already at the table with a bottle of wine before her. She knew enough French to chat, if in faltering style, to the waitress: this was unusual for an American.

Over the first course, Steven learned that she had studied

law at the University of Oregon and had already been married and divorced twice, once to a Frenchman.

'Yeah, I'm thirty-two years of age and I'm a lousy judge of men,' she said wryly. 'No more mistakes, I'm going to concentrate on my career.'

'In television?'

'Sure. I want to go all the way. President of Sports at AAN or one of the other networks. That's how I see it.'

'Ambitious.'

'Like you.'

In the gloomy, candle-lit restaurant Steven noticed again how her eyes glittered. She was attractive and tough. Even better, she had some business for him and was more or less handing it to him on a plate. Was there a catch?

They both ordered lamb, which was pink and delectably moist, and Eva insisted on their having a good red wine with it. The *maître d'hôtel* recommended a bottle of Léoville-Barton. It cost more than his father ever earned in a month, Steven thought.

'Let's enjoy the perks,' Eva said, as if reading his mind. 'Here's to us and to our little tournament.' They clinked glasses. 'What I'd like is four mixed doubles teams who'll play off in a league. That's six matches plus a final. We could do it over a couple of days. You provide the players and I'll provide the money.'

'Eight players over two days come expensive, especially when Ray Gerrard's involved.'

'How expensive?'

He pretended to do some calculations in his head, although he knew exactly how much he needed for eight players. He named his figure, which included an overall commission for himself for the package.

'No problem,' Eva Rosen said. 'I've got a sponsor who'll put up the guarantees and the prize money.'

'Who?'

'Just between you and me, it's the Kooler people.'

'Soft drinks. That's good.' Steven had a sudden image of Charlie Tomlin, cool and sardonic. He hadn't seen him for over a year, though they kept in touch. His father was the boss at the Kooler Corporation. But he didn't mention his connection, tenuous thought it was, to Eva. It might come in handy in the future.

'So, what d'you want me to do, apart from deliver eight players for the Kooler Mixed Doubles?' he asked.

'Why don't you package the whole deal? I don't particularly want to do it, but you could do it and make some extra fees.'

Eva was looking at him expectantly and once again Steven wondered when the hit would come. When would she ask him for an introduction fee? It was bound to be couched in some euphemistic way but what it always meant was clear enough: 'I want some money.'

'Eva, I'm a business manager, not a tournament organiser.'

'Don't worry. I've already got the venue in Florida and I can put you in touch with a good tournament director.'

He shook his head doubtfully and Eva said, 'Wise up, Steven, there's big money in television especially if you control rights to events. Effectively, that's what you'll do with this Kooler tennis thing. AAN will pay you a good fee for the privilege of showing your event, it's simple.'

'What's in it for you, Eva?'

'Not money, if that's what you mean. I'm not after a fee. No, I want to get shot of all the detail, and you're the best person to take it off my hands.'

For a moment Steven couldn't believe his good fortune. 'You're very straightforward, aren't you?' he said at last.

'Sure. That's always been my trouble.' She tipped the last

of the red wine into their glasses. 'I'll send you a draft contract. Now you can take me home and I'll make us some coffee.'

As the taxi bumped across the poorly maintained streets towards the fringes of Greenwich Village, Eva Rosen moved close to Steven, took his hand in hers and laid her head on his shoulder.

When they entered her apartment, she made a cursory offer to make the coffee, but instead they headed for her bedroom.

In later years Steven acknowledged, if only to himself, that Eva Rosen was the person who exposed the rich seam of business that televised sport represented and then showed him how to exploit it.

The Kooler Tennis Doubles Tourney, as it was eventually called, taught him a lot, including how to orchestrate an off-beat sporting event so that it attracted a wider audience. The tennis was presented as a showbiz spectacular. Rock music entertained the crowd before the matches and during the intervals, and a television celebrity compered the show; the players, clad in jazzy, multi-coloured outfits, were introduced like prize-fighters to fanfares of trumpets; above all, the spectators were encouraged to join in the fun, to shout and cheer while the points were being played. It was a far cry from the cathedral-like hush of Wimbledon, and it made great television and attracted a huge new audience for the game.

The event also revealed, to Steven's startled eyes, the vast amounts of money which washed through the television companies. By the time that he'd skimmed his commission off the top of the money put up by the sponsor, taken his usual percentage from the eight tennis players, and pocketed the rights fee from AAN, his agency had earned a healthy six-figure sum; a great deal more than the star of the show, Ray Gerrard. And the Kooler Tourney was only a minor event on the AAN sports schedule.

Thereafter, Steven applied the formula to package a mixed foursomes golf event, and a trial of strength competition between a team of field athletes and a team of American Football stars. The latter series was broadened to become 'All-Star-Sport' in which practitioners from a diverse range of sports competed against each other in a number of disciplines – some of which were serious, such as the 100-metres sprint, weight-lifting and swimming, and some more frivolous such as throwing a golf ball and target shooting.

Eva's and Steven's affair blossomed during the autumn and the long New York winter. Nobody seemed to think it remarkable that they spent so much time together; after all they were organising a number of televised events and there was a lot of negotiating and planning to be done. They were able to meet at many sporting occasions without any suspicion being aroused. Most of these occasions were outside New York and this suited Steven since he felt safer in pursuing the liaison away from the city.

One of his preoccupations was that Eva exercised discretion in public. Whereas he had thoroughly schooled his emotions, he was not sure about his mistress. He had learned to remain detached, especially when under stress during a negotiation, and to probe for the weaknesses of others, and he carried this over into other areas of his life.

He was fond of Eva. She was sharp-witted and alluring, funny and perceptive, an ideal person with whom to have both a business and a sexual relationship. But business came first. Steven frequently reminded himself that his ties to the Lynaghs were of prime importance, especially in the immediate future, and must not be endangered. He had a nagging fear that someone might learn of his extra-marital affair and use the knowledge to embarrass him. For the moment, however, the risk was justifiable because of the benefits Eva had brought to his business.

For her part, although she understood the need for prudence, Eva wanted everyone to know that Steven Shaw was her lover. He had all the attributes she had ever sought in a man: exceptional looks, an unforced charm, intelligence and strength of character. She longed for the public signs of their love – a special look, a hand held, a kiss – that Steven eschewed.

Eva was convinced that Shaw's agency was destined to be a major player in the ever-expanding business of sport. What a team they would make!

But he wasn't hers, neither in practical terms, because he was married to Suzi, nor, Eva suspected, in other less tangible ways. There was a hidden core of reserve in him, something she couldn't reach. Perhaps his wife and his child made it impossible for him to commit himself totally. But, one day, maybe . . .

# Chapter Ten

It was only a few months into the second year of Shaw Management's existence when the first significant milestone was reached. To Steven's delight, the commission earned by the agency passed the one million dollars mark.

Without revealing the reason, except to Suzi, he invited the Lynaghs to dine at their favourite neighbourhood restaurant and then made his announcement. It was an uplifting moment for Steven and just as satisfying when he handed a cheque for $50,000 to Joe. It was the first repayment on his father-in-law's loan.

Steven was immensely grateful for Lynagh's part in setting up the agency. It wasn't just the loan of a quarter of a million dollars, but his prescience in seeing a business opening of such potential. Although Steven had five years in which to pay off the debt, he wanted to be free of it as soon as possible. He guessed that the impulse had a lot to do with his mother's attitudes to borrowing money: 'never be beholden to anyone', she used to say with severity.

When the debt was paid, Joe Lynagh would retain his 25 per cent share of the company and Steven was happy for him to do so. Joe was full of ideas for the agency, and the legal support which his firm provided was always available and was invaluable.

After the congratulations and the toasts to the future of Shaw Management had been concluded, Lynagh waved his cheque at Steven and said, 'Are you sure about this? You'll soon need more staff, bigger offices. Fifty grand might come in handy and I'm in no hurry for the money.'

'I can always borrow it back, can't I?'

'Sure you can, son, nothing easier. Look, I can find you a bigger suite of offices in our main building, if you like.'

'That's a thought, Joe, but I've got my eye on a place a few blocks away, closer to Central Park.'

Lynagh shrugged. 'As you like. You want to spread your wings and so you should. Steven, I think about the business a lot. I love it, as well you know. The sports you're in are the international ones, as we agreed when you started out. That's good because you've got to think international, just as we do in our firm. OK, so you're a Brit, and there must be some rich pickings among the sportsmen in your home country. Have you thought about setting up in London? You should go and have a look around there, see if you can tie up with an agency over there. And you could take Suzi and young Adam to see your folks. They'd surely love to see their grandson.'

'And I'd like to see my parents-in-law,' Suzi said firmly. 'Steven hardly talks about them but I know I'm going to love them.'

Steven had thought at length about the European market, and on various fronts. First of all, he knew that the sponsors of golf tournaments in Britain had only a handful of world-class players available to them. To add class and a touch of glamour to their events they liked to invite American stars; and they were prepared to pay handsomely for the privilege. The guarantee was often as high as the first prize, plus first-class travel and accommodation for the star and his family. Steven reckoned that it would be Sam Rhodes who would open doors for him in Britain. Though only in his second full year on the professional Tour, he would win a major tournament soon. It could be the US Open or even the Masters at Augusta, a course which Rhodes loved. What an asset he'd be then!

Lynagh was right to point out that there were clients to be picked up in Europe, too, and London was the obvious base from which to campaign. Steven had heard about a young French golfer who, although he was still a student at the Sorbonne in Paris, was being described as potentially the best French golfer ever. Not that there was much opposition, Steven thought. Nevertheless, Patrice Barbier had won the World Under-25 Championship by a margin of ten shots from some very good pro golfers.

In addition, there were the television rights. The Wimbledon Tennis Championships and the Open Golf Championships were still two of the jewels in the world's sporting crown, and Steven knew that the AAN network, which bought the rights to show the action in the USA, paid way below the real market value. The BBC, who covered both events and sold the overseas rights, obviously needed some expert help. He would persuade them that he was the man to provide it. When he found the right man at the BBC, he would try to sell him some packaged events like the Kooler Tennis Doubles as well.

'You're right, Joe,' Steven said. 'There's a big, untapped market there and I ought to investigate it. I don't know about taking Suzi and the boy. I'll be on the go a lot, seeing people, and so on.'

He tried to avoid the subject of his parents and, as Suzi had noticed, was reticent whenever she asked him about them. Since they didn't possess a telephone he communicated with them by letter. He sent them money occasionally and photographs of Suzi and their baby. Stilted and formal, his mother's replies never went beyond thanking him, enquiring how he and his family were and stressing how much she and Dad would love to see their grandson.

It was Sam Rhodes's performance in the US Open which prompted Steven to make a trip to Britain. The championship was once again played at Winged Foot in New York State, a club which was founded in the 1920s by members of the New York Athletic Club.

In the weeks leading up to the event, Rhodes had not been playing at his best and Steven encouraged him to take some time off in order to see his old coach at the University of Texas. In the tournament that preceded the Open, Rhodes finished equal twelfth but his scoring improved every day and his final round was five under par. Steven had a premonition about his client and, though he rarely placed a bet (except on his own abilities on the golf course), he wagered $100 on Rhodes to win. Joe Lynagh went further and wagered $1,000.

The key to Rhodes's victory in the great tournament was his superlative play of the final five holes. All over 400 yards, they had been designed to test the golfer's nerve and judgement to destruction. The picture of the architect, A.W. Tillinghast, showed a kindly looking man, but he was clearly a sadist whose aim was to reduce the ablest golfers to jelly.

Golfing pundits, especially when pronouncing upon the major championships, invariably say that the tournament really begins over the final nine holes on the Sunday afternoon. At Winged Foot there was a variation, in that the judgement was applied to the final five holes. On this occasion they added that Rhodes was 'too young' to win; he 'hadn't been through the fire'; he'd be 'left for dead by one of the old hands'.

He wasn't. Steven watched with increasing excitement as

his client, two behind the leaders after thirteen holes of the final round, pulverised the finishing stretch. Rhodes seemed to be in a different world as he thrashed his drives great distances down the fairways and hit towering iron shots into the greens. Even as he stood on the tee of the tantalisingly difficult seventeenth hole, Rhodes was smiling and waving as if he knew his destiny. He birdied it, as he had the preceding three holes. Now two ahead of the nearest challenger, he made his par four at the final hole to win his first major championship in ebullient style.

After the presentation, Steven, with Joe Lynagh in his wake, pushed his way towards Rhodes through a throng of journalists, cameramen and well-wishers. They grinned at each other and embraced. Well, you'll certainly be a millionaire now, Steven thought, as he added up the bonuses which would now be due. Most of the contracts would have to be renegotiated. He would start tomorrow.

Someone thrust a bottle of champagne into Rhodes's hand. As he prepared to tilt it and drink, Steven carefully turned the label away from the cameras. 'No free advertising, Sam,' he whispered. 'We'll do a deal with them tomorrow.'

Rhodes's triumph was well and truly celebrated with the assistance of a large and happy band of family and friends at a nearby restaurant. The new champion was too busy shaking people's hands and signing autographs to eat much but, as midnight approached, the party broke up. Only Rhodes and his parents and Steven Shaw were left.

The newly risen star of golf grabbed a bottle of champagne from the table and said, 'Come on, I want to take one more look at the eighteenth. I want to remember it.'

'Oh, you'll never forget it, darling,' Mrs Rhodes said. 'Anyway, I'm for my bed.'

She looked enquiringly at Harry Rhodes, who nodded

and rose to his feet. 'We'll see you in the morning, son. I'm really proud of you.'

A few minutes later the two men had convinced the Winged Foot security guards that they really were looking at the new US Open champion and that all he wanted was to stand by the eighteenth green and drink a toast to his recent victory.

In the soft moonlight the grandstands encircling the green were skeletal and uneasily silent. Some pennants flapped briefly and busily in a sudden breeze and then also fell quiet.

Rhodes drank from the champagne bottle and handed it to Steven. 'This is the first of my dreams come true,' he said.

'How many more do you have?'

'There's no limit. If there was, there wouldn't be any point in going on.'

'The British Open next.'

'And the Masters.'

'And the Grand Slam.'

'Why not?'

There was a pause as both men looked back down the rolling fairway.

Then Rhodes gestured at the course and said quietly, 'This means more to me than anything: a great championship and I won it honestly. You'll keep me honest, won't you, Steven, you'll look after me? All the other things are secondary. The money, the deals. Sure, I want us both to benefit from my successes but it's out there that really counts.'

'I'll take care of everything. You just get out there and win.' Steven patted his client reassuringly on the shoulder. 'By the way, what were you up to on the seventeenth? You were acting as if you'd already won, waving and grinning. I was waiting for some malign spirit to hammer you for your presumption. A thunderbolt maybe.'

'I can't even remember doing that. All I could see was that fairway and it looked a mile wide. So did the greens.'

'Long may it remain so.'

Just after six o'clock on the next morning, Steven Shaw was sitting at his desk. With a mug of coffee in front of him, he summarised all Rhodes's contracts, the bonuses that his win would attract and the probable increases when the main agreements were renegotiated. He knew that all sorts of other offers would pour down the telephone lines during the next few weeks. However firm were his client's wishes to concentrate on his golf and especially on the major championships, Steven was keenly aware that this was his first big chance to capitalise on the name of a star sportsman. He would be discriminating and try to keep Rhodes's commitments to a minimum, but something would have to give. He knew that exhibition matches on behalf of companies which were entertaining important clients was a lucrative source of income for professional golfers. It was easy money, too. More important, such occasions gave Steven a chance to make contact with the chief executive of the business and sell other clients and other ideas.

The outer door of the offices opened at just after seven o'clock and he heard the sounds of Jay Melville's arrival. He had recruited him from a small advertising agency and he liked him. Melville was full of energy and ideas and had the naturally abrasive humour of a native New Yorker.

The trouble was that Steven didn't trust him. On several occasions in the last few months his arrival in Melville's office had caused his employee abruptly to terminate telephone conversations. Steven wondered if he were doing deals for the clients on the side; or if he were planning to set up his own agency and take some of the clients with him. Steven insisted on seeing a copy of every letter that went out of the office and Melville was certainly as assiduous and enterprising as Steven expected. But his unease remained and the thought of leaving Melville at large in the New York office while he spent nearly two weeks on the other side of the Atlantic worried him even more.

He had to make the trip and wondered how to keep watch on Melville. He'd talk to Joe Lynagh about the problem.

'Hey, what a win! Has the boy got class or what?' Melville, well over six feet tall and brawnily built, filled the doorway. There was a wide grin on his square face and his thick mop of fair hair looked as though it hadn't seen a comb for days.

'The phones should start ringing in about an hour,' Steven said. 'Let's be ready. We'll set his personal appearance fee at a minimum of forty grand. All other deals will be considered carefully. We don't want to swamp Sam.'

'No. But we want to make him rich. Us too.'

As well as a good salary, Melville benefited from a substantial bonus which was paid at the end of the year. He had no inhibitions about talking about money and that was another aspect of his character that Steven liked.

One of the first calls was some minutes before eight o'clock from an Englishman who was opening a new golf course near Bristol. Could Sam Rhodes do the honours on the Sunday before the British Open began? There was silence when Steven told the man his fee and he sensed that he was weighing the dent in his budget against the publicity he would reap for his course. He agreed the fee.

In the middle of the morning Steven called Rhodes at

his hotel and, after congratulating him again, suggested that they meet on the following day.

'We've already written half a million dollars of business for you, Sam. The phones are red-hot.'

'That's great, Steven, but let's only take the cream, eh? I don't want to be covered in logos like some of the guys. You know, the Mid-life Crisis Insurance Company, the Bank of Usury and Commerce—'

'Gnat's-piss beer . . .'

Rhodes laughed and Steven said, 'There're lots of offers to play exhibition matches and I want to run one of them past you. It's in England, the Sunday before the Open.'

'Steven, I don't know about that. I need to spend a lot of time in Sandwich. St George's is meant to be a helluva course and I've never been on a links.'

'You'll be fine. You learned to handle the Texas winds, so you'll handle them at Sandwich.'

'Where is this appearance?'

'Near Bristol. It's not far from London,' Steven lied. 'Let's discuss it tomorrow.'

As soon as he had finished speaking to his client, Steven dictated a confirmation of the appearance near Bristol; it was on its way, along with a contract, that evening.

The business pace was furious over the next couple of weeks and Steven had the added distractions of concluding the negotiations for the new office and planning his visit to Britain.

All sorts of approaches were made for Rhodes's services, although many of them could not be taken seriously. However, Steven couldn't help being interested in an offer from the organisers of the European Classic. The tournament was scheduled for the week after the Open Championship in Paris and the suggested fee for Rhodes, irrespective of the prize-money he won, was in excess of $50,000.

His client had planned to have a week's rest after the Open, but Steven guessed he could persuade him to play, especially since the venue was Paris.

Rhodes agreed to do so and added, 'You'll have to get a formal release from the PGA for me. Remember that it's the New England Classic that week.'

'But you're not down to play in that.'

'Doesn't matter. Call the Commissioner, Carl Lansky, and ask for a release.'

Lansky had guided the American Professional Golfers' Association to unanticipated levels of prosperity during the preceding few years. He had become the most influential administrator in the game and his strength of purpose was legendary. Steven had met him briefly at the US Open and remembered his imposing figure and his supremely confident manner. He had come into golf after making millions in the oil business.

To Steven's surprise he was routed straight through to Lansky when he called the PGA headquarters in Florida.

'What can I do for you, Mr Shaw?' His tone was courteous, but brisk.

'Just a formal request for my client, Sam Rhodes, to be released to play in Paris in the week after the British Open.'

'There's a conflict, as well you know. We have a tournament on the east coast that week.'

'But Sam isn't scheduled to play in that.'

'You miss the point, Mr Shaw. What will my sponsors say when they see he's playing in some third-rate European tournament in preference to theirs? He's our Open Champion. He should support his domestic Tour.'

'He's not under contract to the American Tour. He can make his own choices.'

'How much money did it take to persuade him to choose that tournament in Paris?'

'That's my business,' Steven said swiftly.

'And mine, because we don't condone such payments. Rhodes is a full member of our association and ought to know better.'

'Are you going to release my client?' Steven persisted.

'I'll see. Write to me, Mr Shaw.'

'I'm taking that as a yes, Mr Lansky, because it would be irrational of you not to agree.'

'I trust that you won't be taxing me with too many demands for releases. You should know, Mr Shaw, that I abhor the activities of so-called agents like you. Your influence is insidious and we don't need you in golf.'

'Well, I'm here to stay and my clients will pursue their careers in the ways that suit them best. You're no doubt aware of the legislation in this country which covers restraint of trade. Good day to you.'

Putting the telephone down, Steven realised that his face was warm with anger. Christ, it was a simple request and yet he'd been harangued by that bastard as if he were an errant schoolboy.

During lunch with his assistant, Lansky spoke of his contretemps with Steven Shaw.

'I wouldn't bother too much about him,' the assistant said dismissively. 'Agents are like fleas on a dog, they come and go. He'll probably be history by next year.'

'I wonder,' Lansky replied.

The recasting of Rhodes's existing contracts was not taxing because in most cases a formula had already been agreed. The exception was his agreement to endorse Parbreaker golf balls.

Steven hadn't forgotten how dismissive Jack Burrell had

been about Rhodes's prospects of winning a major championship, and it was his chance to take his revenge. He enjoyed making the man pay for his arrogance. He knew that the Chief Executive badly needed a young star like Rhodes and he jacked the price up by a factor of three.

Joe Lynagh's suggestion that Steven should try to link up with an agent in London was sensible and he spoke to a journalist at *Sports International* magazine about the likely candidates.

Joe Moser was a skinny and laconic man in his midforties who drank Scotch whisky in copious quantity and laced his golf articles with quotations from many diverse sources: from Shakespeare and Salinger, from Robert Lowell and Henry Longhurst, from Auden and Zola. He had struck up a cautious relationship with Steven in the course of researching some of his pieces and had been promised access to Sam Rhodes for a full-length feature in the magazine.

'Yeah?' His voice on the telephone suggested that he'd seen the shallow end of a bottle on the previous evening.

'Shaw. D'you know any agents in Britain?'

'Ah, Steven. I know of one agent in your fatherland but he's just a glorified travel agent. Even though we've broached the eighties, the business isn't a business over there as yet. Why are you interested?'

'Because I might need some representation over there.'

'I can't help, but you should call our stringer in London. He's English like you but he can't help that. Frank Lawford, he knows the scene pretty well. The things I do for you,' Moser grumbled. Steven heard a clunk from the telephone, a profane exclamation and the scuffle of pages being turned. 'Here you are, Lawford's number in London. Now it's my turn: what about my interview with young Rhodes?'

Steven reached Lawford on the following day and his

plummy voice reminded him of someone. It was that shit,
James Macaulay, the man who had made his father redundant after nearly thirty years of faithful service. He hadn't
thought about him for ages, which didn't mean that the
slights his father had endured would ever be forgiven.

'Any friend of Joe Moser's is a friend of mine,' the voice
said down the line. 'As for agents, I know most of them. In
fact, I've penned the life stories of many of their ghastly
clients. What can I tell you?'

'Is there anyone bright, ambitious and honest that you
can recommend?'

'Good God, no. They're mostly insurance salesmen and
second-hand car dealers who like to hang around soccer
players. What are they called in America? Jock-sniffers, isn't
that the expression?'

Steven laughed. It was a cruel and apt description of the
men who were besotted with a particular sport and set
themselves up as agents to acquire the spurious glamour of
being 'on the inside'. He had met several of them. Then
there were the former sportsmen who, ageing and frightened at the prospect of being cast adrift into an alien
environment, realised that one way to stay in their sport
was to set up an agency and gather a few clients together.
In addition there was the smattering of lawyers and
accountants who saw sportsmen as a means to promote
and expand their main business. Few of them had any
idea how to market their clients. Steven had been amazed
at the lack of professionalism shown by his competitors.
They seemed to see it as a game, as a way of making some
easy money.

'There's Mark Drummond.' Lawford broke into his
thoughts. 'He's in golf. Well, dabbles in golf. His family
own a merchant bank and his wife's filthy rich anyway.
Adrian Hartley, he does cricket and football, I wouldn't

recommend him. Oh, and Marcus Strawn, he's into rugby and squash.'

'Christ, how can he make a living from squash?' Steven said. 'You can only get three men and a dog to watch a squash match and it doesn't work on television . . .'

'It's a great participant sport.'

'So's jogging but you don't want to watch it. As for rugby, it's still amateur, isn't it?'

'Yes, but—'

'Lots of squat little Welshmen, I seem to remember. They sing when they win and weep whether they win or lose.'

'Yes. The Welsh are appalling losers and even worse winners. Look, Steven, I have a suggestion for you. Why don't I try to place an article about you, get you some publicity. After all, you're English and you represent the American Open Champion and several other fine players. And you have a stable of tennis players, not least Ray Gerrard, a Wimbledon finalist. You're news. If I can get you half a page somewhere—'

'In *The Times*, somewhere like that?'

'No, no. Probably one of the London evening papers. Send me photographs of your clients. I'll say that you're planning to set up shop in London. You might be surprised at the people who will offer their services.'

'It's worth a try.'

'And you have no objection to paying me a fee?'

'Won't you be paid for your piece by the newspaper?'

'Yes, but a pittance. I'll try much harder if you pay me as your press consultant. I could be very useful to you in Fleet Street.'

Excited by the prospect of visiting England and, above all, of meeting Steven's parents and showing off their grandson,

Suzi began to make a series of lists of the items they would need during their stay. Steven reminded her that there were shops in England and doctors available if Adam became ill.

A visit to the Lynaghs for Sunday brunch gave him a chance to take his father-in-law on one side and tell him of his doubts about Jay Melville.

'Why don't you have it out with the young fella?' Lynagh said. 'He seems straightforward enough and you might be able to clear the air.'

'I haven't got much to go on.'

'No, which suggests to me that you're mistaken.'

'It's just a nasty feeling that he's up to something, Joe.'

'What about some surveillance?'

'A private eye?'

'Sort of. But things have moved on from wise-cracking tough guys in snap-brimmed hats. I do mean surveillance. A tap on Jay's telephone, maybe a bug in his apartment. I can introduce you to a very discreet security firm, we use them a lot.'

'OK, Joe, let's do it.'

A few days later Steven went to the offices of Earlybird Security and talked to a man called Corky Price. A rangy man with a shock of grey hair and a goatee beard, Price had been a professional basketball player until a knee injury ended his career. As he shook hands, Steven couldn't help but notice their size; they were like shovels.

It was agreed that, just before Steven left New York, Price would be let into the office and would tap Jay Melville's phone.

'We'll monitor his conversations while you're away, Mr Shaw. Just a first step. It should tell us what he's up to.'

The day before Steven's departure for London, Charlie Tomlin called him. He was in New York for a couple of days and was Steven free that evening?

'Well, I've got some packing to do.'

'That's what Suzi's for, isn't it?' Charlie said with a laugh. 'No, I don't mean it, how is that beautiful girl? Look, let's play squash at the club and then have dinner. My dad'll be there but afterwards we can go out and chase some pussy, how's that sound?'

'Good, except that the last time we did some chasing, I ended up marrying the girl.'

'You don't regret that, do you?'

'Certainly not, Charlie. Anyway, I'd like to meet your father. I do a little business with the Kooler people.'

# Chapter Eleven

Charlie Tomlin had been the one firm friend that Steven had found at Harvard. Each class comprised nearly a hundred people who would stay together for most of the two years of the course. Steven had been open and friendly with all his classmates but he held a little in reserve during the first weeks. He wanted to observe everyone, try to pick out the interesting people, avoid the bores. Most of all his priority was to pick out the winners, the ones who would go all the way to the top of their corporate trees, the ones who would help him in his future business life.

After the formalities of the teaching process at London University, Steven was initially apprehensive of the free-wheeling approach of the Harvard system. The emphasis was placed on group discussion and the importance of individuals combining to analyse and solve problems. Everyone was well advised to make the effort to be open-minded and he realised that any remnants of British reserve that he possessed should be banished. As his supervisor stressed, half his course marks would be earned on the basis of his performance in class – it was vital to make positive and reasoned contributions.

'You don't get any points for hanging back,' he said. 'Get yourself noticed, get your share of air time.'

Steven had his first major opportunity during the opening week. Much of the Harvard Business Administration course was based on the case method. Students were presented with a description of a business problem in terms of the limited information available to the organisation's executives at that time and were asked to suggest solutions.

The problem under discussion in the marketing class that week was the competition faced by a leading manufacturer of nappies, or diapers as they were called in America.

Dreading his first 'cold call' from the professor, Steven was determined not to be caught with food in his mouth. On their second day, one of the class had nearly choked on a mouthful of doughnut when singled out to start the discussion. It was amazing how much food and drink was taken into the first class of the day: there was enough to start a substantial snack bar business.

Without warning, Professor Perlitz, who could identify all his pupils from the labels on the front of their desks, pointed at him and said: 'Steven, will you enlighten the class as to the competitive situation in the diaper market and suggest how the major manufacturer should try to protect his position?'

Steven hastily put down the cup of coffee which was halfway to his lips and tried to compose his mind. At least the first half of the question was clear-cut and, after some hesitations, he managed to give a lucid account of the problem and suggest some tactical moves in the marketplace. Afterwards he was glad that he had opened his account, and within days he was clamouring with the best of them to advance his arguments. It was reminiscent of his grammar school days when the keener pupils waved their hands high and shouted 'Sir, Sir' to get the teacher's attention.

With just over a dozen classes a week, Steven knew how important it was to be well prepared. It was an intensely competitive atmosphere and he was determined to be a leading light in his class, whatever effort it took.

Nevertheless, he remembered the dictum of his English teacher, Jeremy Knight, that a university was there to be enjoyed on all levels and he checked out the various clubs that existed.

The soccer club was an obvious one to join and he became a regular member of the School's team, which pitted their unsophisticated skills against other business schools such as Yale, Columbia and the neighbouring Massachusetts Institute of Technology. Steven took it upon himself to drum some elementary tactics into the team and, with the help of a first-year student from Brazil whose skills would have been welcomed at most leading European clubs (he was inevitably nicknamed 'Pele'), the Harvard Business School side proved too powerful for their opponents.

This was when he met Charlie Tomlin, who was the team's goalkeeper. He had been impressed by Tomlin's interventions in class. Tall and thin, he assumed a rather grave demeanour for his years and his comments were invariably incisive and assured.

On a trip to play against the graduate school at Princeton, Steven learned that Tomlin had been an investment banker in New York for several years. 'Why did you stop?' Steven asked. 'Why leave the gravy train at your age?'

'Because I was pissed with gambling on other people's talents and ideas. I want to gamble on my own. That's why I'm here. I want to get into the real business world like my old man.'

'What does he do?'

'He's Chief Exec of the Kooler Soft Drink Company.'

Steven raised his eyebrows. Kooler was one of the biggest companies in the world.

'Are you going to join his company?'

'No chance. I want to be like him, not with him.'

In contrast to his cool and analytical behaviour in class, Charlie Tomlin, whenever he donned his goalkeeper's jersey, showed a different side of his character. He was the gesticulating and screaming proof of the dictum that goalkeepers are crazy. Tomlin kept up a running commentary on the failings of his team-mates throughout the game and, if the ball came within thirty yards of his goal, he issued a frenzy of commands and exhortations to his defence. After a couple of games they learned to ignore him and, since he was such an amiable person off the field, they forgave him all the insults he threw at them.

As well as soccer, Steven played tennis and squash with Tomlin, who also introduced him to racketball. As they showered after a game, Steven said, 'Where did you learn your squash?'

'The New York Athletic Club. I'll take you there for a game. It's kinda dull but at least they have tennis courts up in Westchester. We go there a lot.'

'Expensive?'

'Exclusive, I think is the word.'

Over the year the two men became close friends and, at the end of the first academic year, Tomlin invited him to spend a few days in New York. His parents were in Australia and they would have the freedom of a massive apartment on Park Avenue.

Charlie set out to show his guest all the sights of New York and they did it on foot.

'It's the only way you'll get the feel of the city,' Charlie insisted. 'You can't see anything from inside a cab.'

They tramped up and down the Manhattan streets from Battery Park to the fringes of Harlem. At night they went bar-hopping and poured themselves into a cab in the early hours.

*

It was an exhilarating few days, and when Steven landed at Heathrow he felt as wan in spirit as he'd ever known. He was grateful for the vacation job which Dick Seabrook had arranged for him at his accountancy firm, but the summer months stretched ahead interminably. The highlight seemed to be the Captain's Day at his father-in-law's golf club.

Telephone calls to Clare were met only by her impersonal voice on the answering machine. Steven didn't leave any messages and wondered whether he really wanted to resurrect the affair. Maybe he would see her at the golf club sometime and he could try again. No doubt she had a lover but they might have a quickie for old times' sake. He felt the need of her cheerful brand of love-making as an antidote to Beverly's missionary-position-only efforts.

Although Steven went through the motions of the dutiful husband and father, it did not come naturally to him. He felt awkward, a feeling that was augmented because both he and Beverly knew that the question of whether she and Emma would return with him to Harvard had to be resolved. Both of them avoided the subject, with the connivance of her mother. Their possible departure was difficult for Louise Seabrook to contemplate: it would leave a void in her life.

For his part Steven tried not to enthuse about any aspect of his life at Harvard. He stressed the long hours of hard work and his commitment to the demands of his course. In some respects it was a genuine expression of his feelings, since he had noticed that, despite its size, his class had achieved a corporate identity. The diverse personalities, drawn from all parts of the USA and dozens of other countries, had developed a rapport. It was a marked contrast to his own family atmosphere, where Steven felt himself ever more an outsider.

Dick Seabrook had visited Boston a couple of decades before and had pleasant memories of it, and Beverly had gone as far as buying a guidebook about the city. But Steven avoided any mention of the fun he had had on his occasional forays south into Boston. He loved its understated charm: the stately buildings in Back Bay, the fine houses on Beacon Hill, the galleries, smart shops and cafés in Newbury Street, the cheap restaurants in Chinatown and the fizz of the Italian North End. He and Charlie Tomlin also loved to watch the people in the Public Garden.

It began as an innocuous conversation on the terrace one Sunday morning. Dick Seabrook had gone to play his usual fourball game and his wife was paying her monthly visit to the local church.

As Beverly poured them both another cup of coffee, she rattled a section of the newspaper at her husband and remarked, 'There's a piece about Boston here, they call it the most European of American cities. It sounds lovely.'

Steven, with one eye on the cricket scores and another on Emma, who was trying to reach up for his coffee cup, replied: 'It's OK, but I live at Harvard. That's a different matter.'

'Even nicer, I would imagine.'

'Very quiet.'

There was silence for a moment and then Beverly said quietly, 'You don't want me and Emma out there, do you?'

Steven looked up from the newspaper. 'Of course I do, you're my family. But it would be awkward. Accommodation is limited, we might all have to make do with one room, a studio flat.'

'I thought they provided apartments for married people,' Beverly said. 'You're graduates – there must be lots married, with children.'

'Well, they do, but they're bloody expensive. We couldn't afford it.' This was a guess because Steven hadn't bothered to check such details.

'Daddy would help.'

'He's done enough,' Steven stated firmly. 'He's keeping you, and I'm not asking him for anything more. It's not fair.'

'And you have your pride,' Beverly said sarcastically.

Steven said nothing and Beverly repeated, 'You don't want us with you, do you?'

'I'm just being practical.'

'I'd use another word.'

'I'm doing this for all of us,' Steven said heatedly. 'For our future.'

Beverly put the cups on a tray and walked silently out of the garden. In her heart she was glad that she wouldn't have to interrupt her comfortable existence and go to live in a new environment with very little money and few comforts at her disposal. If she suspected her husband's real motives she consoled herself with the thought that he belonged to her and she had a marriage certificate to prove it.

In bed that night, Steven put his arms around her and began to caress her. She moved away from him and hissed her refusal.

It was Charlie Tomlin who inadvertently caused Steven to meet Suzi Lynagh.

Although there were plenty of girls in residence at the business school, Steven single-mindedly poured his energies into his work. At the end of his first year he had been assessed in the top twenty per cent of his class and he wanted to do as well, if not better, in his final year.

Steven had a brief liaison with a girl from Paris but it ended in sharp recriminations.

'You're not serious about me,' she said and he agreed.

Charlie had several girlfriends in New York and occasionally, when in dire need, took the one-and-a-half-hour flight home to see one of them.

It was a Friday evening when Tomlin knocked on Steven's door. He was reading the case history of how Texas Instruments took the calculator market by storm. His tall American friend leaned on the door frame and said with a smile, 'Time to chase some pussy.'

'Oh yeah. Where? Money is a problem as usual.'

'I heard an interesting bit of news. Some of the nice young gals from the University go dancing on a Friday night. It's only five dollars to get in.'

'I'm interested,' Steven said, as he reached for his jacket. 'Lead me to them.'

'It's at the end of the subway line. It's called the Dreamland Ballroom.'

'Christ, what are they doing slumming it up there?'

'It's their current fad. Ballroom dancing.'

'The real thing?' Steven asked. 'The waltz, foxtrot, quick step and so on?'

'Exactly.'

'It's not really my style, but I'll have a go.'

The Dreamland Ballroom had acres of car parking available and the building was the size of several aircraft hangars laid end to end. Steven and Charlie stood in line to pay their five-dollar entrance fee; they were the youngest people there by a good thirty or forty years. The six-piece band was playing a waltz in strict tempo. It reminded Steven of the radio music his mother used to listen to when he was a child.

The two men went through the swing doors into the hall and saw the dance floor in all its glory. Steven was astonished by the vast expanse of polished sprung flooring:

it was bigger than a football pitch. On the ceiling above, a huge glitterdome of sparkling glass revolved majestically. There were at least a hundred couples on the floor and they would hardly have filled one corner of the place. The customers were aged and came in all shapes and sizes, but had one thing in common: they could dance. Tubby men with white-haired grandmothers in their grasp were swooping and gliding with easy grace along the floor.

Steven, admiring, stopped in his tracks to watch, and Charlie bumped into him. The American grabbed him by the arm and whirled him around with a bellowed 'Shall we dance?'

Shrugging him off, Steven said, 'Bloody hell, have you seen the dresses?'

The women had dressed up for the occasion in extravagant flounces, layers of lace and tulle and a profusion of flowered motifs. The men were mostly in blazers, though some wore suits; and all wore ties.

'Where's the crumpet?' asked Steven.

'They'll be here. Don't be impatient. Let's go and have a drink.'

They entered the long bar which was crowded with at least another two hundred people. Two policemen stood near the door in their full regalia which included a baton, handcuffs and a handgun.

Steven nudged Charlie and said, 'What are Boston's finest doing here? And all tooled up, too. I wouldn't forecast any trouble from tonight's clientele, would you?'

'No. They're earning some spare cash on the side and it's easy money tonight. It's far from easy, apparently, on Spanish night when there're two or three thousand spics crammed on to the floor. You can hardly breathe for the fumes of after-shave, cheap scent and marijuana, and at least one knife fight is guaranteed.'

Tomlin raised his bottle of Budweiser to his lips and nodded towards the door.

'Here they come,' he said.

Steven looked through the glass panes of the door and saw half a dozen young girls saunter around the perimeter of the dance floor and seat themselves at a table. Like the older women they were dressed to kill in satin and silk, with multi-layered frilly skirts. He wondered if it was a deliberate parody and decided that it was.

Within minutes the girls were being whirled around the floor by eager, blazered old gentlemen.

The band stopped for a few minutes between dances. Tomlin drained his bottle of beer and said, 'It's time to cut one of those girls out from the herd. Are you on?'

Steven nodded. 'My dancing's not really up to this, but never mind. Which one do you fancy, Charlie?'

He hoped that his friend didn't have his eye on the dark-haired girl with the gorgeous eyes and the ready smile.

'The blonde with the prominent frontispiece,' Tomlin replied with a lecherous grin. 'She looks about my speed.'

The music began again and the two men moved swiftly towards the girls' table as a phalanx of potential dancing partners approached from the other direction. Steven stopped in front of the dark-haired girl and consciously exaggerating his British accent said, 'I'm Steven Shaw. Would you care to have the next dance with me?'

The girl rose from her seat and gave him several hundred watts of her smile. She was surprised to see someone so young at the Dreamland. She and her friends visited the ballroom for the fun of the dancing; they knew that the elderly gentlemen whom they partnered wouldn't make the crude advances that their fellow students invariably made. But at least Steven Shaw was handsome and had an agree-able accent, even if his dancing was decidedly clumsy.

Steven had to concentrate hard on the steps his wife had painstakingly taught him but, during their two dances, he discovered that his partner was Suzi Lynagh and that she was in her final year at the Harvard Law School.

'I thought America already had too many lawyers,' Steven said.

'Too many *bad* lawyers,' Suzi replied. 'My father happens to be a very good one. He works in New York and I'm his only child. I know he'd like me to follow in his footsteps.'

'You don't look like a daddy's girl.'

'I hope I'm not, but he's a partner in a big legal firm with all sorts of clients and one day I'll find a niche there. I don't see anything wrong with that, do you?'

Hastily, Steven agreed with her. Don't blow your chances with this lovely girl, he thought. He handed her into her seat and offered to buy her a drink. When he returned with a bottle of Coke, she was already being spun elegantly around the floor by a tubby man in a toupee. Its bronze colour did not match the silvery wisps around his ears.

Steven waited patiently for her return and said, 'Can we meet again?'

'I'll be in Boston tomorrow,' Suzi replied. 'Meet me on the bridge in the Public Garden. Is six o'clock OK?'

Steven smiled his agreement and went off to find Charlie Tomlin. Suzi wondered whether she had done the right thing. A few months before she had vowed to avoid any romantic entanglements for a while. Her affair with a fellow student at Harvard had brought nothing but misery to her life and she had terminated it when she found out that Peter was two-timing her with his room-mate. At least Steven looked straight; but then, so had Peter.

At six o'clock sharp, Steven was standing on the bridge. He

watched the Swan Boats being pedalled around the lake but watched even more carefully for Suzi Lynagh. At last he spotted her as she swung down one of the many paths which crossed the park between the stately trees. With her shoulders back and her head up she strode, graceful and carefree, towards him. Her wave, when she saw him, was allied to a vivid smile.

Steven waved back and walked towards her. She put out her hand to greet him and he grasped it, pulled her towards him and kissed her on both cheeks. An old couple sitting on a nearby bench smiled in their direction and then mistily at each other, stirred by a memory of distant and exuberant youth.

'What would you like to do?' Steven asked.

'Let's walk around the Garden and then we'll have a meal. I'll take you to a very cheap Italian restaurant. We'll split the tab, of course.'

Steven didn't bother to argue and they strolled between the trees for half an hour. Suzi then led them to a car park and found her vehicle, a bright red BMW.

'A present from Dad when I got into Harvard,' she said defensively.

'Why apologise?' said Steven. 'If you've made it, spend it, that's what I say.'

He was beginning to like Suzi Lynagh more and more. Not only was she beautiful and friendly but she was obviously rich too. It was another incentive, a compelling one, to persuade her into bed.

They ate their way through mountainous plates of pasta and Steven learned more about his companion. Suzi had lived in New York all her life, except for the time she spent away at school. A few generations back her father's family was Italian and he was true to his roots by becoming a member of the Board of the Metropolitan Opera.

'Dad loves the opera nearly as much as golf,' Suzi said. 'He bought a house in Pebble Beach because of the golf.'

'That's a long way to go for a game.'

'His firm's got an office in LA, so it's convenient. They have a lot of clients in Hollywood.'

'It sounds glamorous.'

'It's demanding, Dad says. You wouldn't believe the complexities of some of these film and TV contracts.'

'It sounds like fun to me,' Steven insisted and then he allowed himself to be questioned about his own background. He eliminated Beverly entirely from his thoughts and spoke only of his life in Brighton and in London.

When Suzi stopped near his hall of residence, Steven leaned across and kissed her on the lips.

'I've had one of the nicest evenings I can remember,' he said in her ear.

'And me,' she replied.

'Won't you come in and have coffee?'

'No, I think I'd rather leave it a while before . . .'

'Before what?'

'Before . . . before I accept your invitation for coffee.'

Steven smiled at her and said brightly, 'All I'm offering is some coffee and a night of unparalleled delight.'

Suzi laughed. 'I'd like to see you again. Do you like jazz? We can go to a club next week, if you like. I'll pick you up.'

So it continued in the weeks that led up to Christmas. Their relationship blossomed in every sense except the physical: Suzi refused to make love to Steven and he eventually dragged out of her the story of her unhappy affair with Peter.

'Love is like falling off a horse,' Steven said persuasively. 'If it happens you should get straight back on and try it again.'

'That's a rather crude and typically male analogy,' Suzi

replied testily. 'I fell very heavily for Peter and I'll have to be very sure of my feelings before I let such a thing happen again.'

Steven changed the subject because he knew he had wandered on to dangerous ground. He would conduct his campaign without haste. He knew he would triumph eventually.

By the time he left for Christmas in England, Suzi's defences were still firmly in place and he began to have doubts for the first time. Steven thought about her through most of his waking hours. To his family, he blamed his vagueness and lapses of attention on the demands of his academic schedule.

He was very relieved when Beverly told him that it was pointless for her to join him in Harvard since his time there was almost at an end.

After several weeks of his final term, Steven decided that his relationship with Suzi was likely to go no further. They were close friends and enjoyed each other's company but the final bond of physical intimacy was denied to him. He had confided his problem to his friend, Charlie Tomlin, whose verdict was unequivocal.

'Forget her,' he said. 'Suzi's lovely but if she's been taken in by a faggot there must be something wrong with her. There's a sexual screw loose somewhere. Don't waste your time.'

With some sadness, Steven acknowledged that Tomlin's view, cynical though it was, was probably correct. In his pragmatic way, he wrote Suzi off and put even more of his energies into his studies.

Nevertheless, when Suzi invited him to a party one weekend, Steven agreed to go. It sounded fun. A friend of hers had the run of a house on the coast at Marblehead while his family were away for a few days. The plan was to have a dinner party for a few friends, to eat and drink, to listen to music and maybe dance a little; it was to be a relaxed and informal evening.

The two of them left Harvard late on Saturday afternoon and Marblehead was an enchanting sight to Steven. The community straggled along the coast and Suzi drove slowly along the meandering roads between a series of detached, eccentrically shaped clapperboard houses.

She pulled the car into a car park by an old and redundant lighthouse and they walked, chilled by the stiff breeze, to the rocky point. In the fading light they huddled together and gazed along the shore.

Suzi pointed down the coast at a huge house which stood alone on a bluff about a mile away. It was an extraordinary building to find in such a setting, a granite folly with round and pointed towers at each corner. It reminded Steven of a small Scottish castle.

'That's where the party is,' Suzi said. 'Quite a sight, isn't it?'

'"When shall we three meet again, In thunder, lightning and in rain",' quoted Steven. 'Is it real? Does it have ghostly presences and cause dire imaginings?'

'It was built in the thirties by Tom's grandfather, so I doubt it,' Suzi replied. 'He was proud of his Scottish ancestry.'

'Obviously.'

When they entered the house, their host, Tom Douglas, pressed glasses of champagne in their hands and said, 'We are but twelve this evening, darlings, so there is a bedroom for each couple. Suzi, my love, you are in the Glenfiddich room.' He turned to Steven and said, 'My grandfather named each room after a famous whisky and there's always a bottle of the appropriate brand in each room. Help yourself.'

Steven smiled his thanks and looked with amazement at the entrance hall, panelled in dark oak, with suits of armour in each corner and ancient weapons festooning the walls: pikes, claymores, dirks, flintlock rifles and pistols, shields and helmets. A broad staircase led up to a gallery which ran around three sides of the hall. It looked like Hollywood's idea of Bonnie Scotland. Kevin Costner would no doubt play Prince Charlie.

'Grandfather was raving mad,' Tom said. 'Now come and meet the others.'

He led them into a huge room where more oak panelling could be seen between the swathes of tartan material which was draped on the walls. A window took up most of one wall and looked out over the garden to the dark rocks and the sea below. To Steven's eyes the other guests appeared to be around his and Suzi's age and it transpired that the majority were at various faculties at Harvard; one of the men was at MIT and one of the girls at North Eastern University.

Tom and his friend, who was called Terence and was a novelist, circled the room with magnums of champagne in their hands. After some prolonged drinking, Tom clapped his hands for quiet.

'Thank you, darlings,' he shouted. 'Terence and I have things to do—' There were whistles from some of the guests and he continued, 'The final touches to our meal. We'll reconvene in an hour. So, until then . . .'

He strolled out of the room with Terence in his wake and it was a signal for the guests to disperse to their bedrooms.

Steven and Suzi found the Glenfiddich room, which was suitably ornate for a bedroom in a fake Scottish castle. It had a king-size bed and Suzi put her overnight bag on its extreme edge.

'Do you mind if I use the shower first?' she asked.

Her question sounded stilted and Steven sensed her awkwardness.

'Can I no scrub your back for ye, lassie?' Steven said in an appalling Scots accent.

'No thanks, I like to be private,' Suzi said primly as she headed for the bathroom door.

Steven heard the key turn in the lock and thought gloomily that he might as well get drunk at dinner and then pass out in bed, rather than get balls-ache trying to seduce Suzi.

The food, served with panache by Tom and Terence, was outstanding. Steven didn't dare ask whether the seafood terrine was home-made but, if it wasn't, Tom had access to a brilliant supplier. The rack of lamb was served pink and accompanied by bottle after bottle of first-growth claret. Steven noticed that Suzi drank little wine but he didn't hold back.

When the cheese was served, bottles of brandy and vintage port were placed on the table and a large cupboard in a corner of the dining room was opened to reveal shelves of liqueurs. Several rounds of charades were played and then the guests returned to the sitting room where 1940s music was playing loudly. Tom and Terence danced together very well.

Several of the guests were smoking and Steven recognised the sweet smell of marijuana. Tom, his arm around Steven's shoulder, said, 'Do you want a smoke?'

Steven shook his head.

'Anything else? Terence can provide all sorts of exotic tablets or, for very special guests, a line or two of the finest coke.'

'I don't use drugs,' Steven said doggedly.

'You don't know what you're missing,' Terence said.

Steven smiled and pulled away from Tom's encircling arm. 'I'll stick to wine,' he said.

As he began to refill his glass, Suzi said quietly to him, 'Steven, I'm off to bed. Will you be long?'

'It depends what you have in mind,' he said.

Suzi smiled but made no reply. She bade good night, with a kiss and a hug to all the guests and Steven watched her walk gracefully away and through the door.

Suzi was glad to be finished with the party. They were so superficial, so obsessed with having a good time; they seemed on the verge of hysteria. Steven had something that the others would never have. He had joined in the fun; he had been charm itself. Suzi noticed he had been careful to ask the other guests about their families, what their fathers did, what their plans for the future were. But what made him so different to the others? He was self-contained, that was certain. A hard core of self-assurance? A proper sense of reserve? An idea of his own value? It amounted to the same thing, Suzi thought, as she threw her clothes off and stood briefly under the shower. She cleaned her teeth thoroughly and eased herself under the bed covers. Whatever it was about Steven, she had made her decision. She would surprise him.

Downstairs, Steven finished his glass of wine and decided that he didn't want another. He'd had too much to eat and drink; he needed some sleep. That was undoubtedly all he could anticipate upstairs. He reckoned he was as far away as ever from making love to Suzi. Maybe he should use a little forceful persuasion. Assault with a friendly weapon. No, why bother, there were lots of willing women in the world. At least he'd made some good contacts that night. Especially the guy at MIT, Andy. His father ran one of the biggest marketing consultancies in America. Based in

New York. An introduction had been promised.

The door creaked as Steven opened it. Quietly he took off his clothes and saw, in the shadowy light through the window, that Suzi was lying on the edge of the bed. That was a clear enough signal. He sidled into bed, sighed as his limbs relaxed and willed himself towards sleep.

Moments later, Steven registered Suzi's body beside him and her mouth on his. Then she was astride him and their bodies merged. It seemed so simple and Steven wondered why it hadn't happened long ago. But Suzi could have told him why; she could also have told him why she knew that their time had come.

Over the next few weeks Steven and Suzi made love on many occasions. Despite the uncertainties imposed by the imminence of their final examinations, they spent as much time in each other's company as possible. They even revised together in Steven's room. He was careful to destroy any letters that he received from Beverly and hid the photographs of his daughter, Emma.

At the beginning of April, with the examinations only weeks away, Suzi met Steven for a snack lunch just off Harvard Square. As they ate their sandwiches, she reached into the pocket of her jeans and placed an envelope on the table between them.

Steven saw the airline logo and looked at her smiling face. 'Plane tickets,' he said. 'Where're you off to?'

'Where're *we* off to.'

'Don't understand,' he said, through a mouthful of BLT. 'No money for air fares, no time to go anywhere. Tell me I'm wrong, that we've fast-forwarded to a more prosperous time.'

'We're going to New York next weekend. Dad has sent the tickets. The break will do us good, we've both been working at full stretch.'

'Why should your father send a ticket for me?'

'Because he wants to meet you. I've told him all about you.'

Steven had looked quizzically at Suzi and wondered how he would explain Beverly. Better not try, he thought, I'll run with this for a while and see what happens.

As arranged, Steven met Charlie Tomlin at the New York Athletic Club.

Though they were both rusty the two friends played five sets of competitive squash and then hoovered several glasses of beer. While they waited for Charlie's father they caught up on each other's lives.

Walter Tomlin was a tall man, like his son, but where Charlie was stringy and had a perpetually playful light in his eyes, his father was portly and had a look of solemnity.

While they tackled their steaks, Walter Tomlin quizzed his son about the progress of his telecommunications company in Houston.

'We're doing fine, Dad, the bottom line is healthy and there're new markets opening up all the time. We'll make out like bandits in a coupla years.'

Steven noticed that, whereas he and Charlie were drinking claret with their steaks, Tomlin senior stuck to water.

He fixed Steven with his brooding eyes. 'My son tells me that you already do some business with my company. The tennis doubles. I couldn't be at the event but I believe it worked well for us first time around. We'd like to keep it going.'

'I wish you'd tell your marketing director that, Mr Tomlin,' Steven said boldly. 'He's still sitting on my proposal. We want to proceed with Kooler, it's a clean, quality product but we do have alternative sponsors waiting in the wings.'

'Well, I love tennis, as Charlie has probably told you. I'll talk to Don on Monday about it. It's his budget of course, his decision.'

'I'm asking for a three-year commitment, Mr Tomlin.'

'Can you guarantee that Ray Gerrard will play? Now, he is some player and he seems to be a fine young man. I believe he's a member of my church, he's at the branch in Santa Monica.'

'Would you like to meet him?'

'Wouldn't I just?'

Steven saw Tomlin's eyes light up for the first time. Got him, he thought. Another bloody jock-sniffer.

When they parted in the club's hallway, Steven promised that, on his return from Britain, he would fix a meeting between Walter Tomlin and Gerrard. That same evening, the Chief Executive of the Kooler Corporation placed a call to Don March, his Marketing Director, and told him to conclude the Kooler Tennis Doubles contract as swiftly as possible.

As the two young men walked around the corner to a nearby bar, Steven said, 'I didn't realise your father was a God-botherer.'

'Eh? Oh, I see. Yeah, born again when he was in the Marines. He's very proud of being a Marine; but don't ask him about it unless you have two hours to spare. He's got very firm views on America's role in the world and on pretty much every other subject.'

# Chapter Twelve

Steven and his family arrived in London during the week before the Open Championship. He had booked them into a suite in a stately Knightsbridge hotel that overlooked the park. The recent substantial growth of his business and his newly acquired status as the manager of a golfing superstar required him to use a prestigious address, as did the oft-stated precept of Joe Lynagh: 'Always go first-class, people take you seriously then. Anyway, it's more comfortable.' Steven did a quick calculation of the likely bill over the duration of their fortnight's stay and it made him gulp for a moment or two. Christ, it was nearly as much as his father used to earn in a year.

He had written ahead to his parents to tell them that he, Suzi and Adam would meet them in Brighton on the Sunday for lunch. He had booked a table at a large hotel near the pier. He was dreading the prospect.

Once they had settled in their room his first call was to Frank Lawford. He had his doubts about the man's effectiveness and was pleased when the journalist told him that an article about his agency would appear in the *London Evening Times* on the following day.

'All settled, Steven. It'll do you the power of good.'

They arranged to meet for a drink. Steven guessed that Lawford would want his money.

Next on the list was the Head of Sport at the BBC. After several attempts, he at last got through to his department and asked for Paul Davis. His line was engaged, would he like to hold on?

'No, I'll leave a message.'

'If you like, but Mr Davis is very busy and he may not call back for days,' the woman said in a bored tone. 'Why don't you write in?'

'Because I'm only here for a few days.'

'You could try again tomorrow.'

Steven did and was told that Davis was at the Test match.

Since Suzi was playing with Adam in their suite when Frank Lawford arrived that evening, Steven met him in the bar. The journalist was a short man with a prominent belly and his face showed the high colour of the habitually heavy drinker. Whereas Steven ordered a beer, Lawford asked for a mineral water.

'Dieting?' Steven asked.

'No, I don't drink. Well, I can't, I'm an alcoholic,' Lawford said cheerfully. 'I've been off it for three years, thank God.'

He waved a copy of the *Evening Times* at Steven and opened it at a page near the back. 'Here's your article,' he said triumphantly.

Photographs of most of Steven's important clients looked out at him and the headline read: 'SPORT'S SUPERSTAR AGENT IN TOWN'. The opening paragraph was as follows:

In only a couple of years, Steven Shaw, born in Brighton 28 years ago, has built up a stable of brilliant young sporting stars. From his palatial offices in New York, Shaw guides the careers of such luminaries as the US Open Golf Champion, Sam Rhodes, and future Wimbledon winners like Ray Gerrard.

Shaw, married to an American girl and with a baby son, has come back to Britain to cast his eye over the sporting scene here. 'I would like to open an office here in London,' he told me, 'and try to assist the sporting talent of Britain to realise their commercial potential. I'm here too, to support my client, Sam Rhodes, in his bid to become the double Open champion. Above all,' said this assured young businessman, 'I'm here to see my parents and show them their grandson.'

'Well, what d'you think?' asked Lawford.

'I think you've done a bloody good job. And I like the quotes. That's your expertise as a ghost-writer, I suppose. Now what about the money I owe you?'

'Cash, old boy, if you can manage it.'

Steven reached into his wallet and extracted several notes. 'What can you tell me about Paul Davis at the BBC?'

'Not a great deal. He rose without trace, as someone or other said. He went to the BBC from some obscure job in ITV sport. He likes the good life, or so it's said, but don't we all?' Lawford swirled the water in his glass reflectively. 'He was an athlete. Went to Loughborough College and ran in the Olympics. Four hundred metres. I think he got a medal, possibly in the relay. That would have been in the sixties.'

'How old is he?'

'Oh, forty-odd, but looks younger.'

On the following day Steven tried once more, without success, to reach Paul Davis by telephone and then wrote a brief letter to him explaining why they should meet and had it delivered to the BBC's sports department.

During the day, the switchboard operators at the *London Evening Times* re-routed several calls to Steven from people who aspired to work for him in London.

A few minutes' conversation told him that none of them could be taken seriously. The exception was Adrian Hartley, of whom Frank Lawford had spoken. Steven did not like his voice which had the lazy undertone of the London sub-urbs. He knew he mustn't be prejudiced; after all, he and Beverly had worked hard so that he could assume a classless accent. But could Hartley open boardroom doors for him in Britain and, more important, persuade directors to open their cheque books? Despite his reservations, he arranged to meet him that afternoon at his office near Shepherd Market. He could learn a lot by seeing the man's working environment.

It was a fine afternoon and Steven strolled through the park. Yes, it was definitely Hartley's voice which had put him off. Steven hadn't realised how important accents were, until Beverly taxed him with it.

After a quiet wedding, with only the immediate family and close friends in attendance, Steven and Beverly had had a two-week honeymoon at a congenial hotel in Crete. They had lazed in the sun, swam in the sea, ate and drank without restraint and made love several times a day. It was an idyllic period in their lives and neither wanted it to end.

One of their favourite moments of each day was sitting on their verandah before dinner. Glowing from the effects of the sun they sat, pre-dinner drinks before them, and watched the sun decline in the velvet sky.

Beverly chose one of those early evenings of languorous relaxation to tackle her husband about his accent. She knew that she was on dangerous ground. For generations webs of petty social snobbishness had been entwined around the perception of regional accents. George Bernard Shaw had put an incisive mark on the problem when he wrote: 'It is impossible for an Englishman to open his mouth, without making some other Englishman despise him.'

GBS had managed to write a play around that assertion, but Beverly had to find a simpler solution. She was aware that Steven had a Brighton accent. The inhabitants of the town, close to the capital and sometimes called 'London by the sea', spoke in the lazy way that native Londoners do: consonants were slurred and vowel sounds undifferentiated. Steven had inherited some of this laziness, and Beverly, who loved him in his entirety, knew that she must try to improve his diction. Her husband was ambitious in business and, like it or not, a standard English accent was an asset. She knew she had to exercise caution; it was more politic to criticise an Englishman's love-making than his accent.

Her chance came when Steven asked about a trip they had planned to take on the following day.

'Steven,' she said, 'I'm not having a go at you but you sometimes sound as if you were born in Stepney and have never been near a university.'

'What d'you mean?'

'"When are we due to be collected?" It sounded more like "When we Jew be c'lect".'

'It's my lower-class upbringing, darling,' Steven said, every syllable clear and in a parody of the clipped accent used in British films of the forties and fifties.

'That's a lot better,' Beverly said, 'even if you're taking the mickey.'

'You want me to go all la-di-da, do you?'

'No. Don't be offended. You've got a lovely voice and

you use the English language well, but you're lazy. With a little effort you could speak so much better.'

'Why should I bother?' Steven asked.

'Because you're ambitious, you want to make your way in business. You look the part. I know I'm biased but you're handsome and lively, you've all the attributes. But your way of speaking isn't right. Business is run by the middle classes and, well, your accent is slightly off.'

Wondering whether Steven would simply reject her words out of hand she smiled uncertainly at him.

To her great surprise, he said, 'You're probably right, Bev. Fortunately, I can't hear myself. What do I do?'

Each evening thereafter they spent a few minutes on a series of exercises which Beverly knew from her days of amateur theatricals. Guests on adjoining verandahs were intrigued to hear such phrases as: 'the Jew paid the money due to the duke before the dew was off the grass on Tuesday'; 'red lorry, yellow lorry'; and 'although no bones were broken they both told him to go so he slowly drove home'.

Beverly introduced a tape recorder into their sessions, which were punctuated by the laughter induced by the various tongue-twisters she made Steven try. By the end of the holiday his sub-cockney twang had been well on its way to being usurped by the standard tones of home counties England.

After crossing Park Lane, Steven found the entrance to Hartley Sports Management Limited next to a pub. On the first floor he passed the locked door of a travel agency and found Hartley's office above.

The door was open to a small room with one window which overlooked an alleyway. Most of the space was filled by a desk and a fair-haired man lolled behind it; his chair was tilted back, a telephone was cradled under his chin and his feet lay on top of the desk which was crowded with pieces of paper and bits of merchandise: a miniature football, a children's cricket game, a sample football boot, as well as several magazines, a chipped coffee mug and a can of cola.

Hartley grinned and waved Steven to a seat. He was roughly the same age as his visitor and was wearing a striped shirt with several of the top buttons undone. Steven could see a gold medallion resting on his chest, and it seemed to match the bracelet on his right wrist. As he listened, Hartley twisted one of the rings on his left hand.

After a couple of minutes of Hartley's 'yeahs' and 'OK mates' Steven became restless and looked pointedly at his watch.

'Must go, mate,' Hartley said. 'My American agent's just blown in. See ya, mate.' He held out his hand and Steven touched it briefly. 'One of the boys, having trouble with his contract – I'll sort it before the new season starts. Now, what can I do for you?'

With an inward wince, Steven decided to get out of Hartley's seedy office as quickly as possible. 'I'm looking for someone who's got an established set-up and knows the golf and tennis markets. I really need a sizeable office so that I can expand.'

'No bother, Steve, there're plenty of offices we can move to. Tennis and golf, eh? Big numbers I suppose. That Lee Trevino, now I love 'im. Oh yeah, I could get interested. You see, Steve, there's not enough dosh in the football game. You need a Bestie – Georgie Best are you with me? – to make out. Christ, if he was playing now he'd be mega, it's the only word, mega. And they just ain't around anymore.'

'What do you know about the golf market, Adrian? The sponsors, the manufacturers?'

'Well, you'll clue me up, matey, and I'll do the deals. I'm great at closing a deal, even my best enemies would acknowledge that.'

For a few minutes more, Steven went through the motions of polite business discussion and said he'd get back to Hartley after the weekend. He declined his invitation to 'join the boys for a few at opening time'.

As he walked back to his hotel, Steven wondered about the calibre of the agency business in Britain if someone like Hartley could make a living at it. The market must be wide open.

Suzi had been looking forward to her Saturday morning with Steven. She had planned a shopping expedition in Knightsbridge followed by lunch in the Harvey Nichols restaurant, which her mother had recommended.

They had lazed in bed that morning and made love. After breakfast in their room, a nanny, arranged by the hotel, reported for duty and the Shaws prepared to leave. Adam, a placid child, was already absorbed in a game with his new friend, a cheerful Australian girl.

The telephone jangled. Steven picked it up and listened for a few moments. Suzi pointed at her watch and mouthed at him as he sat down and began to make notes on a pad. To her irritation, she heard her husband say, 'In that case, why not come round to the hotel for coffee. In an hour? That's fine.'

Suzi glared at him as he replaced the receiver. Steven held up his hand defensively. 'I know what you're going to say but this is important—'

'It's always important—'

'He sounds interesting, he wants to work in the sports

business. And, darling, you know how I hate shopping. You'll be better off without me.'

'That's not the point.'

'He's only got this morning free, Suzi, and I am here to work. I'll see you in the restaurant at twelve-thirty.'

With a muttered 'damned work', Suzi left the suite.

Steven shrugged. He'd side-stepped the shopping neatly and all in a good cause. Dean Aultman sounded very interesting. Twenty-five, marketing executive with an American multinational, Oxford graduate. And he sounded good; he was confident but didn't overdo it. Maybe Steven should take a chance and set up his own operation in London in the near future. It was a risk, but if he could find the right man . . .

After half an hour of talking to Aultman, Steven thought that he had found the right man. Solidly built and fresh-faced, Aultman, although casually dressed for the weekend, looked smart and he had an excellent background in marketing. The American firm for which he worked was renowned for its management training programme and Steven remembered that one of their executives had lectured at Harvard. Aultman was articulate and interested in most sports.

Having explained a little about the workings of his business, he arranged to meet Aultman again in the following week.

Steven had not seen his parents for over two years, and he prayed that they would not spend their time bickering, as in his childhood. To be accurate, it was his mother who did most of it; his father usually took it on the chin.

The worst arguments had blown up over Steven's education, and they had begun as soon as he passed his Eleven Plus and was offered a place at Dean Grammar School.

Steven was pleased with his own good fortune but disappointed that his friend from next door, Danny Kyle, had been routed to the Secondary Modern.

'Oh well,' Danny's mother said, 'he can be a motor mechanic like his dad. He'll always have a job if he has a trade.' Alice Kyle reflected the optimism of the middle years of the 1960s. Britain was prosperous and brimful of energy; England had won the World Cup at football and the Beatles were at the top of the world's hit parades. British was best once again and weren't the barriers of class finally crashing down? Prime Minister Harold Macmillan's famous quip of a few years before that Britain 'had never had it so good' was beginning to appear prophetic rather than supercilious.

For several days Mary Shaw was carried along on a small cloud of euphoria and pride. People who normally received no more than a brief nod were accosted in the street and engaged in conversation. The merest hint of an interest in Mary's family brought out the news: 'Oh, you probably haven't heard about my boy. Steven's going to the grammar school in September.' All the shopkeepers with whom she dealt received the news and she wrote to all her relations to tell them of her son's success.

The Reynolds family, the Shaws' neighbours on the other side, were invited to high tea on the Sunday: not just sandwiches and cake but a ham and tongue salad and fruit trifle. Mrs Reynolds gave Steven a fountain pen.

It was on the following Friday evening that the discussions began. His father had arrived home from work with a bag of fish and chips, as was his custom. When they had finished their meal and were lingering over cups of tea, Bill Shaw had, as usual, opened his brown wages packet and handed some pound notes to his wife.

'Are you set on Steven going to the grammar school?' he

asked quietly. It was an opening gambit, a rhetorical question, as both parents knew.

'Set?' replied Mary Shaw sharply. 'He's going, that's already decided.'

'How are we going to pay for all the extras?' Bill Shaw still spoke quietly and, as his wife began to speak, he held up his hand and continued: 'I know it's all free, the lessons and so on. But there's a school uniform to be bought, sports gear, the boy will want to play all the games, and there are the trips they go on. It all adds up. I suppose we can get second-hand stuff—'

'Steven is not having second-hand stuff. The very idea. Letting us down. What're you saying? That we can't afford to send him?'

Mary Shaw looked at Steven, who was studying his mug of tea, embarrassed but fascinated by the conversation. 'Steven, your father and I have things to discuss. You'd better go upstairs and get on with some homework.'

'But, Mum—' he began, because he usually did his weekend homework on Sunday.

'No buts. Off you go.'

He went unwillingly up the stairs, shut his bedroom door loudly so that his mother thought he was in his room, but sat at the top of the stairs within earshot of his mother's next fierce words: 'Nobody's going to spoil Steven's chances, Bill Shaw. We may not have much but we can give him a good education, something you and me didn't have. Steven can make something of himself, get on in the world.'

As she paused for breath, Bill Shaw seized his opportunity. 'You know how much I earn and how little is left when I've given you the housekeeping money. How do you think we'll pay all the extras for Steven? Where d'you think we'll find the extra cash? Under the paving stones in the back garden?'

There was silence for a few moments and Steven had to crane his head and listen hard to hear his mother say, 'You could cut out the boozing and the cigarettes for a start.'

'Three fags a day and a couple of halves on a Saturday night.' Steven could hear the anger in his father's voice. 'I'm not giving that up, not even for Steven. You can bloody well give something up. That sodding bingo of yours for instance.'

'There's no need to swear,' his wife said primly. 'Yes, I can do without bingo and I'll go out and get a job. Part-time. My shorthand typing may be a bit rusty but I'll soon get it back. Or I'll work in a shop, there're plenty of new ones opening.'

'Good God, Mary, you're forty years of age. These new shops are called boutiques, they play pop music, it's the swinging sixties in case you haven't noticed. They want young girls serving, in mini-skirts and tight sweaters.'

'All right, I'll go back to a solicitor's office, they always need typists.'

Bill Shaw sighed. 'There's a vacancy at work. Assistant manager in the soft-furnishings department. Another few quid a week. I'll try for it.'

The disagreements were even more bitter when Steven passed his O-Levels. The congratulations were sincere but the euphoria did not last long. Then the discussions about his immediate future began.

'I've been talking to Mr Bamberger,' Bill Shaw began tentatively early one evening when Steven was safely out of the way. He was playing cricket for the Sussex Young Amateurs team.

'Who's he?' Mary Shaw asked without discernible interest.

'One of our managers and he's an associate director of the firm. He'll be on the board one day. Anyway, he tells me that they're looking for some bright young people to join Macaulay's. I think I could get Steven in, he's the right age, he's got his O-Levels. It's a golden opportunity.'

His wife made no reply for several seconds and then her normally quiet voice seemed to hiss. 'Our son is not going to work in a store. He's staying at Dean Grammar School to take his A-Levels and that's that. He's not going to be a shop assistant.'

'Like me, you mean,' Bill Shaw said bitterly.

The continuous presence of the television had taken away the need and the pleasure of conversation in the Shaw household; but, when he returned that evening, Steven noticed that his parents were even less communicative than usual. His father asked him how the cricket went.

'OK, Dad,' he replied. 'Out for a duck, but I took a couple of wickets.'

His father nodded and turned his gaze back to the television screen, which was showing a futuristic series about spies, who seemed to spend most of their time in the arms of women with ludicrous names rather than actually gathering information and causing mayhem.

Steven sat down in a chair while his mother went to the kitchen and reappeared with a plate of fish and chips and a mug of tea.

'Mum, we ate after the match. I don't need it.'

'Eat it up, it mustn't go to waste. Where are your cricket things? I'll wash them in the morning.' Steven gestured at his bag, dropped near the front door. 'Your father and I have been talking.' So that was it – they'd had a row. 'About your future. We know that you want to do well and get your A-Levels, so that's how it will be. Two more years at the Grammar School and you'll be well on your way.'

Although he grimaced, it suited Steven. He wanted to

stay on at school, although he envied Danny Kyle sometimes. Now apprenticed at a garage, he told Steven that
there was good money to be made, and with money you
could get the birds. Oh well, two more years of school it
was to be. That was fine. Within a few minutes he found
that he had, after all, eaten all the fish and chips.

# Chapter Thirteen

Bill and Mary Shaw were already in the reception area of the Brighton hotel when Steven and Suzi arrived. His parents looked smaller and more stooped than Steven remembered and it seemed to be an effort for his father to raise himself from his chair. Bill Shaw was dressed in the same type of grey suit that he had always worn, and Mary Shaw had put on a high-necked floral dress. Steven knew the agonies of indecision which would have afflicted her before she made her final choice.

Any awkwardness which might have overlain their first moments was dispelled by Suzi, who gave both parents-in-law smacking kisses, called them by their first names and gave Adam to them to hold.

As they meandered slowly towards the dining room, Steven asked his father how he was keeping.

'Not so bad, Steven, can't complain. I'm looking forward to retirement. Not that the old age pension is much of a prospect, it'll just about keep me in beer and pay for your mother's bingo.'

'Don't worry, Dad, I'll do what I can to look after you both.'

'That's good of you, son, but you've got your own family to worry about.'

The lunch was dominated by Adam, whose every gurgle and gesture was a source of great delight to Mary Shaw and, to Steven's surprise, to his father. To his horror, Suzi asked a series of questions about his boyhood and his mother answered them in detail. Steven's main function was ordering the food and keeping his father's glass topped up with beer; he refused to drink any wine.

Over coffee in the lounge, Suzi decided that she and Adam must spend more time with his grandparents.

'Well, we'd put you up, dear,' Mary Shaw said doubtfully, 'but there isn't enough room in our little flat . . .'

'I'll soon fix that,' Suzi said. 'I'll book Adam and me in here for a few days. We'll have some fun, while Daddy's at the golf, won't we, Adam?'

She strode off towards the reception desk and Bill Shaw said, 'You've got a fine girl there, Steven, you look after her. Not that I had anything against Beverly . . .' he finished hastily.

'No, I know that, Dad. Now, look, I'm going to make arrangements for you to have a phone in the flat, so that I can call you now and again. I'll pay for it. And, Dad, what about moving to somewhere more comfortable, bigger? I can help you out, pay the difference.'

'That's all right, Steven, it's fine for us.'

'Fine for him, he means,' Mary Shaw said. 'He spends most of his time in the pub on the corner. He wouldn't want to move too far away.'

'Well, the offer stands,' Steven said.

Suzi returned and said that she'd booked herself and Adam in from Tuesday through Friday and that she'd drive down in a hired car. Steven was secretly pleased; it would leave him free to get on with his work. He wondered briefly if Araminta Macaulay still had her flat in Kensington. Maybe it would be worth a telephone call.

Steven had to spend some time with Sam Rhodes before

the Open Championship began, and he hired a car and drove to Sandwich on the Monday.

Everything was more or less in place for the great championship and he marvelled at the scale of the event: the long lines of hospitality tents, the huge tented village where the equipment and clothing manufacturers showed off their wares, the scores of food and drink outlets, the vast stands which were placed on the course and especially around the final green where they resembled a great amphitheatre, the towers and gantries which held the television cameras and the miles of cables which were needed to transmit the pictures to the production unit. Then there were all the people who made the championship work: the stewards, markers and scorers; the policemen and the security men; the boys and girls who collected the litter; and the officials, buzzing importantly around the course on their electric buggies. Finally, there were the players, out in force as they tried to analyse the strengths and weaknesses of the course and plan their tactics for the approaching battle of wits.

Steven caught up with Sam Rhodes as he played the final holes of his practice round and it was clear that his client was hitting the ball with great authority. The ball was whistling off the clubhead and Rhodes's putting stroke was as rhythmic and assured as ever.

When Rhodes had holed out on the eighteenth green, the two men strolled over to the practice ground together. Steven asked him about the previous day's exhibition match.

'It was fine, Steven, but a helluva long day. Six hours travelling and the freeway was all clogged up on the way back.'

Steven shrugged. 'The weekenders returning to London on Sunday night, I suppose. Never mind, you earned some good money.'

'Yeah, but I wouldn't want to do many like that.'

'They're important, Sam. You've got to show your face if we're to market you successfully.'

'Maybe, but winning championships is even more important.'

For a while, Steven watched his client as he worked on his technique; he wanted to hit his shots on a lower trajectory. It was a sensible tactic on a links course where the wind was bound to blow before the championship was over. Rhodes also went through his repertoire of wedge shots: the pitch and run, the lob and the cut-up shot. It was a versatile display and Steven was disappointed to leave but he wanted to scout all the manufacturers in the tented village. He was at the Open to do some business. He would see Rhodes again on Thursday when the Open began.

After having lunch with Dean Aultman on the following day, Steven was certain that he should set up his own office in London. It gave him great satisfaction to think that his first employee in his own country was a graduate of Oxford University. He'd been to Harvard, which accorded him prestige, but Oxford and Cambridge were special in the eyes of the world. If only he could have gone to one or the other.

A call to Joe Lynagh reinforced his decision: his father-in-law was gleeful at the thought of having a London base. 'Betty just loves London,' were his parting words.

Steven rang half a dozen estate agents to enquire about office space and made a reasonably generous offer to Dean Aultman to run Shaw Management in London.

'You'll need a good secretary. Someone classy who'll impress the clients.'

'Are we talking Sloane Ranger material?'

'Whatever you like, Dean. You're the one who's got to work with her and her salary comes out of your budget. All

I ask is that the office is up and running before the end of the year.'

'No problem. But do you have any words of wisdom for me about this business that I'm about to get involved in?' Aultman was hesitant. Steven had spoken at length about the structure of the market and the overall objectives for the agency. But there had been no words about the agency's responsibilities for its clients, no homilies about the ethics of the business.

'Were you expecting some well-thumbed phrases on ethics?' Aultman nodded and Steven smiled. 'Don't sleep with the clients' wives. That's all I have to say on the subject.'

'But, Steven—'

'Let's build the business first. We can worry about ethics later.'

One of the messages that awaited Steven at his hotel was from Paul Davis's secretary. The BBC man would be in the champagne tent at Royal St George's on the following day and could spare him a few minutes. That was big of him, thought Steven, as he dialled a number in New York. Corky Price had news for him.

The security man wasted no time on niceties. 'Your employee Melville has a complicated social life, Mr Shaw. He's banging three chicks, one of whom is a waitress in a bar around the corner and she apparently has a very jealous husband.'

'So he's not on the take or thinking of stealing my clients?'

'No sir. I don't think he'd have the time. He must be a very fit young man,' Price said with a laugh, 'and he has a few personal problems to sort out.'

With relief, Steven put the receiver down and thumbed

through some lists of office property. That evening he
dialled Araminta Macaulay's old number in Kensington –
he had never forgotten it and he could still picture her
handwriting on the card she had given him all those years
ago. There was no reply.

It wasn't difficult to spot Paul Davis. The champagne tent,
at midday on the first morning of the Open
Championship, was not crowded, although one table with
six occupants already showed three empty bottles and a
fourth on the wane. He could see a briefcase with a prominent BBC sticker at the feet of a man who still had the
build, even though he was half a stone or so overweight, of
a 400-metre runner. Davis was over six feet in height and
broad in the shoulder. His long face was topped by thinning, light-brown hair. As he smiled at his female
companion, Steven registered his prominent teeth.

   With a click of his fingers, Davis summoned one of the
waitresses and Steven said, 'Can I get that? I'm Steven
Shaw.'

   'Should I know you?' Davis asked over his shoulder.

   'Your secretary suggested I meet you here. I'm Sam
Rhodes's business manager.'

   'Good for you,' Davis said with a grin towards the girl
who, Steven guessed, was something in public relations.
The curly blonde hair and the ready smile gave it away.

   Before Davis could reach for his money, Steven paid for
the bottle of Veuve Cliquot and filled up their glasses.

   'D'you have a few minutes to talk, Mr Davis?'

   'I'll talk to anybody who buys me a bottle of fizz.' The
girl erupted with laughter, as if he'd said something
uniquely witty. 'This is Lindy, by the way, she's into sport,
aren't you, darling?'

   Lindy jiggled her eyebrows at Davis and Steven said,

'I'd like to put a documentary together about Sam—'

'A young lad like Rhodes wouldn't sustain a documentary. He simply hasn't done enough. It's tough enough to pull a programme off with a genuine eighteen-carat superstar – a Palmer or a Nicklaus.'

'He's going to be *the* golfer of the next decade or two.'

'Yeah, yeah,' said Davis as he refilled Lindy's glass and smiled conspiratorially at her.

'OK. What about tennis? Would you be interested in the UK rights to the Kooler Doubles?'

'Christ, we do Wimbledon and the other big open events. Nobody's interested in a Mickey Mouse tournament like that.'

With a shrug Steven said, 'There're one or two other things, but this obviously isn't the best time to talk. Do you play golf?'

'I hack it around occasionally.'

'Would you fancy a game at Sunningdale? On Monday? With the American Open Champion?'

Davis looked at him with interest for the first time. 'Well, yes, nobody would turn down an invitation like that, would they?'

It was a spontaneous idea and a good one. All Steven had to do was to persuade Rhodes to go along with the proposal.

Luck was with Steven. After a first round score of level par Rhodes was in a contented mood and agreed to delay his departure for the tournament in Paris, in order to play golf at Sunningdale.

'Hell, that was Bob Jones's favourite course in England. He played as nearly perfect a round there as it's possible to play. So I don't mind helping you out, Steven.'

During the succeeding days of the championship, Steven spent his time talking to sponsors and manufacturers. The

ticket provided by Sam Rhodes gave him access to the clubhouse and he was thus able to corner several top American
golfers whom he aspired to represent, and put his case to
them. It was a fruitful occasion, made more so when
Rhodes finished in eighth place to mark a highly satisfactory debut.

During the game on Monday, Rhodes couldn't have
been more co-operative. He gave Paul Davis, who hit the
ball strongly but erratically with an abbreviated action, a
sound tutorial on the mechanics of the swing and, as the
crowd of members following the US Open Champion
grew, he chatted amiably with them. It was a lesson in how
a sportsman should project himself, and it obviously came
naturally to him.

Davis did Steven the courtesy of listening to his comments about the Kooler Tennis event and to his plans to
extend the All-Star-Sport concept to Europe. It was agreed
that they would meet at the American PGA Championship
in three weeks' time to discuss the ideas further.

# Chapter Fourteen

Suzi had enjoyed her time with Steven's parents. The days had flown by as she took them on trips around Sussex and generally cosseted them. They stopped at charming country pubs for lunch and, after a beer or two, Bill Shaw regaled her with his reminiscences of his pre-war days at Macaulay's store. He'd begun work at the age of fourteen as a delivery boy.

'I used to whizz around the streets on my bike. I was a little tearaway, I suppose.'

Bill Shaw had vivid memories of the war years, too, when he had fought in Italy and France. Suzi was surprised when he spoke with affection, rather than horror, of his soldiering days.

'I was with a great bunch of lads,' he said. 'We were either bored or nearly frightened to death. There wasn't much in between, but it was an amazing time and we never doubted that we'd come out on top.' He didn't add that it was the only time in his life that he'd felt really alive, vividly alive, convinced that what he was doing was of value. He taught Suzi some wartime songs and Adam tried to join in. He told her tales of his and his army mates' exploits, which had his wife tutting and pursing her lips and which had Suzi crying with laughter. Bill Shaw felt a happiness he'd forgotten, as his beautiful daughter-in-law hung on his every word and his grandson guffawed and whooped.

Mary Shaw also adored Suzi's lively and open personality and was besotted with her grandson.

On her return to London Suzi was full of her plans for Steven's parents and, above all, was determined to see them housed in a bigger and better apartment.

She had been appalled by their cramped flat on the first floor of a terraced house in a dingy street with a pub on one corner and a newsagent on the other. The rooms looked minute to her eyes and the faded furniture and decorations depressed her. On first entering the place, she had gulped, then smiled brightly and said how charming it was.

'We've got to do something about your parents,' Suzi said to Steven. 'That apartment. My God, it's tiny. Only one bedroom . . .'

'Well, I have been there,' Steven said ironically, 'and I remember two bedrooms.'

'There's something no bigger than a broom cupboard, it's hardly a bedroom. And there's no shower and I don't know how your mother cooks in that little kitchen. Nobody should live like that. Your parents deserve better, Steven.'

'I've offered to help but my father didn't seem all that keen on moving.'

'I know your mother would like to, but she's too proud to push you—'

'Too long-suffering, you mean.'

'And you can leave your father to me. I've never met a man like him, Steven. And he's so funny. I can't wait to have them both visit us. I can take them down to Florida, they'd love that.'

Steven looked blankly at her, wondering if she were talking about the father he remembered. 'Er, fine. I'll do something about their flat but it'll take time because I'd prefer to buy them a place in a smart area of town. I'll get around to it as soon as I can.'

The father whom Steven remembered carried an air of defeat like a cloak that was too heavy to bear. Few people understood how deep his dejection was, but Steven had seen its causes at first hand when he became a temporary employee at the Macaulay store.

Bill Shaw had managed to secure a holiday job for Steven, after he had completed his A-Level examinations, in the packing and despatch department of Macaulay's. 'It'll bring some money in, and he can see how the other half lives and works,' Bill Shaw had said to his wife.

Macaulay's department store, built at the end of the last century, covered a whole block not far from the seafront. It sold everything, and the Macaulay family had another smaller store in the London suburb of Croydon.

As they walked to work that morning, father and son were striking in their differences. The older man was stooped, his faded look emphasised by his shabby grey suit, discernibly shiny at the elbows; fortunately nobody could see just how worn was the seat of the trousers. Bill Shaw was a defeated man and it showed. He had given up thinking about his future. He knew that he had reached his plateau at Macaulay's: the Assistant Manager of the soft furnishings department – and destined to go no higher. In the past year or two, he had frequently said to his wife that he was marking time until his retirement. Roughly twelve years to go and counting; counting every rotten, depressing day.

Steven Shaw stood several inches taller than his father and his straight back and broad shoulders emphasised the different scale of their physiques.

When the two men reached the main doors of the store,

Bill Shaw paused and delivered a brief homily, which he had clearly rehearsed.

'Now, Steven, you're an intelligent boy, so just get on with the work you're given and be polite to everyone. If a manager speaks to you, it's safest to call him sir. If any of the Macaulay family are around they're called Mr Charles, he's the Chairman as you know, and Mr James, he's the Managing Director. But I don't think you'll set sight on either of them. So there we are, don't let me down.'

Bill Shaw pointed Steven towards the far corner of the building and told him where the packing and delivery area was. 'Report to Sid Granger. He's all right. I'll see you tonight.'

As they scuttled towards their Monday tasks, some of the employees wondered about the identity of the young man with the shock of dark brown hair and the bright grey eyes. Surely he couldn't be old Bill Shaw's son?

Sid Granger showed Steven the rudiments of the job in less than ten minutes and then went off to find himself a cup of tea. He left Steven in the care of a lean and taciturn man called Joe, whose bare arms were completely covered with tattoos. As soon as they'd loaded one of the Macaulay vans with a morning's deliveries, Joe decided that they needed a brew of tea. That was more or less the pattern of the succeeding days.

During the second week Steven's responsibilities were expanded to include expeditions to various parts of the store to collect packages for later delivery by van. It was a welcome break in his undemanding routine; he also relished the opportunity to explore other parts of the store. It was a rare day that he was unable to make a detour through the cosmetics department, which was staffed by dozens of young women in tight black skirts and sheer white blouses. Steven was soon on nodding and chatting terms with several of them and had suggested to his old friend and neighbour, Danny Kyle, that they should make up a foursome with a couple of them in the near future.

'Yeah, me and the boys sometimes have a wander around there on a Saturday afternoon,' Danny said enthusiastically. 'Some great bits of crumpet. I'll bet they bang like drums.'

One morning, as Steven and Joe were sorting out a stack of parcels for later delivery, the telephone on Sid Granger's desk rang. The two men heard him grunt a few times into the receiver and then he said: 'I've not got a sodding delivery going anywhere near there. It'll have to wait.' The caller talked a little more and Granger finally said, 'It'll cost you a couple of pints' and put the telephone down.

He walked towards his two assistants, muttering to himself and shaking his head. 'Steve,' he said, 'get upstairs and see your dad, he's made a bollocks of some curtain samples. They're for Mrs Gough-Tempest, the old cow. It would have to be her. Personal friend of Mr James Macaulay and she's been on to him. The samples were promised for last week. So, there's a panic on, and I've got to divert a poxy van to deliver them to her. Very high and mighty she is, and mean as spit. Never been known to give a tip, even at Christmas.'

Granger paused and dragged on his cigarette. 'Off you go, Stevie, we'll try and keep your old man out of trouble.'

Steven jumped to his feet and took the back stairs two at a time up to the soft furnishings department. He couldn't understand what the fuss was all about – a few samples for some old woman who probably didn't have anything better to do. What was the problem? Still, he didn't want the old man getting into trouble. He'd give the cosmetics girls a miss on this trip.

Steven found his father checking the labels on a sheaf of

material samples. Stooped over a table, his scalp with its thin covering of hair shining under the bright strip lighting, he looked smaller than ever. He gave his son a wan smile.

'Hello, Steven, a bit of a panic. Sid said he'd help me out—'

His words were cut short by the thump of a hand on the other end of the table. Steven turned and saw a tall and heavily built man in a pinstriped suit; his waistcoat emphasised, rather than disguised, his large stomach. His fleshy pink face was crowned by straw-coloured hair, which was cut short and had a strict parting low down on the left side. 'For Gawd's sake, Shaw,' the man said, 'haven't those damned samples gone out yet? What on earth are you playing at?'

The words came out as a drawl, but so penetrating that everyone within twenty yards could hear them.

Bill Shaw turned and mumbled: 'Mr James, yes, I'm very sorry, the samples are almost on their way. They'll be with Mrs Gough-Tempest this afternoon.'

'And about time, Shaw,' James Macaulay said, his voice even louder. 'She is a valued client.' He lowered his voice as he realised that several customers were listening with great interest. 'She spends enough every year to cover your salary several times over. Her family have had an account here since we opened for business in 1873. Am I coming over loud and clear, Shaw? Who do you suppose is more important to the well-being of Macaulay's, you or Mrs Gough-Tempest?'

Bill Shaw said nothing in reply. He merely repeated, 'The samples will be on their way at once, Mr James.'

Steven, the pain evident in his eyes, stood helplessly alongside his humiliated father. The pain turned to anger as he looked across at James Macaulay, who caught his stare and asked abruptly: 'And who are you? Do you work here?'

Before Steven could form any words, his father said swiftly: 'This is my son, Steven, Mr James. He's doing a holiday job in packing and delivery.'

'Really,' Macaulay replied. Then he turned and strode away.

'Dad, who the hell does he think he is, talking to you like that?' Steven began furiously.

Bill Shaw turned and gripped his son's arm hard. Tears rimmed the older man's eyes. 'Leave it, Steven, leave it. Just take these down to Sid. Tell him I'll see him later.' He released his grip, turned back to the table and picked up a sheaf of orders. Steven headed for the exit and walked slowly down the stairs and towards the basement.

Bill Shaw returned home a little later than usual and Steven could smell a mixture of beer and whisky on his breath when he sat down at the table to eat his sausages and mash.

'You're late,' Mary Shaw said accusingly.

Her husband shook some tomato sauce on to his plate and said: 'Yes, I owed Sid Granger a drink. Helped me out, Steven knows why.'

Mary Shaw looked questioningly at both of them and Steven said vehemently: 'A great fuss about nothing and that sod, James Macaulay, had no right to speak to you like that, Dad. He's a bully boy and he was enjoying it, the upper-class bastard.'

'Shh, I won't have bad language in this house,' stated his mother. 'Mr James is the boss, he can do what he wants.'

'Well, I wouldn't—' Steven began but his father interrupted him.

'What you would or wouldn't do isn't the issue. That "bully boy" is the son and heir of Charles Macaulay. He's the boss, as your mother says. I need that job; where would

I get another at my age? What would become of my pension? Ask yourself that.'

Bill Shaw's food lay untouched but Steven couldn't leave the subject: 'No one has the right to talk to another human being like that, it's a disgrace.'

His father sighed. 'They're the people who run business, Steven, as you'll find out. They've got the money, they've got the power. They always do all right. When I was young, I thought things would change. When I came back from the war I believed all that twaddle the socialists served up. Equality, a living wage, full employment. What a joke! The same people are still running things and we're still running to do their bidding.'

'The Macaulays of this world,' Steven said quietly.

'Yes. Mind you, Mr Charles is a gentleman of the old school. Always polite, isn't he Mary? He won the Military Cross in the first lot, at Passchendaele.'

'But James Macaulay hasn't done anything,' Steven fumed. 'He's there because he's the only son, one of the family, that's all.'

'Yes and he'll inherit the lot one day. He's rich enough already, with a big house, and a posh wife of course.'

'It's all wrong, Dad.'

'Yeah, and how will the likes of us ever change things? To beat them, you've got to join them and the likes of us don't get to join people like them.'

Steven lay awake in bed that night long after the last drunks had staggered noisily along the street from the pub on the corner, and long after the last goods wagons had been shunted into their places in the nearby railway sidings. He was saddened by his father's defeated outlook. Surely anyone's life should offer more than merely waiting around for retirement and the accompanying pension, which, judging by the Macaulay philosophy, would be meagre. He

could still picture James Macaulay's bullying face, arrogant
and self-indulgent. He wasn't going to let himself be at the
beck and call of anyone like that. And nobody would get
away with treating *his* father like that. James bloody
Macaulay would get his come-uppance one day, that was
certain.

By the time he finally meandered off into a patchy sleep,
Steven had made one important decision. If his A-Level
results were good enough to get him into London
University he would study accounting and finance. The
course would represent the first rung on the business ladder, an important discipline which would show his future
employers that he was a serious person, a man of potential
in their world.

It was fortunate that, during the succeeding days, Steven
saw nothing of the hated James Macaulay. He might have
been tempted to assault him in revenge for his father's
humiliations. But a chance for a first measure of retribution
presented itself when he met Macaulay's wife, Araminta.

During the summer months, when many of the store's
customers were on holiday, the burden on the packing and
delivery department was less than usual. Steven was allowed
to accompany some of the drivers on their delivery runs.

He particularly enjoyed his outings with Kevin, a cheerful and irreverent man in his mid-twenties whose claimed
number and variety of sexual successes would have made
both Casanova and the Marquis de Sade envious. Since he
was a small, though wiry, man who wore thick-lensed
glasses and already had a noticeable bald spot on the top of
his head, Steven discounted the tales of his prowess.

He made Steven laugh, pressed samples of condoms on
him ('they're extra large, my son, because I'm very gifted in
the size department') and showed him some of his fiddles.

'Look, Stevie, my son, every shop, every store, every pub

has a percentage in the books for wastage. Breakages and such like. It's in the books, it's accounted for and it's a shame to mess their figures up, innit?' They had just drawn up outside an imposing house with a curved Regency front in a square not far from the old Brighton pier.

Kevin pulled a case of wine towards the rear of the van and, hidden by the open back door, gave the corner of the cardboard box a hefty smack with a tyre lever. There was a crack of breaking glass and a stain spread across the case. He winked at Steven and said: 'What a pity, the box'll have to go back. Let's deliver the other two, though.'

When they returned to the van, Kevin ripped open the carton and pulled out two unbroken bottles of wine. 'Chateau Cantemerle,' he said, 'very partial to that.' He wrapped them in newspaper and stowed them in a carrier bag. 'One for you, Stevie?'

Steven began to protest but Kevin said: 'Go on, it won't be missed. Share it with a bird, she'll think you're a right toff.'

Nevertheless, Steven was worried about taking the wine. However you described it, it was stealing; he knew that his father would not condone it. He said to Kevin: 'What about stock control, when we get back?'

'I've got a deal with Jack. We look after each other's interests, know what I mean.' He tapped the side of his nose, winked again and shoved the bottle of wine into Steven's hands. 'Come on, we've got a delivery to Lady Muck now. Mind you, I'd love to give her one, I reckon she fancies me.'

Lady Muck turned out to be the Honourable Mrs Araminta Macaulay, the wife of James. On the east side of Brighton and close to the golf course, the Macaulays lived in another of those elegant Regency houses in which Brighton specialises. It sat on the end of a curved terrace and comprised four floors and a basement.

Kevin drew up by a side-door with a squeal of the brakes. 'The tradesmen's entrance, Stevie and that's where I'd like to get the Hon Araminta. How the rich live, eh? They've got a flat in London as well.' He rapped hard on the door, which was opened by a round-faced woman in a maid's uniform.

'Hello, darlin',' Kevin said. 'A delivery for Mrs Macaulay.'

'Don't you darling me—' the maid began.

Araminta Macaulay heard her maid's words and guessed that the delivery was being made by that cheeky little man. Ken, was it, or Kevin? He always stared at her breasts but he was cheerful enough. If only he wasn't so ugly.

'Who's that, Liz?' she asked. 'A delivery?'

She had a languid voice that, to Steven's ears, had echoes of James Macaulay's but with a layer of warmth that his singularly lacked. 'Tell him to bring it all into the kitchen.'

The two men made several trips down the stairs to the spacious basement kitchen and, when Steven first saw Araminta Macaulay, he understood why she had aroused Kevin's uncouth fantasies. She was quite tall and the way her dark hair was swept back and tied emphasised the lean contours of her face. Steven scanned the graceful lines of her body, realised that he was staring and looked bashfully at the floor.

'Thank you, Kevin,' Mrs Macaulay said, not concerned whether she'd got his name right. She was wondering who this handsome young man was. Lovely eyes, beautiful teeth, good body, looked very fit. And a bit shy.

'Just a moment, Kevin,' she said and scrabbled among some change which lay on top of a dresser. She handed him some money. 'And who is your assistant? I haven't seen him before.'

'Er, that's Steve, Mrs Macaulay. A holiday job,' Kevin replied.

'Steve, thank you, too.' She smiled as she gave him a coin and Steven noticed the deep blue-green of her eyes.

As they drove away towards the next delivery, Kevin said: 'I think she fancies me. Bit of all right, eh? A real goer, I'll bet.'

Steven wondered why she had married the odious and unattractive James Macaulay and remembered one of his mother's oft-quoted maxims: money goes to money. That must be it. He was to meet Araminta again quite soon, in markedly different circumstances.

As August began, Steven took more interest in the morning's mail; he was looking for a buff envelope which would contain his A-Level results. He knew that a place at London University depended on his level of success; but his anxieties were nothing compared to those of his mother.

Around the middle of the month he heard the flutter of the letterbox and his stomach lurched uncomfortably as he saw a brown envelope addressed to him; his mind flicked back to the same moment two years before when his O-Level results had arrived. His mother was in the kitchen and he shoved the letter into his pocket and climbed the stairs to his bedroom. He wanted some privacy in order to face whatever the envelope contained.

Carefully he eased the letter open. High grades for English and History, a reasonable one for Geography. It was fine, his place at London was assured. For a moment he looked out of his bedroom window, over the meagre garden which joined one of the same size from the parallel street. Then he walked slowly down the stairs and turned into the kitchen.

'Mum, the results have come,' he said quietly and with

a neutral expression on his face. Mary Shaw abandoned the kettle that she was filling from the tap, looked wildly around for her glasses, failed to see them and said, 'Well, don't just stand there, how've you done?'

Steven smiled and said, 'Good grades, I'll be off to London in October.'

His mother sat down suddenly in a chair and said weakly, 'That's good, Steven, that's really good.' Later, when the two men had gone off to Macaulay's for their day's work she sat in an armchair and rehearsed how she would tell people of Steven's success. She tended to favour a casual statement. 'You know that my boy's off to London in October. To the university, to study accountancy, actually.'

On the way to work, Bill Shaw said: 'Are you sure you want to go through with this university business, Steven?'

'Absolutely sure.'

'It's another three years without any money,' his father said quietly. 'You'll have to work in the holidays to earn your pocket money.'

'I know, Dad, but a degree will give me a head-start in business, won't it?'

Bill Shaw grunted and changed the subject to cricket and specifically England's performance in the latest Test match at the Oval.

# Chapter Fifteen

Macaulay's annual dinner and dance had fallen during the week before Steven was due to take up residence at the University of London. It seemed an odd time to hold such an event which would have been more suited to the Christmas season, but Charles Macaulay had changed it to the first Friday in October many years ago. His reasoning was that it was his opportunity to thank his senior staff well in advance of the Christmas shopping rush. Since Bill Shaw had become an Assistant Manager of a department he was on the guest list. His wife always attended under sufferance since she was not at ease on such occasions. During the weeks that led up to the dinner Mary Shaw engaged the rest of her small family in a series of discussions about what she should wear and how she should have her hair done. If Steven had nothing to offer in the way of advice, neither did her husband, and Mary Shaw's final recourse was inevitably a series of frantic telephone calls to her only sister who lived in Swindon.

When the invitation was borne home by his father, Steven was surprised to find his name on it and said that he had no interest in going.

'You'll have to go,' his father replied. 'Old Mr Charles likes to see some of the younger generation there. To him, we're all part of one big happy family.'

'What a joke!' Steven muttered cynically.

'You can be there to support your mother,' Bill Shaw said sharply.

Charles Macaulay always hired the same room at the same hotel on the seafront. He stood in the same spot each year at the entrance to the room and greeted his guests. Tall and spare of frame, he stood erect and soldierly and looked as fit as anyone could in his mid-seventies. His white hair was still abundant, cut short and neatly parted, and his eyes looked sharp and humorous above a nose which was misshapen from the days when he had boxed in the army. His wife, small and round, stood alongside him, and next to her was James Macaulay, looking alert and, in the presence of his father, working hard at his smile. By his side was Araminta, in the role of a dutiful wife.

As he waited with his parents to shake hands, Steven found it difficult to keep his eyes off Araminta. Her body was encased in a close-fitting dress whose colour echoed the blue-green of her eyes. After darting yet another glance her way he saw that she was looking directly at him. He turned his head to hide his embarrassment.

The Chairman of Macaulay's greeted each of them by name; he prided himself on his memory, though he did make surreptitious use of prompt cards these days. As they arrived in front of Araminta she smiled widely at them all and said to the simpering Mary Shaw: 'I hope I can borrow your son from you later, Mrs Shaw, for a dance. It's Steven, isn't it? You delivered some wine a few weeks back.' As Steven nodded, she said, 'See you later' and they moved into the room and found their places.

The Shaws had been placed at a table with another Assistant Manager and the Head of the soft furnishings department. The conversation was desultory and confined largely to holidays, Macaulay's and the weather. The food was standard hotel fare but at least Steven knew which knife and fork to use, thanks to some guidance from Jeremy Knight, his English teacher. There was plenty of wine on the table but Mary Shaw refused it and drank water. She gave Steven a warning frown when a waiter filled his glass with white wine, but his father raised his own full glass and winked at him.

After the loyal toast, Charles Macaulay stood up to thank his staff for all their efforts on behalf of the firm and to remind them that it was a store for families run on the same principles as a family. He concluded: 'As you know, I have my immediate family around me, but to me you are my extended family and that is why Macaulay's will always be successful.'

There was much applause for the old man, and then a four-piece band struck up; several couples made their way to the small dance floor. Charles Macaulay and his wife, accompanied by his son and Araminta Macaulay, made a slow progress around the tables. It was an annual ritual during which he asked the same rhetorical questions. Is everything going well in your department? Is there anything I can do for you? He always ended the short conversation with an enquiry about the health of his employee's family. On this evening at least, Charles Macaulay was very much the benign father-figure, parading his concern for his charges.

The table at which the Shaw family were sitting was almost the last on the itinerary and as the old man approached, with his family retinue, Bill Shaw and the other men, including Steven, clambered respectfully to their feet. The women, not really knowing whether to remain seated or stand up out of respect to the Chairman, half rose and hovered awkwardly until Charles Macaulay waved his hands and said: 'Please, sit down, no formalities. This is a party, you're my guests.'

After the standard enquiries, the Chairman fixed his expressive eyes on Steven and said: 'Now, you must be Bill's son, is that right?' He had studied his prompt cards assiduously. 'What are your plans for the future, young fella?'

'I'm going to London University, to study accounting and finance,' Steven replied.

'Very good, very good. Come and see me when you've got your degree.'

Steven mumbled his thanks and, amid some more genial enquiries from Mrs Macaulay, James said to his wife, Araminta: 'Christ, another boring accountant at another second-rate university.'

The remark was intended for her ears only, but Steven's hearing was acute enough to catch his words and his wife's reply: 'Darling, they can't all scrape into Oxford on two very dodgy A-Levels and end up with a third, can they?'

She smiled at Steven and said loudly: 'Steven promised me a dance, and that's the best offer I've had so far this evening.' She raised her eyebrows expectantly and he got quickly to his feet, although he was dreading the ordeal of trying to dance with this elegant and attractive woman. His knowledge of dancing was based on half a dozen visits to discos with his neighbour, Danny Kyle; he could jig about in a semblance of a disco dance and knew the rudiments of jiving. He had thoroughly mastered the technique of the last waltz, his arms locked around the girl and his groin pressed into hers. But this wasn't disco music or a disco setting.

Fortunately, as they reached the dance floor, the quartet increased the tempo a little and went into a medley of sixties music.

'That's better,' Araminta said, 'I didn't suppose you were a dab hand at the foxtrot. Can you jive?'

'Only just,' admitted Steven.

'Just grab me on the way round, you'll be fine.'

Araminta was right. She made the dance look easy and he even had time to admire her curvy body and slender legs. As they walked off the dance floor, she said quietly. 'So you're off to London, are you? That'll be good for you. I go shopping in town every Thursday. Would you like me to take you to dinner?'

'Well, I er . . .' Steven tailed off in confusion and nodded dumbly at her.

'Thank you for the dance,' Araminta said with a smile.

She held out her hand. Steven grasped it and felt a piece of paper pressed into his palm. 'Just put the card in your pocket. My number in London is on there. Ring me a week on Thursday.'

Steven glanced anxiously to his left and right but nobody could hear her amid the music and the general hubbub. He thanked her, pocketed the card as casually as he could and sauntered back to his table. He felt ten feet tall.

'You look pleased with yourself,' his mother said sharply.

'Why shouldn't he?' said Bill Shaw. 'He's been dancing with a beautiful lady.'

'A married lady,' Mary Shaw corrected him, 'who ought to dress herself as if she's a Macaulay, not a barmaid.'

'Oh come on, Mary,' replied her husband, 'she looks marvellous.' He drank copiously from his glass of red wine and puffed on a large cigar. 'Anyway she's an Hon.'

'What d'you mean, an hon?' asked his wife.

'She was the Honourable Araminta Lamb, daughter of a viscount, that's what I mean. I thought you, of all people, would have known that, Mary.' Bill Shaw occasionally teased his wife about the close interest she took in the activities of the royal family and the aristocracy.

Mary Shaw looked away in irritation just as there was a

stifled cry from the nearby top table where the Macaulay family and the other directors were sitting. The scrape of chairs hastily pushed back was heard, and one of the directors was seen running towards the door.

Steven stood up and, between the people gathered around, could just see the white head of Charles Macaulay cradled in his wife's arms. Araminta was loosening his tie and his collar. There were several subdued shouts of 'What's happening?' and, as the band stopped playing with a last ripple of discordant notes, the room grew hushed.

'It's the old man,' Bill Shaw said quietly. 'A heart attack, I suppose.'

It seemed a long time before the ambulance siren was heard approaching and then two men hastened into the room with a stretcher. Charles Macaulay was carried out, his family following behind.

On the following day it was announced that Charles Macaulay had died of heart failure. The staff were issued with black armbands and the funeral took place eight days later. It was confirmed that his son, James, would be Chairman as well as Managing Director of the company.

In his second week in London, Steven rang the number which Araminta had given him, and her voice, its upper-class timbre exaggerated by the telephone, answered almost immediately. Arrangements were made to meet on the following Thursday at a Kensington restaurant 'for a meal and a chat'. Steven wondered what they would find to chat about.

He arrived at the restaurant nearly half an hour early and walked to the nearest pub to kill time. He was startled by the cost of half a pint of beer, compared to the generously subsidised prices in the student bars.

Araminta was waiting for him at a corner table in the

busy Italian restaurant. She was glad that she'd dressed down for the occasion in jeans and a black sweater which did full justice, however, to her figure. When Steven walked across to her table she could see how nervous he was. He tried to shake hands formally with her but she pre-empted him by rising from her seat and kissing his cheek.

If Steven felt awkward in the company of an attractive older woman in a London restaurant, Araminta dispelled his tension by saying, 'Don't be bashful. Just pretend I'm your rich auntie who's taking her student nephew out for a square meal. It doesn't matter what anyone else here thinks, even if they have any interest in us, which I doubt. So, enjoy yourself.'

Any doubts which Steven had about their facility to chat were groundless since Araminta took charge and talked entertainingly about her days as a secretary in London and about life within the Macaulay family. When the bill arrived she paid by credit card and said: 'Some coffee at my flat, perhaps?' It was more of a statement than a question and she smiled as Steven nodded. 'Come on then, it's just around the corner.'

The apartment was on the third floor of a Victorian mansion block and the windows overlooked a small square with a garden in the middle. Araminta took Steven's coat and threw it on one of the many easy chairs which were scattered around the sitting room. There were books in profusion and the walls were hung with prints, paintings and photographs.

'This is very nice,' Steven said politely and realised that he sounded like his mother.

'I kept this when I got married,' Araminta said. 'It's nothing to do with the Macaulay family, it's mine. James rarely visits it and only if I'm with him.'

She took Steven by the hand and said, 'Let me show you

my bedroom.' It was nearly as large as the sitting room and contained a huge bed in one corner. Araminta grasped Steven by both hands and pulled him towards her. He could smell a discreet perfume and he heard the thud of his heart.

She looked him in the eyes and said, 'Do you want me?' As an answer he put his mouth to hers and she responded with her lips and tongue.

As they paused for breath, Araminta drew her sweater upwards and dropped it on the floor. 'You, too,' she said and began to unbutton his shirt.

'I'll do it,' he said huskily, eagerly.

Steven couldn't match Araminta's ease and lack of inhibition. Within moments she was standing naked by the bed, her smooth limbs glowing in the soft light. As he pulled at his underpants, he turned modestly away. Araminta caught his arm and turned him towards her. 'You've got a beautiful body, Steven. Come here,' and she led him to her bed, where she began to teach him how varied sex could be. Steven joined in Araminta's acrobatics as his inhibitions fled and his confidence grew.

During the next few months they rarely missed their Thursday evening assignations and Araminta ensured that each meeting was an occasion. They hardly ever went to the same place twice; the only exception was the Italian restaurant where their affair had begun. Araminta rang the changes. She was enthusiastic about the theatre and, as well as attending West End plays, she took Steven off to suburban pubs and clubs to see fringe productions of obscure plays and reviews. One evening they went to the first night of a Pinter play and then to an expensive restaurant. Steven wondered about the chances of bumping into someone who knew Araminta and her husband, but she didn't seem to care. Sometimes they merely saw a film and had a curry afterwards.

Although Araminta was too sensitive to give Steven money, she was generous with her gifts. She improved his meagre wardrobe substantially by giving him several sweaters and shirts, a couple of jackets and a stylish suit. She waved away his protests over the latter gift with a casual, 'I want you to look nice.'

Any unease which Steven had felt during their first encounter in London had long since been replaced by a feeling of pride when he was out with her. She was beautiful and elegant; above all, she was interesting. Steven liked the way people sometimes looked at them, as if they were trying to assess their relationship.

Until he went to bed with Araminta, sex to Steven had been a quick and fumbling experience, something you did after much persuasion and cajoling; it had overtones of discomfort and haste. He had lost his virginity in the back of a van which Danny Kyle had borrowed from the garage where he worked. The girl, who was about his own age, had told him to hurry up and make sure he didn't leave the Durex inside. It was hardly the most romantic of sexual encounters but at least he'd done it for the first time. Since then Steven experienced many hasty fumbled sessions in the back seats of cars, standing up in the lavatory at parties and occasionally on the floor of Danny Kyle's house when his parents were out.

With Araminta the whole process was a teasing, leisurely and exhilarating experience, and on Thursday nights he could hardly wait to explore her supple body and to meet her inventive requests. He hadn't realised how many routes there were to heaven.

They met twice in London during the Christmas vacation; on the first occasion so that Araminta could give him his present. It was an expensive watch which Steven had to leave in his room in London, along with her other gifts. He had no wish to start his mother's antennae quivering; she would immediately want to know how he had acquired such things and would imagine the worst. It was a bleak prospect to know that he would not be seeing Araminta until the latter part of January. For the first time, he felt a real jealousy, not just for her husband but for all the other people who would be enjoying her presence over Christmas.

Steven had daydreams of taking Araminta home to tea. On the rare occasions in the past when he had taken a girl home or bumped into his mother when he had one in tow, she had always been dismissive. There was always something wrong with the girl: her teeth were dirty, she wore too much make-up, 'the hussy', her skirt was much too short. The final condemnation was usually, 'She's a bit common, isn't she? She's not really good enough for you, Steven.'

He was bumptious enough to agree with her but fantasised about Araminta's presence in their little terraced house. As his mother poured the tea he would say: 'This is the Honourable Araminta, Mum. Is she good enough for me, d'you think? We're lovers, Mum, she takes me out and buys me presents. Oh and by the way, I've entered every one of her orifices that can be entered. Is that OK, Mum?'

Steven had gone back to work at Macaulay's for the Christmas holiday and was again with Sid and Joe in the packing and delivery department.

One Saturday morning he was surprised to be waved over to the telephone by Sid: 'Steve, it's someone on the blower for you. From the university she said.'

Steven said a tentative hello into the receiver and was surprised to hear Araminta's voice. 'Darling, I know this is short notice, but I need to see you. In London. Can you catch the nine o'clock train tomorrow?'

He had no plans for the following day except to have a

beer or two with Danny and watch the football on television. Nevertheless, he said quietly: 'Is there a problem?'

'No, except that I need to see you. For a fuck, please darling.'

Steven blushed but no one was paying any attention to him and he mumbled, 'I'll be there.'

There was hardly anyone on the train but Araminta had told him not to speak to her if he saw her; they would meet at the taxi rank at Victoria. During the short journey to her flat they held hands and said very little to each other. But when they entered the flat, they left a trail of clothing from the hall to the bedroom. Their love-making surpassed in passion anything that had gone before.

In the sudden calm that followed, they lay, glowing and contented, their bodies touching. Steven turned his head and found her smiling at him. 'Bliss,' she said. 'The only way to spend a Sunday morning.'

Revived by occasional cups of coffee, they spent the morning making love and, after giggling in the shower together, they had a four-course lunch at a nearby brasserie. The morning's intense sexual activity and a splendid meal, fuelled by wine, induced them to abandon any discretion and travel back to Brighton together. There was no one in their part of the train carriage. As they approached the town, their euphoria began to dissipate.

'When will I see you next?' Steven asked. 'Can we do another Sunday?'

'I don't think so. Christmas, all those family commitments. We'll go back to our Thursdays when term starts again.' She kissed him lightly on the cheek.

'I don't think I can last that long,' he said petulantly.

'I'm sure you've got plenty of girls who are willing to oblige.'

'Maybe, but it's you I want. I'm not interested in other

girls.' It was a lie, since he was taking out a girl from the cosmetics department on the following Tuesday; she was pretty, friendly and known to be 'a sure thing'.

'Why do you stay with your husband?' Steven asked suddenly.

'Because it suits me,' Araminta said sharply. 'He's rich and, despite appearances to the contrary, I'm not. All I have is that flat, no income of my own and no inheritances to come.'

'My dear, how dreadful for you.' Steven tried to mimic her accent.

'Grow up, Steven. I married James because I'd had my fill of being one of the impoverished aristocracy. And I'm not giving up my easy life. I like my expensive clothes. I like my holidays in Sardinia and South Africa.'

'So it's a marriage of convenience, is it?'

'Yes, if you like. We're friendly enough and I expect we'll have children eventually. I'm only thirty, so there's plenty of time. We go our own ways, up to a point. I suspect that he has a girlfriend. And I have you. So why worry?'

'What a way to live!' Steven said primly.

'You're on very dangerous ground, if I may say so, Steven, and I'm not interested in hearing your second-hand and naive views of morality.'

'I'm sorry.'

'So I should think.' They were on the outskirts of Brighton and she kissed him hard on the lips. 'Let's not quarrel. We've had a lovely day and we'll have many more. Just contain yourself until January.'

'Araminta, it's just that I—'

'No, you don't,' she interrupted him. They were approaching the station and she picked up her handbag. 'I'll walk down the train. Best not to be seen together here. Have a lovely Christmas, darling.'

On Tuesday evening he took Kim from cosmetics to the cinema. Afterwards, on the living-room sofa of the flat she shared with her friend, Cathy, she enjoyed some of the expertise Steven had acquired with Araminta. Steven insisted too that she give him pleasure as, with surprise and growing interest, she learned that lips weren't just for kissing and a penis didn't just fit neatly between her legs. On the following Friday, for good measure, he had repeated the experience with Cathy.

# Chapter Sixteen

Although preoccupied by his plans to establish his agency in Britain, Steven was eager to return to New York. There was much to do and, to his surprise, he also found that he was missing Eva Rosen. It wasn't just her body that he craved, it was the power of her personality. Whereas Suzi was the more beautiful woman, her preoccupations were the conventional ones of someone of her upbringing: her own immediate family, Adam and Steven and her parents, and her other relatives, who now included her husband's parents, her charity work and the doings of her many friends.

In contrast, Eva was hounded by other motivations, some of which were obscure even to her and certainly hidden from Steven. As a result, her behaviour was unpredictable. But she had a dynamic spirit, a muscular resolve and therein lay her fascination.

The day after his return to New York, Steven left his office in the late afternoon and met Eva in her apartment. He usually avoided visiting her there but his need for her overrode his caution.

When they had made love, they lay drowsily together and listened to the staccato noises which came from the perpetual traffic jam below the apartment.

'I've missed you,' Eva said. 'Terribly.'

'Me too.'

'I was jealous of Suzi. I should have been with you, not her.'

'She's my wife.'

'Not for much longer, I hope.'

Steven said nothing. In recent months Eva had nagged him about the validity of their relationship. He was aware how keenly Americans observed people's relationships and analysed their own. It was a national obsession. Eva had taken to asking him when he would leave his wife and live with her. Despite his non-committal attitude she had begun to assume that he would, one day, leave Suzi. All Steven wanted was to keep things as they were, to balance one relationship with the other. Stability and familial content on the one hand: stimulation, both intellectual and physical, on the other. Above all, Eva gave him an inside track at AAN Sports.

'How's the wide world of television sport?' Steven asked cheerfully, in an attempt to change the subject.

'Don't change the subject. But the answer is shitty. That bastard, Jake Richardson, has been promoted. He's now a senior producer with responsibility for football. I was up for that job and I've got the talent to do it properly,' she finished fiercely.

'He was a big name, Eva. A star quarterback with the New York Giants. He knows the game.'

'So do I. But I'm a woman, so what chance have I got against one of the boys? Even if his IQ doesn't quite reach room temperature level.'

'You'll make it,' Steven said and hugged her to himself.

'Yeah, but first I'm going to fix Jake bloody Richardson and I'll fix him good.'

'How?'

'Because he's on the take.'

'What d'you mean?'

'I've analysed some of his programmes over the last few months and it's obvious that certain brand names and logos are getting a lot of extra exposure.'

'Come off it, Eva, how could he fix that?'

'Easily, that's how. There're lots of breaks in the action in any sportscast and it's the director's job to call the shots. He's got cameras everywhere and he wants colour shots, of the crowd for instance and the scoreboard of course. Jolly Jake has been producing some of the baseball and you'd be amazed at how often the camera lingers on a certain brand of beer which is shown on the scoreboard.'

'So you think Jake's in cahoots with the director.'

'Sure and he's cut a deal with the brewery. And it's the same technique when he's been involved in the golf broadcasts. The brewery has several brands and some of the players have the names on their bags and on those bloody stupid visors they wear. And guess what? The camera seems to be in love with those brand names.'

'If you're right, that sort of exposure is worth millions to a brewery.'

'Yeah and you can bet that Richardson's getting his share.'

'Can you prove any of this?'

'Not yet but I'm working on it. I've got myself a mole in the marketing department of the brewery. I worked with him when they sponsored a volleyball tournament. He's a straight-up guy.'

'Oh really,' Steven said. 'I've got a rival, have I?'

'Never,' Eva said, as she moved on top of him. 'When are you going to leave your wife and live with me?'

As he jolted back towards his own apartment in the care of a swarthy cab driver who seemed to have not a word of English nor any knowledge of the New York streets, Steven reflected on what Eva had told him. Jake Richardson seemed to have taken hold of a brilliant idea. What if he, as a business manager, could guarantee manufacturers and sponsors some extra exposure on television? There was a real business opportunity there – as long as Eva didn't act impetuously and blow it all away.

In the week before the PGA Championship, the tipsters had promoted Sam Rhodes as a possible winner. But, as he flew to California for the event, Steven was not convinced; his client seemed to have lost his edge. No doubt it was a temporary loss of form, but Rhodes had confessed that his timing was slightly awry; his approach shots were not quite carrying up to the flag and his putts seemed to lack that extra bit of roll that took them into the cup instead of stopping short. As always when a golfer's touch eludes him, so does his luck run out. The ball topples into bunkers at the last gasp and wayward shots always finish in deep trouble rather than rebounding into open spaces. And Riviera Golf Club was no place to be if your game was off colour: the penalties were too harsh.

In such circumstances Steven decided to spend only a couple of days at the tournament. He would watch Rhodes, encourage his other clients who were playing, and talk to the manufacturers and sponsors. He had to be seen there but his main objective was to meet Paul Davis and secure him as an ally. In the short term he knew what that would entail: some generous hospitality with a pretty girl or two thrown in. At least Davis appeared to be heterosexual – no complications in that area.

But if he were to uncover the rich sources of income that the BBC represented, how would he lock Davis in over the long term? Although the Head of Sport obviously liked the good life, an endless parade of women, expensive dinners and vintage champagne wasn't the answer. Money or money in kind had to be the solution; and it had to be carefully documented, just in case Davis got frightened or tried to be too clever at some future time. In the first instance, Steven wanted merely to sound Davis out and he invited him to lunch.

One of Joe Lynagh's clients, a film producer, had put his house at the disposal of Sam Rhodes for the duration of the tournament and Steven had been invited to use it too. Not far from the Riviera course, the house was in one of the canyon roads, the notorious 'slide area' where land-slips regularly destroyed opulent residences.

It would have to be some slide to take out Mike Lescher's house, Steven reflected as he waited by the swimming pool for his guest. It was a crescent-shaped, stucco building on two storeys, arranged around the huge pool. There were a few acres of garden, which included a sizeable putting green and a practice bunker. There were no prizes for deducing that the owner was a rabid golf fan.

Lunch had already been laid out under a canopy near the pool. The weather was hot and Steven eyed the various ice buckets which contained bottles of champagne, white wine, beer and mineral water. As he reached for a beer, a cab turned in through the gates. Paul Davis was wearing a white summer suit with a faint blue stripe in the material, blue shirt, and black loafer shoes without socks. A panama hat completed his ensemble.

'Wow,' said Davis, 'what a scorcher! I'll take a beer before we hit the fizz. It's a nice spread you've got here.'

'It belongs to a client of my pa-in-law.'

'Ah, were you clever enough to marry into money? I always intended to do that,' he said wistfully.

'Are you married, Paul?'

'Oh yeah. Wife and two kids tucked away in west London. Suburban man, that's me.'

'Hardly. You're one of the most influential men in sport.'

'Influential, maybe, but that's not reflected in my standard of living. You know how mean the BBC is.'

Steven was expressionless as he opened a bottle of champagne, carefully ensuring that the cork gave only a discreet hiss and a pop. He was surprised that Davis was already dropping hints about how little he earned. But he knew he must be careful: maybe the man was merely having a conventional grumble and his remarks meant nothing beyond that.

They talked sport as they ate their buffet lunch and, after one of Mike Lescher's staff had cleared the remains and served coffee, Steven prepared to get down to business.

Davis took him by surprise. 'There's been a bit of a change of heart in the BBC since I last spoke to you. I'm conscious that I treated your ideas a bit lightly. I wasn't taking the piss, I assure you.' The Head of Sport raised his glass of brandy towards Steven and bared his prominent teeth in a smile.

'But the top brass have decided to make the dear old Beeb more populist, to go after a bigger market, to target young people and that sector of the great British public which watches darts and wrestling on commercial TV.'

'You mean the lager louts with the tattoos and the sleeveless T-shirts that don't quite cover their beer bellies?'

'They're the ones,' Davis laughed, 'and that's just the women. Anyway, to be serious, this new approach spills over into my department. As you know, we've always been very conservative about our sport. It's got to be the real thing or nothing. Tennis is played on grass, cricket means five days at Lord's, golf is the Open and the Masters at Augusta, football is the Cup Final at Wembley and so on.'

Steven was waiting intently for the punchline and it came when Davis said, 'We've been told to jazz things up, cover more sports. Well, we've always had a wide brief actually – athletics, all the horsey stuff, badminton, squash, motor racing – but I've been told to look at fun events, and this is where you can help us. I'm thinking first of all of the Kooler tennis thing and your All-Star-Sport concept. I can run with those now and maybe other things in due course.'

'That's a great start,' Steven said enthusiastically and, in his turn, he raised his brandy glass in a toast. 'You'll want to use British sportsmen for the All-Star-Sport, I take it? We can handle all that through our London office.'

As he talked, Steven's mind gathered in the implications of the All-Star-Sport deal. It would give the London operation a very healthy start. More importantly, Shaw Management would be selecting the leading British sportsmen for a popular television series and Dean Aultman would have the opportunity to poach the best of them as clients. If they already had agents, the offer of participation in All-Star-Sport would prise them away. In Steven's experience, limited though it was, most sportsmen were whores: if the money was right, they'd do anything. There were exceptions like Sam Rhodes. Maybe.

The outlines of the two deals were quickly sketched, and Steven, conscious that he needed to snag his man firmly on the hook, said boldly, 'So what can I do for you, Paul, apart from taking you to a very smart bar I know in Beverley Hills tonight . . . ?'

'Nice girls?'

'The best and very friendly. And I've got the use of a suite at the Beverly Hills Hotel.'

'Is that pa-in-law again?'

'Yeah. His firm always has one available.'

'Nice.'

'Quite. Look, Paul, I won't beat around the bush, we'll do a lot of business in the next few years. In a way, you'll be a valued partner of mine and under normal circumstances I like partners to share in the rewards.'

There was silence for several seconds and all Steven could hear was the hum of distant freeway traffic and the slow ripple of the water in the pool. It was a deep aquamarine colour and he had an urge to throw his clothes off and jump in.

'The Beeb don't allow us to accept any, er, outside consultancies,' Davis said slowly.

'They wouldn't know.'

'No, but it's tricky.'

'Maybe, but you'd probably like to take a holiday in the sun some time, wouldn't you? In January, say, it's usually a vile month in England. The West Indies or the Seychelles perhaps? California? You and your family would enjoy that and I'd be happy to arrange it.'

'Well, not necessarily with my family. I'd be on a research trip, and Lindy is very necessary to me when I'm working on a complex project.'

Both men grinned simultaneously with relief. The parameters of their business relationship had been defined.

'It's a start,' Steven said. 'I'll deal with it. Now, a question for you. Who sells the overseas TV rights for such events as the Open golf and Wimbledon and, in particular, the American rights?'

He already knew the answer but didn't want to seem omniscient; Davis had to be played along a bit.

'We deal with them in-house.'

'OK, well you're not doing yourself any favours.'

'That doesn't surprise me. Tell me more.'

'AAN have usually bought the rights for both events, haven't they? And they've got one more year to go on a three-year deal. Is that right?'

Davis nodded. Eva Rosen had told Steven every detail of

the agreements and she had also told him that AAN would pay at least double the price of the last contract in order to secure the two events for a further period.

'The British Open and Wimbledon are two of the biggest events in world sport,' continued Steven. 'And I think I could increase your take by at least fifty per cent. I know the people at AAN and I know their two competitors. I'm on the spot in New York and through my London office I'll be able to liaise easily with you. Why don't you let me handle those rights? I'll do it well and I'll only charge you ten per cent of the deal.'

'If it was up to me, Steven, no problem. But there's a committee, and we have to consult another committee at Wimbledon, and the Royal and Ancient run the golf and they have a committee. The whole sodding country seems to be run by committees – no wonder nothing gets done.'

'But you're on the BBC committee?'

'Sure.'

'And you're the Head of Sport, so you could swing the deal my way.' Steven leaned forward earnestly. 'Paul, let me offer an incentive. If I can't increase the fees for the two events by more than fifty per cent I won't take any commission. I'll do it for free, how's that?'

'It shows a lot of confidence. Why don't you send me a proposal?'

'I will, and something will come your way.'

Davis put up his hands deprecatingly and shook his head. 'Not necessary. The best interests of the BBC and all that.'

The two men arranged to meet later at Davis's hotel and Steven got busy on the telephone. Despite the late hour in Europe, he had no qualms about calling a director of a Zurich bank on his private line at home. Arrangements were made for an account to be opened in the name of Paul

Davis and Steven instructed the banker to transfer an initial deposit of $10,000 from his own account.

The man had been well and truly hooked, gaffed and landed. Delighted with his coup, Steven went into the house, changed into some shorts and ploughed strongly up and down the pool for half an hour.

# Chapter Seventeen

Since Steven had arranged the installation of a telephone in his parents' flat, Suzi had no difficulty in making all the arrangements for their trip to America. They would be in New York at the end of September which would coincide with Adam's first birthday and then she would take them to the family's Florida condominium for a few days. She insisted that Steven should write the dates in his diary and she checked with his secretary that he had done so.

It was unfortunate that Steven was faced with a more than usually severe schedule of work when his parents arrived in New York. Apart from looking after his ever-growing list of clients – and his spade-work amongst the golfers at the PGA Championship had been productive – another series of All-Star-Sport was being produced for AAN in California, the final details of the Kooler Tennis Doubles were being negotiated and he had four other tele-vision projects in various stages of development.

As a result, Steven was unable to be present at his son's official birthday party, which took place during the after-noon, but he hosted a dinner that evening for his parents and Joe and Betty Lynagh. Despite Steven's misgivings, it was a jolly affair: Bill and Mary Shaw, encouraged by Suzi, responded to the natural ebullience of the Lynaghs.

With no wish to spoil the evening, Steven kept the news of his imminent departure to California until the following day. As he finished his cup of tea, he said, 'Bad news, Suzi,

I've got to fly to LA today. Problems with the All-Stars series.'

'But your parents—'

'I know, it's a real bind but I'm needed there.'

'Why don't you send Jay? He's competent, isn't he?'

'Yes. But a major contractual problem has cropped up and they want me. I'm the person who put the package together, after all.'

'You're indispensable, are you?'

'In this case, yes,' Steven said impatiently. It was true. A nasty dispute had arisen because the sponsor had used photographs of the competitors in his advertising. It had prejudiced some of their individual endorsements or so they claimed.

He might have resolved the issues by telephone, but Steven knew that it was far safer if he were there in person. There was a great deal of money at stake and he would leave nothing to chance. And there was a bonus: he would spend some time with Eva.

'I'm sorry, Mum,' Steven said, 'but I'll be with you for several days in Florida and that'll be nice.'

When Steven had left his mother said, 'He works very hard, doesn't he, Suzi? In and out of aeroplanes.'

'Yes, he's building up his business and it's a very tough business.'

'You must be proud of him. We certainly are. Aren't we, Bill?' she said sharply to her husband.

Bill Shaw nodded. His mind had been far away, trying to recall the taste of a creamy, full-headed glass of Bass. He was dying for a pint.

'He's doing famously,' Suzi said. Let's hope he doesn't forget who he's doing it for, she thought.

After spending four days on the west coast and acting

successfully as a mediator between the sponsor and the All-Star competitors, Steven flew to Florida and joined his family in West Palm Beach. The regime of going to the beach with Adam and talking inconsequentially with his parents soon began to pall.

His peevishness was compounded by the way his parents doted on Adam. His mother deluged the boy with love and affection. Steven could not remember being treated like that. Of course she had cared for him and watched over him. For instance, there had been the rituals that preceded important examinations. When he was revising, there were little treats such as steak and chips on an evening when sausage and mash had always been the rule . . . the night before his first examination his mother would sponge and press his jacket and trousers and shine his shoes to Coldstream Guards standards . . . a cup of tea was brought to his bedroom in the early morning . . . and he was served a special breakfast of fruit, bacon and eggs and toast while his father made do with toast and tea and a carefully rolled cigarette.

His mother had been excessively proud of all his successes. But it had all seemed an anxious, tight-lipped business. Where was the warmth, the hugs and the kisses that Adam received?

After a couple of days Steven made an excuse to visit Kenny Crane at the tennis academy. After all, as he explained to Suzi and his parents, his company had made a big investment and he needed to keep a close eye on it. It wasn't far from West Palm Beach, so he wouldn't be gone too long.

Steven had raised nearly a million dollars in sponsorship and the money had been ploughed into new buildings and two new tennis courts. Crane, still wearing his green and gold tracksuit, showed him the new administrative block, the new gymnasium and the well-equipped first-aid room which doubled as Dr Rexel's office when he was at the academy.

Although Steven had seen Fran Zanini win a junior tournament six months before, he was astonished once again at the change in her physique. She now looked like a fully developed woman and was well above average height. She was due to make her debut on the women's professional circuit before the end of the year.

'Is she ready?' Steven asked.

'She'll win tournaments within a few months,' Crane said confidently.

'And you'll travel with her?'

'Sure. If only to keep Mauro off the poor kid's back.'

On the following day Steven called his New York office to ask if all was well. He was told that Dean Aultman was desperate to talk to him. Although he had only just begun working officially for Steven, he had been busy on the agency's behalf for several weeks.

Impatient though he was to contact Aultman, Steven delayed the call until it was eight o'clock in London.

The receiver was picked up on the second ring and he heard his London executive's agreeable voice.

'Hello, Dean, is there a problem?'

'Sorry to break in on your holiday. Not a problem, more of a great opportunity. Have you heard of a Swedish firm called Larssen? They make skis and bindings but they're also dabbling in tennis rackets?'

'Can't say I have. Tell me more.'

'I read an item about Larssen in the *Financial Times*. Apparently they have an American subsidiary that's involved in the defence and space industries, all very high-tech. Anyway, to get to the point, I phoned the company in Sweden and they claim they've developed an over-sized tennis racket that'll knock spots off anything else in the market.'

'There's nothing new about over-sized rackets. What's so different about theirs? Mind you, I'm still using a Maxply. I haven't even graduated to steel.'

'Well, Larssen's technical director says his rackets will leave all the others for dead. It'll be like a Porsche against a VW. No contest.'

'So what's the secret?' Steven asked, sceptical of such technological miracles.

'It's bigger and stronger.'

'Which means it'll weigh a ton,' Steven said, remembering how his arm ached after wielding a Maxply for five sets. 'You'll need someone built like King Kong to get the best out of it.'

'How heavy is your Maxply?'

'About thirteen ounces.'

'The Larssen will be no more than eleven ounces.'

'Oh, come off it, Dean—'

'But it'll still have sixty per cent more hitting area – in other words a much bigger sweet spot. And of course, because it's lighter and has a stiffer frame, a good player will generate much more racket speed. Just think how hard Ray Gerrard could hit the ball with a racket like that,' Aultman finished enthusiastically.

'He already hits it bloody hard.'

'I dare say. What's his service timed at?'

'Over a hundred mph.'

'OK, the Larssen people claim that a top player will get twenty to thirty per cent more power out of their racket.'

'So, what's the magic ingredient? Rocket fuel?'

Aultman laughed. 'That's the first problem. They won't tell me. They're in the defence business, remember? So they keep everything close to their chests; it's second nature.

From what the FT article said it's some sort of composite – graphite with glass fibre or maybe some titanium. Anyway, they convinced me that they've got something.'

'What's the second problem?'

'I floated the name of Ray Gerrard at them and they told me that they're about to sign Nils Ryberg.'

'Why? He's ranked fifth in the world and Ray is number two. Anyway, he's an all-court player and they need a serve-and-volley man, a real power merchant like Gerrard.'

'Ryberg is Swedish, it's as simple as that, and he's available.'

'It's a pity we didn't sign him up, isn't it?'

'I pitched hard for Ryberg, Steven. But his uncle has managed him since he was a teenager and they're a very close-knit family.'

'Yes, I remember. Have you seen a sample of the racket?'

'No, but I'm meeting them tomorrow at the Sports Trade Fair in London and they'll show me one.'

'Can you divert them from Ryberg, d'you think? Give us time to persuade them that Gerrard's their man. His racket contract's up for grabs at the end of the year and he'll be the favourite to win Wimbledon.'

'I don't know, Steven, they seem very committed to Ryberg.'

'Would it help if I met them?'

'Of course. But aren't you on holiday?'

'Not any longer. I'll get a plane tonight. Meet me at Heathrow in the morning.'

As he put the phone down and began dialling the airport Steven turned and saw Suzi in the doorway. Adam was clinging happily to her leg.

'I gather that's the end of the family holiday,' she said drily, 'as far as you're concerned.'

'Darling, I'm sorry, but this really is an emergency. It's

just too important to miss, it could make the agency's fortunes.'

Steven tried to explain the potential impact of such a revolutionary racket.

'If the racket works as the Larssen people say it does, we need Ray Gerrard's name on it. We could keep it under wraps until Wimbledon and when he wins, the whole world will want to buy it. He'll be made and so will we. Tennis is such a vast market, the most valuable one in terms of endorsements.'

'There seem to be lots of ifs, Steven. If the racket works, if you can elbow Ryberg in favour of Gerrard—'

'That's why I've got to get on the case, Suzi.'

'I suggest you get on the case for your family, Steven. They'd all appreciate it.' She scooped Adam into her arms and walked out of the room.

The Larssen brothers, Jan and Olle, were difficult to differentiate. Both were of medium height and medium build, with thinning fair hair and narrow faces which were slightly pock-marked. Steven noticed that Jan, the Marketing Director, had a slightly larger nose. They both had slow and monotonous voices.

In the hospitality booth of their modestly sized stand at the British Sports Trade Fair at Olympia, the brothers showed Steven one of the prototype rackets. Used as he was to the conventional shape and dimensions of a wooden racket, it looked ugly and unwieldy with its thick frame and its huge surface area. He gripped it and swung it gingerly in the confined space of the little room and was surprised at how light it felt.

'Very light, eh, Mr Shaw?' Olle Larssen said.

'Yes, but how strong is it?'

'It'll last for years, it's made from a space-age material.'

'Easy to make?'

'Only if you have the technology, the bonding techniques. And we're a long way ahead of any other manufacturer. We're ready to go into mass production.'

'After Nils has won Wimbledon,' added Jan Larssen, with a confident nod.

The remark encouraged Steven to go through his sales pitch on behalf of Gerrard: he was a higher-ranked player than Ryberg, he was acknowledged as the man most likely to win Wimbledon, and the racket was ideal for his powerful game. Very important, Gerrard was one of the most exciting players in tennis; he was handsome and articulate, the ideal package to front a world-wide advertising campaign. He refrained from saying that Ryberg, in his opinion, was a boring, anonymous, squinty-eyed journeyman.

'We admire Mr Gerrard,' said Jan Larssen, 'but he won't beat Ryberg if he's armed with our racket, I can assure you.'

'Why not go for the best available player?' Dean Aultman said.

'Because we would like a Swedish player to benefit. It'll be good for our company and good for Swedish tennis. And anyway we've more or less agreed terms. Nils loves the racket and we hope to sign him officially next month.'

'Can I borrow one of the rackets?' Steven said suddenly.

'Well, they're to show to the big retailers. We're preparing the ground for the launch next year,' one of the brothers said doubtfully, 'but, if you bring it back within the hour—'

'I promise,' said Steven. 'Come on, Dean, I want to try it out. Where's the nearest public tennis court?'

Ten minutes later people walking their dogs in a Kensington park were treated to the unusual sight of two men playing tennis in what were obviously the bottom halves of their business suits. After skidding about in their shoes they decided to play barefoot.

It didn't take long to convert Steven to the virtues of the Larssen racket. Even the bald tennis balls that they had rented were singing off the strings. He positioned himself at the net and asked Aultman to try and pass him; the larger surface of the racket ensured that any off-centre hits became respectable volleys.

After going through his repertoire of services, Steven called a halt and, as they replaced their socks and shoes, he said, 'This is a peach of a racket, Dean. I could get really interested in the game again with this in my hand. It's got all the extra power the Larssens boasted about but it's so bloody forgiving as well.'

The two men gathered up the tennis balls, returned them to the caretaker, who grunted but did not look up from his study of the *Sporting Life*, and walked to their waiting taxi.

On the way back to Olympia, Steven inspected the racket from all angles.

'We've got to do our damnedest to get this deal for Gerrard. He'll walk Wimbledon with this. What do we know about Ryberg? Apart from the fact that he's the Swedish number one and has a great all-round game.'

'He's in his mid-twenties,' Aultman replied, 'ranked in the top ten for several years. Married to an English girl, one small child. Nothing much else.'

'Booze, drugs, extra-maritals?'

'I doubt it. He's a committed Christian, does charity work for refugees, that kind of thing.'

'Shit,' said Steven with feeling.

From his hotel later that day Steven called Earlybird Security in New York and asked Corky Price if he had a trustworthy and intelligent associate in London. 'But I want somebody who knows his way around the tabloid newspapers, who knows the best place for a nice juicy bonking story.'

'Let's think, the best operator in that area is Dan Fisher. I'm told he can fix anything and that his past isn't exactly spotless. He was with the security forces in Northern Ireland and now he calls himself a public relations consultant. His job is keeping people out of trouble.'

'Or putting them into it?'

'Maybe. Call him and mention my name.'

Throughout the rest of the evening and during the first part of the following morning, Steven rang the many journalists he knew and asked their opinion of Nils Ryberg. Was his public image the reality? Was he straight? Reliable? The family man that he appeared? To Steven's astonishment, none of his contacts had a word to say against the man.

Dan Fisher came to call just before lunch. Unobtrusively dressed in a suit with a faint tweed pattern, he looked about forty years of age. Spare of frame and with neatly cut brown hair, his main distinguishing feature was a thin moustache. His voice was quiet and Steven could just hear a faint accent. Was it Scottish? Maybe it was Belfast.

After a few questions which elicited cautious replies, Steven came to the point. 'I need to discredit someone, dig up the dirt on him and make sure the public knows about it. Is that your line of work, Mr Fisher?'

'As long as it pays well, sure.'

'The problem is that the subject seems to have an untarnished reputation.'

'Nobody has an untarnished reputation. Who is he?'

'Nils Ryberg, the tennis player.'

Fisher gazed towards the window and picked gingerly at

a tooth. 'Tennis. Not as good as football or showbiz but not bad. The press give it a whirl at Wimbledon time, don't they? All those dykes. Yes, I could run with that. Where does he live?'

'All over. He's in the States at the moment but he's got a house not far from here. An English wife, you see.'

'I wonder if she's got any form. We could embarrass him . . . guilt by association. Tricky. We'd have to catch her in bed with half a dozen boy scouts. No, no . . . We'll have to concentrate on Ryberg, set him up, get someone to spill the beans.'

'"My nights of love with Swedish tennis star", that sort of thing,' Steven said.

'Exactly. It'll cost a packet but the tabloids will lap it up.'

'How much are we talking about?'

'Ten to twenty grand to do it properly.'

'But we'll get some of it back from the paper, won't we?' Steven pointed out. 'They'll pay handsomely for a story like that.'

'Agreed. But that normally comes to me, that's how I make my profit.'

After a few moments of thought, Steven nodded his agreement. 'OK. But don't the gutter press ever try to verify these stories?'

'They don't give a toss as long as they sell more newspapers. If they get done for libel occasionally, so what? The costs are worth it in terms of publicity.'

'It's as simple as that, is it?'

'Look, the tabloid scum hate success. They hate the sportsmen and the showbiz crowd because they've made it – they've got glamour and money and they can put two fingers up to the rest of the world. And they hate the royals because they've been born with unrivalled privilege. But they're only reflecting the bottom-of-the-heap instincts of the yobs and illiterates who read their rags. They're exactly the same, they hate the toffs most of all but they're also longing for their heroes – the pop singers and the footballers – to be dragged back down to their level.'

Fisher spoke in a matter-of-fact way, without any discernible heat. 'I've just had a better idea,' he continued. 'We won't go down the pussy route, we'll send him down queer street. There's nothing the tabloids and their readers like more than a bit of queer-bashing. It appeals to their favourite prejudices.'

'Can you make it look genuine?'

'Of course. We can fake some photos and a tape. I've done it before, for one of the minor royals.'

'You'd better be quick,' Steven said, conscious that the Larssen brothers intended to sign a contract with Ryberg within a month. He looked at the tennis schedule and confirmed that the Swede would be in London for an indoor event in ten days' time.

'That'll do. It's nice when the subject is around to issue his denials,' Fisher said with relish. 'I'll need a recorded interview with Ryberg so that we can cobble up a tape, the two lovers arranging a tryst or something. I think I'd better involve our mutual friend, Corky Price. He can get some tame journalist to interview Ryberg before he leaves the States, and I already know who I can use over here. An actor. The photos are no problem. Leave it to me.'

Steven returned to New York just in time to see his parents off on their flight home. Within a week he was on his way back to London, having been told by Fisher that the Ryberg story would begin to break on the first day of the tournament.

# Chapter Eighteen

It didn't worry Nils Ryberg when his wife, Jenny, wasn't at Heathrow to greet him on his return from Dallas. She'd said she'd try to be there but sometimes the demands that their daughter made on her time intervened. There was also the work that Jenny did for a refugees' charity. Ryberg, who travelled as light as possible, took a taxi towards his home in Wimbledon.

He'd played reasonably well in Dallas, even though it had been disappointing to lose to Gerrard in the final. Never mind, when he got his hands on that new racket, he'd show him and the rest of them.

At seven o'clock in the morning Ryberg did not expect to find a reception committee by his front gate. As he paid off the taxi, they crowded around him and pushed microphones at him. He didn't know any of them but the jeans and bomber jackets told him that they weren't from one of the 'heavies'.

They shouted questions which he couldn't quite hear. '. . . Oliver Dickson . . .', '. . . your wife? . . .', '. . . divorce . . .', '. . . you're gay . . .'

The cameras clicked as Ryberg, angry and bewildered, pushed his way through the crowd. A gentle man moved to fury can be dangerous and Ryberg was no exception. Extremely strong and fit from the long hours on the practice courts and in the gym, Ryberg sent one persistent journalist flying with a flat-handed thump to his chest.

With his head down, he shoved onwards towards his front door; it opened and he slipped gratefully inside while Jenny slammed it behind him. The letterbox opened and a microphone was pushed through. Its owner shouted, 'Would you like to make a statement, Nils?'

Jenny backed away from the microphone and Ryberg put his arms out to comfort her but she backed away from him too. He had never seen her face show such a mix of doubt and fear.

'What is it, Jen? What's this all about?'

'They've been here since dawn. There've been phone calls – dozens of them.' She thrust a newspaper at him. 'Look.'

As Ryberg read the brief item which was headed 'Mystery of tennis star's love life' Jenny felt a flood of shame that she had doubted him and rushed to embrace him.

Suddenly he bent his head to bury his face in her neck. 'Why? Why? Why?' he muttered. 'Why do this to me?'

Jenny tightened her arms around him. Now he was back, her faith in him was renewed. She had seen how other players were coarsened by the demands of professional tennis, how their vision was narrowed and their personalities reduced. But Nils had remained true to himself, a gentle man, honest and with a broad appreciation of life. Together with his friend, John Winter, he worked for refugee charities and had involved her too; he organised exhibition matches for them and quietly donated a proportion of his prize-money every year to their desperate cause.

In a crisis, Jenny always tried to emphasise normality and she led her husband into the kitchen and began to make coffee.

The telephone rang and, before Jenny could stop him, Ryberg picked it up. The conversation was brief and he told her that it was Uncle Bjorn, his agent. He had asked a lawyer, who specialised in libel cases, to act for him.

The stories of Ryberg's illicit relationship, carefully phrased in most cases, appeared in the press over the next two days until halted by the libel lawyer, who plastered the Fleet Street newspaper offices with injunctions.

In the indoor tournament, Ryberg won his first-round match as if playing on autopilot, but it was no surprise when he succumbed in the next round to a Czech whose only apparent asset was a service of stunning power. Ryberg seemed anxious for the match to be concluded quickly so that he could retreat from the public gaze.

On the following day Steven Shaw visited the Larssen factory which was about forty miles outside Stockholm. In his briefcase he carried a sheaf of recent newspaper cuttings about Ryberg; as back-up he had some photographs which had been carefully manufactured by Dan Fisher. They showed Ryberg and Oliver Dickson, both naked, in a series of obscene positions.

It wasn't necessary for Steven to show any of the items. Jan Larssen, the Marketing Director of the company, at once confirmed that he had abandoned his plans to use Ryberg to endorse the new range of rackets.

'It's a tragedy,' Larssen said. 'I can't comprehend how he got involved in such a thing. He called me to say that, in the circumstances, we shouldn't go ahead with the contract. It was too important to the company to take any risks.'

Jan Larssen shook his head sadly. 'He's a gentleman. I didn't know what to say to him. He said that God was the only judge.'

'Well, I don't know about God but he's right about the contract,' Steven said quickly. 'You can't pin your future to someone who might be involved in a scandal, it wouldn't be very smart.'

By the end of the day the two men had negotiated the main points of the contract for Ray Gerrard to endorse Larssen rackets. Steven's client was guaranteed several million dollars a year over a four-year period. When Gerrard became the Wimbledon singles' champion, Steven estimated that the royalties would amount to at least $30 million over the same period. It had been worth all the effort and the subterfuge.

Tormented by doubts about her husband, Jenny Ryberg above all needed someone who would take a dispassionate view of the whole affair. A call to the BBC elicited a telephone number for John Winter, who was in Africa working on a documentary about refugees.

After several tries she heard Winter's comforting voice. To her surprise, the line was clear of any extraneous noise. Winter listened, without interruption, as she told him about the vile rumours that were afflicting their lives. His words gave her comfort and his faith in Nils's integrity made her feel better.

'I'll talk to Nils,' Winter ended cheerfully. 'You don't need to doubt a man like him. I'll ring you back.'

Two days later, Nils Ryberg returned home after playing an exhibition match in Madrid and told Jenny that he'd spoken at length to Winter. 'He helped me a lot, Jenny. It'll all blow over, as he said. I told him there wasn't a problem.'

The affair with Eva Rosen had meandered on throughout that year and into the following one. On one level Steven was content – it was good for business. But he had grown increasingly perturbed at Eva's persistence that he should leave Suzi and set up house with her. He had pleaded caution, as married men usually do; he had to pick his moment and he had to consider the happiness of his son, Adam. He was also worried by her carefree treatment of him in public. More and more, it seemed to Steven, Eva behaved as if he were her acknowledged lover. It was dangerous, and he dreaded the idea that word of his liaison would be carried back to Suzi. He told himself that he still loved her and that he was only having an affair of convenience. Maybe it was time to part from Eva.

It was a couple of weeks before the Masters at Augusta when Eva called him at his office. There was nothing unusual in that, since they dealt with an endless stream of detail in connection with the various AAN series which were in the planning, production or post-production phases.

That morning the final piece of evidence that would enable her to pin Jake Richardson to the wall had been delivered into her hands. Her mole at the brewery had at last penetrated some confidential files in the Chief Executive's office and had found a letter to Richardson. It outlined the basis of the deal between them: apart from Richardson's handsome retainer he was to be paid bonuses for any extra on-screen exposure for the brewery's products. A copy of the letter lay snugly in Eva's handbag.

Eva didn't attempt to keep the note of triumph from her voice. 'I've got the bastard.'

'Who?' asked Steven.

'Richardson. But I can't say more on this line. Come to the flat, I need your advice.'

'I can't. Dinner with the Lynaghs tonight.'

'Come early then, five o'clock. It's important.'

'OK, but it'll have to be quick.'

'Any way you want it, lover.'

With the seed of an idea germinating in his brain, Steven rode down to Greenwich Village a few hours later. Eva greeted him enthusiastically, thrust a glass of champagne in his hand and waved a letter at him. 'Take a look at that.

The final piece in the jigsaw and it'll destroy Jake Richardson. I've analysed a whole series of programmes which he produced and I can show how he's been favouring that company's products. It's a flagrant abuse of his responsibilities and the corrupt bastard has accepted a bribe to do it. He should be kicked out of the industry on his ass. I'm seeing the AAN Chief Exec tomorrow.'

'Eva, slow down. Don't give the information away just for revenge. Hold on to it. We can squeeze him until he squeaks.'

'No, Steven, I want the bastard out, out of television for good. He's a miserable cheat.'

'Everybody cheats. I'm cheating my wife by being here.'

'That's different,' Eva said, as she put her arms around him.

'Be careful, Eva. Jake's popular and you might not be if you're the bearer of bad news.'

'I'll be the judge of that, Steven. Now, what about that quick one you mentioned earlier?'

Half an hour later, Steven stood briefly under the shower, threw his clothes on and kissed Eva goodbye. She was only half-awake and he closed the bedroom door quietly behind him. In the living room he crossed quickly to the table by the window and found the copy of the incriminating letter. He put it in his pocket and left the apartment.

As she heard the apartment door close, Eva, physically content, stretched and smiled drowsily. She was looking forward to tomorrow.

Steven knew that he hadn't much time to spare since he was due at Joe Lynagh's house for drinks at 7.30. He entered a bar on the corner of the street and dialled the AAN number. He ignored the appraising looks of the clientele, a mixture of middle-aged men in conventional office attire and younger men who favoured sleeveless T-shirts and black leather gear.

He got through to Jake Richardson's office. He had just left.

It was worth trying Mickey's Bar. Big and bustling, it was a favoured after-work hang-out for the AAN sports people and Richardson was as permanent a fixture there as the showcases with the New York Yankees shirts.

While Steven headed up town in a taxi, Richardson, in his favoured seat on the angle of the bar and facing the entrance, was buying a round of drinks in Mickey's. He'd had a good day. His lawyer had finalised the details of his third divorce for one thing; it was costly, just like the other two, but it was nearly over. Secondly, he had collared the new receptionist for a drink. She was just his speed: long legs, big tits and a great ass. Anne-Marie batted her long eyelashes at him and accepted another tequila sunrise. A few more and he'd take her for a quick meal near his apartment and then screw that great ass off her.

He clinked glasses with her, smiled and winked at her. Over her shoulder, Richardson saw the door swing open and a man he knew paused and looked quickly around the bar. It was that agent, he was becoming big-time, doing a lot of business with that tight-assed bitch, Rosen. Steven Shaw. The rumour was that he was sleeping with her. Well, he wouldn't mind himself, but he'd make sure she didn't enjoy it. The guy was heading towards him and Richardson wondered why.

'Steve, how're you doin'? What can I get you?' Jake Richardson got up and clapped a meaty hand on his shoulder.

'Nothing thanks.' Steven nodded at Jake's companion and waved at some of the other AAN people who were scattered down the bar. 'Look, Jake, I need to talk to you.'

'Take a seat, my man, and talk.'

'No. It's urgent and, er, personal. Can we find a quiet corner?'

Richardson kissed Anne-Marie on her full red lips, told her he'd be back and led Steven to a corner table at the far end of the bar.

'OK, what's the problem, Steve? Let's be quick 'cause I've got pressing business with that little girl back there.'

'It's your deal with the brewery, Jake. Someone's on to you.'

'What fucking deal? What fucking brewery?'

'Look, no bullshit, Jake, I haven't got the time. If you like I can quote the letter sent to you over a year ago by the Chief Executive of the Big Apple Brewery Corporation.'

Ticking the points off on his fingers, Steven ran through the conditions outlined in the letter and the amounts which were to be paid to Richardson. He'd memorised the details during the taxi ride and the letter was now in his wallet. He would put it in a safety deposit box at his bank on the following day.

Richardson's formidable tan, kept constant by regular sessions on a health studio's sunbed, turned a waxy yellow. Steven noticed that his fleshy lower lip jutted out, like a small boy who'd been caught doing something naughty. 'How did you find that out? It's that bitch, isn't it? Rosen?'

'Yes. She reckons she's got you by the balls, Jake, and she's going to yank them right off.'

'She's got the letter?'

'And a lot more. Or she did have.'

Steven was enjoying the man's discomfiture. The hale and hearty jock was frightened and it really showed.

'I can help you. I can make that letter disappear,' Steven said quietly.

'Yeah?' Jake looked across the table, an eager gleam of

hope in his eyes. 'You can call Rosen off?'

'No, but we can remove most of the evidence. There are conditions, of course.'

'Of course. What do I do?'

'You make sure, Jake, that all my current projects go through and prosper. You can do that because you're a senior producer and in a couple of years you'll no doubt be a vice-president of AAN Sports. Now, I have certain clients and certain sponsors and I'd like you to arrange a little extra exposure just as you do for the Big Apple people. Nothing too obvious, but there's a logo on Sam Rhodes's golf bag for instance and a logo for Kooler soft drinks on Ray Gerrard's sleeve. Just make sure we have an edge, that's all I ask.'

'It's done,' Richardson said, 'but what about the evidence you mentioned?'

'Forget about the letter that Eva had. It's safe with me and it'll help to cement our relationship, won't it?'

With a nod, Richardson silently acknowledged their accord. 'What you've got to do, Jake,' Steven continued, 'is destroy any shred of evidence that links you to that brewery. Any letters, memos, notes of meetings and so on. And, first thing tomorrow morning, ring your friend at the brewery and get him to destroy anything in his files. OK? And what about your bank accounts, Jake? Eva could shop you to the IRS if you haven't declared the money.'

'No problem, Steve, it's all off-shore.'

'It's Steven, actually, that's my name.'

'Right, Steven.'

'Good. You'll be in the hot seat tomorrow because Eva's got a meeting fixed with your Chief Executive. She's hoping to blow you out of the water. You know what to do, just deny everything because her one concrete bit of evidence is no more.'

'OK. I'm grateful, Steven, but why're you doing all this? My guess was that you and Eva were screwing each other, so . . .'

'You're the one who seems to do all the screwing,' Steven said. 'But what I'm interested in is our business relationship. That's the future. I've got to go, and I suggest you get back to your office and deal with anything that looks remotely incriminating. Good luck tomorrow, it could be bumpy.'

Richardson hurried out of Mickey's Bar and paused only to tell the neglected Anne-Marie that he'd catch her some other time.

Steven was a few minutes late at the Lynaghs' house. He'd done himself several favours. He had a new ally in a more influential position at AAN Sports, and the letter from the brewery made the alliance much more secure than one based on tenuous emotional ties. He knew that Eva would tomorrow discover how he had betrayed her. That would be the end of their affair, which suited him. But it might be very messy, especially if she decided to tell all to Suzi.

Steven was very attentive to Suzi throughout the evening. So much so that Betty later remarked to her husband how much in love they were. She was hoping that they'd have another grandchild for her and Joe in the not-too-distant future.

The Chief Executive Officer of AAN was not looking forward to his meeting with Eva Rosen. He had looked up her performance reviews, which spoke of her commitment to the company and of her clear ambitions to rise up the corporate ladder. But Harvey Sobell did not like pushy women. They irritated him with their obsession about equal opportunities. Why couldn't they accept the limits of

their status in big business, be content to work industri-
ously under the direction of men, be happy to be
decorative?

At 11 o'clock, Sobell's secretary announced Eva Rosen
and brought her through to his office. To take the formality out of the meeting, Sobell ushered her towards a sofa in
a corner of the gigantic office and sat opposite her in a
leather armchair.

After a polite enquiry about her job, Sobell asked Eva
how he could help her and she launched into an account of
how Jake Richardson was exploiting certain sports programmes to increase the exposure for the Big Apple
Brewery's brands. She had spent hours in measuring the
amount of time that the brand names were on screen and
handed Sobell a complete analysis.

'This is a very serious accusation,' he said, 'and I've never
had cause to question Jake's integrity.' He had admired
Richardson when he was a football player and liked his
style as an executive. 'What other evidence do you have?
This breakdown is hardly conclusive, is it, my dear?'

For over an hour that morning, she had searched her
apartment for the letter. Every drawer, all her pockets,
her handbag, her briefcase and the rubbish bins: she had
even looked under her bed and under all the mats.
Nothing. So she had repeated the exercise even more
thoroughly.

In her despair she wept and then wondered if Steven had
taken the letter by mistake. Not by mistake, it suddenly
dawned upon her. She ran to the bathroom and retched
into the lavatory bowl.

Before Eva left for AAN that morning she telephoned
her informant at the brewery and, in desperation, asked
him if he could get her another copy of the letter.

'No chance, Eva,' he replied. 'There're security men

crawling all over the executive offices. There's a real panic on and I think you know why.'

Eva knew that her campaign to unseat Richardson had foundered before it began and she thought hard about cancelling the meeting with Sobell. But she decided to have her say, whatever the cost.

'I did have some more evidence, Harvey,' she said, 'but somehow it's gone missing in the last twelve hours. It's a letter from Big Apple Brewery to Jake Richardson and I can tell you how much he's being paid.'

With his hands held up to silence her, Sobell said, 'Eva, please, I can't allow this. If you have the evidence, I'll look at it. Otherwise, you're simply blackening a colleague's character. It's inexcusable. I want to make a suggestion, my dear. If you want to walk out of this office now, we'll both forget this conversation ever took place. But if you want to pursue your allegations, I'll have to give Jake a chance to give his side of the story. And, depending on what he says, one of you will have to leave the company.'

Knowing she was beaten, Eva stood up and said, 'I won't withdraw, Harvey, but I know my position is untenable. Jake Richardson is corrupt, whatever you think of him. I'll bring my letter of resignation to you before lunchtime.'

Earlier that day, Eva had tried to reach Steven at his office but was told he was out of town. It was true: he was at the Westchester Golf and Country Club. He had decided to make a tactical withdrawal in the expectation of Eva's unbridled rage. He needed the practice anyway, since he was making a rare appearance in a pro–am golf event in the following week.

After lunch, Steven called Jake Richardson on his direct line.

'What's happened, Jake?'

'Our friend has resigned. She's cleared her desk and she's

already outta here. I had a mild balling-out from Sobell. Told to be careful about doing any favours, that kinda thing.'

'Sounds fine.'

'It is. A small celebration is called for. A few of the boys. Mickey's Bar at six. Are you on?'

Occasions such as the one presided over by Jake Richardson – a gathering of people whose only connection was work – were not favoured by Steven. He had to go in order to emphasise his new alliance and he was relieved to think that he would be among Jake's cronies: Eva might not have attracted great affection at AAN but she had certainly commanded respect, and Steven hoped that his role in her departure would not be widely known.

He had been fond of the woman but she was making his life impossible; it was best for both of them that he'd taken the initiative to end the affair and force her back to reality – both on the emotional and the business front.

Half a dozen of the AAN sports people were clustered around Jake, who seemed to be in perpetual motion as he gesticulated for more drinks and waved his arms to illustrate one of his stories. Mister Personality, thought Steven.

'Hey, hey, Steven, what would you like, my man?' Jake greeted him with a bear-hug.

He was halfway down his second beer when he saw Eva pushing her way through the throng of drinkers towards them.

'Here's trouble, Jake,' he said and moved quickly to intercept her.

'Eva, I'm sorry, I couldn't let you make a fool of yourself,' Steven said as he gripped her by the arm.

'You're the real fool around here,' Eva said as she tried to move past him.

Since she had left the AAN building at lunchtime, Eva had fantasised about the many varieties of revenge she could inflict on both Jake and Steven. They included a call on Suzi Shaw to whom she would describe all the ways she and her husband had made love and all the locations. But it didn't comfort her. She would only bring misery into the life of another woman, against whom she bore no grudge. Steven would no doubt suffer for a while but such a tactic was unsatisfactory, even demeaning.

Ever wedded to the idea of direct action, Eva impulsively decided to confront Jake. She would embarrass the bastard in his favourite bar in front of his hangers-on. But she hadn't expected to find Steven there, and now he was trying to make excuses and stop her getting at Richardson.

'Eva, let's go and have a drink somewhere else and talk—' Steven began.

She kicked him as hard as she could in the shin. He went pale and dropped her arm but Eva noticed that he made no cry of pain. Later, she thought wrily that she should have kicked him in the balls. Much more appropriate.

The crowd around Jake Richardson went silent as she reached them. Eva noticed one or two nervous grins and, for a moment, Jake affected not to notice her.

Then, with a wide smile that didn't reach his eyes, he said, 'Hey, little lady, good to see you. Let's have a friendly drink together, huh?'

'Jake, I wouldn't drink with you if you were the last man on earth. You're lower than worm-shit. You're a cheat, you're corrupt and you're a fucking coward.'

Eva's first words were resonant enough to still the noise in the immediate vicinity and the silence spread as the drinkers realised that they had some drama to enjoy.

'Hey, lady, watch the language,' a barman said.

'You shut up,' Eva replied. 'Civilised behaviour is wasted on trash like Jake Richardson.'

She picked up a full glass of beer which lay on the counter and, with studied contempt, poured the contents over his head. Then she turned and almost bumped into Steven who was standing behind her. His face was still pale. 'As for you, Steven, you're just a fucking Judas. I trusted you, I loved you . . .'

The tears started to flood her eyes and Eva ran for the door. A nearby group of drunks clapped her heartily as she passed.

Busily patting himself dry with a bar towel, Richardson grinned savagely at his colleagues. 'Holy shit, that woman sure can't take it. All I did was defend my position. It was her or me, and I won. Come on, let's get some more drinks in.'

Jake clapped Steven, who had rejoined the group, on the back. 'Say, fella, I don't know what you did to the little lady but I don't think she'll be sucking your cock tonight.'

Forcing himself to smile, Steven said, 'Well, you know the problem, Jake, a woman scorned and all that . . .'

For a moment he wondered whether he'd made the base Indian's mistake and thrown a pearl away richer than all his tribe. Then he thrust the thought aside.

# Chapter Nineteen

When Sam Rhodes won the Masters at Augusta with the lowest score ever recorded there, Steven knew that his client's status as one of the world's best golfers was secure. His victory in the US Open had not been enough: it indicated his quality, but the Masters' win had confirmed it.

Steven now knew that Rhodes had the ability to win many more major tournaments and the next priority had to be the blue riband of golf, the British Open.

He was thrilled by Rhodes's success but just as pleased to see three more of his clients finish in the top ten at Augusta. He also noted that Patrice Barbier, the French player, who was making his first appearance, finished in third place.

Steven had watched him for a few holes on the third day and was captivated by the young Frenchman's play. By no means overawed by the occasion, his clear intention was to batter the course into submission and he had power in abundance to do it. If his policy of all-out attack got him into trouble, Barbier had such an assured and inventive short game that he inevitably retrieved matters.

Above all, Steven realised that the crowd, although they wanted an American winner, identified with Barbier. They warmed to the uncertainty inherent in his uncompromising style of golf; he was an instant antidote to the careful tactics of the anonymous journeymen who haunted the American tournament scene. And with his extravagant Gallic gestures and emotional reactions, he couldn't help but involve the crowd with his play; he brought a sense of theatre to the occasion.

It was riveting stuff, and Steven was aware that the Frenchman attracted a considerable female following. It was hardly surprising. Like Sam Rhodes, he had the build of a true athlete; and with his dark complexion, deep brown eyes and glossy black hair, he had the dashing good looks of the archetypal Gallic heart-throb.

Steven knew that he'd seen the future superstar of European golf and he was determined to add him to his stable.

Later that day, he found him drinking iced tea on the clubhouse lawn and introduced himself.

'You're English but based in America?' Barbier said with only a faint trace of a French intonation. When he became a client, one of Steven's first suggestions would be that he cranked the accent up a little. It would turn the women on.

'Yes, but I have an office in London and several European golfers as clients. Perhaps we could talk about representation. You'll need it. In fact, you need it now, in my opinion.'

'It's kind of you to offer, Mr Shaw, but I'm new to the professional game. Who knows, I might not like it and then I go back to Paris and into my father's bank.'

He shrugged and it dawned on Steven that he might have a rich kid with whom to deal. They could be difficult.

'You were at the Sorbonne, weren't you? What did you study?'

'Law. According to my father the lawyers run things these days. Unfortunately.'

'What does your father do at the bank?'

'He owns it, Mr Shaw.'

'That must be nice for him,' Steven said with a smile.

'I'm sure he knows the value of good advice, which is something I could provide. You should have your interests properly protected, even at this early stage in your career. It's never too soon.' Steven grimaced. 'Sorry, Patrice, I sounded like an insurance salesman. But why don't you consider a short-term contract with my agency?'

'Let me think about it. I'm not in a hurry to decide anything at the moment.'

They shook hands and Steven wished him luck in the final round. He would talk to Barbier again at the US Open and try and get his signature on some sort of a contract, however loosely written.

The first few months of the tennis year had seen a decline in Ray Gerrard's form. Although he had signed a contract to endorse the Larssen rackets from the beginning of the year, it had been decided that the maximum promotional momentum would be generated by unveiling the range at the Wimbledon Championships. Because the rackets were so distinctive in shape, Gerrard was only able to test them in secret and he was reduced to playing tournaments with his old rackets repainted in the Larssen livery.

It was little wonder that the regular swapping of his equipment dulled the edge of Gerrard's game and a crisis duly arrived in the third round of the singles at the French Championships at Stade Roland Garros on the edge of the Bois de Boulogne in Paris.

Gerrard liked the event. It was civilised; and it was true what they said about French women. They were elegant, in a way that Americans could never match, even if their male escorts looked rather stuffy in their formal suits and staid shirts. He didn't like the clay courts but you had to learn to win on all surfaces and he wasn't complaining; that is, until a dodgy line call gave his unranked Australian opponent the third set and a two-one lead. Gerrard remonstrated with the umpire, to no avail, and lost his concentration enough to allow his opponent to win the first two games of the fourth set.

Fickle as all sporting crowds are, the spectators on Court One suddenly got behind the Aussie. Gerrard felt their change of mood and so did his opponent. What had started out as a polite interest in seeing the American star's inevitable progress to the next round *en route* to an eventual clash with Ryberg became a highly charged urge to see the underdog triumph. Gerrard underwent the rare experience of an early defeat and the way was left clear for Ryberg to win the event.

Furious at losing, Gerrard insisted that he would use his new Larssen racket at the Queen's Club tournament which always preceded Wimbledon. Otherwise, he told Steven, he would pull out of the contract, whatever the cost. It didn't take Steven long to convince the Larssen brothers of his client's determination. After all, if Gerrard failed at Wimbledon, their marketing campaign would have an innocuous beginning.

Gerrard progressed to the final at Queen's but, still unused to the feel of the Larssen racket, he fell victim to Ryberg who wielded his steel racket to forceful effect. The Swede went to Wimbledon full of self-belief and hope.

Although he acknowledged the pre-eminence of Wimbledon in the pecking order of tennis, Steven disliked the place. It was hard to move around in comfort and the food was lousy and grossly over-priced. Nevertheless, Wimbledon beat Flushing Meadows, the home of the American Tennis Championships, hands down. It was bizarrely located near the end of a runway at New York's La Guardia Airport. The noise was nerve-wrecking and the permanent stink of hamburgers turned the stomach.

The atmosphere at Wimbledon irritated Steven. All those middle-class women talking loudly at one another and braying with laughter at the players' rare attempts at humour, however juvenile. He had many invitations to the hospitality tents but they seemed to be full of members of the moronic classes: merchant bankers and property dealers, no doubt all married to loud women.

Above all, there were the officials. He detested the way they enforced their petty rules with brusque officiousness. Nevertheless, he countered their rudeness with studied politeness.

One rule at Wimbledon which severely tested Steven's patience was the use of the Competitors' Lounge: visitors were allowed in there for no longer than 45 minutes and on three occasions only each day. All passes were minutely inspected and the holder was officially clocked in. It was an irksome rule for Steven who had over a dozen clients at the event and found it easiest to see them in their lounge. When he turned up on the third day to see one of his clients, Francesca Zanini, the man guarding the door looked familiar. His memory searched for the reference. Margate, when he was a boy; the tennis tournament he'd won; the official. Captain Wycherley, that was him. The thin hair, the pale eyes and the dandruff on his blazer.

'Captain Wycherley?' he said doubtfully.

'Er, no, that's my brother. He's here somewhere. Enquire at the tournament office.'

'Thanks.' But no thanks, he thought. So Wycherley was here, no doubt ordering the spectators about, and no doubt working some sort of fiddle.

Unlike Steven, Suzi loved the atmosphere and joined him for the second week of the championships. She had left

Adam in the care of her mother and missed him as soon as the aircraft left the runway in New York.

As soon as she arrived in London, Suzi invited Steven's parents to spend a day at Wimbledon and she booked them into a room at their hotel. Despite his promises, Steven had not found time to visit them during the previous week. Business had to come first but he felt guilty about his omission and even more guilty that he had done nothing about moving his parents to a better flat.

He knew that Suzi would berate him and she seized her opportunity when he told her he was trying to buy offices for the agency in order to take advantage of the boom in London property values.

'I don't believe I'm hearing this,' she began. 'You're talking about expensive offices here in London when your parents are living in a hovel.'

'They're happy enough, Suzi. Dad likes the pub at the end of the street—'

'Do you ever talk to your mother? Do you love your parents? They've earned some peace and quiet and you can afford to provide it. So, show them you love them.'

Suzi was right, he could certainly afford it. Or, rather, Shaw Management could, through an off-shore company. It would be a good investment. He called Dean Aultman and asked him to contact estate agents with properties for sale on the east side of Brighton, in the really exclusive part. Where the Macaulays used to live, he thought. Maybe they still do. It would be amusing to own a property near them, especially with his father in residence. He didn't suppose that James Macaulay even remembered Bill Smith, but Steven would never forget the trauma of his father's redundancy.

Halfway through his first year at London University, the

Easter holiday had presented a bleak face to Steven. He had little prospect of seeing Araminta since her plans were vague: she thought she might be going to the south of France for a few days with James but wasn't really sure. The one bright spot in the vacation was an indoor tennis tournament in which he had been chosen to represent the university. He had arranged to do a couple of weeks' work at Macaulay's to supplement his grant.

Steven arrived home on the last Friday of the month, during the latter part of the afternoon. He was surprised to find his father already in the house. Bill Shaw was sitting silently at the kitchen table, his shoulders slumped even more wearily than usual. Mary Shaw was standing at the other end of the table with a cup of tea in her hand.

Steven's cheery greeting was scarcely acknowledged by either parent and, having dumped his suitcase on the lounge floor, he said: 'Well, that's a nice homecoming. Where's the champagne and the caviare?'

'Your father's had some bad news.'

'What's happened, Dad?' Steven asked. His father gestured towards a letter that lay on the table and said, 'Read it, son. It won't take long.'

He picked up the sheet of paper which was headed with the Macaulay name. It read:

Dear Employee,

With effect from 30 June this year, Macaulay Department Stores Limited will cease trading. All those employees who are eligible for redundancy payments will be informed of the terms by their department managers. The Board of Directors wishes to thank you all for your loyal service.

It was signed by James Macaulay.

238     **Malcolm Hamer**

'I spoke to Mr Bamberger.' Bill Shaw's voice was shaking. 'He told me that bastard has sold the store and the one in Croydon to a property developer. He must've had it in mind as soon as old Mr Charles died. The bastard.'

Bill Shaw put his head in his hands and his wife didn't tell him not to swear. Steven put his hand lightly on his father's bony shoulder and said: 'What will you get, Dad? In terms of money? Enough to retire?'

Mary Shaw spoke bitterly. 'Enough to retire, you must be joking. Mr high and mighty James is the only one who'll have enough to retire. We'll get a pittance.' Such was her agitation that her cup began to tremble and rattle on its saucer. She put it down on the table.

Steven pursued his original question. 'Dad, do you know what you'll get?'

'Mr Bamberger said a hundred pounds for every year of service. Three and a half thousand quid. No pension rights, of course. I'll have to get another job. I'm fifty-four – fat chance I've got of a decent job.'

'Surely they've got to pay you off properly,' Steven insisted. 'You've spent your life there, it's not right.'

'Right doesn't come into it, son,' Bill Shaw replied. 'This is business, big business and big money. People like me don't matter. Macaulay is going to walk away with millions – I'll have to go looking for a job.'

'So will I,' Mary Shaw said grimly, 'we'll never pay our way otherwise.'

'Well, you'll have the three and a half thousand, that'll help,' said Steven.

'That's going in the building society for a rainy day. We'll probably have to move, get a little flat. The landlord wants us out of here, anyway. He wants to sell the place, they're fetching good prices.'

Steven sought relief from the depressed atmosphere of

the house by going for a long walk along the seafront. He hoped it would calm his mind, mitigate the fury of his resentment at the treatment meted out to his father. It was the final blow to the dignity of a sadly downtrodden man. Looking at the grey sea pounding the shore, Steven thought about the futility of his father's life. What a waste!

His anger gathered around James Macaulay. He and his kind were to blame. They had the power over little men like his father. Privileged, self-indulgent slobs. At least he could laugh at the bastard behind his hand: he was sleeping with his wife, giving her a lot more than Macaulay could manage.

Steven grimaced as he thought about Araminta. She must have known that the stores were going to be sold and she hadn't said a word to him. No, he couldn't believe that, she would have warned him. They were lovers. Maybe she could help, maybe she could intervene on his father's behalf. He would talk to her.

He turned for home and the long waves, battering at the land, seemed to mock him. His father's words echoed in his head, 'It's business . . . big business . . . big money . . . people like me don't matter . . .'

On the next morning Steven restrained his impatience. He wanted to telephone Araminta as early as possible but forced himself to wait until a civilised hour.

As Steven had assumed, the maid answered the telephone and he had his story ready. He asked for Araminta and was told that madam was away for the day.

'Who is that?' the maid asked.

'It's Steven from Macaulay's,' he replied, 'about a delivery.'

'You can call back tomorrow.'

It was Thursday. Araminta was probably in London.

A glance at his watch as he left the telephone kiosk told

Steven that it was just after nine; he'd hop on a train to London in an hour or so and go straight round to her flat. It would be better than ringing her up, and there might be the opportunity to spend some time in bed with her.

He went straight from Victoria Station to Araminta's address. The porter came out of his office and intercepted Steven before he reached the lift. They had exchanged greetings on the many occasions that Steven had visited the flat with Araminta but now there wasn't a glimmer of recognition on the man's face.

'Can I help you?' he said gruffly.

'I'm looking for Ara— Mrs Macaulay,' Steven stated.

'You're out of luck. She left for lunch some time ago. You can leave a message if you like.'

Steven declined and said he'd try again later. The porter shrugged and turned away. To kill time he wandered around the shops, had a beer and a sandwich in a crowded pub and eventually returned to the apartment block.

After he re-entered the building, Steven received a brief nod from the porter and a jerk of his thumb in the direction of the lift. He assumed it meant that Araminta had returned.

The apartment bell rang out and Steven heard someone move towards the door. His wide smile died on his face as Araminta opened the door no more than a foot.

'What the bloody hell are you doing here, Steven?' she hissed at him.

'Who's that, darling?' asked an unknown voice from inside the flat.

'It's my nephew. He's taking some things to Brighton for me.' Araminta glared a warning at Steven who noticed, as she opened the door wider, that she was bare-footed and wearing a T-shirt. Her usually immaculate hair was dishevelled. 'You'd better come in,' she said to Steven.

A very tall man, only a few years older than Steven, stood in the sitting room. A mop of blond hair crowned his head and he wore a dark pinstriped suit. He was shrugging his way into his jacket as Araminta gestured towards him and said, 'This is Sandy, who helps me with my investments. Steven, my nephew.'

Sandy nodded briefly at Steven, kissed Araminta on the cheek and headed for the door.

'I'll be in touch,' he said vaguely and was gone.

Although Araminta was angry at Steven's intrusion, she recognised the hurt and confusion on his face. He stood silently, hardly knowing what to say. On the one hand he was there to ask a favour of Araminta, that she should plead his father's case for a more generous settlement when the store stopped trading; on the other hand he was angry and upset that his woman apparently had another lover.

'I'm sorry,' he said tentatively.

'So I should bloody well think,' she replied.

'I needed to see you urgently.'

'Obviously.'

Steven sat down on a sofa and tried to compose himself. 'It's about my dad,' he said. Araminta looked blankly at him and he continued, 'He's been fired by your husband.'

'Not fired, Steven. He's redundant, along with the rest of the staff. He's been offered a pay-off, I presume?'

'Yes, that's the problem. It's not enough, he hasn't got any money saved. I sort of wondered if you'd have a word and try and do better for him.'

'A word? With James, do you mean?'

Steven nodded and Araminta sat down opposite him and shook her head in amazement. 'Look, Steven, my husband's business has got nothing to do with me. I've never taken any interest in it and I'm not going to start now. If I tried to intercede on your father's behalf it would give the game away somewhat, would it not?'

She looked at Steven, her eyebrows arched. He couldn't think of anything to say and she added, 'How would you suggest I tackle James? Along the lines of "there's this young man who's fucking me, James, and I'd like you to double his father's redundancy pay, as a favour to me." Some chance, Steven. Just forget the idea.'

'I already have,' he said bitterly, 'together with the stupid idea I had that I was your only lover.'

'If you're referring to Sandy, that's my business,' Araminta said fiercely. 'I don't enquire about your other girlfriends, do I? I'm really not interested.'

'And I'm not interested in taking my turn after upper-class twits like Sandy.'

Knowing that she was about to lose her temper, Araminta, in an effort to compose herself, rose and strode to the window. Who the hell did this boy think he was? Just because they'd had some fun in bed, he wanted her to get involved in his life. She spoke over her shoulder. 'You're being foolish, Steven. I know that you're upset about your father but, in all the circumstances, I think we shouldn't see each other any more. It's been fun, I've enjoyed it. Now, I think you should leave.'

Without another word, Steven walked to the door and closed it quietly behind him. He felt the deep misery of total rejection. He'd thought they had a strong relationship, but all along he'd been no more than her bit on the side. It hurt him even more to think that a creep like Sandy would enjoy her favours instead.

Back in her apartment, Araminta sat for a while and wondered whether she had done the right thing. If she encouraged Steven any more her life would get too complicated. Better to break it off now. It would be very stupid to prejudice her position as the wife of James Macaulay just as he became seriously rich. There were plenty of other young men just as eager and pretty as Steven. He was special, though.

Briskly Araminta walked over to her desk and wrote a note to him.

On the following day Steven received Araminta's letter. It was brief and ended: 'Let's remember the lovely times we had and I've enclosed a little something as a thank you. Buy yourself a present and think kindly of me.' The little something was a cheque for £200.

Steven's thoughts of Araminta were far from kindly and his first impulse was to tear the cheque into little pieces. But £200 was a lot of money to an impoverished student. Why not have it? he thought. He'd earned it. This wasn't a time for moral posturing.

During a night disturbed by dark thoughts of both Araminta and her husband, Steven made a decision to confront his father's employer. At least he could plead his father's case without any embarrassment. He knew it would probably be hopeless but he had to try.

At six o'clock that evening Steven was in the store's car park, in position by James Macaulay's Mercedes. As the bulky figure of the Chairman approached, Steven braced himself. He said politely, 'Mr Macaulay, I apologise for approaching you like this but could I have a word with you about my father?'

'Your father?' Macaulay paused, his key hovering by the car lock.

'Yes, Bill Shaw. It's a question of his settlement when the store shuts down. It doesn't seem fair—'

'Fair, fair? What are you burbling about?' Macaulay snapped. 'The Board of Directors has been more than generous. We owe nothing to people like your father, I can assure you. Now if you'll excuse me.'

Macaulay tried to shove Steven away from the car door but he stood firm and said, 'My dad has worked for thirty-five years for your firm and all you're offering him is a lousy hundred quid for each year of service. I don't call that generous.' Steven knew that the discussion was heading nowhere, especially when Macaulay pushed him hard and shouted, 'Get out of my way, you little yob.'

Stronger and fitter, Steven responded by throwing the heavier man hard against the side of his car. Some customers watched from several yards away with interest.

'Don't push,' Steven said through clenched teeth. 'Bastards like you have been pushing people around for too long. You're a mean and miserable shit and it may interest you to know that this particular yob has been fucking the arse off your wife for several months. She was grateful, she couldn't get enough.'

Steven stepped back as Macaulay finally got his key in the car door. The man laughed contemptuously at him and said, 'My wife has an unfortunate penchant for bits of rough and it doesn't worry me one iota.'

Macaulay drove off with a squeal of tyres and Steven was left in the car park. His fists were bunched hard together and his body trembled. He had been a fool to appeal to someone like James Macaulay. He had let his father down and, even more, himself. He should have kept the liaison with Araminta to himself – a secret that might have been used for his own benefit, not cast away in a fit of anger.

As he walked home Steven had sworn that he would make himself more than the equal of the likes of James Macaulay – richer, more successful and more powerful.

During the early rounds at Wimbledon, Ray Gerrard experienced few difficulties with his opponents, and his confidence increased markedly as he learned, under competitive conditions, to harness the extra power provided by the Larssen racket. His first real test was in the quarter-finals, and he was within a point of losing to another American player, who won the first two sets, was 5–4 up in the third and serving for the match at 40–30.

As in Paris, Gerrard felt the crowd's support ebbing away from him. As he turned to face his opponent's service at match point, he caught sight of a young girl near the front row in the corner of the court. It was her bright yellow dress that drew his eye. She was staring at him, the knuckles of her one hand pressed hard against her mouth and her face screwed up in anguish. At least he had one supporter who really cared. He'd play the point for her.

His opponent, over-tense on the brink of an unexpected victory, served too long and then too short with his second ball. Gerrard hit it fluently away for a winner and then turned and gave a wave to the little girl in the yellow dress. From that moment on, his confidence flowed back; he took the set on a tie-break and cruised to victory.

In contrast, Ryberg won his quarter-final in straight sets without any strain. He looked invincible and the pundits installed him as the clear favourite to take the title.

That evening Steven telephoned Dan Fisher and arranged to meet him in a pub near Sloane Square. Fisher chose it because it was invariably crowded and the two men were unlikely to be overheard.

They settled themselves in a corner of the high-ceilinged saloon bar. With its bare boards, circular bar area, huge patterned mirrors and eclectic array of wooden furniture, it was an archetypal Victorian pub, busy and noisy both with the after-work drinkers and the pre-dinner drinkers.

'How're your contacts with the gutter press these days?' Steven began.

'As sound as ever. You probably didn't read the saga of

the Tory minister and the Argentinian call-girl, did you?'

Steven shook his head and Fisher grinned. 'All down to me. Lovely stuff. We bugged her flat, got the pictures, everything. It was a set-up, someone in the Cabinet took rather a dislike to the man.'

Conscious suddenly that the conversation at the next table between two pretty girls who were sharing a bottle of white wine had ceased, Steven moved his chair closer to the table and leaned towards Fisher.

'More than just a passing irritation, by the sound of it,' he said quietly. 'Anyway, Dan, I feel our old friend, Ryberg, has had too easy a time of it during Wimbledon, don't you? Considering he's a raving poofter, that is.'

After a long pull at his pint of bitter, Fisher said, 'Are you thinking that young Oliver Dickson might appear from the woodwork again? With some heart-breaking revelations about his affair with Mister Ryberg?'

'I think the public has every right to know about such things, don't you?'

'Of course. Let's see, it's Wednesday night. You'd want young Oliver's sad story to hit the headlines on the morning of the final, I suppose. I've got the pictures. It's no problem to set it up, no problem at all.'

'Let's hope Ray Gerrard wins his semi,' Steven said grimly.

He did, and the scene was set for a classic Wimbledon men's final: Gerrard's power versus Ryberg's versatility. The experts all picked the in-form Swede to win easily.

Early on Sunday morning, Steven strolled across to a newspaper vendor on the corner opposite his hotel and bought a copy of the *Sunday Chronicle*. The banner headline read: 'MY TENNIS STAR LOVER'. Alongside there was a photograph of Ryberg and a thin young man in a T-shirt and shorts. They were smiling at each other and the caption read: Nils Ryberg with Oliver Dickson in happier days.

As he waited for the traffic lights to change, Steven scanned the report.

Nils Ryberg, Sweden's top tennis player who is scheduled to play Ray Gerrard in the Wimbledon men's final, is at the centre of a sex scandal that will rock the staid world of tennis to its foundations. Some months ago there were rumours of a homosexual liaison involving the Swedish star, who is seemingly happily married to an English girl. They have a daughter aged 18 months.

Now Ryberg stands accused of abandoning his lover, out-of-work actor, Oliver Dickson. Oliver, whose last acting part was as a chorus boy in a revival of *The Boy Friend* at an Ipswich theatre, said last night: 'I met Nils at Queen's Club last year and we were instantly attracted to each other. It was love at first sight. He swept me off my feet and we even went through a form of marriage in Amsterdam. He promised to divorce his wife and I thought we'd be together for ever. A few months ago, I was stunned when his lawyer told me that it was over and I wasn't to contract Nils again. I cried for days but wanted to be dignified and try to forget him. But, seeing him on television this last fortnight has brought it all back and I had to speak out about our love for each other.'

The bottom of the page was splashed in red: 'EXCLUSIVE, READ OLIVER'S STORY INSIDE'.

It was one of the most one-sided finals in the history of Wimbledon. From the start, the crowd was muted; the buzz of heightened expectation that attends such great sporting occasions was absent.

Ryberg received a sympathetic reception and, after the players had warmed up, Ray Gerrard walked to the net, called Ryberg over and shook him warmly by the hand. It was a spontaneous gesture that appealed to many of the crowd and was one of the few memorable moments of an anti-climactic finale to the championship.

Nerves reduced both players to mediocrity during the first set, so much so that it seemed they were both doing their best to lose it. Gerrard eventually won it and, for the rest of the final, Ryberg merely went through the motions. It took Ray Gerrard just over an hour to win the match.

Three days later, Nils Ryberg left his home by taxi for Heathrow, ostensibly to catch a flight to Monte Carlo, where he was due to play an exhibition match. He kissed his wife and his daughter farewell and told them that he loved them.

On the way to the airport Ryberg posted a package to Jenny. As well as a letter, it contained his wedding ring and a watch she had given him on their second wedding anniversary. When the taxi neared Heathrow he instructed the driver to drop him at a large and anonymous hotel, where he booked himself in as Mr Laver. The receptionist hardly noticed the sad-looking man who paid cash for his room.

In his room Ryberg lay down on the bed and once more reviewed his decision. The last few months, since the false rumours of his homosexuality had surfaced, had been tough. There were the inevitable sneers and the pointed turning of backs by people he had known for years. Even worse perhaps was the well-meaning heartiness of those who wanted to demonstrate how unaffected they were by the innuendoes. Several of his endorsements had been cancelled.

The hate mail had been unsettling and the constant presence of the journalists around the house, jostling him and Jenny and shouting questions, was a nightmare. There were the long-range lenses to contend with and the video cameras; Ryberg knew that lip-readers were employed to decipher their conversations. Worst of all was the inquisition by Jenny when she received some photos showing himself and Oliver Dickson together, naked and intimate, and the terrible silences that followed.

At first Ryberg thought that he could defy all the problems. Memories fade and he knew the truth. He had the love of God to see him through and he thought he had the love of his wife, too. He could face the lies and the injustice, but only with Jenny's help. Her uncertainty had finished him.

He checked that the 'Do not disturb' notice was in place on the far side of the door and he ran a warm bath. Then he knelt by the bed and made his peace with his God.

Modestly, Ryberg left his underpants on as he lowered himself into the bath and then swallowed half a dozen strong sleeping pills; one of them was usually sufficient to send him to sleep on a long-haul flight. He grasped a Stanley knife and sliced the veins on his right wrist and then on his left. He was surprised at the lack of pain and quickly fell into his final sleep.

At midday on the following day, the chambermaid, unable to gain access to Ryberg's room, called the Head of Security. When he found the dead body, he identified Ryberg from several items in his wallet. He locked the room and used a public phone in the hotel lobby to call the *Chronicle* with the news. For a fee of £1,000 in cash he agreed to give them an exclusive interview about finding the body and to let them take photographs of the hotel room.

In Luanda, the capital of the People's Republic of Angola, John Winter looked sorrowfully at a five-day-old copy of *The Times*. The front page told of the suicide of Nils Ryberg.

Winter was near the end of filming a documentary about Angolan refugees for the BBC. Thank God it was nearly the end; he was anguished as never before by the misery he recorded. It was the children that affected him most deeply.

In nearly two decades of film-making, Winter had seen more than anyone should of man's inhumanity to man: Biafra, Vietnam, Ethiopia, Angola, Mozambique, Nicaragua. The list went on. He had thought that he would become hardened, even immune to the human agonies he saw. But that hadn't happened; the effects on him became worse.

It was the interventions of people like Ryberg which served to renew his faith. Here was a man who might have used the demands of his life as a professional sportsman to ignore the misfortunes of others. But he had taken the time to raise funds for refugees whenever he could and had donated significant amounts of his own earnings to their cause.

'I'll give all the time I can to them,' he had told Winter, 'and as much money as I can afford. I've been lucky and I should share that luck.'

Nils had become a steadfast friend and now he was gone. With a heavy heart, Winter sat in his hotel room, a sheet of paper before him. He wondered what he could write that would comfort Nils's widow.

*

During the calendar year after Ray Gerrard's victory at Wimbledon, over 100,000 Larssen rackets were sold; in the following year over 300,000 rackets were snapped up by eager tennis players around the world. Gerrard's royalties made him extremely rich and his commission made a significant contribution to the profits of Shaw Management.

# Chapter Twenty

Alone in the graceful surroundings of his London house, Steven Shaw swallowed the remainder of his cup of coffee. He was due at the Television Centre in an hour for an interview. As he waited for his car to arrive, he made a mental audit of his progress. His first couple of years had seen spectacular success, ignited by his comprehensive marketing of two sporting heroes, Sam Rhodes and Ray Gerrard, and his penetration of the television sports market both in the USA and Britain. He raised his glass in a silent toast to Eva Rosen, who initially lighted the way for him in television.

If his progress during the first two years had been remarkable, the growth of Shaw Management's business in the following years had been astounding. Steven's brilliance in exploiting his clients' fame and in securing sponsors for the many events he created and controlled had brought new clients and new sponsors to his doors in ever-increasing numbers. With offices in London, New York, Los Angeles and Sydney and well over one hundred employees, Shaw Management was the largest and most professional sports agency in the world.

Steven felt most at ease in London. His office, converted from two sizeable mews houses, was close to a quiet square in Kensington. His own house lay a mere ten-minute walk away. What was that slogan on the women's tennis tour? 'You've come a long way, baby'? Something like that. Yes, he had. The quarter-million dollar loan from Joe Lynagh had been paid off within three years, not five. His father-in-law still owned 25 per cent of the company but he had already told Steven that he'd left it to his grandson, Adam, so it was safe in the family.

He'd looked after his parents, too. Having moved them from their poky flat a couple of years back, he'd recently bought them an even bigger and smarter one overlooking the sea in east Brighton. As before, his company had bought the flat. It was a superb investment; and it wasn't far from where the Macaulays used to live. His most significant investment in property, however, was in New York. He gave up the rented apartment and bought one of the coveted brownstone houses not far from where the Lynaghs lived.

Steven Shaw heard the clunk of a limousine's door outside his house. He took one last look in the mirror, adjusted his tie slightly and smiled into the mirror. He wanted to look relaxed and urbane during the interview and was satisfied that he'd achieve that look.

After ringing the doorbell Terry Parkin stood to attention outside the house. Straight of back and square of shoulder, he looked every inch the former soldier and his smartly pressed grey uniform and the cap sitting firmly on his head emphasised his military demeanour. People assumed that he had been in the army and he never corrected them, even though his asthma had disqualified him from the career he fancied. His clients liked the military bullshit and Mr Shaw was one of his firm's best clients. Parkin liked Mr Shaw. There was no nonsense with him. If he wanted to talk, he talked; if he wanted to get on with a bit of work, that was what he did. He was very generous with his tips and always remembered your name. He was a real gent, always smartly dressed, not like some of his clients. Tennis players worth millions travelling about in torn jeans and sweat shirts: it wasn't right.

Steven threw open the door, smiled as Terry Parkin saluted him and said, 'Good morning, Terry. How are you?' His secretary had telephoned the car hire firm earlier that day to confirm that Terry would be the driver.

'The wife and children well?' asked Steven, as Parkin held open the back door of the Daimler.

'Very well, thank you, sir.' Parkin noted with approval the dark grey suit. From Savile Row, no doubt. 'Off to the Television Centre, are we, sir?'

'That's it, Terry, one of those in-depth interviews. I hate them,' he finished modestly.

As they entered the heavy Knightsbridge traffic and began to crawl westwards, Steven flicked through a wad of papers. The volume of correspondence generated by his four offices did not deter him from seeing a copy of every letter written by his executives. A few years ago he'd taken a course in speed-reading and his eye was trained to isolate the important points. Time and its management were vital, as he regularly reminded himself and his employees. His own itinerary was mapped in outline form for several months ahead and in detail over a thirty-day cycle. Every day was broken down into time slots of fifteen minutes, with the meetings and the telephone calls all listed.

By seeing all the letters which went out Steven could keep hold of the direction and tempo of his business. It was also a method of assessing how busy his employees were and how competent. If in doubt he used other ways of checking them out and dealt swiftly with anyone found wanting.

Not that Steven did anything but encourage his people to use their initiative. He gave them all a loose rein to sign the clients they thought they could best exploit, but within the limits of the company's overall strategy. Dean Aultman had done particularly well in trawling the waters of British and European sport for likely clients. Like Joe Lynagh he had a huge enthusiasm for all types of sport. The agency's control of All-Star-Sport gave him an unrivalled opportunity to seek clients – the television series was very popular and sportsmen were eager for the money it provided and the exposure – and he had fruitful contacts of his own. He had taken the agency into new pastures by representing a couple of German skiers, several runners, television presenters and a fashion designer.

As the Daimler edged its way into Shepherd's Bush, Terry Parkin gave his customer a quick look in the internal mirror.

'Sorry, Mr Shaw,' he said, 'the traffic's diabolical today. Road works in the Hammersmith Road, it's fouled the whole area up.'

'No problem, Terry,' Steven replied.

The BBC's Head of Sport had the bright idea of proposing Steven Shaw as a fit subject for 'Insight' – a television series which took the form of recorded interviews with people in the public eye.

The first problem was that Paul Davis had to trespass on the Head of Features' turf. He overcame the latter's initial resistance by stressing how Steven straddled the worlds of sport and business and how important to the BBC was his goodwill. A bigger difficulty was to ensure that Steven had a 'soft' interview: the programme's reputation was founded on a hard-edged, investigative style. A promise of a trip to the Masters at Augusta for the Head of Features had sealed the bargain.

It was a small price for Davis to pay. It was a tradition that agents in show business and sport were shadowy figures, but Steven loved publicity. Davis was happy to indulge him because he had brought him so many successful sports programmes in the last few years. The BBC man had benefited way beyond the bounds of his paltry salary: there was his villa in an idyllic spot in the south of France and as for his Swiss bank account . . . Lord Reith would turn in his grave.

Davis promised Steven that there would be no tough questions, no controversy. 'It'll be a nice bit of PR for you, Network television. On BBC2, admittedly, but in prime time. Eight o'clock on a Monday night. They're all shagged out after the weekend, they'll watch because you're in sport. You're news.'

Steven's car edged the last few hundred yards towards the Television Centre. Steven smiled momentarily as he recalled the array of trash-sport that he had unloaded on them in the past few years: truck racing on ice, the strongest woman in the world, pro–celeb tennis with broken-down professionals and showbiz celebrities desperate for some exposure, synchronised swimming, underwater hockey, kick boxing, skins games between ageing golfers for preposterous sums of money, drag racing. He was amazed at the shit he'd sold to the Corporation, once renowned the world over for the quality and integrity of its output; but not amazed at all by the huge fees he had negotiated nor by the viewing public's appetite for it. Some of it had paid for the Head of Sport's French villa and the crates of vintage champagne for which he had developed a taste.

The security man on the gate had been told to expect Steven and, when he saw the Daimler, he walked over to the passenger window which hissed quickly down as he approached.

'Morning, Mr Shaw,' he said briskly. 'Very nice to see you, sir.'

'Hello, Jack,' Steven replied. 'How are you? How's your golf?'

As the car hummed up the incline towards the front door, Jack Walker was reminded how pleasant Mr Shaw was; always a smile, always interested. Yes, a real gentleman.

When Steven had been asked to do the programme his secretary, the invaluable Lucy Howard, had stressed that his time was precious. He was met at the front desk and taken straight into a make-up room. A blonde-haired woman, whose professional skills could not quite conceal the crows-feet around her own eyes, applied a small amount of powder to his brow.

'You don't need any help,' she said and gave him a wide-eyed smile. 'I need a trowel for some of them.'

Another blonde, clad in a short black skirt and a shirt with a vivid red and green geometrical pattern, led him down a corridor towards the studio. Steven's dark suit, cream shirt and plain maroon tie made a sober contrast. He knew well that simple clothes looked best on television and his image was critical to him. He was an agent in sport and that was why he dressed like a banker; not like one of those spivs who masqueraded as agents. You could see them coming: flashy, casual clothes, gold bracelets and demotic accents. Most of them looked and sounded like pop music promoters and were about as trustworthy.

He strolled towards the set, careful to step over the trailing cables. He greeted as many of the cameramen and other technicians as possible: a nod, a smile, a hello, a how are you. Then the producer of the programme was grasping him by the hand. Simon Grant was a worried-looking man with glasses. Yesterday, on the telephone, he had taken Steven through the questions he could expect. They were couched to give him an easy run, an opportunity to promote himself and his business to the BBC audience; they

were questions he had answered a hundred times, on radio
and television and in magazine and newspaper interviews.

Now Steven was shaking hands with the 'Insight' interviewer, Sally Wyatt. He noticed the lack of warmth in her
greeting; a nod and a tight-lipped smile was the best that
she could manage. That was a pity, since she had an attractive face, good bones, eyes of a deep blue colour, and long
auburn hair. Like him she was dressed simply and elegantly.
A tailored black jacket was worn over a dark green blouse.
The only hint of decoration was a heavy gold necklace,
half hidden inside her blouse. Sally Wyatt was tall and he
studied her legs as she resumed her seat; he kept his eyes on
them long enough for her to notice.

Was there room for one more up there, he wondered.
She was certainly attractive enough for him to try, and he
had always liked the challenge of tough, composed women.

She reminded him a little of the Honourable Araminta
Macaulay whose intentions towards him had been emi-
nently and emphatically dishonourable. He recalled how
she had taken him on a crash course in sex. An eager pupil,
he had learned that there was more to the activity than a
quick grope and a hurried conclusion. She had educated
him in many ways.

Steven smiled briefly as he remembered one of her
admonitions. 'Napkin, darling, not serviette. You're not a
second-hand car dealer who's trying to be grand.'

He looked again at Sally Wyatt, assessing her. One of his
London people had done the research on her. Steven knew
that she had a lawyer husband and a young daughter; and
she was sleeping with one of the researchers on her show.
He also knew that she was a very competent and ambitious
television journalist, with a reputation for an unambiguous
line of enquiry. She was tough enough to keep on asking
until politicians and businessmen actually answered her

questions. He hoped that the Head of Sport had been as unambiguous as she was, that he had marked her card very heavily.

Sally Wyatt had already had several discussions with her producer about the fourth programme in the new series of 'Insight'. As soon as Simon Grant had handed her a list of 'suggested' questions, she had realised that the programme was to be a fraud. She was used to devising her own lines of enquiry, not foisting these anodyne queries on her public, who expected controversy and a harsh approach to the ethics of business and politics.

'What's all this shit?' she had asked Grant. 'These are the sort of questions you hear from those semi-literates on "The Big Match". I'm an investigative journalist not a fucking sycophant.'

Grant had winced. He hated bad language; it reminded him of his father. But he knew that Sally Wyatt was right. 'Darling, please don't rock the boat. Orders from on high, a favour called in, that sort of thing.' He fluttered his hands nervously.

'I want to see the Head of Features.'

'It won't do any good.'

It hadn't, even though Wyatt put her point of view fiercely. An important issue of business ethics was at stake, she said, as well as her own journalistic integrity. Her interviewee represented many leading sportsmen but he also ran tournaments in which they participated; and then he sold the television rights on behalf of the various governing bodies.

'For Christ's sake, he's selling to himself. He's got some areas of some sports completely under control. There's an unhealthy little monopoly going on here, and I can't even ask him a question about it? Where's my integrity gone? Down the fucking plughole.'

The Head of Features was unmoved and Sally Wyatt
looked over the edge of the cliff: it was toe the line or
resign. The latter was not a reasonable option for her, even
though she had been courted by one of the ITV companies.
She was doing very well with 'Insight'. In only its second
series it had climbed the ratings significantly, from a starting point of less than two million viewers to nearly four
million. In his persuasive way Grant had pointed out that
her current subject would add viewers. 'Good for the ratings, love. Sport is sexy at the moment and he's a very big
wheel in sport.'

'Insight' was just a stepping stone for Sally Wyatt: she
had much wider ambitions, starting perhaps with the Head
of Features' job. On a practical level, her home was in west
London and she didn't fancy a more demanding journey
south of the river to work. Her lover lived in west London
too, not far from the BBC. It was convenient.

As they settled in their seats she could hardly fail to
notice Steven's pointed inspection of her legs. Was he trying
to look up her skirt out of interest or was it a bit of male
intimidation? At least he was attractive; not like most of the
businessmen and politicians she interviewed with their
crumpled and badly cut suits, and their overblown bellies
straining their shirt buttons. No, he was positively handsome. He had a lean and suntanned face, grey eyes and a
prominent nose which saved his face from mere prettiness
and added to its strength and charm. He looked relaxed but
she noticed that his eyes flicked guardedly about him, from
her to the producer, to the technicians, to the various cameras. He looked fit and she knew from her researchers that
he played tennis and golf and 'worked out'. He was well
dressed; his suit was well cut. She wondered briefly how
he'd look stripped.

They each spoke some sentences so that the sound engineer could adjust to their voice levels, the director called for quiet and Sally Wyatt launched into her introduction and first question.

'Today I will be talking to one of the leading entrepreneurs in international sport. In just a few years he has built up an agency which represents many of the leading sportsmen of our time, great champions in tennis, golf, motor racing and athletics. He organises tennis and golf tournaments and, through his offices around the world, he sells television rights to all the major networks, including the BBC.'

Sally Wyatt leaned forward in her seat and, in her slightly husky and well-modulated voice, continued, 'Steven Shaw, you were born in Brighton just over thirty years ago. First would you tell us about your early years? I believe that you had humble beginnings.'

Steven smiled at Sally Wyatt and made sure that the cameras had the benefit of his even white teeth. 'You're quite right, Sally, about my relatively humble beginnings,' he replied. 'My father was the manager of a department store in the town and my mother, in the days before women had careers . . .' he paused and raised a quizzical eyebrow '. . . was content to be a housewife. We owned a small house in Brighton, money was not plentiful but I can't remember lacking for anything because the one thing that was in plentiful supply was fun. We were a happy family and my strongest memory of childhood is a house filled with laughter . . .'

There were several distortions and some unadulterated lies in Steven's first sentences. Over the years he had rewritten his past, not radically but enough to satisfy his own instincts.

With a flick of her tongue Sally Wyatt moistened her lips and recrossed her legs. The bright studio lighting seemed to emphasise their elegance. Steven wondered how she'd look in suspenders. Perhaps one day he'd find out. Concentrate, this is important, he reminded himself.

Sally Wyatt said: 'So you had the poor but happy childhood that is almost traditional for the self-made businessman . . .' Supercilious bitch, Steven thought and smiled at the camera. '. . . indeed it was almost idyllic. Tell us a little about your school days. You started in the local primary school and ended up at the Harvard Business School. That's quite a progression, isn't it? What were the factors that elevated you from a potentially humdrum existence? Was it ambition suddenly unleashed, an inspirational teacher? What?'

Steven clasped his hands in front of him and looked serious. 'It's difficult to analyse at a distance of what? . . . fifteen years. I'm sure that there wasn't a sudden unveiling of the way ahead for me, a sort of Road to Damascus experience. No, my parents were just ordinary middle-class people, with a struggle on their hands, but they expected me to go on to university and I suppose I reacted to their expectations and got on with the job. My teachers were excellent but there was no Svengali amongst them. It was just solid hard work, I suppose. And my parents were very supportive.'

That was another of Steven's convenient distortions. Although his mother had been fiercely ambitious for him, she had to overcome the resistance of his father, who wanted Steven settled in a job as soon as possible so that some extra money came into the house.

The studio manager interrupted Sally Wyatt's next question by waving his arms and shouting, 'Hold it, everyone. Camera four is on the blink. We'll be with you as quickly as possible.'

Steven stretched in his chair, took a sip of water and

leaned towards his interviewer: 'Is it going OK?'

Sally Wyatt shrugged: 'You've done this before, you're coming across fine.'

Try not to be so enthusiastic, you cold bitch, he thought. But he smiled. 'Thanks, that's encouraging. By the way, who's your agent? You do have one, I assume?'

He already knew the answer to his question but, even as she gave him the name, he resolved to find out more about the agency. Maybe there were clients there whom Aultman could poach.

The studio manager waved his arms once again and they were off and running with her next comment and question.

An hour later and the interview had been concluded. Despite her resentment, Sally Wyatt stuck to her brief. Although she suspected Steven to be a cold and calculating, twenty-four-carat bastard, she admitted to herself that he was a charming and very polished interviewee.

On the following day Steven arranged for a bunch of flowers to be sent to Sally Wyatt, along with a thank-you note. A few weeks later he sat down with a 'television consultant' and went exhaustively through the interview to assess his on-camera technique. One or two gestures and phrases had, as a result, been eliminated from his repertoire.

# Chapter Twenty-one

There was just enough time, if the traffic was in their favour, for Terry Parkin to drive Steven to a lunchtime meeting on the outskirts of Coventry. Steven had only agreed to go because there was some big money at stake. He needed a sponsor for one of his television series: truck racing on ice. It was real trash-sport, but Jack Hemmings, self-made millionaire and owner of a chain of DIY stores, was interested.

The car picked up speed on the motorway. Prompted by the interview, Steven's mind flicked back to his childhood. What had he said to Sally Wyatt? A happy family . . . a house full of laughter . . . What a joke!

The house was set in the middle of a terrace of identical buildings just a few hundred yards from the railway station. He could still hear the clunk and rattle of arriving and departing trains. In the summer he used to wander down to the station forecourt and watch the weekenders and the holidaymakers arrive. Some of them were in a state of near-panic, worried that a piece of luggage or a child might go astray; others arrived in a holiday mood, bright and smiling. He liked to look at the younger people, the ones with the more colourful clothes, young men and women hand-in-hand, down in Brighton for a good time, enjoying their new-found freedom as the 'Swinging Sixties' raised its pace.

They were noisy and friendly. One day, a man in a strange suit which was very tight and didn't seem to have any lapels on the jacket asked him for directions. Steven didn't dare look at the man's giggling girlfriend; her legs were bare above her knee. His mother called such girls hussies. He was able to tell the man where to find the street he wanted; the man found a coin in his pocket, flipped it into the air and handed it to Steven. 'Here you are, mate, half a dollar. Buy yourself something.'

The couple swayed off, arms entwined. Half a dollar? Steven looked and found half a crown in his hand. He didn't tell his parents about his reward.

Even to a child the house seemed cramped. Right off the street you entered the living room which was crowded by a mock leather settee and two matching armchairs, a table and a cabinet with a few pieces of china; eventually, a television set took up even more space. There was a meagre dining room and an even smaller kitchen. The mean back garden was mostly covered by cracked paving stones, but there was a tiny, tired patch of grass. The dustbin and the washing line were useful items in Steven's make-believe games.

Sometimes he played with Danny Kyle from next door. Danny was rough and noisy and always seemed to have some money in his pocket to buy sweets. He was the eldest of the four Kyle children. Mr Kyle sometimes gave Steven sixpence for sweets, too, and Mrs Kyle, who seemed only to inhabit the kitchen, always had a chocolate biscuit and some lemonade for the boys.

Steven's mother used to scold him for playing with Danny. 'They're common.' It was her favourite phrase of denunciation. 'Irish, of course. I don't suppose they'll stop breeding even though they've got a houseful.' His mother's lips were pursed tightly in disapproval but Steven didn't understand what she meant. 'He's a mechanic, he's not a professional man,' she added. 'You should make friends with Jane, next door. They're a nice family.'

Jane was the only daughter of Mr and Mrs Reynolds, and was about a year younger than Steven. Whereas Mary Shaw would only nod to the Kyles and pass quickly by, she felt the Reynolds deserving of her friendship. The husband was a supervisor in the Post Office and, in Mary Shaw's hierarchy, was therefore a professional man. The families occasionally took Sunday tea together; there were sandwiches of fish paste and of ham, followed by Battenburg cake and a jam sponge. Steven and Jane used to sit there, silent and bored, as the adults discussed the weather and the other neighbours.

It was a relief to be allowed, after a suitable interval, to go out to play. Except that Jane, since she was a girl, didn't know how to play and cried when she fell over.

Mr Kyle worked for a big garage in the town and there was usually what he called, in his soft and rolling voice, 'an old banger' outside his front door. There weren't many cars in the street at that time: a few motor-bikes, some with side-cars. On a Sunday morning Mr Kyle would either be under the car, his legs sticking out, or craning over the engine, his backside in the air.

It seemed to Steven's young eyes that, despite his mother's disfavour, his father liked Mr Kyle. He often stepped outside the front door to talk to him when his Irish neighbour was tinkering with his car. Within minutes, Mary Shaw would call her husband in to attend to something: to change a light bulb, see to the fire, or peel the potatoes for the Sunday lunch.

One Sunday in December, near Christmas, when Mary Shaw had gone next door to borrow some gravy browning from Mrs Reynolds, his father had been chatting and laughing with Mr Kyle on the pavement. Steven stood by the open front door and listened.

Mr Kyle, a broad-shouldered man with crinkly black hair, flecked with grey, and a rosy face had said: 'Come on, Bill, let's go down to the Red Lion for a jar.'

His father looked doubtful. 'I don't know, Martin. Sunday dinner in an hour, you know what she's like. One o'clock on the dot.'

'Ample time, Bill, we'll just have the one. Christmas is a-comin'. It'll do you good.' Mr Kyle put his huge hand on Bill Shaw's shoulder. 'I'll get my coat. Just a couple of small ones and you'll be home for your dinner.'

Bill Shaw looked nervously at the Reynolds's front door, as if his wife would burst through at any moment, breathing fire and vengeance. 'OK,' he said, 'I'll have to be quick.' He turned to Steven. 'Tell your mother that I've gone for a walk with Mr Kyle, there's a good boy.' He winked at his son and the two men strode quickly away down the street. As they turned the corner, Steven saw his father look quickly back and then walk on.

Several minutes later Mary Shaw returned to the house. 'Mrs Reynolds had some good news,' she said. 'Mr Reynolds has been promoted. Where's your father? I must tell him.'

Steven gave her the message and watched his mother's face, which bore the merest sign of animation, settle back into its disapproving mien. 'Well, he knows that the dinner is on the table at one o'clock.'

Bill Shaw didn't return for his dinner at one o'clock, nor at two o'clock. Steven, sitting by the fire with a copy of *Hotspur*, heard his father and Mr Kyle arrive at the front door at around three.

'Ah, now that was a lovely little session, Bill. We'll do it again sometime.'

The front door opened slowly and Bill Shaw fumbled his way in, several bottles in his arms. Steven looked at them later and saw they had a funny name on them. Guinness. He didn't know how to say it. He noticed that his father was red in the face and that he stumbled a little as he headed for the table to put the bottles down. Crash, they went and one of them rolled on to its side. His father caught it as it fell from the table. "Owzat', he said and grinned at his son. Mary Shaw stood watching silently from the kitchen doorway.

'Hello, my dear,' Bill Shaw said. His voice was odd, the words seemed to run together.

'Don't you "my dear" me.' Her voice was quiet and seemed very chilly to Steven. 'You've been out with that Irish lout and you're drunk. Disgustingly drunk. Your dinner's in the oven. Get it yourself.'

Steven watched his father push the grey beef and dried-up vegetables around in the congealed gravy. He didn't eat much. Suddenly he leapt to his feet and rushed for the stairs. They both heard the sounds as he retched in the lavatory.

'Disgusting, absolutely disgusting,' his mother said, as she turned on the radio to block out the noise of her husband's vomiting.

During the next few days there was no conversation between husband and wife. His parents spoke separately to Steven, who soon got tired of relaying their requests. He let them use him as a sort of conversation exchange: 'Steven, would you ask your father to get me some more Christmas cards from the store?'

'Steven, would you ask your mother how many more Christmas cards she needs?'

It seemed very silly to him. The Kyles seemed to argue all the time but it always ended in laughs and hugs and pats.

It was a long time before Mary Shaw could bring herself to speak to anyone in the Kyle family but Steven thought that they didn't even notice her displeasure.

In the following year, the Kyles had planned a trip to Hayling Island for Whit Monday. Mr Kyle had managed to borrow a van from his firm and, a week before, Danny was sent round to invite Steven. 'Mum says there's plenty of room,' he said. 'It's a nice beach and we'll go to the fair.'

'That's very kind of your mother, Danny,' Mary Shaw replied as if that was the last thing it was, 'but Steven is going to tea on Whit Monday.'

'But Mum—' Steven said.

'No buts, Steven. We have accepted an invitation to the Reynolds for tea.'

Steven thought he hated his mother for a moment or two. He'd only been to a fair once; his mother said they were too noisy, too expensive and very dangerous. He appealed to his father and, as the week progressed, he heard snatches of discussions between his parents: 'I don't want him seeing too much of that family,' said his mother.

'Danny's a nice young boy.'

'The father's no better than a tinker. In the pub the whole weekend.'

'He works hard and enjoys himself.'

'And she's no better than she should be. Can't say no. All those children.'

'The boy will enjoy the company. He doesn't go on many days out.'

'And whose fault is that? If you pushed yourself at work and got a better position . . . Look at Mr Reynolds, he's getting on at the Post Office. We'll never have any money.'

'God Almighty, Mary, I'm doing my best.'

Mary Shaw began to speak but her husband overrode

her. 'The boy is going on the trip and that's final. I'll tell the Kyles now.'

It was rare enough that either of his parents used the other's name, so Steven realised that his father must be mighty annoyed; and he'd never known him brush aside one of his wife's decisions. Steven felt a great surge of love for his father, who had stood up for him and granted him a day which was to be the highlight of his young life.

Very early on the Monday morning Steven was ready and waiting by the front door. In a bag he had his swimming trunks and a towel, and he was neatly dressed in his jacket and school tie. On the previous evening his mother had pressed his short trousers and brushed his shoes until they shone. That morning, with a martyred look, she had given him a ten shilling note with the warning: 'Make sure you offer to pay for things. Don't be beholden to them. And don't spend too long in the sun.'

Just after seven o'clock there was a rat-a-tat-tat on the front door. Danny, grinning, grabbed him by the arm and pulled him towards the van. Steven waved goodbye to his mother and climbed into the back of the Bedford van. A chorus of 'Hello Stevie' greeted him from the assembled Kyle family. 'We're off,' said Mr Kyle, as he let out the clutch and the vehicle rattled and bumped to the end of the road. His wife sat alongside him with the youngest child, Daisy, on her lap. Along with Danny and the two middle children, Alan and Jack, Steven tried to make himself comfortable on the wooden seats which ran down the sides of the van. As they turned corners, metal tools and little boxes filled with odds and ends scuttered across the floor.

Soon they were heading west towards Chichester and Portsmouth. All the children were dipping into bags of sweets provided by Mrs Kyle and, after driving for about forty minutes, Mr Kyle pulled off the road and parked in front of a café.

'Time for breakfast,' he said. 'Got to keep body and soul together.'

Steven felt nervously in his pocket for his ten shilling note. How much would it cost? Would he have enough money?

Mr Kyle led the way into the café. There were a dozen or so tables, mostly occupied, but the Kyles found enough room at one near a window.

The one waitress, skinny and harassed, her grey hair awry, took their order. 'Six full breakfasts, please, my love, and a spare plate for the little one,' he nodded towards his young daughter who had resumed her position on her mother's lap. 'Lemonades for the kids and a big pot of tea. Thanks, love.'

The waitress went off at speed and yelled the order to the man and the woman behind the counter. Steven had never heard his father call anyone 'love'.

It was the biggest breakfast Steven had ever seen: sausages, several rashers of bacon, two eggs, mushrooms, tomatoes, fried bread and some round black stuff that he didn't like. Mr Kyle took care of it. 'Anyone who doesn't want their black pudding,' he said, 'pass it over.' There was a huge stack of toast in the middle of the table which disappeared swiftly.

The waitress had plonked the bill down in the middle of the table and Steven eyed it warily, wondering when he should offer to 'pay his way', as his mother had sternly put it. His opportunity came when Mr Kyle said that they should get on the move, Mrs Kyle took Daisy off to the lavatory and the boys moved towards the door.

'I'll settle up,' said Mr Kyle, as his broad hand closed on the scrap of paper with some figures scribbled on it.

Steven fingered the ten shilling note out of his pocket, held it out and said nervously, 'Mr Kyle. My mum said—'

The large hand ruffled his hair briefly and Mr Kyle said: 'You save that for a rainy day, Steve, my boy. You're with us, enjoy yourself.'

They bowled westward in the old van and Alice Kyle started the singing: 'Nellie the Elephant', 'Knick Nack Paddawack', 'One Man Went to Mow' and 'Ten Green Bottles'. Everyone joined in and it seemed no time at all before Mr Kyle was announcing that 'he had a bit of a thirst' and he reckoned that they all needed to stretch their legs anyway.

When they resumed their journey there was more singing in which Mr Kyle joined even more lustily than before.

At last they got to Hayling Island and the joyful group of running, jumping and yelling children piled on to the beach. The first objective was the sea, and the four older children were soon skirmishing in it, splashing each other and showing off their inexpert swimming techniques. Mr Kyle did handstands in the water and swam through the waves with each of the children in turn on his back; Mrs Kyle paddled sedately on the edge of the sea with Daisy.

Some races were organised on the grass behind the beach – with handicaps, but Steven beat everyone anyway. Cricket followed, with a piece of driftwood hung with Mr Kyle's cardigan as the wicket.

Later, a feast of a picnic was laid out on a tartan blanket by Mrs Kyle: veal and ham pie; pork pie; a tower of sandwiches including ham, egg and cress, cheese and pickle, sardine, and corned beef; tomatoes, spring onions, sausages, crisps, fruit cake, jam sponge, marshmallows, Turkish delight and lemonade. There were several bottles of light ale for Mr Kyle.

Steven, like Danny and the other three children, ate enough to burst and there was plenty left for later, just in case anyone was worried about going hungry.

The final treat was the visit to the fair. To Steven's eyes the Big Wheel seemed higher than the pictures he had seen of Mount Everest. No wonder they screamed when they reached the top. The younger children were not allowed on it and Steven, intimidated, hung back when Mr Kyle looked up at it. 'I'll go, if Danny and Steve will hold my hand. What d'you say?'

Danny jumped in delight and Steven, his legs trembling already, nodded in agreement.

'I'll look after them, Alice,' said Mr Kyle. 'Don't you worry.'

They sat three abreast in one seat and the wheel slowly cranked upwards as the other seats were filled. Then were away. Mr Kyle's arms clasped both the boys to him and Steven could hear his stomach rumbling and gurgling. After a turn or two he dared to open his eyes and watched the sky and the ground hurtling towards him in turn.

They tried the merry-go-rounds and the bumping cars and Mrs Kyle screamed loudly in the ghost train. Mr Kyle rang the bell on the trial of strength machine and won a goldfish in a bowl, and Steven gave Mrs Kyle the coconut he won at the shy.

All the children were given lollipops and candy floss and suddenly it was time to start for home.

'We'll stop halfway,' Mr Kyle said. 'It'll break the journey and stop a thirst developing.'

When the van jolted into the car park of a pub in the early evening most of the children were asleep. They all sat in the garden while Mr Kyle had 'just a couple of halves to keep him going'.

After leaving the pub, he sang one or two songs in a soft

tenor voice: 'Danny Boy' was one, 'I'll Take You Home Again, Kathleen' and 'How Can You Buy Killarny' were others. As they neared the outskirts of Brighton there was merely a contented silence in the van, with an occasional snort from one of the sleeping younger children. Steven noticed that Mrs Kyle had her arm around her husband and her head on his shoulder. He couldn't remember seeing his mother do that to his father.

Then he was home, his skin taut from the effect of the sun, the sea salt and the sand. Tired. Blissfully happy.

# Chapter Twenty-two

During the 'Insight' interview, Steven had also been non-committal about his various teachers. One of them had stood out, but Steven had had no intention of making a public acknowledgement of his considerable debt to the man.

In his second year of A-Level studies, Steven and his fellow pupils moved up to the Lower Sixth Form and were confronted by an English literature teacher who was new to the school. Jeremy Knight had taught at several public schools, and the boys learned that he had been educated at the nearby Lancing College and then at Oxford University, where he had been awarded a first class degree.

'What's he doing here?' the cynics among the boys had asked. 'D'you think he's a poof?'

The first thing that Steven noticed about Jeremy Knight as he stood before them at the start of their opening lesson was his clothing. The average schoolteacher's uniform of grey flannels and a baggy sports jacket, its elbows patched with leather, was not assumed by him. Knight wore a grey checked suit, which, even to Steven's inexperienced eye, looked well-cut and expensive. A bright yellow shirt and a patterned bow tie made up his ensemble. The teacher was quite tall and slim and his thin face was verging on emaciated. Deep lines ran down either cheek and seemed to emphasise a pair of glowing, deep brown eyes; his hair, cut short against the current fashion, was black and shiny and swept straight back from his forehead.

'Good morning, gentlemen,' he said, in a clipped voice that might have issued from a newsreader on BBC radio, 'I'm looking forward to our year together. We're going to read and enjoy and explore some of the greatest books in our, or anybody else's, language. "All of human life is here", to quote one of those tabloid newspapers with which I'm sure you do not sully your young and impressionable eyes.' Knight smiled around at his class and there was a nervous laugh from one or two boys. 'If we're reading Shakespeare, we've got it all,' he continued. 'Murder and every other kind of violence, lustful sex, romantic sex, rape, comedy both low and high, incest, thunderous rhythm and startling beauty.'

There was silence in the room as Knight paused and looked out through the window. 'Talking of incest,' he said, 'we have Lord Byron in the syllabus. Who termed him "mad, bad and dangerous to know"? Does anyone know?'

A boy in the second row put up his hand: 'Lady Caroline Lamb, was it, sir?'

'Exactly. Good. She was his mistress. It is said that he had an incestuous relationship with his half-sister, Augusta Leigh. It was frowned upon then, of course, as it would be now. He was one of the great romantic poets. "Yet Freedom, yet thy banner, torn but flying, Streams like the thunder-storm against the wind." He had idealistic views of human liberty and he died in their cause. Every poet should die in such a way, I suppose.'

Knight looked sombrely above the heads of his class. 'He lived dangerously, as poets should. That's why the British are not at ease with such men. Byron was more honoured abroad than he ever was at home.'

The teacher pointed at Steven and said: 'The young gentleman with dark hair by the window. I'm sorry, I'll learn all your names in due course. Open your copy of *Childe Harold* at page one hundred and fifty-four. Stand up and read the second stanza on that page.'

Although the class was used to reading aloud, Steven went pink with embarrassment in front of this stranger who talked about incest and threw quotations at his class. He mumbled and stumbled through the verses and when he had finished, Knight said, 'You can do better than that. They're fine words, with an easy rhythm. Let them ring out proudly. Stand up and let rip.'

When he had finished, Knight congratulated him and said that they would all get used to declaiming verse in the coming term. He told them a little more about Lord Byron's life and his philosophy, and then, to Steven's astonishment, the bell rang to end the lesson. He checked his watch to make sure that there hadn't been a mistake: the time had raced by.

In common with several of the other boys, Steven began to look forward eagerly to Jeremy Knight's lessons. Casual and eccentric though his teaching seemed to be, his form surged on through the syllabus.

During that first term Steven found that he spent more time than ever before in the school library and in the town's public library. Knight's off-the-cuff remarks about books and writers sent him hurrying to read them: Hemingway and Raymond Chandler, Amis and Albert Camus, Scott Fitzgerald and Graham Greene, Isherwood and Koestler, Salinger and Paul Scott, Waugh and Wodehouse. With the zeal of the converted, Steven devoured their works.

In their second term the class were taken to the theatre in the care of Jeremy Knight. There was a visit to a touring version of *The Importance of Being Earnest* at a Croydon theatre, and to Paul Scofield's *Macbeth* in London.

"'I have a journey, sir, shortly to go;
My master calls me – I must not say no.'"

Jeremy Knight paused and surveyed his class, his habitual smile, partly encouraging and partly sardonic, on his face. 'All you young men have a journey ahead of you and it's only just beginning. I will try to light the way for you, to help you. I'm sure that your parents see my job as trying to ensure that you pass your exams, and I'll do my level best to fulfil their ambitions for you. Despite your gross idleness and inattention,' he grinned quickly at his pupils, 'you're all capable of sailing through, if you put in the time, master the syllabus. You can all get good enough grades, in English and your other subjects, to find a place at a university. That's important.'

Knight paused. There was no sound from his pupils and he continued, quietly and emphatically. 'But to me, that's only a small part of my task, the essence of which is to show you all how to educate yourselves during the rest of your days. Only you can do that, you alone can open your minds and your hearts and welcome beauty and truth, clutch it, foster it, love it and see it flourish. That is education and that is my real task.'

The quiet was interrupted by the sound of a book hitting the floor. Carl Gibson, a tall and gangling boy with carroty hair, muttered an apology and tried to cover his embarrassment by groping for the fallen tome. The spell was broken and Knight's musings ended.

'OK,' he said, 'it's back to the bad Lord Byron. Page eighty-five. Let's read his thoughts about Venice.'

Any thoughts of continuing his education at a university had scarcely entered Steven's mind; the wisdom received from his mother was that he would find a good and respectable job, 'with prospects'.

A few days after Jeremy Knight's encouraging comments about the possibilities that lay ahead for his pupils, Steven broached the subject with his parents. They were chatting about a forthcoming interview with the careers master at Steven's school.

'Have you any idea what you want to do after you leave school?' his mother asked.

'Not really,' Steven replied, 'but Mr Knight says that I might get into a university if I get reasonable A-Levels.'

Both his parents looked up sharply. The thought that her son could go to a university had only been a vague fantasy to Mary Shaw. What a feather in her cap that would be! Telling everyone that her boy was off to the Grammar School had made her glow with pride, but the university . . .

Bill Shaw said automatically, 'We can't afford it. University, that's another three or four years, isn't it?'

'Yes, Dad, but I'll get a grant, it's not going to cost you any money.'

'Oh no, and who's going to keep you during the holidays? You can't live on fresh air, or does Mister bloody Knight have the answer to that as well?'

Mary Shaw ignored her husband's outburst and said quietly: 'Do you think you've got a chance to get a university place, Steven?'

He fidgeted with his empty plate, looked at his father who had buried his face in the evening newspaper, and said, 'I think I can get the grades. Well, Mr Knight thinks I can and then it's a matter of applying to places.'

'And you'll get a grant?'

'Yes and I'll get a job in the holidays to cover my pocket money.'

'Well, you can start in the summer at Macaulay's,' his father said grimly. 'They always need extra people in the packing and delivery department. I'll put your name down and have a word.'

As the spring term wore on, the burdens of the work at school became more intense. Even Jeremy Knight seemed less inclined to be side-tracked from the syllabus. Instead he settled on a group of half a dozen boys, Steven and Carl Gibson amongst them, who were invited to events outside the school curriculum. These augmented the occasional class trips to museums and the theatre and encompassed an eclectic choice of activities.

They saw the musical, *Hair*, and, to the boys' astonishment, Mr Knight was one of the many who danced on the stage during the finale; they visited *The Mousetrap* and their teacher giggled audibly through much of it; and they were all entranced by a play about two minor Shakespearian characters called Rosencrantz and Guildenstern. During the short Easter holiday, Mr Knight took them to hear the Bournemouth Symphony Orchestra and to a film directed by Jean Cocteau.

After the film, Steven walked part of his way home with Carl Gibson.

'He lives in a different world, doesn't he?' Carl said.

'Who? Knight?'

'Yeah. He rattles on about the real purpose of education but he's never had to earn a living. He's one of those people who's always had money.'

'We're lucky to have him as a teacher,' Steven said loyally.

'Oh, yeah, I agree and let's take advantage and make sure we get our grades because that'll get us to university. Get a degree, that's what it's all about these days. I'm gonna do business studies at Birmingham, then it's into the old man's firm and earn some bread.'

Steven knew that Carl's father owned a small chain of electrical retailers on the south coast. 'There's more to it than that, surely?' Steven said doubtfully.

'Just humour the old bugger,' Carl said with a laugh. 'He can be useful, as my dad says. He can open a few doors for us at the universities, if needs be. The old pals' act, that's what it's about these days. A nudge here and a wink there.'

'Yeah, I suppose you're right. It's who you know, isn't it?'

Steven understood clearly the springs of his friend's motivations: a blend of muted ambition heavily overlaid with materialism. But Carl Gibson was right, you needed money to foster idealism. Steven was determined to do well in the forthcoming examinations to further his own ambitions, but also for the sake of Jeremy Knight.

As the summer term began he worked harder than ever, and even refused several opportunities to play cricket. He was in demand for the Young Amateurs of Sussex team, which was seen as a stepping stone to the county's second team, but he had little hesitation in putting his revision first.

After one of Jeremy Knight's classes, the teacher called him over and said: 'You're not playing for the Young Amateurs these days, Steven. Why not?'

He shrugged and pointed at his books. 'Revision, sir.'

'Too much makes Jack a dull boy. Enjoy your cricket, be balanced. Play in the match next weekend, it's a good one. It must be, because they've called upon me to umpire it. You can always put your Dickens or your Shakespeare in your cricket bag and read between innings. Understood?'

Steven nodded his assent and, that evening, rang the secretary of the team to confirm that he would play. Playing against a Surrey Schools Eleven, Steven had a successful day: he scored forty quick runs when they were badly needed and took a couple of wickets.

At close of play he accepted a lift home from Jeremy Knight and as they drove towards Brighton in his old and comfortable Aston Martin, his teacher said: 'You've applied for some of the universities, I believe, but how would you fancy London? To read English?'

'Well, sir, I was thinking of studying accounting or maybe doing a business course. Something that will be of use to me afterwards.'

'Poppycock, Steven. You go to a university to stretch your mind, to continue your education, not to win a few merit badges to flourish in the face of some money-grabbing potential employer.'

Knight swerved sharply around a van and continued, 'You're good at English. I know you'll do well in your A-Levels, so I've had a word with an old friend of mine at London. It's an excellent English department, so would you be interested in a place there?'

Steven's mind flicked back to his conversation with Carl Gibson some weeks ago. It's who you know.

'The sport's good there, too, Steven. Not as good as Oxford, of course, but you can play all the sports to your heart's content. And so you should, you have a special talent.'

'Well, if you can help me, of course I'd love to go there.' But not to read English. He'd stick to his plan to do a business or accounting course.

Knight said: 'Get a good grade in English and reasonable ones in your other subjects and you can consider it done.'

On the day before the examinations began, Jeremy Knight spent the whole of a double-length English literature lesson in talking about twentieth-century novelists and the effects of authoritarian philosophies such as communism and Roman Catholicism upon them. It was one of his favourite themes and, during the one and a half hours of the lesson, he managed not to mention any of the set books on the English literature syllabus. At the end he said: 'Enjoy yourselves in the next few days, let the ideas flow and put in plenty of quotes so that the examiner knows you've mastered the texts. They fill up the page, too.'

There was a little nervous laughter from his pupils and Knight held up his hand for silence. 'Now, it's much too late for any last-minute revision and I don't advise it. I want you all outside the Pavilion Theatre at seven o'clock sharp. I've booked for us to see *Charley's Aunt*. Don't be late.'

Despite the relaxing nature of *Charley's Aunt*, Steven slept badly that night. At least a dozen times he woke up, his mind fumbling for a quotation from Byron or Shakespeare, or his subconscious groping for the date of some important treaty or other. His mother made her traditional exam-day fuss over him and even gave him the briefest of embraces as she wished him good luck. She rarely touched him or any other human being and Steven noticed that her face was white and seemed even more drawn than usual. He was happy to get away from her edgy concern and even happier when he confronted the first of his A-Level examination papers. At last the game was on; all the preparation and planning and speculation were over. This was the real thing.

The end of the school year, not long after the conclusion of the A-Level examinations, was an anti-climax for Steven and his fellow pupils. Very few of them knew what they would be doing in a few months' time, although Carl Gibson was confident that he would be starting his course at the University of Birmingham.

In his parents' presence, Steven had deliberately played down his chances of securing a place at London University.

But, on the second day of his holiday, an innocuous conversation with his parents developed into an argument. In an unguarded moment, he allowed himself to state his real ambitions. The cause was an invitation addressed to him. Steven at once recognised Jeremy Knight's distinctive handwriting, the strokes broad and the loops forthright, on the envelope. A card inside invited him to lunch on the forthcoming Sunday.

'Who's that from?' his mother asked inquisitively.

'Mr Knight. Lunch on Sunday to celebrate the end of term.'

Mary Shaw sniffed in a disapproving way and said: 'Make sure you're back here before four o'clock. The Reynoldses are coming for tea. They're looking forward to seeing you.'

'Mum,' Steven replied with asperity, 'they see me every other day. Why should they be looking forward to seeing me on Sunday?'

His mother said nothing but glared at him and he continued: 'Mr Knight's lunches aren't like his lessons, you know. Start at one, finish at two-thirty. They go on, there's no way I'll be home for four.'

'If you ask me, your Mr Knight takes far too much of an interest in you boys. Dinners and trips to the theatre and lunches in his flat. He's not married, is he?'

Bill Shaw looked up sharply from the morning paper as Steven said, 'What's that got to do with it? As it happens, he's divorced. Mum, you just don't understand, he's fun, he talks about all sorts of things. Poetry, jazz, pacifism, detective stories, the theatre. He says that education doesn't end at the classroom door, it goes on outside. To better effect.'

'Well, schoolteachers didn't behave like that in my day,' Mary Shaw said. 'He's posh, isn't he, a bit far back.'

'He's not a nancy boy, is he, Steven?' his father said hesitantly.

'Christ Almighty, Dad,' Steven yelled, 'you beat the band. He's interested in us, he's a real teacher, does that make him a homosexual?'

'There's no need to blaspheme,' his mother said primly.

'And there's no need to insult Mr Knight,' Steven replied. 'He's interested enough to write to his friends in London about me, he's more or less got me a place there.'

'Oh—' said Mary Shaw.

'To read English,' Steven said spitefully, knowing that it would annoy her.

'What good's English going to be to you, Steven?' his mother said. 'English won't get you a job. Anyway, you already know English.'

'Oh, God, I can't stand much more of this,' Steven said, clasping his head with his hands. 'You wanted me to go to university, didn't you? Now I've got a chance, and it's due to Mr Knight.'

'Leave it alone, Mary,' her husband said. 'It was you who gave him all these grand ideas. If I'd had my way he'd be starting a proper job and bringing some money into the house, but no, you had to push and shove him in other directions.' Moodily, Bill Shaw lighted a cigarette, folded his newspaper and added: 'If he wants to go to lunch with his teacher, so be it. He starts his summer job at Macaulay's on Monday at eight o'clock sharp. He can start learning about the real world.'

'Actually, Dad, I'll start learning about the real world, as you call it, when I go to university because I intend to study accounting. I'm not completely stupid, you know.'

Steven walked out of the room.

Jeremy Knight's Sunday lunch gave Steven a glimpse of

gracious living, which was the worst possible preamble to his job, albeit temporary, at Macaulay's on the following day.

Steven was not surprised to find that Mr Knight lived on the ground floor of a beautiful Regency building on the east side of Brighton. In his eyes and those of his parents this was where the posh people lived, including the Managing Director of his father's store, James Macaulay. It was obvious that Jeremy Knight was posh, too.

The hallway of the flat seemed bigger than the whole ground floor of Steven's house and it was littered with books. They were on shelves, in cupboards and on tables, and where there were no books, there were paintings, prints, photographs, china vases and plates. Knight's sitting room was the same, writ large, and included a huge collection of records. Above the marble fireplace there was an oil painting of a younger Jeremy Knight and alongside it a framed picture of him in athletics garb. Steven peered at the caption which read: 'J. C. Knight, Oxford University Athletics Club, 1949 and 1950.'

The five guests were all from Jeremy Knight's A-Level class and included Carl Gibson. If their conversation was a little desultory when they first gathered, their host quickly scattered their inhibitions to the four corners of the room.

'Today is a little celebration,' he stated loudly. 'Your labours are over, for the moment, and the holidays have begun. There is only one way to begin a celebration and that's with champagne.' With a flourish he removed the cork from a bottle and poured the sparkling gold liquid into long-stemmed glasses shaped like tulips. 'These are proper champagne flutes, young gentlemen, not those saucer-shaped monstrosities that you see at suburban weddings and in third-rate bars. Here's to you: I thank you for making my year with you happy and productive. Good health.'

Self-consciously the boys toasted their teacher and each other. Steven gestured at the painting above the fireplace and said, 'Is that you, sir, the oil painting?'

The teacher nodded and said, 'Done by my first wife. She was a talented painter.'

'And the photograph?' Steven asked.

'Oh, yes, I ran the four hundred for the university. Well, it was the four hundred and forty yards in those days. One tried to live up to the boring old maxim "*mens sana in corpore sano*" in those days.'

Carl Gibson gestured towards another photograph which was propped against the mantelpiece. It showed Knight in the middle of a group of people who were sporting CND badges. 'When was that taken, sir?'

'A few years ago when I was giving my valued support to the anti-nuclear campaign. Alas, Bertrand Russell is no longer with us.'

'You're not one of those, are you, sir?' asked Gibson cheekily.

'You make my wish to support peace sound like a perversion, young Gibson, when the reverse is true. War and its horrors are the perversions and nuclear war is its ultimate expression.'

Knight paused, his face sombre, and drained his glass. 'Never mind, perhaps your generation will show more firmness of purpose than mine. Let's hope so. Now, let's not forget that this is a day for celebration. Let's sit down and enjoy the food and the wine.'

An oval table, covered by a crisp white linen tablecloth, was laid for six people. The heavy silver cutlery glittered, and the glasses, four for each person, glinted in the sunlight which meandered through the tall windows.

Each of the courses was accompanied by a different wine. Like the other boys, Steven didn't have much idea which glass or knife to use, but their teacher had no qualms about telling them.

Halfway through the meal Knight urged his guests to drink plenty of water. 'I don't want the responsibility of sending you home drunk. Your parents would never forgive me.'

'My mum and dad are probably drunk anyway,' Carl Gibson said, 'they spend Sundays at the Conservative Club.'

In the end Steven got home shortly after six o'clock, by which time the Reynolds family had departed. Despite sleeping through most of the television programmes, as his teacher had predicted, he woke up on the following morning with a headache and had to take some aspirin. This did not escape the sharp eye of his mother, who said that Mr Knight was a disgrace, giving strong drink to young boys; she was sure that the headmaster would not approve.

The day after the A-Level results were published, Steven received a letter from Jeremy Knight. Brief and to the point, his teacher congratulated him on his success and ended: 'Please call on me on Friday evening at seven for a celebratory glass.'

Steven considered a diplomatic refusal, partly because he usually played a few holes of golf at the municipal course on that evening. Despite his other sporting commitments he had devoted as much time as possible to the game, and had reduced his handicap to six. The professional at the club, who kept a watchful and enthusiastic eye on the junior members, deemed Steven a natural and encouraged him to play as often as he could. The real reason for his avoidance of Jeremy Knight was that Steven would have to break the news that he would be studying accounting and finance, not English. Nevertheless, he decided to face the problem squarely, however little he relished the prospect.

At five minutes past seven on the Friday evening he rang the bell of Jeremy Knight's apartment. He looked across the road at the quiet swell of the sea and squared his shoulders as he heard the door open and the familiar tones of his teacher.

'My dear boy,' Knight said. 'Come in. A glass of champagne awaits.' He wrung Steven's hand robustly. 'You've done really well, I'm proud of you.'

Steven had expected to find several of his classmates in the room but he was alone with Knight. He had already compared notes with some of them: Carl Gibson, for example, had achieved enough to take him to Birmingham University.

As champagne was poured into his glass, Steven asked politely about Knight's holiday in France. 'As long as you avoid those parts which the middle-class English are busy discovering, it's fine. They're hard at it in the Dordogne, I believe. Cooing sentimentally over broken-down cottages and buying them up in droves.' Knight shuddered dramatically and continued, 'However, I have already spoken to my friend, Christopher, in the English department at London and told him to expect a star pupil. So, don't let me down.'

Steven sipped at his wine and decided that he must seize his opportunity and tell Knight of his change of academic plan. 'I'm afraid I am going to let you down, sir,' he began.

'You don't need to call me "sir" anymore. I'm Jeremy to you now. But what's this about? You're going to take up your place, aren't you?' Knight peered anxiously at him. 'It's not money, I trust – you'll get your grant and you'll manage, like everyone else.'

'No, sir, I mean Jeremy. I've decided I want to do accountancy, not English. It'll be better for me,' he ended lamely.

Knight, his glass halfway to his lips, paused and replaced it on the table. His eyes intent on Steven, he spoke gently: 'Steven, there are, in my opinion, enough accountants in the world already. I see no reason for you to join them. You know my views about university education well enough by now. It matters not one jot what you study as long as it's a real subject, with an intellectual challenge. Physics, English, mathematics, history, chemistry, Chinese, German. They're real objects of study.' He stopped for a moment and gulped some champagne. 'Accountancy is just a skill, you can learn it any time. Don't give in to some dreary advice to learn something useful at university, something to stand you in good stead for your business career. The three years that await you should be a time to glory in your academic freedom, to give full rein to your imagination. You should be like Newton, "voyaging through strange seas of thought, alone", not bothering about profit and loss accounts. That can all come later, what's the rush? You have a flair for English, you should capitalise on it, enjoy it. Get a good degree. You've got the rest of your life to be a businessman, for God's sake.'

In his eagerness to convert Steven, the words had cascaded from Jeremy Knight's lips. It took Steven several moments to compose his thoughts.

'You're right, of course,' Steven said placatingly. 'In an ideal world, I would spend three years reading English. It would be wonderful. It's what I want to do.' He paused and looked out of the window as if seeking inspiration.

'But I can't linger in that way,' Steven continued. 'I've got to get on with my life and my life will be business. Accountancy will be a head-start for me. When I go for a job they'll realise that I'm serious about business. I'm sorry, I've let you down.'

Knight held up his hands, as if in surrender and said,

'You haven't let anyone down, Steven. It's your privilege to decide what you read at university. I can't disguise my disappointment; I think you're wrong. Still, you're ambitious and I'm sure you'll succeed in whatever you choose as a profession.'

'I'm determined to go places,' Steven said emphatically.

'Yes, but they're not my kind of places,' Knight replied sadly.

'We're nearly there, sir.' Terry Parkin broke into his thoughts. 'Hemmings DIY, just off the A45, I've got on my schedule. We'll be on time, sir.'

# Chapter Twenty-three

A glass of claret on a table to his right, Jeremy Knight settled down to watch 'Insight'. He was no fan of television: he had bought one so that he could watch the sport. A drama series occasionally held his attention, as did some of the films.

This evening, however, he was looking forward to seeing one of his old pupils on the small screen: Steven Shaw, who had been so promising. Knight remembered how brightly and eagerly Steven had followed the trail of knowledge he had marked out for him. Such rare students had made his career seem worthwhile. He sipped at his wine and recalled with sadness that his young pupil had abandoned his plans to read English in favour of some dreary business and accounting course.

The measured notes of a cello played over the titles for 'Insight'. The camera panned slowly towards the interviewer and her subject as they faced each other across a table. Steven hadn't changed much. He looked just as handsome as in his youth, Knight thought. Beautiful teeth, smart and understated clothing. He exuded self-assurance. Steven had become a great success in his chosen field of business, as he'd boasted to Knight that he would.

Their last meeting, more than a dozen years ago, had ended badly. It must have been after Steven's first year at London University. Knight had received a letter from

Steven: could he call and see him on an urgent matter? It had sounded mysterious and the schoolmaster hoped that he wasn't in some sort of trouble. A pregnant girlfriend, drugs, money, it was probably one or the other. You're getting cynical, he told himself. It turned out to be money.

Knight had noticed the changes in Steven. Although he had left school only a year before, there was little left of the gawky schoolboy: he looked confident and had no latent hesitation in addressing him as Jeremy.

As he poured them a drink, Knight went through the usual polite enquiries about Steven's studies and his other activities. When they had settled in their seats, Knight said, 'I know this isn't just a social call, so why don't we deal with whatever's troubling you and then we can both relax. What's the problem?'

'Would you be prepared to lend me a few hundred pounds?' Steven asked.

'It depends,' Knight said slowly, 'on the reason. Straightforward debts? Woman trouble?'

Steven laughed. 'No, nothing like that. And I'll pay you back within a matter of weeks. I want to buy into a franchise. A friend at college put me on to it. It'll be my holiday job and it should set me up for the rest of the year.'

'Tell me more.'

'It'll cost me three hundred pounds and then another hundred or so for all the back-up. It's selling soap powder to people. We cut out the middleman and sell direct to the public. Once I'm in, I can appoint other agents and they pay me a fee for the privilege. Then they set up their own networks and I still get fees all down the line.'

Steven smiled hopefully at Jeremy Knight, who said, 'It's called pyramid selling, Steven, and I can think of a much nastier description. I urge you not to get involved. It's just a scam for extracting money from gullible people. You won't sell a spoonful of soap powder to anyone. It's immoral and I cannot encourage you to get involved.'

'It's harmless enough, Jeremy. Everyone makes money—'

'That's the fallacy of the scheme,' Knight interrupted. 'Someone, somewhere down the line must lose his money, that's the whole point. Why don't you find yourself an ordinary job like any other student?'

'Because I want to make some decent money.'

'You'll spend the rest of your life making money. Relax, enjoy your freedom while you can. Money isn't that important.'

'It's easy for you to say that,' Steven gestured around the flat. 'You're well off, I don't suppose you've ever had to worry about money. I've got to start from scratch.'

'True, Steven, because money isn't worth worrying about. If you make the pursuit of money and material things your abiding passion you can only be unhappy. You'll diminish yourself as a human being. Don't fall into that trap.'

'I don't see the Macaulay family as unhappy. They've got money, pots of it. They've made it at the expense of people like my father.'

'Exactly, and that's why you can't possibly admire people like them. I know James quite well, he's rich but he's worthless.' Knight waved his hand dismissively.

Steven finished his drink, stood up and said, 'I didn't say I admired the Macaulays. But I intend to be a lot richer than any of them.'

Knight had been startled by his emphatic statement and had feared for him.

On the way to the front door he asked Steven to wait for a moment. Knight had an impulse to give the boy a present, something significant. He wanted to present him with a reminder of the world Knight held so dear, a talisman perhaps. He went to his bookshelves, extracted a copy of Byron's *Childe Harold* and scribbled a few words on the title page.

'This is for you, Steven,' he said quietly. 'It's quite a rare edition, but that's not the point. The point is that this book, this poetry, this work of genius, is worth more to me than any amount of money. I hope you'll keep it and enjoy it.'

Briefly, Jeremy Knight put his hand on Steven's shoulder in farewell. He shut the door and walked back into his sitting room. From the wide windows he saw the boy stride vigorously away against the backdrop of the sea. Knight watched him until he was out of sight.

A decade and a half later Shaw was once again in his view. Polished and articulate, Shaw had obviously achieved his ambitions. He was rich and a celebrity in the business world. Knight wondered if his protégé still had the book he'd given him.

# Chapter Twenty-four

The following afternoon had been set aside for a detailed review of the activities of the London office. Dean Aultman was doing a great job but one of his clients was causing trouble. Steven was determined to analyse whether Jimmy Burns, football's shining superstar, was worth the agency's time and trouble. Aultman maintained that he had genius in his feet. 'But shit in his head,' Steven replied.

Dealing with the strange ways of sportsmen like Burns was nothing new to the agency: that was its business. It had attained a pre-eminent position in the sporting markets of the mid-1980s by controlling the men and women whose verve and hard-edged talents dominated the courts, fairways, tracks and arenas of the world. It was the London agency's misfortune that even its combined efforts had failed to keep Burns under control.

Dean Aultman had made the first contact with Jimmy Burns. Steven had reservations about football. With its emphasis on team endeavour, it rarely produced individual stars who would appeal to the mass market advertisers. Steven felt at home with golfers, tennis players and motor racing drivers. They were marketable from head to toe; they could be turned into living and breathing billboards for the products which they endorsed.

Nevertheless, Steven recognised that football was big business on a world-wide scale. The quick way into that business was to represent its best exponents. The trouble was that British football in the middle of the 1980s was in the doldrums; it had become a game where mediocrity was hailed as brilliance and childish buffoonery applauded as charisma.

At fifteen years of age Jimmy Burns had been signed by the shrewd manager of Partick Thistle. The club, which was struggling for survival, had pinched him from under the noses of its illustrious Glasgow rivals, Celtic and Rangers. Two years later, Burns played his first game in the Partick colours and his impact was such that the word 'genius' was freely, and for once accurately, used by the media.

When Burns turned twenty years of age, the Scottish manager sold him for several million pounds to a rich London club. Burns's electric skills and especially his ability to score goals from apparently impossible situations enabled the London team to win the First Division Championship.

Soon after Burns arrived on the English soccer scene, Aultman had seen him as a possible recruit to Shaw's agency. He had recognised the special quality of the man, his potential to be the brightest star in the European footballing firmament. Out on the pitch Burns had dynamic skills in abundance and he was brave; he took his daring to the margins of audacity. The crowd identified with the knife-edge quality of his football. Young and old, men and women, they were involved with Jimmy Burns, entranced by him.

The attention focused by the media on the young star was overwhelming and Burns added to it by his propensity for visiting the night-spots of London with a succession of models and aspiring actresses. He was news, he was sexy. His cheeky good looks were enhanced by long, black, curly hair and striking dark eyes. A tough, lithe body completed an exceptional package.

After conferring with Steven in New York, Aultman got busy. He reckoned he had exactly the right man on whose back the agency could charge into the rich pastures of the football business, a client whose appeal went far beyond the confines of the sport. Aultman persuaded Burns to visit the agency, and the reactions of the staff, who were blasé about the sporting stars who passed through, told him that he had the right man in his sights. All of them made excuses to pop into his office to meet Burns. One of them later referred grandly to his 'essential vulnerability'.

'You mean you'd like to give him one, don't you, Julia?' Aultman said.

Aultman had no difficulty in prising Jimmy Burns away from his Glasgow agent. When Burns scored the winning goal in the European Cup Final and was named the European Footballer of the Year, Aultman was convinced that he had a client who would generate bundles of money for the agency.

So it proved, as the mass market purveyors of food and drink, clothing, toys and computer games, cars, magazines and holidays clamoured for his services, and the media hounded him for comments and interviews.

The first of Burns's contracts to be rejigged was that with his club. Despite the archaic rules of the Football Association which denied a player the right to use an agent to negotiate terms with his employer, Steven had arranged an informal meeting with the Chairman of Burns's club. It hadn't taken long for Steven to convince him that the club's most valuable asset was underpaid. Within a few weeks a new agreement was signed which guaranteed Burns millionaire status within three years. The endorsements and advertising deals which followed multiplied those earnings several times.

Burns regarded his newly acquired wealth with

equanimity. He had only met Steven Shaw a couple of times and regarded Dean Aultman, who had assumed total responsibility for the agency's new star client, as his sole point of contact in the complicated world of big business. Burns had met some of the other London staff and hazily recalled screwing one of the girls – Jenny or was it Julia? – after the launch of a soft drink he was now endorsing. But Aultman was his man.

Aultman was delighted with the arrangement. His success with Burns had inflated his bonus enough for him to move from a small flat in a run-down suburb of London to a three-bedroomed mews house in Kensington. Just as important, Burns signed any document that was put in front of him: contracts, share transfers, even a Power of Attorney in favour of Shaw.

'It's OK, Deano,' Burns used to say in his clenched Glaswegian accent, 'whatever you say.'

The problems began no more than a year into the agency's long-term management contract with Burns. Burns's sense of time was sketchy and Aultman ensured that he was picked up at his home or at his football club's training ground well in advance of any engagements. Despite such precautions Burns failed to make his scheduled appearance to open a supermarket in Milton Keynes. The Managing Director of the group, the Mayor, newspaper and television reporters and a couple of thousand devoted fans were disappointed.

Aultman did what he could to assuage their anger and, on the following day, issued a press release which excused Burns's absence on the grounds of a sudden illness. It was a pity that a freelance photographer had snapped the superstar, his arm around his latest companion, as he entered a bar on the same evening. The photograph, which appeared in several newspapers, made Aultman's statement look ridiculous. The Managing Director of the supermarket group described the incident more forcefully and was only placated by the offer of a future free appearance by Burns, plus some tickets for himself and his wife for the men's singles final at Wimbledon.

Burns's contract with Shaw's agency was an exclusive one, and one of its conditions was that all business activities, without exception, would be channelled through the London office. The footballer hadn't even read his management contract and he was astonished when Dean Aultman telephoned him one morning and asked him why he'd opened a sports shop without telling him.

'Come on, Deano,' he said with a laugh, 'Dave's an old mate of mine. I knew him up at Partick. It was no big deal. A grand in my back pocket. There's no point in you being involved.'

'The point is that we do all your deals,' Aultman said emphatically. 'And you don't work for peanuts. Your minimum is three grand, so why spoil the market?'

'Aw, he's a good mate and cash is cash.'

'Not if the Inland Revenue gets to hear about it, Jimmy. Wise up, they keep tabs on people like you and so does my boss, Shaw. He'll hit the roof.'

'He won't know if you don't tell him, Deano,' Burns said naively. 'Anyway, I'll keep your share for you in readies.'

Shaw would know, Aultman thought gloomily, as he replaced his telephone. He had press cuttings sent to him on all his clients wherever they were in the world, and Burns's little favour for his mate had made the national press. Aultman would try to protect his client because he liked him. But, as Steven had often and emphatically pointed out to him, clients were not there to be liked.

Steven's point was rammed forcefully home on the

opening day of the European Sports Trade Fair at London's
Olympia. After months of negotiations an Italian manufacturer had signed up Jimmy Burns to endorse a complete
range of football boots and sports footwear. He was to be
the focal point of their attack on the European market.
The products were stylish and Jimmy Burns provided the
perfect image for their marketing strategy. So perfect that
the Italians had paid an unprecedented guarantee over three
years with a scale of royalties which had made even
Aultman blink. They had wanted Burns badly and he and
Steven had exploited that need until it hurt.

The launching pad for the campaign was the Trade Fair,
and Burns was booked to be on the stand at two o'clock.
Half an hour before, the large and elaborate stand was
already ringed by journalists and photographers. At a quarter to two, Steven Shaw, who had flown in from New York
for the launch, was trying to calm the anxious Italian Chief
Executive when Aultman called him from a restaurant in
Chelsea.

'He wasn't at his flat when I got there,' Aultman said
grimly. 'He was here half an hour ago drinking champagne,
but the owner doesn't know where he is now. He's on the
phone trying to find him. Tell them half an hour. I'm
sorry.'

Signor Capello had started to sweat when the man who
had driven such a tough bargain for the services of his
famous client told him that Burns had been delayed. He
saw Shaw's face tighten with irritation for a moment and
then he was smoothly authoritative once again.

To Capello's relief he said, 'I'll make an announcement
to the press. Jimmy's stuck in traffic. Don't worry, I'll
handle it.'

Steven did so, and made a subsequent announcement at
three o'clock.

By this time, Capello's stomach had knotted tightly and he wanted to be sick.

Just before 3.30 there was a commotion at the main entrance and a ragged entourage of people approached the stand. Steven could see Aultman, who was pushing his way urgently through the crowd. Behind him came Jimmy Burns, a girl clinging to each arm. They were both blonde, their hair cascading around their shoulders. Even over the heads of the crowd and at a distance of twenty yards, Steven could see that Burns was drunk.

He lurched on to the stand, Capello rushed forward to greet him and the company's public relations team went into action.

Aultman began to explain what had happened but Steven cut him short. He nodded at Burns's two companions. 'Get those tarts out of the way, Dean. Put them in the hospitality room.'

'It's lucky I know his haunts, Steven, otherwise I'd never have found him.'

'Don't bother next time,' Steven said icily. He walked off, smile back in place, to join his client and Signor Capello.

Once he was there, Burns gave good value, as Steven later acknowledged. He exchanged jokes with the journalists and praised the product to the skies. 'Great boots, great design,' he said. 'They'll be worth another ten goals a year to me.'

When they eventually gained the much-needed seclusion of the company's hospitality suite, Burns felt his arm gripped securely by Steven. He turned and looked into his business manager's eyes. He noticed that they had the hue of wet granite, harsh and unyielding.

Steven drew him into a corner and turned his back on the others. He spoke quietly. 'Jimmy, don't ever do that to one of your sponsors again. You turn up on time and you turn up sober. And you don't bring any tarts with you.'

'Aw, come on, Stevie, I lost track of time, no harm done. I—'

'Above all, don't ever let me down again. That's the most important thing. You pay me to manage you and you either listen to me or you fuck off. Am I making myself plain?'

Burns realised that his agent still had him firmly by the arm. He didn't understand why Steven was making such a fuss. A few minutes late, why worry? He nodded his agreement and muttered, 'OK, you're the boss. Sorry and all that.'

As they left Olympia together, Steven said to Aultman, 'Dean, I have a feeling that we don't have a great future with our footballing star.'

'He's a genius, Steven.'

'Flawed. Booze and crumpet. Nothing wrong with that in moderation. But a soccer player should steer clear of the booze, anyway. Burns can't handle it, he can't handle his own celebrity status. Let's cash in while we can.'

'I can handle him,' Aultman protested.

'No, you obviously can't. And I've no intention of paying for a full-time baby-sitting service. If he steps out of line again, that's it. I'll cut him off at the knees.'

On that morning, Aultman went into the office very early. He had an endorsement contract to redraft and wanted to go over the many items which were due for discussion with Steven that afternoon. Number one was the problem of Jimmy Burns. He knew that Steven was on the verge of dismissing him as a client, but Aultman wanted to keep him; he was sure he could handle him effectively, whatever his boss's doubts.

At nine o'clock Lucy Howard walked into his office and dropped a magazine on his desk.

'I hope you got Jimmy a lot of money for this,' she said. 'Very revealing.'

The glossy weekly was aimed at unattached, liberated women with money to spend. The front cover was a picture of Jimmy Burns, bare-chested and wearing a pair of jeans. Aultman saw that the description 'stripped to the waist' was inadequate since the jeans were unzipped to give a hint of his client's pubic hair. The caption read 'Jimmy Burns, football's sex symbol, as you've never seen him before.'

To his horror Aultman saw that the logo on the jeans was clearly visible, as it was in the four pages of pictures in the centre of the magazine.

'That stupid bastard,' he said bitterly. 'Bang goes our deal with Freedom jeans.' On cue, a brief call from Freedom's Advertising Director undid months of hard negotiations. 'Shaw will go into orbit,' Aultman said, replacing the phone. 'We've been working on them for nearly a year. Christ, what a cretin Burns is!' He stood silent for a moment and then said quietly, 'Lucy, will you get me another cup of coffee, please, and then try and raise Jimmy on the phone.'

Burns's telephone was continuously engaged and Aultman finally heard his client's rough-edged Glaswegian tones about an hour later. His voice was hoarse and Aultman guessed that he'd had a long night in one of his favourite Chelsea haunts.

'No training today, Jimmy?' he asked quietly.

'Bit off colour, Deano, and why are you ringing so sodding early?'

'Because I've seen the feature in that tarts' magazine.'

'Oh yeah, good isn't it? I meant to tell you about that. They wanted a full frontal but I drew the sodding line at that. Not for ten grand I said.'

'Why the hell are you fucking about like that for a lousy

ten grand, Jimmy? The publicity for the magazine was worth ten times that, but worst of all you've promoted those bloody jeans. For nothing.'

'It was only a morning's work, Deano. And they laid on plenty of booze,' Burns said proudly. He'd enjoyed it. There were lots of pretty girls and he'd ended up screwing two of them. Now that's what he called fun; and he got paid for it, too.

'Jimmy, I talked to you about a deal with Freedom jeans. Do you remember that? We were nearly there, almost a million quid over three years. You've just blown that one right out of the window. Their Advertising Director phoned me an hour ago and she told me to stuff my proposals.'

'Win some, lose some, Deano. That's life.'

'Shaw won't see it that way, Jimmy.'

'Well, stuff him, too. I'm my own man. I do what I want.'

Steven rarely gave way to anger, whatever the provocation. When Aultman showed him the magazine he understood the implications at once and said coolly, 'That Scottish yob is on his way out, Dean. That's between you and me, not a word to him. And you're off the case. I'll deal with him now. Tell Lucy to set up a meeting with Burns's Chairman and the club Manager.'

When Steven discarded a client he planned it as carefully as when acquiring one. He had stayed close to the Chairman of Burns's club and knew that he shared the same disquiet as the Manager over their star's conduct. On several occasions during the previous year Burns had missed training and been fined; the trainer had caught him in bed with a woman in his hotel room on the morning before an important match; and Burns had made a habit of missing

the team bus to games. None of those misdemeanours
would have been regarded as desperate sins in the wider
world. But in the tiny, inward-looking society of professional football they were severe breaches of discipline which
led to large fines and suspensions.

Even worse, Burns had upset the delicate morale of the
team by boasting loudly about how much he was paid – far
more than anyone else.

The Manager, Ron Ambler, who had been a journeyman
professional footballer for twenty years before graduating to
management with a success that surprised him more than
anyone, recognised that time was running out and that a
transfer should be arranged while Burns still had maximum value in the transfer market.

His Chairman, who had made a fortune from a chain of
tyre and exhaust centres, agreed with him. Brian Hannah
knew a declining asset when he saw one.

On the way to Steven's Knightsbridge home for dinner,
Ambler said, 'Shaw probably wants to renegotiate Burns's
contract. We'll refuse and then he can go on the transfer
list. Sporting Milan are still interested. They need a top
striker very badly.'

'How much?' asked Hannah, as he puffed on a howitzer-
sized cigar, despite the no-smoking sign in the taxi.

'They offered nine million, we might get eleven or
twelve.'

'A nice profit. We need the money for new stands. Let's
do it. What about our cut?'

'Ten per cent on top. Into a bank anywhere we like.'

'Nice one, Ron.'

The two men had expected a tough bargaining session
with Shaw but, even while the first glass of champagne was
being sipped, Burns's agent came to the point.

To the surprise of his two guests, who thought that their

initial talks with the Italian club had been known only to themselves, Steven said, 'I'm in favour of doing a deal with Sporting Milan. Burns wants to move, he wants the challenge of playing in Europe.' He winked at the two men. 'And the money, of course. What do you think?'

Hannah knew that there was no point in subterfuge and the three men agreed that Burns, whatever his views, would go.

Ambler in particular felt relieved that he was not to be involved in a wrangle with Shaw. One look at his expensive clothes and his calm, good-looking features and he was immediately intimidated. Where was this smooth bastard coming from? he wondered. The other agents he'd met in football were nearly as stupid as their clients: they had seedy one-roomed offices off Shepherd Market. But not this fellow.

Shaw's surroundings were intimidating as well. Both the sitting room and the dining room were furnished with what looked, even to Ambler's untutored eyes, to be highly desirable antiques. The walls were hung with a variety of paintings and they looked even more expensive than the furniture.

The meal was served by a striking Eurasian woman and such was her grace and beauty that Ambler felt clumsy. Later, in their homeward taxi, he said crudely to Hannah, 'Do you think Shaw's shagging that dark bint?'

His Chairman laughed and said, 'Probably at it already, the lucky devil.'

Burns had not been surprised when Ron Ambler suggested a transfer. Summoned to the Manager's office after training, he had listened to Ambler's lengthy catalogue of his faults, both as a man and as a professional footballer.

'I'm still averaging a goal every one and a half games,'

Burns objected. 'Where will you find a player to do that for you?'

'The team's a bloody mess,' Ambler snapped, 'and you're mostly to blame. You're a bad influence and the Chairman agrees that we've got to bring in a couple of new players and rebuild.'

Burns knew that no British club would pay the amount of money that Hannah wanted for him and guessed what was coming.

'You've done a deal with Sporting Milan, haven't you?'

'Off the record, yes.'

'I don't want to play in Italy. I want to stay in London. I like it here.'

'Look, son,' snapped Ambler, 'It's either first team football and a lot of money in Italy or the reserves in London.'

Burns knew he was bluffing but he also knew that Ambler could make life very unpleasant for him if he refused to bend to his wishes.

Aultman reinforced Ambler's position by stressing the financial advantages to his client. 'Double your current salary, Jimmy, and three million up front to sign. It's serious money. We'll invest it for you and you'll be secure for life.'

Within a week the various contracts were signed. On the following Sunday, before a match against Lazio, Jimmy Burns was introduced to the Sporting Milan crowd as their new star forward.

As soon as Steven's Swiss bank confirmed that Burns's signing-on fee of £3 million had been deposited in one of Steven's accounts, he telephoned Burns's hotel in Italy. It was 6.30 in the morning and his client sounded drowsy. Good, he had woken him up. He didn't apologise.

'This is Steven Shaw here, Jimmy,' he started coldly. 'A letter is on its way to you by courier. It will formally terminate our representation of you. I thought it was only fair to warn you.'

Burns was jolted awake by the harshness of Steven's tone, as he gave a graphic summary of Burns's failings.

'You can stuff your contract and your fucking deals,' Burns yelled.

Steven overrode the string of obscenities. 'I could take you to court, Burns, and ask for damages. And I'd get them, believe me. But I'm glad to say that your signing-on fee, which I negotiated, is now in my bank. I'm keeping it, every penny. You can do what you like. I hope you sue me because I can then ruin you, you stupid drunken bastard.'

There was a click in Burns's ear as the line went dead. He held the receiver in his hand for several moments as he tried to come to terms with what Shaw had said. He had never felt so lonely.

Steven smiled briefly to himself; he'd taken his revenge. Later, he marked the occasion by buying himself half a dozen cases of the 1978 Chateau Latour.

# Chapter Twenty-five

When Aultman had talked of signing up British athletes as clients of Shaw Management, Steven had been more than a little sceptical. The sport had cast aside its trappings of amateurism early in the 1980s and athletes were allowed openly to receive the money that had previously been paid in secret.

'What can they endorse?' Steven asked. 'Running shoes and tracksuits? That's a limited market, I'd say.'

'Listen, Steven, athletics has a healthy image and the TV boys are promoting it like mad. And the best middle-distance runner in the world is Ben Naylor. He's British.'

'Athletics healthy? Dean, it's riddled with drugs.'

'I daresay. But the various organisations, like the Olympic Committee, will keep the lid shut tight on drug abuse. There'll be the occasional scandal despite all their efforts. They'll sacrifice someone, a minnow, a weight-lifter from Eastern Europe or a third-rate sprinter from Taiwan. Then they'll turn round and say how well they're policing the sport when everybody knows that's a pile of crap.' Aultman strained forward in his seat in his eagerness to convince his boss. 'The gravy train marked "athletics" has arrived at the platform, Steven. Huge fees for TV rights and bundles of money from the sponsors. They're not going to spoil their chances of making big bucks by exposing drug abuse in the sport.'

'OK, Dean, understood. Tell me about Naylor. All I know is that he won the Olympic eight-hundred last time out.'

'That's right and he holds the world record for the fifteen-hundred. Should win both in the World Championships next year, and they are the glamour events. The TV boys love the middle-distances because they're the right length. Two to four minutes of drama. The sprints are over in a flash and the longer distances are boring – there's no action until the last couple of laps. Now, Ben Naylor is Mister Clean, nice to everybody, talks well and he's a very stylish runner. I knew him at Oxford and he's as mean as muck: he's motivated solely by money.'

'He sounds ideal for us then,' Steven said cheerfully.

To Steven's surprise, Aultman swiftly proved his point by uncovering the substantial amounts of money to be made in athletics. Naylor's fee to race was established at around £25,000 and a long-term deal to endorse a health drink was a real coup.

Other athletes and several racing drivers were added to the London office's list of clients. Although Aultman wanted to sign up more footballers, their recent experiences with the uncontrollable Jimmy Burns had been a salutary lesson. As Steven pointed out, they'd turned the stupid bastard over comprehensively and made a lot of profit but it was a trick that couldn't necessarily be repeated. Anyway, Steven thought he saw a better entry to the fecund pastures of football: he would represent the major First Division clubs and show them how to exploit their names and capitalise on their appeal to sponsors. The BBC's Head of Sport, Paul Davis, would give him the edge he needed in that market – he'd make sure that the chosen clubs got extra exposure on the box. Davis had really come up trumps, he was the puppet who danced when Steven pulled the strings. Apart from buying hundreds of hours of sports programming, Davis's appointment of Shaw Management to sell the rights to Wimbledon tennis and the Open Golf Championship around the world had been critical. It was good business for both of them, but especially for Steven Shaw.

At six o'clock precisely, Lucy Howard tapped on Steven's door and went in. She loved her job with Shaw Management. There was so much going on, in marked contrast to her last job in a London publisher's publicity department. She had felt frustrated since the Head of her department had limited her to sending the books to a standard, and sometimes inaccurate, list of media people. When a friend had introduced her to Dean Aultman, who was looking for an energetic person to work with him and also with the agency's founder, Steven Shaw, she had accepted the job eagerly. Lucy loved sport and had been a good all-rounder at her boarding school, albeit most successful at tennis.

She liked working with Dean: he was full of ideas but needed to be organised properly and she was good at that. In contrast, Steven was organised down to the last minute and it was her job to keep him that way.

At first, Lucy had been in awe of her employer. The first time she had met him at Heathrow off his flight from New York, he stood apart from the rest of the passengers who shambled into the arrivals area. Although it was just after six o'clock in the morning, he looked spruce and rested. He was freshly shaved, and dressed in an elegant light-grey suit and a crisp blue shirt. Steven was ready for work and began dictating letters to Lucy as soon as they settled in the back of the chauffeur-driven car. She was nervous and fumbled some of the unfamiliar phrases and he repeated himself, at her request, without any impatience.

Later, when she assessed her initial feelings about Steven, she realised that he had most of the attributes she wanted in a man: not only was he good-looking, with the build of an athlete, but he had all the self-assurance that success brings. If his composure was complete enough to make him seem austere at times, his occasional smiles, which lit up his face and his wide grey eyes, showed a different aspect of his character.

She fantasised a little about his falling in love with her, but knew he had a glamorous wife and a young child. She had looked at the photographs of them in his office.

When she entered his office that evening, Steven looked up only briefly from a magazine article he was reading. Lucy knew that it was not rudeness; she was used to his preoccupied ways. He seemed able to deal with several matters simultaneously.

'How's the schedule for tomorrow, Lucy?' he asked, his eyes still on the newsprint.

'All done. You start with a breakfast meeting with Paul Davis. It's all here for you.'

'Fine. Can you be in at seven? The letters and memos have piled up.'

'Of course.' She saw the pile of correspondence he had read.

Steven looked up and smiled at her. She was a pretty girl, tall and with the soft peaches-and-cream complexion for which English women were envied. She dressed smartly and had an agreeable voice, low-pitched and devoid of any accent. Aultman had told him that she was from a solid middle-class home: her father ran a successful packaging company in Bristol and her mother did some charity work. Lucy was typical of the class which used to be called the backbone of England; such people were reliable, cheerful and hard-working and were getting rarer every day.

Steven wondered what her love life was like. Maybe Dean was slipping her one. No, he was involved with a girl from an advertising agency – Chrissy, or Lindy or Jacqui. They all had names like that. Dan Fisher's reports on Aultman hadn't mentioned any involvement with other employees.

For once, Steven had no business engagements that evening. He planned to catch up on his reading: there was a whole bundle of magazines to scan before he had an early night. He would call Suzi in New York but not his parents in Brighton. His father would be on his nightly visit to the pub and, in his absence, his mother would spend her time complaining about him. There was no one else he wanted to call; if only Charlie Tomlin were in London, he'd love to chat to him over a few drinks.

On an impulse he said, 'How about a quick drink, Lucy? I hardly know you, and yet we've spent quite a bit of time together since you joined the agency.'

Lucy smiled her agreement and Steven said he'd be in the reception area in half an hour.

Having dealt with the pile of letters and memos, Steven wanted to finish a golf magazine article by a young writer called Toby Streeter. 'Anatomy of a Golf Tournament' described how Shaw Management organised the CTC Fourball Championship which began in a few days' time.

The Editor of the magazine was happy to use the material because it helped to maintain his good relations with Shaw's agency, a powerful force in the golf business.

Streeter, with the benefit of an interview with Steven, had got most of the facts right. Eight pairs of golfers, all clients of the agency, were to do battle. The sponsor rightly boasted about the prize fund of over £600,000; the winners would share £150,000 and even the last pair would be paid thirty grand. What Streeter didn't know was the scale of the appearance money for some of the players, although he'd made some educated guesses. Sam Rhodes was getting £50,000 from the Continental Tobacco Company just to turn up, for example. As the creator and promoter of the tournament, Steven had negotiated with himself for the services of his own client. That was the sort of business he really enjoyed.

Nor did Streeter know how much money came flooding Steven's way in the wake of the tournament. The extent of the television coverage, which was the dominant factor as far as Continental Tobacco was concerned, was crucial and generated a small fortune. The BBC, AAN in the USA and stations in Australia, New Zealand, Japan and several European countries covered the event.

Shaw's agency profited in many other ways: by publishing the programme which was sold at the tournament, and above all by keeping the gate receipts. The concept had originally been sold to CTC as television coverage for one of their brands. Steven had minimised the importance of the spectators and had magnanimously agreed to handle that aspect of the event in return for the gate money. From the start, the fans loved the tournament. It was different, and the format encouraged the pros to go for their shots with panache. It was fun; it was the form of the game which club golfers most enjoyed.

Steven was expecting around 40,000 spectators over the three days of the tournament. It was big money.

Pleased with the article, well-written and reasonably accurate, he put it aside. Perhaps he could find a niche for Toby Streeter somewhere. He had been thinking of starting a sports magazine of his own but had realised that the generalised approach didn't work. Only *Sports Illustrated* had overcome that problem. In a smaller market like Britain he'd have to specialise, and golf was the obvious area. Steven reckoned that he could make money and the magazine would give the right kind of publicity to his clients; and, more important, to his agency and to himself.

He had been astute enough to turn the normal concept of a sports agency on its head. The clients thought that Shaw Management worked for them and that's how he had originally thought of his role. Now the clients worked for him and that's how it would stay.

Yes, he liked the idea of having his own magazine. Steven Shaw, publisher. It had a nice ring to it. But he would keep his usual stringers in place to plant favourable stories about him and his clients in the press. Frank Lawford, who had been the first to write about him for a British newspaper, had been invaluable in generating positive publicity for him. But Steven also had on his payroll the sports columnist of a middle-of-the-road tabloid newspaper and the golf writer on one of the posher dailies. The latter had an unfortunate gambling habit and Steven's retainers just about kept him solvent.

At the time when Steven Shaw left his office in the company of Lucy Howard, a meeting of four of the directors of the Continental Tobacco Company broke up. It had taken place in the boardroom, whose windows looked out over the Thames to St Paul's Cathedral.

As usual, Andrew McDonnell, the Chief Executive, had dominated proceedings. How John Springett, the Advertising Director, hated that harsh South African accent of his. He looked with distaste at the man's thin lips, the jutting chin and the sparse grey hair. Springett supposed he was so aggressive because he was small; everything was a battle to McDonnell, everything was reduced to a contest. 'We've got to screw the competition'; 'I did my best time over five miles this morning'. God, the man was even a fitness bore. And always banging on about the sanctity of family life. With four kids and that dreary wife, he would, wouldn't he?

'I think Shaw is taking the mickey out of us,' McDonnell said. 'He's asked us to pick up the option on the tournament for another four years on the same basic terms but with a minimum ten per cent uplift in prize-money and guarantees each year. We're already shelling out over a million quid for this event and I want something back. I'm going to call his bluff.'

'The exposure we get is colossal,' Springett said. 'The brand name's up in lights in over a dozen countries. Our analysis shows that to get that sort of brand exposure on television would cost several million quid. Even if we were allowed to advertise the product, which we're not. We should stick with it in my view.'

'Figures can be massaged to mean anything . . .' McDonnell said.

'Thanks for putting my job in perspective,' Springett interrupted sharply.

'The point is, John, that Shaw is making too much money out of us. We don't have to support his event, we can create our own or sponsor an official tournament.'

'You wouldn't get anything like the same television coverage. Shaw's a great operator in that market.'

'He's just a goddam sports agent,' McDonnell said. 'We're a multinational company with huge assets. I intend to renegotiate the deal. He can stay on as a consultant for a reasonable fee and we'll use some of his players. But we pay the money and we'll exercise the control.'

Springett shook his head resignedly. He approved of the tournament. He knew it was good for business and, an enthusiastic golfer, he enjoyed rubbing shoulders with the top players each year. He was willing to bet that Shaw would come out ahead of McDonnell in any head-to-head negotiation. The Chief Executive had an exaggerated idea of his skills in that area. Gloomily, Springett anticipated that his boss would cock up the deal very badly.

Settled in a corner of a busy wine bar near Harrods, Steven steered Lucy away from business and lured her into doing most of the talking. She did it in a lively and unaffected way: about her parents, the flat she shared with a friend, her Burmese cat, her two brothers, one of whom was at St Andrews University.

It was a pleasant interlude. He didn't have to sell himself to her or put any pressure on her or try to use her in any way. He felt relaxed, as if he'd known this pretty girl for years. Steven felt that he could tell her anything, although he had no intention of doing so. Should he take her to dinner and then persuade her into bed for an hour or two? She had the right curves in the right places; she looked comfortable, almost maternal.

No, not yet, he decided. He would wait until his appetite was a little sharper. Steven would admit only to himself that the jet-lag was beginning to take its toll.

A message on the answering machine at home asked Shaw to call Andrew McDonnell without delay on his private line. Suddenly the man was in a hurry, after being highly elusive for several days.

'So, you're still alive and well,' Steven said ironically when McDonnell picked up the telephone.

'Ah, Steven. We need to talk about next year.'

'I've been trying to find you to do that. Let's get it done at the tournament.'

'No. Too many distractions. Anyway, I can only be there for an hour on Friday. Let's make it Monday. Late afternoon.'

'Difficult. I'm booked on a plane that morning.'

'I'm sorry, Steven, but that's my only chance to see you before I go off to Australia and the Far East. I take it you want to do another deal?'

There was more than the usual challenge in McDonnell's voice and Steven smelled trouble. He agreed to postpone his return to New York and persuaded McDonnell to meet him at his house. It would be easier to deal with him there. Next Steven had to call Suzi to explain that he'd be delayed in London and would miss his son's fifth birthday.

The transatlantic line was very clear and Steven heard his wife's gasp of irritation. 'For God's sake, Steven, Adam's talked of nothing else but his party and the fact that his daddy's flying all the way from London to be with him. Do you know how much that means to a little boy of five?'

'I do. But there's no way out of this one. Darling, you can explain to him, he'll understand.'

'No, he won't, Steven, he won't. Let me ask you something. How much time have we spent together in the last year?' A few days before, Suzi had gone through her diary and checked.

'I've no idea. But about fifty-fifty, I would think.'

'Wrong, we've spent less than ninety days together. I really feel that I'm married to Shaw Management, not to you. Thank God I've got Adam and the rest of my family.'

Suzi was not soothed by her husband's remarks and soon wished him goodnight. She omitted to ask him how often they'd made love during the last year. Rarely, was the answer. She thought she'd accept that invitation to dinner on Saturday night after all. She'd always liked Greg, who'd been a contemporary of hers at Harvard. He wasn't handsome but he was witty and engaging; and if he asked her nicely to go to bed with him, well, why not?

# Chapter Twenty-six

On the following day, Steven made his scheduled telephone call to his parents. He felt guilty for not visiting them and was irritated that he couldn't shake off the feeling. Perhaps it was Suzi's fault. She demonstrated a degree of affection for them which he couldn't approach. But he'd looked after them, hadn't he? A lovely flat, and a monthly allowance. He toyed with the idea of inviting them to the tournament, which began on that day. But neither of them was interested in golf. His father might watch the highlights on television and that was it; his first love was football and he still went to watch his local team.

He decided to invite them to next year's pre-Wimbledon party at his office. His mother would like that. She'd be nervous but Suzi would look after her and she'd be able to tell her friends about it afterwards; he would keep a wary eye on his father and try to ration his intake of booze. When he put the phone down, he asked Lucy to send a Harrods' hamper to his parents.

His next call was to Sam Rhodes to wish him luck. Steven felt that he had a special relationship with his first client and this was one of the ways in which he marked it.

One of the staff in the house in which Rhodes was staying answered the call. All the players were accommodated in luxurious homes near the course; it was one of the perks on which Steven insisted. Rhodes was in a palatial mansion alongside the first fairway and it amused Steven to think of his unmarried and unattached client being watched over by a staff of four.

The two men chatted about the state of the course for a few minutes and Rhodes, who had teamed up with an Australian client of Steven's called Vince Holman, said, 'I'm going to enjoy myself, Steven. You can't imagine what a relief it is to escape the grind of a normal stroke-play event. Vince is like a machine, he's always down the middle, so I can really go for it.'

'Make sure you win, I'm paying your agent a very large appearance fee, you know,' Steven replied with a laugh.

'How about next year? Are we on again?' Rhodes took a keen and friendly interest in the agency's affairs.

'Ninety-nine per cent sure. I'm seeing McDonnell on Monday. It's a bind, I'll miss Adam's birthday party.'

'Hey, that's too bad. Anything I can do? I'll be in New York. I could take him a present from London, if that's any help.'

Steven despatched Lucy to Hamley's to buy Adam an extra present and Sam Rhodes agreed to deliver it on the Monday.

To Steven's irritation, Jack Hemmings had proved reluctant to commit his firm to sponsorship of the truck driving on ice series. Steven decided to force the pace by inviting him to London, since he guessed that some persuasion in the form of an expensive dinner and some female company might do the trick.

Girls had never been a problem for Steven. He was good-looking and confident, dressed well and assumed an easy charm which appealed to women. Many of them sensed something different about him, a concealed strength, and this made him even more attractive.

In his early days as a sports agent, Steven had occasionally

rounded off an evening with a business contact by taking
him to a bar and picking up a couple of women. He was
usually successful in those free and easy days and such a
process, especially if his companion got laid, usually
cemented his business relationship. A night on the town, all
paid for by Shaw, and some sex at the end of it: few men
were able to resist such a sales pitch.

The time arrived when Steven decided to control such
situations more closely. Why not take out the hassle while
maintaining the illusion? His solution was to place two
tarts in a bar and then go through the process of chatting
them up, safe in the knowledge that they had already been
paid to take care of his customer. It was easy enough for
one of his 'consultants' to find two professionals intelligent
enough to act out their roles as enthusiastic amateurs.
Sometimes they really were part-timers who wanted to earn
some extra money: resting actresses or poorly paid secretaries – and Steven preferred them.

He used the technique in most of the big cities including New York, Los Angeles, Sydney and London,
particularly the latter where he felt most at home.

During the latter part of a testing afternoon in his
London office, Steven again went through his sales pitch in
his efforts to persuade Jack Hemmings to sponsor his series.
Truck racing on ice had already been shown on American
television and had attracted a considerable audience. The
BBC had agreed to produce yet another Shaw Management
trash-sport series for British viewers and to run it over
Christmas. Steven had negotiated a handsome fee for the
project.

It hadn't been a difficult sale to make, since an appropriate slice of the fee had been deposited in a Swiss bank
account for the benefit of Paul Davis, the Head of Sport.

The pitch had been made several times in different

forms to Hemmings, who hailed from the Midlands and had founded his empire a dozen years before.

Steven looked with distaste at the man. His white shirt gaped where his sturdy paunch strained at the buttons and his ready-made suit was badly creased. The tie of his local rugby club sat awry on his chest.

'A quarter of a million,' Steven said with a winning smile, 'is nothing to a firm like yours. Think of the exposure you'll get. The Hemmings DIY Trophy. The punters will see it all over their screens at Christmas. Four times. I couldn't even begin to add up how much it would cost if you tried to buy that sort of publicity. The customers will be beating on your doors to be let in.'

'It's all right for you big-money boys, but a quarter of a million quid is a lot of dosh to a firm like mine. I made it the hard way and I don't give it away easy.'

The monotonous drone of Hemmings' Midlands accent grated on Steven's ears but he nodded his agreement.

'And then there's your fee on top. Fifty thou. It all adds up.'

It was a good job that Hemmings didn't know how much commission he planned to take out of the prize-money: 25 per cent off the top and then another 25 per cent from each of the drivers, who were contracted to his agency for the series.

'Could your lovely lass give me a refill, Steven?' The lovely lass was Lucy Howard, and Hemmings was drinking champagne.

The discussions ended a few minutes later without Hemmings committing himself to the deal. A chauffeur-driven car was waiting to take him to an apartment in a quiet street near Harrods. Both had been put at his disposal by Steven, who knew how much weight businessmen like Hemmings attached to such favours. He confirmed that he would pick Hemmings up at around seven o'clock for dinner.

'Think about it, Jack, it's one of the best deals you'll ever make,' were Steven's parting words.

Having steeled himself to take a proper interest in Hemmings's stories of his many brilliant business coups, Steven coasted through the meal on mental autopilot. The excellent food, at an expensive French restaurant, was wasted on his guest. Steven managed to make the appropriate admiring comments on the man's commercial acumen and he didn't even falter when Hemmings gave a long-winded account of his plans to revolutionise his local rugby club.

Over the coffee and large brandies, Steven's patience was rewarded when Hemmings agreed to put the sponsorship proposal to his board of directors. Steven calculated that the deal was almost done. A visit to a nearby wine bar would clinch it.

At just before ten o'clock the customers in the wood-panelled bar were in full swing. It was a haunt of property developers and the property market was doing famously. Champagne corks were being popped every few seconds by the frantic bar staff, and the noise generated by the drinkers was near the level of pain.

Steven had spotted the two girls as soon as he entered the bar. They were sitting at a corner table, just visible through the throng of drinkers. He was glad to see that one of them was Chrissy, a bright blonde girl who was one of his favourites. He hoped that Hemmings would go for the other one, a busty brunette whom he hadn't seen before.

'Champagne, Jack?' Steven bought a bottle of Veuve Cliquot and edged them both into a space not far from the girls' table. Chrissy gave him a barely perceptible nod.

As they clinked glasses, Shaw said, 'There're a couple of

very nice chicks over in that corner. Why don't we try and buy them a drink? You never know your luck.'

'Well, if you think so, Steven. I can't say I get on with these smart London lasses, they're a bit stuck-up aren't they?'

'They look friendly enough. Come on, we'll have a go.'

As always, Chrissy played her part well, with a nice blend of friendly reserve. She could have been an actress but Steven knew that her business was providing meals for lunchtime gatherings in City boardrooms. He was not so sure about her companion, an Australian girl called Pat, who said she was a receptionist in an advertising agency. She looked as though she'd had plenty to drink already. But he was glad to see that Hemmings was ogling her prominent breasts with evident enthusiasm; he would be able to have Chrissy after all.

After a further bottle of champagne, Steven 'persuaded' the women to join them for a nightcap at the flat. Hemmings needed no encouragement to go into the main bedroom with Pat, and Steven went into the bathroom, slid a panel aside and switched on the video camera which was trained on Hemmings' bed. It was nice to have some insurance in case the man had second thoughts about the deal.

It had been a long day, made longer by the ennui induced by Hemmings's company, and Steven wondered whether he wanted Chrissy after all. He needed some rest, but she coaxed him into a little gentle love-making. What a sweet girl, he thought, as they lay back and chatted drowsily. But they both sat up when they heard Pat's unmistakable Aussie voice at the door.

'Steve, Steve,' she shouted. 'Is up the arse in the contract?'

While Steven fell back on the bed with helpless laughter, Chrissy threw open the bedroom door and took charge.

Steven had a full view of Pat's breasts and they were magnificent. Hemmings, clad only in a sleeveless vest, was standing in the middle of the lounge. As the two lovers were ushered by Chrissy back into their bedroom, Steven, with a resigned shake of the head, began to dress. He hoped Pat hadn't undone the work he had put in on the man . . .

Determined to repair the damage caused by too much food and drink on the previous evening, Steven was in the gymnasium at seven o'clock the next morning. He worked hard for nearly an hour and entered his office at around 8.30. He wondered when Hemmings would call him and what his attitude would be. Steven didn't have long to wait. Hemmings telephoned from the railway station.

'We're in business,' he said. 'I like your style, Steven. A great night out, thanks for the loan of the flat and, er, everything. Send me the contract, the board will approve it.'

The Rhodes/Holman partnership duly won the CTC Fourball Championship with a blaze of eagles and birdies and the provisional gate receipts showed, to Steven's delight, a 10 per cent increase on the previous year.

Despite the undoubted success of the event and its growing importance in his business portfolio, Steven was irritated that, despite all his efforts, the final gloss was lacking. Patrice Barbier, who had already won the British Open twice, plus a string of tournaments around the world, had turned down his invitation. To secure the most dynamic European golfer, Steven had offered an appearance fee beyond that received by Sam Rhodes. It had been a verbal offer only and he could always deny it, but he prayed that his foremost client would never find out. Barbier had sent him a note to say that he had elected to play in an event in New Orleans because he 'rather enjoyed the city'. It was charmingly phrased but was, nevertheless, one of a long succession of snubs. Steven was as far from securing the Frenchman as a client as he had always been.

An extra and unscheduled day in London gave him the opportunity to review the full scope of the agency's activities with Dean Aultman. At the top of the agenda was Patrice Barbier.

'I don't understand it,' Steven began. 'I've shown him what we can do on the contractual side and I've offered him stacks of appearance money. And I'm getting nowhere. Where's he coming from, Dean?'

Aultman drained his cup of coffee and stared past his boss through the window. 'I don't get it, either. We've made all the right moves but he just goes his own way, that's all there is to it.'

'There must be something he wants. How the hell do we buy the bastard?'

'It's not money.'

'I didn't mean that literally, Dean. He's human, like the rest of us, so what does he want? Drugs, women, small boys, power? What is it?'

'Whatever it is, we don't have it,' Aultman said slowly. 'His family is rich anyway and so is he. He's young and I've seen him with some devastating women, so there're no hang-ups there. Maybe it's very simple. He's happy and he doesn't want to be hassled by anyone, much less by a bunch of business managers like us.'

'You sound as if you're on his side, Dean.'

'I admire his independence. He's certainly his own man.'

'Maybe, but I need him, he's the only missing link in the golfing chain. Look at the field last week, we had sixteen of the world's best golfers, all clients of Shaw Management. We've got another thirty or forty clients in golf and a bunch of sponsors begging to give us money. Dean, we're in a position to call the shots, to set up the beginnings of a world circuit.'

Now pacing up and down his office, Steven continued. 'Within a few years we can have a network of events around the world, all controlled by us. We've got the sponsors, the players and the ability to sell the television rights. But we need Barbier, otherwise the European events will lack credibility.'

'There isn't enough space in the official schedule to add many more events,' Aultman protested.

'Sod the official schedule. We'll be putting up so much money that the players will ignore the Madrid Open or the Greater Milwaukee Classic or the Tokyo Challenge. They'll be Mickey Mouse events compared to ours.'

'But the players are committed to their home Tours. They have to play so many events or lose their exemptions. You can't fight the American Tour and the European Tour – they control the game.'

'Why should they? Professional golfers should have the right to play whenever they want. Anybody who wants to prevent that ought to be bounced for restraint of trade.'

'Try telling that to Carl Lansky.'

'Oh, he'll come to heel one day,' said Steven confidently, although he knew that the Commissioner of the United States Professional Golfers' Association was one of his most formidable opponents.

'I think we've got to try and work with these people,' Aultman said. 'You can't take them on and win.' More conservative by nature, he was worried by Steven's eagerness to confront the might of the golfing establishments. Aultman thought that the game was well run, in marked contrast to all the other sports, which were in the hands of incompetent fools and charlatans. Steven's attitude was uncharacteristic since he usually relied on persuasion and subterfuge.

'Christ, Dean, I've tried to work with them. Lansky shat on my idea for an official world championship.'

Steven recited again Lansky's behaviour eighteen months earlier when Steven had sent his proposals for such a championship to both Lansky and the Chief Executive of the European Tour. Closely reasoned and detailed, the proposal had run to thirty pages and the Chief Executive had sent a detailed and polite rejection but had left the door open for further negotiations. Lansky, though, had totally ignored Steven's approach and his several subsequent telephone calls and when cornered by Steven at an American tournament had called him a privateer with no place in golf. 'And the arrogant prick hadn't even read my proposals.'

'Yes, I know all that, Steven,' Aultman persisted, 'but—'

'But nothing. I'll run my world championship, whether it's sanctioned by the PGA or not. And I'll schedule it where it'll really fuck Lansky.'

'Be careful. Lansky might hurt you more than you can hurt him.'

'No, Dean, the Commissioner has begun to believe his own publicity. He's done great things for pro golf in America, but he's an arrogant shit and the sponsors don't like him. He's tough on the players, too, and treats them like schoolboys. They have to jump when he says so.'

'He's got to keep control, hasn't he, or he'll lose his sponsors and his television ratings.'

'Fine, but he's overreaching himself, trespassing on those areas where the pros make their endorsement money. The PGA is putting its logo and its seal of approval on clubs, clothing, balls, shoes, golf trolleys and there's now an official PGA car and an airline. It's quite an operation and it's taking money from the pros' pockets. So, as I said, he's vulnerable. The pros don't like it.'

'But they can't stop him.'

'Maybe not,' Steven admitted, 'but Lansky is heavily into golf resort development. It's done with PGA money and it's very high risk. You wait till some of those projects go belly-up and the PGA pension fund takes a hit. Then you'll hear the pros squeal.'

'I've heard some are already up in arms about Lansky's life-style.'

'That's right. The new offices in Florida cost a fortune and already they're too small. He has a rented apartment there and another on the west coast and a private jet. His salary's not far short of a million dollars plus a generous bonus. So, what do the players do? They say "Hey, this guy's doing better than us and we employ the bastard."'

'If he's a smart operator, he deserves everything he gets, doesn't he? He's the Chief Exec of a big operation. What's the turnover? A hundred and fifty million dollars?'

Steven nodded and Aultman continued, 'You and Lansky shouldn't be in opposition. You should have him as a client.'

'Some chance. Things have gone too far for that, Dean. Lansky will get his, I promise you. But first of all I've got to sort out Andrew McDonnell.'

At five minutes past six a large Mercedes stopped outside Steven Shaw's house. As he got out, McDonnell told the chauffeur to be back in one hour. This won't take long, he thought. I've got the money and I'll call the tune.

Neither man was in the mood for any gentle verbal sparring: Steven because he'd scented trouble and McDonnell because of his self-confidence.

After refusing a drink, the Chief Executive of Continental Tobacco said, 'If we're to continue our fourball event, changes have to be made. Fundamental changes. We must redefine our objectives and our business relationship.'

'Redefine what? It's all been clear enough in the past,' Steven protested. 'What's the problem?'

'Money. It costs too much to put on and I personally think that the benefits to our brand are marginal.'

'Springett wouldn't agree and nor would I,' interrupted Steven. 'You couldn't buy the television exposure I provide and that is a literal statement, as you well know.'

'There are many ways of promoting fags, Steven. Television is just one part of the promotional mix and we have an on-going assessment procedure. By the way, and between you and me, Springett's opinion doesn't matter to me one way or the other.'

Steven shrugged. He guessed what was coming but asked the question anyway. 'So what do you have in mind?'

'More control, Steven. We wish to organise the event and decide which players take part. We would retain you as consultant, of course—'

'Thanks a million,' Steven said drily.

'But we would want the lion's share of the television revenue and the gate money to amortise some of our considerable investment.'

'It's not your tournament, Andrew. I created it, put it all together and sold it to the networks and then to you. There isn't much that's negotiable there as far as I'm concerned.'

'We're putting up the money, and without us you don't have a tournament.'

'There're plenty of other sponsors around, Andrew.'

'Not who'd put up our kind of money.'

'What do you mean by the lion's share of television and gate money?'

'We would pay you the agent's normal commission of ten per cent. And a retainer as consultant. I had a sum of thirty thousand pounds in mind.'

Steven leaned across the table and poured himself another cup of tea. McDonnell sat back comfortably; he knew that Shaw had to accept the terms. After all he pocketed all that commission on his clients' guarantees and on their prize-money, too. It was still very good money for any agent and Shaw wouldn't have time to find another heavyweight sponsor in time for next year's tournament. McDonnell was looking forward to the meeting he had called for tomorrow when he would tell his directors about the new terms. He would wipe the superior smile off Springett's face.

Expecting some protests from his adversary, McDonnell enjoyed the pause as Steven settled himself in his seat again and sipped his tea. No doubt he was trying to think of a way of accepting the proposal without losing face.

'I want to settle all this, Steven, before I leave for my trip tomorrow,' McDonnell said, savouring the moment.

Steven nodded. This Formosa Oolong tea wasn't half bad. It was McDonnell's favourite brew, apparently. The data in his file covered his other likes and dislikes: he didn't eat red meat but was keen on shellfish and he drank little, just an occasional glass of white wine. His hobbies were jogging, squash and sailing. But Steven remembered well that McDonnell had shown a reasonable capacity for vintage champagne on an occasion a few months before.

'Do you remember our little party?' Steven asked with a smile. 'Just before Christmas last year?'

'Let's think,' McDonnell said warily. 'I go to so many.'

'Oh, let me remind you. We had drinks at the office and then just a few of us went back to a flat I use occasionally not far from here. There was Nigel from your advertising agency and that TV presenter and a few girls. It was a rather jolly affair, I thought. You took quite a shine to that dark-haired girl: slim waist, big hips and splendid breasts? You remember, Andrew?'

With a clinical interest, Steven saw McDonnell's eyes swivel past his shoulder; a slight tinge of pink had appeared on his cheeks.

'I'm a sociable person, Steven. I try to take an interest in people; I try to join in.'

'You certainly did on that night.'

'What's that supposed to mean and what is its relevance to the business under discussion?' McDonnell looked pointedly at his watch.

'I seem to remember that you went home with the lovely Anthea and I don't think it was to discuss the future of the tobacco industry.'

'We left together and I gave her a lift because her flat was on my route home, that's all there was to it. Now, let's get back to this contract we're discussing.'

A raised forefinger silenced McDonnell and then Steven flicked a switch which lit up a large-screen television in a corner of the room. There was a hiss as a videotape began to run. The first scenes were innocuous enough: about a dozen people were seen drinking champagne in an elegant, high-ceilinged room. McDonnell saw himself chatting to a tall woman with dark and flowing hair.

'That's Anthea,' Steven said enthusiastically, 'what a pair of knockers she's got.'

The scene then switched to a room which was extravagantly decorated in scarlet. The centrepiece was a king-size bed, with a huge heart-shaped headboard.

McDonnell's face went pale and he felt on the verge of vomiting as he watched himself being led to the bed, stripped of his clothes and handcuffed to the headboard.

Anthea, already down to her scarlet knickers and black suspender belt but with her pendulous breasts revealed, donned what looked like a PVC mask, climbed on the bed and went to work on McDonnell's penis.

'She's a real trouper, isn't she?' Steven said admiringly. 'I can turn the sound up if you like.'

'That's enough,' McDonnell croaked.

Steven continued to smile at the screen, 'I can give you some stills, too, if you wish.'

'That's enough, enough,' McDonnell whispered, beseechingly.

Briskly, Steven opened a file which lay on the table and produced a single sheet of paper from it. 'Here's the memorandum of agreement for you to sponsor my tournament for a further four years. The terms are the same as in my original proposal. Sign it. I'll have Dean Aultman send the formal contract to your deputy within a few days. Make sure he has the authority to sign on your behalf.'

With a nod, McDonnell acknowledged his agreement. 'Steven, can you just give me one or two minor concessions,' he said hesitantly, 'so that I can show the directors something in my favour.'

Shaw stood up to signal the end of the meeting. 'Fuck you,' he said in a level voice. 'Just do it.'

'You bastard, Shaw.'

'That's right and don't you forget it. Did you think you could come swanning in here and take my tournament away from me? How the fuck you ever got to be chief executive of anything, I don't know.'

Adam's birthday party had gone as well as any such gathering of five-year-olds could. There was a great deal of noise and fun, occasional tantrums and some tears caused by over-excitement. Suzi had been surprised when Sam

Rhodes turned up at her front door with an extra gift for Adam from his absent father.

Invited to join in the fun, Rhodes had done so with enthusiasm. He had acted as a willing stooge for the entertainer who did a series of conjuring tricks, juggled and sang, and asked for his autograph when he had finished his act. Some of the mothers and nannies who arrived to collect their children also requested his autograph and hung eagerly on his every word.

When the last guest had left, Betty Lynagh took charge of the clearing-up operation and insisted that Suzi sat down and had a quiet drink with Sam.

They sat in Steven's study and sipped at their glasses of wine. They had met on many occasions during the past few years but had done little more than exchange social pleasantries. This time, exhausted by the demands of overseeing a boisterous children's party and not constrained by Steven's presence, they relaxed and gabbled away like close friends. They finished the bottle of wine and Betty Lynagh put her head around the door to remind Suzi that they were both due at the Lynaghs' home for drinks followed by dinner. On his way to the door, Rhodes said how much he'd like to take her and Adam out for the day, maybe in Florida, since their homes were so close. Suzi said she'd like that.

In London, Steven Shaw, exhilarated by the manner of his victory over Andrew McDonnell, could not settle down. However, he decided that he would definitely buy a seventeenth-century oil painting which a dealer had offered to him. It was by a Dutch master and showed a primitive form of golf. It was good and would no doubt appreciate in value.

For the second time he watched the video which

featured McDonnell; the real star was the girl. Excited by her, he thought of ringing a discreet agency whose business was supplying high-class tarts to businessmen. But he wasn't quite in the mood for that kind of evening, the stilted conversation over an expensive dinner and the joyless and mechanical sexual act.

No, he needed a chat with a friend, someone to whom he needn't pretend. He dialled Charlie Tomlin's business number in Houston. His secretary told Steven that Mr Tomlin was out of town on business for several days, but could she have him call Mr Shaw?

Steven declined the offer and, after several minutes' thought, dialled another number.

With a contented sigh, Lucy Howard sank back into an armchair and watched the titles of the situation-comedy programme fill the television screen. It was one of her favourite evenings of the week. Her flatmate had gone to do her Highland dancing and she could watch some undemanding television and then go to bed. She lifted her tray on to her lap, careful not to dislodge her Burmese cat, Juniper, from the arm of the chair, and took her first forkful of salad. Lucy was slightly worried about her weight; she didn't want to get pear-shaped before her time.

Bugger, she muttered, as the phone rang. It was probably someone for Sally. She hoped it wasn't that young stockbroker who thought he was God's gift.

Lucy recognised Steven's voice as soon as he spoke.

'I'm sorry to ring you at home,' he said, 'but I wonder if you can help me out, Lucy? I'm tied up in the morning and then I've got to catch my flight home and there are a few things that I want to pass on to Dean. Do you think I could tell you? This evening? It's important.'

For a moment Lucy wondered why Steven didn't call

Dean; he was flying to Glasgow tomorrow but could be reached by telephone easily.

'Will you have dinner with me?' she heard him ask. 'There's a little bistro around the corner. Ma Maison, I expect you know it. Meet you there in half an hour. Come as you are.'

Thoughtfully, Lucy covered her salad with foil and put it in the refrigerator. She had a shower, put on clean clothes and headed towards Knightsbridge.

Later, Lucy realised that her intuition had been correct. Steven, dressed informally in a pale green cashmere sweater and casual trousers, had told her that, as a result of his meeting with Andrew McDonnell, Dean should send out a new four-year contract for his signature. The deal was of great importance to the agency but nothing could be gained by briefing her about it that evening. It occurred to Lucy that her boss, despite his aura of steely composure, was lonely, and she warmed to him.

She was flattered that he'd picked her when he must know dozens of beautiful women, and he was so entertaining, too, without any trace of the brisk and hardened businessman that she knew during the day.

'Shall we have coffee at the house?' Steven said, as they finished their second course. 'You've never been there, have you? It's just a stroll away.'

# Chapter Twenty-seven

A visit to London in January would not usually have been Steven's choice. It was better than New York but he tried to be in California or Australia for much of it. But London in January it had to be because he had a lot of business to conclude with Paul Davis. It was the Head of Sport's suggestion that they combine the negotiations with a visit to his villa at Cap Ferrat. It was owned by a company registered in Liechtenstein, so that nobody would be able to establish that it was a gift from Steven Shaw.

However, Steven could not waste time on a trip to the south of France. Apart from all the deals he had to oversee, he wanted to spend some time with Lucy. Friendly, sympathetic Lucy, undemanding fun both in and out of bed.

Against his instincts, Steven had agreed to meet an independent television producer for lunch. Paul Davis had recommended John Winter, and Steven knew that Winter had built a reputation for integrity; all those harrowing features about the disasters in Africa, which Steven avoided watching. But he had seen one or two of Winter's subsequent programmes. Commissioned by Davis, they took quirky looks at some of Britain's pastimes: women's cricket, polo, bowls, fencing and squash. Now he was putting together a film about women's tennis.

Seated in the grill room of the Parkside Tower Hotel at his favourite table, Shaw looked out to the trees and the manicured lawns of the square alongside. An occasional figure, muffled and bulky against the depths-of-winter bleakness, hurried down the pathways.

He saw the *maître d'hôtel* intercept a tall man and lead him towards his table. Winter's height made him stoop a little, as if he were used to craning to hear other people's words; dressed in corduroy trousers, a woolly-looking shirt and a tweed jacket, he looked like a caricature of a vague academic. As Steven rose to shake his hand, he noticed a pair of very bright blue eyes in the man's craggy face and a topping of unruly mouse-brown hair.

When the business of ordering food was finished, Steven asked Winter how he could help him with his latest project.

'Fran Zanini,' Winter replied. 'She seems to be the archetypal teenage tennis player. Favourite to win Wimbledon in a few months' time. Trained by her father for tennis glory since her cradle. Straight on to the tournament treadmill on her fourteenth birthday, poor soul.'

'It's not against the rules,' Steven said. 'Anyway, girls are well-developed physically at that age.'

'But what happened to her childhood? What will happen to her when she starts asking herself questions about her life?'

Steven laughed. 'She'll count her money and say to herself that she's a multi-millionaire and bloody lucky. I must try and be there, John, when you lead Fran into these deep philosophical waters. If I were you I'd stick to her cosmetics and clothing contracts and her favourite pop stars.'

'Well, OK, but it seems to me that tennis, especially women's tennis, embodies many of the evils of westernised society. It's capitalism grown ugly and deformed, isn't it? These ridiculously inflated rewards for a talent that doesn't have a lot of social merit. Rather like the currency dealers in the City, they've got a knack and they get their ludicrously high bonuses and they're burned out at the age of thirty.'

'A good parallel, John, but we live, thank God, in what's called a free society. Fran and others like her have the right to exploit their talents in any way they can. What's her alternative? A dead-end job behind a supermarket check-out? Married at eighteen and twelve kids to bring up in the backstreets of Milan by the age of thirty? At least she's rich, I've made sure she's capitalised on her ability and I'll make sure she keeps her money.'

'Shouldn't she give some of it away?'

'That's a personal decision. As a matter of fact I encourage all my clients to participate, if their schedules allow it, in charity events. As you know, sport raises a lot of money for the disadvantaged. And some of my clients invest in ethical funds.'

'Can girls of fourteen cope with the tennis environment? The drugs, the lesbians?'

'She has her father to watch over her.'

'OK, but what about drugs? Steroids for strength, amphetamines to boost performance levels – would you turn a blind eye?'

'No chance,' Steven answered emphatically. 'I want my clients to have long careers.'

'I notice you don't comment on the moral aspects of these problems.'

'They interest me,' Steven said carefully. 'But my job as a business manager is to maximise the clients' income. I also encourage each of them to make their own decisions. I only guide them: they must take the ultimate responsibility.'

'OK,' said Winter, 'let me get to the nub of things. Can you give me some access to Zanini? I'd like to talk to her initially and then, a few days later, film an interview for the programme.'

'Two things, John. First, you'll have to pay a fee.'

'As long as it's reasonable. You know how tight documentary budgets are, I'm sure. It'll be good publicity for her.'

'Come off it, the only publicity she needs is winning titles. But, secondly, have you any idea what Fran Zanini's schedule is like?' Steven held out his left hand, the fingers spread and ticked off his client's commitments.

'The final stages of the Australian Open are on now, then she's got an exhibition match in Perth, on to Tokyo for a corporate date for her clothing company. Hong Kong for another exhibition match, then there's an event in Oklahoma, back to the West Coast to do a breakfast cereal commercial, then Chicago for a magazine feature, then Florida for another tournament. Shall I go on?'

'I'm impressed by your instant recall of your client's schedule. Can you do it for all of them?'

'We have well over a hundred clients but I can do it for the major ones and also for myself.'

'OK, what are you doing a week tomorrow and a month tomorrow?'

'A week tomorrow I'll be in Hardelot to have lunch with Patrice Barbier and maybe play a few holes of golf with him. A month tomorrow?' Steven laughed. 'Lunar month or calendar month? Today's the fourth and on the fourth next month my main meeting is with the Head of Sports Programming at the Australian Broadcasting Corporation in Sydney. How's that?'

'I'm even more impressed.'

'Good. So let's say I can give you some access to Fran, what other programmes are you planning?'

'I'd like to do the women's golf tour, when I've finished with the tennis.'

'From lesbos in leggings to dykes in spikes, eh?' Steven said.

'Ah, you obviously don't have many lady golfers on your books.'

'None, they're not great earners. Whereas the tennis players are, as you've discovered. In fact they're the highest paid sportswomen by a street. I can get a hundred thousand dollars for a logo on Zanini's right sleeve.'

Winter took a long drink of wine. 'There's another tennis project that interests me. You remember Nils Ryberg?'

Steven looked up slowly from his fillet of sole, trying not to betray any interest in the subject. Nevertheless, Winter wondered if he saw a warning flicker in his host's eyes.

'I remember Nils very well, of course. What a tragedy! He was obviously a good man, a committed Christian, I believe.'

'Yes. I got to know him very well. He became a good friend of mine and so did his wife, Jenny. He was no more a homosexual than you or me. I can't understand where those stories started. Anyway, I want to interview Ray Gerrard.'

'Why Ray Gerrard?'

'Because I believe he had most to gain from the hatchet-job done on Ryberg. He got the racket deal that was going to Nils. Isn't that so?'

'I know some of the details, John, because I represent Gerrard. That deal fell into my lap. I didn't even know about the Larssen rackets until one of the brothers who owns the company called me. Naturally, I grabbed the chance with both hands. It was manna from heaven. I was actually weighing up the racket endorsements available to Ray and, wham, here was a revolutionary product. I couldn't believe my luck, it was every agent's dream situation.'

'And Gerrard's made millions and Ryberg is dead.'

'That's hardly Ray's fault. He was a good friend of Nils's. He was terribly upset.'

Steven poured the last of the wine into their glasses, paused while a waiter cleared away their plates and said, 'Look, I'm not keen that Ray should be involved in a programme raking up the past. Ryberg's death was regrettable, but these things happen. Better not to rekindle his family's anguish. I've got a suggestion for you. The history of golf. It's a lovely project, six hours of it and I've already got a provisional approval in the States and over here. Let me send you the outline and we'll talk it through.'

Because of the time change, Steven had to wait until late that evening to call Ray Gerrard in Australia. The tennis superstar had just got back to his room after spending the night with the star of one of the country's best-loved television soap operas. The fact that she would never see fifty again hadn't worried Gerrard. Her daughter was next on his list.

His client's voice sounded hoarse to Steven, who said, 'Ray, are you OK? You sound a bit croaky. Not flu or anything?' Gerrard's schedule over the next four weeks included three exhibition matches and a two-day shoot for a car commercial. There were nearly a million dollars to be earned.

'No, no, I'm fine. Just got in from my morning run, that's all.'

'Look, Ray, there's an English guy who's poking around the Ryberg story. John Winter, he was a friend of Nils. Says he wants to interview you. I want to counsel you to steer well clear. The story can't go anywhere and I'd rather you didn't get involved, OK?'

'Yeah, that's fine.'

'And, Ray, what about our contract? You've been sitting on the renewal for over four months. It's a formality, isn't it? So just sign it, fella, and send it to me.'

'Yeah, yeah, Steven, but I want to discuss one or two points with you.'

Some warning sounds clanged in Steven's head. Gerrard would normally do anything rather than discuss a contract – he left everything to his agent.

'Ray, you're the richest tennis player the world's ever seen and the main reason for that, apart from your natural talent, is talking to you now. But if you want to discuss things, that's fine. I'll catch you in Monterey in a couple of weeks, OK?'

It was a mystery to Patrice Barbier why Shaw was still deluding himself that he would become a client of his agency. Certainly, the man had put some business his way, some exhibition matches and a promotion for French wines in Britain. It was good money and not too time-consuming, but he had turned down enough of the other deals which Shaw had offered him to make it plain, surely, that he wanted to remain a free spirit. Barbier knew how good an operator Shaw was, and he had offices in all the strategic places, but he wanted to control his own life. Not for him the rigid schedule of appearances and the hellish regime of air travel which Shaw Management imposed on its clients. If he wanted to take a girl to Rome or Rio for a few days, so be it, and a modification to his diary would be made. *C'est la vie, c'est l'amour.*

With a shrug, Barbier concentrated on the outline plans for a second course which he had been commissioned to design for the Hardelot club. He loved the existing one, a challenging lay-out which threaded its way through avenues of stately trees; he'd won his first amateur tournament of any note there when he was thirteen years old.

Shaw was arriving by private plane at Le Touquet and then making the short drive to Hardelot. Barbier would play a few holes with the man, give him a good lunch and explain, for the final time, why he had no wish to be his client.

Although it was January, the two men were lucky with the weather; a watery sun welcomed them and printed the patterns of the trees palely on the rich green turf. With no other golfers in sight, Barbier and Steven played their nine holes in just over an hour, and the Frenchman was impressed by his guest's golfing skills. Although he was using borrowed clubs and was clearly rusty, he dropped only a couple of shots and birdied the demanding ninth hole.

'I think you missed your vocation,' Barbier said, as they strolled towards the clubhouse. 'You should have taken the game seriously and become a pro.'

'That's very kind, Patrice, but I never had the dedication. The Harvard Business School sent me in a different direction.'

'Nevertheless, I say you should play more, have some fun with the game.'

'Like you?'

'Like me, even though I'm a pro.'

From their table in the restaurant, they looked straight down the eighteenth hole to the tunnel of trees which hemmed in the tee 500 yards away.

'It's beautiful, isn't it?' Barbier commented. 'And my new course will be just as pretty.'

'You should do more design,' Steven replied. 'You've won four major championships, you're as well known as Sam Rhodes. There's a huge world market for you as a course designer. We could franchise your name in the States and Japan and Australia.'

'But how would I cope with all the work?'

'It's your name we'd be selling, not your time.'

'Ah, I do not want that, Steven. I want to build my

courses, one by one if necessary. That's what interests me.'

'You'd oversee everything that we did on your behalf, I promise you.'

'No, it's not the same. It's a matter of my integrity, and I would not compromise that, you understand?'

'I do,' Steven said warmly, though inwardly his teeth were grinding in irritation. To compose himself, he looked through the windows and saw an elderly golfer lurch nervously at the ball and thin it through the green.

'Patrice,' he continued. 'I've made no secret over the years of my wish to represent you. We have everything you need, all the contacts, all the expertise, all the energy. You've done a few deals with us and you must know how efficient we are and how we always get top dollar.'

From the clients, too, Barbier thought.

'We will be doing things in golf over the next few years which you should be part of,' Steven said earnestly. 'As you know, we already run several tournaments. We'll increase our commitment in that area so that we'll control maybe eight or a dozen events each year. We want the top players and we're prepared to pay handsomely for the privilege.'

'I've heard about your plans but I've got enough on my schedule. There are the four majors and the French Open and the Spanish Open, five or six events in America, a few in Japan, and I like to play in Britain in September. I like that event at Sunningdale.'

'Our schedule would lead into a world championship in December with all the leading players. At least half a million for the winner and a huge bonus fund if you play in all the other tournaments.'

Barbier twirled the wine in his glass, drank and then speared a piece of cheese from the assortment before him. 'Difficult. I take a break over the winter, go skiing, do some travelling, you know how it is.'

Steven smiled, convinced that Barbier was merely adopting a tough negotiating position. His integrity would disappear like a puff of Gauloise in a high wind when the Frenchman was told just how much money was on offer. In francs, it sounded even better. He decided to press ahead with his sales pitch.

'I can promise you a really formidable guarantee for your services over, say, a three-year period. How does ten million francs sound? There is, of course, a condition that we get to handle your endorsements. Since it's you, we'd take a lower commission, only fifteen per cent.'

The Frenchman lifted his cup of black coffee to his lips and gazed thoughtfully out of the window. Got him, thought Steven.

'I'm very happy with the endorsements I already have. My clubs and balls, OK, they're not made in France but in Japan. Nevertheless, I've signed a contract for seven years and the products will carry my name. Clothing – that's French and has a good design – classy and doing well in America and Japan. I have a deal with Citroën and, Steven, I actually like their cars, and I promote Air France. I have the deal with the French wine people through you, but I also give a little push to French cheese.'

Barbier spread his palms before him. 'What more do I want? It's all under control. I don't want flashes on my beautiful golf clothing promoting some disgusting fast food company or a visor with Kooler Cola all over it. Anyway, I don't wear the bloody things. If it's wet or cold I wear my nice cap from Lock's of St James. Very chic, very practical. And you know, Steven, I don't want to go dashing around the place to do this appearance or that appearance just to earn more money. I've got enough, I'll never spend it, I'll have to give a lot of it away.'

The Frenchman, however, omitted to tell his visitor that

he was setting up his own golf company to initiate and promote tournaments in Europe.

'But, Patrice, I would like you to play in my tournaments. I want the best players, you must realise that.'

'Sure and I'll look at the dates on an individual basis. If I can fit them in, I'll play, you understand?'

As they walked to Steven's hired car Barbier told him how much he admired him as a businessman and how much he appreciated his interest and his frankness. As Steven opened the car door, Barbier said, 'And I'd play golf with you anytime, especially in pro–ams. You and I'd clean up.'

'Thanks, Patrice, that's a great compliment and one which I'll treasure,' Steven replied.

As Steven drove across the car park he heard Barbier shout 'Au revoir', his handsome face alight with a dazzling smile. Steven rolled his window down, and waved his farewell, as he turned on to the road. He thought grimly to himself: I'll screw that supercilious French bastard somehow, somewhere, and the sooner the better.

At Hardelot, Steven had made a note of Patrice Barbier's hat size and, on the following day, he sent Lucy along to Lock's. When she returned, he composed a letter of thanks for the Frenchman's hospitality and sent it, together with the new cap, to his home in Paris.

# Chapter Twenty-eight

The comparative warmth of Monterey was a relief to Steven after London's bleak weather. Ray Gerrard had been booked for a tennis exhibition match in an area of California that was more familiar to Steven as the home of several illustrious golf courses, including Pebble Beach, Cypress Point and Spyglass Hill.

Gerrard had suggested a game at one of those courses but Steven wanted to get the business done without distractions. He suspected that his client was planning to put pressure on him for more lenient contractual terms or even to leave the agency altogether. Therefore, he arranged the meeting in Gerrard's hotel, a luxurious colonial-style building in the centre of the city.

At least Gerrard was waiting for him, sprawled on a white leather sofa and watching a re-run, on video, of one of his recent matches.

'Look at that backhand again, Ray, in slo-mo,' his coach, Al Strawn, was saying when Steven entered the room. 'Look at the balance, look at the weight-shift. You're just a bit off in that area at the moment. Hey, Steven, how ya doin'? I'll leave you boys to it. I'll catch you later, Ray.'

Gerrard felt ill at ease as he led his business manager to the balcony and poured the coffee from the vacuum flask. He knew that he was about to be embroiled in an unpleasant discussion. He wanted to cut his ties to Shaw Management. Gerrard was grateful for the contracts that had come his way: Shaw was a brilliant negotiator and the whole agency ran like clockwork. The trouble was that he was expected to perform in the same way: go here, fly there, be nice to him, be extra-nice to her. He wanted some control over his life and, hell, he'd more or less promised to sign up with that agency in Hollywood. It was an actor's agency, and big-time, and he really liked the girl who was setting up their new sports division. Luisa. She was a hell of a good fuck, too.

'Right,' Steven said, having laid a copy of Gerrard's new contract on the table, 'let's go through this, Ray. I'm sure we can iron out any problems.'

His eyes half-hidden behind his sunglasses, Steven watched his client closely and saw him swallow hard. Here it comes, he thought.

'Look, Steven, we've had a great business relationship. I've got no complaints about the contracts; I'm richer than I ever believed possible but, you know, I want to slow down a bit.'

'Thanks for your vote of confidence,' Steven said sarcastically. 'So, you want to play fewer tournaments? Not so many appearances? Come on, Ray, you're still in your twenties. You're at your peak. We can slow things down a bit, but this should be the time when you really capitalise on your success.'

Leaning back in his chair and running his hands through his glossy black hair, Gerrard grimaced. 'Steven, it's more that I'd like to run things a bit more myself, you know how it is.'

'You mean, more consultation?'

'Not exactly, I mean I'd really like to run the show myself.'

'You're going into the agency business, Ray? Come off it, you stick to what you know. Tennis.'

Stung by Steven's dismissive comment, Gerrard looked straight at him and said, 'I want a change, I don't want to dance to your tune for the rest of my career. So I won't be signing a new contract with you.'

Removing his sunglasses, Steven looked steadily at his client. 'Why didn't you say so? I suppose you've had an offer from another agency?'

'Over in Hollywood, yeah.'

'That must be Luisa Ebbers. I've seen her at Flushing Meadows. She's very pretty, isn't she? She's starting up a sports side for one of the talent agencies. I saw something about it in *Sports Illustrated*.' Steven was playing down his knowledge; he was aware that Ebbers had already signed up several footballers, basketball players and tennis stars.

Gerrard nodded and Steven continued. 'There's a bit of a problem, Ray, if you want to switch agents. Some of your major contracts have to be renegotiated during the next few months. Number one is the Larssen racket deal and we've already talked numbers to them. They're very big numbers – the biggest endorsement deal I've ever done. Now, I'm betting that Ms Ebbers has her eyes on a slice of that. Am I right?'

'She says that, in those circumstances, you should share the commission.'

'Really. Well, if I were you, I'd show her a copy of your representation agreement with us and direct her pretty little eyes to clause forty-eight. That states quite clearly that any contracts initiated by Shaw Management remain under our control, and extensions or renewals will be negotiated by us, and that you will pay us our full commission on all the income derived from such contracts.'

'That's not how Luisa reads the agreement.'

'She probably needs a bit of help with her reading in that case.'

'Help she has, Steven, in plenty. Those Hollywood lawyers know a thing or two.'

'I'm really disappointed to be having this conversation with you. Why weren't you frank and open with me? We could've sorted things out without resorting to lawyers, and we still can, I'm sure. Ray, we're the best business managers for you: we've already proved that in a hundred ways. I took some heavy risks to land that Larssen deal, I promise you, and I won't let some Hollywood tart reap the benefits. Fuck her, by all means, but don't let her fuck up your career.'

Both men stood up and Steven shut his briefcase carefully. 'Think about it,' he said. 'Very thoroughly, please. As for the contracts that've made you a multi-millionaire and that I negotiated, they're not going anywhere except to my office. If you try to take them away from me, you'll have a lawsuit on your hands that'll wipe you out financially. That I promise you.'

As he strode towards the door of the suite, Steven thanked Gerrard for the coffee. 'I'll be in touch,' he added in an even tone.

When he got back to his Los Angeles office Steven telephoned Corky Price in New York and talked to him at length. Price promised to assign the best man he had on the west coast to help. 'Don't worry, Mr Shaw,' he said in conclusion, 'the firm's been up to its elbows in these kind of deals since the early days in Hollywood. We're used to operating in the sleaze factory.'

One of Earlybird Security's trusted employees went into action and bribed a temporary secretary in Luisa Ebbers' office to keep him informed of her movements. When he knew that Ebbers was away in San Francisco for a few days, he got his informant to contact Ray Gerrard and arrange dinner with Luisa in Bel Air.

It didn't worry Gerrard when Luisa wasn't in the restaurant to greet him. Her time-keeping was nearly as bad as his, and he settled at a corner table, feeling safely anonymous behind his sunglasses. There were so many celebs in there anyway that he'd hardly be noticed. No doubt that was why Luisa had chosen the place. Safety in numbers.

He was enjoying a second glass of beer when a waiter appeared at his side and told him that Ms Ebbers had just called to say that she'd been delayed in San Francisco and therefore couldn't make it for dinner. That was strange: why hadn't they brought a telephone over to his table so that she could speak to him direct?

Gerrard was philosophical. He'd have some pasta and a rocket salad and head for home. Maybe he'd give Lauren a call – she might come over for an hour or two.

Idly, he read through the menu while he toyed with the remnants of his beer. Then he became conscious of someone standing by his table. The girl was really gorgeous. Long blonde hair, an oval-shaped face with deep-blue eyes, and what a body. 'I hope I'm not being rude,' she said in a quiet and well-modulated voice, 'but you look as though you've been stood up, just like me. I feel a bit embarrassed on my own in here and wondered if I could join you.'

Gerrard stood halfway and waved her into the chair opposite him. 'Nothing I'd like better. Who's the idiot who let you down?'

'Another in a long line of television producers with a star part that's going begging for the right girl.'

'Oh yeah, I think I know that scenario. Anyway, I'm Ray Gerrard.'

'The tennis player! Oh, my God, you'll think I'm one of those groupies! Now, I'm even more embarrassed.'

'Look, let's order some food and enjoy our dinner. That's all we need to do, OK?'

It turned out that Maria was a model who was trying to break into television and films. She'd had a few minor parts but was one of the army of aspiring actors who lived in the hope of that one big break that would bring them fame and fortune.

Maria asked Gerrard a series of questions about his life on the international tennis circuit and clung eagerly to his every word. She liked him. He was an extremely attractive hunk of man and she had no hesitation in accepting his invitation to have a final drink at his home.

It was only a couple of miles to Gerrard's home and the journey, in his Porsche, was swift. Maria refused his offer of a drink and delved into her handbag. She brandished a small packet of white powder at him. 'D'you use this stuff?'

'Coke? Hell, no. Some of the guys on the Tour do, but I'm straight on the drugs front.'

'D'you mind if I do?'

'Go ahead.'

Gerrard had no idea what the cocaine did to his new friend's head, but it made her do some remarkable things to both their bodies. When he awoke in the early dawn, he stretched gingerly on the bed; he felt as if he'd played several five-set matches in one day – and lost them all. Where was Maria? Gerrard made his way slowly to the bathroom. She wasn't there, nor in the living room. Christ, had she stolen anything? He'd heard of tarts ripping off their customers when they went off to sleep. No, his wallet and credit cards and the keys to the Porsche were all where he'd left them. He threw himself back on the bed and went to sleep.

As arranged, Jack from Earlybird Security was waiting for Maria at a discreet distance from Gerrard's home and he drove her back to her mother's apartment.

At ten o'clock on the following morning Joan Lister

dialled Ray Gerrard's telephone number and waited for nearly two minutes for the receiver to be lifted.

'Yeah,' said a weary-sounding voice.

'Is that Mr Gerrard?'

'Yeah.'

'This is Joan Lister, Maria's mother. I think you and I should meet.'

'Why's that?'

'I want to know what you've got to say for yourself before I go to the cops.'

'The police? What are you on about?'

'I'm on about you screwing my fifteen-year-old daughter, you bastard.'

'Fifteen? Oh yeah? And I'm Arnie Schwarzenegger.'

'We'll see whether you've got a sense of humour, Mr Gerrard, when you're in court and my little daughter gets on the witness stand in her sweet little dress, no make-up, hair in plaits, flat shoes and white ankle socks—'

'This is a set-up. Your daughter picked me up.'

'No. Wrong. The waiter saw you feeding booze to Maria and the doorman saw you drive off with her in your car. Then you persuaded her to try some coke and then you forced her to have sex with you, you stinking pervert.'

'It was Maria who had the cocaine—'

'Don't you lie to me, you bastard. There're enough offences there to put you away for a long, long time. And the guys in jail will like a pretty boy, a rich and successful boy like you. You'll be their pin-cushion.'

The light sweat on Gerrard's brow suddenly went cold and he felt himself go pale. He was in the middle of a nightmare: this couldn't happen to him, surely not to him.

'I don't know who the hell you are, lady, but you're wasting your time trying to shake me down,' he said hoarsely.

'I'm Maria's mother and I'll tell you what I'm going to

do. You'll get a messenger at your door in less than an hour. He'll have a copy of Maria's birth certificate, OK? That's just for openers, to show I'm serious. Then we'll talk.'

The line went dead. Gerrard raced to the bathroom and was violently sick.

At least they hadn't gone to the police yet, that was something to cling on to. Who could he turn to? Luisa? No. There was only one person who might handle this for him.

When the first call came from Ray Gerrard, Steven told his secretary that he'd get back to his client within the hour. He left it for two hours. Let the bastard suffer, he thought. Corky Price had told him that the first phase of the operation had been accomplished.

By the time that Steven returned his call, the birth certificate had arrived and Gerrard saw that Maria Lister had been born a mere fifteen years, two months and a few days before.

His business manager's voice was cheerful. 'Hello, Ray. I expect you're calling about our contract. You've had second thoughts? I knew you would.'

'No, Steven, well, I mean I haven't had any thoughts. Look, this is personal. I'm in trouble and I need some help.'

'What kind of trouble?'

'Girl trouble, an under-age girl.'

In a series of stumbling and disjointed phrases Gerrard told him the story of the previous evening.

When he finished, Steven said, 'And you're sure they haven't gone to the police?'

'Her mother says not. She wants to talk.'

'OK, you sit tight and do nothing. I'll get somebody over to help you. Unless, of course, you'd prefer one of Luisa Ebbers' hot-shot lawyers to handle it for you. They are on the spot, after all,' Steven said playfully.

As soon as he broke the connection to Los Angeles, he contacted Corky Price and told him to start the second phase of the project.

Steven was in a mood which was sufficiently buoyant to last through most of an evening with Walter Tomlin. The Chief Executive of the Kooler Corporation had grown ever more dogmatic over the years that he had known him. It was difficult to believe that his old Harvard friend, Charlie, sharp and high-spirited, could be Tomlin's son.

They were due to discuss an extension of Kooler's sponsorship of the tennis doubles event and several other proposals. Tomlin professed to enjoy good food and it suited Steven to conduct the negotiations in an informal atmosphere over dinner. He found that men like Tomlin were easier to handle when they were divorced from their own environments, when they were not surrounded by the reminders of their own power.

Steven took him to the French restaurant where he and Eva Rosen had enjoyed their first meal together. In a sentimental moment, he ordered a bottle of Léoville-Barton in her memory. He wondered where she now was. Steven knew that his guest would only have one glass at the most. He wondered how Tomlin got his kicks: it couldn't just be from attending church on Sunday. Maybe he'd put some surveillance on him some time.

The Kooler Tennis deal was rapidly concluded in principle. One of Steven's people, Jay Melville, would work out the subordinate details with the Kooler marketing executives, and the show was on again for a further three years.

'As long as we're guaranteed Ray Gerrard,' Tomlin said through a mouthful of *gigot d'agneau*. 'What a fine young man! I still remember our dinner together. Though I gather he doesn't go to our Santa Monica church anymore.'

'No, he's living around Bel Air now, Walter. I'll be seeing him shortly and I'll pass on your best wishes.'

Over the coffee, Steven persuaded Tomlin to guarantee some money for one of his golf tournaments, and he exacted a promise that Kooler would use a racing driver called Angus Gray to promote their brand in Britain. Gray had been signed by Dean Aultman, who was convinced that the Scotsman would one day win the Formula One championship.

In return for the deals, Steven had to listen to Tomlin's homilies about the problems of the world: from drugs to Northern Ireland, from education to the state of the New York streets.

A lawyer called Mike Russo went to see Gerrard the day after Joan Lister first made contact. Russo was an ebullient man of Gerrard's age, dressed in a sharp suit and an open-necked shirt.

He went through Gerrard's story once again and told him to carry on his life as normal. 'You've got this invitation event at the weekend, right? So, get in there and try and win it. And you've got a tournament starting in about ten days. OK, we'll try and sort this thing out before then. We're on the case. We've got the Listers under surveillance and we're investigating their background. If they're on the level, we've got a problem.'

'On the level! For Chrissake, Mike, she looked about twenty-five. She was snorting coke right here, she fucked me half to death, man. She did things I've only read about.'

'Lucky you. But it doesn't matter how old she *looked*, Ray. That isn't the point. You've seen her birth certificate and we've checked it out and it seems legitimate. That is, unless they're impersonating some people called Lister.'

'Let's pray that the press don't get wind of this.'

'You bet. Don't let this get you down. We're going to intercept all your calls and I'll try and negotiate with this woman. OK? I'll call you on a regular basis.'

Mike Russo did as he promised but had nothing to report. Gerrard played in the invitation event and, to his and the sponsor's chagrin, lost all his matches. Tuesday brought a message from Russo to say that 'he was getting there' and Steven Shaw telephoned to say that he was flying to Los Angeles at the end of the week. His business manager's final comment was unequivocal. 'If we work it out and it's a big if, it's going to cost you, Ray. You'll need a hundred grand in cash and you'll have to authorise me to draw at least as much again from one of your accounts to meet fees and expenses.'

The money didn't worry Gerrard in the slightest. All he wanted was to sleep at nights again and to be freed of his perpetual feeling of nausea.

On Friday morning Russo picked Gerrard up and took him to a bank where a hundred thousand dollars in cash was waiting for his collection. Then the two men drove to a nondescript building in downtown Los Angeles, not far from the Dodger Stadium. The name of Earlybird Security was just discernible above the door.

The other people present at the meeting were Steven Shaw and Joan Lister. Steven didn't bother to make formal introductions which was just as well since Gerrard could hardly bear to look at Lister, a tall and attractive woman, who was probably still on the right side of forty. She was dressed in a sombre, dark-grey outfit, relieved by a green silk shirt. Her only sign of nerves was the way she pecked quickly at the cigarette which she kept between her fingers.

Steven took charge of the meeting and began by telling everyone that an accommodation had been reached between Joan Lister and Ray Gerrard through the good offices of Mike Russo. A formal agreement had therefore been drawn up which absolved Gerrard from any action against him for having unlawful relations with Maria Lister. In return, he was donating the sum of one hundred thousand dollars to the Listers.

The formalities of signing the legal document were presided over by Russo, who then handed over a package containing the money to Joan Lister. She opened the envelope, looked quickly inside and nodded her approval. It struck Gerrard that she hadn't spoken a word during the meeting.

She left the room, escorted by Russo and Steven said sympathetically, 'OK, it's over, Ray. You can resume normal life. You won't hear from her again.'

'Thank God.'

'Yes, it was a pretty expensive fuck, wasn't it?'

Russo walked back into the office and both men thanked him for his help. 'Just send the account to me in New York, Mike,' said Steven. 'You did a great job.'

When the lawyer had left, Steven put the agreement in his briefcase. 'I'll keep that document safely locked up in the bank, Ray.'

'How do I know that bitch won't try it on again one day, blackmail me?'

'Because she's a realist. Mike has made it plain that things could get very, very rough if she tries anything.' Steven delved in his briefcase. 'Now there's one other item, your representation agreement. If you'd like to sign both copies.'

As Gerrard scrawled his signature, Steven smiled his satisfaction. 'That's great, Ray, we're back in business. Tomorrow I've arranged for us to play golf at Riviera. It'll be a change for you and it'll do us both good.'

Mike Russo and Joan and Maria Lister were already

heading north towards San Francisco when Gerrard was signing his new contract. Even after Earlybird had taken their 50 per cent cut, it had been a good hit for the three of them.

When he got back to New York, Steven arranged to meet Corky Price in order to congratulate him on a very smooth and successful operation. They had a cup of coffee in the airy café attached to the Pierpont Morgan Library. Steven liked to browse in the shop and he bought a word-game for Adam.

The two men sat in a corner of the café, a pot of coffee between them.

'I've got another pussy trap for you to spring,' Steven said with a smile.

'You sure like the technique.'

'It works, that's why. Let's make it the week before the Masters. Our target will be playing in the New Orleans event.'

Price shrugged. 'OK. Gimme the details. I'll handle it.'

# Chapter Twenty-nine

Ray Gerrard's new contract with Larssen contained the biggest numbers Steven had ever seen for such an endorsement deal. He was proud of himself, especially since Gerrard was locked in for another five years. He was determined to exploit every aspect of his client's earning capacity.

Steven felt it was diplomatic to keep Joe Lynagh informed of any major developments in the business; he was, after all, the other shareholder and he was also his father-in-law. Abetted by the Larssen publicity department, he knew that the sporting media would seize on the story with relish and he made a point of going over the figures in Gerrard's new contract with Joe. With the sports journalists Steven was outwardly coy but he dropped enough hints to feed the rumour machine which as ever was highly susceptible to a potent mixture of big money and glamour.

At eight o'clock one evening Steven was still in his office. He was looking at the agency's income projections over various periods of time. The business could hardly be more vigorously healthy, but at regular intervals he liked to review his overall progress. Although the long-term forecasts were academic exercises prepared by his financial staff, they helped to concentrate his mind and spurred him to think in a free-wheeling way about the future.

The telephone rang and he recognised at once the ebullient tones of Joe Lynagh. 'I love this headline,' Joe said, '"Super-agent does super deal". How about that?'

'I'll settle for that any time.'

'I'll bet, and I suppose you've got half the tennis stars in the world asking you to represent them.'

'We've already got the cream, but some of the others have approached us. The grass is always greener. We'll pick one or two but we're close to saturation in the tennis market.'

'So you're looking for fresh fields to conquer? But not boxing, I hope, nor American football.'

'No, Joe, real football. Soccer, as you Americans call it. There's a real opening in Britain.'

'I'll have to take your word for that. How's your plan for a world circuit in golf?'

'So, so. Lots of battles to come.'

'Well, I know you're a battler, Steven. I saw that as soon as we met. You were prepared to go the extra mile for Suzi, weren't you?'

'To the end of the line.'

'You two are OK, are you? No problems?'

'None. Happy as larks.'

'Great. What else is happening?'

'Well, very long-term, I want to get involved with the Olympics.'

'It's only every four years. Isn't that a bit limited, Steven?'

'No. It's the biggest sporting extravaganza of all. It's truly international and there're massive amounts of money involved. I want my share.'

'That's my boy. Come to lunch on Sunday, will you? Tell me more then.'

His train of thought broken, Steven decided to finish work for the evening. Suzi and Adam were away and he craved some company or, even better, some excitement. He dialled a number. If he asked for Carrie-Jane, the excitement was guaranteed. She was the antidote to the dullness of his sex life with Suzi: 'meat 'n' potatoes' sex, that's what they called it in the old days in Brighton. Nowadays he had a much more sophisticated palate.

While Steven was playing the numbers game in New York, Suzi was enjoying good weather at her parents' home in Florida. Sam Rhodes's apartment was only a few miles away and, although he was playing in a tournament, he had contrived to spend much of the early part of the week with her and Adam, who was delighted with his new friend. They talked and played ball together and, at Adam's insistence, a toy golf set had been bought and Rhodes had given the child his first rudimentary lessons in the game.

If Adam adored Sam, it was nothing compared to Suzi's feelings for him. After some soul-searching on Rhodes's part, because he liked and admired Steven and valued their relationship, he had made love to Suzi, and their affair had been going strong for several months. There had been no hesitations on Suzi's part. She had had several liaisons in the last year or two, including a very satisfactory one with her old Harvard friend, Greg. That had been real fun, but Sam Rhodes was different. Attentive and courteous, tender and loving, he aroused feelings in her that she thought she'd forgotten in her years of marriage to Steven.

Suzi was in love with Sam and, every hour of every day, wished that she could devote herself to him. But they had to be careful, as Sam often stressed. He maintained his pose as the family friend and Suzi was always careful to introduce him as 'a client of my husband, Steven'.

'In fact, Sam was my husband's first client and therefore very special,' she sometimes added, and then ensured that she talked about Steven at some length, as any proud wife would.

The two of them made no secret of their meetings and it

would have been foolish, as they had decided after they first made love, to try to cover up their social relationship. They were good friends, and it was apparent to everyone who saw them together that Adam had adopted Rhodes as a substitute for the real father he rarely saw.

Suzi hated the subterfuge which surrounded their relationship, but knew they had to maintain it. The need to confide in someone was always present but she could not burden her mother, who in the past had been her confidante, with such a revelation.

At first, Suzi had found excuses for Steven's neglect of her. He was busy, he was building a business, he was working day and night for her and Adam. But it wasn't for them, it was all for the greater glory of Steven Shaw. She began to wonder if he had ever loved her. His love-making had become not only infrequent but also perfunctory. Suzi didn't care. She felt only relief when she finally admitted to herself that her love for him had run out.

For his part, Steven didn't concern himself with the structure of their marriage, as long as they presented a united front to the world. He occasionally wondered if she was sleeping with anyone; she was beautiful and wouldn't be short of offers. He'd heard her mention Greg, who took her to the theatre occasionally. Perhaps he was throwing his leg over. There was Sam, of course. He spent some time with her, but he was too much the gentleman.

A couple of weeks later, John Winter was also in the Sunshine State. He had a time and a date in his diary for a preliminary interview with Francesca Zanini. It had been organised by one of the executives in Shaw Management's New York office. Winter reckoned he would be in and out of Fort Lauderdale within two days.

After checking into his hotel, where Zanini, her father

and her coach were also staying, Winter called his interviewee on the internal telephone but there was no reply. No
sweat, she was obviously out practising. Maybe he would
catch her that evening; an interview over dinner would be
better than his appointed time at ten o'clock on the following morning. It would be more informal, and possibly
more productive. Winter called her room several times
between five and six o'clock without any luck. With a gin
and tonic by his side he sat in the lobby in the hope of
intercepting her but there was no sign of her.

At seven o'clock he called her room number, but once
again got no answer; he also telephoned her father and her
coach with the same result. Winter gave up, ate a tasteless
meal in the hotel's coffee shop, watched an hour of television and went to bed.

After breakfasting early, be began the same routine.
There was no response to his calls and Winter went up to
Zanini's room and knocked on the door. Nobody answered
so he pushed a note written on a page torn from his diary
under her door: 'Looking forward to seeing you at ten
o'clock, Yours, John Winter.' Some bloody chance, at this
rate, he thought. At midday, he called Holly Baer in Shaw's
New York office and asked why Francesca hadn't showed up
for their meeting. She'd get back to him immediately, she
said, but it was three o'clock when she did.

'I'm so sorry, Mr Winter,' Holly Baer said. 'Frannie had
a scheduling problem but she could see you tomorrow.'

'Tomorrow? When? I'm booked back to London. Could
we make it nine o'clock in the morning?'

'Well, your best bet is to speak to Mr Zanini, he'll fix
everything. He's aware of your interest.'

Aware that his irritation had reached a dangerous level,
Winter decided it was better to act than to brood. He
squeezed into a courtesy car with three journalists and

headed for the practice courts. He found Zanini hitting volleys to a constant stream of instruction from her coach, Kenny Crane. 'C'mon, Fran, balance, lightness, hit the spot, that's good.' His shouts of encouragement were, however, overlaid by what sounded like a stream of invective from a squat, middle-aged man who stood at the side of the net; it was in Italian and Winter therefore couldn't be sure. That must be Mauro, her father.

'Mr Zanini?' Winter said tentatively.

'Yeah. What you want?'

'John Winter. My interview with your daughter—'

'Interview, you must pay. We talk about the fee later.'

'No. Mr Shaw arranged it. For ten o'clock this morning, do you remember?'

'OK, yeah, but we busy. It must wait, I think.'

'I only need an hour or so.'

'That's what they all say.'

'The fee has already been agreed with Shaw Management, so I need to talk to Francesca soon.'

'OK. Seven o'clock tonight. At hotel.'

Annoyed by the delay, Winter used a telephone in the clubhouse to rearrange his flight home. He bought himself a cup of coffee and, as he headed for the terrace, he nearly bumped into Terri Calvin, a lanky American player who had reached several important finals without winning any of them. Outspoken and controversial, she rarely hesitated to air her views on the game and Winter had already interviewed her for his programme.

'Hey, John,' she drawled at him, 'who are you pursuing this time?'

'Fran Zanini. I'm supposed to interview her tonight.'

'That shouldn't take long. Make sure you use words of one syllable. Come on, let's sit at that table. Nice to see you.'

'Tell me more about Zanini,' Winter said.

'Could be a great player. I might put a few dollars on her to win Wimbledon this time. It'll be her best chance, I guess.'

'How come?'

'I doubt whether she'll still be around in, say, five years. A lot of people in the game are worried about burn-out. Franny was on the tournament scene so young and always with that father of hers barking at her, bullying her. What a shit he is! Pressure, pressure and no fun. She won't last. Also, she's gotten so big in the last coupla years.'

'What d'you mean?' Winter asked, suddenly alert.

'Look, John, I'm a big girl but I was born that way. My dad is six-four and my mom is tall for a lady. But Fran hardly came up to my shoulder when she arrived on the scene and her father is the shape and consistency of a tub of lard. But now she's nearly my size. How come?'

'Is she on something? Human growth hormone, for instance?'

'Who knows? But some of these loving parents will stop at nothing. They're a menace. But, John, don't quote me on the drugs thing, it's too hot an issue at the moment.'

'OK. So, to change the subject, tell me about Fran's manager, Steven Shaw.'

Calvin shrugged. 'Oh, he's great at making deals, he's clever. But I see an unscrupulous man, an amoral man. I don't think he's got any concern for his clients, they're just merchandise to him. You should see Franny's schedule. Christ, he really hustles her, she's here, there and everywhere like a grasshopper on speed. OK, she's earning big bucks, but she needs to rest occasionally. But Shaw wouldn't give a damn about that.'

'So, he's a tough businessman, but that doesn't mean he's amoral.'

'No? I can dimly remember when tennis was fun, when it wasn't solely about money and deals, deals and money. Some of the players managed to perform with a smile on their faces. Not any longer. And it's mostly the fault of the men in the suits with the briefcases. Men like Shaw. They're running the fucking game, John, and it shows.'

'You've got an agent, haven't you?'

'Sure, but she does what I tell her to do. Shaw makes his people into robots. Look at Ray Gerrard. He was a super guy a few years ago. Real fun to be with. The more money he's made the more miserable he's become.'

'And you blame Shaw for that?'

'Yeah. I wonder sometimes whether Gerrard is haunted by what happened to Nils Ryberg. He dies and Ray gets the big contract and becomes a multi-millionaire.'

'Oh, come off it, Terri. Shaw told me about that. He dived in there when Ryberg died. He has to do the best he can for his own clients.'

'Agreed, but Shaw has too much influence in tennis for comfort. It always seems to be his clients who get the interviews, especially on AAN and BBC programmes. Well, OK, he does a lot of business with those people, but he's really got things sewn up there. There's something about the guy that gives me the creeps.'

A few minutes later, Terri Calvin hauled her long limbs out of the chair, smiled, sketched a kiss to Winter and went off to practise.

It was just after eight o'clock that evening when Winter finally caught up with Francesca Zanini. Terri Calvin was right, she was a big girl; almost a head taller than her father who was close by her side. She was clad in a black and green velour tracksuit. The headphones of a personal stereo were around her neck, but at least she had turned off the music. That was nice of her. When they shook hands,

Winter noticed the roughness of her palm, the legacy of her long hours of practice.

'Jus' tennis,' Mauro said. 'No questions about money or boyfriends, things like that.'

'This is only a preliminary chat, Mr Zanini. We'll film your daughter in Paris for the programme.' Winter set his tape recorder running and asked her about her training programme with Kenny Crane. 'I believe he's trying to make you faster about the court, quicker to the net and so on.'

'Yeah, I've got to take control, force the pace more, you know.' Zanini spoke in a sing-song voice with little trace of her father's Italian accent.

'She a natural athlete, she get it from me,' Mauro said firmly.

Winter soon exhausted his list of questions about her tennis, since Zanini answered all of them with abbreviated comments.

'What about Wimbledon? Can you win the title?' he asked.

'Uh-huh. They're fast courts. Good for my game.'

'OK. What d'you do when you're not practising or playing?' Holly Baer had told Winter that her client was interested in clothing design.

'Oh, listen to music, you know, watch a little television. Sleep a lot.' She smiled wanly.

'Your agent said you're interested in designing clothes. You have some ideas for the firm that makes the Zanini tennis gear, is that so?'

'Oh, yeah, right.'

Winter waited for more but that was all she was willing to volunteer on the subject. He halted the tape and said that they'd fix up the filmed interview during the French Championships. 'Do you like Paris?'

'Sure,' she replied. 'It's really neat.'

'What do you most like about it?'

'Oh, you know, the museums and that tower thing.'

'Which museums have you visited?'

'Well, I haven't yet, you know. But maybe this year.'

As he played the tape back later that evening, Winter wondered what was the point of interviewing the girl. Maybe he should just concentrate on action sequences of her. But he'd agreed a fee and had to make the most of his access to her.

The New Orleans branch of Earlybird Security had received some bizarre requests in its time, but the one from Corky Price took some matching. He wanted them to find a really classy tart, someone who could pass as an actress or a model and who would be capable of picking up and sustaining the interest of a well-known sportsman.

'The last bit shouldn't be difficult,' the New Orleans man said. 'The average sportsman thinks through his dick.'

'Not this one,' said Corky Price. 'He's French, he's civilised and he's discerning. And, by the way, she's got to have a dose of the clap to pass on to our French lover-boy.'

'Shit,' said the other man with feeling.

He'd allowed a good round to slip away from him and Patrice Barbier knew that the main problem had been his putting, the game within a game. If he were to do well in the Masters during the following week, he knew he must regain his touch. He didn't dwell on his mistakes, but spent nearly two hours on the practice green in order to try and eliminate them. That evening he would have a nice dinner, listen to some jazz and relax. Tomorrow was another day.

Barbier liked New Orleans. It had one of the highest crime rates in America but was bursting with fun, and he loved the music: bar after bar with live traditional jazz. He ambled along Bourbon Street for a while and then sat in a noisy restaurant. In theory, soul food wasn't to his taste but he enjoyed the spicy chicken, seared black but tender. Some ice-cold beer went down well with it.

With thoughts of visiting the Preservation Hall for a full blast of New Orleans jazz, Barbier wandered out on to the street again. Amid the bustling crowds, he didn't notice the couple who were tracking him about fifty yards back. As he passed the open windows of a bar, he heard the pure notes of a trumpet prancing exquisitely high above the accompanying instruments. Now there's a man who can really play, he thought, and he went through the door to hear some more. The place was cavernous and crowded and he eased himself into a gap by the bar and ordered a beer. After a couple of gulps he became aware of a woman just behind his left shoulder. She was gesticulating in the direction of the barman. Barbier looked again. She was beautiful. Her tanned face was framed with dark curls and she had widely spaced dark eyes and a generous, smiling mouth. Her simple dress showed off her lissom figure.

'Let me do it,' he said and waved a barman over. 'What would you like?'

'That's kind,' the woman said. 'A beer would be fine.'

'You're English? On holiday?'

'Yes, I'm from England and I'm on a working holiday. Fortunately, the work's finished, and I've got a few days left to enjoy myself.'

After they exchanged names, Barbier learned that Caroline was an actress who'd been shooting a commercial in New Orleans and he told her that he played golf for a living. The jazz was invigorating and Caroline was easy to talk to; she also had a superb body. The time rattled by and, when midnight approached, Barbier realised that he must get back to his hotel. Although his starting time was not until midday, he nevertheless wanted at least an hour's practice before that.

He finished his beer and said, 'It's been a delightful evening, Caroline, great fun, but I must get back to the hotel. Can I drop you off anywhere?'

'Oh, Patrice, it's not late. The fun is only just beginning.' She smiled her brilliant smile at him.

'No, it isn't late but I've got a big day tomorrow, I must be at my best, if possible. It's boring, I know.'

'Not at all. You can give me a lift, I'm staying at the Commodore Inn.'

In the taxi, Caroline snuggled up against him and she felt his wiry arm around her shoulders. This was no hardship, the Frenchman was attractive, not like the flabby and sweaty businessmen she usually had to service. She was expensive anyway and was being paid three times her normal rate. Of course, she was off-limits really with a dose, and she wondered why he'd been set up. A jealous husband, probably. Oh well, this was one time when she could really enjoy the sex.

When they reached the entrance to the Commodore, Barbier walked around the car and opened the door for Caroline.

'You must come in and have a night-cap,' she said. As he hesitated, she added, 'Please.'

'Of course,' he said, with a smile. 'It wouldn't be very polite to leave you on the doorstep.'

They sat in a corner of the lounge while Caroline had a brandy and Barbier confined himself to a cup of coffee. After half an hour, he glanced at his watch and said he must be on his way.

'You don't have to go back to your own hotel, you know,' Caroline said. 'There's room upstairs for both of us.'

A sporting superstar, handsome and charismatic, Patrice Barbier was never short of such invitations. But she was special, beautiful and eager. Why not seize the moment? Tomorrow was just another round of golf. Then his mind flicked ahead to the Masters, the first of the four majors and only a week away. The New Orleans event was a vital part of his preparation.

'Let's meet on Saturday,' he said. 'Tomorrow will be tricky for me, I must make sure I qualify for the last two rounds of the tournament.'

'I understand, but will you do me a favour? Take me up to my room. I don't like these lifts and the long corridors, they frighten me.'

When they reached her door, Caroline thrust herself against his body, entwined her arms around him and whispered in his ear, 'I'll make sure you sleep well, Patrice.'

He eased himself slowly out of her arms, kissed her firmly on the lips and said, 'I'll call you on Saturday. There's no rush, is there?'

Caroline went into her room, had a shower and sat in an armchair to think things over. She'd had half her fee from Earlybird, who had used her several times in the past for these special assignments. She'd never let them down and she knew that it wasn't their practice to set up surveillance in her room. Well, they'd done that once but they'd warned her so she could make sure that the fat slob's face was easily identifiable. This was a time to lie. She'd say that Barbier had insisted on wearing a rubber. She was glad that the ruse had failed. She liked the man. If she ever saw him again she'd give him one for free.

It was a good omen, in Steven's eyes, that Sam Rhodes finished fourth in the New Orleans event; he was obviously in good form just before the Masters. Patrice Barbier also

finished strongly to get into a tie for sixth place. He would
be one of the danger men at Augusta, but not if he were
infected with venereal disease, and the medical book he'd
consulted had told him that the incubation period could be
as short as three days.

On the Tuesday morning, just before he left for Augusta,
Steven met Corky Price in their favoured spot in the
Pierpont Morgan Library café.

'How's our French friend?' Steven asked.

'As happy as a dog with two dicks, I should imagine.'

'Yes? Did he do his stuff with the girl?'

'Oh yeah, she picked him up, no trouble, and got him
back to her room. And he put the wood to her, as they say.'

'Great, so he'll be feeling pretty sorry for himself in a day
or two.'

'No.'

'What d'you mean?'

'The girl admitted that he was well rubbered-up. He
used a condom, a French letter.'

'Very appropriate,' Steven muttered. 'Bugger.' He
paused and then continued. 'OK, Corky, it's plan two for
Monsieur Barbier. Whether he's in a position to win or not
after the third round, we'll disturb the bastard's Gallic sang-
froid.'

# Chapter Thirty

Every year, the first of professional golf's major tournaments took place early in April at the Augusta National Golf Club in Georgia. Invariably it caused an epidemic of purple prose among the journalists who felt obliged to churn out painfully lyrical descriptions of the beauties of the course: its towering pines, the fruit-bearing trees, the flowers and shrubs after which the eighteen holes were named: flowering peach, yellow jasmine, camellia, dogwood, azalea, red bud. Then the scribes would extol the great traditions of the Masters, the undoubted quality of its champions, and the dramas which had unravelled at Amen Corner, the stretch of holes from the eleventh to the thirteenth. Then there was the founder of the Masters, the legendary Bobby Jones. Steven occasionally fantasised about the deals he could have done for the man.

Steven recognised the event as a unique golfing occasion and he had enjoyed the course when he played it as Sam Rhodes's guest. But to him, the tournament was primarily an unequalled opportunity to do business. The stately old clubhouse, its veranda and the immaculate lawn, shaded on one side by an ancient and massive oak tree, were the places where some of the most influential businessmen in the world gathered. The equipment manufacturers, the sponsors of tournaments around the globe, the public relations people, the media men and the business managers rubbed shoulders there. Outwardly sedate, it was a marketplace, which hummed to the music of ideas chasing money. Steven Shaw, the most powerful agent in sport, loved it.

One of his first meetings was with the man who owned a fast food chain with tens of thousands of outlets around the world. Bobby Rossner had got interested in golf late but had the fanaticism of the true convert. Very small in stature and so thin that Steven reckoned he never ate his own fast food products, Rossner had a neat moustache on an anonymous face. 'Neat' summed up the man, and his only notable characteristics were an incisive, clipped manner of speech and a way of wagging his right index finger in order to emphasise a conversational point.

The omissions in his personality had not prevented Rossner from building up a company with a turnover that was measured in billions, and Steven knew that he was eager to spend some of that money on golf. The two men had discussed various schemes, and Rossner, whose enthusiasm was always tempered by caution when promotional money was concerned, wanted to test the water first by placing his company logo on the shirts and golf bags of several of Shaw's clients.

It was a start, albeit a conservative one, but Steven was confident that it would lead to much bigger things. Earlier that day he had arranged for Sam Rhodes to present Rossner with a new set of his own Parbreaker clubs. They had been custom-built: the shafts were one inch shorter than standard to account for the recipient's height. The gesture had cost Steven nothing and he knew that the goodwill it engendered would give him an edge in the negotiations to come. The gift was documented in the file on Rossner that he was steadily building.

They met at eleven o'clock on the clubhouse veranda and, for once, Rossner had eschewed his normal dark business suit for a pair of cream trousers and a green blazer. Its

colour was dark enough not to be confused with that worn
by the members of Augusta National; nevertheless, one or
two of that patrician band looked askance at it.

When he had ordered a pot of coffee from one of the
white-jacketed waiters, Steven asked Rossner how he liked
the new clubs.

'Thrilled, Steven, absolutely thrilled. I chipped a few
balls around the garden this morning. They're just great,
and as for your client, well, he's a real gentleman. I'd love to
have a game with him.'

'That can be arranged, Bobby. After all, you're going to
be one of Sam's sponsors, along with several other fine
golfers. We'll set up a fourball in the near future. That'd be
fun.'

'It sure would. Now, you are guaranteeing Rhodes as
part of the package, aren't you, Steven?'

'No problem.'

'What about Patrice Barbier? I'd like him for Europe.
Can you deliver?'

'He's not a client, officially, but we do a lot of business
together. The trouble is, Bobby, that he's tied up with some
French food consortium and there might be a conflict of
interests. I'll see what I can do.'

'OK, here's my idea.' Rossner sat erect in his chair,
straightened the knot in his tie and smoothed his moustache. 'I'd like six of your clients, who must include Sam
Rhodes, on a one-year contract, with an option for a further two years. The company logo on their shirts and their
bags, two personal appearances by Rhodes and one apiece
by the others. What's the ballpark figure, Steven?'

Shaw had watched Rossner's finger ticking off the points
as they were made. He knew how much he wanted but, as
usual, jotted some figures on a small pad and kept his
adversary waiting. After a couple of minutes he gave

Rossner a sum well in excess of a million dollars, which was the figure he was actually expecting to get. 'Plus all the usual expenses, Bobby,' he added.

'I want to pay less than a million,' Rossner replied, knowing that he could afford a little more than that. 'It's the other directors, they'd have a fit.'

'Sam Rhodes comes expensive. But I want to do business with you. So, with a bit of give and take, I'm sure we can get there.'

'As long as I'm not doing all the giving and you all the taking,' Rossner said, with a smile. 'Of course, if you can arrange that fourball . . .'

'I'll give you some possible dates by the end of the week.'

Rossner nodded his satisfaction. 'I can put one of our aircraft at Sam's disposal for any work he does on our behalf. And, Steven, if you need an executive jet to take you somewhere, give me a call. Now, is Sam going to win this week?'

'I sincerely hope so,' Steven said with feeling, as he thought of all the bonuses which would automatically become due if Rhodes donned the famous green jacket once again on Sunday night. Whatever happened, Shaw Management had made a good start to the Masters: he'd take $200,000 off the top of the Rossner deal and then charge his clients the usual commission as well. Yes, it was a very good start, like having two or three birdies in the first half-a-dozen holes of a round.

It had become a tradition that Steven invited Sam Rhodes to dinner at his hotel on the eve of the championship. Steven had reserved his usual table in a corner of the utilitarian dining room and knew that his client would order roast chicken, as he had done on the same occasion when he had first won the Masters.

As always, the tablecloth, the place settings and the menu were in Augusta green. When they had both ordered from the set menu, Rhodes said ruefully, 'I expect you're as sorry as me that I won the par three competition.' This was an informal event which preceded the championship proper.

'Why should I be?'

'Because the winner has never gone on to take the green jacket.'

'Well, you're the man to beat the jinx. Remember, the four-minute mile was just a dream until Bannister dared to do it,' Shaw said comfortably and went on to outline the main points of Rossner's proposals.

'We should have contracts within a month, so I'll send yours on to you for signature.'

'I don't know, Steven. I'm no great lover of fast food, as you know—'

'You don't have to eat it,' Steven said with a smile. 'I don't think Rossner dines out much at his own restaurants.'

'What I mean is, there are ethical problems with these fast food chains. I'm not sure I want to encourage people, especially young people, to eat junk food.'

'They'll go to them, Sam, whether you encourage them or not. And anyway, Rossner does a range of veggie burgers and there're lots of salads.'

'Maybe, but the business was built on burgers, on the American obsession with meat. And that obsession has cost the world dear.'

'I'm not with you, Sam. I'm proposing a simple business deal which will earn you a lot of dollars and you're waving your ethics in my face.' Steven smiled to soften his words and continued. 'Business isn't run on an ethical basis, we all know that—'

'More's the pity.'

'You can hardly say professional golf is, can you? It's very simple: the best player gets the biggest prize. It's straightforward law-of-the-jungle capitalism.'

'We're getting off the subject,' Rhodes said. 'There are environmental considerations, too. All this meat that chains like Rossner's use is factory-farmed. All those cattle devouring vast quantities of grain so that the industrialised countries can grow fat on burgers. That grain could go to feed the Third World. It's all wrong.'

'I agree with you, Sam,' Steven said gently, though he'd have liked to scream at him, 'but I have a responsibility to you and my other clients to maximise your income. You won't always be a hot favourite to win the Masters, you won't always be winning tournaments. I just want you to be totally secure when you retire.'

'I'm secure now, Steven.'

'That may be so but many of my other clients are not. Like young Billy Grayson. He's supporting two brothers and two sisters through school and college and he's a part of this deal with Rossner.'

Steven had suggested Grayson merely as a bit of filling in the sandwich; after all he didn't want to use too many of his powerful clients on this initial deal with Rossner. He had originally had high hopes of the young player, who'd had a brilliant record as an amateur, but he hadn't yet come to terms with the demands of the professional game. Steven liked him and sympathised with his problems but was only prepared to give him one more year as a client; he'd have to start winning or go.

Aware that Grayson's name had caught Rhodes's attention, Steven pressed home his advantage. 'I didn't want to tell you this,' he said earnestly, 'but if you don't participate, it kills the deal. And Grayson needs the money, it'll give him a real boost just when he needs it. So, will you think about it?'

'Yes, Steven, I'll think about it.' I don't have any option but to agree, Rhodes thought gloomily.

'OK, I'll accept your decision, whatever it is,' Steven said cheerfully. He knew he'd done the trick by appealing to the philanthropic side of his client's nature.

Later that evening Sam Rhodes called Suzi at her New York house. After asking what she and Adam had been doing during the day, he told her about Steven's proposals for the Rossner deal. Suzi was unequivocal. 'Don't do it if you're unhappy with it. I know how you feel about these fast food joints and you've told Steven often enough that you want to remain selective about your endorsements. Well, don't waver, darling.'

'You're right, Suzi, but I do feel awful sorry for young Billy Grayson.'

'That's exactly how my husband wants you to feel. He's conning you.'

'Maybe, but he's a helluva good agent, whatever you feel about him. He's looked after me real well. Anyway, let's change the subject. When will I see you?'

Since his starting time for the first round was not until after lunch, Sam Rhodes spent a part of the following morning on routine matters. He made inroads, first of all, on his correspondence. All fans received handwritten replies and he made a point of writing to thank the sponsor of the previous week's tournament. He also called Steven and told him that he would go along with the Rossner deal.

'I'm not that keen, Steven, but I couldn't possibly blow it out of the water, not with those other players involved and especially Billy.'

'That's good news. I'm grateful.'

'I'll probably give my share to some environmental charity. Greenpeace, maybe?'

'Conscience money?'

'Exactly what it is, Steven.'

He could do what he liked with it, Steven thought. His own end of the deal was now safe and sound.

After the first three rounds of the Masters, the leader board had a cosmopolitan look: Barbier led the field, with Rhodes in second place, along with the Australian Vince Holman and a little-known South African. The scene was set for an almighty struggle on the last day. The smooth power and elegant touch of the American would be pitted against the aggression and inventiveness of the Frenchman.

Barbier had spent more time than usual on the practice ground that evening and, after a quiet dinner with his parents, he went to his room and watched the television. He hopped the channels for a few minutes, found a Clint Eastwood film and settled down on his bed. The telephone beside him woke him about an hour later and Barbier heard a rough American voice say, 'Don't try to win tomorrow, you French motherfucker.'

'That must be Sam Rhodes,' Barbier said with a laugh. 'Now come on, Sam, it's only a game. May the best man win and all that.'

'Very funny,' the voice said. 'You won't look so fucking funny with a bullet in your head. You'll look fucking messy. I'll make sure it's done on a good hole, let's say the sixteenth.'

'But that's one of my favourite holes,' Barbier began to say as the line went dead. '*Va te faire foutre*,' he muttered to the receiver as he replaced it.

Most people in the public eye are subject to nuisance calls and sportsmen are more vulnerable than most. Barbier had received his share of them and had always shrugged them off. They were sick people who rarely, if ever, attempted to carry out their puerile threats. He wondered whether to report the call to the police, but what could they do? Form a human shield around him? That would make it difficult to play his shots. He tried to be flippant but he was unnerved. He checked the locks on the door and the windows and then told himself not to be childish. It was some deranged American chauvinist. Maybe he could tell the cops and ask them to keep the whole thing low-key. But he guessed that Georgia's police didn't do low-key and he had visions of gun-toting policemen in body armour all over the course. That wouldn't be conducive to producing his best golf. Barbier decided not to mention the threatening call, not even to his parents. He didn't want to spoil their day.

But their day, and the day of everyone connected with the great tournament was spoiled anyway when an anonymous call to the Press Association alerted the world to the threat to Barbier's life.

Steven enjoyed the headline in the *Atlanta Journal*. 'DEATH THREAT TO MASTERS CONTENDER', it read, followed by 'YOU WILL BE KILLED ON 16TH HOLE, SAYS MYSTERY CALLER.'

The news dominated the television screens and the local Chief of Police promised a massive security operation. No, he would not disclose any details for obvious reasons. A spokesman for the Augusta National club said that the Pinkerton Agency's security force was being reinforced and their operatives would mingle with the crowd to look for anything suspicious.

'Well, that's one way of getting a ticket to see the Masters,' the programme's presenter said jocularly.

Barbier stayed in his room throughout the morning. He and his parents chatted in desultory fashion and eventually, in order to ease their tension, his father went down to the hotel lobby and bought a pack of cards. They played three-handed poker for matchsticks until midday when Barbier, with six policemen for company plus a few hundred journalists, headed for the practice ground. He looked as composed and as cheerful as usual and, when a journalist asked him whether he was worried by the prospect of the sixteenth hole, Barbier replied, 'Yes, it's a tough hole, lots of water and a difficult pin position.'

'Aw, come on, Patrice,' the man persisted amid his colleagues' laughter, 'what's the plan?'

'I'm going to ask my caddie and Sam Rhodes to stand very close to me. That's all I have to say. OK?'

As Patrice Barbier was announced on the first tee there was a massive and prolonged round of applause. Then an eerie silence. Policemen, with their backs to the tee and to the fairway, scanned the spectators for any suspicious movements. The television pundits decided that the Frenchman, regrettably, had no chance of winning the Masters; nor had Rhodes who was caught up in a disturbing situation through no fault of his own. Vince Holman was the popular choice to win. One of the commentators wondered melodramatically how Barbier would even manage to get his clubhead back from the ball, such was the tension.

After fifteen holes of shifting fortunes Rhodes and Barbier were level, four shots in front of their nearest challenger, Vince Holman. The destiny of the Masters was in their hands as they approached the fateful sixteenth tee.

Ringed by policemen, Barbier noticed that, despite the apparent danger, his caddie and Rhodes walked shoulder to shoulder with him. More policemen were spread out at intervals down both sides of one of the most famous short holes in golf and several were perched in the trees that ran to the left and the right. Barbier gestured at the expanse of water that ran from the front of the tee almost to the back of the green on the left.

'Maybe there's a guy in a mini-submarine waiting for me,' he said.

'It's your honour, Patrice,' said Rhodes, to indicate that his opponent was to play first. 'I'll stand close to you, if that's any help.'

'No, Sam, you've done enough. Nothing will happen. Let's play golf and forget that lunatic.'

As Barbier placed his ball on a wooden tee-peg, the thousands of spectators made no discernible sounds. Only the breeze disturbed the silence, as it brought a shallow sigh from the trees and a placid ripple from the water. Barbier threw some wisps of grass in the air to test the strength and direction of the wind. Some onlookers later claimed, as the years passed and reality became myth, that the grass hovered near Barbier's shoulder for minutes rather than seconds.

Trust your swing, Barbier told himself, relax, let your mind go blank. With a beautifully rhythmic action he flowed down and through the ball and watched it take wing into the succulent blue of the sky. At the top of its ascent it seemed to hover for a moment and then plunged into the green. The cheers of some fans were stifled as the ball stopped dead, clinging to the top edge of the green, a long way from the flag. Then, as gently as a teardrop, it began to move and the fans shouted with excitement and joy as it rolled inexorably on and on towards the hole.

Patrice Barbier had a tap-in birdie of less than a foot to give him the lead. Victory was his less than half an hour later. With a beaming face he hurled his ball into the crowd and stood, arms raised high in triumph, as the crowd's applause erupted around Augusta. Sam Rhodes was the first person to congratulate him, closely followed by Barbier's caddie.

Barbier's parents pushed their way through the throng of

excited spectators and kissed and hugged their son. Steven Shaw was right behind them and made sure that his congratulations were suitably fulsome; he pumped the Frenchman's hand ostentatiously for several seconds. The new Masters Champion was so overcome that he lapsed into his native language. '*Vous êtes mes invités, ce soir,*' he said to Steven and Rhodes. 'I'm sorry – please join me for dinner this evening. We will have a little celebration.'

'Love to, Patrice,' Steven replied. 'But I've got to get back to New York. Some other time. You played fantastic golf in very difficult circumstances. It was a stunning display.'

# Chapter Thirty-one

It was Steven's practice to arrive in London a few days before the Wimbledon Tennis Championships began but a call from Kenny Crane forced him to fly to London a day earlier than usual.

The two men met in Steven's office and Steven studied the face of the man on the other side of his desk. It was still a good face, lean, and with humour never far from the surface; it was tanned and creased from daily exposure to the elements.

They had a problem on their hands: Francesca Zanini. Now eighteen years of age, she was the holder of the French title, the losing finalist at Wimbledon in the previous year and the favourite to win it in three weeks' time. She would be Kenny Crane's first real champion and a huge amount of money was riding on her talents.

The hidden tape recorder was running in Steven's office. If necessary, he would have the conversation edited so that what remained of his own questions and comments would sound harmless. Fortunately, he knew a BBC sound recordist who was a genius at manipulating audiotape. You couldn't see the join.

'Just because her poxy father played football in the back streets of Milan,' Crane said quietly, 'he thinks he knows about training a tennis player. He's just a fucking nuisance.'

'He did coach her when she was young,' Steven said mildly. 'He's bound to take an interest.'

'His main interest is lining his own bank account. And that's not the only thing—'

'I know,' Steven said quickly. 'He's doing deals for her on the side.'

'It's a bloody sight worse than that. Fran tells me, on the quiet, that he wants to manage her. He doesn't see why they should pay you twenty-five per cent of the take. Especially when she wins Wimbledon.'

'Will she?'

'Yeah, best chance she'll ever have.' Crane reached into his trouser pocket, found a packet of chewing gum and popped a piece into his mouth.

'Is she a stayer? How many more major titles? Will she still be around in five years, ten years?'

'No chance, mate. She's a big girl and her body's already had too much stress. That crazy bastard of a father had her doing hundreds of sit-ups and press-ups every day from the age of six. He pushed her each day of her life. The poor little cow never had a childhood, and what's worse is that she never had an education.'

'Does she realise what she's missed?'

'No way. She can't think past her next training session. But the trouble is she's injury prone and the strains are beginning to hurt. She's never been given time to recover properly in the past and it's beginning to catch up with her. And Christ knows what that crazy bastard of a doctor, Rexel, has been feeding her. I made sure I didn't ever ask, but I can guess. Anyway, all that wear and tear is taking its toll and when her body's fucked her mind'll go at the same time. It'll all become too much for her, mate.'

'So, we've got a year or two,' Steven summarised, 'and we don't want any problems from papa. We've got to get him out of the frame.'

'How? He's her father, for Chrissake.'

'Any abuse? Physical? Sexual?'

'Naah, I think he's whacked her occasionally but it's the verbal abuse that Mauro is really good at.'

'Lesbian or straight?'

'Oh, she's straight enough.'

'Good, that makes it simpler. Boyfriend?'

'No.'

'OK, Kenny, this is where you step in.'

'Step in? What d'you mean?'

'Screw her and keep on screwing her.'

Crane laughed. 'Don't be bloody stupid. Anyway I don't like girls with big arses.'

'Well don't give it to her from the back then.'

'Are you serious?'

'Do I look as if I'm joking? Look, Kenny, we've got to get rid of this jerk, Mauro. He annoys you by interfering with Fran's training and, even worse, he's trying to mess up my business relationship with her. If we let him, he'll bugger us on both fronts. You're her coach, she trusts you. She probably hates her father but she's used to relying on him. You're her real father-figure and she's probably longing to open her legs for you. You get into bed with her and that's Mauro on the sidelines.'

'I'm a coach not a fucking gigolo.'

'What's the difference? Most of the other coaches and ball-hitters are doing it – with the ones who aren't dykes, that is.'

Crane looked at the floor for a few moments and chewed rhythmically on his gum. He had given up cigarettes several months ago and the chewing helped to allay his craving for nicotine.

'Steven, I don't care what the other fuckers do, it's what I want to do. Coaches should have ethics. How can I act in

Fran's best interests, advise her, bollock her when necessary, if I'm in her pants. I can't do it.'

'Smarten up, Kenny, this is in her best interests. You can worry about ethics in a few years' time when you're counting your money. Remember that I've got a big stake in your tennis academy. You've had some good players under your wing but if Fran Zanini wins Wimbledon it'll make you as a coach and it'll put the tennis academies on the map in a big way. At the moment, you're earning good money from her and from Ferraris, and you'll get a helluva bonus if Fran wins Wimbledon. But that'll be nothing to what you'll make when we build you up as Zanini's guru. She'll be your protégée, your champion. We'll really expand the academies. We'll open up all over the world. Shit, you'll be in clover for the rest of your days.'

Crane began to speak but Steven cut him short. 'You screwed everything that moved when you were on the circuit, so what's the problem?'

'That wasn't the same.'

'Well, it's up to you, Kenny. You're a client of this agency and you'll be an important one and a rich one if Fran stays with us. You know the form, you know how much work we've put in for that girl. If she wins Wimbledon, she's worth millions in endorsements, I've got deals in the pipeline worth more than ten big ones.'

Steven stood up to emphasise the point he was making. 'I'm not going to let that Italian clown of a father fuck us about. This is when I capitalise on my investment, when the money really rolls in. For both of us. Come on, Kenny, see some sense.'

'If I start screwing her, she'll ditch me eventually. I'd give it a year. If she gets emotionally attached to me, her coach, it'll be too much for her.'

'So it's a short-term solution. Who cares? You and I'd

better pray that she wins Wimbledon. You say she'll be washed up soon afterwards anyway. And there'll always be another superstar for us, someone scratching and clawing her way up the rankings.'

With a shrug, Crane got up, said he'd think about it and left the office. Steven rewound the tape, labelled it and put it in the safe. It would end up in one of his banks, secure under lock and key.

On the following day, Crane subjected Fran Zanini to physical and mental pressure that she had rarely experienced. At one point, even her father protested at the barrage of demands and criticisms.

Crane walked over to the squat, grey-haired Mauro Zanini, put his sweating face close to the Italian's and snarled, 'You want your daughter to be a champion? Well, either shut up or piss off out of here, I don't need your interference.'

At the end of the practice session, Fran Zanini slumped into a chair, put her hands over her face and sobbed. Crane knelt in front of her, put his hands on her shoulders and gripped her hard.

'Come on, Frannie,' he said, 'you did great. I've got to push you, it's the only way. You get back to the hotel and rest and then we'll have an early dinner tonight. Just the two of us. We'll relax, have a few laughs. OK?'

She nodded her agreement and her father busily ushered her off to the courtesy car.

During their meal in a bistro at the unfashionable end of the King's Road, Crane did not pay any attention to a man who sat alone in a corner and read a newspaper throughout his meal. Nor did he register the man's presence in the hotel corridor when he accompanied Fran Zanini into her room.

Earlier that day the man had placed a miniature

transmitter in the girl's room. In his own room just down the corridor, he switched on his receiver. After a few minutes, he heard the sounds for which he was waiting.

From a telephone box in the hotel lobby the man called Steven Shaw's London house.

'They're at it,' he said and put down the receiver.

Steven smiled and rejoined his guests.

# Chapter Thirty-two

When he reviewed the work of his London office, Steven was delighted to see how prosperous it had become. As well as the staple business in golf and tennis and the agency's thriving trade in television rights, Dean Aultman's forays into athletics and motor racing were bearing dividends. Angus Gray had already won two grand prix races and was now being touted in the newspapers as the next world champion. In the past, Gray had been forced to beg his drives in the grand prix races but now he was being courted by two of the most successful teams in Formula One. The time was near when the agency would begin to make real money from him. Aultman was already talking in terms of a multi-million-pound contract for the next season.

The Friday before Wimbledon was the day on which Shaw Management held its annual party. The evening was an opportunity to entertain clients and sponsors in one fell swoop, and one of Steven's favourite social occasions of the year. He was the focal point of the affair, an immensely successful entrepreneur at the heart of a web of business arrangements that spread densely through sport, the media and industry. It delighted him to think that the managing directors of major public companies waited eagerly for their invitations and amazed him how easily those hard-headed and powerful businessmen succumbed to the heady attractions of being in the presence of a sporting superstar.

His clients' fame rubbed off on Shaw himself. He carried his own aura of glamour and knew how to exploit it: the boardroom doors were flung open wide for him.

How he would have liked to rub the Macaulays' patrician noses in the sweet smell of his success. Shaw, who never forgot or forgave his enemies, had instructed Dan Fisher to keep tabs on James Macaulay, but had been told little of interest. He must remind Fisher to dig deeper.

With some apprehension he had invited his parents to the party. He was counting on Suzi, who was arriving in London with her mother on the day before the party, to look after them, and he would have to keep a very wary eye on his father's drinking.

Whenever the work-load became excessive, Dean Aultman took on temporary staff from a nearby employment agency. As soon as Steven caught sight of Lesley West he decided that it would be fun to add her to his list of conquests. She had an aloof manner which very attractive women sometimes affect and the unmistakable vocal intonations of the English middle class. But it was her tight, taut behind that caught his eye. He wondered how aloof she'd be when he sank his teeth into it.

Steven knew that the only gap in his schedule was that evening. After he finished dictating some letters to Lucy Howard, she said, 'Are we getting together this evening?'

'I don't think so, Lucy.'

'There's nothing in your diary, so I thought . . .'

'I've got a few things to do, we'll find some time together next week maybe.'

'But your wife will be here.'

'Love will find a way,' Steven said, with a reassuring smile. 'Can you send that temp in, please – Lesley, I think her name is.'

Disappointed, Lucy left his office. She thought she was in love with Steven and it was obvious he was going to try his luck with Lesley West. Stuck-up bitch. Never mind, men like him were restless, competitive: you had to make allowances for them. Lesley was just a one-night stand. Steven would be back in her own arms soon, and she'd welcome him, as always.

Although she had another date that evening, Lesley West had no compunction in cancelling it in favour of a drink with Steven. For one thing, he was rich and handsome, and for another it would annoy that cow, Lucy Howard. She hated the way she lorded it in the agency as Mr Shaw's personal secretary. She had such a dewy-eyed devotion to the man; it was really sickening.

Steven took Lesley to a nearby wine bar and they shared a bottle of champagne. She liked him. He was amusing and attentive, nothing like the serious and purposeful person she had been told he was. As they finished the bottle, Steven suggested that they ordered a meal to be sent round to his house.

'It'll be more comfortable,' he said, 'and I use a gourmet service for take-away meals. Anything you fancy. French, English, Thai, Italian, Chinese . . .'

She was impressed by the house and looked forward to dining in style. He was bound to ask her to go to bed with him and she hadn't quite decided whether to do so or not.

Lesley was startled when Steven said, 'Shall we eat afterwards?'

'Afterwards? After what?' She was admiring one of Steven's paintings in his sitting room.

'It's a Jasper Johns,' he said in her ear and folded his arms around her. She leaned her head back towards his. He spun her round and bent to kiss her. Lesley responded and his kisses became fiercer. She felt his hand stroking her buttocks. 'Let's have some fun in bed,' he murmured, 'then dinner and then some more fun.'

Lesley pushed him away. 'You're being presumptuous, Steven.'

'No, just straightforward,' he said with a grin and, sure of his charm, took her in his arms again, though more gently this time. Lesley felt she had regained control and returned his kisses. She allowed him to unbutton her shirt and caress her breasts, but when he bent his mouth to her nipple she felt again that he was moving too quickly. She tried to break away but he held her tightly and she felt a sharp pain as he sucked hard at her breast. His attentions were now decidedly unwelcome and she tried harder to struggle free. He pushed her on to a sofa and she became aware of just how helpless she was against his weight and strength.

'Steven, Steven, please don't,' she pleaded as he pushed up her skirt.

He paused and pulled back to look at her. 'Come on, Lesley, you and I know why you're here. You like to fuck, don't you? What if I give you a couple of hundred pounds? How about that?'

He tore at her panties and she felt panic at her inability to defend herself. Lesley felt his fingers prying between her legs and suddenly found some strength. She managed to push him from her and drove her knee into his groin. Steven gasped with pain and staggered back, but only for a moment. 'You bitch,' he said furiously and lashed her across the face with his open hand. Partly stunned, Lesley found herself thrown on to the carpet. Face down, with Steven's hand tight on the back of her neck, she couldn't cry out. His knee was in the small of her back and, with his free hand, he was tearing once more at her underclothes. Desperately afraid, she stopped her futile struggles and went limp. To her intense relief, she felt him release his grip.

Lesley rolled over, scrambled to her knees and then to her feet. She was sobbing. Watching her from an armchair, Steven wondered why he'd allowed himself to lose control. Why hadn't the stupid bitch just got on with it? She'd probably screwed half the hooray Henrys in London, so why make a fuss?

'I'm sorry,' he said. 'We both went too far. Why don't we start again from square one? Let me get you a drink. A brandy would be best, I think.'

'Start again? You bastard, you hit me and then indecently assaulted me. I'm going to the police.'

'I wouldn't bother. It's your word against mine. And I must tell you that I have an associate here in London who'll dig up every scrap of dirt on you if necessary. If there isn't enough, he'll invent it and he'll make it stick to you. So, let's be sensible about this. No harm was done.'

'No harm was done?' Lesley said, aghast. 'No harm? You just assume that women are there for the taking, whenever you fancy a quick fuck, don't you? Well, I'm not, and certainly not for an arrogant jumped-up shit like you.'

Steven shrugged. Now that she was talking he knew she was unlikely to go to the police. If she did, Dan Fisher would fix her. But, better to resolve things now. 'As I said, let's be sensible, Lesley. We've had a misunderstanding and I'm sorry. Why don't I make up for that? I'll make you an *ex gratia* payment. I'm sure that would be better than some silly court case, which wouldn't do either of us any good.'

'How much?'

'Two thousand pounds in cash, as long as you don't come near me, this house or my office again. Don't try and come back for any more because unpleasant things will happen to you if you do. Agreed?'

'Agreed.'

'Fine. Go to this address tomorrow at noon and a man called Dan Fisher will give you the money.' He wrote down the address of a nearby flat which he used for 'business entertaining'. After Lesley West had left the house, Steven called Fisher and made the arrangements for her pay-off.

'By the way, Dan,' he concluded, 'make sure the transaction's on video, won't you?' He knew that Fisher would keep his face out of camera shot. 'And put some surveillance on the bitch, just for insurance. I want to know where she lives, where she goes, who her friends are.'

Fisher replaced his receiver. It was the second pay-off he'd been asked to make on Shaw's behalf. There'd been that whore last year. He'd knocked seven bells out of her. One day he'd go too far.

The offices of Shaw Management, though spacious, could hardly contain the throng of people who attended the pre-Wimbledon party. The food had been prepared by a chef whose restaurant was the proud possessor of a Michelin star and the champagne and the wines had been carefully selected by Dean Aultman, in consultation with his own wine merchant. Aultman had not only secured a substantial discount but had also negotiated a gift for his own use of two cases of vintage champagne. In deference to the presence of Steven's father and, more so, of several representatives of the Rugby Football Union, he had also ordered a barrel of beer. The waitresses were all attractive and many of them were willing to make freelance arrangements with the guests for later in the evening. Steven had earmarked a discreet number of important guests to continue the party, together with some girls, at the apartment he rented nearby. It had five bedrooms, four of which had both video and still cameras to record whatever happened therein.

Steven guessed that Suzi would leave him free to continue the party. She would be happy to shepherd his parents back to their hotel and then go back to his house with her mother.

As he and Suzi stood in the reception area of the London office and waited for the first guests to arrive, Steven knew that they appeared to be the perfect couple. He looked at his wife with a dispassionate eye and realised that she was, in her greater maturity, more beautiful than ever. Betty Lynagh looked fondly at them as their photograph was taken by Rory McCall, whose usual beat encompassed the higher strata of the city's society. What a beautiful couple: a man who had reached several pinnacles of business success but was pressing on to greater heights, handsome and assured; and her stunning daughter, smiling and relaxed. Surely her doubts about their marriage must be unfounded.

The cameras clicked again as the first guests arrived at the door. Steven knew that several of the newspapers would carry items about the party in their gossip columns and the invaluable Frank Lawford, still at large on his behalf in Fleet Street, had secured a feature in a London evening newspaper.

Andrew McDonnell was among the first arrivals, and the Chief Executive of the Continental Tobacco Company had brought his wife with him. As he smiled at them, Steven remembered how Continental's Advertising Director described McDonnell's wife. Dreary. Christ, that was doing Mary McDonnell a favour. Dressed in a dark grey and shapeless smock and devoid of make-up, she looked like a caricature of a provincial earth-mother. John Springett, the advertising man, was also expected at the party. He now received an annual retainer from Shaw Management and was an invaluable source of information on the company and on McDonnell.

The trickle of guests soon became a flood. Steven and Suzi stood firm in the hall and greeted every person. Remembering old Charles Macaulay's habit of using prompt cards when he greeted his guests at the department store's annual dinner and dance, Steven used the same technique. He'd committed the details to memory but had the cards in his pocket just in case.

Paul Davis, the Head of Sport at the BBC, arrived with his new girlfriend, Jacqui Bryson, whom he introduced as one of his assistant producers. Steven knew that they had been sleeping together for several months and that she was a former student of the London School of Economics; she had played for a few unsuccessful years on the professional tennis circuit.

After more than an hour of greeting his guests, an eclectic mix of sponsors, media people, publishers, sports equipment manufacturers, clients and sports officials, Steven decided that it was time to do the rounds in earnest. Suzi went to look after her mother and his, whereas Steven joined Angus Gray, who was not, as expected, talking about motor racing but about fishing in Scotland. Gray had a pleasant voice, without a trace of a Scottish accent. Steven thought that, if his client could win the Formula One Championship a couple of times and stay alive, he could have a wonderful long-term career as a television pundit. Gray spoke eagerly about the pleasures of fishing on the Tweed as a guest of dukes and other aristocracy. He had good connections and that was a helpful asset for a client to have.

Out of the corner of his eye, Steven could see his father, strategically positioned close to the barrel of beer, drain his glass of bitter and pour himself another. He was talking to several large men in dark suits, all of whom were wearing crested or striped club ties. They were the rugby officials whom Dean Aultman was cultivating; he wanted to handle their television rights which would be big business one day, especially with the Rugby World Cup in the offing.

Steven made his way slowly through the animated throng towards his father. He put his arm lightly and affectionately round his narrow shoulders. 'Hi, Dad, are you enjoying yourself? Is the beer OK?'

'Fine, son, fine.'

'Your father's telling us about his days in Macaulay's store,' one of the burly men said. 'He's had us in fits.'

'Well, don't let him start on the war,' Steven said with a smile, as he moved on. So far, so good; the old man seemed well in control.

The decibel level was now so high that the guests had to shout at each other. The waitresses moved swiftly around the room in a valiant attempt to keep up with the demand for wine and food.

Across a gap, Steven spotted the slender figure of Toby Streeter, the Editor of his golf magazine. He was standing close to Jacqui Bryson and they were laughing and talking at the same time. Steven wondered just how well they knew each other. Maybe they were planning to get really well acquainted, although Fisher's inspection of Streeter's past had not revealed any sexual adventures. Maybe he preferred men, but there was no evidence of that either. A few minutes later, Steven intercepted Streeter and said, 'Is Jacqui Bryson a friend of yours?'

There was surprise in Streeter's blue eyes and he brushed his long hair nervously back from his forehead. 'We were at LSE together. Why?'

'Nothing. She's helped us with a few things at the BBC.'

Within half an hour, some of the guests began to drift away and it became possible to talk in comfort again. Steven made a strict effort to talk to all those people to whom he had not paid enough attention. He was chatting about the possibility of doing Angus Gray's diary of the Formula One racing season with a wild-eyed publisher with unkempt black hair which, though thin, had deposited copious flakes of dandruff on the shoulders of his weary blue suit, when a commotion started in the corner of the room where the beer barrel had been set up. Two of the rugby men were hoisting Bill Shaw on to one of the tables and were calling for quiet.

'Bill Shaw will now give his rendition of "Trees",' one of them announced with gusto.

His mother was a few yards away and Steven saw her lips purse in disdain and her face tighten with embarrassment. He wanted to intervene but it was too late as his father, half-full pint pot in hand, launched into the first verse.

'"I think that I will never see
A poem lovely as a tree."'

At least he knew all the words and he got the tune more or less right, even if his intake of alcohol caused him to waver occasionally.

When Bill Shaw finished there was an outburst of applause, orchestrated initially by the rugby men but then spreading throughout the room. Steven felt deeply embarrassed and wondered why his father, however much he'd drunk, had done such a thing in front of his clients and guests. His mother was looking rigidly at the floor but Steven forced himself to walk across the room and hug his father. Then he turned and held his father's arm aloft like a triumphant boxer.

'If he performs like this,' Steven shouted, 'I'll have to take my father on as a client.'

Suzi kissed Bill Shaw and said, 'That was wonderful, Pop, wonderful. And now I'm going to take you and Mary back to your hotel for a rest.'

Steven knew that his father would be in for a fearsome dressing-down from his mother: she would tell him in several different ways how he had let her and his son down in front of all those people. On the following morning, Steven said so to Suzi, but she and Betty Lynagh protested that it had been one of the highlights of the evening.

'It was nice and spontaneous,' Suzi said. 'Giving the other guests a song came naturally to your pop. Everyone enjoyed it. You shouldn't be so stuffy.'

Nevertheless, Steven vowed not to let his father near one of his parties again.

# Chapter Thirty-three

It was a highly successful Wimbledon for Shaw Management. Three of the men's and four of the ladies' quarter-finalists were clients of the agency. Once again, Ray Gerrard powered his way to the title, and Francesca Zanini, motivated as never before by her coach, Kenny Crane, who not only supervised her by day but made love to her by night, won the ladies' singles title.

It was to be Zanini's one and only Wimbledon crown. During the following year, she suffered a number of injuries. She dismissed Crane as her coach and her father, Mauro, took over.

John Winter captured Zanini's moments of glory with his cameras and skilfully intercut the action sequences with the interview she had recorded for him just before the Championships began. He also managed to speak to Ray Gerrard for a few minutes. Winter intercepted him as he pushed his way off an outside court during the first week. Gerrard had just had an easy win over a qualifier from Sweden.

With a bag over his shoulder, rackets under his one arm and surrounded by fans clamouring for his autograph, Gerrard wanted to keep on the move. But this tall and craggy man, dressed in old corduroy trousers and a rumpled shirt, barred his way.

'Mr Gerrard, I'd like to talk to you some time. I'm John Winter.'

'Fix it through my agent.'

'Steven Shaw?'

'Yeah.'

'I'm working for him. I'm a television producer. But I really want to talk to you about Nils Ryberg.'

It was his wish to get away from the fans, to have a shower and return to his hotel that motivated Gerrard to take the easiest way out.

'Why don't you call me at my hotel?'

'Thank you. I'll call you this evening.'

Gerrard knew that he could avoid Winter if he so wished. But maybe he would talk to him. He'd always been puzzled by Nils's suicide; he just wasn't the kind of guy to give up the ghost like that. It wouldn't surprise him if Shaw had had something to do with it, somewhere along the line. Gerrard was now convinced that Shaw had set him up earlier in the year with that under-age tart in Los Angeles. He'd been so terrified by the whole bizarre situation that he'd gone along with everything that he and that lawyer, Mike Russo, had told him to do. Later, it had occurred to Gerrard that Russo had never given him a business card or an office telephone number; everything had been handled through Shaw's office. Was he really a lawyer or just a part of the plot?

Gerrard hadn't dared to contact Luisa Ebbers, who had been so keen to secure him as a client. He had simply written her a note to say that he had signed up again with Steven Shaw. At tournaments thereafter, they avoided each other but, after a while, Gerrard took courage and asked her about the January night she had failed to appear for their dinner. She had denied all knowledge of the arrangement; it was a misunderstanding. Some misunderstanding.

The telephone rang. It was John Winter and could he see Mr Gerrard? Well, maybe tomorrow. Why not now, since he was downstairs in the lobby?

'Hell, why not?' Gerrard said. 'Come on up.'

Winter accepted a beer from the fridge and Gerrard sipped at his habitual can of cola. The tennis was still being shown on the television but the American turned the sound down.

'Bloody tennis,' he muttered.

'You sound disillusioned,' said Winter.

'Yeah. It's a treadmill but every step has a pot of gold on it.'

'So, why complain?'

'I don't. Well, not very often, anyway.'

'Tell me, Ray,' Winter said, after taking a sip of beer, 'do you think Ryberg was a homosexual who committed suicide out of remorse because he was "outed" by the press?'

'No. I saw a lot of Nils. There was no sign that he was gay, no rumours, nothing. He was a sincere Christian, happy with his wife and his child.'

'So, what went wrong? You, after all, were the main beneficiary. The Larssen contract and a Wimbledon title went to you.'

Gerrard looked sharply at him. 'It sounds as if you're condemning me for doing my job. I won the championship fair and square, even if it was one of the lousiest finals for years.'

'I didn't mean that. But it was very convenient, wasn't it? A revolutionary racket, a huge endorsement contract up for grabs and the front-runner for both is suddenly taken out. Was it a conspiracy to discredit him, d'you think?'

'That's a shade elaborate, isn't it?' But worthy of Steven Shaw, thought Gerrard.

As if reading those thoughts, Winter said, 'Too elaborate for your agent? I wonder. I had a curious conversation recently with Terri Calvin. She categorised Shaw as clever and utterly unscrupulous. She also made the point that his clients always seem to get the air time with AAN and BBC—'

'Well, he does have the best players.'

'Agreed, but she was suggesting that he has *undue* influence. She also said that Shaw gave her the creeps.'

Gerrard laughed. 'That sounds like Terri, always ready to have a go.'

'Is she right?'

'Shaw's tough and ruthless,' Gerrard said guardedly. 'The best agent in the business. You'd want him for you, not against you, that's for sure.'

'What if he'd been for Ryberg? Would he still be alive? And perhaps as rich or richer than you?'

'I can't answer that, John, but I'd advise you to stay on the right side of him. It could be very dangerous otherwise.'

Steven Shaw was in a confident mood when he entered the City of London offices of the Amalgamated International Banking Corporation. AIB was one of the biggest financial conglomerates in the world, with branches in every country. One of its greatest strengths was its credit card operation which spanned the world, and he was attending a meeting to finalise a deal whereby Sam Rhodes would front a world-wide campaign to promote the AIB credit card. Three years, up to five television commercials a year plus advertising in other media, six personal appearances a year; it all added up to a multi-million-dollar deal with a blue-chip company. Just what Sam Rhodes liked, but, above all, what Steven Shaw liked.

AIB had undertaken some extensive research which concluded that a sportsman like Sam Rhodes embodied the image that the corporation was trying to project. He was a winner; he had integrity; he had class and charisma.

It was a comparatively easy sell for Steven, but he had acquired a bit of insurance cover by inviting the Advertising and Media Director to one of the tournaments run by Shaw Management. It took place at the end of the year in the West Indies and the Director, who apparently lived a blameless married life in Surrey, had revealed a copious appetite for black rent-boys. It was reassuring to have an edge, Steven had reflected at the time.

All the hard work had been done and the meeting was a formality, called to tidy up some loose contractual ends. The real motivation was to have a celebratory lunch; Steven was to join the Advertising Director, the Marketing Director and the President of the International Division of AIB in the boardroom. Perched on top of the towering office block, it was a sumptuous octagonal room, with wide windows on four of the sides. In between, there were oak panels carved by Grinling Gibbons and rescued from a building long since demolished. From the windows could be seen the other priapic City buildings, thrusting themselves brutally skywards, symbols of the gross materialism of the decade. Steven felt at home in such a cityscape and he sparkled on such occasions. He was there by right, accepted as an equal by businessmen with real power. He felt more equal since his business peers hung on his every story of this client or that client. Jock-sniffers all, that's what they were. Or maybe jock-suckers was a better word for them; it certainly described their women.

As Steven had predicted, the remaining details were quickly resolved. Everyone wanted to get into the boardroom for lunch, which was long and convivial. He promised the President that he would have the contract ready for signature by the time that Sam Rhodes arrived in Britain for the Open Championship in a few days' time.

Perhaps they could arrange a formal signing at the Open itself, which was to be played at St Andrews.

As he landed in Edinburgh, Sam Rhodes was unhappy at the thought of a confrontation with his business manager. A few days ago, he had received a letter in which Steven outlined the proposed contract with AIB. It was a clever concept and it would align him with an international company of great repute; and Steven had emphasised, as always, the rewards, which were huge even by the standards set by him in the past.

But Rhodes didn't want any part of the deal. As he settled back in the limousine for the short journey to St Andrews, he wondered what ace Steven had up his sleeve to win the hand. There was bound to be one, as there had been when he had manoeuvred him into the contract with the fast food company.

As soon as St Andrews had been confirmed as the venue for the Open Championship, Dean Aultman had booked forty rooms in an hotel that overlooked the course. They were for Shaw Management employees and clients. Steven had also rented a large house not far from the centre of Edinburgh, which was fully staffed and liberally stocked with alcohol. He had recruited one of Scotland's best chefs for the week, along with half a dozen tarts from London. This was to be Shaw Management's entertainment centre.

Within an hour of his checking into his hotel suite, Rhodes received a call from Steven, who asked to see him.

'I need some sleep, Steven. Jet-lag.'

'No you don't. Jet-lag doesn't exist. It won't take more than a few minutes. I want to take you through the AIB deal.'

With a sigh, Rhodes agreed. He might as well get this over with and then he could concentrate on his golf.

Within minutes, Steven was at his door. He looked relaxed and cheerful, although Rhodes noticed the dark smudges of tiredness under his eyes. He knew what his schedule was like, as he covered his markets from New York to Los Angeles to Sydney to Tokyo to London. Rhodes shook his agent's hand and ushered him to a chair by the window. 'How are you, Steven? How's your golf? Are you playing much?'

'I haven't had the time, Sam. I'm too busy setting up deals for you.'

'You should make time. For instance you're within an hour's drive of one of the world's greatest courses, Carnoustie. Why don't you take some of the boys up there? Dean would love it and so would a New Yorker like Jay.'

'Sure, sure. You should see my schedule and theirs. Tomorrow begins not with one breakfast meeting but two.'

'You should slow down,' Rhodes said, hoping to postpone the inevitable disagreement. 'Suzi says so, too. I saw her and Adam in New York. They send their love.'

'Fine. Lucy Howard's booking me some time with Adam next week. However, to business. Here're the main points of the AIB deal on this sheet of paper. No problems there, I hope. It's just a matter of fitting the dates into your diary.'

'I'm not sure I want any more dates, Steven, and certainly not for AIB. Look, I've already got eight main sponsors. What with the photography and the TV commercials and the personal appearances that's a lot of time out of my year. And then there're the exhibition matches, you send me on a few of those, too.'

'They're bloody good business, Sam. Easy money, as you know.'

'Maybe, but it's out there that counts.' Rhodes gestured towards the expanse of the famous St Andrews course that lay beyond the windows. 'I'd trade an Open victory at St

Andrews for all the deals in the world, Steven.'

'You're a professional golfer, so the deals and the glory go hand-in-hand.'

'But if the deals get in the way, they have to go. And there's a danger that they are getting in the way, taking up too much of my time and energy. Jack has warned me not to dissipate my energies by chasing the dollars and I agree with him.'

Steven looked blankly at his client. 'Jack Shelley may be one of the best coaches in the game but he knows sod-all about business.'

'I grant you that, but he's got my best interests at heart. He's been there, Steven, he won the US Open and he knows the exhilaration of competition. You must know what that means, you've played good golf and good tennis.'

'I'm coming from a different direction, Sam. I get my kicks from setting up things like this AIB deal. It fits you like a glove, everybody's happy with the concept, so what's your problem with it?'

'The nature of AIB's business.'

'They're in the money business, they're a bank and a credit card business.'

'Yes and they've got huge investments in some of the most totalitarian regimes in the world. Chile, for instance, and South Africa. And they lend money to the Third World countries on ruinous terms that those countries simply can't afford.'

'That's their business. They lend money.'

'Come on, Steven, you must have some grasp of business ethics. It's not all grab, grab, grab, surely?'

Steven shrugged. 'We're getting well away from the subject.'

'No, it's very much on the subject. Even if I could give

AIB so much of my time, I wouldn't. I don't want to get involved with the company.'

'I can negotiate your commitments down, I'm sure. Fewer commercials, fewer appearances.'

'That's not my point and you know it. I don't like their moral stance.'

'Christ Almighty, how can you turn down all this money? There're millions of dollars at stake. And I've more or less committed you to the deal. What the hell do I tell the AIB President?'

'How about the truth? Now, Steven, I know you don't believe in jet-lag, but I'm a mere mortal and I need some rest.'

Steven got to his feet. 'Let's sleep on the problem, Sam, I'm sure we can work something out.'

'There's no point. You won't move me on this one.'

Sanctimonious bastard, Steven thought bitterly, as he strode away down the corridor. Did he really believe that turning down big bucks would help the Third World? Rhodes's tender moral scruples were going to deprive him of a million and a half dollars' commission at the very least. Christ, he reminded Steven of his wife – Suzi was getting very socially conscious these days. Collections for this worthy cause and that deserving charity. He stumped up the money and smiled but it was too much of a good thing when his clients went all righteous. Sportsmen were not supposed to think. They were there to tough it out in the arena while he made money out of them.

Steven didn't even have any holds over Rhodes. For one thing he'd never had him under surveillance, or bugged his telephones or his apartment. The bastard seemed to lead a blameless existence. His sex life was conventional enough: Steven had seen him with a succession of attractive women, who all seemed to fall in love with him but were eventually traded in for next year's model. Mind you, he seemed to be having a bit of a fallow period at the moment; Steven hadn't seen his client with anyone special recently. Rhodes wasn't greedy or flashy in any way. He had his condo in Florida and a modest apartment in New York. He'd even refused to put any of his money off-shore. It was all declared to the IRS and invested in conservative ventures. Shit, the man was too good to be true and Steven even liked him.

On the following morning, Carl Lansky, the Commissioner of the United States Professional Golfers' Association, was in the hotel lobby trying to locate his missing copy of the *Wall Street Journal*, when he saw the athletic figure of Steven Shaw issue from the elevator. The Commissioner, who presided over a Tour with purse money of around $50 million and additional revenue of roughly twice that amount, felt a surge of distaste and of unease when he saw the man. They had fought a guerrilla war for over five years. Lansky had instructed his staff to be as obstructive as possible when Shaw tried to obtain releases for his clients to play in tournaments outside America. But the agent had responded with more and more requests for such releases and had backed them up, when necessary, with the threat of legal action.

Initially, Lansky had expected him to overreach himself. But he now managed many of the top golfers and had become more and more powerful. Shaw was the unacceptable face of sporting capitalism. Lansky made no secret of his opinion that business managers should be drummed out of golf.

In the meantime, Lansky had to tackle the problem because some of the sponsors of the US Tour events were restive. The big golfing names were playing in Shaw's tournaments instead of the official events. What the hell was going on? they asked the Commissioner. Why did Sam Rhodes's schedule only encompass the minimum fifteen appearances on the Tour when the sponsors were clamouring for a superstar like him?

Never a man to side-step a problem, Lansky, a tall man with a square face and closely cut grey hair, decided to intercept Shaw, who was undoubtedly on his way to a breakfast meeting. Maybe an unofficial approach would help to dissipate the poison that infected their relationship.

Giving up his enquiries about the missing newspaper, Lansky hailed Steven. 'You're on your way to a meeting, I guess, Steven, but can you spare me a minute or two?'

With an ostentatious look at his watch Steven shrugged and led the way to a table in the corner of the reception area.

'I'll be frank with you, Steven. I'm a little grieved by the number of exemptions your clients are taking from the American Tour. We've got two important events following the British Open and we would've liked Sam Rhodes and several other fine players who also happen to be clients of yours to be there. But they're playing in Europe instead.'

'That's their privilege. They're freelance professional sportsmen and they play where they choose,' Steven replied with relish. 'As long as they fulfil their obligations to your Tour. Fifteen tournaments, and that's too many in my opinion.'

'The American Tour is the richest and best in the world. People like Sam Rhodes owe a great debt to it and I hope they feel obligated to support it fully. I know Sam is conscious of his duty to encourage the sponsors.'

'Yes, Sam's an honourable kind of guy. But he's also aware that there's a wider world of golf than the American

Tour. The Open, for instance. It means more to him than any of your tournaments, Carl.'

'That's understandable. The British Open is special but you can't say that for those Mickey Mouse tournaments he's playing in Europe.'

'Thanks for the compliment, Carl. One of them is run by my company, as you know. The sponsor is paying Sam a handsome fee to appear and both he and my client are very comfortable with the arrangement.'

'What about the other event? I hear that you're providing a nice little package deal – your clients turn out for the sponsor so long as you get to handle the TV rights. Isn't that so?'

Steven wondered who'd tipped Lansky off about his negotiating techniques. 'I market a wide range of services to sport.'

'Services,' Lansky said with a humourless laugh. 'It sounds more like blackmail.'

'Like the way you manipulate the tournament sponsors? The people with the most money get the best dates. At least I put the interests of my clients first. They're all on hefty guarantees to play.'

'Appearance money is just a scam invented by agents,' Lansky said bitterly. 'Thank God we don't allow it on our Tour.'

'So you say. But I thank God that we've got a free market over here in Europe. The sponsors want the superstars and I provide them, at a price. Not that my business arrangements are anything to do with you.'

'They are if you foul up my arrangements with my sponsors. Rhodes and Vince Holman are members of the American Tour and that's where their duty is—'

'Bullshit, Carl. They're free agents. I offered you the chance to co-operate with me to create a world circuit but you were too one-eyed and chauvinistic to listen. You wanted to keep all the power to yourself. But I intend to go on setting up tournaments wherever and whenever I can.'

'Especially if you can schedule them against important tournaments on my Tour.'

'You're getting paranoid.'

'Not at all. But does Sam Rhodes realise what his absences do to tournaments? If players like him are not there, the gate receipts suffer and the contributions to charity are less. And the sponsor is pissed into the bargain.'

'You talk grandly about contributing to charity, but it's the tournaments themselves that raise the money. Your organisation contributes very little to charity. Your revenues and prize-money have gone shooting up but the Tour's charitable contributions haven't kept pace.'

'That's crap,' Lansky said. 'The PGA is a non-profit organisation, we're tax exempt. You don't think the Internal Revenue Service would allow that if we weren't genuine contributors to charity, do you?'

'You spoke earlier, Carl, about agents running scams like appearance money,' Steven said, as he rose to his feet. 'But they pale in comparison with what you're doing. You're running the biggest scam of all.'

With a nod to Lansky, he strode off towards the coffee shop. He would talk to Joe Lynagh about the PGA's tax-exempt status. One of the law firm's taxation hot-shots would cast his beady eyes over the regulations. Steven might be able to threaten Lansky's position, even if it meant making representations to the IRS. Or he could merely threaten to do so, that would make the bastard sweat. He'd also talk to the Federal Trade Commission again and emphasise that Lansky's restrictions on golfers amounted to restraint of trade. Anyway, Steven had some plans for the following season that would really rock him.

*

The conditions at St Andrews that year were miserable. The temperature dropped, the wind blew hard and there were squalls of heavy rain. Steven was thankful to spend his time in the hotel, the clubhouse and the hospitality tents. He had much to occupy himself. First, there was the question of his continuing to sell the overseas television rights for the Open. With a vigorous recommendation from Paul Davis, the relevant R&A committee rewarded Steven with another four-year contract to represent them. He wondered if they would ever ask him to become a member of the R&A. He rather fancied that distinction.

Although Steven had over a dozen executives at the championship, he went through his familiar routine of visiting every manufacturer of note in the massive exhibition tent. His own magazine had a small stand in a corner of the tent and, on two or three occasions each day, he went along to gauge the degree of activity there.

On the second day he found Dean Aultman chatting to one of the girls on the stand.

'Steven, I'm glad I've caught you,' he said. 'You obviously haven't seen the press release yet. From Patrice Barbier.'

'No, what's it about?'

'Competition, that's what. He's gone into the tournament business. He's scheduled a new event for May next year. The French Masters, to be played in Paris and all under the control of his own company. It's to be the first of many, he says.'

'Where's Toby Streeter?'

'The Editor's taken one of our advertisers for a glass of champagne,' the girl said helpfully. 'The Bollinger tent, I think.'

'Thanks,' Steven said. 'I want to make sure he covers the news correctly.'

Steven's umbrella didn't give him much protection against the driving rain and he ran the hundred yards to the champagne tent. It was doing a brisk business; many of the fans had decided to take refuge there and watch the golf on the television screens. The tent was also a haven for journalists, equipment manufacturers, many of the show-business people who haunt golf tournaments, sponsors and officials. Steven recognised several of the faces and, with a smile here and a greeting there, he advanced on Toby Streeter who was standing at the end of the bar with a stocky man in check trousers and a blue blazer. Shortly after being introduced to Steven, the man drained his glass and wandered off to join some friends at a table near one of the television screens.

'He spends a lot of money with us,' Toby said cheerfully. 'A good bloke.'

Steven grunted. 'How are you going to play this Barbier business?'

'Give it lots of coverage. It's good for golf. A new big-money event in Paris in the spring – and all run by the most charismatic figure in the game.'

'Is that really how you see it, Toby? Don't you think that's rather naive?'

'Naive? I'm sorry, I'm not with you.' Toby stood up straighter and looked at Steven sharply. 'I'm a journalist and I have to interpret the news for the readers. That sounds a bit pompous but I think Barbier's initiative is great for European golf.'

'I see it from a different angle, Toby. My company runs events in Europe, and Barbier has now set up in opposition. I don't want to hand him any publicity at all, no favourable comment. We'll treat it as a minor news item.'

'It's not a minor news item, Steven, it's headline news and I shall treat it as such.' Steven noticed that Toby's voice had risen and that his lean face had flushed. 'How can I run a reputable golf magazine if I have to kow-tow to someone else's opinions?'

'Because I'm the proprietor and you're just the sodding Editor.' Steven's voice had risen in response to Toby's and several heads, quickly attuned to the possibility of a row, turned towards them.

'Yes, I am the Editor and I take the responsibility for what goes in the magazine. I'm not your fucking lackey, you've got enough of those working for you. If you don't like it, you know what you can do, don't you? You can write the magazine yourself.'

'There are plenty of hacks to do the writing,' Steven shouted. 'You're fired. Get the hell out of my sight.'

'Glad to,' Toby said. He picked up his umbrella and his briefcase and strode out of the tent.

His fists clenched and his face tight with anger, Steven realised that a dozen or more people were looking intently at him. A portly man in his sixties got up from his table and walked over to him. He smiled at Steven and pressed a business card into his hand. 'Len Hardy. I run a news agency. Sounds as if you'll need a good editor. Ring me. I've got just the man for you.'

Steven gave him a nod and a barely civil 'Thank you' and turned away from the bar.

'Excuse me, sir.' Steven heard the urgent voice behind him. 'Your friend's bill, sir.'

Steven threw a £50 note on the bar and walked quickly out of the tent with as much dignity as he could manage.

# Chapter Thirty-four

A hundred yards on from the champagne tent, Steven met Dean Aultman coming the other way. He was talking animatedly to a tall and attractive dark-haired girl. Aultman stopped and the girl walked on.

'I'll catch you later,' Aultman said. She waved an acknowledgement. 'She plays on the women's tour. Could be a useful golfer one day. But you don't look in the mood to discuss potential clients, Steven. What's up?'

Steven forced himself to smile; it wasn't his habit to confide his feelings to his employees. 'I've had to fire Streeter. He refused to see my point of view over Barbier's tournament.'

'That's a pity. He's a good journalist.'

'There are plenty who're just as good. It's a minor irritant, whereas Sam Rhodes has really pissed me off. Despite all the pressure I put on him he's turned down that deal with Amalgamated International.'

'Why?'

'Principles, for Christ's sake. He doesn't approve of their investing in countries with totalitarian regimes. So all that commission has gone down the tubes. And we can't substitute another client. AIB want Sam Rhodes. No one else will do.'

'It's ironic, isn't it?' Aultman said with a thin smile. 'He's one of the few sportsmen around with any ethical sense and what's more he's prepared to stand by his beliefs.' Aultman admired Rhodes both as a golfer and as a man. In his heart he was glad that there was at least one client who was prepared to stand up to Steven.

'More's the pity,' Steven muttered. 'What with him, Streeter and Carl Lansky this hasn't been my most enjoyable Open ever.'

Steven's exasperation at Rhodes's rejection of his cleverly engineered contract with AIB was heightened as he witnessed his client's serene progress to victory in the Open Championship. But the resulting deluge of bonuses was a source of consolation. Coupled with the commission on his prize-money and that of the other clients, the money earned not only covered the agency's expenses during Open week but showed a handsome profit.

A few weeks later, Steven received a telephone call in his New York office from Paul Davis. The BBC's Head of Sport told him that John Winter had recently approached him with a proposal to do an investigative programme about the events surrounding Nils Ryberg's death.

'Is this your idea, Steven? I'm worried about his deadline on the "History of Golf" project. That's far more important.'

'Too true, Paul. I'll speak to him. We don't want him getting side-tracked. I take it you didn't bite on the Ryberg idea?'

'No, no. I told him I had to speak to you.'

Steven managed to reach Winter a couple of days later. He was on location at Prestwick, where the Open Championship began. He responded optimistically to Steven's enquiries about his progress with the 'History of Golf' series.

'Can you meet the deadlines?' Steven asked. 'AAN over here in the States want to schedule it for next autumn. Is that a problem?'

'I don't think so. It was getting bogged down at one stage but I've taken on a bright young journalist. One of your ex-employees, actually. Toby Streeter.'

Alarm bells started up in Steven's head but he merely said, 'Ah, Toby. We had an unfortunate disagreement. I found him a little unstable.'

'He's an excellent writer, Steven.'

'Yes. I'm sure you're a better judge of such matters than me. John, I hear that you're still dabbling in that Nils Ryberg project.'

'Hardly dabbling. Actually, I've got quite a lot of material. I want to do the project. D'you think it's got a market in the States?'

'I don't think it's got a market anywhere. Not even at the BBC.'

'In view of our golf series, I thought it polite to offer the programme to Paul Davis first.'

'Why don't you forget it? For one thing, it's old hat. Who could possibly be interested in the death, several years ago, of a rather sad Swedish tennis player?' Why don't you stop meddling, you stubborn bastard was Steven's actual thought. 'And for another thing,' he continued, 'have you considered Ryberg's wife? She surely doesn't want the old wounds to be probed again. I'd advise you not to pursue the idea. Your priority is to deliver six hours of the "History of Golf". The BBC and AAN and my company have made a considerable investment in that series and we don't want you going off at a tangent.'

'OK, don't worry. You'll get your series, I promise you that.' Winter decided not to argue with Shaw about the Ryberg project; but he was even more determined to carry on with his research – quietly. Shaw was so adamantly opposed to any re-examination of Ryberg's death that his journalistic instincts were fortified. There was a real story to be told and perhaps Shaw would play more than a minor role in it.

Over dinner that evening he mentioned his suspicions to Toby Streeter. The two men had already forged a close friendship and Toby had happily spread his creative wings in the wider world of television production.

'I've been wondering about our mutual friend, Steven Shaw,' Winter said. 'I have no complaints about him, he's put some nice business my way. That's why we're sitting here in Scotland, after all. But I've had some less than admiring comments about him. Terri Calvin doesn't like his business methods and even one of his leading clients, Ray Gerrard, was very guarded about him. He almost warned me not to cross Shaw. A good friend but a very nasty enemy, that sort of thing.'

'He certainly didn't pull his punches when he kicked me out,' Toby said. 'He's a powerful presence in several markets, especially tennis and golf. And there are all those sports programmes he packages, trash-sport, but they're seen all round the world. He's got a very unhealthy grip on golf. In my opinion it's close to a monopoly. He represents most of the top players; only Patrice Barbier has refused to be drawn into the net. And by the way, that really bugs Shaw. He's almost irrational about it – that's really why he fired me.' Toby smiled ruefully. 'As you know, Shaw has complete control over a number of tournaments: he organises them from A to Z. He gets the sponsor, sells the television rights, puts his own clients in the event, does the programme, he even keeps most of the gate money.'

'He'll be doing the television commentary soon,' Winter said with a laugh.

'I wouldn't put it past him. The trouble is he'd probably do it very well.'

'Yes, he's a clever bugger,' Winter mused. 'It's not really

possible to like him, he's too guarded, too cold. But he's miles brighter than most people in sport.'

'That wouldn't be difficult. But I agree with you.'

'Perhaps we should broaden our approach to Ryberg and his death. Maybe his story should be the story of how top-class professional sport is really run. Who really pulls the strings? What's the role of people like Shaw?'

John Winter pushed aside his plate, its dreary vegetarian lasagne mostly uneaten. He took a healthy swallow of his wine. 'Yuk. Vin de Strathclyde. I think I'll switch to whisky. Terri Calvin said something very interesting to me. She implied that Shaw had undue influence both at AAN and the BBC. Why don't we look at that? You've got a friend at court, haven't you? Jacqui Bryson. Doesn't she work for Paul Davis?'

'I knew her at LSE, but I wouldn't call her a close friend.'

'Well, it's a start. Cultivate her. Ring her up when we get back to London. Take her out for a few drinks or a meal. See what she knows about Shaw.'

'Plenty, I would think. Paul Davis is sleeping with her, I'm told, and he's very matey with Shaw.'

'I don't think anyone is really matey with Shaw, but I take your point.'

Two weeks later, Toby Streeter met Jacqui Bryson in a west London pub not far from the BBC's sports department. An unpretentious place, whose merits were its excellent beer, generous doorstep-sized sandwiches and cheerful staff, it was a favoured watering-hole for many of the Corporation's employees.

When Toby arrived, Jacqui was leaning on the bar with several colleagues. She was a tall girl, with an elongated face that just stayed on the right side of prettiness, and it was softened by her abundant black hair. Her jeans and a bright red T-shirt showed off her slim figure to the maximum effect. She was halfway down a pint of bitter, and when she saw Toby, she waved energetically at a barman and ordered more pints. Jacqui seized him around the waist, kissed him firmly on each cheek and introduced him to her friends. It was only six o'clock and Toby wondered how many drinks she'd had.

Over the course of the next hour, the group had three more pints of bitter and swapped stories about the arcane working practices of the BBC and the sexual peccadilloes of its stars. When one of the men, who sported a moustache and seemed to have a roll-up cigarette permanently burning between his fingers, proposed another round, Toby said that he'd promised to take Jacqui for a curry.

'Super idea,' Jacqui said. 'Are you going to join us, boys?'

To Toby's relief, they declined and he and Jacqui walked a few hundred yards to a spacious Indian restaurant. Since it was not yet eight o'clock in the evening, the place was almost deserted and they sat in a corner by the window.

By the time that they had snacked their way through several poppadums each, they had exhausted their recollections of the London School of Economics. Jacqui, on her first visit to the lavatory, wondered why Toby had made a point of asking her out. She liked him a lot. He was good company and did not bother with that boring male process of sexual innuendo. But she hoped he wasn't going to suggest sex, because she really didn't fancy him.

When the main course arrived, Toby ordered more lagers for them and said, 'Are you still involved with Paul Davis?'

'Yes, if you call having a quick one before he goes home to his wife being "involved".'

'His wife probably would.'

'That's a bit censorious, Toby, isn't it?'

'It's not meant to be, love. But there must be more to it than a quick poke now and again, surely?'

'Of course there is. There's more to Paul than most people see. He's a bit flash, all that champagne and expensive meals, but there's another side as well.'

'He's really a sensitive and vulnerable creature, is he?' Toby smiled.

'Cynic.'

'Anyway, how can he afford the good life on his salary? He's got a wife and a mortgage and the kids' education to pay for. He doesn't strike me as a man with a private income. Is his wife rich?'

'I don't know and I don't ask,' Jacqui said firmly. 'Now, Toby, you've asked me some personal questions, what about your love life?'

'Nothing special. I had a friend until recently but he went off to Australia.'

Jacqui looked up sharply, her glass of lager poised on the way to her lips. 'I didn't realise . . .'

'That I'm that way inclined? Why should you? I don't broadcast it but, on the other hand, I don't hide it.'

'Very wise. Come on, let's settle the bill and you can walk me home. It's not far and I'll provide brandy and coffee.'

No longer feeling uneasy about Toby's sexual motives, Jacqui welcomed him into her neat one-bedroomed flat on the second floor of an ornate Victorian house which overlooked a small park near the River Thames. Comfortable with each other, they sat in her kitchen while the coffee brewed. They clinked their large glasses of brandy.

Several times Toby tried to introduce Shaw into the conversation but Jacqui veered away from the subject. In the end he asked her bluntly what she thought of him.

'No real opinion,' she said carefully. 'I don't know him that well.'

'But he does loads of business with Paul,' Toby pressed her.

'Yes, too much.' She finished her brandy in one long gulp. 'He's got Paul by the short and curlies and it worries me.' She refilled her glass but her hand was so shaky that the bottle collided with the rim of the glass and knocked it over. The brandy spread over the pine table.

'Oh, shit,' Jacqui said and buried her face in her hands. Toby jumped up, grabbed some kitchen towel and mopped energetically at the spilled liquid. He deposited the paper towel in a bin and turned to Jacqui, who was sobbing.

'Darling, what's the matter?' He went to her and put his arm around her. 'It's only a drop of brandy. No harm done.'

Jacqui hugged him and thrust her face into his chest. 'It's not that, it's Paul. He's in too deep with Shaw. Those horrible parties, for instance.'

'What parties?'

'You know, lots of champagne, other substances discreetly available if required, the tarts who'll satisfy any request from Shaw's important sponsors. Paul's been to them, though he claims he hasn't done any screwing. But it's all so insidious. Shaw has got these people exactly where he wants them, including Paul.'

'Why don't you tell him to walk away?'

'It's not that simple. Paul is . . . he's . . . I'm sure he's taking money from Shaw and I don't mean a few fivers in a brown envelope.'

Gently, Toby disentangled himself, returned to his chair opposite Jacqui, took her hand and said, 'Jacqui, love, if it helps, tell me about it.'

Toby handed her some kitchen towel on which she dried her eyes. She blew her nose vigorously. 'Look, Paul has got a villa in Cap Ferrat. I've been there. His story is that it's owned by some Swiss company he does consultancy work for. He has the run of it whenever he wishes. It's pretty bloody obvious that it's one of Shaw's companies. And Paul is always flush with money, with cash. I'm convinced Shaw pays him.'

'But you've no proof?'

'No . . . Yes . . .' Tears once again filled Jacqui's eyes. 'I've been such a fool. I was approached by some man who said he had an interesting proposal for me. A bit of extra work, well paid. Well, I arranged to meet him and he asked me to keep my eye on Paul, on all his business dealings at the BBC, except for those with Shaw. Two hundred pounds a week, in cash, if I did. I'm always short of money but I told him to go to hell. He was a horrible sod, very self-contained, very cold. To be honest, he scared the shit out of me. So then he produced some photographs of Paul and me together.'

'What sort of photographs?'

'They were pretty harmless but he said they were just the hors d'oeuvres, I think that was his expression, for Paul's wife.'

'You should've called his bluff.'

'I did and he told me that he had the really juicy ones available too, ones of Paul and me having it away. He actually named dates and places and described what we did. It was all very clinical and he was obviously enjoying himself. It was vile, Toby, vile.'

'Who is this bastard?'

'Whoever he is, I'm convinced he works for Shaw.'

'So you agreed to work for him?'

'Yes. What could I do? Wreck Paul's marriage, break up his family? The marriage is still holding together, for the sake of the kids, so he says.'

'How often have I heard that?' Toby said wearily. 'And Davis knows nothing of all this?'

'Christ, no. The whole situation would blow up in our faces if he knew what was going on.'

'So now you're both on Shaw's payroll. What a Machiavellian bastard he is.'

'Yes. The trouble is, I've got used to having the extra money.'

It was a beautiful autumnal morning, crisp and clear, when Steven next arrived in London. As always, Lucy Howard met him at Heathrow and they went through his schedule as the limousine joined the traffic jam into the centre.

'Paul Davis needs to talk to you urgently,' Lucy said.

'But I'm seeing him tomorrow. Lunch at the Caprice.'

'Yes. But he asked that you call him this morning.'

'Did he say why?'

Lucy shook her head and Steven noticed afresh how attractive she was. Not only that, but she was a reassuring presence in his life. For once, he had failed to sleep through the transatlantic flight from New York. It was never normally a problem; he had his meal, stretched out, shut his eyes and woke up in London. But not this time. For the whole journey his mind had been occupied in reviewing the fierce row that had erupted between him and Suzi just before he left.

It had started innocuously and had centred on the lack of time that Steven spent with his family, and particularly with his son, Adam, who was appearing in his school's concert during the following week. Steven had promised to be there, but Dean Aultman had arranged some extra appointments for him in England and now he would have to miss Adam's musical debut.

'As usual,' Suzi said bitterly, when Steven told her of his

change of plan, 'business comes before everything. Adam will grow up hardly knowing you.'

'That's nonsense, Suzi.'

'Is it? When did you last come to his birthday party? When did you last read him a bedtime story? He wants to play golf, like his daddy, but have you ever given him any encouragement, taken him down to the range?'

'The last year or two haven't been easy. I've been running hard just to keep the agency under control because it's growing so fast.'

'And you're doing it all for us, I suppose, Steven?

'As a matter of fact, I am.'

'What bullshit! You're doing it for you. More and more money, more and more power, fewer and fewer scruples and zero regard for others.' Suzi sat down on the arm of one of the many sofas in their expansive sitting room. Staring at the floor, she continued. 'I was once under the illusion that you loved me. I certainly loved you. But now I think you saw me as a very convenient step on the ladder to success. You saw a wealthy family and a doting father. It really was a marriage of convenience.'

'That's a terrible thing to say.'

'Yes, it's been terrible to face up to it, but I haven't had a husband for a long time and Adam hasn't had a father.'

'Well, no doubt you've found some acceptable substitutes among New York society,' Steven said with a sneer. 'What about what's his name, Greg? I assume he slipped you one.'

'Yes, Steven, he did. But I'll tell you what else he gave me. Warmth and tenderness. I wonder if you're familiar with either concept? On the evidence of the last few years, no. And Greg wasn't the only one. The only thing I can say is that I'm sure my total of extra-marital affairs is minuscule compared to yours. I regretted every one because every one was a betrayal of our marriage but now I don't give a row of beans.'

Shaken to his roots, Steven stared at Suzi. 'Am I to assume that my favourite client, Sam Rhodes, is one of your lovers?'

'No, you're not. You probably can't understand this but he's far too moral,' Suzi lied. 'He's a true friend, both to me and Adam.'

'Do you want a divorce?'

'No, because it would break my parents' hearts, especially Dad's.'

'So, we'll go through the motions, eh?'

'Yes and, by God, you'd better make it look good,' Suzi said fiercely.

The Daimler crawled slowly down the Cromwell Road and Steven turned to his secretary and said, 'Let's go straight to the house. I haven't spent much time with you recently.'

Lucy smiled at him, without artifice, without calculation. He wanted to crawl into her arms and lose himself in her body. What was that line in *Under Milk Wood*? His old teacher, Jeremy Knight, who played the part of blind Captain Cat in their classroom reading, proclaimed it with such feeling. 'Lie down, lie easy. Let me shipwreck in your thighs.' That was it.

# Chapter Thirty-five

Steven's first task of the day was to spend half an hour with Dean Aultman while they reviewed the work of the London office. He noticed that his Chief Executive had put on a bit of weight and, with approval, how smartly dressed he was. That was a bespoke suit and an expensive silk tie. Steven paid him handsomely, in accord with the man's success. He hoped that would keep him honest. It was an occupational hazard that people left agencies to set up on their own and took important clients with them. Steven didn't want that to happen. Even though Aultman had signed a non-competition agreement, both of them knew it would probably be deemed illegal in a British or European court on grounds of restraint of trade.

Aultman was eager to talk about his motor racing client, Angus Gray. 'He's on a roll, Steven, after winning at Silverstone. You should've been there – the reception the crowd gave him was fantastic. They're saying he's the best driver since Jim Clark. The offers are pouring in, and if he wins next time out in Spain I can't see anyone stopping him from being world champion.'

'That's good news. What about next year? Same team or does he move on for more money?'

'I'm playing a waiting game at present. You've no idea how political Formula One is. It's like playing poker blind for millions of pounds. Fortunately, Angus will have the strongest hand in the game.'

'Good. Now, what about these football club chairmen? I see you've lined me up with a dozen meetings. These are the leading clubs in the First Division, with one exception. What's happened to Salford United? That's the one I want to hook. That club's got one of the best followings in Europe. What's the problem?'

'The problem is Derek Mason. He's the Chairman, as you know, and he says he's happy with the way his club is marketed.'

'You gave him the hard sell?'

'The lot, in spades. But he refuses to believe that we can have any influence on which games are shown on television or that we can better his sponsorship deal.'

It had been a simple concept. Steven knew that much of the big money in football came from the fees paid by the television companies to the clubs. When a club knew that its games would be on national television the value of its perimeter advertising increased dramatically. It seemed obvious to Steven that this was an area where he could make his influence felt, and therefore generate a lot of money for his client. He already had Paul Davis in his pocket; if he could bribe the man within ITV who picked the league matches for the Network, Steven would be in a position to exercise a fair degree of control over which clubs were seen on the television screens. He would then have something of great value to sell to the various chairmen of the leading First Division clubs.

The man who was charged with the responsibility for selecting ITV's live matches was Wayne Travers, and Steven had been surprised at how easily he had been persuaded to co-operate.

Dan Fisher had researched Travers's background and forecast that he wouldn't pose any problems. 'Football writer on a provincial newspaper, then on one of the

national tabloids. Worked for Central as a fixer on their
sports programmes and then got this job with ITV football.
A semi-literate yob with expensive tastes, a skirt-chaser, no
moral judgement, basically corrupt.' That was Fisher's succinct appraisal and he had been proved right. A
down-payment of £50,000 into a nominee account in the
British Virgin Islands and a promise of a share of the
income generated by Shaw Management from the scheme
had done the trick.

'You're sure that Wayne Travers is well and truly
hooked?' Steven asked Aultman.

'No problem. He's as happy as a pig in shit.'

'And these chairmen are ready to play ball?'

'Of course. Anything that makes them and the other
directors some more money is OK by them. And the managers will get a cut too.'

'"The game that fell off a lorry",' Steven said. 'It was a
newspaper headline I saw the other day. And it sums up the
game very neatly, don't you think?'

'It sure does. Money is the only thing that matters. And
the players themselves will say anything if there's some
serious cash about. I've been doing a brisk business
recently in footballers' memoirs, though that's far too
grand a term for them. You've probably seen the figures
we're getting from the tabloids. Kickers and knickers
stories, I call them.'

Steven laughed and Aultman said quietly, 'Not that our
hands are very clean, are they?' He knew how Steven had
masterminded his forced entry into the rich football market
and felt great disquiet. But he had grown used to an expensive style of life and was loath to give it up.

Steven sensed his misgivings and knew it was just as
well that Aultman didn't know the extent of his machina-
tions: the story behind Nils Ryberg's suicide, for instance.

'We're only reacting to the market conditions, Dean. We didn't create the corruption but we've got to work within that culture in order to be effective. So, if we need to bung a few managers and directors some money, so be it. That's nothing compared to what goes on in the City or in the corridors of power at Westminster.'

'So what will we do about Salford United?'

'I'll put Dan Fisher on to it. He can find out what makes Derek Mason tick.'

It was the middle of the morning when Lucy Howard put Paul Davis through to Steven. By that time he had already agreed outline terms with the chairmen of two of London's most important football clubs for Shaw Management to act as their marketing consultants.

'Hey, Paul, what's the rush? We're meeting for lunch in about twenty-four hours' time.'

'I thought you should know about this right away. Somebody at Channel 4 tipped me off that John Winter has got some seed money to develop a programme about Ryberg's death. Not only that but he's looking at your role as an agent.'

'Winter loves to meddle, doesn't he? I've handed him a really prestigious series on a plate and he goes off at a tangent. What the hell is he up to?'

'Well, he was a great friend of Ryberg's and of his wife.'

'I daresay. Paul, I don't want him poking his nose into my business. And I don't suppose you'd want that either, would you?'

'Well, I—'

'No, is the answer,' Steven said curtly. 'I'm going to put pressure on him to get on with the golf series. I'll bring the deadline forward. If he can't deliver, I'll find another producer who can.'

'He might sue you for breach of contract.'

'I hope he does take me on because I'll bankrupt the bastard.'

'Steven, that series must come in on schedule. I don't want any problems.'

'It will, don't worry. But let's review all the material he's put together. Get someone in your office to contact him. Send a car round for it. And Paul, you make bloody sure that Winter never works again for the BBC. Never. Is that clear?'

'Of course. See you tomorrow at the Caprice. Lovely, one of my favourites.'

As soon as he put the telephone down, Steven called Lucy Howard in to his office and dictated a letter to Winter in which he shortened the delivery date for the 'History of Golf' by three months. He knew that it would be impossible for Winter to meet such a deadline. Aultman was set to work to find a replacement producer.

The foundations of the Mason family's wealth had been laid generations before when their company had become one of the major producers of industrial engines in the north of England. Derek's grandfather had been prescient enough to realise that Britain's days as the 'workshop of the world' were numbered and he diversified into the manufacture of motor car components. The next tactic was to distribute the cars themselves and, in the two decades after the Second World War, the family constructed a thriving business in the selling and servicing of both British and foreign cars. In Derek Mason's tenure as Managing Director of the company, the emphasis had been firmly placed on German and Japanese models.

Grandfather Mason had been a keen sportsman and had played as an amateur for Salford United before the First World War. As one of the more important employers in the area he had been asked to become a director of the club and been rewarded with a modest shareholding. When the old man died, Derek's father, John, succeeded him and had bought more shares from the unwieldy collection of trade and professional people who sat on the club's board. By the early 1970s he held nearly 40 per cent of the equity and set about acquiring more, because he realised that the club represented a gilt-edged asset. The game was popular and, every other week during the season, cash flowed through the turnstiles. Not only that, but Salford United actually owned the freehold of its ground. Shrewdly, John Mason went in pursuit of the little parcels of shares that were held by individuals. In return for their shares, widows were offered what they regarded as bountiful cash payments and elderly men were granted season tickets to the ground for the rest of their lives.

Within a couple of years, Mason had become the major shareholder in Salford United and, when he died at the beginning of the 1980s, his controlling interest passed to his eldest son.

Derek Mason had led an easy and uneventful life, confident in the knowledge that he would succeed his father at the helm of the Mason business empire. So he did, with his two younger brothers installed as managing directors of the car distribution and the engineering divisions. Derek had inherited his father's invaluable knack of picking able managers to run their businesses but he was vain enough to assume most of the credit for their successes. Most of all, Mason loved the social distinction that his prominent position in commerce brought him. Encouraged by his wife, Hilary, the daughter of a wealthy Cheshire farmer, he allowed himself to be co-opted on to numerous committees. He became a trustee of his local golf club; he served as a magistrate; and was an important member of the

Chamber of Commerce. But the jewel in his crown was his chairmanship of Salford United. It brought him priceless prestige at all levels in his community.

Towards the end of the 1970s, John Mason had been faced with the recurring, and difficult, problem of choosing a manager for his football club. Most of the candidates seemed to be taciturn former international players with impenetrable Scottish accents. Mason wanted someone with fresh ideas, with some vision of what a great football club should represent. His eye eventually fell on Brian Hurley who had taken an almost bankrupt team, made up of part-timers and ageing professionals, from the lowest reaches of the Fourth Division to somewhere near the top of the Second Division within three seasons. Hurley had had an undistinguished career as a footballer but was known as a great motivator of players, as a man of great integrity with firm socialist principles. Salford had prospered under his management and Hurley had become a familiar figure on television, a pundit always ready with a telling phrase.

Wary of Hurley at first, Derek Mason had quickly discovered that his manager's image as a caring football-man-of-the-people was as bogus as his socialist principles. Hurley took a substantial cut of every player's transfer, whether into or out of the club, and he and Mason, along with the club's Financial Director, refined John Mason's practice of skimming a proportion of the gate money at every home game.

It was little wonder that Derek Mason dismissed the approach he received from Dean Aultman. Why should he bother with a marketing consultant? He had his own Commercial Manager to handle all the sponsorship and advertising contracts and the man structured them in the way that Mason wanted. As for Aultman's claim that Shaw Management had a say in which matches were seen on television, that was nonsense. Salford United was the most charismatic team in Britain, with fans in every corner of the country and all around the world, too. Mason believed that his team was on the box too much. Television needed his team more than he needed television.

Mason was surprised to hear again from Shaw Management, but this time it was the boss himself who called, not some underling. He'd read about Steven Shaw and heard a rumour that he'd orchestrated Jimmy Burns's transfer to Italy for the maximum profit to his own agency. Apparently Shaw had rolled Burns over and well and truly flattened him. Served the bugger right. It sounded as if he and Shaw were kindred spirits.

With a show of reluctance, Mason agreed to meet the agent. 'We've got a League Cup match on Wednesday evening,' Mason said. 'Down at Luton. A God-forsaken ground but you're welcome to join the directors, if you wish. We can talk then.'

'Where are you staying?' Steven asked, since he had no interest in seeing a second-rate cup-tie. 'Why don't I drive over? We can have a chat in private before the match.'

Armed with the information about Mason and Hurley which had been gathered by Dan Fisher, Steven set out for the Markley Arms Hotel on Wednesday afternoon. The Georgian façade with its clusters of Virginia creeper, which had assumed their vivid autumnal hues of bronze and red, was delightful. But, as he turned past the front of the building into the car park, Steven saw the havoc which the philistine owners had wrought. A concrete block of bedrooms, grey and depressing, had been tacked on to the back of the building and alongside was the obligatory leisure centre which looked better suited to a low-cost municipal housing project than a 'secluded and exclusive country house hotel'.

A chirpy receptionist told Steven that Mr Mason was waiting for him in the lounge. She bustled out from behind the desk, her full bosom bouncing gently, and pointed him towards a broad-shouldered man who was sitting in a corner of the high-ceilinged room. As he approached, Steven registered Mason's crinkly auburn hair and a pair of very pale blue and protruding eyes in a round, fleshy face. He wore a dark, double-breasted suit with a chalk stripe and a brightly coloured silk tie. Steven could discern no trace of a northern accent in his voice. He sounded and looked like a prosperous southerner, someone who had worked in the City all his life. Steven knew that he had been educated at a middling public school in Lancashire and had studied law at Leicester University.

The preliminary courtesies were disposed of during the first cup of tea and Steven opened his campaign by saying, 'I realise that Dean Aultman has already said this, but we believe that Shaw Management could generate a lot of extra income for Salford United.'

'We're already very successful,' Mason countered, 'and so we should be. League champions four times in the last decade. FA Cup winners three times, European Cup winners.' He ticked the achievements off on his fingers and Steven noticed the bushy red hairs on them.

'We have a first-class sponsor,' continued Mason, 'we have good relationships with the TV people, our Commercial Manager handles all the perimeter advertising very ably and all our merchandising activities – we really are very sound on all these things. I'm flattered that you should be interested in us, Mr Shaw, but I can't see where you can possibly assist us.'

'We do major sponsorship contracts every day and we could increase your fees substantially. As for merchandising, you haven't even scratched the surface. There are millions to be made from Salford United products.'

'We have an excellent rapport with our main sponsor. It's a northern brewery, as you know. It's very successful, it's local and it's a family concern and that's why we have a good relationship. Quite frankly, I don't want to rock the boat, Mr Shaw. I know it must sound very naive to you, as a wheeler-dealer in international sport, but our local relationships, one family concern to another, are very important to us. We're not ruled by money, you see, even though Salford is the best-known football team in Britain. Integrity has always been the watchword, since my grandfather became Chairman. He played for Salford, and both my father and I played amateur football. I like to think that we've brought some of the true-blue amateur ethos, the Corinthian spirit if you like, into the harsh milieu of professional football. We manage things professionally but we don't lose sight of our sporting integrity.'

What a hypocritical bastard, Steven thought. But he said, 'We're very experienced in television, Mr Mason. After all, we sell rights all around the world, including the Open golf and the tennis at Wimbledon, and All-Star-Sport is one of the most successful sporting series ever done on TV. So we could be of great help in that area.'

'I don't think so,' Mason said comfortably. 'Would you like some more tea?'

Steven shook his head and Mason continued, 'We get enough coverage already and the fees are laid down in the overall contracts with the television companies. It's so much per appearance. How can you help us there?'

'Because I can make sure that you do actually get that coverage. If you didn't your sponsor would be unhappy and so would the people who advertise at your ground.'

Carefully, Mason put his teacup down and spoke very

quietly. 'I haven't made myself clear, have I? We don't need you. Everything ticks over very smoothly.'

'Very smoothly for you, I think you mean. Do the other directors know how much the brewery pays you in consultancy fees? Or rather, how much they pay to a company with nominee directors in the Isle of Man? But I just happen to know that you and Brian Hurley control it.'

Steven watched with interest as Mason, his eyes bulging even more, forced himself to maintain eye contact. He gulped. 'It's a legitimate business arrangement. Not that I have to justify anything to you.'

'It doesn't quite square with Hurley's image, does it? And does the Inland Revenue know how much you and your saintly manager skim off the gate money and from all the transfer deals? I wonder where all those briefcases bulging with money end up? Where do you launder the cash, Mr Mason? Jersey or the Cayman Islands? No doubt it ends up in a Liechtenstein Trust?'

Enjoying himself immensely, Steven sat back in his chair and smiled at Mason, who wiped his damp forehead and then stood up. 'You've been reading too many tabloid newspapers. They're full of rubbish like that. That's all I have to say to you on the subject.'

'Just one moment,' Steven said, as he also rose to his feet. 'The team's at home a week on Sunday, isn't it, and it's live on television?'

Mason nodded reluctantly. 'One of the Sheffield teams. Not the most appealing of matches.' He seemed to gather himself and said spiritedly, 'That's why the TV boys need us. When there isn't an obvious stand-out fixture, they plump for us every time. We're manna from heaven to them. And that's why we don't need you, we've got it all sewn up.'

'Really,' Steven replied, as he straightened his tie and

smiled at Mason. 'By the way, I'd keep a close eye on those tabloid newspapers over the next few days if I were you.'

For several days, Mason felt uneasy about his conversation with Steven Shaw. The man was a smart-arse. He obviously had a very high opinion of himself and his remarks had been too near the mark for Mason's comfort. Nevertheless, he couldn't prove a thing and, if he tried any tricks, Mason would hit him with a libel writ as quick as blinking.

# Chapter Thirty-six

The Ian Westwood column appeared twice weekly in *The Journal*, a middle-of-the-road tabloid newspaper which was trying to hang on to its middle-class readership with increasing desperation. In his earlier days as a journalist, Westwood had pursued legitimate sporting stories with vigour and had turned his phrases with flair. The demands of his Editor for more sensational material had dulled his skills. His talents were, however, welcomed on television where he played the roles of sporting jester and controversial critic with ease.

Westwood had been on the payroll of Shaw Management for several years and was rewarded for planting positive stories about the agency and its clients. Because of his activities in television, he had himself become a client of Dean Aultman's, who had put him forward as a possible narrator of the 'History of Golf' series.

The Monday morning column contained Westwood's musings about the weekend sport and, in addition, a tailpiece which was headed 'Trouble at Mill'.

> Rumours reach me that not everything is coming up roses at Salford United, the club which has been in the sure hands of the patrician Mason family for several decades. The Inland Revenue are said to be taking a beady-eyed look at the club's transfer dealings over the last few years. Those tax-chasing terriers are also wondering who are the real owners of a nom-

inee company in the Isle of Man. The Chairman, Derek Mason, was not available for comment. Perhaps he was counselling his high-principled Manager, Brian 'the saintly socialist' Hurley, who was said to have become extremely tired and emotional after United's unexpected defeat at Leeds on Saturday.

I'm sure Mr Hurley wouldn't become involved with any financial malpractices, nor would the Mason family, one of the North's best-connected business families. They even own United's ground. The idea that they would sell the famous stadium to a supermarket chain just to top up the family pension fund is obviously ridiculous.

The telephone lines to Jeremiah Mason Limited, which was the holding company for all the family enterprises, were busy throughout the morning. Derek Mason refused to take any calls unless they were from members of his family or close friends. He made an exception for Wayne Travers from ITV Sport: he assumed that Travers wished to discuss some of the details of the coverage of Salford's forthcoming match.

'Nice piece in *The Journal*, Derek,' Travers said with a coarse laugh. Mason loathed the man's uncouth tones but forced himself to chuckle.

'All rather silly, Wayne. My lawyer is having a word with Westwood's Editor.'

'Old Charlie? He'll do sod-all. Controversy sells papers, you know that. But I hope you don't have trouble with those boys from the Revenue. I'd a bit of bother with those bastards over expenses. Blimey, did they turn me over. Bastards.'

'What can I do for you, Wayne? It's about Sunday, I assume.'

'Yeah, there's a slight hitch, a change of plan. We're going for the Leeds game, not yours, my old mate. They're on a winning streak and you're not. Sorry and all that, but that's showbiz.'

Mason was about to protest when the line went dead. Shit, that was a substantial facility fee that had suddenly gone west, plus all the premiums that the sponsor and the perimeter advertisers paid for television exposure. But none of that was as serious as the allegations made by that hack, Westwood. The trouble was that it would be very difficult to prove libel, or so his solicitor had told him. He'd also told him that newspapers thrived on libel allegations and that legal action would cost him a bundle of money. His final warning was that if he were Derek Mason he wouldn't want anybody prying into certain sensitive financial arrangements.

It was on the following Monday morning that Mason heard once again from Steven Shaw. He was about to leave for his office when Hilary called him back into the break-fast room. 'Someone called Shaw, darling. That's all he would say.'

'How did you get my home number?' Mason asked sharply.

'That didn't present a difficulty, Derek. Nor did finding out how you get your cash away from the ground and out of the country.'

Dan Fisher had master-minded the operation. Every turnstile at the club's ground and every exit had been covered by one of his freelance associates. Two security vans had been tailed to their destination, a bank in Manchester which opened its doors on match days specifically to take possession of the gate money. An unmarked van, with cash on board, had been followed to Holyhead and thence by boat to the Isle of Man.

With his wife's eyes upon him, Mason felt singularly uncomfortable. 'I don't know what you're talking about,' he mumbled.

'I'm talking about a proportion of the gate money being diverted to your company account in the Isle of Man. We've got the number of the van and we know the driver's name. I'm sure that the money will be transferred electronically to Jersey this morning and then on its merry and rewarding way to another destination. Difficult to track, but the Inland Revenue will be interested in what we have to tell them, don't you think? I think you're getting careless,' he ended playfully.

With a shifty look at Hilary, who was watching him closely, Mason said, 'I'll have to call you back. Give me your number, would you?'

Mason scribbled a number down on a pad and replaced the receiver. Hilary saw that he'd gone very pale, except for matching spots of colour, lurid red, on each cheek.

'Are you all right?' she asked. 'Sit down, I'll get you some coffee. Is there a problem?'

'No, no. I'll have to get into the office. Just a transfer deal that's fallen through.'

When her husband had left, Hilary Mason used a soft pencil to sketch over the indentations left in the writing pad. Eventually she was able to read what her husband had written down. At nine o'clock she dialled the number in London and when a girl said 'Shaw Management', she broke the connection. It wasn't that she didn't trust Derek but it was as well to be certain.

On the way to his office, Mason used his mobile telephone to call Brian Hurley. He tracked him down to the office at the club's training ground and gave him an outline of his conversation with Shaw.

'Tell the prick to get stuffed,' was Hurley's succinct

advice. 'He won't be able to prove a thing.'

It was all right for him to be so belligerent, thought Mason. Hurley only had a job to lose, whereas he had his position in society to worry about. He'd already had some funny looks and some pointed remarks at the golf club over Westwood's confounded article. What would Hilary think if his name were plastered all over the newspapers for tax evasion, for fraud even? There'd be more than funny looks then at the golf and the tennis clubs. And what would they think of him at the Lodge?

'I'll try to sort him out,' Mason said. He would take a firm line with Shaw, call his bluff a bit; the man was only a sportsmen's agent after all. Smoother than most of them, agreed, but just a middleman. But when he contacted Shaw at his London office, his first words put Mason back on his heels.

'You ought to know, Derek, that Ian Westwood is preparing a series of articles on corruption in football and Salford United is top of the hit list. Interesting, don't you think? Of course, if we were to reach an agreement. . . . Why don't you take the mid-morning shuttle to Heathrow? I'll send a car for you and we'll thrash everything out over lunch.'

Steven took his quarry to the grill room of the Parkside Tower Hotel and had his accustomed table overlooking the square. Mason noticed that the *maître d'hôtel* paid close attention to his host and addressed him by name, as did the wine waiter.

As soon as the first courses had been served, Steven got down to business. 'I can be of enormous help to you, Derek, if you'll let me. I have expertise in the television and merchandising areas that would prove invaluable to you and the club. And, of course, I have contacts in the media which are second to none. You're probably wondering why your game isn't on television at the weekend and you're certainly worried that a paper like *The Journal* is taking an interest in your finances.'

Steven spoke quietly, like a friendly doctor who was about to break some bad news and Mason merely nodded docilely in response.

'I can give you and your club a very positive image,' Steven continued, 'if you will allow me to. You mustn't be narrow-minded. My company's commission, twenty per cent of what we generate for the client, will be outweighed by the extra income that our expertise will bring in. You're a businessman, you'd understand that, I'm sure. And as a businessman and, I believe, a pillar of society in Lancashire, you'll understand how much harm those pariahs of the gutter press can do to you.'

By the time that the two men had finished their second courses, an outline agreement had been reached. Shaw Management would handle all Salford United's advertising, promotional and merchandising contracts including all dealings with the television companies. In addition, Steven would participate in all the negotiations for the transfer of players. He advised Mason to stop skimming the gate money. It was a dangerous practice, and especially so when the time came to float Salford onto the stock market. Then, all the activities of the club and its directors would come under the closest scrutiny.

'That particular source of easy money is nearly over anyway,' Mason said resignedly. 'What with all the season ticket holders and people who pay by credit card. Then there are the safety officers and local authority licensing officials crawling around. There'll be computerised turnstiles in the not too distant future and then we'll have to be very careful. The good old days are finished, more's the pity.'

After lunch the two men went their different ways, a chastened Derek Mason to Heathrow by car while an ebullient Steven Shaw strolled back to his office. His well-tried tactics had worked yet again. The most prestigious club in British football was now his client and would be the spearhead for his penetration of another lucrative market. He had turned the same trick in golf and tennis where his representation of Sam Rhodes and Ray Gerrard had been the foundations of his success.

Steven now had agreements with five other English clubs as well as Salford United, and with a leading Scottish club. The rich pickings of football were within his grasp.

What a pathetic creature Mason had turned out to be. All that crap about integrity and the Corinthian spirit and he was just another small-time crook, like most of the other people who battened on the sport. He hadn't even put up much of a fight. No, Mason was like most of those who'd been handed their wealth and social position on a plate: he was more worried about what people thought of him than about his business. Steven didn't give a damn about that – unless it was very important that someone liked him.

Three years later, when Salford United became a public company, the Chairman, Derek Mason, was praised for his shrewdness in appointing a professional marketing agency, with an international outlook, to oversee all aspects of the selling of the club's name. Those activities had made a significant contribution to Salford's financial success, as they had to that of Shaw Management. Fortunately, the substantial commissions levied by Shaw (and also by Mason and Hurley) on the transfers of players did not appear in the accounts. The money was safely hidden in anonymous off-shore accounts.

The account Toby Streeter had written of his conversation

with Jacqui Bryson had reposed in the Ryberg/Shaw file in
John Winter's office for several weeks. He had discussed its
implications with Toby on several occasions: not only had
Shaw contrived a secure hold on televised sport in Britain
(and in America they assumed), but he was prepared to
defend it by blackmail, bribery and any other dubious
methods that he thought necessary. Winter knew that his
continuing curiosity about Ryberg's death and Shaw's part
in it could not stay unremarked for long. Winter was outraged when he received Shaw's letter imposing a new
delivery date for the golf series. It was a unilateral decision
and was unacceptable. He spoke to Dean Aultman, who
told him that the decision was final and Paul Davis echoed
Aultman's words.

To call their bluff, Winter told Aultman that he would
have to withdraw as the producer of the series. To his astonishment, his resignation was accepted and on the following
day a letter from Aultman arrived which summarised the
ungenerous severance terms. For a while Winter played
with the notion of challenging Shaw Management in the
courts. But good sense prevailed over his anger. Why throw
good money away on greedy lawyers?

He realised that Shaw had outflanked him with ease and
was at first depressed. Soon he became elated. His instinct
that there was a big and very dirty story to be told about
Steven Shaw had been proved right, and the tale began
with Nils Ryberg.

The Winters' rambling Victorian house lay on the west
side of London. It had been a home for their expanding
family for over a decade and, though comfortable, looked a
little jaded from the attention of the four children. Toby
Streeter had been asked over for a meal, but primarily to
talk about the Shaw project. All of the Winter family liked
Toby, starting with John's wife, Penny, and ending with

the youngest of his four children, Matthew. It was an early meal because of the varying ages of the Winters' offspring and, when it was over, Winter grabbed a bottle of wine and took Toby upstairs to his study.

'There's no hurry on this Shaw story,' was Winter's first remark, as he pulled the cork from the bottle. 'We've got the development money to do the programme but there are other projects to crack on with meanwhile. Losing the golf series was a blow but there's enough work and money to keep us going for a year or more. Nevertheless, we need a clear plan of campaign. We need a lever to lift the lid on this story. If Shaw is the sort of man we think he is, he'll have enemies and they should be eager to do the dirty on him. So, where are they? Who are they?'

'We start with Jenny Ryberg, don't we? Not that she's got anything concrete to tell us.'

'No, but she'll make a terrific contribution to the programme. She'll give a hefty tug on the viewers' heart-strings. How much she loved her husband, his work for charity, his integrity. How her one small moment of doubt unhinged him and made him commit suicide.'

'But she can't say that Shaw set Ryberg up. Can she?'

'No. We can only show how he benefited and let the viewers form their own conclusions. Toby, we've got to dig deep into Shaw's background and into his business activities. We've got to do our detective work, if you like.'

'Well, let's do a list,' Toby said. 'Shaw's clients, his employees, his family, the sponsors and so on.'

'Agreed. There are obvious names, like Ray Gerrard. He knows plenty about Shaw but he won't tell.'

'That seems to be the problem. People won't risk upsetting Shaw. Maybe we could get at Paul Davis. After all, we do have Jacqui Bryson's evidence. Let's confront him.'

'Not yet, Toby. Jacqui's very useful where she is. We don't want to blow her cover.'

'Maybe she can help us prove that Davis owns a villa on the French Riviera, courtesy of Steven Shaw.'

'Not a chance. If it's owned by a Swiss company, that's the end of the trail, I'm afraid. Nobody gets anything out of a Swiss banker. They take their secrets to the grave. What about the London office, Toby? Is there anyone there who harbours a grudge against Shaw? What about his secretary or this Aultman fellow?'

'Dean Aultman is the only person in the London office who really knows how Shaw works. He's bright and Shaw rewards him well. He's also discreet. As for Lucy Howard, I don't think she knows much. A sweet girl, actually, and I've heard the rumour that she sleeps with Shaw. For that reason alone I don't think we'd get very far with her.'

'What about the sponsors? They can't all love Shaw.'

'You wouldn't think so, the way he screws them for money. But they keep coming back for more.'

'Maybe because he delivers?' suggested Winter.

'Yeah, he puts their name up in lights, you've got to hand it to him. A year or so back, Continental Tobacco were going to pull out of their sponsorship of the Fourball Tournament but suddenly they were in for another four years. The MD, Andrew McDonnell, was supposed to be thirsting for Shaw's blood but he signed up again, quiet as a lamb.'

'Aren't we missing something pretty obvious, Toby? These parties that Jacqui mentioned. Shaw provides the tarts for his guests and you remember that he photographed Jacqui with Paul Davis. It's logical to assume that he uses concealed cameras to record the fun at the parties. Documentary evidence for later use. No wonder nobody's prepared to slag him off, he holds all the aces.'

'Rory McCall,' Toby said decisively.

'The photographer? What about him? He does the royals, doesn't he? I seem to remember he's the brother of an earl.'

'Yes, and rumour has it that he's got a drug habit to go with his addiction to gambling. In other words he's perfect for someone like Shaw to manipulate. He was taking the snaps at Shaw's pre-Wimbledon party.'

'Let's take a look at him. Now, what about Shaw's family and friends?'

'Friends? What friends?' Toby said scornfully. 'He's got acquaintances by the train-load but I can't think of a friend. Lucy Howard might come into that category, I suppose. And he once mentioned a guy he knew at the Harvard Business School. That's it. His parents live in Brighton and I could get at them, I'm sure. I'll say I'm writing an article about their beloved son. There's the gorgeous Suzi, of course. She plays the part of the devoted wife to perfection. But I wonder.'

'So do I. What would she think of Shaw's parties and his relationship with Lucy Howard? I'll try and talk to her when I'm next in New York. The same pretext as you, Toby. A magazine article. And I'll have another crack at Ray Gerrard. You, Toby, should have a go at Sam Rhodes.'

'Difficult. He's very well-protected by Shaw. His first client. How he laid the foundations of his agency with a handshake. All that bullshit. I'll try Rhodes but I don't think it'll lead anywhere. I really like him, he's the genuine article. Anyway, we've got the basis of a plan.'

'Yes,' Winter said. 'But first things first. Let's get our final presentation ready for that series about the Olympics.'

# Chapter Thirty-seven

As Dean Aultman expected, Angus Gray won the Formula One championship in style. He followed his victory in Spain by winning the Japanese Grand Prix with a nerveless display of high-speed driving in torrential rain. He won the final race in Adelaide, too, and made the process look more like an extended victory lap than a real competition.

Steven knew little about motor racing and wanted to keep it that way. All that noise and the technical drivel that obsessed the spectators and commentators alike. To him, the sport was just a branch of the advertising industry. The drivers were covered from head to toe in patches and flashes promoting a dozen different brand names and so were the cars. The way the winner sprayed champagne over everyone on and around the podium actually offended him – what a waste of a good drink! It was great business, though.

He was content to allow Dean Aultman to conduct the negotiations for Gray's services during the following season. In the middle of January, Aultman telephoned him in New York with the news that, despite a very competitive bid from an Italian team, Gray was to continue with his original outfit.

'Christ, it was heavy in Milan,' Dean said cheerfully. 'I was sitting in this office the size of a football pitch and was face to face with the President of the company. When I say face to face, that wasn't strictly true because there was about thirty feet of carved mahogany desk between us. He had a bodyguard outside the door and two more outside the windows. They were all toting Uzi machine-pistols. It was just a bit intimidating, like suddenly being on the set of *The Godfather* and you've forgotten your lines.'

'But you set your jaw and thought of England.'

'No. I thought of all that lovely money. Six million quid. But then our British friends topped his offer.'

'You've done a great job, Dean. I'll be over in a couple of weeks to congratulate you in person. We'll have to take another look at your bonus.'

Lucy Howard felt awful when she woke up that morning. She had all the symptoms of 'flu, including a harsh pain in her stomach. She attributed it partly to jet-lag and partly to the food on the aircraft during her flight home from India on the previous day.

Nevertheless, she stuck to her routine and met Steven at Heathrow. He looked fresh and bouncy, as he usually did whatever the duration of the overnight flight. He asked her about her holiday and then began to run through his itinerary for the next few days.

For a while, Lucy thought that she'd conquered her queasiness but, as the Daimler slowed down and joined the queue of commuter traffic crawling into London, the pain in her stomach gripped even more fiercely.

She opened the window a little. 'Steven, I don't feel well.'

Steven looked up sharply and noticed how pale she was. 'What's the problem?' He slid across the seat and gently put his arm around her and took her hand. Christ, he thought, as soon as I arrive one of my staff gets sick. I'll have to get a temp to help out. He looked past Lucy out of the side-window and a man at the wheel of a Vauxhall Cavalier alongside gave him a lecherous grin and a thumbs-up sign. If only you knew, Steven thought.

Lucy scrabbled in her handbag and found some tissues. 'A touch of food poisoning. I'll be all right once I get to work.'

'No, you won't.' Steven slid the glass partition aside and told the driver to go to Lucy's flat. 'You're going to bed and we'll call a doctor.'

Fortunately, Lucy's flatmate was still at home and, to Steven's relief, she volunteered to take charge. A couple of hours later she left a message at his office to say that Lucy had a mild form of food poisoning and should stay in bed for at least a couple of days.

Later that day Steven sent a huge bunch of flowers to her and his 'Get well' note instructed her to take off as much time as she wished.

Several audiotapes were included with the letter, which ended: 'Just a couple of non-urgent reports on the tapes – in case you get bored. Love from Steven.'

There were no kisses underneath his name, Lucy noted.


It was Steven's habit to skim rapidly through the main national newspapers wherever he was in the world. He wasn't particularly concerned about the key issues, because they were easy to track, but more about the fleeting fashions and ideas of the day. They were important pointers in his business. The newspapers' coverage of his clients' activities was also of great interest.

An item in the Thursday edition of the *Financial Times* caught his eye. It announced the interim results of a small property development company, Macaulay Estates Limited, and commented that its Managing Director, Mr James Macaulay, was pleased with the firm's steady progress after its recent problems. Steven put the newspaper down and wondered if that was the James Macaulay who had ruthlessly sold the family department stores for a quick profit some fifteen years ago: the man who had dismissed loyal employees like Bill Shaw without a thought for their future.

Steven focused again on his past. The images were still sharp in his memory – his fury at the way his father was treated, his confrontation with the arrogant James Macaulay, his passionate affair with Araminta. He remembered her body with an extraordinary clarity, despite the hundreds he'd since enjoyed. She'd be in her mid-forties now. He even remembered the telephone number of her flat. It was Thursday, the Honourable Araminta's usual day for shopping in London.

Steven dialled an internal office number and asked one of his accounting staff to get him a copy of the latest accounts for Macaulay Estates.

At just after eleven o'clock, Steven picked up his telephone and punched the digits of Araminta's number. He remembered the voice that answered so well, its upper-class timbre leavened by a warm undertone. To his surprise, Steven felt his heart thudding as if he were once again a nervous and inexperienced youth confronted by a sophisticated woman.

'Is that Araminta Macaulay?' he asked. Deliberately, he deepened his voice to emphasise the classless quality he'd worked so hard to attain.

'It is. Who's that?'

'A voice from the distant past. Cast your mind back to Brighton in the early seventies. I'm Steven Shaw. I hope you don't mind my ringing you, Araminta. It was just an impulse. Please forgive me.'

Araminta nearly dropped the phone, such was her surprise. That gorgeous boy with the beautiful teeth. And the stamina.

'Good heavens. Steven. I've read about you. I've even seen you on television. There's nothing at all to forgive. How are you?'

For several minutes they exchanged their news. Then Steven asked the vital question.

'Yes,' Araminta replied. 'I'm still married to James. Well, sort of.'

'It was always sort of, I seem to remember.'

Araminta laughed. 'We've had our good times, you know. When he sold the stores we lived in southern Spain for years. It was lovely, but too many Brits arrived. Of the wrong sort. Professional footballers with permed hair and their ghastly wives and children, third-rate television personalities. You know the scene, darling. So we came back to England.'

'And James has a successful property company, I believe.'

'Yes. He nearly went under a couple of years ago but things are looking good now.'

'May I take you to dinner tonight, Araminta, for old times' sake?'

'Well, I—'

'It's my only chance. I'll be on a plane back to New York on Saturday morning.'

Araminta thought quickly. She was supposed to go to the opera with the boring estate agent, Nigel. He could only just get it up at the best of times. She'd put him off. It would be fun to see Steven again. He used to get it up and keep it up.

They met at Rossiter's in Knightsbridge. Restaurants of various persuasions had come and gone on the site but the latest venture looked set to maintain its initial success under the direction of one of the new breed of inventive and publicity-conscious English chefs. David Rossiter-Jones had become a client of Shaw Management and had already recorded his first television series for the BBC.

The soon-to-be-famous chef himself greeted Steven and Araminta. He was small, dark and ebullient and fitted his lively restaurant perfectly. He showed his two customers to Steven's favourite table in the rear corner of the room and a complimentary bottle of Veuve Cliquot was already waiting in its ice bucket.

It was one of the most entertaining and relaxing evenings Araminta had experienced for years. She remembered Steven as beautiful in his youth and he had matured into an assured and civilised man. He still looked lean and fit, she was glad to note, but there was a watchful look in those sharp, grey eyes that was new. Without the hint of a boast he made her aware that he was a powerful and very successful international businessman. He knew his way around a wine list, too.

Towards the end of the meal, Steven surprised Araminta. 'I may have a little business venture soon for James. I've been looking at some property developments on behalf of a few of my clients and I need some expertise in that area. Your husband sounds just the man.'

'I'm sure he'd be delighted.'

'Fine. But, Araminta, will you promise me something?' She nodded her agreement. 'When I contact him, will you make sure that you don't mention my connection with him from the old days? There's no reason why you should, I realise that, but I'd be a tiny bit embarrassed if James knew who I was. I'm sure he'd feel slightly uncomfortable, too. Is that a deal?'

'Of course, Steven, darling. We never discuss business anyway.'

Steven called for the bill and said, 'For old times' sake again, will you invite me back to your flat for coffee? I'd really like that.'

'Steven, would you like to come back for coffee?' replied Araminta.

On the following morning Steven arranged for a bunch of red roses to be delivered to Araminta's flat. It seemed to be his week for sending flowers.

He also instructed one of Dean Aultman's assistants to start the search for a suitable piece of real estate, which could be developed for offices or houses and should be less than ten miles from central London.

# Chapter Thirty-eight

It was shortly after Easter that Toby Streeter finally had some time to devote to the 'Shaw Imperative' as he and Winter lightheartedly called their project. He scanned his list of names and decided to begin with Bill and Mary Shaw. He telephoned them and requested an interview in connection with a magazine article he was writing about Steven.

'Just the early years,' Toby said comfortingly to Mary Shaw. 'I want to know about him as a boy, as your son.'

The Shaws' flat was on the first floor of a tall and elegant Regency building which overlooked the sea on the east side of Brighton. The late afternoon sun struck across the façade which was painted a pristine white. Once inside Toby was surprised by the size of the flat. The living room, into which he was ushered by Mary Shaw, was on the grand scale. Plush sofas were scattered about, a large chandelier hung from the lofty ceiling and several oil paintings adorned the walls. Very few things in the room seemed to be personal to the Shaws, beyond a few framed photographs on the baby grand piano of Steven with his wife and son. Mary Shaw seemed ill at ease. She waved Toby towards a broad bay window which gave an expansive view of the sea.

A tray, laden with sandwiches, biscuits, cake and a large teapot, lay on an ornate table by the window and she urged him to tuck in. Toby settled into a chair while she perched on the edge of the padded window-seat, her back to the view.

'Bill will be along in a moment,' Mary Shaw said.

'Tell me about Steven,' Toby said. 'What was he like as a lad?'

Mary Shaw didn't need any encouragement to list the virtues and achievements of her son. Toby, with no need to prompt her, took a few notes, although the bare bones of Shaw's early life were familiar to him from the various articles which he'd read. A good selection was in the file in Winter's study.

After several minutes, Toby heard the door open and close and Bill Shaw walked over to the table. As he got to his feet to greet him, Toby saw a small, round-shouldered man. Shades of grey was his immediate impression: grey trousers, grey cardigan and a grey face, highlighted by the broken veins on his cheeks and nose. Toby remembered his unscheduled performance of 'Trees' at Steven's smart pre-Wimbledon party; the old man had enlivened a routine occasion.

When they had all settled again and Toby had accepted another cup of tea, he said, 'What about Steven's wife, Suzi, and her family? How d'you get on with them?'

'They're a lovely family,' Mary Shaw said carefully. 'They've been very kind to us, and our grandson, Adam, is a wonderful boy. He reminds me so much of Steven.'

There was a rattle as Bill Shaw replaced his cup in its saucer. Toby noticed that his hands were none too steady. 'Suzi's a grand girl,' he said animatedly. 'She's really beautiful, and Steven should thank his lucky stars that he found her. They're a rich family, you know. Joe Lynagh's a lawyer and he really gave Steven a leg-up, he started him off in his business.'

'Steven didn't need a leg-up from anyone,' Mary Shaw

said sharply. She smiled at Toby. 'What he means is that Mr Lynagh lent him some money but it's all paid back. We would've done the same if we'd had the wherewithal.'

Toby gestured at the flat. 'You seem to be nicely off, if I may say so, Mrs Shaw.'

'We are now. Steven looks after us. He does us proud.'

'One of his companies owns this,' Mr Shaw said. 'He's got property all over. I don't know how he keeps track.'

'In the south of France?' asked Toby.

'I don't know. You'd have to ask him about that.'

After a few more questions, which were answered by Mary Shaw, Toby concluded the interview. As he got up to leave, he saw her husband glance at his watch. He said, 'I'm popping down the road for an hour, Mary.'

The old man had left the talking to his wife who had assumed the conventional pose of a proud mother, delighted by her son's success. Maybe Bill Shaw, especially over a pint of beer or two, would be more revealing, perhaps even indiscreet. It was worth a try.

'I'll drop you off, Mr Shaw, if you like,' Toby said quickly.

'Thanks, lad. That'll save me waiting for the bus.'

'Don't be long,' Mary Shaw said, a warning in her voice. 'Your dinner will spoil.'

Bill Shaw's favoured pub lay on the other side of the town and was a cramped and dingy place on a street corner. No one had attempted to jazz it up and it probably hadn't changed much since the war; it was still very much a 'local'. Bill Shaw was well known to most of the other customers, who nodded or spoke a greeting. As soon as they entered, the landlord began to pull a pint of Bass, which looked in superb condition. Toby confined himself to a half-pint of shandy because he had to drive back to London.

The two men talked about sport for a while and Bill

Shaw told Toby how he'd hoped that his son would have played professional football. 'He had the talent but his mother wouldn't have liked it. She had other ideas.'

'Presumably, so did Steven.'

'Yes, he was always ambitious. He was going to be an accountant. He worked for his first wife's dad but then he decided to go to Harvard.'

Toby hid his look of surprise by fetching another pint. 'Mr Shaw, I didn't know he'd been married twice.'

'Call me Bill. No, Mary doesn't like it known. A shotgun wedding, as we used to call 'em then. Nice girl, Beverly. They met at university. We still get a card from her every Christmas but Mary doesn't want to know. Beverly's parents were very good to our Steven.'

'He seems to have a knack for charming parents, doesn't he?'

'For charming anyone, if you ask me. He's been a great success, Toby, hasn't he?'

Toby nodded. 'Who could I talk to, Bill, about Steven? I need another angle. What about a close friend? Someone from his boyhood, perhaps?'

'Well, there was our neighbour, Danny Kyle. But he's long gone. He went to live in Australia. Steven never really had any best friends. I suppose he was always so busy.'

You bet, thought Toby. 'What about Beverly? I'd like to talk to her. Just for the record.'

'Well, I don't know.'

Toby changed the subject rather than press the man too hard. After another pint, Bill Shaw said, 'Beverly's married again. She's called Beverly Marriott now. Lives in Wiltshire.'

'Wiltshire. Nice county. Whereabouts?'

'Malmesbury way. But not a word to my missus about this. She'd kill me.'

'Let me give you a lift home.'

'No need, Toby. I'm going to have a game of dominoes with the boys and a couple more pints.'

Toby struck lucky with the third Marriott he contacted in Wiltshire. The telephone was picked up on the second ring and Beverly announced herself in an agreeable, evenly pitched voice. Toby explained why he had contacted her and there was a delay of a moment or two.

'I really don't want to talk about Steven. It's a part of my life that I'd rather forget. He upped and left me and our young daughter, as you obviously know.'

'You and I have something in common then,' Toby replied cheerfully, 'because he fired me on the spot as well. I used to edit one of his magazines.'

'Yes, that's Steven all over.'

'When did you last see him?'

'About eight years ago, on a street corner in New York. The Upper East Side. Park Avenue and 83rd it was. The scene is still crystal-clear in my mind.'

'And that was it?'

'Yes, we were still married. But not for long.'

'What happened?'

'The Lynagh law machine went into action. A quickie divorce. A settlement on Emma. That was that. I've never seen him again.'

'Does he see your daughter?'

'No. That was one of my conditions of the divorce.'

'I see. D'you regret all this? Steven is immensely successful, immensely rich.'

'No. Rich is what matters to Steven, but not to me. It's all he ever wanted. That's why he dumped me. Suzi Lynagh was a better prospect.'

'You make him sound like a monster.'

'He is a monster, though he wouldn't recognise his own failings. He's amoral, he doesn't have any finer feelings. I think he'll do anything to ensure his own success. That's his sole motivation. I hated him at the time. I felt betrayed. My whole world was in ruins. But now I'm glad I don't have any connection with him. My husband is a good man and I'm happy.'

'And Steven? A sham?'

'You could put it that way. I met his present wife, Suzi, you know. She's beautiful and she had the sort of class that only lots of money can bring. But I'll bet you two things . . .'

'Go on.'

'That she has an unhappy marriage and, one day, Steven will trade her in for an even better model. It's Suzi you should talk to, she could tell you much more than I can.'

'I'll try and arrange it.'

'If you quote me, Mr Streeter, will you promise me one thing?'

'If I can.'

'Don't make me sound bitter because I'm not. I was at the time, but not now. I count myself lucky.'

The day before the Masters Tournament began at Augusta, Steven Shaw called a press conference to announce his tournament programme over the next eighteen months. His events division now ran fifteen tournaments in various parts of the world. As in previous years, Shaw's events inevitably took leading players away from the America Tour, but there was consternation when some of the assembled journalists realised that his 'World Classic' was scheduled in direct opposition to one of American professional golf's most important championships at the end of November. Not only that but his 'European Classic' was to be played in southern Spain at the end of the following March, when the Players' Championship, which Carl Lansky was trying to promote as the fifth 'major', took place. In both cases, Shaw's prize fund outreached that of the American tournaments by several hundred thousand dollars.

The first shouted question came from the golf correspondent of the *Los Angeles Times*. 'You're in competition with two of American golf's blue riband events. What are you trying to prove, Mr Shaw, that you're bigger and better than Carl Lansky?'

'Not at all, Mr Martin. These are the dates my sponsors requested.' There was some disbelieving laughter in the room and some derisive comment but Steven overrode them. 'I've tried to co-operate with Mr Lansky but he wants to run his own show. He's made it plain that he doesn't need me.'

'So you're going to twist his tail and set about destroying the credibility of the American Tour, is that the big idea?' someone asked from the body of the room. 'There's no chance of Lansky releasing players, anyway,' someone else shouted.

'Golf is an international game, just like tennis,' Steven replied. 'The players are free agents, within the limits of the obligations they have to their domestic tours. I've said that to Lansky on many occasions. Now, if he tries to restrict my players' freedom of action, I'll go to the Federal Trade Commission and, if necessary, I'll go to the law courts.'

'Is Sam Rhodes going to play in your tournaments?' It was Jim Martin again.

'I hope so. We haven't worked out his schedule yet.'

'Are you talking to his agent?' someone shouted amid laughter.

'OK, boys,' Steven said. 'Thanks for your time. Drinks

next door. You can ask me or my executives or the sponsors' representatives anything you like in there.'

Steven had said nothing specific about television coverage of his events because a final decision had not been made by AAN, to whom he had offered his golf package.

To general surprise the Masters was won by the Australian, Vince Holman, who was reckoned to be a veteran even though he had only recently turned forty.

Three days later Steven attended a meeting at the New York offices of AAN. He always liked to linger for a few moments in the reception area and count how many of his clients featured among the action photographs on the walls. Plenty, including Sam Rhodes, Ray Gerrard and the recent addition of Vince Holman. The receptionist, a tall black girl with a classically beautiful face, also caught Steven's attention. He had no doubt that Jake Richardson would already have used his well-practised seduction routine on the woman.

His meeting was with Jake, now a Senior Vice-President of Sports, and his immediate boss. Al Isaacs had been brought in by the parent company to make sure that AAN's sports division showed a profit, and the hatchet-men at head office didn't care how he did it. They had their own seven-figure bonuses to worry about.

One of the areas of concern was certainly golf, the coverage of which entailed a formidable investment in equipment and people. The ratings were falling and didn't justify the expenditure. Steven knew that this was a priceless opportunity to secure AAN's long-term support for his tournaments. Jake had already recommended his package; it was now a question of convincing Isaacs that the deal would be in AAN's best financial interests.

Jake Richardson made his familiar noisy entrance, grinned lecherously at the girl behind the reception desk and gave Steven a vigorous double-handshake.

'Hey, Steven, we're all set, my man. It shouldn't take long. Hi, gorgeous.' He waved at the receptionist, put his arm around Steven's shoulders and urged him towards the double doors into the sports department. The man's brand of bonhomie, demonstrative and tactile, irritated Steven. But Richardson was an important ally. He needed him on the inside at AAN, just as Richardson needed the steady flow of income which came his way from Shaw Management.

Al Isaacs was a small and slender man of an indeterminate age. Steven knew that he must be well into his forties since the obligatory photographs on his desk showed a family which included four children, two of whom were teenagers. Isaacs shook hands briefly and suggested they got down to business. He wiped his spectacles thoroughly and replaced them on his narrow face. Steven wondered, not for the first time, whether his wavy ginger hair was entirely natural. If it wasn't, Isaacs had spent a lot of money on his toupee.

'As you know,' Isaacs began, 'Lansky is asking a whole lot of money for a package of tournaments over the next three years. We'd like to look at alternatives. For some reason, the ratings are dropping. We'll put in a bid but we've got to be realistic.'

'It's obvious why the ratings are down,' Steven said. 'The public are disenchanted with these anonymous golfers they see every week. They come off the college production lines and they can all hit their drives two hundred and eighty yards and they all putt well. They all look the same, as far as you can tell under the visors they all wear, and they're about as interesting as robots.'

'There's something in what you say.'

'The viewers and the spectators want heroes,' Steven

said firmly. 'They identify with Sam Rhodes, he's got charisma. They get involved with Patrice Barbier because he brings fire and adventure to the game. They're fed up with these journeymen golfers with the personality by-pass.'

'And you can deliver some top-class events with the best players in the world?' Isaacs asked.

'I represent the best players.'

'With the exception of Barbier.'

Steven shrugged. 'I can deliver him, nevertheless. Jake's shown you our programme. The World and the European Classics are natural for AAN. You already cover the Masters and you buy the British Open from my company. That's a helluva good hand to be holding in international golf and I can add on some other goodies from our schedule.'

'He's right, Al,' Richardson said. 'With that sort of coverage, we don't need Lansky. Let the other two networks fight it out.'

'As long as the figures work,' Isaacs replied.

'Jake and I will make sure they work,' Steven said. He meant it because he was ready to undercut Lansky to ensure network coverage of his events.

Within a few weeks the contract with AAN was signed and Shaw was able to twist Carl Lansky's tail by announcing the news on the eve of the US Open Championship.

# Chapter Thirty-nine

The middle months of the year were always extremely busy for Steven Shaw because of the confluence of the major sporting events: the Masters, Wimbledon, the American and the British Open Golf Championships. The Olympic Games, scheduled for Madrid at the end of July, added to the intense activity at the agency since Dean Aultman had signed up several British athletes, in addition to his star middle-distance runner, Ben Naylor.

A few weeks before the Olympics, the major sponsors of the British team got together to host a dinner at a prestigious hotel in central London. They made much of their wish to raise money for various charities, but their real objective was to trumpet their involvement with the Olympics. The cream of British sport had promised to appear, both performers and media; they were heavily out-numbered by the hangers-on. Jock-suckers all, as Steven Shaw contemptuously called them.

Steven had encouraged Dean Aultman to reserve a table to demonstrate their power in the British sporting market. Paul Davis, BBC's Head of Sport, Andrew McDonnell of Continental Tobacco and Derek Mason, the Chairman of Salford United were invited.

On the morning of the dinner, Dean Aultman spoke enthusiastically of the agency's chance to wave the flag. 'We'll have the two athletes most likely to win gold for Britain. Ben Naylor for sure and Cheryl Anderson.'

'Are you that confident of Naylor?'

Aultman paused. 'Six months ago I would've said you could bet everything you possess on him. He's a great runner. He's got speed, strength and a beautiful style. But now I'm not so sure.'

'Why not?'

'You've probably read about Zak Ravelli?'

'Italian?'

'No, American. He's young and he's suddenly started to win races. He's a real battler and his times are within a whisker of Ben's. The eight-hundred final shouldn't be a problem for Ben. That's about raw pace; it's almost a sprint now. That suits Ben because he's got plenty in his tank. But Ravelli will be a major threat in the fifteen hundred. Mind you, Ben's always one step ahead when it comes to, erm, performance enhancement.'

'What do middle-distance runners use?'

'Oh, steroids for strength and aggression, and he's not averse to a bit of blood-doping as well. He's got a man in Germany who oversees his programme. The best in the business, Ben calls him the Count.'

'The Count?'

Aultman grinned. 'A joke. Count Dracula.'

'Tell me more about the blood-doping.'

'About six weeks before a big competition they'll take a pint of blood from him, extract the red blood cells, and store them. In the meantime his body replaces the lost blood. Just before the competition, they'll re-infuse the extra blood cells into his body. More red corpuscles in his body means more oxygen available. He'll have a great chance of taking both titles.'

With a thoughtful look at Aultman, Steven said, 'Maybe I'll get to Madrid for the fifteen-hundred final. It'll be good to see the Olympics close up. You've booked plenty of rooms?' Aultman nodded. 'I might bring Corky Price. A bit of extra help. We'll call in a favour and get him a press pass.'

Steven didn't want to leave anything to chance and, between them, he and Corky Price should be able to provide some insurance for Ben Naylor.

'What does Ben do between training sessions?' Steven asked.

'He's interested in politics. He bangs on about the enterprise society and all that crap. When he's won his gold medals, he's going to try and get a safe Tory seat in Parliament.'

'One day he should make the perfect Minister for Sport. You know, Dean, we should try and sign the Count. What a book he could write.' Aultman laughed and Steven continued, 'Make sure you brief me about Cheryl Anderson. All I know is that she's a middle-distance runner, too. Tell me about her family, all the deals in the offing and so on. And can you seat me next to Angus Gray, please?'

Steven had been to dozens of such dinners. They were usually marked by dreary food, grossly over-priced wines and boring speeches. On this occasion, however, he was entertained by the main speakers, both former prime ministers, one from each wing of the political spectrum and both witty and irreverent.

It was just as well that Angus Gray, a lively talker, was next to Steven, since his other neighbour, Cheryl Anderson, would only answer questions or react to comments which were directly addressed to her. Well prepared by Aultman, Steven went through a catalogue of questions about her family, her training and the forthcoming Olympics. He didn't even have the consolation that Anderson was pretty. Far from it. She was sturdy with a pale, square face and close-cropped, mousy hair. Although she was heavily made-up, Steven could discern signs of facial hair, and she had quite a deep voice for a woman. He wondered what she was on. No wonder people were calling the Games the 'Freaks' Olympics.

Ben Naylor sat opposite Steven. Already a sporting multi-millionaire, he was smooth and self-assured. He would make an excellent politician. Aultman had done well to sign him up for the agency.

On his other side, Angus Gray talked about his future. 'One more season after this, I think, Steven. I should win the championship again this year and maybe next as well. Then I'll retire.'

'To do what?'

'Commentate and do all the promotional and consultancy stuff that Dean's lined up for me. But I'll get involved in other sports. As you know, I love the field sports – fishing, shooting, though I don't go hunting. Too dangerous. But my wife is very keen on horses. She's into the three-day eventing scene and I love watching polo. One day I'll get involved. So should you, Steven – they need help to raise sponsorship money.'

'That's not my area at all,' Steven replied quickly. 'There's no money in it for a start.'

'It's very high profile. You'd get to meet some interesting people. You know that the royals are into polo in a big way, don't you?'

It was a fine evening and Steven and Aultman decided to walk back towards Kensington. They used an underpass to cross Park Lane and walked quickly past several homeless people who were begging for loose change from the occasional passers-by.

'Why don't the Government clear these beggars off the streets?' Steven asked impatiently as they went up the steps on the other side and cut across Hyde Park towards Knightsbridge.

Aultman shrugged and Steven continued, 'What the hell is our client, Cheryl Anderson, doing to herself? She looks like an experiment that's gone wrong!'

'Some sort of anabolic steroid. Anadrol I expect – it only stays in the system for a couple of days.'

'Christ, you've only got to look at her to see she's on drugs. If she was a horse they'd take her away and shoot her and then ban all her connections for life.'

'The officials don't see it that way. They've got their testing programme and she's clean.'

'Some testing programme, Dean. It's a complete farce.'

'Agreed, but nobody wants to rock the boat. The boat was listing very badly, by the way, at the World Championships. In fact, it was shipping water, one might say. One of the athletes tested for drugs was Ben Naylor and the test was positive. And he wasn't the only one. Several of the other big names were caught out.'

'I thought you said the Count was infallible.'

'He's supposed to be. But Ben was, for once, careless. It was all rather amusing. With hindsight, that is. Ben had been on a course of anabolic steroids, which as usual ended several weeks before the championships. But the bloody fool had his pint of blood removed before his system was clear of the drug. An oversight. So, just before the championships, the blood was taken out of storage and re-infused in his body. Whoops! Traces of the steroid show up in his test.'

Steven laughed. 'What happened?'

'As I say, nobody in athletics wants to stop the gravy train rolling. All that lovely money that keeps the officials and the promoters in luxury. They don't want to catch the Ben Naylors and the Cheryl Andersons. So, someone spread some money about and the offending urine samples went missing from the laboratory. It was all blamed on the cleaners. Can you believe that?'

'Dean, I'll believe anything to do with sport. If Naylor goes into politics, he'll find it all very tame after international athletics.'

'Yes, but we've done famously by representing him and we'll make big money from Cheryl Anderson too.'

'Maybe. But Dean, I wouldn't go after any endorsements for cosmetics and clothing. Maybe she could promote one of the electric razor brands.'

Aultman laughed and, as they parted at the junction of Sloane Street, said, 'By the way, I think we've found a property that you might be interested in. It's in west London, the site of a school that's gone out of business. I'll tell you more tomorrow.'

While Steven was in London, John Winter was in New York, primarily to seek out archive film of the Olympics for his series. Winter established where Shaw was by the simple expedient of telephoning his office and asking. Since he was safely out of the way, Winter felt more relaxed about contacting Suzi.

After trying her number on several occasions during the course of two days, Winter at last found her at home and asked if she would allow him to interview her.

'Who for?' she sounded wary.

'One of the British golf mags.'

'I don't know anything about Steven's business, I assure you.'

'I'm interested in Steven's family, in you and your son, that sort of thing.'

'I'm sorry to disappoint you, Mr Winter, but our private life is exactly that and will remain so.'

Suzi Shaw was polite and Winter could discern the charm in her manner. But she was also very firm. He thanked her and hung up.

Suzi sighed. At the best of times, she rarely gave way to the temptation to talk about her private life. Her mother was her only confidante. She didn't even want to talk to her about her recent problem. Suzi was late with her period and, since she was normally as regular as the tides, she assumed that she was pregnant. She hadn't made love to Steven for several weeks. The putative father could only be Sam Rhodes.

That evening Toby received a call from John Winter, who told him of his lack of success with Suzi. He suggested that they should turn their attention to Shaw's tame photographer, Rory McCall.

'Why should he tell us anything?' Toby replied. 'Or are you thinking of using a length of rubber hose on him?'

'It's sometimes surprising what people let slip, Toby. I've met him. We were on a chat-show together a few years back.'

'That's hardly the basis for an intimate discussion about Shaw, is it?'

'No. But if I pretend I want to talk about a collaboration on a book that'll get us through the door, won't it? Let's have a bash. I'll be back on Tuesday.'

McCall's studio was located in a narrow street of smartly decorated cottages which were tucked away behind the main thoroughfare in the Notting Hill Gate area of west London.

The two men were greeted by a cheerful girl in jeans and a T-shirt and Toby registered the main features of the ground-floor office: a couple of desks, a sofa, some leather armchairs and two large filing cabinets against one wall. Photographs taken by McCall were the main form of decoration on the hessian-covered walls.

They heard McCall coming. He bounced noisily down the stairs, threw open the door to the office and exclaimed how delighted he was to see John Winter again. Winter remembered him as small and energetic and he was little changed, although he seemed much slimmer. His crinkly black hair had thinned, especially at the front, and was now tied back in a ponytail. It accentuated his sharply drawn features. Winter wondered why incipient baldness usually prompted people to resort to that hairstyle. McCall led them up the stairs, paused at a refrigerator on the landing to extract a bottle of white wine and ushered them into his office-cum-studio. He waved them into a couple of easy chairs.

'This is where I spend most of my time,' McCall said. 'The dark room is through that door.' He gestured to his right. 'All the tools of my trade are in there.'

He wandered about the room until he found a corkscrew and then slopped the wine carelessly into three glasses. Having taken his seat behind the desk, he seemed unable to settle. As the three men traded gossip about their respective professions he kept shifting his position, one moment lying back in his chair with his hands laced behind his head and the next leaning forward to drum his fingers on the desk. Toby was nervous just looking at the man.

After a few minutes McCall looked eagerly at Winter, and said, 'OK, John, you've got a project in mind for me and I'd be happy to work with you, if the price is right.' He grinned at his two visitors. 'The price always has to be right.'

'It depends what you mean by the right price,' Winter said cheerfully. 'We're not in Steven Shaw's league, for instance. You do a lot of work for him, I'm told.'

Fidgeting with his wine glass, McCall said, 'I work for lots of people.'

'But you do special assignments for Shaw, don't you?' Toby suggested quietly.

McCall stood up and wandered over to a cabinet and leaned against it. 'What's all this Shaw business? I thought you came here, John, to discuss a publishing project?'

'I'm interested in Shaw because we're researching a story about him and you can help us.'

'That depends on the story.'

'It's not the usual whitewash,' Toby said, 'that sycophantic slush that people like Ian Westwood on *The Journal* spew out. You'd probably know how much Shaw pays him, wouldn't you, Rory?'

'I don't know anything about his business.' McCall looked quickly around the room as if seeking an escape route.

'Are you afraid of Shaw?' Toby asked.

'Afraid? Why should I be?'

'You look agitated, that's why,' Toby countered. 'I used to work for him and I began to realise that he's a first-class bastard, but I wouldn't say that he scared me. So what's the problem, Rory?'

'There's no problem except that you're here under false pretences. I do a bit of work for Steven Shaw and, as you rightly said, he's a very good payer and that's it. End of story.'

'Why won't you help us?' Winter asked quietly.

'Because I can't,' McCall replied as he walked jerkily over to the door and opened it. 'I've got a lot of work to do. You'll have to excuse me.'

With pints of bitter in front of them, John Winter and Toby Streeter settled into a corner of a dingy pub not far from McCall's studio.

'Where do we go from here, I wonder?' Winter said. 'McCall's a dead end, I'm afraid.'

'Not at all. Let's not give up. He's twitchy and he's scared. Scared probably that if he upsets Shaw he'll lose the money that feeds his costly habit.'

'Habit?'

'Yes. That sniffing isn't caused by a common cold, you know.'

'No. What's he on? Cocaine?'

'Probably. Some cynic said that cocaine is God's way of telling you that you've made too much money.'

They both drew thoughtfully on their beer and Toby said, 'If I could get into that studio and have a nose about . . .'

'That's what I was thinking.'

'I'll bet we could find something. Maybe not directly about Shaw but something we could use to pressure McCall. And he'll crack under pressure, believe me.'

'I know someone who might help us,' Winter said. 'I use him for, erm, more sensitive enquiries. If I call Harry Bevan, will you go and see him while I'm in Berlin?'

Harry Bevan had a small office near the Oval Cricket Ground and could not have looked and sounded less like a private investigator. Tall and tubby, he had a rubicund face and a pronounced Lancashire accent. To Toby he looked like a typical publican rather than London's answer to Philip Marlowe

When Toby had explained the service he required, Bevan was silent for a few moments and then said, 'Breaking and entering. Very dodgy that, lad. Not normally my cup of tea. It's only because Mr Winter is involved that I'd even consider helping you. Fraught with problems. What sort of alarm system does the subject have? Is there a safe? Does he live on the premises? And so on.'

'He rents a studio in Notting Hill. It's in a mews. I don't know anything about the security.'

'And you need to gain access? You need to have a look around for something, is that the idea?'

'Yes, I've got to get inside.'

'OK. I'll call you tomorrow. You need an expert and he's got to be reliable.'

The call from Bevan came late on the following afternoon. 'You'll meet a man called Lenny in the Addison Arms tomorrow a quarter of an hour before closing time. He's thirty-ish, has a beard, will have casual clothing on, dark clothing for obvious reasons, and will be reading a copy of the *Sporting Life*. Drinks Guinness. Lenny could get you into Fort Knox if you wanted, but this place is a doddle, lad. A Mickey Mouse alarm and so on. It's a good time for this sort of thing, after throwing-out time in the pubs. Lenny will deal with anything that needs opening inside and then you can both leave discreetly.'

'Do I have to pay him?'

'No, we'll do all that. And, by the way, I'll be keeping an eye on the subject. To make sure he doesn't take it into his head to visit the studio. This little lot is going to cost Mr Winter. I hope it's worth it.'

Toby found Lenny in the Addison Arms without any difficulty and at closing time they walked the half-mile to McCall's studio. Even though the night was cool, Toby found that he was sweating. He kept checking his jacket pocket to make sure that the plastic carrier-bag was still there. He wasn't sure what he would find in McCall's studio, if anything, but he wanted to be prepared.

Lenny, lean and assured, said little to him, and when they arrived in the mews, it took him just a few seconds to open the front door of the studio. If anyone had been watching, it would have seemed that he was merely

fumbling with the keys to the entrance. He knew where
the control box for the alarm was and turned off the system.

'They always leave the key by the box,' he said with a
satisfied smile.

With his heart thudding, Toby followed Lenny through
a door into a ground-floor room. His companion in crime
walked over to the window, closed the venetian blinds and
put on the lights. Toby headed straight for the cabinets,
neither of which was locked. They contained a conventional system of files listed by client, among whom were all
the national newspapers and many of the leading magazines. He seized a slender folder marked Shaw Management
and was disappointed that it held nothing more interesting
than a few invoices for moderate amounts.

Toby turned his attention to the desks but they revealed
nothing except a disorderly array of stationery. By mutual
consent the two men headed for the stairs to the first floor
after Lenny had switched off the lights and reopened the
blinds.

McCall's dark-room had only one cabinet. It held several
boxes of film and a variety of chemicals. Lenny gestured at
the lower shelf which held several cameras. He squatted
down to look. 'Shit, a Hasselblad and a couple of Leicas
and a Nikon. And I can't touch them,' he said wistfully. 'I
could nip back sometime, I s'pose.'

'No, you bloody can't.'

Toby looked around the office and a cupboard revealed
several shelves of box files, neatly labelled. He delved into
the S to Z box and found, after a folder marked
'Sandringham', one for Shaw Management. All it contained
were photographs of the agency's clients.

Irritated by his inability to find any hidden treasures,
Toby sat behind McCall's desk and tried the central drawer.

It was locked but did not survive Lenny's skilled persuasion for more than a few seconds.

'Why did he bother to lock this?' Toby asked as he sorted through the unpromising muddle of the drawer. 'Pens, pencils, visiting cards . . . nothing of any interest.'

He slammed the drawer shut.

'You'll never make a burglar,' Lenny said as he reopened the drawer, felt around for a moment and almost immediately drew out an envelope which was taped to the underside of the desk top. He handed it to Toby who emptied out the contents – a couple of dozen black and white photographs. All were crystal clear, as he would have expected from Rory McCall's lens, and the faces of the male participants were clearly shown. In some of the pictures, where more than two people were involved, Toby found it difficult to work out who was doing what to whom. The important thing was that he recognised most of the men as business associates of Steven Shaw and they included Paul Davis, Andrew McDonnell of the Continental Tobacco Company and many other captains of commerce.

'Bingo,' Toby said quietly to himself. As he shuffled through the photographs, he was conscious of Lenny looking over his shoulder.

'Blimey,' Lenny said, 'he's got a weapon on 'im, ain't he?'

Toby put the pictures back in the envelope and shoved them into his carrier-bag. It was interesting that the Chairman of one of Britain's largest High Street banks seemed to like boys, and the blacker the better.

'Let's go,' Toby said quietly.

'Not yet.' Lenny was pointing at a rack of video-cassettes. 'There could be lots of good stuff there.'

Most of the cassettes had company names written on

their spines, and several had events – Henley Regatta and Ascot Races, for example. Lenny pointed Toby towards three or four marked with dates and switched on a television and a video machine in one corner. He turned the volume right down and, grinning, shoved a cassette into the player.

The live action sequences covered the same ground as the still photographs and with many of the same people. Toby did not identify all of them but he did recognise a former Wimbledon tennis champion, Francesca Zanini, bucking away astride her erstwhile coach, Kenny Crane.

It was an intense disappointment to realise that neither in the photographs nor on the video was there a sign of Steven Shaw. Not that Toby was surprised by that.

'OK, I've got enough,' Toby said, as he put the cassette in his bag.

'Just one more,' Lenny said. He'd really entered into the spirit of the occasion, thought Toby. Lenny grabbed a video-case from the end of the rack and tried to remove the cassette. Several small sachets fell on to the carpet. Lenny picked them up, walked to McCall's desk and shook the video-case.

'What a naughty boy,' he said, as over a dozen sachets containing white powder fell out.

'And rather careless,' Toby said. 'You'd better put them back.'

'Well, yeah, but minus a couple. I'm not a user but I know where to sell this stuff. And I was a good boy over the cameras.'

'Make sure you don't come back for them, Lenny, won't you?'

'I wouldn't do that. Mr Bevan wouldn't like it.' With a grin, he pocketed three sachets and Toby urged him out of the room. They checked that all the lights were off and the internal doors shut. Lenny turned on the alarm and the two men ducked out of the front door. To Toby's relief, there was nobody in the street and they took different directions away from the building. A glance at his watch told Toby that he'd been in McCall's studio for less than twenty minutes. It had seemed like a lifetime. But what a result! What prizes to show to Winter when he returned to London!

# Chapter Forty

With commendable speed and efficiency, the ten-acre site of the old school in west London earmarked by Dean Aultman as suitable for his employer's purposes, had been acquired. The surveyor who acted for Steven was a friend of Aultman's and helped him refine his plan.

The first step was to persuade James Macaulay that a genuine business opportunity existed and, to this end, Steven invited him to lunch at the Parkside Tower hotel. Steven had been anxious that he should not have any inkling that their paths had once crossed in Brighton. He judged that Macaulay would not see any parallel between the wealthy entrepreneur with the classless accent and the expensive tastes who was entertaining him in one of Europe's best hotels and the reckless, underprivileged youth who had confronted him in a Brighton car park some fifteen years before.

Steven recognised the man as soon as he entered the dining room. For a moment all the security induced by his successes drained out of him and his hatred of Macaulay and what he represented flooded through his body.

The intervening years hadn't improved him. The dark, double-breasted suit could not hide his bulk as he waddled in the wake of the *maître d'hôtel*. The superior look, which Steven remembered so well, still stained his face. It was even fatter, its characteristics obscured by the ample folds of flesh. Greed and self-indulgence on two legs, Steven thought, as he rose and greeted his guest with a wide smile. Despite the air conditioning, he noticed that Macaulay's face was damp from the effort of walking across the dining room. How on earth could Araminta let him near her? She probably didn't.

'Your usual bottle of Veuve-Cliquot, sir?' asked the *maître d'hôtel*.

'Would some vintage champagne suit you, Mr Macaulay?' Steven asked, as he handed him a sixteen-page brochure about Shaw Management.

'Oh, yes, it's my favourite tipple.' The man's voice hadn't changed and Steven remembered how he'd humiliated his father all those years ago.

'That booklet tells you a little about the company,' Steven said. 'As you see we are the world's leading agency for sports celebrities, we package a wide range of sport for television and sell the rights for the blue riband events around the world. We have a huge business in books about sport and we represent some of the top football clubs in Britain. We're involved in most aspects of most of the major sports around the world.'

'I'm very impressed, Mr Shaw—'

'Call me Steven, please.'

'Thank you. I just wonder why you're entertaining me to lunch. You mentioned a property deal on the phone. You need some advice. With your contacts, I'd have thought you could afford the best that's available in London.'

'I can but that's not how I want to do business, James. You see, I read about your company in the *Financial Times*. You're doing fine and, like me, you run the show. You're in charge of your own destiny and therefore you're the sort of person I prefer to work with. I'm not interested in some old-established firm in Mayfair where the partners take six weeks to answer a letter.'

Macaulay's face wobbled with misplaced pride as he drained his glass at a gulp. Steven refilled it. What a waste of good champagne, he thought. 'The point is this, James, that my clients have considerable funds to invest. I'd like to diversify a little, test the temperature of the property market in Britain. But I need a partner, someone with drive, someone I can work happily with. And when I read about you, I thought it was worth a call, worth a lunch.'

'What sort of property are you looking for? Commercial? Residential?'

'I'd like to do some small-scale development. In the south-east of course, preferably in the London area. One of my executives has been looking around and he's unearthed one or two sites that would bear a second look. Maybe we could start there, examine their potential.'

'You're going too fast for me,' Macaulay said, as he crammed a piece of lamb into his mouth and chewed vigorously. A dribble of sauce worked its way down his chin. 'The property market is unstable. You can spend a lot of time and get nowhere, and my time is worth money, Steven, just like yours. I can't work on a promise of jam tomorrow.'

'Of course not.' Steven reached into the briefcase by the side of his chair and handed Macaulay a single sheet of paper. 'The main points are there for discussion. We'll pay your daily rate as a consultant whatever happens. It'll be seen as an advance against your twenty-five per cent share of the profits. We'll formalise everything as quickly as possible. But why don't you give your expert opinion on these various properties?' Steven handed him some more sheets of paper. 'Do we have the basis of a deal?'

Shaw recognised the shifty flutter of greed on his guest's face. Christ, he'd make a lousy poker player. Macaulay raised his glass and said, 'It looks OK to me. I'll have to consult my lawyer and accountant, of course.'

'Now what about some cheese and a glass of port?'

Macaulay's lawyer was germane to Shaw's scheme. Dan Fisher had investigated Mark Brandon and had described him as 'a cheapjack, lazy and incompetent'. He had told Shaw that he was also vain and had the illusion that he was a really sharp operator. He was perfect for Steven.

When they parted outside the hotel entrance, Steven held up his hand and Terry Parkin, in his firm's biggest limousine, glided to a halt.

'Please take Mr Macaulay wherever he wants, will you, Terry?' Steven shook hands heartily with Macaulay. 'I'll wait to hear from you, James. I'm off to Hong Kong tonight but I'll be back in town in about ten days. Lucy Howard always knows where I can be contacted.'

Got you, you fat, stupid bastard, Steven thought as the car eased its way silently into the early afternoon traffic.

James Macaulay had begun his work early on the following morning. By eleven o'clock he had scouted all the properties whose details Steven Shaw had given him and he had returned to the one which had the clearest potential for development. Macaulay peered through the fence at the site of the school. Houses encircled it on three sides and a substantial Georgian building took up one corner. It was perfect for conversion to flats and the rest of the property could take at least forty houses. Outline planning permission had been granted for such a scheme. He hurried away to talk to the estate agent whose board was fixed to the fence.

In the estate agency office a vigorous young man gave him the details of the property in Langdale Road and confirmed that it had planning permission for housing. Macaulay knew that the price being asked was slightly below its true market value but he said, 'The price is a bit steep, isn't it? I was vaguely interested but not at this figure.'

'You can try an offer, sir,' Marcus Lane replied. 'The owner wants a quick sale, so I'm told.'

With a grunted promise to think about it, Macaulay headed for his office near Olympia. His first call was to his bank manager to request a bridging loan of several million pounds. The manager acquiesced 'in principle'. He neither liked nor trusted Macaulay, but the family account had been at the bank for over a century. He reckoned that James would bite off more than he could chew one day. When that happened his only regrets would be for Araminta Macaulay. He still savoured the memory of the knee-trembler he'd had with her at the bank's Christmas party a few years ago.

Macaulay's second call was to a building company in Sussex which undertook some carefully considered property development. The firm was shrewdly managed and had ridden the recession well. Macaulay had completed one successful project with them and knew that the Langdale Road site was perfect for their conservative outlook. Yes, said the Managing Director, it sounded very interesting. Would Macaulay send the details by fax?

It was all very simple. Macaulay would buy the property himself and sell it on to the Sussex company. It was under-valued and he saw himself making a quick profit of around half a million pounds. As for Shaw, he'd tell him they'd missed the boat on the best of the four sites and he'd look around for other similar properties.

While Macaulay was speaking to his bank manager, Marcus Lane was on the telephone to Dean Aultman.

Under instructions from Steven Shaw, who had promised generous bonuses all round, Macaulay's offer for the Langdale property was rushed through. Processes that normally took weeks were abbreviated to a matter of hours. Macaulay couldn't believe his luck and he browbeat his solicitor, Mark Brandon, into reacting as speedily as the representatives of the vendor, a company registered in the Isle of Man.

When John Winter returned from Berlin, Toby Streeter resumed his habit of having an evening meal with him and his family. They had much to discuss.

Comfortably ensconced in Winter's study, a bottle of wine before them, Toby went through his adventures with Lenny and told Winter what they had found.

'Where's the, ah, evidence?' Winter asked.

'In the safety deposit box at your bank.'

'Won't McCall miss it?'

'Maybe, but he's so bloody careless. And what can he do if he does miss the photos? Call the police?'

'I take your point, Toby, but I'm wondering how we can use what we now know. You say that Shaw is nowhere to be seen on the videos or in the photos.'

'No, but they're his clients who are playing the starring roles.'

'It's inadmissible evidence as the lawyers say, especially since you obtained it illegally.'

'Maybe we could get some of the girls to talk. It must be Shaw who's paying them.'

'Not necessarily,' Winter said thoughtfully. 'He'd have a middleman, a gofer to do his dirty work.'

'So we'll put the squeeze on McCall. He's as weak as water. We'll tell him that we found some of his property and want to give it back. I've made copies, of course.'

'You're really on the case, aren't you, Toby?'

'Yes. We know how Shaw works. What a corrupt bastard he is.'

''Twas ever thus,' Winter said, '"Money makes the world go round, the world go round",' he sang.

'And sex.'

'Of course. But let's not get tarnished by Shaw's brush, however pure our motives are.'

'We'll have to get our hands dirty, John. You think of your friend, Ryberg. Doesn't that whole incident have Shaw's obscene stamp on it? Wouldn't you bet that he dreamt up that story about Nils's homosexuality? Well, we'll use a bit of blackmail of our own. On McCall. If the drug squad found that much coke in his possession they'd put him away for several years.'

'I don't like it,' Winter said. 'But you're right. We'll pressure him and see what happens.'

Suzi Shaw had not mentioned her pregnancy to anyone, least of all her mother. Betty Lynagh had already taken to asking Suzi 'how things were' with Steven. She had observed how much time she spent with Sam Rhodes and how little with Steven. Suzi was afraid that her mother would jump to the right conclusion.

Mrs Lynagh had voiced her worries about the state of Suzi's marriage to her husband. He was familiar with the demands of international business and told her that Steven had to run hard just to keep abreast of the challenges that faced his firm. 'It comes with the territory,' Lynagh said. 'And by the way, Betty, the one thing you don't do is interfere in someone else's marriage, and certainly not your daughter's.'

Suzi knew that any confession that Sam Rhodes was the father of her child would devastate her parents. She didn't care what Steven would think because she neither loved him nor felt anything for him. But she didn't want their marriage to end yet. The status quo suited her; one day she would make the break but only when she was ready. There was only one way to resolve the problem.

Steven arrived in New York, via Hong Kong, Sydney and Los Angeles and confirmed what Suzi already knew: that he was booked on a flight to London four days later. She had little time.

Steven was surprised when Suzi suggested that they had dinner together. It was Saturday night and for once they had no social engagements. In public they still presented themselves as the devoted couple, but in private they led separate lives, divided by Suzi's antipathy on the one side and Steven's complete preoccupation with the affairs of business on the other. They were polite to each other for the sake of Adam but their aloofness extended to their occupying separate bedrooms and often to taking their evening meals at different times. Not that Steven was often at home for dinner. He realised that his marriage had ironic echoes of that of his parents.

'Let's have dinner together,' Suzi said. 'Just the two of us, for a change.'

'We eat out all the time,' Steven replied. 'I'd like to stay home. I've got masses of correspondence to look at. Some contracts to read.'

'What is it your pop says? "All work and no play . . ."'

'Yes, well my dear old dad never had to run a large and complex business.'

'Steven, we never spend any time together.'

'Whose fault is that?'

'Both of us. And I think we should try a little harder to be nice to each other. I've booked a table at a new restaurant a couple of blocks away. How about it? Let's put our differences aside or should I say our indifference?' Suzi smiled at him and arched her eyebrows expectantly. Steven shrugged his agreement.

A basement whose starkly decorated while walls were relieved by a few abstract paintings housed the restaurant. The clientele was fashionable – Steven recognised a television producer and Suzi said hello to several people she knew on the charity circuit – and so was the cooking. The emphasis was vegetarian and the approach to the few meat and fish dishes was minimalist; everything was 'quickly seared'.

If the food promised more than it delivered, it didn't seem to matter because Suzi made a resolute effort to be attentive to everything that Steven said. Always vivacious and interested in other people, she had developed her skills considerably in the last few years and used them on her husband. His initial wariness disappeared and they were soon chatting animatedly. Steven gave his wife an edited version of his campaign against James Macaulay. Since she was so fond of Bill Shaw, she approved of the principle of Steven's getting even with the man who had humiliated his father. But she questioned the extent of the revenge. She did not voice her doubts because her objective was to humour and flatter Steven, not to provoke him by criticism.

When they arrived home, Suzi tried to sustain the cheerful mood of the evening by suggesting that they had a night-cap. 'Let's take a bottle of champagne to bed, darling, like the old days.'

'I don't want to be churlish, Suzi, but I've got an early start tomorrow. Golf with Jake Richardson and some sponsors at Westchester. You know how it is.'

'That never used to hold you back.'

'Times change. We've changed. Anyway, I didn't imagine you were interested in me any more.'

Suzi moved closer to Steven and put her arms around his neck. 'That's where you're wrong. Go along to bed, darling, and I'll get the champagne.'

What a cold bastard you are, Suzi thought, as she put the bottle and two glasses on a tray and followed him upstairs. But she had a job to do, just like a high-class whore. She steeled herself for her task and thought back to the time when Steven had been the centre of her world. She had adored him, and for the next few minutes she must pretend.

When Steven returned to London, one of his first calls was to James Macaulay to check on his progress.

'A problem, Steven, old boy. Only one site was really viable, the old school, and a sharp little property company got in ahead of me. They probably heard I was sniffing around and that was good enough for them. They dived in and bought it. Not to worry, I'll find something even better for us. You're top of my action list, believe me.'

Two nights later, Steven took Araminta out for dinner again. He had never forgotten the location of the Italian restaurant where they had first dined together and Lucy Howard discovered that it still existed. When she booked a table she wondered why Steven had chosen such a modest place to dine; perhaps his parents had received one of his rare invitations to visit him in London. They had been his guests at Wimbledon but that had been at Suzi's insistence.

To Steven's eyes, the restaurant looked as if time had passed it by. It seemed to have the same decor, and maybe even the same head waiter. Only a few tables were occupied and Steven, who had deliberately arrived several minutes early, secured the table at which he and Araminta had dined together for the first time.

When she arrived, Araminta smiled widely at him and said, 'What a romantic you are, Steven! I wouldn't have put money on your remembering this place.'

'There are things about you I'll never forget.'

'Can you remember what you ordered on that first occasion?'

'Of course. Veal milanese. Very suitable for a hungry student, and that's what I'm going to have tonight. The menu hasn't changed much, has it?'

'Nor have you, darling.' Araminta laid her hand on top of his. 'You're still as gorgeous and you look even more sexy, if that's possible.'

'I'll drink to that.'

Nor had Araminta changed much, Steven later reflected. Perhaps her hips were a little more fleshy but her physical needs were as sharp and varied as ever.

On the Friday morning, Macaulay received a disquieting telephone call from Bernie Haywood, the oldest of the three brothers who owned the Sussex building firm. The purchase of the Langdale Road property had been completed by Macaulay and the money paid, by virtue of his bank's bridging loan. Haywood had agreed to buy the site and Macaulay was looking forward to a nice profit of over £400,000. He'd take a holiday but not with that bitch, Araminta. Maybe he'd go to Thailand and enjoy some of the talent out there.

'Bernie, how are you?' Macaulay said heartily. He despised the man, even though he acknowledged his shrewdness. 'When will you be ready to complete the deal?'

'When you've got clear title to the whole property.'

'What on earth d'you mean? What's the problem? My lawyer did all the searches and so on.'

'Well, he's a prat,' Haywood said bluntly. 'Because you haven't bought the whole site. There's a strip of land at the front. It covers the grass verges on both sides of the fence. You can hardly see it on the plan, it just looks like a slightly thicker black line. But my surveyor spotted it and checked it out. It's still owned by some company registered in the Isle of Man.'

'I'll sort it out. Just a technical error, Bernie.' Macaulay tried to keep the panic out of his voice.

'I hope so. Otherwise, it's no deal, because whoever owns that strip of land can deny access to the site. Some technical error, eh, James.'

His face running with sweat, Macaulay contacted Marcus Lane, the agent who had sold the land to him. 'Now look here, Lane,' he began, 'there's been some sort of cock-up over Langdale Road. It was my understanding that I'd bought the whole site, but your vendor seems to have retained a small and insignificant area. It's obviously a mistake but I have to say that there seems to be some negligence on your part.'

'Not at all. You were given the plans and all the relevant documents. Didn't your solicitor check everything?'

'Of course, but—'

'Good, then I suggest you sue him for negligence.'

'Don't be bloody ridiculous. He's a one-man-band with a small practice in Richmond. His insurance wouldn't cover this kind of thing.'

'I'm sorry to hear that,' Lane said, trying to keep the glee out of his tones.

'Well, who are these Isle of Man people? Who's their representative in London?'

'It's a Mr Steven Shaw. Here's his number.'

Macaulay put the telephone down without a word. A sudden attack of nausea sent him lumbering towards the lavatory.

Steven refused to see Macaulay until the following Thursday. He'd let the miserable bugger sweat it out until then. When Macaulay arrived promptly at six o'clock for their meeting, Steven kept him waiting for nearly an hour. The concealed tape recorder was running when he at last admitted Macaulay to his office.

'Hello, James,' Steven said in a friendly fashion. 'I expect you want to talk about Langdale Road.'

'Yes. There seems to be a slight misunderstanding about the site.'

'It's crystal-clear to me. You see, James, I did my research very thoroughly. You copped a bundle of money back in the seventies and you lived in Spain. You did a few property deals but got your fingers badly burned a few years back with some developments and you paid the price.'

'I was let down by my partners.'

'You were let down by your own stupidity. And that's what I was gambling on when I set you up. On your greed and your stupidity. I looked at your accounts and they told me what I was expecting. You do all your trading via bank loans. You don't have any real assets, aside from your house and the apartment at Sotogrande. I'm just bloody amazed that any bank would trust you with their money, but then the banks are hardly renowned for the quality of their judgement, are they?'

'I run a reputable property company, that's why the bank trusts me.'

'Not for much longer, they won't. I guessed that you'd go behind my back and try to make a fast profit. You're just a cheap spiv, Macaulay, that's all you amount to.'

Macaulay stood up and tried to assert himself. 'I'm not taking any more of these vile insults. It was always my intention to deal fairly with you but things got out of hand. I had to move fast and you weren't around.'

'Sit down,' Steven said fiercely. 'And don't lie to me, you miserable shit. I set you up. I already owned Langdale Road and we set the price low to drag you in. I knew you wouldn't be able to resist such a bargain. And we guessed that stupid, lazy solicitor of yours, Mark Brandon, wouldn't do his job properly, that he'd miss the ransom strip.'

'Ransom strip? What d'you mean?' Macaulay was sweating heavily and he wrenched a silk handkerchief from the breast-pocket of his suit and mopped his face.

'The ransom strip is that bit of land either side of the front fence. I own it, and that arsehole of a lawyer you use didn't spot it.'

'But surely we can do a deal,' Macaulay said hoarsely. 'We could share the profits, if you like.'

'A deal?' Steven said softly. 'A deal? You still don't get it, do you?'

'We can both make some money, old boy. That's what this business is all about.'

'That's where you're wrong. You won't be making anything out of the deal. Because the ransom strip has a hell of a price on its head.'

'How much?'

'I want two and a half million pounds for it.'

His mouth gaping in horror, Macaulay looked helplessly at Steven. 'That's bloody preposterous, it's laughable. No one would pay that kind of money.'

'And you're stuck with a worthless piece of real estate, aren't you? No access, no profit. It's very simple. Remember, I've already got my money, courtesy of your bank, and can afford to wait. You can't.'

'Why are you doing this to me?'

Steven swivelled his chair and, with his face in profile to Macaulay, gazed out of one of the windows. 'Cast your mind back to the days of Macaulay's department stores and specifically the one at Brighton. You'll remember when you sold the business, when you sold the people who'd worked hard for your family down the river. You do remember, don't you?'

'I had no alternative,' Macaulay blustered, as he dried his face yet again with his handkerchief.

'You kicked a lot of people out of their jobs just to line your own pocket and you paid them a miserable pittance even if they'd spent their lives working diligently for Macaulay's. One of those people was Bill Shaw. Do you remember him?'

'Well, I can't be expected—'

'Soft furnishings. You shat on him from a great height in front of the customers and in front of me. I'm his son, as you've probably realised, and I never forgot how you spoke to him that day. You wouldn't remember because I imagine you spoke to everybody like that. And I tried to intervene when you sacked my father. I waited for you in the car park and tried to beg some more money for my dad but you treated me like shit, too.'

'I'm really sorry, Mr Shaw,' Macaulay stuttered. 'I'm sorry about your father, believe me. It was all so long ago. Surely you can't bear a grudge for so long. It's water under the bridge now.'

'No. I can remember it as if it was yesterday.' Steven stood up. 'The deal is on the table. Two and a half million for my interest in Langdale Road. Let me show you out.'

Steven escorted the man out of his office, down the stairs and along to the front door. He ignored Macaulay's outstretched hand as they paused on the front step. 'By the way,' Steven said, 'Araminta was a wonderful fuck for an eighteen-year-old like me back in Brighton. It was nice to find that she's still as good as ever and that she still likes it up her arse. Give her my love, won't you?'

He shut the door on Macaulay and watched with glee from a window as he walked, his shoulders hunched, down the street.

On the following morning, Steven met Macaulay's bank

manager and gave him a succinct account of the position with regard to the Langdale Road property. 'In effect, Mr Thomas,' he concluded, 'the site your client has bought with your money is worthless.'

'But you're here to offer some kind of solution, I take it.' Alan Thomas was already anticipating some very unpleasant questions from his regional manager if he had to write off yet another bad property debt, but the confident, well-dressed businessman in front of him might perhaps offer a lifeline. But what was his angle?

'There is a solution, an easy one at that. My company will buy the property back from the bank at the price Macaulay paid for it, less ten per cent. You pay all the fees connected with the purchase, of course.'

'Of course.' Thomas couldn't believe his luck.

'On condition that the bank first calls in Macaulay's guarantee. He's put up something, I assume?'

'Yes. His house in London and an apartment in Spain.'

'And they're owned by him? They're not in his wife's name?'

'Owned by him. Mrs Macaulay still has her own flat in Kensington.'

'What's the value of Macaulay's properties?'

'A little short of a million pounds.'

'If you call in your guarantee first, you'll be well covered. And we'll have a deal.'

'You want us to bankrupt him, in other words.'

'That's it, Mr Thomas.'

Alan Thomas did not delay in telling Macaulay the bad news. He almost felt sorry for the man, and then remembered how arrogant he had shown himself to be over the years. At least Araminta still had her own flat. If she had any gumption, Thomas thought, she'd kick Macaulay out and get herself a toyboy.

That evening Macaulay arrived home drunk, much to Araminta's disgust. Tearfully he told her of his imminent bankruptcy which disgusted her even more. She didn't tell him that, earlier in the day, a courier had brought her a package from Steven Shaw.

He remembered the farewell note that he'd received from Araminta and her gift. Many years later he echoed it but Araminta didn't register its significance. The note read: 'Thank you for the good times we had. Don't think badly of me. Please buy yourself a present.'

Steven had enclosed £2,000 in cash.

# Chapter Forty-one

'Toby, why don't you show Rory some of those items you recently acquired?' Winter said.

The three men were back in McCall's first-floor office. It had taken a great deal of persistence on Winter's part to persuade the photographer to see them. He had finally agreed to a meeting during the early evening when his staff had gone home.

Toby opened his briefcase and put a large brown envelope on the desk. 'Take a look, Rory. Excellent camera-work, if I may say so.'

McCall grabbed the envelope and spilled the video-cassette and the photographs onto the desk. He shuffled through some of the latter and surprised them with his spirited response. 'Jolly interesting but I'm not into sleaze and blackmail. I've never seen these before in my life.'

'Cut the crap,' Winter said sharply. 'Those snaps were found in your desk, the video on your shelves. You're not too hot on your security, are you, Rory?'

'I don't know how you got this material but I ought to call the police.' McCall's hand hovered uncertainly over his telephone.

'We're merely returning your property,' Toby said, 'but we have kept copies. How much does Shaw pay you for this kind of work?'

McCall shook his head wearily. 'Shaw, Shaw. You're

obsessed with the man. Is he in any of those photos? Are
any of his staff to be seen? No, is the answer.'

'You're right,' Toby said, 'but all those men have business
links with Shaw. And the video shows one of his clients getting her rocks off. Fran Zanini, Wimbledon champion, no
less.'

'It doesn't prove a thing,' McCall insisted. 'Those men
have business links with many other people, as well as
Shaw.'

'Maybe we should talk direct to Shaw,' Winter said
thoughtfully. 'He would assume that he has the only copies
of this stuff, the exclusive rights, one might say. He
wouldn't like this rather sensitive material floating around.
What if the tabloids got hold of it? I don't think you'd be
Mr Shaw's favourite photographer then, Rory, do you?'
Winter, watching McCall closely, saw his face pale.

'It was Fisher's idea to make copies. A bit of insurance.'
McCall tried to fight against the panic that threatened to
overcome him. Shaw's money was crucial to him, but his
fear of Dan Fisher was even more compelling.

'Who's Fisher?'

'Dan Fisher, a middleman for Shaw, does surveillance
and security, sells sleaze to the tabloids.'

'Invents it, perhaps?' Winter said.

Sensing McCall's imminent collapse, Toby said, 'D'you
supply Shaw's clients with drugs? Cocaine, for instance?'

'For God's sake, what is all this?' McCall protested.
'Pantomime time? I'm not into drugs. At the slightest whiff
of this kind of thing, the royals would drop me. Instantly.
And where would my business be then?'

Quickly, Toby walked across the office and pulled an
unmarked video-cassette cover off the shelf and up-ended
it. Two sachets dropped into his hand.

'Purely for my own use,' McCall said swiftly.

'You must be a big user,' Streeter said. 'When I last looked there was enough coke to get the whole of west London stoned.'

'You obviously had a bloody good snoop around my office.'

'For good reason. You threatened to call the police, Rory. Why don't you go ahead? Or would you prefer to help us with some information about Shaw?'

'I'm just a photographer,' McCall whined. 'I set up the video cameras and operate the still cameras when needed. That's it. He pays me bloody well.'

'Did you have anything to do with Nils Ryberg?' Winter asked.

'The tennis player? He topped himself years ago, didn't he?'

'Yes. Did you do any pictures of him?'

'No. I didn't know Shaw and Fisher then.'

'Perhaps we ought to talk to Fisher.'

'Don't waste your time,' McCall said. 'He's a real bastard, the last man you should cross.'

'Will you agree to talk on camera about Shaw's interesting parties?' Winter asked.

'Not a chance,' McCall said. 'It's more than my life's worth.'

When his two visitors had left, McCall sought relief by ingesting a line of cocaine. He felt better, but not for long.

The two men tried a different pub in the neighbourhood. It was packed with tourists and a juke-box was playing music loudly. They found a corner of the bar on which to lean.

'We know a lot about Shaw's business methods now,' said Winter, 'and can surmise a lot more, but . . .'

'But, as you told me before, it's hearsay.'

'Exactly. So how do we pin the bastard? Above all, how

do we get at the truth about Ryberg?' Winter drank some of his beer and continued. 'We could try flushing Shaw out.'

'How would we do that? Send him copies of the photos and a letter telling him we know he's a naughty boy.'

Winter swallowed some beer. 'This beer's rubbish, isn't it? I doubt the landlord's cleaned the pipes for months.' He grimaced as he drank some more. 'Anyway, I think we should twist Shaw's tail, make him imagine that we know a whole lot more than we really do. He might over-react, do something stupid.'

'How?'

'First of all, Toby, you could write a piece for one of the golf magazines. It will tell the readers how brilliantly successful our friend Shaw has been, not just in golf but in other sports as well. Then you will touch upon his remarkable hold not only on a distinguished array of sponsors but also on the BBC and AAN in America. Your piece will be full of innuendo but will not actually accuse him of any misconduct because you don't want to attract a writ for libel.'

'And you think that'll flush him out?'

'I don't know but we'll have some fun running with it, won't we?'

It took Toby Streeter less than a week to write his article about Steven Shaw. Then he contacted the Editor for whom he used to work at the *Golfer's Magazine* and, in response to his cautious expression of interest, took it along to his office.

It was some days before Jim Maloney got around to reading Toby's piece, which was headed, 'Is Shaw good for golf?' He skimmed rapidly over the introductory material which told the familiar story of Shaw's dominance of golf through his representation of most of the world's best players, by his control of tournaments around the world and by his influence over the sale of television rights. Toby then showed how he had used the same techniques in other sports including tennis, football in Britain, and, to a lesser extent, in motor racing and skiing.

There's nothing new here, the Editor thought, but his attention was fully engaged when he reached the next paragraph.

What amazes many observers of the sporting scene is the loyalty which Shaw commands from his many sponsors. He delivers the goods in terms of television coverage but sponsors have never been known for loyalty. Some might call them promiscuous, as they flit from one publicity concept to another, like starstruck adolescents.

But not Shaw's sponsors: they remain faithful. Shaw is attentive, of course. His parties are lavish and his presents are generous, and that comment is not meant to suggest any impropriety. Shaw would not step into the gutter along with the pop music promoters and the politicians where favours are secured by bribery, by the provision of willing 'models' (of all three sexes), by the supply of recreational drugs to make the party swing, or, in very special cases when long-term favours must be secured, the gift of a Côte d'Azur villa and a Swiss bank account which is kept nicely topped up. If all else fails, the record made by the hidden cameras of the sexual peccadilloes of the rich and famous can later be used for a spot of blackmail.

These kind of malpractices would never be condoned by Steven Shaw. He is simply a remarkably talented man. But should he have such a dominant position in golf? A position which he intends to strengthen when his dream of a world circuit, peopled mainly by his own clients, becomes a reality.

Maloney liked Toby, both as a writer and a man, but there were two important considerations which prompted him to call Dean Aultman about the article. First, his magazine derived important advertising revenue from Shaw's tournament division; secondly, he relied on the agency's goodwill to give his journalists access to their star golfers for comments and interviews.

By insisting that the call was important, Maloney eventually spoke to Aultman, read him some parts of the article and then sent him the whole piece by fax. From London it was sent to Steven in New York and he spoke to Aultman on the following day.

'Kill that article, Dean. It's rubbish, of course, but mud of that kind sometimes sticks. Maloney's in our pocket, isn't he?'

'Yeah, he knows that he needs us more than we need him.'

'OK, call the other magazines and persuade them not to have anything to do with Streeter. Tell them he's bitter and twisted because I had to dismiss him for malpractice. We advertise with all of them, don't we? Fine, we've got our lever. If they seem reluctant, then stress the libellous aspects of the article.'

'If I do that, they might get interested.'

'No, magazines like that don't want to get involved in litigation, they don't have the money. And Dean, get hold of Dan Fisher, will you, and ask him to call me.'

Toby was not surprised by Jim Maloney's rejection of his article. But when the other three golf magazines he approached expressed a total lack of interest he realised

that their editors had been suborned by one of Shaw's min-
ions in London.

He and Winter shrugged off their disappointment,
although Toby was still musing about Shaw and his machi-
nations a few evenings later in his 'two-up-and-two-down'
house on the end of a Fulham terrace. Not that it was two
down any more, because the couple from whom he'd
bought the house had removed the dividing wall to make
one large living area.

It was Friday evening and Toby was not going anywhere.
He'd eaten his chicken casserole and was on his second
glass of Australian chardonnay. As the light began to fade,
he closed the curtains and tried to decide what to watch on
television. Should it be the last in the series about a morose
Cambridge detective or the Louis Malle film? Just as he
decided to watch the detective and record Louis Malle, the
doorbell pinged. Toby had very few casual visitors and
wearily assumed that it was a door-to-door salesman of
double-glazing or garden sheds or something else he didn't
want. He always felt sorry for them, however, and always
listened politely to their sales pitch.

As Toby opened the door he knew that he must not
linger since his programme started in a few minutes. The
man, neatly dressed in a dark suit, certainly looked like a
salesman but Toby was surprised when he greeted him by
name. 'I'm a colleague of Steven Shaw's,' he continued,
'and I have a proposition for you.' So that was it.

When Toby failed to show up for Sunday lunch, Winter
was surprised. His friend was always well organised and
would have telephoned if a problem had arisen. Maybe his
mother was ill again and he'd raced off to Derbyshire to see
her. That evening, Winter telephoned Toby's house but
there was no reply.

On the Monday morning Toby was due to join Winter at a meeting to discuss sponsorship of a skiing series they were planning. When he did not turn up, Winter took a taxi to his house. There was no answer to his knocks on the door and the curtains were drawn. Now worried, Winter shinned up the garden wall and dropped down to the patio on the other side. The curtains to the French windows were also drawn and he could see nothing untoward through the keyhole of the back door which led into the small kitchen.

Something was wrong. John Winter climbed back over the wall and startled an elderly lady who was walking by. He stopped her and asked if she knew Toby Streeter.

'No, love,' she replied. 'I live at the other end of the road.'

Winter walked round to the front of the house in the hope that he might speak to Toby's neighbour. The house was empty and the 'For Sale' sign told him why. He walked to the main road, saw a telephone box and called the police. A car with a uniformed officer arrived at the house within ten minutes and Police Constable Spencer elected to try and gain entry through the French windows. 'You wait by the front door, sir, I won't be a minute,' he said as Winter gave him a shove up the wall. He heard the crash of glass as he walked away.

Much more than a minute passed before Spencer opened the front door. Impatient, Winter was about to ask what the hell had kept him when he noticed the policeman's white face. Spencer gulped and said, 'Don't go in there, sir. Your friend's in a terrible state. I've got to radio for help.'

Winter pushed past him into the narrow hall and then paused on the threshold of Toby's living room. Amid the chaos of overturned tables, broken ornaments and a wine bottle on its side on the floor, he saw the body of his friend, naked from the waist down. His smashed head had oozed blood blackly on to the carpet.

'Don't touch anything, whatever you do, sir,' said Spencer's voice behind him. 'That is Mr Streeter, is it?'

'Yes,' Winter said, only just audibly, as he turned away. He sat on the stairs, his head in his hands, and wept.


'Are you sure you weren't seen?' Steven looked intently at Fisher. They were sitting in the lobby of a huge and anonymous hotel in Manhattan on the Monday evening. Fisher had declined to visit Steven's office because of his suspicion that the conversation would be recorded and Steven had avoided Fisher's room for the same reason.

'I expect I was seen but not noticed,' Fisher said impatiently. 'It was nearly dark when I knocked on his door.'

'Why the hell did you do it? I told you to bribe him. Violence was supposed to be a last resort. For God's sake, Dan, did you think you were back in Belfast?'

'Things got out of hand.'

'I'll say. I thought you could deal with these situations.'

'I can, but Streeter came on too strong. I thought you told me he was the weak link in the partnership with Winter. Some fucking weak link! I offered him the ten grand to leave you alone and he laughed at me. Said that the bribe would make another juicy episode in the exposé of Steven Shaw.'

'So what happened? Get to the point.'

'He told me to leave and I thought I'd rough him up a bit. It sometimes works. So I went for him, smacked him in the mouth. But he came straight back at me, he knew some karate and I had to use the persuader.'

'The persuader?'

'A cosh I carry for jobs like those. Well, I hit him too

hard and when I checked his pulse, he was a gonner. So I hit him a couple more times, to make it look good. You told me that he was supposed to be a queer, so I took his trousers off and left him there. The police will assume that Streeter picked up some rough trade and got more than he bargained for. I took all his cash and his credit cards to make it all look authentic.'

'I hope the police buy it, Dan, for your sake.'

And yours, Steven, thought Fisher, but he said, 'The police will go through the motions, that's all. They don't try too hard if a queer's been topped. If it's a child or a so-called respectable married man or woman, they pull out all the stops. They need a result, it's important for their public relations. But queers don't mean lots of brownie-points.'

'I hope you're right,' Steven said quietly.

'What about Winter?' Fisher asked.

'Stay well away. This is when we keep a very low profile indeed.'

'Fair enough, Steven, but who's been blabbing to him and Streeter? That article was bloody near the knuckle.'

'It could be one of our sponsors, but I doubt it. Maybe they got at McCall. He's flaky, he's got a cocaine habit. Though come to think of it, Streeter knew Jacqui Bryson and he obviously knew about Paul Davis's villa. You'd better keep a discreet eye on her.'

# Chapter Forty-two

When Corky Price had been forced by injury to retire from basketball, he thought his real life was over because he loved playing the game above all else. To his surprise, he soon discovered that there was nearly as much fun in watching; his enthusiasm extended to nearly every sport.

He was thrilled when Steven asked him to fly to Madrid to watch some of the Olympic action. His ardour cooled suddenly when Steven told him what he was planning to do.

It was the penultimate day of the Games. As he waited for the start of the Olympic 1500-metres final, Price looked with awe at the magnificent stadium which the city of Madrid had built for the Games. The steeply raked seats soared above the arena. Price had to crane his neck to see the topmost tiers; he hoped that the spectators up there didn't suffer from vertigo. He waved to Dean Aultman whom he could see two rows behind. Dean was an OK guy and he was crazy about sports. So far, his predictions had been right. Cheryl Anderson had won gold in her 800-metre final and so had Ben Naylor. He'd burned the rest of the field off over the two-lap distance. Zak Ravelli had finished third; nevertheless, many of the pundits saw the young American as the potential victor in the 1500 metres.

They were sitting in some of the best seats in the stadium, right opposite the finishing line. Price prayed that all their efforts would prove successful.

As the runners were lined up by the starter, Price glanced at Steven sitting alongside him. He grinned briefly back. How could he be so calm, so bloody assured?

Price had felt uneasy from the moment he arrived in Madrid. When he had checked into the press centre, clutching his accreditation to an obscure news agency in New York, he had felt himself sweating under the inspection of a tall official with a cadaverous face and thin lips. Dressed in a white shirt and with the obligatory dark glasses, the man had studied Price's press credentials and his passport very closely. There were 15,000 media people at the Games, so why was this Spaniard so interested in him? 'Please complete the forms, Mr Price,' he said finally.

There were several forms in triplicate and Price duly worked his way through them. In return, he received an identity card, an armband, a badge ('to be worn at all times,' the official admonished) and a bundle of tickets.

'Have a nice visit,' the man said, with the warmth and sincerity of a piranha.

They had arrived two days before the 1500-metres final and, therefore, had very little time to carry out their plan. Steven had sent Price off to the competitors' compound in the Olympic Village but, despite brandishing his press pass and telling the officials on the gate that he was a friend of Zak Ravelli's family, he could not gain admission. Security had become tighter and tighter at the Olympics ever since the murder of the Israeli athletes at Munich in 1972. The Spanish authorities, mindful of the continuing threat from the Basque separatist movement, were taking no chances.

The officials allowed Price to scribble a note to Ravelli but he was resigned to the fact that it would not elicit a reply. He was relieved because he didn't relish trying to bribe one of his own countrymen to lose an Olympic final.

\*

Steven put the telephone down, took a satisfied swallow from his glass of beer and said, 'I've got a contact number for Ravelli's coach. A guy called Wes Dannen. Have you heard of him?'

Corky shook his head. 'The journalist who just gave me Dannen's number says he's been around. He's coached quite a few athletes, negotiates their race fees and so on. He's a dealer in other words.' Corky looked at him expectantly. 'So, why don't we deal? We haven't much time, have we?'

An hour later, a compact man of medium build walked into Steven's suite. Wes Dannen had what looked like two days' growth of stubble on his chin and an unlit cigar jutted from his lips.

He grinned at Steven, 'So you're the famous agent. I've heard a lot about you over the years. And you want to manage my boy Zak, is that right?' His voice was harsh, the words staccato. He's seen too many Jimmy Cagney films, thought Corky Price.

'I could be interested,' Steven said. 'He's got talent.'

'He'll win the fifteen hundred tomorrow,' Dannen said challengingly.

'Maybe.'

Dannen jerked his thumb in Price's direction. 'Who's the big guy?'

'I'm sorry,' Steven said. 'Meet Corky Price, one of my consultants.'

Dannen gave an abbreviated nod in Price's direction and then spoke to Steven.

'If I point Zak your way, what's in it for me?'

'Fifty thousand dollars in cash,' Steven said calmly.

'Not bad for openers.' Dannen sat down opposite Steven. 'And a percentage of what you make for him in the future.'

'No chance.'

'No deal.'

'OK, Mr Dannen,' Steven said. 'I'll increase the front money but it must be a once-and-for-all payment. We'll double the offer.'

Dannen nodded slowly and Steven continued, 'But Ravelli doesn't win tomorrow, is that understood?'

'You're fucking crazy. Zak is up for that final, he knows he's got a great chance of winning.'

'Well, you'd better stop him, Wes.'

'Stop him? What do I do? Tell him it's not his day, that he's gotta wait another four years for his chance?'

'No. You tell him how to run his races, don't you? You're his coach, you give him a tactical plan. For instance, you could tell him that the only way he'll win is to force the pace from the start, to dictate the race from the front, if necessary. That's logical because everyone knows that Naylor has the best finishing burst, that no one can live with him over the last two to three hundred metres. So, you make sure, Wes, that your boy burns himself out in the first three laps.'

'He might not go for it.'

'I'm sure you can persuade him.' Steven opened a briefcase and handed an envelope to Dannen. 'Here's fifty grand on account. You'll get the rest after the final. If anything goes wrong, Mr Price will be calling round to see you.'

There was a collective sigh as the starting gun fired for the start of the 1500-metres final. Then the cheering began as the athletes charged at the first bend. Price could see Ben Naylor in the pack, as the runners jockeyed for position. When they reached the far side of the stadium a Kenyan runner hit the front, closely followed by Zak Ravelli.

At the end of the second lap, the two runners had opened up a gap of about fifteen yards on the rest of the field.

Naylor was in fifth place and running easily with his effortless style. With a lap and a half to go the Kenyan began to slow and Ravelli had no option but to take up the pace.

'It's going like clockwork,' Steven said in Price's ear. 'Ben'll make up the ground at the bell.'

But he didn't. Although Naylor lengthened his stride and broke away from the three or four runners in pursuit of Ravelli, he had made up no more than a few yards halfway round the final lap. The noise from the spectators had reached a rolling, thunderous crescendo, as they urged on the brave American runner. With two hundred metres to go, Naylor, flying along in a flat-out sprint, had cut the gap to about five metres. Inexorably he began to make up the ground on Ravelli.

'He'll do it, he'll do it,' Steven yelled. As the two runners entered the straight, Ben was on Ravelli's shoulder.

Price realised that he was on his feet, like everybody else in the stadium, and was screaming his encouragement to Ben Naylor. Steven had his arms in the air and was bellowing, 'Ben, Ben, come on, Ben.'

Twenty metres from the tape, it seemed that Ravelli had somehow found another turn of speed with which to hold Naylor off. But the Englishman responded once again and drew level. A few yards from the line both men threw themselves desperately at the tape.

'Christ, what a race,' Price muttered.

'D'you think Ben won?' Steven asked hoarsely.

The cameras showed that Ben Naylor had won the gold medal by little more than an inch in what was undoubtedly one of the most exciting finishes ever seen at the Olympic Games.

As they walked out of the stadium, Price said quietly to Steven, 'That was too close for comfort. Dannen nearly blew his delivery fee.'

'No, he earned it.' Steven nodded his satisfaction.

In his place by the side of the track, Dannen heaved a huge sigh of relief; Shaw would never know that he had done nothing to influence the outcome of the race.

# Chapter Forty-three

During the next few months, John Winter learned how much he had relied on Toby's sharp judgements and enjoyed his good fellowship. An hour rarely went by without his thinking of him: to wonder how he would have reacted to this idea, how he would have enjoyed that television programme, or to recall some remark of his.

Winter couldn't believe in the manner of Toby's death. It was the lack of dignity – and he couldn't see his friend as the victim of a casual dalliance with a bit of rough. The detective-inspector who had interviewed him had made his indifference plain, and Winter loathed him for it. Was Mr Streeter a homosexual? Did he pick up strange men in the pubs or the parks? Or perhaps in public lavatories? He had lost his temper at that point and told the man that Toby had a degree of integrity and dignity that a poxy policeman would never understand.

'I'm only doing my job, sir,' he replied, drawing himself up like an outraged spinster. 'We want to find your friend's murderer. Please try and co-operate.'

It wasn't difficult for Winter to put aside the Shaw project. He didn't have the heart to go on and he had other preoccupations, the chief of which was a pressing need to earn money. A family of six was a demanding obligation. He was relieved when Channel 4 decided that his programme about Nils Ryberg should be shelved.

Winter suspected that Shaw Management had exerted

some influence and he was correct. The agency had a football package that Channel 4 wanted: 'match of the day' from Europe, the best of the action from Italy, Spain, Germany and Holland. It would be shown on Sunday afternoons. It was a big coup for the Controller of Channel 4 and the favour that Steven requested in return was only a small one.

To resolve some of his immediate financial problems, Winter accepted a very lucrative commission from an international publisher to edit a comprehensive book about the refugee problem. Sometimes this big man, with the attractively craggy face, found his eyes brimming with tears as he scanned the photographs of forlorn refugees. He realised that his tears were for Toby and that his period of mourning had not yet ended.

In comparison with Winter, money posed no problems for Steven because he and his various companies were rolling in it, his profits compounded by the successes of his many clients. Sam Rhodes won the US Open again, his sixth triumph in the major championships, and the agency's tennis clients did a clean sweep of the major titles during the year. In the Olympic Games, Dean Aultman's judgements had been proved sound as Ben Naylor took both the middle-distance gold medals and Cheryl Anderson won the 800-metres title.

It was well into the autumn of that year when Penny Winter, who had mourned Toby's death almost as keenly as her husband, decided that it was time that he once again got to grips with Steven Shaw.

She took a pot of coffee up to his study and laid her hand gently on his shoulder. 'You're not going to let Shaw get away with it, are you, John?'

'I've been wondering when you'd ask that. But I've felt hopeless, helpless without Toby.'

'I know.' She massaged his shoulders gently. 'But not any longer. You're getting stronger, back to normal. And you'll do it. Not just for Nils Ryberg but for Toby, too.'

'Where should I start?'

'Start where Toby started. With Jacqui Bryson.'

The Pembroke Restaurant was Jacqui's choice, and Winter met her there a week later for dinner. The restaurant, in a quiet street near Hammersmith, had a reputation for ambitious food at reasonable prices – an unusual concept for a city like London. As Winter waited for his guest, his unobtrusive survey of the room revealed an eclectic mixture of customers: businessmen, elderly and middle-aged couples, pairs of lovers and a table of eight young men and women who were clearly having some sort of reunion. The owners hadn't wasted money on the furniture which was wooden and functional and the waiters and waitresses were young and alert.

Just as Winter was finishing his first glass of wine and beginning to get impatient, Jacqui appeared in the doorway, spotted him and waved animatedly. 'Sorry I'm late, John – a bit of a panic in the office. You know how it is.'

'That's showbiz.' He rose and kissed her lightly on each cheek. As he poured her a glass of wine, she fumbled in her handbag and lit up a Gauloise. Winter looked warily to his right where three women were about to begin their main courses but they made no signs of disapproval, despite their close proximity. While they chatted about television and the various friends they had in common, though without mentioning Toby, Winter had time to study Jacqui Bryson. She was a striking woman, with beautiful blue eyes; his mother would probably have called her handsome. She was rather neurotic, fidgeting and lighting one cigarette from the stub of another. Winter noticed the puffiness under those velvety eyes: too much booze and too many late nights, he assumed.

The food was superb, the chef's ambitions fully realised. Halfway through his main course of Orvieto chicken, Winter was feeling relaxed enough to talk about Toby but Jacqui beat him to it. 'You must miss Toby,' she said.

'Every day. He was so bright.'

'And courageous, I think.' Jacqui put her knife and fork down. Winter noticed that she'd eaten little of her braised oxtail. 'I can't believe he was killed by some sick yob he picked up in a pub.'

'It wasn't his style, was it?'

'No. Maybe it was a burglar. His credit cards and his wallet were taken, weren't they?'

Winter nodded. 'But not much else. He wore a nice watch, quite expensive. That was still there, and a couple of cameras.'

'Someone on drugs?'

'I'm not buying that, Jacqui. I've always been wary of conspiracy theories but I wonder if he died because he was getting too close to the truth about our friend Shaw. He wrote an article about him, you know, but none of the golf magazines would run it. It was full of innuendo, and Toby intended it to cause trouble, to flush Shaw out. I suspect that it was uncomfortably close to the truth and that Shaw sent someone round to Toby, to apply a bit of persuasion.'

Jacqui twisted her wine glass and pushed her plate aside. She reached for another cigarette, saw that Winter hadn't yet finished his food, and stopped herself from lighting up. Half a dozen stubs already lay in the ashtray. 'Look, John. I can't believe that Shaw would condone violence.'

'Why not? He bribes people, he threatens them and he blackmails them. Why stop there?'

'I can't believe it.'

Irritated by her apparent obtuseness, Winter looked hard at Jacqui. Despite the challenge in his words, his voice remained even. 'Why not? Because you take his money. Because your boyfriend has accepted a villa in Cap Ferrat and God knows how much in bribes from Shaw? A man who sees nothing wrong in that will see nothing wrong in sending a heavy round to beat some sense into someone. Toby was a danger to Shaw so he had to be put in his place. I don't say that Shaw wanted him dead. I suspect it all got out of hand.'

Winter realised that, in his vehemence, he had leaned far across the table towards Jacqui. They must look like lovers. He could see the hurt that had spread across her face. 'I'm sorry, Jacqui, I'm getting a bit out of hand too.' He smiled at her.

'No, you're right to have a go. I haven't covered myself in glory in the last few years.'

'Well, you did provide some ammunition for Toby.'

'And I wish I hadn't. He might still be alive.'

'Are you and Paul Davis still, er, seeing each other?'

'Oh yes,' Jacqui said wearily. 'You're going to ask why, I expect. And the answer is that I haven't found anyone else.'

'It's odd how nobody wants to cross Shaw, isn't it?' Winter said quietly. 'If they do, they end up in trouble. Or dead. Like Nils Ryberg and Toby. But it'll all come out one day.'

'So it should.'

'D'you mean that enough to help me?'

'That depends.'

'It's for Ryberg's family but most of all for Toby. Please remember that, Jacqui.'

Her hands shook as she helped herself to another Gauloise. Her face tight, she dragged deeply on the cigarette, blew the smoke out, and with a sigh, said, 'OK, John, what do you want from me?'

'You tell me everything that you told Toby about the bribes paid to you and to Paul Davis. You speak up about the villa Shaw has provided. You tell everything you know and everything you suspect but you tell it to camera.'

'Shit.' Jacqui drew hard on her Gauloise. 'You're going to do that programme after all, then?'

'I have to. But I won't show the sequence when your lover-boy Paul has his cock sucked by a whore.'

'That's nice of you. Where did you find that edifying bit of *cinema-vérité*?'

'Toby, er, acquired a video and some photographs of many of Shaw's business acquaintances in action.'

'Hard evidence, I suppose you'd call that.' She smiled wanly at Winter. He knew that in her attempt at humour she was committing herself to their cause.

'Very good, Jacqui. When will you do the interview?'

'As soon as you can book a studio.'

It was no surprise to John Winter that he found it difficult to arrange a meeting with Channel 4's Head of Documentaries. As far as Hugh Jensen was concerned, Winter's project had been shelved, and just as well. Steven Shaw's influence in broadcasting was powerful and he preferred to have such a man on his side. He certainly didn't fancy the prospect of a libel action against Channel 4; they'd had their fill of those recently.

Nevertheless, the interview with Jacqui Bryson was a fascinating piece of television, even if Jensen thought it a wildly improbable piece of fiction. 'We can't recommission the project on the basis of one interview, John,' he said. 'Much of it is libellous, anyway. You'd have to provide some real proof. I'm sorry.'

On the same day, one of Jensen's assistants, who had also watched the Jacqui Bryson interview, had a pub lunch with a secretary from Channel 4's sports department. He was hoping to get her into bed when his wife next went to see her mother up in Edinburgh and he decided to impress her with the story of Paul Davis and the bribes which were purported to have been paid by Steven Shaw. Because the girl was sleeping with one of Dean Aultman's assistants who had conducted some of the negotiations for the European Match of the Day series, the news of the interview was relayed to Steven on the following day.

Steven was in Florida to watch over the first day of filming of a golf skins game and he called Davis on his home number. Briefly, Steven outlined what he had heard from Dean Aultman.

'Your girlfriend has become an embarrassment, Paul. You'd better get rid of her. Warn her off any more revelations to Winter. They'll only get her into trouble, deep trouble.'

'I'll do my best, but—'

'But nothing,' Steven interrupted. 'She's dropped you right in the shit.'

'The interview will never see the light of day. Jacqui's OK, just a bit mixed-up.'

'Not too mixed-up to accept two hundred quid a week from me.'

'What d'you mean?'

'A little retainer. To keep her eye on you and your department and report back.'

There was silence from Davis and then he said, 'Christ, what have I got myself into?'

'Into lots of women and a very rich life-style. Courtesy of me and don't you forget it, Paul. So, get rid of that bitch first thing tomorrow.'

Steven's next call was to Dan Fisher, who was

unavailable. A message left on his answering machine, however, brought a response from him within the hour.

'It's time to terminate our arrangement with Jacqui
Bryson,' Steven said.

'It was a waste of money anyway.'

'It depends on your view of insurance, Dan. We've had
one or two snippets from her, haven't we? Anyway, she's
become difficult, she's been shooting her mouth off about
Paul Davis.'

'What d'you want me to do?'

'Go and see her, tomorrow if possible. She'll get her
marching orders from Davis in the morning. Impress on
her that we won't tolerate her blabbing her mouth off about
our business. Suggest that she retracts all that stuff about
bribes. We might make her an *ex gratia* payment then and
help her find another job. If she proves difficult, apply a
little persuasion. But, Dan, go easy. Just do enough to
frighten her. We don't want a repetition of the Streeter incident, do we?'

Jacqui knew that her days at the BBC were numbered,
but she was unprepared for such a sudden dismissal. At
ten o'clock Davis called her into his office and handed her
a letter which terminated her employment on the grounds
of improper conduct. A cheque for three months' salary
was attached. He didn't look at her as he asked her to clear
her desk and leave the building within an hour.

'You really jump when Shaw says jump, don't you, Paul?'
she said bitterly.

Davis shrugged. 'Don't get involved with Winter.
There's no future there.'

'Perhaps he'll offer me a job.'

'He'll be lucky to work in television again, so I wouldn't
count on it.' Davis got up from his chair, walked around his
desk and crouched in front of her. He took her hand.

'Jacqui, please, please forget all this. It's not worth it. You can't win, not against Shaw.'

Without another word, Jacqui wrenched her hand away, stood up and strode from his office.

After a long lunch with two friends in a wine bar, Jacqui went home, turned on the television and fell into a heavy sleep. When the doorbell woke her, a black and white movie was flickering on the screen. She thought she recognised George Raft. The doorbell rang again insistently. Woozy from the lunchtime alcohol, Jacqui stumbled to the front door and opened it to see Fisher. She tried to shut the door but he put his foot in the gap and then shoved his way inside.

'Not a very polite greeting, Jacqui,' Fisher said. 'Where're your manners?'

'What do you want?'

'To notify you of your second sacking of the day. My employer no longer needs your services.'

'Shaw, you mean?'

Fisher shrugged. 'What does it matter? But my employer's prepared to make a final payment if you renounce all that nonsense, that trash you recorded for Winter.'

'Get lost, Fisher.' Jacqui gripped her arms around the front of her body to stop herself trembling.

'Don't be a fool, Jacqui. Walk away from it, that's a good girl. There can't possibly be anything in it for you.'

'Nothing that you'd understand. But I don't like to see my friends threatened, my friends murdered.'

'You mean Streeter? One of his bum-boys killed him,' he said contemptuously.

'Why don't you leave? I've said all I want to you.'

'Now, now, Jacqui. I've got a proposal for you. You're out of a job, right, out of two jobs actually. I can't manage two hundred quid but I could go to a hundred a week for your services.'

'My services? What services?'

'What you're best at, Jacqui. A couple of fucks a week, that's all I ask. I've seen the pictures, remember, you're really good at it.'

Jacqui knew it was a mistake to spit in his face. The first blow knocked her backwards on to a sofa and then Fisher dragged her upright by her hair and smashed his fist into her ribs. She dropped into a ball on the floor but he hauled her upright and pounded her body. When she had almost lost consciousness, the violence stopped. As if from a distance she heard Fisher hiss at her, 'If you go to the police, slag, I'll come and finish you off. And that's a promise.'

After a long interval, Jacqui tried to drag herself upright but the pain in her ribs stopped her. Something must be broken. Sobbing with pain, she crawled towards the sofa. Her handbag was there and inside it was her mobile phone. She called an ambulance.

After one night in an emergency ward at the Charing Cross Hospital Jacqui was as keen to leave on the following morning as the administrators were to get rid of her. They needed her bed for another patient. Her face was bruised and puffy from Fisher's punches but the real damage had been done to two of her ribs which were cracked. Despite the strapping it was uncomfortable to breathe. She doubted she'd be laughing for a while but guessed how painful it would be if she did.

When she got home she swallowed some painkillers and contacted several friends to tell them that she'd had an accident and would be out of circulation for a few days. She rang John Winter and told him the truth.

'I'll be round this afternoon,' he said. 'With a camera.'

Jacqui's account of her beating at the hands of 'a known associate of Steven Shaw' didn't take long to record and the camera homed in on her technicolour face and the strapping on her damaged ribs.

When the cameraman had left, Jacqui poured drinks for both of them. As they clinked glasses they heard the door-bell; one long and two short rings.

'That's Paul,' Jacqui said. 'Don't answer it.'

Winter was already on his feet. 'I think he should see how his friend Shaw treats people.'

Davis was discomfited when Winter opened the door. 'Oh, is Jacqui in?' he said, with a weak smile.

'Come in and see Dan Fisher's handiwork.'

Striding into Jacqui's living room, Davis stopped short when he saw the livid marks on her face. 'What happened? Helen, in the office, mentioned that you'd had an accident. What on earth . . . ?'

'Why are you here, Paul?' Jacqui said harshly. 'It's over. So why are you here?'

'I was worried about you.'

'Yeah, well don't. One of Shaw's playmates came round to see me. To persuade me to retract all I've said about you and Shaw. When I wouldn't be persuaded he beat me up. I've never been so bloody scared. He's called Dan Fisher.' She looked hard into the face of her former lover and spat out, 'He used to pay me to spy on you. You see, your friend Shaw likes to cover all the exits.'

'Steven told me about the money,' Davis said. 'How could you do that to me? I was devastated.'

'Devastated,' Winter said disgustedly. 'You have the nerve to say that. How much money have you had from Shaw over the years? How can you afford a villa in Cap Ferrat on a BBC salary?'

'That's my business.'

'It'll be the business of the Director-General before long,' Winter said. He wanted to punch Davis in the face. 'You're a fucking disgrace, you've been Shaw's creature for too long. You're just a whore, you'll screw anybody for some easy money.'

Staring hard at the floor, his head down and shoulders slumped, Davis was on the brink of tears. His voice quavered. 'I wouldn't ever harm you, Jacqui, I promise.'

'Maybe not,' she replied. 'But you're up to your eyeballs with the people who did.'

'In way above your head, I'd say,' Winter added. 'Why d'you think Toby Streeter was killed?'

'He was done in by some queer, wasn't he?' Davis muttered.

'Was he hell!' Winter said. 'He was killed to keep him from broadcasting the truth about Shaw. Those are your business associates, Paul.'

Davis moved towards the front door. 'I'm really sorry, Jacqui. About everything.'

She didn't reply but Winter followed Davis into the hallway. 'I'm not going to let go of Shaw. He's corrupt and I'll prove it.'

# Chapter Forty-four

The World Golf Classic was due to begin in Australia at the end of November. It was Shaw Management's showpiece, the richest tournament in the game and the fulcrum of Steven's effort to dominate the sport. Less than a month before the first round the two foremost golfers, Sam Rhodes and Patrice Barbier, had failed to confirm their participation. Neither player had formally declined, and Steven continued to tell the media that he had assembled the best players in the world for his event. But if he failed to deliver Rhodes and Barbier his own reputation and the claimed status of the championship would be diluted. Carl Lansky, the PGA Commissioner, would love it. He would make the maximum capital out of Steven's failure, particularly since Rhodes was his client. The World Classic was in direct opposition to the American circuit's International Tournament. Steven had secured eight of the top ten players in the world rankings, of whom only two were American. He had paid handsomely for their services even though they were both clients of Shaw Management. That left Barbier and Rhodes. He needed them both and didn't even wish to contemplate the possibility of their playing in Lansky's event.

Steven couldn't understand what made Sam tick any more. He'd become worse since the confrontation over the Amalgamated International Bank deal. Every proposal which was put to him was assiduously screened. Was the company concerned environmentally correct? Did they invest in any totalitarian countries? What was their policy towards the Third World? Steven didn't want all that shit: he was in business to keep the financial wheels turning. On the rare occasions that he was at home with Suzi he got the same kind of comments. It must be the baby. There were three months or so to go before it was born; Suzi was vague about the exact timing. The Lynaghs were ecstatic; both were hoping for a girl.

Steven was due to meet Rhodes on the following Monday; his client had agreed to come over to the Shaws' house in New York for dinner. He'd told Steven that he was really looking forward to it because he hadn't seen Suzi and Adam for several weeks. Steven hoped he realised that the purpose of the meeting was business not pleasure.

Comfortably settled into a deep leather armchair, Carl Lansky prepared himself to negotiate with Patrice Barbier. His staff had been hard-pressed to find the Frenchman but Barbier's father had given them the telephone number of a villa in Sardinia. He was staying there with a few friends.

Ill at ease with most foreigners, especially those who did not speak American, Lansky hopefully repeated Patrice Barbier's name several times to the woman who answered the number he dialled in Sardinia. The line seemed to go dead and he was on the point of hanging up when a voice said, 'Carl, how are you? How's Florida?'

Lansky recognised Barbier's voice with its slight Gallic inflections. 'Christ, Patrice, you're hard to track. What the hell are you doing in Sardinia? Where's that?'

'It's an interesting island in the Mediterranean, Carl. A complicated history. My mother is related to the Savoy family who used to own it. As for what I'm doing, well, a little tennis, and cycling and sailing. Then there are the wines, books to read, my friends to talk to.'

'Sounds like my kinda town.'

'Yes, you should take more time off, Carl. Life isn't just business. If you make the mistake of thinking that it is, it will pass you by.'

'You're in a philosophical mood, Patrice, but I'm afraid I've called you about business. Specifically the International Tournament. I need you in that event, as I've told you before.'

'Ah, yes, but Mr Shaw has made me a tempting offer.'

'What sort of offer?'

'You can guess. Lots of francs.'

Lansky sighed. 'Look, Patrice, I won't jerk you about. I want your participation in that tournament and in the Players' Championship in April. If you guarantee to play in them both for the next three years I'll give you an exemption on our Tour until you're fifty. Play as much or as little as you like.'

'That is generous. Are you sure you mean it? What will the other players make of it?'

'Let me worry about that.'

'I've got quite a long exemption already, Carl. Nearly ten years, as you know. Maybe I won't want to play much after that. There are other things I want to do.'

'For Chrissakes, Patrice, I'm sticking my neck out for you.'

'I appreciate it, but it's something else you're sticking out, isn't it, because you want to screw Shaw? *Tant pis.* I'll give you an answer within a week.'

When the connection was broken, Lansky wondered bitterly what the hell he had to do to get the Frog on his side. He'd offered to break one of the cardinal rules of the American PGA and still the guy was hedging.

Late on the Monday afternoon Steven was startled when

Sam Rhodes strode into his office. Unannounced and smiling widely he said, 'I was shopping near by.' He held up several carrier-bags. 'So I thought I'd catch you for a lift.'

Steven never saw anyone without an appointment, and only Rhodes would have been allowed to get away with such casual behaviour. 'Well, that's just great, Sam. The limo's on its way. While you're here, there are a couple of contracts for you to sign.'

'But not one for the World Classic, I trust.'

'No, Sam, we'll discuss that later. Though I've never seen much need for all this talk.' He stared hard at his client.

'As you say, Steven, we'll talk it through later. Let's enjoy the evening first.'

As he passed through the main office towards the exit, Rhodes stopped to exchange a few words with every employee. Even though sporting superstars made up the common currency of the agency's business, Steven noticed how they reacted to the warmth of Rhodes's personality. Whatever they called it – star quality, or charisma, or the X-factor – he had it in abundance. The girls couldn't help but flirt with him; even one of the book-keepers, a plain girl whom Steven couldn't imagine having a sex life.

The stretched limousine took them in silence and comfort to the Shaws' brownstone house off Park Avenue. When they entered the hall, the place was quiet except for the muted sound of a television on an upper floor.

'I expect Suzi's having a sleep,' Steven said.

'When's the baby due?'

'Some time in the New Year. Go on in and I'll get us a beer.'

While Steven went towards the kitchen, Rhodes strolled into the sitting room and stopped when he saw Suzi. She was dozing in a chair by the French windows. She looked beautiful, at peace. He moved to within a few feet of her and smiled. As if on cue, Suzi came out of her sleep and registered his presence. 'Oh, God,' she cried. She hadn't seen Sam for some time, as he had truthfully told Steven. When she became pregnant she had maintained the fiction, even to Sam whom she loved, that the baby was Steven's. Sam had said that it was diplomatic for him not to see her so much, but she had known that wasn't the real reason.

Seeing Sam so unexpectedly, she felt a lurch in her stomach as she rose to greet him. She put her hands protectively over her belly.

'How's the baby doing?'

'Fine.'

With glasses and cans on a tray, Steven came into the room and pecked his wife on the cheek. She went to the door and called out, 'Adam, Adam! Daddy's here with Sam.'

There was a pounding of feet on the stairs and the figure of the seven-year-old Adam whirled into the room. 'Hi, Adam' was stillborn on Steven's lips as the boy rushed past him.

'Sam, Sam, Sam,' the boy shouted as he hurled himself at his friend.

'Whoah, steady there,' Rhodes said, crouching down to embrace Adam and then lifting him up in the air. 'Hey, you're getting to be a big fella, aren't you?' He put Adam down. 'How're those golf clubs I sent you?' He'd recently arranged for a half-set of boys' clubs to be delivered.

'They're great, Sam. Can we go and play somewhere tomorrow?' Adam clutched at Sam's hand.

'I'm sorry but I'm off on a plane tomorrow. Your daddy'll take you to the range.'

'Oh, Dad'll be too busy.'

'I'll see what I can do at the weekend, Adam,' Steven said.

Delighted though she was to be in Sam's company again, Suzi went to her bedroom shortly after nine o'clock. She was genuinely tired and knew that the two men had business to discuss.

They remained sitting at the dining-table, a large pot of coffee between them.

'I hope you're not going to hassle me about your World Classic, Steven.'

'When have I ever hassled you?' Steven smiled at his client. 'We've had a very good relationship over the years, haven't we?'

'Of course. But you have a way of, well, getting your own way.'

'Maybe that's been one of my strengths as an agent.'

'You're much more than an agent, Steven, and that's fine by me. But what you're trying to do in golf worries me. You're going to cause a civil war. And there's no need for it. You didn't have to pitch your tournaments against some of the important US Tour events. What's your problem with Lansky?'

'He's trying to create a sort of monopoly and I want people like you, Sam, to have freedom of action.'

'I'm happy with the way the Tour is run. The established tours here and in Europe and Asia give our business stability. I don't want to undermine it. I don't want anarchy. I don't want golf to get like boxing with several different Mickey Mouse federations battling it out. It would diminish our sport.'

Steven poured more coffee. 'You're very conservative, Sam.'

'Yes, I'd rather conserve. Golf has great traditions and I want to guard them. It doesn't matter how much prize-money you offer, Steven, you can't ever equal the prestige, the glory of the two Open Championships, of the Masters, even the PGA Championship.'

'Are you saying you won't play in the World Classic?'

For several seconds, Rhodes looked silently at the table. 'This is what I mean about civil war. You and Carl Lansky are forcing a choice on me. I want to support the Tour but I don't want to let you down either.'

Despite what he knew of Steven's ruthless approach to business, Rhodes still liked him. He'd been the agent he'd needed to capitalise on his intense talent; Rhodes also realised that he'd been one of the clients who'd propelled Shaw Management to unparalleled success. So, everything was even there. But he had betrayed Steven by falling in love with his wife. He could never make amends for that.

'I really need your support on this one, Sam,' Steven said quietly.

'And you'll get it. I'll play for you. I'll be there.'

On the following day Steven was still elated by Sam Rhodes's decision. He merely needed Patrice Barbier's participation in the World Classic to inflict substantial damage on Carl Lansky's reputation. But he was taken aback when he received a call from the Florida headquarters of the US Tour. Lorne Scheider was one of two middle-ranking executives who were paid retainers by Shaw Management to feed the agency sensitive information about the policies and activities of Carl Lansky.

Scheider called Steven from a public telephone in a shopping mall. 'I'll be quick,' he said. 'Lansky's offered Barbier one helluva deal. Exemption on the tour until he's fifty. Can you beat that?'

Steven wondered whether he could but at least he had to try.

Three days later Steven at last caught up with Barbier at

his Paris apartment. He offered him $1 million plus expenses to play in the World Classic; the money to be paid into an account anywhere in the world.

Such an offer made even the insouciant Frenchman pause. 'Wow,' he said finally. 'That's some proposal, Steven. Hard to refuse, truly. I'll fax you a reply within forty-eight hours.'

On Monday morning both Steven and Carl Lansky found almost identical faxes waiting for them in their respective offices. Steven's read:

> I must thank you for your generous offer to play the World Classic. You will know that I received an equally generous proposal to play in America during the same week. If only I could be in two places at once. Alas, I found it impossible to choose between the two offers and decided the only honourable course was to refuse them both. I am deserting the golf course for the skiing slopes until after Christmas. Best wishes, Patrice.

You French bastard, was Steven's first reaction. But at least he hadn't thrown in his lot with Lansky. As Steven admitted, albeit with a degree of bitterness, Barbier had been shrewd; there was an element of the wisdom of Solomon in his decision.

# Chapter Forty-five

Jordan Samuel Shaw was born in the middle of January, a little later than Suzi anticipated. She was grateful for the timing and told Steven (and everyone else) that the baby was slightly premature: just in case he got around to thinking about the date that they'd made love.

In London, Jacqui Bryson began a new job with an independent television producer who specialised in situation comedy. John Winter strove to finish his book about refugees. He also tried to make contact with all the people whom he and Toby Streeter had listed as having special knowledge of Steven Shaw and his business methods. His efforts proved barren since many of them refused to talk to him and the information garnered from the others was of little interest. He recorded the interviews on videotape but merely for the sake of balance – if his programme ever came to fruition, which he doubted.

In desperation, and as a shock tactic, Winter used the material in Toby's unpublished article about Shaw to produce a scurrilous piece for a gossip-sheet called *Nosey Parker*. It was written and produced by two young men who had been at Winchester School together. Their headquarters was the Kensington garage of the parents of one of them. The fortnightly magazine amounted to eight smudgily printed pages in which corruption and pomposity in all its disguises were vigorously attacked. The royal family, politicians, show-business personalities and businessmen were primary targets of ridicule. Libel was their stock in trade; since they had no discernable assets there was little point in their victims pursuing them in the courts.

Despite the meagre resources of *Nosey Parker* and its inept production, it had built up a notable following, especially in London and the south-east, and represented a perfect medium in which John Winter could twist Steven Shaw's tail.

After cataloguing Shaw Management's influence on several major sports, Winter's final paragraphs read:

Ever since David, equipped with superior weaponry by some clever promoter, upset the odds by beating Goliath, competitive sport has had its share of villains and conmen. Sometimes they call themselves agents. Steven Shaw has risen above them all to become the Godfather of sport, his briefcase bulging with offers that the sponsors and the television moguls cannot refuse. Or dare not. It's truly remarkable how receptive are the BBC and American's AAN to Shaw's blandishments. Of course the key men, Paul Davis in London and Jake Richardson in New York, are real chums of Shaw and he looks after them as a doting godfather should. His bounty extends to the 'loan' of a villa to Davis in Cap Ferrat, the French playground for the very rich; and bouncy Jake Richardson, with three ex-wives to support, pursues a life-style which is the envy of the New York media-trash.

Shaw's influence is pervasive and it's amazing how close-mouthed his many associates can be. If you do break the code of silence you might encounter a mild form of retribution. Like Jacqui Bryson – a few cracked ribs and a black eye. But the friends of Toby Streeter are still wondering why he died in such mysterious circumstances. Was it because he dared to voice some criticisms of Shaw's methods? Was it because he had evidence of Shaw's intimate parties for top decision-makers where good champagne and willing girls are always available? And little Rory McCall, photographer to the royals and the aristocracy, records it all for the Godfather rather than posterity.

To go back further, the family and friends of Swedish tennis star Nils Ryberg wonder if he stood in the way of one of Shaw's big deals and paid the penalty by being driven to suicide.

With glee, the editors of *Nosey Parker* printed the piece and waited for the reprisals. They did not materialise because Shaw's lawyers advised him to ignore the article rather than draw attention to it by beginning a libel action.

Winter followed up his first broadside by contacting a magazine in New York with similar preoccupations to those of *Nosey Parker*. *Public Eye* published another version of the article which was adapted for its American readership.

Eva Rosen was content with her job and liked her life in Boston. When a cable television company in New York approached her to take on the job as Head of Features, she was at first reluctant to return to the city, despite the opportunity that the job represented. Within days, however, she had adjusted to the pace of life in New York. She realised how much she had missed it.

Eva's job demanded that she was aware of any news item that might be expanded into a longer story for the network and she combed all the newspapers and magazines, the radio shows and other television programmes for ideas. When she read the piece about Steven Shaw, all sorts of emotions crowded into her head. The first thing she did was to contact the editor of *Public Eye* and ask her for access to the author of the article. Eva tried to telephone John Winter and left a message on his answering machine. Two hours later she received a fax which told her that he would be in New York within a month and would be happy to meet her.

It was less than two weeks later that Winter arrived in New York. It was bitterly cold and he thanked his luck that the heavy fall of snow which was forecast had not yet arrived. He had refugee statistics to check at the United Nations headquarters, but much more interesting was the thought of talking to Jake Richardson and Suzi Shaw.

While engaged on the 'History of Golf', Winter had met Richardson who, despite some reservations, agreed to meet him at Mickey's Bar which was still his favoured haunt. On their first meeting, Winter had not enjoyed the man's noisy and ostentatious brand of bonhomie; on their second meeting he took to it even less, especially the way Richardson broke off their conversation to shout loud greetings to every other person who entered the bar.

Winter decided to get the encounter over as quickly as possible. 'I'm interested in Steven Shaw,' he said. 'His reputation, his business methods, why he's so powerful in sport, why he's so powerful in televised sport.'

'I wouldn't say that,' Richardson replied. 'He does zilch in baseball, American football and basketball. They're our major sports.'

'But they're not international sports. You look at tennis and golf and even motor racing and Shaw is the man. Look at all the trash-sport he sells around the world.'

'The public love it.'

'They'll watch anything if it's hyped enough,' Winter said contemptuously. 'What I'm interested in is why Shaw's got such a grip on televised sport. Hell, you people at AAN take hundreds of hours from him and so does the BBC.'

'There you've got it, John. The guy's got great ideas and he fuckin' delivers. In his field he's got the best clients and the best properties. We buy the British Open golf and the Wimbledon tennis from him, so of course we look favourably on any other ideas he brings in. That's show business.'

'It's not just that, is it? He has an edge over his competitors, that's what I've heard. He looks after his business associates well, very well.'

'That's how it works. You buy from people you like.'

It was time to jab at Richardson's bubble of pretension and Winter said, 'Particularly if they invite you to good parties, Jake, with lots of pretty girls.'

'I've never needed any help in that department.'

'I'm sure. Maybe Steven helps you in other ways.'

'What the fuck's that supposed to mean?'

'You have expensive tastes, I believe, Jake. Three ex-wives don't come cheap, for a start. I imagine Shaw would help you out – for services rendered.'

Richardson stood up and said, 'John, I don't know where you're coming from and I'm sure you didn't mean to be insulting. But you were and that's why this conversation's over.' He drained his beer, walked to the other end of the bar and noisily joined a group from AAN.

Winter hadn't expected to gain much from talking to Richardson. But the man's air of affronted dignity confirmed his feelings: he was in up to his eyeballs with Shaw.

Suzi remembered Winter and that she had refused his request for an interview some time ago; and she had read his article in *Public Eye*. It was obvious that he had Steven's number. Now that she had safely negotiated the problem of her pregnancy she felt able to talk to him. Winter claimed that he wanted to focus on her role as Shaw's wife, but no doubt hoped she would be indiscreet. And so she might, Suzi thought mischievously. She might drop a few hints. She liked the sound of him: he had a nice manner.

However, she reminded Winter sharply that she had a life of her own before agreeing to see him. 'Why don't you come to the house tomorrow at around four?' she said. 'You might have to share the conversation with my children and my mother but no doubt we'll cope.'

After arriving at the Shaws' imposing house, Winter was greeted by Suzi, Adam and Betty Lynagh. Muffled against the New York cold, he removed his sheepskin coat, a long woollen scarf, thick gloves and a tweed cap, which was admired by Mrs Lynagh. She then took Adam away to watch television. Since the baby was asleep, Suzi and Winter were able to talk undisturbed.

Though keenly aware of how attractive she was, he didn't miss the wariness in her eyes when he began to ask her about her husband's business. She confessed that she knew little about it, although she had always taken an interest in tennis.

'Did you know Nils Ryberg?'

'No. He was that poor guy who committed suicide, wasn't he?'

Winter nodded. No reaction there. But that was to be expected.

'My real favourite is Ray Gerrard,' Suzi volunteered. 'He was such a great player and such fun when Steven first took him on as a client.'

'But not so any more?'

'I guess it's the strain of staying at the top for so long. He's become rather serious, morose even. The last time I saw Ray, all he talked about was retiring from the game.'

Winter asked Suzi about her own interests and she

talked enthusiastically about her work for charity. After half an hour, she glanced at her watch and said that she must feed her baby.

'What's his name?'

'Jordan Samuel.'

'An unusual first name.'

'It was my maternal grandfather's name.'

'And Samuel?'

'That's for Sam Rhodes. He was Steven's first client.'

Suzi rose to her feet suddenly and Winter wondered why she looked agitated. He also got up and thanked her for talking to him. He looked around the elegant sitting room and ventured a final, more personal question. 'You must be a very happy woman, Mrs Shaw?'

She followed his eye. 'You mean my beautiful home, my two sons, a rich and successful husband. How could I not be happy?'

Suzi smiled and Winter wondered if he caught a discordant note. 'Who should I talk to about your husband's early days as an agent?' he asked. 'I've tried Jake Richardson but are there any friends I could see?'

'There's Charlie Tomlin but we seem to have lost touch with him. Unfortunately.' Suzi led Winter into the hall and paused by the front door. 'Steven was very involved with a woman called Rosen. Eva Rosen. I mean in the business sense, of course.' She smiled. 'There was a profile about her in a magazine the other day. She's at the cable network. PNE. You should try her.'

Suzi hadn't planned to mention Eva Rosen. As Winter walked away into the gloom she realised that she'd done it to help him. He was so English and so transparently honest. Quite a contrast to Steven. The sight of Eva's name in the magazine had reminded her of her old suspicions. In the past she hadn't wanted to face the ugly truth of Steven's affair with her. Now it seemed so obvious and it didn't matter any more. Suzi remembered how the woman had suddenly left AAN. No doubt Steven had buggered her in more ways than one.

Winter was intrigued that the name of Eva Rosen had surfaced. He'd had no idea that she had a previous connection with Shaw. It made it even more imperative that he saw her before he returned to Britain.

Three days later Steven returned to New York from Dallas, where he had been negotiating sponsorship for a series of exhibition tennis matches. As soon as he entered the office, Jay Melville asked to see him. His second-in-command in New York, normally ebullient, looked sombre as he settled himself into an armchair opposite Steven.

'A problem?' Steven asked.

'Yeah, several. I've been beaten to the punch yet again. You recall that we lost out on that young tennis player a month ago?

'Nancy Perez?'

'That's her. Well, we've now missed out on the two young golfers I was after. The ones at Wake Forest. They've both got a helluva reputation and I thought they were as good as signed up. But no, they've gone to another fuckin' agent.'

'Faber?'

'You've got it. Archie Faber. Hell, he's really active, Steven. It's not just the youngsters he's signing, either. He's stepped in and signed three or four of our clients who've come to the end of their contracts with us.'

'Nobody big, though.'

'No, but he's getting a good stable together.'

'Tell me more about him.'

'He's smart, Steven, we shouldn't underestimate him. A

graduate of USC, a Walker Cup golfer. He's bright and personable and he knows the business. His dad is a TV producer in Hollywood.'

'Has he got money?'

'Some, but he's got a wife and a baby to think about.'

Steven paused and then said quietly, 'I'm not about to underestimate him. On the contrary, I think we should put him out of business.'

'I wouldn't go that far. Let's just watch him carefully. There's room enough for both of us, and all the others. What about Luisa Ebbers? She's a competitor but we haven't got after her with a hatchet.'

'She's in a different market, Jay. Mostly football, baseball and boring basketball. You will recall that I kept her away from Ray Gerrard. With him as a client she could've become a significant competitor in tennis.'

'Yeah. So what do we do about Faber?'

'First, you make a list of all the people with real potential in golf and tennis and athletics. Contact them and find out if they've been approached by Faber. If they have, sign them up. If necessary, offer them guarantees to join us.'

'How much?'

'Whatever it takes, Jay. Two, three, four hundred thousand dollars. Just put the block on Faber. And approach his key clients. Same tactics, offer them guarantees to join us.'

'What about their contracts with Faber?'

'Get hold of a copy. You know what these representation agreements are like, they can always be broken if you look hard enough. Get our lawyers on to it, and offer free legal counsel to get these guys out from under Faber. And another thing, lean on all the equipment manufacturers we know. Ask them politely to avoid Faber's clients. We'll offer better equivalents to his people at a lower cost. We'll bust Faber, I promise you. I don't want him on my patch.'

'I'll need some more help.'

'Jay, hire whoever you need.'

'Right.' Jay paused. 'One other thing, Steven, I heard from Fran Zanini the other day. She wants to talk to you.'

'I haven't got anything to say to her, Jay. She cancelled her contract, didn't she? And she's hardly played in the last year. I saw a picture of her the other day, when she was busted for drugs. She's as wide as a beer truck.'

'She needs help. She wants to go into a drug rehabilitation clinic, a private one. But it costs.'

'What's the problem? She earned millions for God's sake. Where's it all gone?'

'It was invested by Mauro. I think we know what that means.'

'Let me think about it. We might be able to help. Dean could probably get some good money from a British tabloid for her story and then there'd be some syndication here and there. Yeah, we might run with it and there'd be enough money to pay her fees. Where can I reach her?'

When he had played back Eva Rosen's message on his answering machine in London, Winter had found her strong, low voice attractive. As he waited in the PNE reception area, he wondered whether the woman would match the voice. When she came out to greet him he was not disappointed. Her striking good looks were enhanced by her elegant clothes. For a moment, Winter felt clumsy in his battered tweed jacket and corduroy trousers but Eva's vibrant smile of welcome put him at his ease.

As they settled in her office and a pot of coffee was brought in, Eva wasted no time. 'I liked your piece about Shaw. But why did an English television producer go to the lengths of getting it published in New York?'

'Because I think Shaw's a crook. Because I believe he

may have engineered the deaths of two of my friends. One day I'm going to do a programme about him. To answer your question, though, the article was designed to shake him up a bit.'

'The writer as *agent provocateur*?'

'That's it.'

'What hard evidence d'you have of Shaw's misdeeds?'

'Photographs of businessmen in compromising positions and a video. The sort of thing he'd use to blackmail people. And let me show you this. It's a witness who tells how Shaw's got a key man at the BBC under his thumb.'

From his briefcase Winter produced a video-cassette. When he had run Jacqui Bryson's testimony for Eva, he elaborated on the points he'd made in the *Public Eye* article. In response, Eva summarised what she knew about Steven's hold over Jake Richardson and his influence at AAN.

'The irony is that I threw open the doors for Steven in television. I encouraged him to package events, I showed him how to capitalise on his clients' fame.'

'And he took you for a ride, no doubt.'

'Didn't he just, John? But I fell for him in a big way. I thought all the usual foolish things, like assuming he'd leave his wife for me. You know the scene, I'm sure.'

Winter nodded sympathetically and she continued, 'And then the bastard betrayed me. He cut my legs from under me just as I thought I'd got Jake Richardson by the balls. They've been big buddies ever since. God knows how much Jake has earned from Shaw over the years.'

'Would you say all this to the camera for me?'

'For your programme?'

'Yes.'

'On several conditions.'

'Well . . .'

'Don't worry, John, you'll like what I'm going to say.

First of all I'd like to bid for the programme. In fact we might find some development money for you. I know we're not AAN or one of the other networks but our cable coverage is wide. It's not just America but most of the world. Second, I'd like to run a little item about our mutual friend in one of our magazine programmes.'

'You won't pre-empt me, will you? I don't want to spoil the story.'

'Not at all. It may help you. I'll go for his soft spot and see what happens.'

'Does he have a soft spot?'

'His marriage. He's always maintained the façade of having the idyllic marriage. The glamorous and successful businessman in a high-profile job. The rich and beautiful wife. It's a glossy fantasy.'

'A sham.'

'Yeah. He carried on an affair with me for over a year. No doubt there were other girls then and plenty more since. OK, despite all the feminist ideas, many people wouldn't look askance at him. It's a man's world, he's a hunter, all that bullshit. But what if we focus on Suzi? She's beautiful, isn't she? I don't suppose she's been short of offers to jump into bed.'

Frowning apprehensively, Winter said, 'I wouldn't want to harm Suzi, you know. She's a nice person. She's not our target.'

'You want to get Shaw, don't you?' Eva's voice was insistent and Winter nodded in reply. 'Well, this is a way to unsettle him. Suzi's been seen around town with other men. In the last year or two specifically with her husband's top client. Sam Rhodes. What's in my mind is a gossip piece in one of our programmes along the lines of "Super-agent's marriage on the rocks". A few facts, some speculation and a large helping of innuendo. How does that sound?'

'Nasty.'

'Like your piece in *Public Eye*?'

'Yes, but they had another baby not so long ago. Their second son. It doesn't look as if the marriage is in trouble, does it?'

'They may have made a baby to try and save the marriage. Some couples are naive enough to do that.'

'Naive isn't a word that I'd ever apply to Steven Shaw.'

'No. Maybe there's another explanation.' Eva smiled widely at Winter. 'What do you say, John, to a couple of drinks and some lunch? Between us I think we can take that bastard Shaw apart.'

# Chapter Forty-six

PNE's Wednesday morning magazine programme, 'People in the News', had been on the brink of extinction when Eva Rosen joined the company. It was a worthy programme which wheeled in the usual band of social and political commentators to discuss the issues of the day. She jazzed it up and made it a gossip column of the airwaves which concentrated on short and punchy items which were of interest to New Yorkers. It became a virile mixture of fashion, sport, local politics, entertainment, the arts and especially scandal. Studio-based discussions were punctuated by on-the-street interviews.

A regular viewer, Betty Lynagh had only half an eye on the television while she poured herself a second cup of coffee. Her attention was fully engaged, however, when the presenter, just before a commercial break, announced a juicy story about the supposedly idyllic marriage of Steven Shaw, agent to the sporting superstars, and his beautiful wife, Suzi. Mrs Lynagh had the presence of mind to record the item.

She watched with mounting horror and embarrassment as the reporter dwelled on the rumours of an irreconcilable breakdown in the Shaw marriage. It was said that Steven had had a string of extra-marital affairs and that Suzi had retaliated by having a liaison with a well-known golfer. To Mrs Lynagh's relief, the golfer was not named. But there was a further sting in the tail.

'It is alleged that the Shaw marriage has foundered on doubts about who really fathered their recently born baby, Jordan Samuel. The buzz in jock-sniffing circles is that a pro golfer was the lucky man.' With a last smirk at the camera, the female reporter said, 'Not that we would give any credence to such a scurrilous and unfounded rumour. But it's worth a bet on Jordan Shaw to win the US Open in two thousand and something.'

These final remarks had been one of Eva's ideas and she had no evidence for the insinuation.

Shortly after Betty Lynagh had told her husband about PNE's disclosure, the video was on its way by courier to his law firm's offices. As soon as he had viewed it, Joe Lynagh tracked Steven down to the head office of an insurance company in Chicago.

It didn't take Lynagh long to summarise what had been alleged in the programme and Steven said, 'Will you handle it personally for Suzi and me? Let's hit PNE with a writ and ask for punitive damages.'

'I take it that there's no truth in what they said. No extra-marital affairs on your part? Or Suzi's for that matter? Well, I suppose you wouldn't know about that, Steven.'

For a moment or two Steven did not reply and Lynagh pressed ahead. 'You have to be very careful in these cases, Steven. Mud sticks, and the PNE lawyers will sift your private life through a fine mesh. It won't be pleasant.'

'I've got nothing to hide, Joe, and the baby is mine.'

'I'm sure the baby is yours. I'd trust my daughter to the end of the line. But it's foolish to say you've nothing to hide. We all have skeletons in our cupboards, Steven. They'll rake up your first marriage and they'll make it look as if you abandoned Beverly and your child. It won't be pretty.'

'I won't be libelled, Joe, and I won't be made to look foolish. Anyway, I owe it to all of us to protect my family's reputation.'

Lynagh was worried. If the potential litigants hadn't been a part of his own family, he would have rubbed his hands happily at the thought of a protracted legal tussle which would bring in huge fees to his firm. But he knew well how messy such a case would be and he did not want his beloved Suzi to become involved. No doubt Steven could handle it, but not his daughter. Even more difficult was the fact that his firm represented PNE's interests in the USA and he had known the President of the company, Ron Palmer, for many years. He knew that Palmer would defend such an action to the wire and he was one of the richest men in the world.

'Let's be practical,' Lynagh said. 'You don't need this kind of hassle and PNE isn't the sort of outfit to front up against. They're big-time and they won't back off because they'll love the publicity. It'll bring in more subscribers. What'll it do for you, Steven?'

'I've dealt with PNE. Who's the executive in charge of "People in the News"? We're bound to have something on him.'

'Her. She's called Eva Rosen.'

There was a delay of several seconds before Steven said, 'That explains a lot. She was forced to resign from AAN and she blamed me. Joe, I want you to go for the jugular.'

'In that case, I'm afraid you'll have to find yourself another lawyer. First, because I believe you should take limited action only. Go after PNE for an apology and nothing more. Second, because PNE is a client of mine, an important client. You're family, but business is business and I have a responsibility to my partners.'

'Well, that's just great,' Steven said bitterly. 'Now I see

what's behind your advice.'

'It's good advice. Please listen to me. Anyway, there's Suzi and the children to consider. I'll talk to her tonight.'

'So will I. I'll be back in New York tomorrow.' Steven put down the telephone.

Suzi returned from a charity lunch to find several urgent messages from her mother, whom she called at once. When Betty Lynagh told her about the 'People in the News' item, Suzi felt ill. She slumped into a chair and nearly dropped the telephone.

'Are you OK, darling?' asked Mrs Lynagh.

'Yes, Mom, just dropped the phone.'

'As soon as Joe gets home we'll bring the video over. It's best that you see it for yourself.'

'If you must.'

Suzi made herself a cup of coffee. How could anyone know that Sam was the father of her child? It was her secret. She hadn't told a soul. So it was a guess. Somebody had taken a guess and hit the jackpot. Thank God Sam was out of the way in California, though it wouldn't be long before the rumours got to him.

By the time that Suzi had fed Jordan, her parents had arrived. She left the baby and Adam in the care of the nanny.

Joe Lynagh was as breezy as ever as he attempted to play down the significance of the broadcast. 'It's just gossip, Suzi. Malicious, yes, but we shouldn't build it up into a feud.'

'It's disgraceful,' Mrs Lynagh said. 'Why do these television people do such awful things?'

'To increase their ratings.'

'At the expense of other people's feelings?' Mrs Lynagh said. 'It's not right.'

'Steven wants to go for the jugular as he put it,' Joe Lynagh said quietly. 'But I advised caution. What d'you think, Suzi?'

She shrugged. 'Steven will do whatever he wants, as usual.'

Mrs Lynagh looked at her sharply. 'There's no truth in these rumours, is there, darling? You do see an awful lot of Sam, don't you?'

'That's not really our business, Betty,' Lynagh said. 'Except inasmuch as it affects our view of the case,' he ended lamely.

'The baby is definitely Steven's,' Suzi said flatly.

Her father noticed Suzi's evasion of the question about Sam Rhodes, while her mother did some mental arithmetic. The baby had been born in January and Steven had been abroad for much of the previous March and April.

'Let's all go out for dinner,' Joe Lynagh said decisively. 'I'm going to talk to Steven tomorrow and stop him doing anything stupid. Libel cases are just a load of trouble for everyone concerned and we don't want that, do we, Suzi?'

Suzi guessed that her father had made all the correct deductions and was offering her a way out of the problem. 'Please do your best with Steven, won't you? Because I will refuse to have any part of a libel action,' she said.

Lynagh had a chance to speak alone to Suzi while his wife supervised Jordan's bathtime. 'This Eva Rosen,' he began tentatively, 'do you think Steven had an affair with her?'

'Yes. And dozens of other women.'

'You seem very unhappy, Suzi. Are you going to leave him?'

'No. I married him for better or worse and I'll stick by him. At least, until the children are grown up.'

Before Steven contacted him late the next morning, Joe

Lynagh had already spoken to Ron Palmer in Johannesburg. The owner of PNE laughed when his American lawyer explained that Steven Shaw was determined to take him on in a libel action. 'Let him,' Palmer said. 'We'll take him to the cleaners, you know that, Joe. Even though he's your son-in-law.'

'I'd rather you didn't.'

'It'll be good for business. We need more subscribers in your country.'

'It won't look good, Ron, when Steven Shaw tells the court that he had a brief liaison with Eva, then broke it off and she manufactured the story about Suzi solely to get revenge.'

'Is that true?'

'More or less. But I have a suggestion which'll get all of us off the hook. If I persuade Steven not to take action against you for libel, will you broadcast an apology?'

'Well . . .'

'I'd recommend it, as your lawyer.'

'Speaking as Suzi's father, you mean,' Palmer said. 'OK, Joe, it's a deal. We've known each other for a long time. We don't need all this shit. Christ, that lovely lady, Eva Rosen, will hit the roof but I'll deal with her. You deal with Steven.'

Joe Lynagh's office had changed very little over the years. He sat behind the same enormous desk and the grandeur of the painted ceiling and the ornate chandelier was undiminished. Whenever he entered it, Steven remembered his first sight of it when he was fighting to retrieve his relationship with Suzi. He still felt at a slight disadvantage whenever he went there.

'I'm going to instruct a lawyer tomorrow to issue a libel writ against PNE,' Steven began aggressively.

'Don't,' Lynagh replied. 'It's not worth it. I know you're

a very rich man, Steven, but Ron Palmer can buy and sell you a dozen times over.'

'It's personal. That bitch Rosen has libelled me and she's got to pay for it.'

'I thought you were a tough and sophisticated business-man and such people never let nonsense like this get to them. Why spend millions on a battle you can't win? Your dirty laundry will be exposed to the public gaze and you won't like that. Neither will Suzi. Have you talked to her yet?'

'Not yet.'

'Well, I would and quickly. She's not going to like the story of your affair with Eva Rosen being recounted for the titillation of the public.'

'What affair?'

'Don't give me any bullshit, Steven. I don't care what you've done, who you've screwed but you're not going to upset Suzi. You have obligations to her and your children, you remember that.'

Lynagh paused and Steven noticed that he was flushed and his hands were tightly clenched.

'OK, Joe, what do you suggest?'

'An on-air apology from the PNE people and you forget the matter.'

'You've done a deal with Ron Palmer, I presume.' Lynagh nodded. 'What about Rosen? I want her bounced out of that job.'

'I'll mention that to Palmer but I wouldn't bet on him doing anything. He'll do exactly what he wants and noth-ing more.'

'Maybe I'll deal with that bitch myself, in my own time.'

A week later Eva walked into her office shortly before eight o'clock in the morning. She would have an hour to demolish some paperwork before the others arrived. She grabbed a coffee from the machine in the outer office and strolled into her own room. Her heart seemed to drop into the pit of her stomach when she saw Ron Palmer, neat and compact, behind her desk.

His terse fax had instructed her to apologise for the item about Steven and Suzi Shaw's marriage. 'And make it sound good' had been the final sentence. She had shrugged off her irritation. Palmer was the boss and she had already achieved her first objective, which was to trash Steven Shaw. The subsequent retraction didn't fool anybody. John Winter had made that point when he contacted her, after receiving a transcript of the programme.

Nevertheless, she wondered if she had gone too far. She had heard nothing more from Palmer and now, here he was, unannounced, in her office. As usual, his grey hair was cropped close and once again she noticed the brilliance of his dark-brown eyes. She wondered whether she was about to be fired.

'Sit down, Eva.' Palmer waved at one of the chairs and stayed put behind her desk. 'I wanted to talk to you.' Despite having emigrated with his family to South Africa in his youth, Palmer had never lost his English accent. 'Steven Shaw asked me to fire you. I'm surprised at you, Eva, for pursuing a personal vendetta like this in such a public way. It's unprofessional.'

Here it comes, Eva thought. 'There's a very big story about Shaw and I'll be the person who'll tell it.'

Suddenly Palmer smiled at her. 'Good, that's what I'd hoped to hear. You'll get all the backing you need. Nobody tells me how to run my business. Nobody. I'd been meaning to talk to you anyway, Eva. I've been really impressed with what you're doing here. Matt Engelman is going to be moved upstairs as President of the American company.

How d'you feel about taking on the job of Chief Executive Officer?'

'How do I feel . . . ?'

'I'll double your salary, of course, and we'll work out a bonus package and some share options.'

'Wow, I accept—'

'Good. That's settled then. Now, let me explain why I decided to settle with Shaw. For one thing, Joe Lynagh was talking sense when he advised me to steer away from a libel case. But the real reason is that there's a bigger game to be played. Shaw is a big operator in sport and that is one of the key areas for our future expansion. At present we buy rights all around the world to events. Football, golf, basketball, volleyball, tennis, speed skating, drag racing, body building, any kind of crap. You name it and we show it.'

Palmer reached across the desk and took a sip from Eva's cup of coffee and grimaced. 'Shaw has created a lot of events for television and he retains control. He sells rights for many of the blue riband events and he represents some of the top talent in golf and tennis and athletics. So, I want to buy him out. With all his properties we can produce a massive amount of programming for our network. That's why I walked away from this libel nonsense, Eva. That's the reason.'

'Shaw owns the company.'

'He owns seventy-five per cent of it. My friend, Joe Lynagh, owns a quarter of it.'

'OK, but why should Shaw sell out?'

'Because everyone has a price.'

'Not necessarily, Ron. Shaw's like you. Would you sell your company?'

'I have sold some of it, recently. To a fellow in Hong Kong. Jimmy Chung. He waved the sort of money at me that made me blink. It wasn't just the money, of course. He was able to give me access to other markets because his cable company's footprint spreads throughout Asia. Chung also sees the logic of acquiring an outfit like Shaw Management.'

'I'll bet you that Shaw won't sell,' Eva said firmly.

'Well, we'll have to persuade him somehow, won't we? Any ideas?'

'We could give a man called John Winter some money for a start.' Eva told Palmer about his plans to make an investigative programme about Steven Shaw and how it might undermine his reputation. Palmer agreed to put up some money for Winter's project.

That would be a revenge to savour in itself, thought Eva. But if her company took over Shaw Management . . .

# Chapter Forty-seven

In the weeks leading up to the Wimbledon Tennis Championships, Fran Zanini told her harrowing story to the Sunday tabloid newspaper with the largest circulation in Britain. It was a tale of physical and mental abuse by her father in her childhood and of drug dependency from an early age. She claimed that, from twelve years onwards, she had been fed hormones and steroids. Doctor Rexel had assured her that they were vitamin tablets and tonics. However, she made the point emphatically that her coach, Kenny Crane, had no knowledge of what was going on. In fact, he was one of the few men who had shown her any love and kindness.

Zanini also praised her business manager, Steven Shaw, for his steadfast support despite all her problems. She would be eternally grateful for his generosity in paying for her treatment at the drug rehabilitation clinic. She intended to repay him by getting her life back on course and winning another Wimbledon title.

The fees that Aultman negotiated in London and the subsequent syndication of the story left Shaw Management with a healthy profit, even after the considerable costs of Zanini's treatment were deducted.

Her subsequent attempt at a comeback ended in a miserable and tearful failure.

Kenny Crane went from strength to strength as a coach

**Malcolm Hamer**

and his chain of tennis centres flourished. Occasionally he thought about that uneducated and vulnerable girl whom he had coached and motivated to win Wimbledon; but he was busy with too many other aspiring champions, all of them clients of Shaw's agency.

Steven hardly thought about her again. There were dozens of Francesca Zaninis to be nurtured and then exploited. He would have been amazed to hear that Kenny Crane wept when he read, a few years later, of Zanini's death from an overdose of drugs.

In the middle of the first week of the Wimbledon Tennis Championships Steven took Angus Gray, twice the Formula One motor racing champion, to sit in the Royal Box. Such invitations were rare, even to a man like Steven who had sold Wimbledon's television rights around the world with such success. They watched Ray Gerrard scrape a victory over a lowly ranked German player.

'Ray looks as if he's lost interest,' Gray said.

'He's talking of retiring,' Steven replied.

'If he's talking of it, he should do it because he obviously doesn't have the will any more.'

'Maybe, but he still has a lot of obligations.'

'You mean, Steven, that he's earning vast sums of money from his endorsements. But they can carry on even if he retires.'

'Not for long. The public forget. There's always another Ray Gerrard for them to worship.'

'And I expect you represent him,' Gray said with a laugh.

Steven shrugged. 'You're retiring too, I gather? Dean Aultman tells me this is your last season.'

'Yes, but I've got lots to do, as you know. Commentaries, books, consultant to companies in the motor racing business. And I'll have the time to get involved with three-day eventing and with polo. Dean's going to help me with some sponsorship projects and I was hoping, Steven, that you'd give me some help, too.'

'I've told you before, Angus, it's not my scene. There's no real money in it. I'm surprised that Dean's got the time to bother.'

'Well, it's a favour to me, actually.'

'Agencies aren't built on favours.'

'Don't be narrow-minded, Steven, and don't give Dean a hard time either. Polo's a great game, very high profile as they say. So is three-day eventing. You know that the royals are involved in both sports.' Gray lowered his voice since they were sitting a few seats away from some minor royals.

The two men watched as a tall American player served successive aces to his opponent. Gray said, 'I want to convince you about polo. There's an international match at Windsor on Sunday and I want you to come. We'll have lunch with the sponsors and you can get a feel for the game.'

'Who're the sponsors?'

'Valentino Fragrances.'

'I've never really understood the perfume business. Coloured water that's sold for ludicrous sums of money. Those bloody awful ads.'

'They're selling dreams, Steven. Just like you when you sell an endorsement for me or Ray Gerrard or Sam Rhodes. So, will you come to the polo? You should bring Suzi.'

'She's not coming over this year. I should be seeing my parents in Brighton on Sunday. My father's not too well.'

'Oh, I'm sorry. In that case . . .'

'No, Angus, I'll take a look. Since it's you.'

A Daimler, with the soldierly Terry Parkin at the wheel,

picked Steven up at his house shortly after midday on
Sunday. They made the short trip to Angus Gray's flat
and drove to the Guards Polo Club in Windsor Great
Park.

Steven told Terry Parkin to let them out by the huge
public car park and to pick them up later near the sponsor's
tent. 'I want to assess the appeal of the sport,' he said to
Gray. 'So I need to look at the people, look at their cars,
look at what they're eating and drinking.'

The spectators were taking proper advantage of the sunshine. Their vehicles were drawn up in orderly ranks under
the instructions of the Scots guardsmen. Steven took stock
of the expensive machinery: there was a preponderance of
Mercedes and BMW models, with a smattering of Range
Rovers and their Japanese copies. In the generous gaps
between the cars the picnics were in full swing. Many of the
spectators had made elaborate provision in every way:
tables and chairs were in place, tablecloths, ice buckets for
the champagne and tempting displays of cold food. Some
of them had brought playthings for their children; one
enterprising party had erected a slide and a swing. The
middle classes were at play, Steven reflected, their conversation uncontroversial, their preoccupations conventional.
On the surface, that is. An occasional shriek of laughter or
an admonition to an errant child punctuated the chatter.
The men were mostly in casual and inelegant weekend
clothes. Many of the women seemed to have dressed for a
home counties wedding rather than a sporting occasion,
although Steven looked with interest at the younger women
in their revealing cotton shifts.

'Interesting?' Gray asked. As Steven nodded his agreement, a tall, slim woman, with a flamboyant mane of
blonde hair, swayed past. Her skin-tight, white skirt finished just the right side of decency. It was decorated with a

broad gilt belt; above it she showed a bare and suntanned midriff. A low-cut green silk top, tightly fitted over ample breasts, completed the ensemble.

The two men grinned in unison. 'Now that *is* interesting,' Steven said. 'Is she your typical polo follower?'

'Euro-trash,' Gray said, 'but let's not be small-minded.'

As the girl made her way between the lines of picnickers, the men stared at her with lascivious appreciation under the disapproving eyes of their women.

Gray led Steven past the tents which sold beer, hamburgers, sandwiches, champagne, Pimms, clothing, saddles, garden furniture and souvenirs. They skirted the polo field and entered the sponsor's marquee. Over a hundred tables were set with white linen tablecloths and silver cutlery and each had a centrepiece of flowers. One of the sponsor's hostesses, her smile firmly glued in place, led them to their places and introduced them to the other guests. With an inward groan, Steven shook hands with a merchant banker. Christ, he'd probably bang on about foursomes being the only real form of golf and how he could get round Royal St George's in two hours flat. He was tall and cadaverous, clothed in a three-piece, pinstriped suit, and his only merit seemed to be a very attractive wife. Steven gave her the full wattage of his smile and held his handshake with her just a little longer than necessary. A former international polo player, Robbie Downes, and his wife, and the Valentino Publicity Director, Simon Lacey, made up the table. There was a vacant seat on Steven's right.

'It's for Lady Louise Flint,' Gray said. 'She's always late. You'll like her, I think. She's a three-day eventer, knows my wife.'

'Where is Kate?'

'Gone to see some aged relative in Dorset.'

The second course was being served when Lady Louise

arrived. As Lacey introduced her, Steven was able to study her. Her face, with its deep-blue eyes and full mouth, suggested generosity and the light scattering of freckles implied a sense of fun. Dark-brown hair with a tinge of auburn crowned a shapely head. Initially, Steven's gaze rested approvingly on Louise's tight and rounded bottom; but it was her natural physical grace that really held his attention. He caught the merchant banker's wife watching him and smiled discreetly back.

As everyone settled into their seats and resumed their meal, Gray leaned towards Louise and said, 'Steven Shaw is my business manager, Louise, and knows more about sponsorship than anyone. He's promised to help me raise some money for some of the equestrian sports, especially three-day eventing.'

Steven gave Gray full marks for manoeuvring him into this situation. But he would put Dean Aultman to work to ferret out sponsorship while he worked on Lady Louise. She chatted agreeably to him throughout the meal. He noticed that she ate very little and assumed that she was trying to keep her weight down. He learned that Gray went shooting with her father, the Earl of Wenlock, and that daddy also had a stretch of fishing on the Wye.

'What do you do when you're not riding horses?' Steven asked.

'Oh, some public relations. For Simon for instance. I've worked for years for Valentino's. But I'd like to concentrate more on my eventing.'

'So you need some sponsorship?'

'Yes. Despite his castle in Herefordshire and the shooting and the fishing, Daddy can't afford to pay for my hobby, I'm afraid.'

'Let's discuss this in more detail,' Steven said quickly. 'Over dinner tomorrow?'

Louise nodded her agreement and handed him a business card.

The band of the Scots Guards led the two teams on to the field and the players were introduced to the crowd. After a seemingly interminable rendition of the national anthem, the match began. Gray explained some of the finer tactical points to Steven, who admitted to himself that polo had its moments of thunderous excitement. After an hour, however, he'd had enough. There were contracts and a mass of other material to be read. As Terry Parkin drove him home, Steven looked ahead with pleasure to his date with the attractive Lady Louise.

Steven had noticed how Louise had the priceless knack of making the person to whom she was talking appear to be the centre of her world. It was a flattering attribute and he savoured it to the full during their meal at Rossiter's.

During the day, one of Dean Aultman's assistants had researched her background as thoroughly as possible. Lady Louise Flint was 27 years of age and the eldest daughter of the Earl and Countess of Wenlock. She had been educated at Benenden and at a college in Switzerland but had only a moderate academic ability. From an early age she had shown a great interest in horses and eventually specialised in three-day eventing. She had been on the verge of the 1984 Olympic team but had been passed over – unfairly, said some of the experts. Louise had been engaged to be married on two occasions, once to a middle-aged American financier and once to a French diplomat. She was currently unattached. She was said to have inherited her parents' fondness for alcohol and had been arrested once for possession of marijuana. No charges were made by the police.

It was an enjoyable evening and Steven was determined

to take it to its logical conclusion by sleeping with Louise. It would be his first full aristocrat. Araminta had been an Honourable, but the Wenlock title had been granted in the seventeenth century and Louise's mother was related, albeit distantly, to the Queen. Louise was the real thing.

Steven would have been surprised to hear that his own background had been scrutinised by his dinner companion, even if Louise were not as thorough as Steven's employee. Telephone calls to some of the media people she knew had sufficed. When she heard that he was one of the most influential men in sport and that his fortune was estimated in the hundreds of millions, she decided he was too good a prospect to spurn. He was sexy, too.

When they returned to Steven's house, he poured two glasses of Armagnac and suggested that they watched the highlights of the day's play at Wimbledon. One of Shaw's clients, yet another young female prodigy from Kenny Crane's production line, was playing a singles match. From the first rally it became a war of attrition played by both competitors from the baseline.

'I can think of better things to do,' Louise said as she knelt on the floor in front of him. Slowly she unzipped his trousers and felt caressingly for his penis. 'Yum,' she said and went to work on him.

After several minutes they decided to continue their encounter in the comfort of the bedroom. If Araminta had shown the young Steven the many different and diverting routes to heaven, Louise knew them and a few more. Her body was as graceful and inviting as Steven had imagined and her sexual appetite was sharp. It must be the way the toffs are brought up, he thought happily.

At seven o'clock in the morning Steven dragged himself out of bed and towards the bathroom. He looked over his shoulder at Louise, who was sleeping fitfully, and smiled.

As he threw cold water at his face to revive himself, Steven noticed a few grains of white powder on the top of one of the bathroom units. That's odd, he thought, the cleaner had visited the house on the preceding day and she was very thorough. He looked at the powder again and picked up some of it on a damp forefinger. Gingerly, he tasted it. His tongue went numb. Well, well, so that was it.

Steven padded downstairs and made two mugs of tea. He awoke Louise by stroking her forehead. Drowsily she reached out for him, one hand around his neck, the other gently stroking his penis. Rather than the eager, gymnastic couplings of the night before this was a gentler exercise in sexual fulfilment. Afterwards they lay back, smiling with pleasure.

'Don't forget your tea,' Steven said. 'Or do you prefer coffee.'

'I prefer what I've just had.'

'Every morning?'

'If I can get it.'

After a shower, Steven waited downstairs for Louise. He was in no hurry; fortunately, he had no breakfast meetings that morning. When she appeared she refused his offer of another cup of tea and said she had to be on her way. 'A meeting with Simon Lacey at midday. When shall I see you again, darling?'

'How about tonight?'

'That'll be lovely.'

'One question, Louise, before you go. Who d'you get your coke from?'

'Oh, er, mainly someone called Rory. Why d'you ask?'

'Rory McCall, the photographer?'

'Yes, but I don't use it much.'

'Just recreational? It's best to keep it that way. Rory is an old friend of mine. I'll have a word with him and I'll look after your bills in the future. Within reason, that is. You're sure you can control the habit?'

'Of course, darling. You know, you're really sweet. See you later.'

During the succeeding months Steven spent more time than usual in Britain, and as much of it as he could in Louise's company. They attended the major sporting events together and Louise even inveigled him into going to watch horse-racing and to the Henley Royal Regatta. They usually met up with groups of her friends and Steven invariably found that he paid for the champagne and the meals. But he didn't mind.

He tried to keep a check on Louise's consumption of cocaine. It was difficult because McCall was responsible for procuring the drug for Shaw Management's business contacts and Louise's expenditure became lost in the agency's overheads. Steven told himself that she was just an occasional user who would not become addicted.

Ever wary of revealing any weaknesses that might be used against him, he was careful to maintain the fiction that Louise was a consultant in equestrian sports to the agency. He put her on the payroll, much to Dean Aultman's annoyance, since her salary affected the London office's profits. Steven saw his point and arranged to pay her from the same off-shore account that funded McCall's activities in the drugs market. Steven also put Louise under occasional surveillance. The reports that came back from Dan Fisher confirmed that she was not sleeping with anyone else.

At a polo match in Windsor Great Park in September, Steven met Louise's mother, the Countess of Wenlock. She was a plump and smiling woman who confessed to him that she'd rather have a good strong gin and tonic in her hands than a cup of weak tea. He warmed to her, especially when she introduced him to one of the members of the royal family. This was the life, he thought. Rich, preeminent in his field and now hobnobbing with the upper classes. As the 1980s drew to a close, Steven reckoned that he'd made the big time in every way.

# Chapter Forty-eight

Despite the backing he received from PNE, John Winter had made limited progress in his efforts to investigate Shaw and ultimately to destabilise him and his agency. Eva Rosen was trying to find an informant in Shaw's New York office and Winter was attempting the same thing in London. One of his most positive allies proved to be Jacqui Bryson, who volunteered to try and foster a friendship with Lucy Howard.

'As far as I know she's still sleeping with Shaw,' Jacqui said. 'She's been his secretary for years. She should know nearly as much about the operation as Aultman.'

As a pretext for contacting Lucy again, Jacqui said that her company was creating a comedy series around a sports promoter and she wanted to hear about Lucy's routine work at Shaw Management. The friendly Lucy was happy to talk and the two women established a routine of meeting at least once a month.

Towards the end of the year, Winter read a long article in *The Times* about Ray Gerrard. It told how his disillusionment with tennis had led him to decide on retirement. He would play a few events in the following year and see whether he was up to playing at Wimbledon again. Whatever happened he would retire after the US Championships. 'The sport has lost its way,' Gerrard stated. 'It's solely about money now and the money available is obscene. The men in suits run it and they run it for themselves.'

Gerrard was playing in an indoor round-robin tournament in Amsterdam, one of Winter's favourite cities. So great was Gerrard's apparent disillusionment that Winter felt he might talk freely about Shaw. He took an evening flight to Amsterdam.

On the following day, Winter used the accreditation provided by PNE to enter the Press Centre and find out where Gerrard was staying. He remembered Winter well and agreed to have lunch with him. They met at a restaurant in the Jordaan district.

When he was halfway through his omelette and salad, Gerrard said, 'I suppose you want to talk about Shaw, don't you? You're still on your crusade, are you?'

'I'm a television journalist, Ray. I'm after a story. Particularly since one of my friends, Toby Streeter, died in very odd circumstances last year. He got too close to Shaw and I believe he paid the penalty.'

Pushing aside his unfinished meal, Gerrard looked hard at Winter. 'You don't really mean that, John, do you?' He took a long swallow of beer. 'Shaw's capable of many things, but not murder, surely?'

Winter shrugged. 'Maybe I'm getting paranoid. Let's ignore my theories. You tell me what you think.'

'As you saw from that article, I'm pissed with tennis and have been for a long time. But it's gotten worse.' After a pause Gerrard said, 'I know a guy called Harry Faber back in LA. He has a brother, Archie, who set up as a sports agent. He's a bright guy but, the way Harry tells it, Steven Shaw is trying to ruin him. He's stealing Archie's clients, warning the manufacturers not to deal with him. For Chrissakes, Shaw's business is huge, he's mega-rich, why should he try and fuck up a small guy like Archie Faber?'

'You tell me.'

'The trouble is, I can't. I didn't major in psychology for a start. But I can tell you how Shaw loused me up.'

'Go on,' Winter said quietly. He did not interrupt as Gerrard, with many hesitations and explanations, told him the sordid tale of his night with the under-age Maria, of the threats by her mother to denounce him to the police, and of the subsequent rescue operation master-minded by his agent.

Shame had prevented Gerrard from mentioning the incident to anyone. His father, a devout churchgoer, would have been hurt and humiliated by his son's revelations and his few friends would have granted him little sympathy. It was a relief to talk to someone like Winter about such a lamentable experience.

'I'm convinced that Shaw set me up. You see, I was about to leave him for another agent.'

'That sounds very much his style, doesn't it? That hardy perennial, the honey trap, but with an unusual and very bitter taste. Shaw's wasted in the sports business, he should've been head of MI5 or the CIA.'

'Or both.'

'Yes.' They swapped wry smiles. 'Now tell me about Ryberg.'

'I can't help you there, John. You already have your own suspicions and they're probably right. It was a variation of how Shaw conned me, wasn't it? Ryberg was all set for that racket contract and he'd have won Wimbledon with the Larssen racket. Suddenly the press are after him. He's gay. He's two-timing his wife in favour of a guy. No manufacturer would touch him after that.'

'Let's go back to your problem with Maria. Would you tell the story again to the cameras?'

'Jesus, no chance, John.'

'We could make it anonymous. Block your face out and disguise your voice.'

'Well, I don't . . .'

'It would simply illustrate Shaw's methods, the lengths he'll go to get his own way.'

'Maybe.'

'Why don't you give me the names of the people involved and we'll try and find them? Maria Lister, wasn't it? And her mother. What about the lawyer?'

'Mike Russo, he called himself.'

'A false name? Was he a lawyer or just playing the part for Shaw?'

'Nothing would surprise me.'

'So you'll help us, Ray?'

The tennis player drained his glass of beer and shrugged. 'Why not? Shaw's made me very rich but I wonder whether the pain was worth it. Let's cause him some pain in return.'

'What'll you do when you retire?'

'Drink some beer. I guess I'll stay in tennis – it's what I know.'

'Commentate perhaps or write about it?'

'I want to try and bring some sanity back into the game. I don't know how I'll do it, but I'll try.'

A few weeks later, the Features Editor of the *Daily News*, a tabloid newspaper whose circulation was diminishing nearly as rapidly as its reputation, was glaring at the middle pages of the following day's edition and wondering how he could find something to titillate his readers.

'Another sodding article about losing weight,' he muttered to himself. 'How to have your baby at home. God Almighty, what drivel.'

Impatiently he flicked through some photographs that had been collected by his gossip columnist. Not much here, he thought. If only they had one of Charlie with his tongue in Camilla's ear, or somewhere, or of Fergie with her tits out. He was about to throw the pictures aside when one at the bottom of the pile caught his eye. He recognised Steven Shaw and Lady Louise. She was into showjumping or some such horsey shit. Anyway, she was the daughter of the Earl of Wenlock. They were coming out of a club together and their body language told him all he needed to know.

'Jeremy,' the Features Editor bellowed at his gossip columnist. 'Here's a nice little bonking item for you. Ideal as the lead in your column tomorrow. Look at this.'

The picture headed Jeremy Marshall's column on the following day and took up a quarter of the page. The caption read: 'Superagent Steven Shaw and his constant companion, Lady Louise Flint, leaving Jezebel's in loving mood.' Marshall's story told his readers how they had been introduced by the Formula One world champion, Angus Gray, and had fallen instantly in love. Several of Louise's friends were quoted as saying how happy they were together. There were no quotes from Steven Shaw. Marshall reminded everyone that he had a beautiful wife and two children in New York.

Such a gossip item is usually dead and buried within days: the wise victim will laugh it off as the product of a journalist's disordered imagination. That was Steven's line when Lucy Howard showed him the article. 'Just a lot of nonsense,' he said. 'We went to the club for a few drinks with some of Louise's friends. She had a few too many and I was helping her out to her taxi. That's it, Lucy.'

'Why don't you sue the *News* for libel?'

'Because that's what they want me to do. Just forget it.'

In fact, Steven was furious that he'd dropped his guard and taken a sucker punch. But he reasoned that the story would soon be as cold as yesterday's soup and that it would

certainly not surface in New York. But the story was kept
on the boil. First, John Winter faxed copies of the article to
Eva Rosen and to *Public Eye*, whose Editor ran a piece
about the Shaw marriage in the next edition of the magazine.

In the meantime, an enterprising young woman in the
syndication department of the *Daily News* sold the picture
of Steven with Lady Louise and the accompanying story to
a magazine in New York. They ran the story, and PNE's
'People in the News' programme commented on it briefly.
Eva played it down because she was mindful of Ron
Palmer's strictures that there was a much more critical game
in progress with Shaw. The real pay-off would come later –
and bigger.

When Steven boarded the morning Concorde flight to
New York, he was unaware that the story of his dalliance
with the Lady Louise was circulating in the city. From the
airport he went straight to his office. The receptionist
seemed startled by his arrival but told him that Jay was
anxious to talk to him. His Chief Executive was sprawled in
his chair, a telephone to his ear; his jacket was off and the
collar of his shirt unbuttoned. He was already well into
the challenge of another long, hard day. He grinned at
Steven and waved him towards a chair. He ended his conversation with a promise to talk his client through the offer
later. 'Well, Steven, you've been busy in London.' He
pushed some newspaper cuttings across the desk. '"People
in the News" have covered it, too.'

'No doubt.'

'I don't blame you. Wow, what a great-looking girl! And
she's a Lady, too. Does that mean she knows the Queen and
Prince Charles?'

'Don't take the piss, Jay. She works for the London office
as a consultant. That's all there is to it.'

'Fine. I'm sure Suzi'll be relieved to hear that. She's rung a couple of times while you've been away. I wouldn't want to interfere but maybe you should call her.'

'I wonder why she didn't contact me in London?'

'I'm single,' Melville said lightly. 'I don't know about these things.'

'I should keep it that way.'

Steven asked his secretary to contact Suzi and tell her that he had various meetings to attend during the rest of the day but would try to be home before six o'clock.

It was after eight o'clock when Steven reached his house. The children were both in bed. Suzi followed him into the kitchen and watched him delve into the refrigerator for a beer. Icily polite, she asked him about his trip and he asked her about the children. Fed up with the tension that filled the kitchen, Steven said, 'Jay showed me those silly stories about Louise Flint.'

'About *you* and her.'

'Yes. It's just a nasty bit of tabloid journalism. You know what the gutter press is like in Britain. Anything for a cheap thrill for their readers. They're the worst in the world.'

'That's OK,' Suzi said calmly. 'There's no doubt in my mind that you're sleeping with her. I've got used to the idea of you sticking your cock into anything you fancy.'

'Suzi, I haven't—'

'Don't even bother to deny it. It's of no interest to me. After all, I haven't remained faithful to you, so I suppose I'm as guilty as you are.'

'Fine. Let's leave it at that, shall we?'

'No, we won't. It's one thing to screw around but it's something else entirely to have it broadcast to the general public. That may sound like a piece of crass hypocrisy but it really matters to me. I've done what we agreed, I've been discreet. But you obviously don't give a damn any more.'

'At least I don't screw your friends, Suzi.'

'What's that supposed to mean?' She felt cold and empty. He might as well know the whole truth now.

'Sam. Sam Rhodes. He was my first client and I thought he was still a friend.'

Suzi shrugged. 'Why deny it? You're right, of course, and we shouldn't have let it happen. If I'd had a husband who gave a damn about me, it wouldn't have happened.'

'Oh yes, it's all my fault,' Steven said sarcastically. 'What makes you think Sam'll treat you any better?'

'Because he's a gentleman in its true sense.'

Steven laughed. 'I wonder how long this dewy-eyed romance will last? Sam's always taken his pick of the women. Why should he change?'

'That's a despicable remark. Thank God Sam's not like you. You're probably jealous of him. All you've ever done is devote yourself to making money. That's where you start and finish. It's pathetic.'

'It's easy for a rich bitch like you to say that.'

'Steven, you're a complete failure as a husband and a non-starter as a father.'

'I've done my best for Adam.'

'Bullshit. You've never done the ordinary things that ordinary fathers do: read him a story, taken him for a swim, gone to a movie.'

'I took him and all his friends on the Circle Line for his birthday treat. I hired the whole fucking boat, and a bunch of entertainers for Christ's sake.'

'Yes, the grand gesture. You don't get it, Steven, do you? That doesn't make up for all the small gestures. Like turning up for Adam's school concert or the prize giving, or his birthday. Your presence meant so much to him. But some meeting or other was much more important to you. Grand gestures don't signify. It's all the little gestures that add up to something. To love. D'you remember the word?'

'Very good, Suzi. Did you rehearse that? With lover-boy Sam, perhaps? I assume all this is leading up to you demanding a divorce?'

'Since you've mentioned it, yes, it's probably the answer. Sam and I will be happy together. The whole family will be happy together.'

Steven stared angrily at her and then smiled thinly. 'You don't really think you're taking my sons away from me, do you? They stay with me. If you want a custody battle, you can have it.'

'You're in no position to be a parent to two young children. You've failed comprehensively with Adam and I can prove it.' Suzi stood up very straight and steeled herself. 'There's another thing you should bear in mind. Jordan isn't your child. Sam is his father.'

Steven started towards her but Suzi didn't budge, though she was afraid. 'I don't believe you, you bitch,' he said, his face inches from her.

Having demonstrated her steadfastness, Suzi turned away and said calmly, 'Think back, Steven. You're so good at remembering dates. Compare Jordan's birth date with the time he was probably conceived. You were out of the country for most of March and the early part of April.'

Heavily, Steven sat down on one of the kitchen seats. 'So that's why you were so insistent on our going to bed that time.'

'I was amazed you fell for that. Male vanity, I suppose. The last thing I wanted was you fucking me. I really had to fake it that night. It was a cover-up and I suggest we keep it that way. For all our sakes, including yours.'

'But especially for the sake of your precious parents.'

'I don't suppose your parents would like to hear the

unsavoury truth, and I certainly want to hide it from mine. The divorce will be bad enough. It wouldn't do much for Sam's public image either.'

'Does he know he's the lucky father?'

'No. I'd hoped it would remain a secret. One day, when I was ready, I would've told Sam.'

Steven left the house that evening and never entered it again. As he settled himself into a suite in an hotel near his office, he found it impossible to order his emotions, which were usually so closely controlled. There was a debilitating sense of betrayal, not so much by Suzi but by Sam Rhodes, his first client, whom he'd guided to stardom and unimagined wealth. He'd deal with him in due time. Not at the moment because he was a potent weapon in his battle with Carl Lansky. But let Suzi beware: she'd tricked him shamelessly. She probably thought she had a claim on the business he'd built so skilfully. Well, let her try. The gloves would then come off with a vengeance. Steven didn't care whose reputations were ruined.

He remained in the hotel until Christmas which he spent in the Bahamas with Louise.

A couple of days after the confrontation with Suzi, Joe Lynagh called Steven and suggested that they met to talk about the divorce. He had had no inkling of how unhappy Suzi had been and the collapse of the marriage saddened him. But it was his wife's appalled reaction that distressed him most of all. Lynagh was determined to do all in his power to ease the pain felt by the two women he loved. Suzi refused to discuss her problems in any detail beyond stressing that the marriage was over and divorce the only solution. Lynagh decided he was the best person to attempt to achieve a settlement.

At Steven's insistence the two men met in the offices of

Shaw Management. He wanted to negotiate on his own territory.

Steven was not going to underestimate his father-in-law. He was a hardened and wily negotiator. Looking friendly enough, albeit rather solemn, Lynagh began by stating that he didn't wish to have a wrangle about the rights and wrongs of the dispute. 'I'm here to set up a deal, Steven. I'll try to be an honest broker, even though I can't tell you how despondent this miserable business has made me. And Betty is terribly upset, as you can guess. But let's not have an acrimonious divorce. No point in handing out millions of dollars to the lawyers, is there?'

If I had my way, I'd screw your ass to the wall, thought Lynagh. But Suzi wouldn't have it.

On cue, Steven said, 'That depends on what Suzi wants. I'll make provision for her and the children but she can forget any claim on my business.'

'Our business,' Lynagh said, a warning in his words. 'I've still got a quarter share. But to keep to the point, Suzi wants out. She doesn't want anything from you. Except the house. It's practical for her to keep that. D'you agree?'

Primed for a battle, Steven was suddenly deflated. He paused as he considered Suzi's motives. She had clearly decided that there was a price to pay for keeping the identity of Jordan's father hidden. Fair enough. Steven nodded his agreement and said, 'I suppose she'll marry Sam. If he hadn't come between us—'

His face stiffening with anger, Lynagh replied, 'Don't give me that kind of crap, Steven. From what Suzi has told me, you've been screwing around for years. OK, it's a man's world, but you should've done my daughter the courtesy of not being caught with your pants unzipped.'

'Hell, Joe! She's been having it off with one of my clients, someone I thought of as a friend. That's courtesy, is it?'

'You can hardly take the moral high ground, Steven. What about Eva Rosen? You can't have been married much over a year when you started sleeping with her.'

'These things happen.'

'They shouldn't. If you'd been a decent husband to Suzi, none of this would've happened. She's a fine girl.' Lynagh realised that he was doing what he had promised to avoid; he was trawling over the past. He smiled placatingly and prepared to apologise but Steven cut him short.

'Save the sermons for your daughter, Joe. She's the one who's had a baby by another man and then tried to con me into thinking it was mine.'

Speechless for a moment, Lynagh then said heatedly, 'What the hell are you on about?'

'Jordan. He's not my child. Sam Rhodes is the father.'

Steven waited expectantly for a reaction but Lynagh's expression remained stony. He's too good a negotiator to let things show, Steven thought.

There was a measure of contempt in the lawyer's voice as he said, 'If you're trying to destroy my faith in my daughter, you can forget it, Steven. That's a really despicable accusation.'

'Why don't you ask her?'

'I shall. In the meantime I'll get the divorce process started. We'll make it quick. The less I see or hear of you the better.'

'I'll want some access to my child. To Adam, I mean.'

'We'll arrange that.'

'One more thing, Joe. It hardly seems appropriate that you should retain your interest in Shaw Management, does it? It could cause problems, in view of the divorce. Will you sell your shares to me?'

'Maybe. At the right price. What's the business worth?'

'Oh, a hundred million or so, I suppose.'

'More than that, according to the last accounts, Steven. I'd reckon my interest is worth at least fifty million dollars.'

'Not a bad return on a loan of a quarter of a million dollars, is it?' Steven said drily. He shrugged. 'We'll let the accountants work it out.'

'That's probably the best course.'

That evening Joe Lynagh called at Suzi's house and told her that the divorce would proceed as planned. There would be no problems. He did not mention Steven's accusation that Jordan had been fathered by Sam Rhodes. However, he did speak to Betty about it.

'What should I do?' Lynagh asked. 'I don't feel I can start asking Suzi such questions. It's not fair.'

'Ignore it. Suzi tells me everything that matters,' Mrs Lynagh said firmly, even though the news confirmed her suspicions. 'Steven's trying to upset us and to get back at Suzi.'

Doubts had never disturbed his love for his daughter and Lynagh said, 'Yeah, well Mister Shaw will find that he's not the only one who can play games.' He had a plan to take a measure of revenge on Steven.

# Chapter Forty-nine

Before January was out, the divorce was concluded with the minimum of fuss, even though the gossip columns of newspapers on both sides of the Atlantic had some predictable fun with the news. In the opening years of the 1990s, Steven Shaw was once again a bachelor. Jake Richardson hosted a lavish party to celebrate the fact and the two men ended the evening's entertainment by sharing the sexual favours of identical twins called Mary-Joe and Mary-Jane.

A formal offer to buy Joe Lynagh's interest in the agency for $40 million was made before Christmas, but he made no response. However, Lynagh knew of Ron Palmer's interest in acquiring a company like Shaw Management. The billionaire from South Africa had not been naive enough to say that Steven's agency was his actual target, but it was to him that Lynagh went with a proposition.

By the end of February, Lynagh had sold his shares in Shaw Management to Chung Enterprises, a company registered in Hong Kong, for $65 million. Ron Palmer was one of the directors of the company. Joe Lynagh put the money into a trust for Suzi's two children; she would have the benefit of the interest on the money in the meantime.

Steven was at first mystified when he received a share transfer form from the Company Secretary of Shaw Management. It showed that a company of which he had never heard, Chung Enterprises, had acquired 25 per cent of the shares in his business. The penny dropped with a resounding clunk. Joe had done the dirty on him.

The first call was to the Company Secretary, whom he asked to find out whatever he could about Chung Enterprises; the second was to Joe Lynagh. Steven tried to keep the bitterness out of his voice. 'Wasn't my offer good enough for you, Joe?'

'It was a fair offer but I did better elsewhere.'

'Why didn't you give me a chance to make another bid for your shares? Anyway, there should've been a pre-emption clause in our original agreement.'

'You're right, Steven, but since you were family I didn't think it necessary. Just as well in the circumstances.' Lynagh gave a quick laugh.

'You should still have given me the option to buy you out,' Steven said bitterly.

'No, Steven, I don't want to do business with you on any level. Whatever you offered wouldn't have been enough. I won't ever forgive you for the way you treated Suzi.'

'So, it's a cheap piece of revenge.'

'You've been let off lightly. Don't you ever forget that. Suzi could've sued you for half of everything you possess. As it is, you still own three-quarters of the business.'

'That wasn't altruism on Suzi's part. She didn't want a court case that would've told the world how she gave birth to an illegitimate child fathered by Sam Rhodes, America's favourite golfer.'

Lynagh replied quietly, almost avuncularly. 'You're all screwed up, Steven. You ought to get yourself some counselling. Like me, Suzi has utter contempt for you and wanted to be free of you with the least possible trouble.'

'Well, you've both managed that, haven't you? Who are these Chung Enterprises people, by the way?'

'They'll make their presence felt soon enough, don't

worry. One of the directors is Ron Palmer of PNE. Your old friend and sleeping partner, Eva Rosen, heads up their American operation. I expect Ron will nominate her to sit on your board of directors. That'll be cosy for you, won't it?'

Lynagh put down the telephone. He'd really enjoyed the conversation. That was a good idea of his about Eva Rosen. He got his secretary to fax the suggestion to Palmer in South Africa.

Early in April, Steven visited London for the fifth time that year. The spring-like weather suited his mood since he had decided to propose marriage to Louise. This would be his ultimate social triumph, to marry into an ancient aristocratic family. Maybe it would be some consolation to his parents, who had been distinctly upset when he had told them of his forthcoming divorce from Suzi. Bill Shaw had been hostile, as he catalogued the many virtues that he perceived in his daughter-in-law. Later that day, conscious that he hadn't written a letter to anyone for many years, Bill Shaw sat down and wrote to Suzi. It entailed several false starts and much mental anguish but Suzi, when she read it, understood the love that had been put into it. She wrote back and asked her two parents-in-law to visit her and the children in Florida later that year.

Having grown used to Steven's lavish hospitality, Louise was unsurprised by his invitation to travel to Venice on the Orient Express. As they settled in their seats for dinner on the first evening, a bottle of vintage Krug was popped open and poured by the waiter. This was the life, Louise thought: a far cry from her parents' obsession with keeping the family inheritance intact. That bloody awful, draughty castle in Herefordshire that never got warm. All the keeping up of appearances. Louise actually liked Steven. It did help that he was filthy rich; he was generous too, and that didn't always follow. He didn't even seem to mind the hangers-on, which was nice. She hoped he didn't notice how much cocaine they were all getting through. The head waiter appeared at Steven's side and proffered him a silver tray on which lay a single red rose. How romantic, Louise thought, as Steven took the flower and presented it to her. A middle-aged couple, seated across the aisle, beamed at the two attractive people.

Taking Louise's hand, Steven leaned across the table and said, 'Louise, will you marry me?'

She was taken aback. She hadn't imagined that he had marriage in mind. 'This is rather sudden, darling,' she stuttered. 'I'm overwhelmed, I really am.' They both smiled at her clichéd response. What the hell, she thought, I'll still have plenty of freedom and the money won't ever run out. 'Of course I'll marry you.' She leaned across the table and kissed him.

Steven put his hand in his jacket pocket and handed her a small jewellery box. Inside there lay a gold ring with a single flawless diamond.

'It's beautiful,' Louise said as she slipped it on her finger. 'There's just one thing you must do before we announce anything.'

'What's that?'

'Ask my mother for permission.'

'I thought it would be your father I asked. Perhaps at his London club. Over lunch he'd interrogate me about my business prospects and, at the end, he'd call for some large brandies and tell me, gruffly, to look after jolly old Louise because she's a good stick. He might have the beginnings of a tear in his eye. Isn't that how it's done?'

Louise laughed. 'Only in Wodehouse stories, darling. I'm not sure that the old boy notices he has a daughter.

Isobelle runs things. She'll be delighted: she thought I was going to be left on the shelf.'

'No chance of that. Here's to us.'

When the tabloid newspapers first relayed the story, with such gusto, of Steven's liaison with Lady Louise Flint, Lucy Howard, blinkered as ever in her love for Steven, consoled herself with the thought that he would eventually return to her. She had discussed the affair with her new-found friend, Jacqui Bryson, who encouraged her to find herself another man. Lucy had begun a half-hearted affair with a man who worked for an American bank. He had responsibility for Shaw Management's account in London. In the normal course of his security activities on Shaw's behalf, Dan Fisher discovered that Lucy was sleeping with Marty Lawson and told Steven.

A month later, after Steven had spoken to the President (Europe) of the bank, Lawson was transferred to a branch in Philadelphia. Steven justified his intervention on the grounds of security, but the true reason was that he didn't want anyone else messing with one of his girls.

Lucy was not particularly perturbed by Marty's sudden departure and she was distinctly heartened when she learned of Steven's divorce. Perhaps her day would yet come.

The day after Steven returned from his trip to Venice with Louise he asked Lucy to call at his house at seven o'clock that evening for a drink. He had something important to discuss with her. She assumed that Steven, his affair over, wished to pick up the pieces with her again. She would give him a hard time, lay down some ground rules, make sure he realised that she wouldn't be treated so casually in the future.

Home a little earlier than usual, Lucy took a shower and

put on some new silk underwear. She donned some casual clothes and, after some thought, exchanged them for a smarter outfit. They might well go out to dinner and she wanted to be at her best. She indulged herself by taking a taxi to Steven's home.

As Steven let her into the house, Lucy thought he looked distracted. It was unusual because he kept everything under control; some business problem must be bothering him. He waved her towards a seat and asked her what she would like to drink. Lucy had imagined that he would have a bottle of champagne ready. She asked for some anyway.

A few minutes later Steven reappeared with a bottle of Laurent Perrier.

'It's good to see you, Lucy.' He meant it; she was a stable influence, thoroughly dependable. Whatever happened, he wanted her to stay in his life. 'Here's to us.' He raised his glass in a toast. 'I've ordered some Thai food, the dishes you like. Let's relax.'

'You look tired,' Lucy said solicitously.

'Not at all,' Steven replied, with a sudden cheeriness.

After the champagne and the food, they made love. Then Lucy watched fondly as Steven went into a doze, his features relaxed and his arm thrown sideways across the pillow. Carefully she began to roll away from him but her change of position awoke him. 'Don't go, Lucy,' he said, 'I need to talk to you.'

She kissed him lightly on the lips. 'There's no hurry. Have a little sleep.'

'No, no. It's important.' Steven sat up slightly and drew Lucy towards him. 'You know how important you are to me, Lucy. You've been a constant in my life.'

Happily, Lucy snuggled closer to him. Was this how proposals happened? In bed, after sex? She'd have preferred some soft music, some moonlight perhaps.

'I told you I had something to tell you,' Steven continued. 'It's not easy. But you should be the first to know that I'm going to marry Louise Flint.'

With great deliberation Lucy sat up. She turned her head away from Steven and managed a barely audible 'Oh.'

'I realise this is a shock,' Steven said. 'You and I have been close for a long time, but Louise has become very special to me. She's right for me.'

'I see.' Afraid she was about to be sick, Lucy sprang out of bed, grabbed whatever of her clothes she could see and ran into the bathroom. For some minutes she sat on the lavatory, her body racked with sobs. When they got too bad she flushed the lavatory to mask the noise. She heard Steven rattling the door and asking if she was all right.

'Fine,' she shouted back and set about patting cold water over her face.

Lucy went back into the bedroom and put on the rest of her clothing. She had to get out; she also had to retain her dignity. 'Steven, I must get home. Things to do,' she said lamely.

'Yes. I'm sorry, Lucy, but I knew you'd understand. We don't need to change anything. You and Louise will get on like a house on fire,' he said cheerfully.

Lucy left the bedroom and clattered down the stairs. She found her handbag in the sitting room and headed rapidly back into the hall.

'I'll get a taxi for you,' Steven said as he opened the front door. She waved his offer aside and he watched her as she hurried, almost at a run, for the main road.

When Lucy got home, she went straight to bed and, between her bouts of tears, sought the oblivion of sleep. On the following morning she telephoned Dean Aultman to tell him that she was unwell. She needed to talk to someone, but to someone other than her flatmate. Jacqui would understand. She'd been through the mill with Paul Davis and she knew Steven. She called her at her office and to Jacqui's cheerful 'How are you?', Lucy responded with a flood of tears.

Gently, Jacqui persuaded her friend to explain what troubled her. 'Come over to my flat this evening,' she suggested. 'Have a few drinks, tell me all about it. Seven o'clock OK?'

Lucy snuffled her agreement, and a few minutes later Jacqui was telling John Winter of her evening engagement. He had recently been under great pressure from Eva Rosen to push the Steven Shaw project to its conclusion but wasn't satisfied that his material was strong enough. He wanted to finish Shaw off properly.

'This is a heaven-sent chance to get some dirt on Shaw,' Winter said eagerly. 'Lucy should know plenty about him and his business.'

'I'm not so sure. She wouldn't have an inside track like Dean Aultman, would she?'

'Let's find out. Tell her about the famous parties Shaw runs, with the tarts and the drugs. We'll see what she has to say. You'll have to tape the whole thing.'

'John, I can't trick her like that. She's become a good friend.'

'You want Shaw and his friends to be well and truly taken apart, don't you? Fine, so this isn't a time for misplaced scruples. I'll send someone over early this evening with some equipment. Make sure you do your stuff.'

It was surprising how much detailed knowledge Lucy had of the Shaw Management operation. In particular, she knew that a Swiss company owned the villa in Cap Ferrat which was for the sole use of Paul Davis. She calculated that the BBC executive had received at least half a million pounds in bribes from Shaw. She could add little to

Winter's knowledge of the Nils Ryberg affair but knew that someone called Dan Fisher had been receiving a monthly retainer as Shaw's security consultant since the early 1980s. Lucy was able to quote the fees which had been paid to directors of firms which sponsored events organised by the agency, and also to a wide range of journalists.

She was particularly scathing about Steven's method of plundering the fees that he negotiated for his clients. 'It's grossly immoral,' she said indignantly, 'and he wouldn't get away with it in most professions.'

Jacqui's voice was heard, asking how Steven did it.

'It works best with a package deal. Let's say four golfers or tennis players do a promotion. The fee is half a million, for the sake of argument. Steven skims a hundred and fifty thousand off the top but he doesn't stop there. He splits the remainder of the money four ways and then takes a further twenty-five per cent from each client. Bingo, he's ended up with over half the money.'

When they had listened to the tape together, Jacqui asked Winter how he was going to use the material.

'It corroborates many of the things we already know,' he replied. 'My first port of call is going to be the Director-General's office. I'll have Paul Davis out of the BBC on his ear.'

'You'll have to tell Lucy what we've done.'

'I will and I'll take her through all the other evidence. Maybe she can rifle the files in Shaw's office for us.'

'I doubt he leaves anything important lying about in a file.'

Most of a day was spent in convincing the Director-General that the evidence Winter had was genuine. He agreed not to reveal Winter's sources and promised an inquiry into how programmes were commissioned and bought by the Corporation. In addition, he said that Paul

Davis would be asked to retire at once from his position as the Head of Sport.

'But Shaw is another problem,' the Director-General said grimly. 'He's got a number of contracts with us and I doubt we can renege on them. He'd have us in court like a shot.'

On the following day, an announcement was made that Paul Davis had taken early retirement to pursue other interests. When a senior executive like Davis retires he is traditionally given a fulsome tribute, well-larded with references to his long and honourable service. On this occasion it was omitted, and the media-watchers wondered why.

Davis cleared his desk and left with the minimum of fuss. Within hours of leaving the Television Centre he reached Steven by telephone and told him of his dismissal.

'What reason were you given?' Steven asked.

'None. It had come to the D-G's notice that there were certain irregularities in the way my department was run. You know the sort of shit these bureaucrats speak while they finger their old Etonian ties. Better if you resign, old chap, we'll pay you off and you'll get your full pension rights at sixty.'

'So, who is it? Winter? You saw his article in *Nosey Parker*, no doubt. But what's he found out that's new? And who from? That's the question.'

'Be careful, Steven. There'll be a BBC inquiry into how the sports department has been run. Cover your traces, for God's sake.'

'You don't have to worry about that. Why don't you take a low profile, Paul, for the next few weeks? Go down to that nice villa of yours and check how your alternative pension fund is doing. It makes the BBC one look pretty puny, doesn't it?'

*

It was fortunate that Winter took the precaution, recommended by Toby Streeter, of putting all the material relating to Steven Shaw in a safety deposit box at his bank.

When the Winter family returned to their house late one Sunday evening from a visit to some relatives in Wales, they found that their back door had been forced open. The intruder seemed to have concentrated on Winter's study, where his files had been thoroughly searched and several computer disks stolen. He had back-up disks so it didn't matter. Otherwise, the rest of the house had been left untouched.

Thereafter, Winter concentrated on putting together his programme about Shaw. Many of those he had targeted refused to be interviewed and he resorted to some crude badgering tactics. One morning he rang the bell of Dan Fisher's front door at seven o'clock. With a video-camera rolling he waited for Fisher to appear. Winter only got as far as saying, 'Mr Fisher, I believe you're a close business associate of Steven Shaw,' when the door was slammed in his face. He rang the bell again and Fisher retaliated by pouring a bucket of water on Winter and his cameraman, who decided that a tactical withdrawal was wise.

The method worked marginally better with Paul Davis. Having established that he was holed up in his French villa, Winter 'doorstepped' him and got some effective footage of him as he denied any impropriety in his business relationship with Shaw Management.

Sally Wyatt, who had interviewed Steven for 'Insight', refused to make a formal contribution to Winter's programme. Poised and incisive, she had achieved her ambition of becoming the Head of Features – her *first* ambition, the cynics stressed: they reckoned that she had the Director-General's job in her sights. However, she told

Winter that she had been ordered to give Shaw a favourable interview on 'Insight'.

'It was disgraceful. I was given an ultimatum. Give Shaw a favourable interview, a whitewash, or pack my bags.'

Her admission in itself was more grist to Winter's mill.

With Eva Rosen's help several of Shaw's clients and business associates were interviewed in a non-controversial way. Eva herself gave a lucid and forceful exposition of how Steven penetrated the television sports market in America. But Winter was surprised and elated when she told him that Suzi Shaw was prepared to talk to camera about her marriage.

'But only about the marriage,' Eva stressed. 'She doesn't know about Shaw's business.'

'How did you manage that?'

'It's a favour to her father, Joe Lynagh. In turn he's doing Ron Palmer a favour.'

'It's a funny old world, isn't it.'

'Shaw's about to find that out. He thought he could outgun everybody.

'Hubris.'

'Yeah, and we'll be his nemesis.'

# Chapter Fifty

Although Brompton House, the London home of the Countess of Wenlock, was no more than a mile from his own, Steven had elected to be driven there. The Daimler slid through the Kensington streets towards his six o'clock appointment with Louise's mother. It had proved unexpectedly difficult to arrange. Steven's own schedule, much of it arranged well in advance, was complex, and so, apparently, was Lady Isobelle's. With Louise's blessing, he left one of his New York secretaries with the problem and at last a time had been found, early in May when Steven had a series of meetings concerning the marketing of the Wimbledon Championships.

Concerned to observe the proprieties by asking formally for permission to marry Louise, Steven had made her promise not to forewarn her mother of their plans. He was looking forward to talking to the Countess, who seemed to be a jolly lady. No doubt she'd offer him a drink, although he was no fan of gin and tonic which was her favourite tipple.

As the car drew to a halt outside Brompton House, Steven reflected on how far he had climbed up the steep incline towards wealth and prestige. Now at home in any boardroom in the world, he was about to establish himself in the higher echelons of society. He would be able to invite his new parents-in-law to his pre-Wimbledon party next year. Their names would look good on the guest-list.

A middle-aged woman, plump-faced and dressed in a shapeless black dress, opened the door. 'You must be Mr Shaw,' she said. 'You'd better sit yourself down in the drawing room. I'll let the Countess know you're here.'

The maid opened a door on to a tall-ceilinged room with a number of sofas and easy chairs ranged around its walls. A heavy oak table sat in the middle, with magazines scattered on its surface. It reminded Steven of a doctor's waiting-room. There was a smell he recognised. It must be furniture polish; probably a brand that his mother used. He wandered over to the window and looked out to the street, now busy with traffic.

The door opened and Lady Isobelle came towards him, smiling politely. 'Mr Shaw. Your secretary made it all sound so urgent. I couldn't think what you wanted from me. I suppose it's about Louise. She doesn't owe you money, does she?'

'No, no, it's nothing like that.' Steven smiled and paused. He had expected to talk to the Countess in more cosy surroundings. This had the feeling of a formal audience. Weren't they going to sit down and have a drink?

'So what can I do for you, Mr Shaw?' Lady Isobelle was showing signs of impatience.

'Well, Lady Isobelle, it is about Louise.' For the first time in years Steven felt uncomfortable, almost gawky. 'I would like to marry your daughter. I'm here to ask your blessing.'

What is this man on about? Lady Isobelle thought. He's totally unsuitable: rich, but the very worst kind of *arriviste*. How could he have imagined that he'd be welcomed into the Wenlock family? She'd start looking again for a husband for Louise, someone solid and dependable. She'd be a different girl when she had a few children to look after.

Steven had expected a smile, even a gracious exclamation

of pleasure from the Countess. But she frowned and said, 'A marriage to you is out of the question, Mr Shaw. I'm surprised that Louise encouraged you in such a fantasy. I recall that you've been married and divorced on two separate occasions. Isn't that so?'

'Yes, but—'

'That means you are unsuitable to marry our daughter. We would not permit it.'

'Millions of people divorce and remarry. There's no stigma attached to it, surely?'

'We do not condone it in our family, Mr Shaw. That's final. I'm sorry. Now, I've got to get ready for dinner. Jean will show you out. Good evening.'

Lady Isobelle walked swiftly away and her maid appeared in her place so promptly that Steven wondered if she'd been eavesdropping in the hall. He trudged the few steps to the front door as if his limbs did not belong to him anymore. Out on the street he looked blankly at the passers-by, at the cars with their drivers and passengers, at a cyclist who weaved past. No doubt they had their own problems but they lived in a secure world. Suddenly his secure world was in bits and pieces, and he couldn't understand why. It was the finality of his rejection that had shocked him. She hadn't given him a chance to argue his case. He was unsuitable, she would not permit a marriage. He realised that his driver, the reliable Terry Parkin, was speaking to him. 'Where to, sir? Are you OK, sir?'

Steven tried a smile but it didn't work. 'I'm fine, fine. I'll walk back to the house. I won't need you again this evening.' He waved a hand towards Parkin and walked slowly away down the street.

For a moment or two, Terry Parkin watched him. He was puzzled. On the way to the house, Mr Shaw had seemed so chipper, jaunty as a spring lamb, you might say.

Now, he looked really down in the dumps. Something must have upset him. Still, he'd bounce back. That sort always did.

Steven had no idea where he went that night. He remembered walking the streets with a great weariness, bumping into other people occasionally because his mind was engaged elsewhere. At one stage he went into a bar and had two large brandies in rapid succession. He grimaced as the spirit hit the back of his throat.

Eventually he found himself in a quiet street near Victoria Station. He walked towards a main road, hailed a taxi and went home. Steven took a sleeping pill and awoke to the same miserable thoughts he'd had during the previous evening. His day was taken up with meetings and telephone calls and he forced himself to concentrate hard on the various issues under discussion.

Occasionally he tried Louise's telephone number but only got her answering machine. When his last meeting ended at around seven o'clock, he toyed with the idea of asking Lucy to have dinner with him. But she had made a point of maintaining her distance from him ever since he'd told her about Louise. No, it wasn't a good idea. Maybe he should call that agency and employ a tart for the evening. Instead, he tried Louise's number once more and she picked the receiver up on the second ring.

'I thought it might be you,' Louise said. 'I gather things didn't go too well with Mother.'

'You've talked to her?'

'Yes.'

'So what should we do?'

'I don't know, darling.'

'Well, I do. We'll get married anyway.'

'No, we can't,' Louise said. 'I won't cut myself off from my family and that's what it would mean.'

'What's this thing your parents have got about divorce? They're not Catholics are they?'

'No, they're Anglicans, but very High Church.'

'So, what's the problem?'

'It's got nothing to do with you being divorced, Steven. My mother has very firm views on who I should marry. He's got to be suitable, you know . . .' She tailed off helplessly.

'You mean someone of the same class.'

'I suppose so. My mother may look a bit vague but she's very shrewd actually. She'll have checked you out, and we did have all that publicity. She hated all that.'

'So she's going to sentence you to a life of genteel poverty, is she, Louise? I can give you a lot more than that, as you know.'

'I know, darling.'

'So, let's get a special licence and get married. Or we can fly to the States and do it. Or Mexico, or Peru, I don't care. Your parents will get over it. They'll welcome us back in no time at all, particularly when they have grandchildren to fuss over.'

'No, Steven, you don't understand. They won't and I couldn't bear to isolate myself from them.'

'So, it's curtains, is it?'

'I'm sad to say that it is.'

After putting down the telephone, Louise looked at it wistfully for several moments. All that lovely money, and she'd just kissed goodbye to it. Why couldn't Steven have just enjoyed their affair for what it was? Why worry about marriage? One of her friends had told her that Steven was the archetypal social climber. She'd thought it a spiteful remark at the time but maybe her friend was right. He wanted to marry her for her connections in high places. Not that it mattered anyway. There were always two sides to a bargain: in this case, his money for her social standing. It was what had kept the European aristocracy going for centuries. And she'd hoped her mother would agree to the marriage for that reason.

The palmy days were temporarily over. Louise would have to start the search for a rich husband who was acceptable to her mother. In the mean time, life had to go on. She made a call to Rory McCall and asked him to deliver several grammes of cocaine. Steven wouldn't notice the extra cost and she and her friends would have one final fling at his expense.

The rhythm of Steven's working day was intensified by the demands of his role as the marketing consultant to the Wimbledon Tennis Championships. As a result, there were whole minutes during the following day when resentful and debilitating thoughts about the débâcle of his marriage proposal to Louise did not intrude on his thoughts. He returned to his home drained of energy and emotion. Thank God he refused dinner with those Wimbledon committee people; it would have been beyond the call of duty.

He realised that during the past thirty-six hours he had hardly eaten; he had picked at a salad during lunch on the previous day and that was all. He ought to have something, even if he had to force it down. He looked in the refrigerator and the kitchen cupboards, which were stocked, when he was in residence, by the agency which looked after the house. There was a selection of sandwiches in plastic containers and he chose one and opened a bottle of sauvignon.

Steven wandered into the living room and flicked through the television channels. The usual dreary offerings: a police series, a situation comedy which featured yet another hapless male being henpecked by all about him, a wildlife series and a game show. He looked at the evening newspaper and abandoned it; he opened his briefcase and took a cursory look at some contracts and then threw them aside. His sandwich and glass of wine sat, untouched, on a side-table. He walked through to his study and selected a video-cassette from his large collection. 'Open Golf Highlights' was written on the case but it contained a compilation of incidents from Steven's parties of the past few years. Open Legs Highlights. What usually turned him on merely looked absurd on this occasion.

Maybe he should go for a walk; perhaps have a quiet pint in a pub and watch the world for a change. As he debated the idea, the doorbell rang. Steven strode to the small television screen by which he monitored any visitors. He flicked it on and saw a man in a dark suit. He was wearing a bowler hat, an unusual item of attire in 1990s London. He didn't know the man. Maybe he was there to serve a writ on behalf of a disgruntled client. He certainly wasn't selling some household product or other that Steven didn't want.

As he went into the hall, Steven wondered if the man bore a message from Dan Fisher, who used a variety of unusual people to run errands.

The man on the doorstep was much too elegant to be running errands or serving writs. His suit was beautifully cut. Despite the warmth of the evening he wore a waistcoat and Steven identified the Old Wykehamist tie, tightly knotted and flush against the collar of his cream shirt. The man removed his bowler hat to reveal his curly light-brown hair which was cut short and had a sharply defined parting. With his regular features and slight tan, Steven thought he looked like an actor, one in constant demand to play the role of a lawyer or a civil servant.

On cue, the man said, 'Mr Shaw, I apologise for intruding like this. I'm Hugh Hornby and I work at the Home

Office. Here's my card.' His voice was light, with just a hint of a drawl; it seemed to imply that what he said should not be taken too seriously.

'What can I do for you?' asked Steven, glancing at Hornby's engraved visiting card.

'You could invite me in. I'm here on Home Office business, albeit in an unofficial capacity.'

Steven stood aside for his unexpected visitor and told him to turn left into the living room. 'Have a seat. What does the Home Office do?'

'Oh, immigration and passports, the police, all that type of thing.'

'I'm a British citizen,' Steven said good-humouredly.

'A distinguished one,' Hornby replied with a smile.

'So, why are you here?'

Hornby crossed one leg carefully over the other. 'It's a matter of your friend, the Lady Louise.'

Noticing his untouched glass of wine, Steven offered Hornby a drink but he declined. 'Louise. Yes. Is she all right?'

'Oh yes,' Hornby replied. 'It's her mother, you see, Mr Shaw. The Countess has, shall we say, friends in high places.'

'Don't they all?'

Flicking at an imaginary speck of dust on his immaculate waistcoat, Hornby continued. 'She is related to the Queen and therefore has the ear of my masters in Whitehall.'

'My liaison with Louise is over,' Steven said firmly.

'Quite, and I am charged with the task of ensuring that, shall we say, a degree of discretion is maintained about the whole *affaire*.' Hornby gave the final word of his sentence the correct French inflection.

'Discretion? What do you expect? Of course I'll exercise

discretion. What other course of action do I have?'

'The Countess and her friends—'

'In high places—'

'Quite. They are concerned that you might be tempted to sell your story, er, to the tabloid press. Anyone remotely connected to the royal family seems to be fair game these days, as you know.'

'The royals haven't covered themselves in glory, have they? They're behaving like living clichés in a badly written soap opera.'

'They have their minor difficulties, I agree.'

'Mr Hornby,' Steven said quietly but emphatically, 'I'm not a professional footballer with a tax problem, nor an out-of-work actor with an expensive divorce looming. Why should I sell a story about Louise and her family?'

'Revenge?'

'No.'

Hornby smiled and rose to his feet, smoothing a hand over his well-groomed hair. 'Thank you, Mr Shaw, for your forbearance. It wasn't a task I relished. I was particularly pleased that you were alone and we could talk in confidence. On the subject of confidences, I should add that, assuming the subject of the Lady Louise is laid to rest, your outstanding work for British sport may well, in the future, be recognised.'

'Recognised?'

'By Her Majesty in some future honours list. Not to be counted on, but a possibility, you understand.'

Hornby headed for the hall, picked up his bowler hat, shook hands with Steven and then placed the hat firmly on his head at a slight angle. As Steven opened the front door, Hornby paused and said, 'You're still putting lots of work Dan Fisher's way, I believe. Give him my regards, won't you?'

With a smile, he walked the few paces to the pavement and strode away in the direction of the Brompton Road.

Steven stared after him, wondering how much he knew.

'I've had this schmuck sitting in my office all morning, Steven, and I couldn't get rid of him.' Jay Melville, a hardened businessman with all the traditional 'fuck you' bounce of a native New Yorker, sounded like an ageing spinster whose virtue has suddenly and violently been assailed.

'Who is he and what is he?' Steven asked. He'd just taken a sleeping pill and wanted to go to bed.

'Eddie Kozoll, he's called. Says he's a consultant to Chung Enterprises. Says he wants to sit in on our American operation to see how it all works. The schmuck said he'd have some valuable input for us.'

'Why didn't you throw him out?'

'Because he's built like Schwarzenegger and twice as ugly.'

'Get Corky Price on the job. He's our security consultant, that's what he's paid for.'

'I've done that, Steven, and he was on his way over until I mentioned Kozoll's name. Then he suddenly got very busy and told me to humour the guy. Steven, you'd better get back here. These people are trouble.'

'So it seems. I'll be on Concorde in the morning.'

Steven was pleased to have an excuse to leave London after the collapse of his plan to marry Louise. He handed Lucy the task of unravelling the rest of his business week and told her to use the excuse that one of his children was ill. He anticipated his meeting with Mr Kozoll almost with relish. It would be a different kind of challenge. The man had put the wind up the normally feisty Jay Melville, but Steven had no qualms about taking him on. The bigger they come . . . His mood was almost jaunty as he boarded the morning Concorde flight to JFK Airport.

When Steven entered his New York offices just before eleven o'clock, Jay was waiting for him in the reception area. He looked agitated and pointed backwards over his shoulder with his thumb.

'He's waiting in your office,' Jay said.

'Kozoll? Fine. Come and introduce me, Jay, will you?'

The man was sprawled in one of Steven's armchairs, with the *Wall Street Journal* spread out over his knees. As he rose to his feet, Steven realised why Kozoll had intimidated Jay. He must have been nearer seven than six feet tall and his shoulders were in proportion; and an awful lot of material had been used to make his light-grey suit. His crew-cut hair emphasised the rounded shape of his large head.

'Eddie Kozoll,' he said in an indeterminate American accent. 'Glad to meet you, Mr Shaw.'

Steven allowed his hand to be enclosed briefly in Kozoll's gargantuan grasp. 'I don't know what you're doing in my office, Mr Kozoll, but my Chief Executive, Jay here, tells me he didn't invite you. So, why are you here?' Determined not to be bullied by anyone, Steven turned his back on Kozoll, strolled over to his desk and sat down. What could the man do? Throw him through the window? Hardly.

'As I explained to Mr Melville, I'm a consultant to Chung Enterprises, which has a considerable stake in Shaw Management—'

'Only twenty-five per cent—'

'A considerable stake. May I sit down?' Kozoll sat down. 'I'm here to help and advise, Mr Shaw.'

'I've done OK on my own, Mr Kozoll, in a very tough business. I won't be needing your help.' Steven looked challengingly at his unwanted visitor.

Kozoll smiled placatingly back. 'OK, Mr Shaw, I don't

mean to be rude. I'm here only to protect Mr Chung's interests.'

'If he had any doubts, why did he buy into my agency? Presumably he was confident of my abilities.'

Kozoll shifted his weight and the armchair creaked alarmingly. 'Can we talk in confidence, Mr Shaw?' He looked at Jay.

'I've got plenty to do,' said Jay. 'Catch you later, Steven.' He was glad to get out of the looming presence of Kozoll, although he was heartened to see that Steven didn't betray any alarm.

Kozoll began again. 'Mr Chung has one or two requests to make of you.'

'He holds a minority interest in my company. He doesn't have any say in the policy of the company, or the way I run it.'

'Nevertheless, he has a couple of requests. Can I run through them?'

Steven grimaced. 'Go ahead. It's all the same to me.'

'Mr Chung asks that you back off Carl Lansky. You're taking top players away from the American Tour and this is harmful. He wants the dispute to cease.'

'I'm creating my own tour, a world tour.'

'In Mr Chung's opinion, there isn't a necessity for a world tour.'

'He's entitled to his opinion.'

'There're good business reasons, Mr Shaw.'

'Oh yeah, what?'

'Mr Chung has a business association with the Commissioner. There are some resort developments, joint-ventures with Lansky and the American Tour. In Florida, California and Texas – not just in the USA but also in Thailand and the Philippines. A great deal of money is involved.'

'Good for him,' Steven said and began looking at his diary to signal that the meeting was over.

'It's rather important that the developments succeed,' Kozoll persisted. 'The prestige of the Tour is an important factor in ensuring that success. But your activities, Mr Shaw, are counter-productive.'

'Not for me, they're not. They're part of my long-range business plan.'

'Mr Chung has a suggestion and he thinks it'll solve the problem you and the Commissioner have. It's very simple.' Once again Kozoll flashed his smile at Steven. 'You will continue to organise and promote your golf tournaments and handle the TV rights but in association with the Tour. Lansky will give you new dates which won't conflict with any of his. How does that sound?'

'Like shit. I'll go my own way, as I've always done.'

'You're making a very big mistake.'

'That's my privilege.'

Kozoll stood up and said, 'I'll let Mr Chung know your views. With respect, Mr Shaw, I would counsel you to co-operate. Mr Chung has a habit of getting his own way.'

Steven remained in his seat. 'So do I. And, Mr Kozoll, don't bother to call again. I don't want to see you in this office. Do I make myself clear?'

Kozoll smiled fleetingly at Steven and walked towards the office door. He opened it and paused. He seemed to fill the doorway. 'I expect Mr Chung will be in touch.'

# Chapter Fifty-one

The buzz of the telephone next to his bed saved Steven from an eerie dream. He was at a meeting, with a complex contract before him. It had to be negotiated, word by word. But the two other people had their heads averted so that he couldn't see their faces; and they spoke a language he'd never heard before.

As he jerked awake, he reached automatically for the bedside light and then the buzzing phone. He was sweating, vague thoughts of panic imprinted on his mind. Shit, it was three o'clock in the morning. It must be one of his parents. Seriously ill or worse.

'Yes,' he said hoarsely into the receiver. 'Steven Shaw.'

'Are your affairs in order, Mr Shaw?' The voice was thin and reedy, and as dry as crushed eggshells.

'What? Who the hell is this?'

'I know you're well insured, Mr Shaw, but is your will entirely as you want it? Any extra bequests? For Lucy Howard perhaps or the invaluable Dan Fisher?'

The man didn't sound his r's.

'How did you get my number, Mr Chung?'

The caller ignored Steven's question and said, 'This is your one and only warning. Do what Mr Kozoll tells you.'

There was a click as the line went dead. Steven noticed that he was sweating. He sniffed, suddenly aware of an alien smell. Christ, it was petrol. He threw the duvet aside, strode to the bedroom door and threw it open. The stench filled his nostrils. Instinctively he pressed a switch and light filled the hall. He went weak with dread as he realised that a slight spark from the switch might have sent the place up in flames.

He looked at the dark stain which covered the carpet at the far end of the hall. Someone had poured petrol through the letterbox. So this was Chung's idea of emphasising his power. The man was serious.

Steven went to the kitchen, grabbed a fire extinguisher off the wall and laid a layer of foam over the petrol-soaked carpet.

What had the security people been up to? They were supposed to provide 24-hour protection. That was one of the reasons he'd bought the apartment. He'd deal with them in the morning. He needed time to think.

Now calmer, he acknowledged that he was wide awake. He might as well read some contracts. There wouldn't be any more shocks that night. He collected his briefcase from his study and went back to bed.

Steven awoke at his usual time of six o'clock, the lights on and a contract clutched in his hand. His neck was stiff from the awkward position he'd assumed. For a moment he wondered what had been going on. The stink of petrol brought it all back with a rush, including Chung's emotionless warning. He'd have to get some protection. He'd talk to Corky Price.

He walked into his living room, pressed a button and the curtains which covered two walls of the expansive room rolled apart. After his divorce, Steven had bought an apartment not far from his old home. It was on the top of an eight-storey building and the windows looked west across Park Avenue. To the south the sky was clear: it would be a beautiful day.

It was time for a mug of tea, and Steven went into the kitchen and switched on the kettle. He had proper English teabags, not the excuses for them that Americans used. He swung the door of the refrigerator open and looked for a carton of milk. As he bent to look at the shelves he saw something furry lying there. What on earth? . . . Taken aback for a moment, Steven recognised Adam's battered teddy bear. How had it got there? Nowadays the beloved teddy never left the house; in fact it rarely strayed far from Adam's bedroom, where it had kept him company for nearly ten years. He'd let him know where it was and give it back when they next met. When was that? He'd have to check whether his secretary had arranged their next get-together.

Steven reached for the teddy bear and one of the legs came away in his hand. Puzzled, he reached in with both hands and realised that all four limbs and the head been neatly severed.

The hair prickling on his scalp, Steven carried the dismembered parts to the kitchen table. His tea forgotten, he stood there for several moments trying to work out what was happening to him. It was another attempt to frighten him. Kozoll had spread some money around. He'd bribed one of the staff of the apartment block to place it in his refrigerator. Simple. Hang on a minute, Steven thought, it wasn't simple at all. Just before he went to bed he'd gone to the refrigerator for some orange juice; the teddy bear hadn't been there then. They'd been in his apartment while he slept. They could have killed him. And the petrol: they hadn't poured it through the letterbox; they'd done it from inside his apartment. And how had they got the bear from Adam? His fear was multiplied when he realised that the threat was not just to his own life but to his son as well.

Although it was not long after six o'clock, Steven had no hesitation in calling Corky Price. To his credit, Price sounded as if he'd been out of bed for hours rather than rudely plucked from a deep slumber. Steven gave the security man a brief account of what had happened that night and asked him to gather all the information he could on Chung Enterprises and on Eddie Kozoll.

'I've told Jay most of what I know,' Price protested. 'These people are trouble, Steven, don't fuck with them.'

'Obviously. But I want you to dig deeper. OK?'

'Yeah, I'll try. I'll ring you later.'

In the middle of the afternoon, Price called to suggest that they met face to face.

'Why?' asked Steven.

'If they can deliver fuel you don't want and stock up your refrigerator without you knowing, maybe they've bugged you in other ways.'

Price insisted that they met in a place they'd never used before, a noisy bar off Fifth Avenue and not far from the Trump Tower. He had commandeered two stools on the corner of the bar and was drinking a bottle of Beck's. Steven ordered the same drink.

'So what's the form?'

'The form is that my people sweep your office and your apartment tomorrow morning,' Price replied. 'If I were you I'd arrange for all your offices and all your other properties around the world to get the same treatment.'

'Are you serious?'

'You bet. These are deadly serious people.' Price swallowed half a glass of beer and waved for another. 'It won't do you much good because they'll replace the bugs in due course. They've probably got some people in place in your organisation. A secretary or two, a book-keeper, or they'll have bribed some of your execs.'

'Shit.'

'Yeah. It's only what you've been doing for the past ten years, Steven.'

'Business is business,' Steven said, with a sharp look at Price, 'but I've never threatened people or their children. Anyway, tell me about Chung.'

'There's nothing much I can add to what you know. He's one of the richest men in the Far East. Origins unknown. He appeared on the Hong Kong property scene nearly twenty years ago and made bundles of money. Nobody really knows what he owns because he hides behind nominee companies. But he's into transport, shipping, hotels, building and engineering. And he owns a brewery. People say he's into prostitution and drugs, and he has a substantial investment company in New York. He's acquired newspapers and television companies and is the man behind one of the biggest cable operations in the world. It covers Asia. Rumours say that he owns a big slice of PNE over here.'

'I thought Ron Palmer owned most of it.'

'He did but rumour has it that he's sold out to Chung and is just a front man to satisfy regulations about foreign ownership of media businesses over here.'

'Palmer's an American citizen, is he?'

'Yeah.'

'What about Kozoll?'

'There are gaps in his CV too. He went to the University of Maryland to study law enforcement, for Chrissake. But he spent his time playing basketball and flunked out. Turned pro but didn't make it. There's a drugs bust on his record. He worked in computers and then went to Australia. There's a gap of ten years and he surfaced in Hong Kong working for Chung.'

'Apart from the drugs bust, no criminal record?'

'No, but I'm told Kozoll has a habit of getting his way.'

Steven swallowed the last of the beer in his glass, grimaced and ordered himself a glass of wine. 'So, what are you telling me, Corky?'

'It's in your best interests to back off. Do what Chung tells you for the time being. There's nothing too terrible involved, is there?'

Steven knew that Price was talking sense. He'd take the chink on in his own time, when he'd made his preparations. Nevertheless, he said, 'I don't want to be ordered about by anyone and I don't take kindly to threats.'

'Think of Adam. D'you want him thrown out from the top storey of Suzi's house? Or worse, kidnapped and then killed in a "snuff" porno-movie. Steven, live to fight another day, when you're ready. Chung is lethal and his tactics are simple – divide, intimidate and conquer. He'll trash you and your agency until you beg him to lay off and let you *give* him what's left of the business.'

Prior to his meeting with Corky Price, Steven had refused to take any calls from Eddie Kozoll. He half-expected some more harassment at his apartment that night and, on Price's advice, booked into a Manhattan hotel under an assumed name.

On the following morning, Kozoll telephoned at nine o'clock and Steven told his secretary to put the man through.

'You've been elusive, Mr Shaw.'

'Busy, Mr Kozoll.'

'We wondered if you'd made any decisions regarding Carl Lansky?'

'I've given it a lot of thought.'

'And?'

'I'm ready to talk to the Commissioner,' Steven said quietly.

'Good news. Mr Chung will be pleased. I'll ask Lansky to contact you.'

With a great deal of anxiety, Eva Rosen had been awaiting the delivery of John Winter's programme about Shaw. She had provisionally scheduled it for the evening before the United States Open Golf Championship in the middle of June. She had sold the British rights to Channel 4, whose Controller wanted to transmit it on the same evening.

Winter had enough material for a programme of several hours' duration. He had, he believed, performed a miracle to compress the Shaw story into ninety minutes. He consoled himself with Kingsley Amis's pronouncement that 'more will mean worse'. When he ran the final cut, he thought it was the best work he had ever done. When she viewed the tape towards the end of May, Eva agreed with him.

Steven and Carl Lansky discussed their differences and, during the course of two meetings, agreed a deal along the lines laid down by Chung. It surprised Steven that Lansky conducted the business in a dispassionate way: no exultation on the Commissioner's part was allowed to intrude, and they agreed not to discuss the matter with the media. Grudgingly, Steven gave him high marks for his conduct, even though he hated every inch of his own enforced climb-down.

Although few people knew of the stake in his agency acquired by Chung Enterprises, Steven felt the need to reassert himself as the prime mover in the business. In the space of two weeks he visited all of his dozen or more offices around the world.

In a series of reviews of the various markets, both geographical and generic, Steven made it clear to his executives how detailed was his knowledge and how intense were his expectations for the agency's growth in future years. He demonstrated his own dynamism and expected it to rub off on his employees.

After his lightning motivational tour, Steven returned to New York to find that the sporting gossip centred on rumours that Sam Rhodes was about to defect from Shaw Management. It was said that golf's superstar was concerned about the public image projected by Steven Shaw, especially in view of the damaging assertions which were to be made in a forthcoming PNE programme about him. Steven had known that John Winter was near to concluding his so-called exposé but not of its transmission date.

When told that PNE were to show 'Manipulator or Manager? Is Super-Agent Shaw Good for Sport?' on the eve of the US Open, Steven wrote a formal letter to the Chief Executive of PNE and asked for the opportunity to see the programme before it was broadcast 'in view of the possibility of libel'.

The reply came from Eva Rosen and began 'Dear Steven'. She told him that the programme was a balanced appraisal of his role in international sport and that it was based on factual information gathered by its producer and his researchers and on interviews with people who knew him. 'It would be inappropriate, therefore,' the letter concluded, 'for you to have access to the programme prior to transmission. Libel cannot be assumed, it must be demonstrated to the satisfaction of a court of law.'

Steven had expected a brusque rebuttal from Eva and he turned his attention to Sam Rhodes. On the one hand he despised his first and most illustrious client and, in a masterpiece of self-deception, put much of the blame on his head for the failure of his marriage. On the other hand he wanted to retain him as a client for a little while longer. When the break came, Steven wanted to initiate it.

Shinnecock Hills, the venue for the US Open, was no more than a hundred miles from Manhattan at Southampton, Long Island, and was one of the oldest golf clubs in the country. Steven decided to go there by car on the Tuesday, a practice day, and talk to Sam Rhodes. In the days leading to a major championship, Steven knew that his client would be more than usually vulnerable. He did his customary tour of the exhibition area and then, to show that old wounds had healed, had a cup of coffee with Carl Lansky. The Commissioner made a point of mentioning the forthcoming PNE programme.

'I don't think you'll find my comments objectionable,' he said, 'despite our past battles.'

'I'm sure. Anyway, it's only television. Here today and gone tomorrow.' Steven wasn't going to drop his guard to reveal how anxious he was about the programme. If they went too far he'd insist on a right to reply. Conveniently forgetting his past activities, he told himself he'd done nothing to be ashamed of, nothing anyway that an enterprising businessman wouldn't do. He was a saint compared to Chung, who was up to his eyes in drugs, prostitution and extortion.

Steven intercepted Sam as he came off the eighteenth green. An outsider who witnessed their meeting would have assumed that they were the closest of friends, as they both grinned and then shook hands warmly.

'Sam, you look in great shape! This course is made for you.'

'I hope so. My putting's a bit off, though.'

'Come Thursday, it'll be fine,' Steven replied. 'I'm glad

to catch you, actually, because there're one or two business matters to talk over.'

'I can't do anything now, Steven. I've got a couple of hours' practice lined up and then some rest.' Sam signed several autographs, in each case thanking the recipient warmly. 'I'm not as young as I was.' He smiled.

'Let's have an early dinner,' Steven offered. 'You know, as we always do at the Masters.'

'Not possible, I'm afraid. I'm already committed.' Sam started to move off, as his caddie urged him towards the practice ground. As he walked he kept signing the programmes, autograph books and scraps of paper that were thrust at him. Always gracious, he thanked everyone for their encouragement. 'Good luck, Sam', 'Go for it, Sam', 'Win it for us, Sam'. Steven admired anew his patience and his mastery of the basic public relations skills.

'Look, Steven, can we leave the business until after the Open? This is the week I need tunnel vision. I'll call you. Where are you staying?'

'I'm at home. I'm being driven out each day.'

'I don't envy you in all that traffic.'

Steven shrugged. 'Why don't I call you, Sam? I assume the office has the phone number of the house you're renting.'

'You can try but I warn you that I turn the damn thing off at night. Catch you later, anyway.' With a wave and a smile, Sam strode in his caddie's wake towards the practice area.

Steven knew that Suzi and the children were spending the week of the Open with Sam in his rented house. Adam had told him and Jay Melville had confirmed it. That was one reason for his client's elusiveness. The other motive was murkier: Steven could tell that Sam had already distanced himself and would very soon sever his association with Shaw Management. He wondered whether Sam had contributed to Winter's programme and, if so, what he'd said.

In sombre mood, Steven was driven back to the city. On the following day he didn't bother to visit Shinnecock Hills. He told his secretary not to put any calls through and busied himself with contracts and correspondence.

At seven o'clock that evening he left his office and walked home. The PNE programme was scheduled for eight o'clock and Steven was in an armchair in front of his television five minutes beforehand. A new videotape was ready in the video recorder.

The programme opened with a montage of sequences: Ray Gerrard winning Wimbledon; Angus Gray, arms aloft in jubilation, crossing the line in Adelaide to gain his first Formula One title; the captain of Salford United receiving the FA Cup from the Queen, and then a dissolve to the mountains of merchandise in the club's shop; Fran Zanini hit her winning volley to take the ladies' title at Wimbledon, and Steven was shown shaking hands with the Prime Minister of Britain; Ben Naylor was seen breasting the tape to take the gold medal in the Olympic 1500-metres final; Vince Holman received the green jacket after winning the Masters, and the joy of Sam Rhodes was shown in close-up as he holed the putt that won him his first US Open Championship; the camera cut to show Steven turning the bottle of champagne that Sam was brandishing so that the label couldn't be seen. Then there was action from several of Shaw Management's many television sports programmes including All-Star-Sport.

'This is the world of Steven Shaw,' the commentary, intoned by a celebrated English actor, ran. 'Through a network of offices around the world, Shaw and his high-powered executives control the lives and destinies of many of the world's greatest sportsmen and sportswomen, household names and heroes in tennis and golf, athletics and motor racing, soccer and skiing. He master-minds the television contracts for many of sport's blue riband events, including the British Open and the Wimbledon Tennis Championships, and produces a multitude of sporting spectaculars for television around the world. His All-Star-Sport series has been seen in over fifty countries.'

Steven was shown getting into a stretched limousine outside his New York office. He was glad to see that he still looked fit: well, he worked at it. The voice of the commentator said: 'Steven Shaw is one of the most powerful men in sport, a man with a briefcase packed full of contracts and a head full of secrets. The question is whether this man, with a semi-monopolistic position in some sports, is good for his industry. Does he have too much power? Are his methods of doing business acceptable? If not, is he a symptom of the ills that afflict sports or is he and men like him the disease?'

Bloody hell, thought Steven, is this programme loaded against me or what? But what could he expect with John Winter and Eva Rosen in league?

The next part of the programme was devoted to interviews with various clients and business contacts, interspersed with extracts from the BBC interview he had done a few years before with Sally Wyatt, who had achieved her ambition, Steven had recently noted, of becoming the Head of Features.

A typical sequence began with his comment to Wyatt: 'I always put the interests of my clients first, it's their peace of mind that counts.' The camera cut to Fran Zanini joyfully receiving the Wimbledon singles trophy from the Duchess of Kent, then some headlines about her injuries, then photographs of her drugs bust and the commentary concluded:

'Francesca Zanini, Wimbledon Ladies Champion, died of an overdose of drugs and alcohol at the age of twenty-four.'

So it went on. Ray Gerrard, his face in shadow and voice disguised, stated his suspicions that he'd been blackmailed into signing a new contract with Shaw's agency. Later, and undisguised, he told how Nils Ryberg (whom the narrator called 'a truly good man in the Augean stable of contemporary sport') had been neatly removed as the main candidate to endorse the Larssen racket range to the immense profit of himself – and of his agent, Steven Shaw.

'There was not a shred of evidence to suggest that Nils was homosexual,' Gerrard said. 'I believe there was a conspiracy to discredit him and that he was driven to suicide.'

'So, who was behind the conspiracy?' asked the interviewer.

'I wouldn't care to say.'

This led on to the death of the reporter, Toby Streeter and, pointedly, Dan Fisher was brought into the story at this stage and categorised as Shaw's 'fixer' in London. There were several shots of him looking either shifty or aggressive.

Fisher had a part to play in Jacqui Bryson's narrative, too, as she related how he had beaten her up. Her main thread, however, was her suspicion of the corruption in the BBC sports department. Aerial and ground shots of Paul Davis's villa in Cap Ferrat were shown, and the narrator focused on his humble background and his official salary at the BBC, moderate by the standards of the entertainment industry. The implications were obvious, especially when the opinion of an unnamed employee of Shaw Management (who was Lucy Howard) was added: that Paul Davis had received at least half a million pounds in bribes from Shaw.

By the time that Eva Rosen had told of her affair with Steven so soon after his marriage to Suzi and of how he had infiltrated the AAN sports department, he was beginning to feel ill. The tales of his off-shore companies, of his parties where designer drugs and sexual favours were freely available, and of his secret payments to high-placed executives of companies which sponsored his events, added to his distemper. He noticed that all the allegations were carefully phrased to avoid any accusations of libel. It was typical media bias: they'd distorted the facts to suit their story. And the exaggerations! For God's sake, he had a business to run, as best he could. Didn't they realise how tough it was in the real world?

The final betrayals emanated from Sam Rhodes, who castigated his business manager for his attempts to establish a world circuit of golf in opposition to the American and the European Tours. 'It's an example of an immensely talented man,' he said, 'being tainted by overweening ambition. Golf is the best-run sport of all, it has a basic decency and a lot of integrity. The boat is stable and, like many others in the game, I don't want it rocked by Steven Shaw.'

Steven saw himself say on screen, 'I'm very lucky to have a stable and happy home life.'

There were some photographs of his London house and of his former family home in New York. Then Suzi, elegantly clad in a simple green dress, filled the screen. Her voice was controlled but wistful. 'At first I was caught up in the excitement of Steven's new company. We'd just got married and I was carrying our first child, Adam. It was all wonderful. I expected him to work all hours, to work hard for each success. And success there certainly was and I felt it was for all of us. Then he opened the office in London, and then in LA, and then in Sydney. I saw him less and less, and life wasn't quite so wonderful. Once I looked at my diary and saw that Steven had spent less than ninety days at home during the year. And if he was at home, he wasn't really. There were the meetings and the dinners and the golf games. There wasn't much time for his family. I didn't know about his affairs with other women then.'

The camera closed in on Suzi's face. She looked near to tears. 'You might say that's the price you have to pay for success in business. Well, believe me, it's not worth it. Steven became a stranger, especially to Adam, our son. I lost count of the times Steven missed his birthday and those other occasions which mean so much to a child. Once gone, they can't be reclaimed, they're over for ever. Usually his secretary phoned. It's no kind of marriage when a secretary makes appointments for you to see your own husband or for a son to see his daddy. It was sad, saddest of all for Adam.'

The camera panned back to show Suzi, alone, sitting in an armchair. She looked almost frail.

'You bitch, you conniving, miserable bitch,' Steven shouted at the screen. 'I'll fucking well get you for this.'

He hardly registered the remainder of the programme which concentrated on the ethical question of whether it was desirable for a man like Steven Shaw to manipulate sport and sportsmen and, in the process, make millions of dollars for himself.

'Who gives a fuck about ethics?' Steven muttered, as he marched over to the windows and looked out over the great city, ablaze with light. Restless, he wandered around the large room. What to do? He looked vaguely at a shelf of books and a leather-bound volume caught his eye: *Childe Harold* by Lord Byron. He must had brought it over from London but couldn't remember when or why. He removed it and flicked to the title page. 'To Steven, with hope, Jeremy,' he read. Jeremy Knight, his English teacher, all those years ago. A sentimental old devil, but at least he'd had style.

Briskly, Steven put the book back on the shelf. He went to his study and telephoned an agency. 'Send me a nice, strong girl,' he said. 'You know the sort I like.' He had to relieve his boiling anger and frustration.

# Chapter Fifty-two

As he buttoned his shirt the next morning, Steven noticed that the knuckles of his right hand were puffy. She'd been a willing girl, although he hadn't liked the insouciant way she'd called him 'big boy'; but he'd given her a couple of hundred dollars extra.

He dressed with great care. It was essential to look every inch the successful international businessman, mega-rich and relaxed. He would go to Shinnecock Hills and behave as if Winter's programme had been a paean of praise rather than a brutal assault on his reputation. Winter would get his in due course, and so would several other people. In the mean time, he would outface all of them. It was business as usual. Steven's clothing was elegantly understated, but his arrival in the clubhouse car park in a stretched limousine with dark windows was not. He knew when it was time to put on a show.

He strolled over to the exhibition tent and greeted every-one he knew with enthusiasm. He saw embarrassment on the faces of some of his acquaintances but dissolved it swiftly with his easy bonhomie. As he was talking to Jack Burrell on the Parbreaker stand, Jim Martin, the *Los Angeles Times* golf correspondent, passed by, waved at Steven and yelled, 'Loved the programme, Steven. What's the sequel? The Shaw Empire Strikes Back?'

'Love you, Jim,' Steven shouted back, with a smile.

He knew that Vince Holman, his Australian client and

former Masters winner, was promoting a new line of clubs that morning and sought him out. It would be interesting to see how a client, and one of an independent frame of mind, would react.

The Australian, who was giving his sales pitch about the merits of the clubs to a group of fans, broke off when he saw Steven. His nut-brown face split in a grin and he shook his business manager warmly by the hand. 'Shit,' he said quietly, 'I'm glad you're for me and not against me. Talk to you later, I've got some clubs to sell.'

One of the early starters, Sam Rhodes had reached the eleventh green when Steven caught up with him. He wished a disastrous round on his client but Rhodes looked in prime form and had already got to three under par. Steven watched him for three holes. At the fourteenth green, however, he thought he glimpsed Suzi in the crowd and he retraced his steps towards the clubhouse. He didn't want to disturb his hard-earned equanimity.

Steven made a point of being much in evidence throughout the championship. He had to grit his teeth hard since Rhodes's good form continued and there was an awesome inevitability about his victory by seven strokes from his nearest challenger.

When he returned to his New York apartment Steven took stock of the alcohol available. He drank a bottle of champagne and then proceeded, for the first time in his life, to get totally drunk, alone; and on brandy. At five o'clock in the morning he woke up, rushed to the bathroom and retched violently. He drank a litre of water, put on a tracksuit and went gingerly out into the early morning. After jogging for half a mile, he was sick into a gutter, but then felt a little better. He persisted and was soon running freely through Central Park.

On his return, Steven drank another litre of water and

had a long shower. It was seven o'clock. He dressed and set out on foot for his office. When he got within a block of it, he went into a delicatessen and had a full American breakfast, accompanied by several cups of coffee. He felt renewed, ready for anything, as if during the last twelve hours he'd poisoned his body but purified his brain.

At just after eight o'clock the office was quiet, although he knew that Jay Melville would soon appear. Despite his life-style, he worked long hours. He played long hours, too; Steven sometimes wondered when he slept.

He glanced at the mail and then sat at his desk and jotted down the bonuses which Rhodes's victory would harvest. Not bad. Well over two million, and new offers for his services would flow in. Not that Sam was easy to please these days: very few endorsements or promotions gained his approval.

There was a buzz from the front door of the office, swiftly followed by a vigorous rapping. A delivery, no doubt. Steven opened the door and saw a man in a smart uniform.

'Shaw Management?' he asked. Steven nodded. 'Two letters, sir. Please sign here.'

They were both addressed to him and marked 'personal'. The first was from Sam Rhodes and the opening sentence was brief and pointed. 'I have decided, with effect from today's date, to terminate our business relationship.' There was more but Steven threw the letter aside and tore open the other. It was from Ray Gerrard and used the same phrases to end his association with Shaw Management.

He turned back to Rhodes's letter. The usual platitudes about how grateful he was for all Steven's help and support . . . their long friendship . . . how he hoped they could reach an amicable settlement over what remained of the contract. Some chance, Steven thought. And he thought he should tell Steven that he was going to marry Suzi in the autumn. Steven had expected it, but it still hurt him; he didn't attempt to quell the bitterness he felt. Rhodes had it all now, the bastard.

There was one more paragraph. 'You, Steven, should be the first to know that I have taken a substantial financial interest in Archie Faber's agency. So has Ray Gerrard, as he has informed you independently. We both intend to be very active in the agency field, and therefore will be in direct competition with you. I trust that the rivalry will always be friendly.'

You sanctimonious fucking hypocrite, Steven muttered. He glanced at Ray Gerrard's letter. Yes, the same shit. He stood up, rested both hands on his desk and stared balefully at the wall. What was the point of it all? He might as well sell the company out to Chung. His share was worth plenty, $150 million dollars at least, judging by what Joe Lynagh had received. Except that Chung, according to Corky Price, didn't work that way; he was planning to use his foothold in Shaw Management to hassle Steven so comprehensively that he'd eventually give up his control of the agency. Chung was an asset-stripper. There were only certain parts of the agency that he wanted: the rights in the successful television series like All-Star-Sport, for instance. He could run them for ever on his cable stations. And maybe some of the tennis and golf talent, but only the big stars.

Whatever Chung tried to do to him, Steven already had enough money in his various off-shore accounts to live like a king. But what would he do? Play golf every day? Screw women? Drink champagne? He could do all those things at will. No, the battle that had begun with Chung wasn't about money. It was about power and influence and prestige. Steven wasn't going to give any of it up to some dried-out Chinese megalomaniac. He'd do his own asset-stripping. He'd take the pick of the clients and the television programmes *he'd* created and transfer their contracts to a different company, one which was a hundred per cent owned by Steven Shaw; and all the agreements that came up for negotiation would go in the same direction. He'd take Chung on and it would be much more than a defensive campaign – he'd take the battle to the enemy. There were other scores to settle too: with Rhodes and Gerrard, with Carl Lansky, Eva Rosen and John Winter, and with Suzi.

Steven heard Jay arrive in the outer office. He put his head around the door. 'Hey, Steven, another great weekend for Shaw Management. Bonuses all round.'

'Not so great, Jay.' Steven pushed the two letters across the desk. 'Look at those.'

He watched Jay's expressive face go still and then sombre. 'Shit, a double whammy. That's serious, coming on top of the PNE stuff.'

'Desperate but not serious, as they say. Our biggest problem isn't losing clients to Archie Faber. Our problem is going to be with Chung. He'll try to break up the agency and pick up the pieces he wants. But I'm not about to let it happen.'

'What's the plan?'

'Better the right hand doesn't know what the left hand's doing, Jay. I'm going to oppose him in my own way, in my own time. No doubt it'll get bumpy at times. You'll have to trust me. OK?'

Jay nodded solemnly and Steven said, 'You hold the fort here today. I'll be out and about. I'll see you at close of business.'

A few minutes later, Jay sipped reflectively at his cup of coffee. He hoped to God that Steven knew what he was doing. He didn't fancy any unpleasantness with Eddie Kozoll, that was for sure.

When Steven returned to his office at five o'clock Jay greeted him with the news that Jake Richardson had resigned his position as Senior Vice-President (Sports) at AAN. Steven shrugged. Richardson was history.

By that time Steven had acquired the use of two offices, one in a side-street in the Garment District not far from Macy's, and the other near the Chelsea Hotel. They were both shabby, and he had paid a year's rent in advance in cash.

On that day Eva Rosen talked to Ron Palmer, who was in Los Angeles. He congratulated her again on John Winter's programme.

'The cracks are appearing,' she replied. 'I hear that Shaw's lost his oldest and best client, Sam Rhodes. Ray Gerrard has cut and run too, and they're putting their muscle behind Archie Faber. He's a bright young agent. He'll do well.'

'Shaw was a bright young agent once. Remember? And look at him now.'

'He's still bright, Ron, and he'll fight back, believe me.'

'I do believe you. You've also heard, no doubt, that Shaw's lost his playmate at AAN. Jake Richardson's resigned.'

'Yes,' Eva said with relish, 'that's one less bastard in sports broadcasting.'

'Things are moving our way. Chung will apply pressure all round until he breaks Shaw and then he'll take what he wants from his agency.'

'Whatever you do, don't underestimate Shaw.'

By the end of the following day each of Steven's new offices had two telephone lines and an answering machine, a fax machine, a photocopier and a small computer. The Garment District office carried the name of a nominee company registered in the Bahamas and the other office the name of a company registered in the British Virgin Islands. Steven awarded himself bonuses of several million dollars from Shaw Management which went into his Swiss account and he deposited nominal sums of $50,000 into the bank accounts of his two new companies. He was ready.

On the Wednesday morning he was in his office near Macy's at six o'clock. He had a lot of calls to make to Europe. With his list of telephone numbers in front of him on the computer screen and a yellow legal pad squared carefully on his otherwise empty desk, he began. His first call was to a man who worked in the Lausanne offices of the International Olympic Committee. A new game had begun.